Born in Hobart, Bruce Venables was an Inspector in the Royal Hong Kong Police Force during the 1970s. He served as a Launch Commander in the Marine Division and was a Platoon Commander in the Police Tactical Unit.

In 1984, Bruce moved to Sydney and began his career as a writer of film and television scripts. He is also well known to Australian and international audiences as an actor. His television credits include *Blue Heelers, Wildside, Water Rats, Minder, Always Greener* and *Murder Call*, and he's appeared in films such as *Paperback Hero* with Hugh Jackman and Claudia Karvan, *Evil Angels* with Meryl Streep, and *On Our Selection* with Geoffrey Rush and Leo McKern.

The Time of the Dragons is Bruce's second novel. His first, *A Necessary Evil*, is a story of vice and corruption, set in Sydney during the rock and roll years of the '50s and '60s. Also well known as a poet, a collection of his works entitled *The Spirit of the Bush* was published in 2003. Bruce resides at Bondi Beach with his wife, actress and international best-selling author Judy Nunn.

THE
TIME
OF THE
DRAGONS

BRUCE VENABLES

RANDOM HOUSE AUSTRALIA

Random House Australia Pty Ltd
20 Alfred Street, Milsons Point, NSW 2061
http://www.randomhouse.com.au

Sydney   New York   Toronto
London   Auckland   Johannesburg

First published by Random House Australia 2004

National Library of Australia
Cataloguing-in-Publication Entry

Venables, Bruce.
The time of the dragons.

ISBN 1 74051 296 0.

I. Title.

A 823.3

Cover illustration by K Chin Galleries, California, USA
Cover design by Darian Causby/Highway 51 Design Works
Typeset in 11.5/14 pt Sabon by Midland Typesetters, Maryborough,
 Victoria
Printed and bound by Griffin Press, Netley, South Australia

10 9 8 7 6 5 4 3 2 1

ACKNOWLEDGEMENTS

I would like to thank, above all, my wife, Judy Nunn; thanks, Jude, you're the best.

I would also like to thank my publisher, Jane Palfreyman, for her trust and patience, my editors, Kim Swivell and Jody Lee, for their marvellous efforts, and all of the staff at Random House Australia for their smiles of welcome and their obvious love of literature, in all its shapes and forms. And thanks also to Colin Julin for his patience with my computer illiteracy.

My gratitude must also go to three mates in particular: Paul Keylock and Les Bird, who provided, at their own expense, books and research material I would otherwise never have located, and Steve Tarrant for the information on triads. I owe all three a beer and a bowl of noodles, which they can collect when next I'm in Hong Kong, or by making an application in triplicate through the proper channels at the Australian Department of Foreign Affairs and Trade.

Finally, my thanks go to Judy's two dogs, Baxter and Lucy, for their silence, which I chose to interpret as critical acclaim.

FOREWORD

I am a storyteller. I write to entertain. In this instance, I hope to transport the readers to a time and place unfamiliar to them, the city of Hong Kong during the 1920s and 30s.

I have used real characters such as Wilhelmina Vautrin and John Rabe of the International Safety Zone Committee in Nanking, General Ch'iang Kai-shek, Air Chief Marshall Sir Hugh Dowding and others to give an historical perspective to the narrative.

I have also taken literary licence with the practices and procedures of the Hong Kong Police during the era in which the book is set. Owing to the destruction of Hong Kong during the Second World War, no records remain of such practices and procedures. In particular, anti-riot drills did not exist; they were created after the formation of the Police Training Contingent in 1958, which became the Police Tactical Unit in 1967.

I have a limited knowledge of the Cantonese language. Throughout this book I have italicised all Cantonese dialogue, in an attempt to capture the wonderful sense of humour and the refreshing candour of the people of Hong Kong, whom I knew and lived with in the 1970s. To those who might find fault, I would explain that I have used it as a device to give the reader a sense of belonging to the time and place of which I write. It is very easy to make a fool of yourself when embarking on a conversation in a foreign language and the Cantonese showed great patience when I did so. They helped me as I stuttered and stammered my way through a linguistic nightmare, and laughed, with great affection I'm sure, at the way I so often abused their language, and for that I remain deeply grateful.

Finally, the years during the 1970s when I served as an officer in the Royal Hong Kong Police Force was one of the happiest periods of my life. The friendships I made then have stood the test of time. I have lifelong friends in Hong Kong, New Zealand, the United Kingdom and elsewhere. To all of them I would like to say, thank you for your friendship and thank you for the memories.

Bruce Venables
Sydney
Australia

Hong Kong Song

There's a city up in Asia
Nestled in the China Sea
It's the mother of all misfits
And a port for refugees
It is known as Fragrant Harbour
'Though it contradicts the name
If you ever chance to go there
You will never be the same

. . . a song of the South China Sea

PROLOGUE

London 1941

The boy was scared. The dragons were a hundred feet high. Every way he turned they roared at him. Snarling and writhing, they leapt at him. And the snakes were everywhere on the ground around him, hissing and spitting. The boy wanted his mother, but he knew that if he moved, the dragons would notice and breathe their fire on him. A snake slid against his foot and he knew beyond all doubt that if he moved even one inch, it would bite his leg and he'd die. Dragons screamed and wailed all around him and people ran for their lives.

'Bloody Hitler! May 'e rot in 'ell!' the boy heard a man say as he ran past. He was a big man dressed in a black woollen suit and wearing a shiny brass hat.

'Keep away from the hoses son,' another man yelled. 'Jesus, Mary and Joseph! Every house in the bloody street's on fire.'

The boy stood in what was once a sleepy street in a London suburb and began to cry. He dropped the teddy bear he'd been carrying and stared at the raging inferno around him. The house he lived in was gone. The dragons had eaten it, along with all the others in his street, and as he watched, they roared and snapped and snarled at each other, fighting over each morsel as their feeding frenzy reached its fevered pitch.

Through tear-filled eyes, the boy looked towards the entrance of the street. A man was standing there. A man in a peaked cap wearing an army greatcoat. A black silhouette in the glow of the flames. Maybe it's God, the boy thought as the silhouette walked towards him. His mum had often told him that if anything bad happened to him God would come and look after him. His fear started to evaporate as God came closer. He knew God was good. God was kind and looked after little boys. God knelt down in front of him.

'What's your name, son?' God asked.

'Jeremy. Are you God?' the boy replied.

'No.'

'Are you an angel?' the boy asked, noticing the wings on the man's hat.

'No.'

'The dragons ate my mum. I was sleeping at my friend's house but I heard the dragons coming, I heard them screaming and Mr Ogden tried to make me stay, but I ran away, and when I came home the dragons were here.' The boy began to sob, pointing a trembling finger at the flames engulfing his house.

The stranger gathered the boy in his arms. 'I'll look after you,' he said. 'I know where you'll be safe.'

William clung to the man's neck as they left the street and, over the stranger's shoulder, he watched the terraced houses in the street he'd known for the six short years of his life disappear. And the dragons watched as the man carried him out of their reach.

The stranger took him to the Sisters of Mercy. A beautiful lady all dressed in black with white wings on her head took him in her arms and cuddled him, while another winged lady gave him a cup of hot soup. It was the best he'd ever tasted and it had vegetables floating in it. Then the first winged lady told him it was time to sleep. She washed his face with a warm cloth and took him into a large room filled with beds and tucked him in between warm blankets.

He was nearly asleep when the stranger returned. The stranger had taken off his greatcoat and the boy recognised the uniform of an RAF fighter pilot. 'The sisters will look after you,' the man murmured softly, and he stroked the boy's forehead. 'I have something for you,' he whispered, kneeling by the boy's bed. 'Something I want you to keep forever. Will you do that?' The boy nodded and the man took a gold chain out of his breast pocket. Attached to it was a small medallion the size of a sixpence. 'You know the dragons you saw tonight?' Again the boy nodded, mesmerised by the shiny medal. 'Well, they were fire dragons. They are evil. But there are other dragons,' the man said as he placed the gold chain around the boy's neck. 'Good dragons. Ones that will be kind to you.'

'Like you?' the boy whispered.

'Yes, like me.'

'Are you a dragon?'

'Yes,' the man nodded and smiled. Then he lifted the medallion in front of the boy's eyes. 'I am a golden dragon like this one. A friendly dragon who will always care for you.'

The boy scrutinised the medallion. On it was a dragon. It was breathing fire and a small pearl sat in the flames coming from its mouth. 'It's a fire dragon,' the boy whispered.

'No,' the man replied softly. 'See how many toes it has on each foot. It has five.'

'Is that good?'

'It is,' the man whispered. 'That means it is a celestial dragon, the most powerful dragon of them all. It comes from heaven and it will always protect you as long as you keep the medal around your neck. You must never lose it. Promise me.'

'I promise,' the boy answered, unable to drag his eyes from it.

'Good. I have to go now.' The man rose to his feet. 'The sisters will look after you.'

'Will you come back?' the boy asked hopefully.

'Perhaps, one day. You never can tell with dragons.' He stood at the foot of the bed and smiled at the boy. 'But even if I don't, you have your own dragon to wear next to your heart. As long as you have him, you will be safe from all evil. And lucky. Very, very lucky.' The man raised his hand, a silhouette to the boy in the half-light of the room. *Joi kin, Sai Loh,*' he murmured.

'What does that mean?' the boy asked, wide-eyed.

'That's dragon talk,' the stranger replied. 'It means goodbye, little brother.'

'Are you my brother?'

'Yes, I am,' the silhouette answered, then turned and walked away.

The boy gazed at the shining image of the golden dragon with the white pearl in its mouth. 'My brother,' he whispered. Then he looked up, but his brother had gone.

BOOK ONE

AWAKENING

CHAPTER ONE

Hong Kong – 1925

Richard Brewster's brain struggled valiantly to assimilate the constant flow of unfamiliar sights, sounds and smells. Every ten paces something new assailed his senses. Spices, aromas, drums, gongs, cymbals, wind chimes, dishevelled beggars, children singing in a tiny schoolyard, the cackle of chickens, the squeals of piglets, the mournful moan of a ship's horn announcing its departure for foreign ports, the shrill scream of a steam whistle as a crowded ferry bustled away from a wharf, while all around him a multitude of people gabbled in a variety of oriental dialects offering him fruit, clothing, poultry and even a monkey on a leash. It was exciting. It was overwhelming. It was Hong Kong. The British Crown Colony of Hong Kong.

'*Chai gwoon?*' he asked occasionally, not expecting an answer as he pushed his way along Des Voeux Road through the sea of oriental humanity.

An Indian Parsee, a fellow traveller on the boat from Bombay, had assured him he would have no trouble finding Central Police Station when he finally set foot on land in Hong Kong.

'All you must be doing, good Sir,' the chap had explained, 'is walking in a westerly direction along the foreshore of Hong Kong Island and you will be saying to all, the Chinese words *chai gwoon.*'

Apparently it meant police station in Cantonese. But for all the good it's done me so far, Richard thought, I might as well be yelling God save the bloody King.

'*Joh san, Dai Loh.*'

Richard turned at the sound of the deep voice and found himself staring into the eyes of a very tall Chinese. The man wore a conical straw hat and was dressed in a green thigh-length linen jacket, green trousers with white leggings and soft-soled coolie sandals. The badges on his white belt buckle and high-necked collar identified him as a constable in the Hong Kong Police.

'I'm sorry,' Richard stammered.

'I say good morning, Elder Brother,' the big Chinese said in heavily accented English, then threw a stiff salute and folded his powerful arms across his chest.

'Elder brother? I don't understand. I don't speak Chinese.' Richard replied. He stared at the policeman before him. Richard was nearly six feet tall and was well short in height to this fellow. Good God, he thought, the man must be six feet two inches at the very least. I thought the Chinese were all small people.

'I speak English very well,' the constable answered.

'Central Police Station?' Richard gasped. He wiped his brow with his handkerchief. The heat of the sun within the confines of the crowded street was insufferable. 'Superintendent Higgins?'

'Higgins *Geng Si*,' the big Chinese nodded wisely. 'Higgins Superintendent.' He grinned expansively and pointed vaguely in a westerly direction. 'Higgins number one bossy.'

'Can we go to him?' Richard was on the verge of fainting. The heat and his overworked senses were combining to make him dizzy.

'Go. Yes,' the policeman grinned and saluted again.

'Yes. Go.' Richard's head began to spin and all of a sudden three images of the giant Chinese policeman appeared before his eyes.

'I think you fall down first, yes?' The constable nodded to himself, confirming his own suspicions.

Richard tried to reply but his tongue was stuck to the roof of his mouth. He knew he was falling but he didn't care. His mind went totally black.

Several times in the next ten minutes he regained consciousness and was aware he was being carried over someone's shoulder, but once again, he could not have cared less and let his mind wander back into peaceful oblivion.

龍

A flood of cold water brought him instantly awake.

'Come on, lad!' a Scottish voice boomed. 'Get off your aaarrrse!'

Richard had spent three years in the Guards as a junior officer and in that time he'd learned to recognise the voice of authority and this voice ringing in his ears was definitely one of authority. He flew to his feet and stood to attention, swaying precariously as the room span around him. Water ran in rivulets down his face.

'My officers do not faint in the street!' the voice boomed again. 'Is that pairrrfectly clear?'

'Yes, Sir!' Richard replied automatically. He looked at the man standing in front of him, another giant, only this time undoubtedly a Scot. He was immaculately turned out in the brilliant white summer uniform of a Hong Kong Police Inspector. On his head he wore a pith-helmet, or solar topee, with a spike protruding from the top and the face beneath it sported a waxed moustache. Ex-military, Richard guessed. Sergeant Major, Black Watch Regiment. I'd bet my life on it.

'Letters?' the Scot snapped.

'Sorry, Sir?'

'Letters, maarn! Letters of introduction and employment from the Colonial Office in London!' The Scot's Glaswegian accent ground against Richard's eardrums.

'Yes, Sir.' Richard snapped into action and rummaged in his suitcase, finally pulling out a crumpled envelope, which he handed to the Scot.

The big man read the documents and looked up. 'Right, lad!' he roared. 'Consider yourself formally employed. You are now Sergeant Richard Brewster of the Hong Kong Police and I am your immediate superior. My name is Inspector

Robert McCraw, but you will call me Sir! Is that perfectly clear, laddie?'

'Perfectly, Sir.' Richard extended his hand. 'I'm pleased to make your acquaintance, Sir.'

'That may well be, lad,' McCraw bellowed as he shook Richard's hand, 'but am I pleased to make yours? That remains to be seen!'

Richard felt his hand being crushed by the big Scot, who was drawing breath to continue his verbal onslaught when he was interrupted by a soft, perfectly modulated English voice.

'I say, McCraw,' the voice purred.

McCraw flew to attention. 'Sir!' he bellowed. Richard remained at attention, unable to turn and inspect the man who entered the room.

'My dear fellow,' the voice continued lazily. 'Whereas I can understand the necessity for discipline around the old place, must you really go about it all in such a stentorian manner? Stand at ease. Both of you.'

Richard relaxed as a tall angular man, prematurely balding and immaculately attired in the white summer uniform of a Superintendent, appeared before him. The man removed his spiked helmet and smiled as he extended his hand.

'Charlie Higgins. How d'you do.' Richard shook the proffered hand. It felt like a wet fish. 'You're the new chum, I take it?' Higgins smiled. 'We've been expecting you. I sent a chap to meet your ship, but he obviously missed you. So you're Binky Brewster's boy, eh?'

'Yes, Sir.' Richard attempted a smile, but with water still dripping from the end of his nose, he withered with embarrassment.

'We met in London, you know, your father and I.' Higgins drawled as his eyes appraised Richard. 'How is the old bugger? Still as tough as boot leather is he, eh?'

'My father is in excellent health, Sir. He asked me to convey to you his best wishes.'

'Yairs, yairs,' Higgins drawled and began to circle Richard. 'Very kind of him. You resemble your father, you know. Same cheek bones, same stiff shoulders.'

A vision of his father appeared in Richard's mind, hands clasped behind his back, standing tall and austere in front of the huge fireplace in Hallowdene, the ancestral home of the Brewsters. 'You've too much of your mother in you, boy!' His father had roared, glaring at Richard over a bushy moustache. 'The army did you no good at all. You're weak! A stint in the Far East will sort you out! Let's hope Hong Kong will make a bloody man out of you!'

'Had a spot of bother on the way here, eh?' Superintendent Higgins continued. 'Fainted dead away, so I hear. The climate takes some getting used to, but you'll manage, I'm sure.' Higgins sat lazily at McCraw's desk. 'Has Inspector McCraw filled you in on the situation here? Paperwork and all that sort of bumf?'

'Well, Sir,' Richard replied, 'the Inspector informed me that I was to hold the rank of sergeant. My father led me to believe this would be an inspectorate appointment.'

'Colonial service regulations, dear boy.' Higgins murmured as he toyed with a quilled pen and ink set on the desk. A mere formality. I'm afraid you'll have to put up with it for several months, but don't worry, we'll pop you up to Sub-Inspector's rank in no time at all.' Higgins smiled at him. 'Of course all officers' privileges will be extended to you immediately and use of the mess goes without saying. Speaking of which,' Higgins got to his feet. 'How about a gin and tonic? Just the thing for a new chum in the Orient, what?'

'It may be a bit early in the day for me, Sir.' Richard replied.

'Rubbish!' Higgins took Richard's arm and led him towards a balcony door. 'In other parts of the world it's already dark.' He stopped and turned to McCraw. 'I say, be a dear chap, would you, Mr McCraw, and arrange induction papers, accommodation and all that other bumf,' he waved his hand airily. 'For our new sergeant, eh?'

'Certainly, Sir,' McCraw replied and saluted stiffly.

'Then join us in the mess for a drink,' Higgins finished and drew Richard along with him out onto the balcony of

Central Police Station, where he stopped and gave a secretive wink.

'McCraw is a Scot. Formerly an RSM in the Black Watch.'

'I guessed as much, Sir,' Richard said.

'Just the sort of man we need around here. He's instilled discipline into the local chaps, but he has a bit of difficulty coming to grips with officer's rank. Regimental Sergeant Majors are a breed apart, as you probably know, so have a bit of patience with him, eh?'

'Yes, Sir.' Richard replied. 'You can rely on me.'

'Enough said.' Higgins nodded then waved a hand in front of him indicating the harbour. 'Well, there she is, dear boy. What say you, eh? Is she not beautiful? Eh? Eh?'

Richard gazed out over Hong Kong. Directly below him, the wharves of Central and Western were hives of industry and across the glittering expanse of harbour the district of Kowloon bathed in the warm morning sunshine, while in the far distance, the farms and villages gave way to the majestic Kowloon Mountains.

'It certainly is a magnificent sight, Sir.'

'Yairs,' Higgins murmured taking in the view. 'Do you know what Hong Kong means in Cantonese?'

''Fraid not, Sir,' Richard muttered, embarrassed.

'It's a bastardisation of the Cantonese words *Heung Gong*, which mean "fragrant harbour".' Higgins looked into his eyes. 'A beautiful name, don't you agree? And the perfect place for a young man like you to carve out a career, eh what? You can make her your mistress,' he murmured seductively. 'You can have her in every conceivable way and she'll sprawl at your feet and beg for more, but . . .' Higgins paused and looked out over the harbour, 'you have to tame her first. She's a wildcat! A slut of the first water!' He turned back to Richard. 'Learn her ways, and above all, show no fear. Then she's all yours.'

'Yes, Sir,' Richard whispered. He felt hypnotised. Higgins' eyes held his with a fierce glare.

Finally Higgins smiled and patted Richard's shoulder. 'And beware of her mother.'

'I beg your pardon, Sir?' Richard was nonplussed.

'*Jung Gwok*.' Higgins laughed. 'China. Hong Kong's mother. Never forget her. She's the boss. The sleeping giant.' Higgins turned and Richard followed him along the balcony. 'There's a saying among the old China-hands out here. When China sneezes, Hong Kong catches a cold.' Higgins nodded, agreeing with himself. 'Don't ever forget that, Richard. Where Hong Kong's concerned, China rules the roost. She always has, and she always will.'

They neared the end of the balcony and Higgins stopped. 'Ah, here we are,' he indicated a set of louvred wooden doors. 'The Officers' Mess. Our little bit of England. Let's have a drink and I'll introduce you around,' he said and went through the doors.

Several men stood up as Higgins entered. 'Relax, chaps,' he said in what Richard thought to be a most condescending tone. 'Just bringing the new chum in for a drink.'

The room was spacious with a high ceiling on which two electric fans revolved slowly. A bar was set at one end and bamboo furniture was scattered about a parquet floor. Several board and dice tables were set up and a dartboard hung forlornly in one corner. But what caught Richard's eye were the trophies and shields adorning the walls; battle standards of several British regiments, swords, bayonets and even a Ghurkha kukri were mounted in various places of pride. Photographs of Marine Police vessels and Royal Navy ships of the line covered every available space. Over the fireplace, set on either side of an honour roll of Hong Kong police officers who had died in the Great War, were two magnificent tigers' heads mounted on wooden plaques.

'They're beauties, aren't they?'

Richard turned towards the man's voice. He was behind the bar, and also in white summer uniform. He placed a gin and tonic in front of Richard and extended his hand in welcome. 'Bertie Pertwee, Inspector. I'm the Station Officer here at Central.'

Richard shook his hand. 'Are they Bengal tigers?' he asked.

'No,' Pertwee replied. 'They're your common, everyday, garden variety Chinese tigers.'

'Really? I didn't think you'd find them this far east.'

'Oh yes,' Pertwee laughed. 'The buggers most probably wander across from Burma or Indochina. There's no shortage of them hereabouts.'

Higgins strolled up and entered the conversation. 'One bit a local chappy, a farmer, just the other day up in the New Territories,' he drawled, resting one buttock on a bar stool.

'Charles here shot one himself back in 1915,' Bertie Pertwee said deferentially. 'Isn't that so, Charles?'

'Yes, I did, actually.' Higgins replied. 'The blighters turn up every couple of years and eat a coolie or two and we have to organise a hunting party and shoot the damned things.'

'Sounds like great sport, Sir,' Richard said enthusiastically, but feeling quite the opposite. He envisaged his father's trophy room at Hallowdene, filled from wall to wall with the heads of animals slaughtered on hunting trips across the globe.

'Not so, I'm afraid,' Higgins drawled lazily, and placed a pipe stem between his teeth. He lit it and puffed. 'Bloody dangerous work, mark my words. I remember that one back in '15, at Tai Po in the New Territories. It bit a police constable's head clean orf! While we were actually killing it.'

'Really?'

'Oh, yairs, yairs. We put no end of bullets into the bugger, but he just kept chewing. Who was that PC, Bertie?' Higgins asked.

'Indian if my memory serves me correctly, Sir, PC Ruttan Singh.'

'Yes, Indian chappy.' Higgins ran another match over the bowl of his pipe. 'So there you go, young Brewster, just hope you don't get posted up into the New Territories. Could get your bally head bitten off, eh, what?' Higgins snorted at his own joke.

'Is there any chance of that, Sir?' Richard inquired.

'Any chance of what?' Higgins replied.

'Getting posted to the New Territories.'

'NT? I'm afraid not, lad. I promised your father I'd look after you and I wouldn't dare cross him. That means you're staying right here on Hong Kong Island. Besides,' Higgins winked at Bertie Pertwee, 'there's tigers enough for you to worry about right here, eh, Bertie?'

Bertie Pertwee winked lasciviously. 'There certainly are, Sir,' he chuckled.

'Two-legged ones mind you, young Richard,' Higgins grinned. 'But tigers none the less, with big cat's eyes and very sharp claws to tear the skin off your back, eh boys?' Higgins laughed and the other officers in the mess joined in.

'I don't quite get it, Sir,' Richard answered, embarrassed.

'No, but you will, boy!' Higgins smiled as the other officers laughed uproariously. He took the pipe from between his teeth and looked at Richard. 'You see, lad,' he continued, 'the tigers hereabouts hunt in packs, but you'll find that out for yourself, soon enough. We'll have to have someone show you where to find them.' Higgins gazed about at his young officers. 'Young Stewart Cameron here, for instance.' He waved his arm and a young man of about twenty-three approached.

'Glad to be of assistance, Sir,' Cameron grinned.

'I'll just bet you are, Sergeant,' Higgins said. He introduced Richard to the young Cameron. When the two had shaken hands Higgins continued. 'Take a couple of days off, Mr Brewster. Get to know the place. Young Cameron will show you around and who knows, you just might find a tiger or two.' Higgins laughed and the other officers grinned and winked at each other. 'No need to report for duty until your uniforms are made up. In the meantime, have some fun. And may I say on behalf of all of us here, welcome to Hong Kong.'

龍

Richard was allocated a large room with double doorway opening onto the station balcony, at the opposite end to the Officers' Mess. It had a single bed with mosquito netting, a ceiling fan, several rattan chairs, a large wardrobe and, much to Richard's surprise, a magnificent rosewood escritoire. Wong jai, the room-boy who was packing away Richard's belongings, explained in broken English that the writing desk had belonged to a previous European Inspector, since transferred to Aberdeen Police Station on the south side of Hong Kong Island.

'Doesn't he want it anymore?' Richard asked.

'No can do,' Wong jai replied as he busily packed Richard's clothing into the drawers of the wardrobe. 'Inspectah what live here before, he makee desk hi'self.'

'Well, surely that's all the more reason for him to keep it?' Richard asked as he struggled to absorb the room-boy's thick English pronunciation.

Wong jai pointed to the door. 'Door too small. Desk no can go out.'

'I see,' Richard nodded. 'The desk is too big, right?'

'No,' the room boy looked at Richard as if he were an idiot. 'Door too small,' he stated with perfect Cantonese logic. Richard was saved from further confusion by a knock at the door.

'All stowed away, are we?' Stewart Cameron asked as he entered Richard's room.

'Yes, thanks,' Richard replied and scratched his head.

'Having a language problem?' Cameron laughed.

'Eh? Oh no. His English is good enough, it's the logic that intrigues me.'

'Was he speaking English?' Cameron asked and stared at the room-boy.

'Yes. It's a bit broken up, but understandable.'

'The cheeky devil!' Cameron snapped and grabbed Wong jai by the scruff of the neck. 'I thought you couldn't speak English, you little bugger. Have you been prattling on in *Ying Gwok wah*?' Cameron yelled.

'*Ngoh m sik gong Ying Gwok wah, Dai Loh!*' the small Cantonese squealed.

'Don't give me that rubbish, Wong jai,' Cameron shook the man. 'Brewster *Sin Saang* here said you were speaking English,' he growled and pushed the room-boy away, then turned to Richard. 'I've been here for a bloody year and never had a word of English out of him.'

'Well, perhaps it wasn't English,' Richard answered hurriedly. 'It just sounded like it to me, that's all.' Stewart Cameron was typical of the boys Richard had attended boarding school with, a bully to those he considered inferior, providing of course they were smaller in size. He was not at all surprised the room-boy had pretended no knowledge of English to Cameron.

Cameron turned to the Wong jai again. 'Look here,' he said pointing his finger. 'If I find out you've been having me on I'll . . .' He raised his fist to strike the boy and Richard interrupted.

'Come on, Stewart,' Richard took the other Englishman by the arm and pulled him towards the door. 'Forget it. I thought you were going to show me the sights?'

Cameron turned at the door and glared at Wong jai. 'Don't play games with me, you little monkey, or I'll have your guts for garters, understand?'

The Cantonese room-boy cowered in the corner. As they left, Richard winked at the lad from behind Cameron's back and gave him a warm smile.

龍

The two young Englishmen walked along the dockside of Central District on Hong Kong Island. The sun had only just dipped below the western horizon and to the north, across the harbour behind the Kowloon Mountains, a beautiful orange glow lit the sky.

Richard looked about at the flurry of activity all around. Chinese coolies struggled with bags of rice being dumped onto their backs by crewmen from a barge, while sampans loaded and unloaded their cargoes of passengers travelling between Hong Kong Island and the Kowloon Peninsula. From all sides came the sounds of industry, people yelling as they bought and sold. Boat engines stopping and starting. A motor car, its horn honking, threaded its way through the mass of humanity surrounding it.

But above all, Richard's senses registered the smells. Perfumes, food aromas, diesel oil, sewage, rotten vegetables, fresh farm produce, fish; all assailed his nostrils as he strolled through the evening with Stewart Cameron.

Earlier, in the heat of the day when his brain had resisted the sensory onslaught he'd fainted, but now, as he allowed it to wash over him he felt a strange sense of elation. It was almost sexual. The warm evening air, the beautiful sunset – his own sweat, which was causing his clothing to cling to his body – were all combining to make him feel vibrantly alive.

Richard's mind went racing back to when he was a child. The same excitement had bubbled within him then as he'd experienced Cairo for the first time. After a wonderful sea voyage from Southampton, he'd arrived in Cairo with his parents and his mother had introduced him to that vast metropolis. It was unlike anything he could have imagined. His senses were overwhelmed as the city and its ancient ways were recorded forever within his memory.

Richard's mother, Elizabeth Ayesha McKenzie, had been the product of a Scottish father and an Egyptian mother, and a woman of rare beauty and refinement. His father had met and married her in Alexandria at the turn of the century.

'Disgusting, isn't it?' Stewart Cameron's voice was filled with loathing.

'I'm sorry?' Richard answered. Stewart's words had broken in on his thoughts like an unwelcome guest.

'Hong Kong,' Stewart continued. 'It's disgusting. Mind you, it's better than Port Said, or bloody Aden.'

'I don't know those places,' Richard muttered as they walked past an old woman who offered him a bowl of steaming hot soup. The smell of it made Richard's mouth water.

'Can't stand the Arabs!' Stewart moaned. 'Filthy people. I'll take a Chine'e any day before an Arab.' He stopped walking and looked at Richard. 'Did you know they eat sheep's eyes?'

'Who?' Richard asked.

'The bloody Arabs!'

'I'm sorry,' Richard mopped his brow with a handkerchief.

'I'm not feeling all that well. Would you mind terribly if I cut short our stroll?'

'Not at all, old man.' Stewart replied. 'Hong Kong does that to you. It takes a bit of getting used to.' He pointed to a large wooden crate on the dockside. 'Sit there for a while and relax. I've got a spot of business to attend to in Central. I'll collect you on the way back if you like. Perhaps you'd like an introduction to the flower boats in North Point, that's where you'll find those beautiful two-legged tigers Higgins was ragging you about. I should only be an hour or so.'

'Don't bother.' Richard sat on the crate feeling the anger rise within him. 'I'll be able to find my way back to the police station. You go on.'

'Are you sure you don't mind?' Stewart looked rather relieved.

'Not at all,' Richard looked at the old woman with the soup.

'Right you are then. I'll head off. I'll see you in the Mess for dinner.' Stewart's tone was one of false apology as he walked off through the crowd.

Richard watched him go, seething inside at Cameron's racist attitude towards the Chinese, and, more particularly, the Arabs. He stood up and dismissed Cameron from his mind. He felt a tingle of excitement run through him. He wanted nothing more than to be alone and explore the docks by himself.

Hong Kong had cast its spell on Richard and it had taken less than one day. His desire to touch and taste everything around him was overpowering. He stretched his arms and breathed in the scented air.

The old soup woman waved at him. Even the action of her hand was unlike anything he was accustomed to in England. She waved, palm downward, like the action of patting a dog, or the head of a small child.

'*Lai ni doh, Dai Loh,*' she coo-ed in the singsong tone of the Cantonese. 'Come this place, Elder Brother.'

Richard went over to the small stall she operated. The old woman gestured for him to sit on a wooden stool in front of a counter and placed a bowl of hot soup in front of him.

'How much?' Richard asked and held some coins up to her.

The old woman held her palms up and shook her hands several times. '*M sai, Dai Loh,*' she said. 'Not necessary, Elder Brother.' She knew how much the foreign devils loved her soup. What was one free bowl if he returned over and over to give her business?

Richard stared at her for a moment, embarrassed, until the smell of the soup became too much for him. He took the small China spoon she offered and ate greedily.

The soup was a revelation to him. He'd never tasted its equal. Beef and vegetables floated in the broth and each mouthful he took was better than the one before, until it was all gone.

The old woman laughed. '*Ho sik ah?*' she said, pointing at the empty bowl. '*Ho sik ah?* Good to eat, eh?' she asked again.

Richard nodded enthusiastically. '*Ho sik,*' he replied. The old woman laughed happily and Richard joined in. '*Ho sik,*' he said again, without the slightest idea of what it meant.

The old woman then produced a teapot and cup. '*Yum cha. Bo lay,*' she sang in high-pitched Cantonese.

'*Bo lay,*' Richard repeated and the woman nodded and grinned.

'Well, well, a fellow Cantonese speaker.'

Richard looked up at the sound of the English voice. An elderly man dressed in a shabby white three-piece suit stood, hands behind him, rocking back and forth on his heels and grinning at Richard. Tufts of white hair sprouted from beneath a grubby white Panama hat perched above a gleeful ruddy complexioned face, which contained the most laughingly mischievous pair of blue eyes Richard had ever seen.

'I only wish I *could* speak the lingo,' Richard said. 'This woman's being ever so nice and I don't even know how to say thank you.'

'*M goi,*' the elderly man answered. 'Make an "mmm" sound as in hum, and quickly add the sound "*goi*". That's Cantonese for thank you. A small thank you.' He took off his hat and sat next to Richard. 'If you want to express a big thank you you must say "*doh jay*".'

'*Nei ho ma 'Effernan Sin Saang*. Are you well, Mr Heffernan', the old woman asked of the elderly Englishman, and placed a bowl of soup in front of him.

'Heffernan,' the man said extending his hand to Richard. 'Quincy Heffernan, scholar, poet, and long-time dweller in the Far East. How do you do?' the old man said as Richard shook his hand.

'Richard Brewster,' Richard smiled. 'Short-time dweller in the Far East. It's my first day here, in fact.'

'Well, you've wasted no time getting into the language. It's good to see an Englishman trying to communicate with the Chinese,' said Heffernan as he tucked into his soup. 'And a rarity, I might add. Are you here on holiday?'

'No fear!' Richard replied. 'I'm here to start a career in the police force.'

'Oh dear,' came the reply and Richard could not help but notice the odd tone in Heffernan's voice.

'Is there something wrong with that?' he asked rather curtly.

'My dear fellow,' Heffernan answered. 'Please, don't misunderstand me, I didn't mean to offend you, but . . .'

'But what?'

Quincy Heffernan placed his soup spoon on the counter and looked Richard in the eye. 'Well,' he began cautiously, 'It's just that some members of the English society in Hong Kong, particularly those in the Colonial Service, look down upon the Chinese and . . .'

'English society in general,' Richard interrupted, 'looks down upon anyone of foreign extraction, Mr Heffernan. It always has done. But that doesn't mean there aren't exceptions to the rule.'

'And you're one of them, I take it?' Heffernan asked.

'My mother was part Arab, Egyptian,' Richard continued. 'She died of a fever during the war. I was only twelve at the time, but I remember all too clearly her being the subject of racist remarks. Especially when my father was not present to protect her.'

'I'm sorry,' Heffernan mumured.

'Don't be,' Richard was silent for a moment. 'My father is a wealthy man, he was able to shield her from most of it.'

But he'd been unable to shield her from himself, Richard thought, remembering vividly the scene in the ballroom at Hallowdene after his father's annual Spring Ball. He'd been ten years old at the time and should have been in bed, but the noise and excitement of the night had drawn him to the doorway of the ballroom after the last noisy guests had departed, just in time to see his father slap his mother across the face and call her a 'bloody wog'. His father had immediately apologised, but the damage had been done, both to his mother and to Richard, for Richard had realised, in that instant, the true shallowness of his father's love.

The quintessential Englishman, Binky Brewster no doubt believed that he loved his wife, but in actuality she was no more to him than a beautiful foreign ornament he'd acquired in North Africa, in much the same way as one might acquire a rare vase or a valuable painting. Richard had recognised that night, despite the tenderness of his years, that the capacity of his father's love could reach no deeper.

'In any event it was ten years ago, Mr Heffernan . . .' He brushed his hair from his eyes and dismissed the subject.

'Call me Quincy, lad,' Heffernan interrupted with a wave of his hand.

'That was ten years ago, Quincy, and I made a decision to never judge a person by race or colour, and I can assure you I will not do so. Neither here in Hong Kong, nor anywhere else,' Richard finished emphatically.

'That makes me doubly happy to make your acquaintance, young Richard Brewster,' Quincy patted his young country-man on the shoulder. 'But I'm afraid it will set you at odds with your contemporaries here in the Colony. Especially some members of the Constabulary.'

'Be that as it may, Sir.' Richard smiled at the old soup woman as she poured him tea. '*Doh jay,*' he said to her and she laughed.

'*M sai doh jay,*' she chuckled and placed a hand over her mouth like a shy girl.

Richard turned to Quincy. 'Did I say something wrong?'

'Not at all, boy.' Heffernan smiled. 'You said a big thank you and she replied courteously, it's not necessary to say a big thank you. You see, when it comes to saying thank you for services such as tea pouring, the little thank you *m goi* is sufficient.'

'Oh, right you are,' Richard nodded and turned to the woman. *'M goi,'* he said clearly.

'Aaai yah!' the old woman gasped. *'Ni goh Ying Gwok yan sik gong Kwang Dung wah, ho ho!'* And pointed at Richard.

'What did she say?' Richard asked turning back to Quincy.

'She said,' Quincy translated, 'this English person knows how to speak Cantonese very good.'

'I only wish I could.'

'Well, you'll find me here every evening at this time, and I'd be only too happy to teach you, providing you pay for the soup.' Quincy Heffernan said affably. 'I always say that anyone coming to live in the Colony should begin Cantonese lessons from day one. Firstly, it's a most enjoyable pastime and secondly, the Chinese will love you for it,' Quincy smiled. 'They'll fall over laughing at your pronunciation, but I can assure you, they'll love you for trying. And of course, if you master it, you'll be afforded great face.'

'Face?' Richard queried.

'Respect. They call it face. Probably the most important single element in Chinese society,' Quincy said between mouthfuls of his soup. 'They hate public embarrassment and if they commit a *faux pas*, they will simply choose to pretend it didn't happen rather than be held up to public ridicule. That gives you the choice of insisting it did happen and making a public announcement of the fact, thereby causing the other person to lose face. Or, you can pretend not to notice, let them off the hook and await the opportunity to voice your real opinion to the person concerned in private.' Quincy finished his soup and went about lighting a cigarette. He puffed gently on it before continuing. 'The same principle applies to achievement. When someone does something good you offer praise publicly, thereby giving them face.' He looked at Richard. 'The same thing occurs in our society, but much more importance is given to it by the Chinese. You'd do well to remember it.'

'I will. Thanks for the advice,' Richard replied. 'Now, about the language lessons, I'd be happy to pay for them.'

Quincy held up his hand. '*M sai bey chin, Dai Loh,*' he replied. 'Literally translated, not necessary pay money, Elder Brother. That's your first lesson.'

'Elder Brother?' Richard queried.

'Yes. It has nothing to do with age really, although it can do, such are the vagaries of the language. *Dai Loh,* meaning Elder Brother, is another way of giving face. The term is used to show deference to any person with a higher station in life. You are about to become a senior police officer, hence, I call you *Dai Loh,* Elder Brother.'

'And what do I call you?' asked Richard.

'*Sin Sang* is the equivalent of Mister and it also means teacher, but it's rather formal. *Pang yau* will suffice,' Quincy held out his hand again. 'It means friend.'

'All right, *pang yau!*' Richard laughed and shook the old man's hand. 'You've got yourself a student.'

龍

The following morning, after a visit to the tailor to be fitted for his uniforms, Richard once again found himself soaking up the atmosphere as he walked up the hundreds of steps that constituted Centre Street. It ran from the Western Docks directly upward into the foothills of Victoria Peak, which towered over the island. It was filled with small shops selling every kind of merchandise and hawkers vending their wares every few feet, much to the anger of the shop owners, whose doorways they blocked.

Richard reached the cross street of Park Road and sat in a small *dai pai dong,* a licensed food stall, and tucked into a bowl of noodles and beef. As he did so, he reflected on the circumstances that had brought him to the Crown Colony of Hong Kong.

When Elizabeth Ayesha McKenzie-Brewster had died, twelve-year-old Richard's life had changed dramatically. He'd gone home to Hallowdene from boarding school for the funeral and had been sent straight back to school the following day. His father had shown no outward signs of grief and had told Richard he was going away to Africa to check on his business interests there and would be gone for six months.

'During my absence, boy,' his father had said to him, 'I want you to reflect upon your character and the weaknesses you've inherited from your mother. You have her beauty, you know? You've got the face of a girl and I want none of that in a Brewster. Upon my death you are to inherit all I own and I'll have no namby-pamby for a son and heir. You will inherit wealth, and with wealth comes power. To wield that power you will need strength of body and mind, something of which your mother had very little. I have instructed your schoolmasters at Banden Hall to toughen you up, and I expect to see the beginnings of a man's man when I return from Africa.'

Richard's schoolmasters had taken old man Brewster, one of their major benefactors, at his word and life at Banden Hall became a living hell. The sensitive boy Elizabeth McKenzie-Brewster had cultivated slowly but surely succumbed to the requirements of harsh school discipline. He played rugby football, mandatory in the winter, and cricket, also mandatory, in the summer and tried to give as good as he got in schoolyard fights, but his heart was never in it. Richard yearned for his mother's love and, faced with the cruel reality of boarding school discipline and the indifference his father displayed at home, he found it best to become ordinary. A face among the crowd. A non-entity, competent in most things but excelling at none.

The year before his mother's death, war had broken out in Europe and dark days of conflict had fallen on England yet again. At first Richard was excited by the tales of battle, but after his mother's death, and as the years dragged on and death touched the lives of all those around him, he became forlorn and introverted. He tried desperately to win his father's affection but nothing he did impressed. He finished school and attended university but was never more than a very average student and eventually his father cut short his education and secured him a commission in the Army.

Military life was nothing more to Richard than a return to boarding school. He hated the back-slapping, moustache twirling, young officer types in his regiment and detested the rules and regulations. He remained in the regiment for three years, his service record anything but distinguished, until finally his Colonel suggested he consider an alternative career.

'A loner!' his father roared. 'That's what your Colonel called you. A loner. He says you're unable to grasp the sense of *esprit de corps* required by an officer! You seem to show no interest in your duties, you've made no friends to speak of, and seem unprepared to accept any form of responsibility.'

Richard had wilted during the fiery confrontation with his father. At first he'd tried to explain that the boredom of army life gave him no desire to aspire towards anything, but his father would not listen.

'You've too much of your mother in you, boy! It's the Far East for you, my lad. I've arranged a commission in the Hong Kong Police. It's your last chance to show me some qualities of leadership! You've got three years to show me you've got what it takes to be a Brewster! We'll see if the Orient can make a bloody man of you! And if it doesn't, by God, don't bother returning to Hallowdene. Nor England for that matter!'

Richard's reflections were interrupted as he suddenly became aware of a small Chinese boy, about six years old, staring at him through a rattan screen.

'*Joh san, Dai Loh,*' the boy said shyly.

'*Joh san, Dai Loh,*' Richard replied politely, realising that the boy had summoned up a great deal of courage to start a conversation.

The boy laughed at Richard's Cantonese and shook his head. 'No, no!' he shrieked. 'You *Dai Loh*, Big Brother,' and pointed at Richard. 'Me *Sai Loh*, Little Brother.'

'You speak English?'

'Yes, of course,' the boy said proudly. 'I speak English number one excellent. All 'a policeman teach me speak.' He came out from behind the screen and sat next to Richard. 'How come you eat Chinese food, *gwai loh*?'

'I like it,' Richard said trying desperately to get the noodles into his mouth using chopsticks. 'And what does *gwai loh* mean?'

'You *gwai loh*,' the boy replied, again pointing a finger at Richard. 'White person. Foreign devil.'

'Ah, I see,' Richard nodded sagely. 'And what does that make you?'

'Me? *Tong yan*,' the boy said proudly. 'Chinese.'

'I thought Chinese were called *Jung Gwok yan*?'

'*Jung Gwok yan*, yes,' the boy said and this time his finger pointed skywards as if to emphasise his point. 'But that is proper word, also you can say *Tong yan*. Issa same fing.'

'Thank you for the information,' Richard said, delighting in the boy's open show of friendliness. 'Do you have a name?'

'You say first,' the boy looked him straight in the eye.

'My name is Richard.'

'Lichard,' the boy murmured as he considered the information. 'Lichard,' he said again and poked his finger into Richard's chest. 'You Lichard. I am called Kwan. Kwan Man Hop.'

'I'm pleased to meet you, Kwan. You are my first Chinese *pang yau*,' Richard extended his hand and the boy shook it gravely.

'*Pang yau*. Friend,' the boy nodded, but before he could speak again he was distracted by shouting and screaming in the street.

Richard turned and saw four young Chinese men wearing red headbands drag an Indian shopkeeper from his shop into the street. Three of the men held the Indian on the ground, and quick as a flash the other Chinese cut the shopkeeper's fingers off with a meat cleaver.

Richard stood up horrified, but before he could move Kwan pushed him back onto his seat.

'Not your *si gon*,' the boy said urgently, mixing English and Cantonese. 'Not your concern!'

'Good God,' Richard whispered. He watched the four Chinese assailants run off down the stepped street, as several Indian women ran from the man's shop and began screaming and wailing.

'You no go to him,' little Kwan shouted. 'Not your *si gon*, *Dai Loh*.'

Richard watched as one of the women wrapped a towel around the man's bleeding hand. The other women helped him to his feet and ushered him back inside the shop. The dozens of Chinese in the street, who had witnessed the assault, immediately resumed their business as if nothing had happened.

Richard, physically sickened by the violence he'd seen, could only stare at the boy. 'What on earth was that all about?' he finally managed to stammer.

'*Hung loh*,' the boy replied. 'Red brothers. They from the *Man Shing Tong*. Do you know what is *Hung Mun*?' Richard shook his head. '*Hung Mun* is triad, they very dangerous. You go near to them, *Dai Loh*, they chop you,' Little Kwan made a chopping motion with his hand. 'Kill you. You understand?'

A female voice shouted from behind the rattan screen and the boy jumped off the stool. 'I must go,' he said and began to leave.

'Goodbye,' Richard called.

The boy stopped and grinned. 'You must say, *Joi kin, pang yau*. Goodbye, friend,' he shouted. 'You come see me again, ah?' and he disappeared.

Richard's eyes returned to the scene of the assault and widened in horror as he watched the only remaining evidence disappear. A skinny, mange-ridden dog consumed the last of the severed fingers and began licking at the pool of blood.

He sat for some time, unable to finish his soup. The joyful excitement he'd felt earlier was replaced by a sickening foreboding. What sort of place had he come to?

CHAPTER TWO

Chang Tse-man hated travelling. He was overweight to the point of obesity and lazy. Ten years of living in the rich man's city of Hong Kong had made him so. He'd left Canton in 1911 not long after Dr Sun Yat-sen had overthrown the Manchus. After serving his time as a Red Pole in the triad known as the Man Shing Tong in several smaller lodges in Kwang Tung Province, he'd been rewarded with the post of *Shan Chu*, or Master, of the Number Two Lodge in Hong Kong.

Tiger Paw Chang, as he was known, because of his obsession with cultivating long fingernails, believed he was born to rule. He'd been a member of the triad since he was a young boy and always dreamed of the day he would be made Master of a Lodge. His awesome fighting skills as a young man had seen him rise quickly through the ranks and his psychotic ability to take human life without the slightest twinge of remorse had made him indispensable to the brotherhood.

Chang had kept his personal life well hidden from the masters he'd served. He was driven by a voice from deep within. Somewhere in his mind there dwelt a devil over which he had no control and when it took command of him he was unable to resist. Had his masters known of his madness he would have achieved little. His sexual proclivity for children was known to very few, and he'd kept his opium addiction a secret until his rise to power was complete. He'd worked diligently as a servant of the brotherhood and carried out his orders with a minimum of fuss always knowing that one day he'd take the reins of power. Then, at forty years of age he'd gained control of the Number Two Lodge, destroyed the Number One Lodge making him supreme ruler of the triad, and then commenced his long slide into the depths of depravity.

Now, as Tiger Paw Chang sat in the back of an ox drawn cart that rocked and rolled its way down a stony path towards the coast, the demon began to whisper in his mind. Why had it been made to suffer this torturous journey? Where was the pipe of opium it so desperately craved? Where was a child to be sucked dry of innocence? Tiger Paw Chang, it screamed and snarled, feed my desires tonight in the village of Hang Hau Tsuen, or you will know my wrath. Your dreams will be filled with the nine horrors of hell!

Lau Fau Shan, on the western extremity of Hong Kong's New Territories, stretched from the Shum Chun River, which forms the border between China and the Colony, south along the shores of Deep Bay at the mouth of the Pearl River. Lau Fau Shan was not a place frequented by law-abiding citizens of Hong Kong. Wild, remote and lawless, it was commonly known as pirate country. Two or three tiny fishing villages including Hang Hau Tsuen, dirty and uninviting, were safe havens to the marauders of the South China Sea.

Pirates don't last long if they don't keep lookouts. The inhabitants of Hang Hau Tsuen were well aware that an ox cart, escorted by a dozen armed men was rumbling down the rocky track towards their village. The flash of a heliograph mirror in the distant hills had forewarned them. Several men who had been lazing under the huge banyan tree in the centre of the tiny town slunk off over the sandy hills to the beach, while others began concealing property better not seen by strangers. A young boy ran off through a pocket of bamboo trees towards the rickety wooden wharf to alert the crews of several junks that it may be high time they put to sea. And women, pirates' women, long used to violence shattering their daily existence, took their babies in arm and stared at the approaching procession with distrustful eyes.

The men of the village relaxed visibly when a yellow banner was unfurled by a man at the head of the procession, but the women shuddered and whispered to each other. They now knew who rode in the ox cart.

'*Aiyah!*' an old woman moaned. '*It is the fat beast, Tiger Paw Chang. He returns to feed on the blood of babies!*'

The mere mention of his name galvanised the women into action. Orders were issued dispatching the younger children into the hills to hide and it was quickly decided to gather the babies together and take them into the sand hills for protection.

'*Shut up!*' There was instant silence as a strapping young man, bare from the waist up, jumped onto a fish crate and glowered at the women. '*You will do nothing!*'

'*But our children . . . ?*' a young woman began to protest.

'*You will do nothing,*' the young man growled and stared the woman down. '*At this moment our Admiral, The One Eyed Woo, he who must be obeyed, is sailing up Deep Bay. He will be here within one hour. Until he arrives you will do nothing!*'

'*Tiger Paw Chang is a defiler of children.*' It was the old woman who muttered ominously.

'*Silence!*' the young man roared. '*You barren hag! You will all listen to me. I am The Young Captain Wong Shik-mei, Captain of the Admiral's Fleet. I alone have authority when the Admiral is gone and I tell you all. You will do nothing!*' The Young Captain Wong stared at the gathered villagers, forcing his will upon them. '*The evil one Chang. He comes to meet with the Admiral, The One Eyed Woo. This meeting is of great importance. It will mean an end to your filthy existence in this place where rats gnaw old bones. It will mean riches for all. It will mean you can go to Hong Kong, the city where rich men eat fat pork. It will mean you can live like mandarins. For now, you will do nothing, except prepare for the banquet in honour of our illustrious guest Tiger Paw Chang and his men of the Man Shing Tong.*'

The Young Captain Wong was no fool. Wise beyond his years, he watched the light of greed in the eyes of the villagers. He knew he need say no more. They would do nothing. They would allow the shit-swallowing dog, Tiger Paw

Chang, to defile their children. The women would fill their vaginas with oil in preparation for their inevitable rape by Chang's entourage and their men would allow it. They would do anything for the promise of escape from their squalid existence.

'*I am the voice of the Admiral, The One Eyed Woo,*' he hissed, holding their gaze for several seconds. '*Tremble and obey!*'

The women, in particular, stared sullenly at The Young Captain Wong, their minds already resigned to the fear and pain they would suffer during the night to come. Rape was no stranger to them. It was always the same when the fleet returned. The pirate crews would drink into the night, laughing uproariously as they divided the spoils of their voyage. Eventually fights would break out and blood would be spilled. The women would be summoned to the inn, the inevitable would take place and when the men had finished, the women would crawl away into the night, the semen of a dozen or more men oozing from their every orifice. Tonight they knew it would be worse. Tiger Paw Chang would be there.

龍

Deep Bay is a misnomer of the very worst kind. Any mariner who didn't know it would assume, because of its name, that it could be navigated with a degree of safety. The exact opposite is the case. Deep Bay is a vast mudbank and to enter it requires a great deal of local knowledge.

The Admiral, The One Eyed Woo, kept his junk well to the west on the Chinese side as he entered Deep Bay. He stood, legs astride, on the poop deck of his motorised junk, *The China Moon*, and set his bow on Black Rock on the Chinese mainland coast. To the west, the last remnants of sunset were fading to blue. To the east, several lights began to flicker on the remote coast of Lau Fau Shan signalling the coming of night.

In the cabin below, three of his men lay dying. He turned, looked up at the main mast and snarled as he saw the machine gun holes in the lanteen sail. The Hong Kong Marine Police, those pig-fucking sons of whores, had caught his fleet off the Sokos Islands as they had attacked a ferry on its way to Macau. The police had been on the ferry. They'd actually been aboard the ferry. With machine guns!

It was only the power of his new American engine that had saved him from certain slaughter. The rest of his fleet had been blown out of the water. Three junks just like that! In the time it takes to light a good cigar! Three junks and sixty men, gone.

Never before had the Admiral seen such firepower. He'd counted six machine guns. They raked the decks of his wooden junks, tearing men and boats to shreds. And on the stern of the ferry, a mounted two-inch naval gun had sent what remained of his fleet to the bottom with a dozen or so well-aimed shots at the waterline.

Such audacity. Such planning. The Admiral could only shake his head in a mixture of loathing and admiration. It was not like the Hong Kong Police to be so clever, or so devious. It could mean only one thing. A new commander. A new foreign devil. He'd bet ten thousand taels of silver on it! A new commander with yet another order to wipe out piracy.

The One Eyed Woo thanked the gods for giving him the foresight to install his new American diesel engine. With its speed of eighteen knots, three times that of any police vessel, he was able to escape into the South China Sea.

'*Go and fuck your mother's smelly cunt!*' The One Eyed Woo roared as he looked back over the Pearl River Estuary. '*I hope your mother's breasts give forth green slime!*' He smashed his fist against the poop rail.

The Admiral lit a Portuguese cigar and turned his gaze towards the Hong Kong Coast. He sighed and the anger ebbed from his system. Civilisation was catching up to him. Soon he would have to move his hideout from Lau Fau Shan. The New Territories was becoming infested with post offices and police stations. Towns were being built all over the place. Before long people would spill over the western hills towards his village and they would bring law and order with them.

He would discuss this matter with his second in command, The Young Captain Wong. They would have to leave British soil. The fact was inescapable. And they would have to do it soon. The China coast to the east of Hong Kong was his best bet. Daiya Wan was a known pirate refuge and he would be welcome there. His reputation in the South China Sea would assure him of that welcome.

His left eye socket began to ache. He removed an egg-shaped ivory eye from the socket and polished it on his sleeve. Many years ago, a woman had taken his eye. A long-nailed tigress protecting her cub had clawed his eye from its socket when he'd attacked a village to the west of Macau. Strangely enough, he'd let her go. He'd stood and watched her run off into the trees, blood oozing down his cheek, shocked by the ferocity of her resistance.

His men had been swarming the village, killing everyone in sight and he'd caught the woman by the hair as she fled past him. She'd screamed and fought him with one arm, while she held her child in the other. Her thumb had torn out his eye, but as he'd roared and raised his knife to slit her throat, the bravery he'd seen in her eyes had stopped him dead in his tracks. For one instant he had witnessed pure courage. He had never seen it since. And that had been twenty-five years ago, at the turn of the century, when the Emperor still sat on the Dragon Throne of China.

The One Eyed Woo puffed on his cigar and sighed. Times were changing.

His mind went back again to earlier days when he'd been the happiest man alive, and piracy had been the easiest of professions. He'd had a beautiful young wife who'd borne him twin sons. She'd died not long after, but his sons were now strong little boys at school in Canton. They would be educated and become rich. They were a part of his future. They would support him in his old age and he would be happy again. But that would be a few years yet.

The Admiral flicked his cigar butt over the side and looked again at the coast. Times were indeed changing. He would definitely talk to The Young Captain Wong about moving their base of operations. But first he would talk with Tiger Paw Chang.

Chang's message, received in Macau, had intrigued him immensely. The great Tiger Paw Chang had offered to travel overland to the wilds of Lau Fau Shan in order to discuss a matter with The One Eyed Woo. It had to mean money. Lots of money.

The Admiral had dropped anchor in the Portuguese colony of Macau two weeks before, several days after his fleet was mauled at the Sokos Islands. There, forty miles to the west of Hong Kong, and out of the jurisdiction of the Hong Kong Police, he'd licked his wounds and brooded on his future, until The Young Captain Wong had arrived with Tiger Paw's message. The Admiral had dispatched The Young Captain Wong to Hong Kong by ferry and tonight's meeting had been arranged.

Black Rock loomed large in the twilight as The Admiral, The One Eyed Woo, altered his course to starboard. The lights of his village, Hang Hau Tsuen, flickered intermittently off the starboard bow. He would soon be home. Within the hour he would be laughing and drinking with the fat pig-fucking, bag of entrails, Tiger Paw Chang.

龍

The smoke of joss sticks mixed with the sweet, sickly smell of burning opium from somewhere below filled the room above the inn in the village of Hang Hau Tsuen, as The Young Captain Wong eased the girl back onto a pile of dirty silk pillows. Below, the drunken singing of the pirate crews was punctuated with laughter and the occasional squeal of a woman's voice.

The Young Captain Wong moved slowly over the breath-less girl. He slid his hands beneath her buttocks and teased the entrance to her gate of jade with his penis, while she tossed her head from side to side in anticipation.

'Stab me, Lord,' she whispered. 'Pierce me with your manroot, Lord Wong.'

The Young Captain Wong watched her eyes open wide as

he moved into her. She reached up and tried to draw him down, but he resisted and withdrew. The girl began to sob and forced her hips up to him and he plunged deeply, embedding his penis to the hilt. The young woman shuddered and cried out in ecstasy.

'*Tell me how much you enjoy it,*' a voice, which was not that of The Young Captain Wong, whispered seductively in her ear.

'Oh, oh, greatly, Lord,' the girl sighed. The opium in her blood was making her mad with joy. She drifted in a cloud of sexual delirium.

'*Tell me of your feelings,*' the voice hissed.

'Oh, oh, Lord,' the girl managed to gasp. '*I am filled with the heavenly shaft of my Lord.*'

'*Do you wish the seed of your Lord to rush into you?*' the voice demanded.

'Yes! Oh yes!' the girl's head thrashed from side to side as her orgasm approached. '*I am dying, Lord! I am dying!*'

'*Yes, you are dying,*' Tiger Paw Chang continued as he placed a dagger on the girl's throat.

'*Enough!*' The Admiral One Eyed Woo reached over and pulled Tiger Paw's hand away from the girl. '*You have had your fun, Chang, let The Young Captain Wong enjoy the girl!*'

Tiger Paw Chang sighed. '*Ah, my dear Admiral, you are too honest and fair for the trade you ply,*' he said, returning the dagger to a sheath strapped to his forearm under his silk sleeve. '*The girl could have left this life under the most perfect of circumstances, writhing, delirious with sexual joy, under a virile young man. True or not true?*'

'*I have indulged you for long enough, Chang,*' the Admiral snarled as he placed his ivory eye in his mouth. He wet it with spittle and put it back into his empty eye socket. '*You requested we meet. You said we could share in a heavenly dream, true or not true?*'

'*True, my Admiral,*' Chang murmured.

'*Is this heavenly dream associated with the fruit of the poppy? Because if it is I warn you, running opium up the Pearl River is too dangerous these days. General Ch'iang Kai-shek is in control of the Army Academy at Whang Po and he hates opium.'*

'*I did not allude to the fruit of the poppy,*' Chang sighed as he watched the young lovers copulate next to him. The girl was moaning incoherently, lost in her opiate dream. He stroked her breasts with his long nails. '*Ah, to be in her mind at this moment would be an experience, true or not true?*'

'*Is it true or not true that you must keep a string tied to the end of your penis, to pull it free from the folds of your fat gut in order to piss?*'

Tiger Paw Chang's eyes flashed with hate momentarily, but he smiled, refusing to rise to the bait. '*Sadly it is true, Elder Brother. It is also true that copulation for me is but a melancholy memory of my youth, but there are other ways to satisfy one's sexual appetite.*'

Like defiling children and babies then slitting their throats, Woo thought. He knew that watching innocents in the throes of death was the only thing that inspired Chang's shriveled penis to ejaculate. '*Such as sucking the pricks of pigs!*' He roared at his own joke momentarily, enjoying the fat man's annoyance, then, just as quickly, his face turned to stone and he cast his good eye upon Chang. '*Do you have, or not have, something to discuss which will bring us great reward in the near future?*'

'*I have.*'

'*Then let us discuss it.*'

'*First a pipe,*' Chang attempted a smile. '*Let us chase the dragon and relax our minds.*'

'*I do not smoke opium, it's a disgusting habit,*' The Admiral said coldly as the girl began to wail again. '*Shut up!*' he roared and thumped her on the forehead with his fist. '*In the name of Tin Hau, Goddess of the Sea,*' he yelled at The Young Captain Wong. '*Ejaculate and shut her up!*'

The Young Captain Wong, with a series of grunts, did exactly as ordered, withdrew and collapsed on top of the girl.

'*The Young Captain has a lance of great proportions, true or not true?*' Tiger Paw Chang giggled. '*Rarely have I seen a shaft so magnificent. He performs like a stallion.*'

'*If my knife were to slit your guts, Fat One,*' the Admiral growled, '*your entrails would spew forth from here to Canton!*'

Chang's eyes glittered with anger at the insult, he placed his palms together in an act of mock obeisance.

'*Forgive my indulgences, Admiral,*' Chang said as he closed his eyes. '*I so longed for a night of pleasure in your beautiful village, but I can see it is time to tell you of my heavenly dream. I call it so because a dream filled with such good fortune and expectation, could only come from the Celestial Kingdom.*' He looked at the pirate's false eye. It never failed to unnerve him. There was an eye painted on the ivory, but the damned ivory rolled freely within the socket and sometimes the painting disappeared and all that was left was a cold, lifeless, stony stare. '*It is a story you will find hard to believe, but I swear on the graves of my ancestors it is true.*'

'*I am listening,*' The One Eyed Woo murmured through clenched teeth as he lit a cigar.

'*Do you know, or not know, of Sun Chung Shan?*'

'*I know! He calls himself Sun Yat-sen. He is a doctor. All China knows him. He is a revolutionary! He had something to do with the fall of the Emperor.*'

'*Something?*' Chang sighed. '*Something, to say the least. Did you know he was dead?*'

'*No, but it is good news. China with no emperor is not China.*'

'*Sun Yat-sen died several months ago in Peking, just after Chinese New Year.*'

'*I am a pirate, Chang,*' The Admiral said. '*I don't need politicians, except to rob them, for they are all rich,*' he grinned, puffing on his cigar. '*It's a pity a few more of them don't fancy an ocean voyage occasionally.*'

'*By all the Gods in the Celestial Kingdom,*' Chang sputtered. '*Do you have, or not have, any knowledge of what has happened in China in the last fifteen years?*'

'*Why should I care what happens in China?*' The Admiral spat. '*I live on the ocean. I heard the Emperor K'ang-hsi*' *and his poor old mother, the dowager Empress Tzu-hsi, died, may they be with their Celestial Ancestors. There was a boy emperor, Pu Yi, I think?'*

'It is important you know some of the facts in order to realise the magnitude of what I am about to tell you. I am talking of riches beyond your imagining,' Chang shook his head in exasperation. It's like talking to a child, he thought.

'Then tell me. And don't confuse me with too many words.'

'Have you heard, or not heard, of the Golden Dragons?'

'Baaah!' the Admiral roared as he spat tobacco leaf from his lip. *'Did you summon me all the way from Macau to listen to a foolish story? A story told by drunken old sailors!'*

'Be patient, Admiral,' Tiger Paw Chang whispered and raised his hand, his long fingernails glittering in the candle-light. *'I tell you it is no old sailor's story. The Golden Dragons exist. True. A man came to me who said he saw one. He actually saw one of the dragons.'*

'In an opium dream, true or not true?'

'Not true, Admiral. I believe he saw a Golden Dragon. I am certain they are in Hong Kong in the hands of foreign devils. I am the only deserving person who knows they exist.'

'What about this man who saw them?'

'Unfortunately he died, several minutes after he told me of his discovery.'

'Ha!' The One Eyed Woo coughed. *'Unfortunately for him! Fortunately for you!'*

'Yes, it would seem so,' Chang smiled. *'Now, please listen to my tale. It is important to us both.'*

'Well, get on with it!'

'Sun Yat-sen, as you know him, was a peasant from Hsiang-shan in the southern province of Kwangtung. As a young man, he joined his brother in Honolulu . . .'

'Where?'

'It is in the Hawaiian Islands...'

'Where?'

'It is of no consequence.'

'Then why say it?'

'He went to Christian schools in Hawaii and learned the ways of foreign devils.'

'Then he was a fool. Christians are fools. They copulate in only one position.'

'That is so, my Admiral.' Tiger Paw Chang was only too aware that he was talking to an idiot, but, he reminded himself, a very dangerous idiot. 'Regarding my story,' Chang continued in a fatherly tone, 'Dr Sun returned to China and the light of revolution found his heart. While the war between China and Japan raged in 1894, he went back to Honolulu and formed certain organisations to strengthen the revolutionary movement and overthrow the Manchus.'

'More triads,' The One Eyed Woo groaned. 'Will no one let the Ming rest in peace?' He puffed heavily on his cigar and blew the smoke into Tiger Paw Chang's face. 'The country is infested with triads. Your society of the Man Shing Tong has been dedicated to restoring the Ming Emperor for three hundred years and where has it got you? And how many other turtle shit societies are there, dedicated to the same offal-eating ideal? This is all beyond my understanding. Speak to me of money!'

'Will you please let me continue?' Chang snapped. He looked at The Admiral's good eye and sighed as he realised he had regained the fool's attention. 'Dr Sun also visited Japan and the United States of America,' Chang maintained a calm tone, 'where he made many influential friendships and huge sums of money were raised by these friends of China. And gold was donated by thousands of Chinese living in foreign lands. The money was easily transferred to Dr Sun via bank accounts, but the gold was a different matter...'

'Why?' The One Eyed Woo interjected.

'Because it came in all forms. Bracelets, earrings, watches, statuettes, plates...' Chang sighed and placed his hand on the Admiral's knee. 'If you want to know the true story of the Golden Dragons, please let me speak. Good or not good?'

'Good,' The Admiral grunted. 'Speak on, but get your child-defiling hand off my knee.'

Chang smiled and removed his hand, but anger seethed

within him. He would love nothing more than to see this pirate scum hacked to pieces by ten thousand knife cuts, but he needed him to hatch his great deception.

'Dr Sun used the money from the foreign banks to fuel his revolution, and eventually, in 1911 at Wuchang on 10 October, that greatest of days, the Manchu government was overthrown. The tenth day of the tenth month on the foreign calendar. The greatest day in the history of China,' Chang placed his palms together. *'I give thanks for that day to all the Gods.'*

'Forget Ten Ten Day,' The Admiral growled. *'Tell me of the dragons!'*

'I will,' Chang growled back. *'But I must tell you the rest of the story. There are unworthy forces in this story you must know of. They all know of the Golden Dragons. And they all search for them!'* Curse you, The One Eyed Woo, he thought. Tiger Paw Chang's temper was at breaking point. *'In order for us to defeat our rivals we must know who they are. Is this not simple logic?'* The fat on Tiger Paw's body quivered as he fought to regain his composure. He took a deep breath and continued.

'A year following the fall of the Manchus, Sun Yat-sen was made president of the new Republic of China with a capital in Nanking. Soon afterwards, however, in order to avoid civil war, he stepped aside in favour of the warlord Yuan Shih-k'ai . . .'

'That semen-drinking runt of a sow's litter!' The Admiral raised his head, his good eye glittered. *'I remember him. He tried to install himself as Emperor. He is the result of a dog copulating with a pig.'*

'He's dead.'

'That's good.'

Chang could only shake his head as he continued. *'Yuan Shih-k'ai outlawed Dr Sun and his party, the Kuomintang and declared he would restore the Dragon Throne. And, you are quite right, declared himself Emperor of China.'*

'Ha!' The One Eyed Woo sneered. *'How could the pus from a boil sit upon the Dragon Throne? But speak again,*

speak again, I am now enjoying your story immensely.'

'Most of the people I have spoken of so far are dead. Now I will speak of people, powerful people, who live. These people still seek the Golden Dragons, therefore they are our adversaries.'

'I am The Admiral, The One Eyed Woo, I fear no one! Speak again, Chang.'

'Sun Yat-sen was in the southern provinces at Canton. He raised an army, the Kuomintang under the leadership of Ch'iang Kai-shek . . .'

'Ah,' The One Eyed Woo stiffened. 'Perhaps I fear him. He is a devil!'

'General Ch'iang Kai-shek led the rebellion in 1916 and soon after, Yuan Shih-k'ai died. Other warlords rose up in the north and controlled Peking, so the Kuomintang Army returned to the southern provinces. Then, two years ago, Dr Sen and General Ch'iang formed an alliance with the Communists and they are now the principal force in China. There are still warlords in the north, but they won't last long.'

'Not against the devil General Ch'iang,' The Admiral laughed. 'Speak again, greatest of storytellers.'

'In 1914, when the Great War started . . .'

'Where was that?'

'Have you never heard of the Great War fought by the foreign nations? It was the biggest war in the history of man,' Chang sighed with disbelief.

'Aaah, yes,' the Admiral nodded wisely. 'I have heard of this war, it was fought by foreign devils, true or not true?'

'True,' Chang sighed again. 'To continue, this war diverted all foreign aid from Sun Yat-sen and he was forced to import his gold from foreign lands.'

'The Golden Dragons?'

'Yes. In 1914, Dr Sun married his second wife, Soong Ching-ling, who was educated in America. She is of the all-powerful Soong family. They are bankers who could hold the world to ransom with their great wealth. Through her family's minions, all the gold held in the four foreign cities was melted down and formed into four statues . . .'

'*The Golden Dragons,*' The Admiral clapped his hands. '*True or not true?*'

'*True!*' Even Chang felt a shiver of excitement run through him at the thought of the Golden Dragons. '*They stand three feet high and are identical except for the eyes. The eyes of each dragon are precious jewels, one has diamonds, one sapphires, another rubies and the fourth has emeralds.*' Chang was aware of the greedy gleam in the Admiral's good eye. '*The stones identify from which city each dragon comes.*'

'*Aaaiyah!*' The Oned Eyed Woo clapped his hands in delight. '*This is a story to rival the Romance of the Three Kingdoms. Which are the cities of the Golden Dragons?*'

'*Honolulu, San Francisco, Tokyo and Sydney.*'

'*Faraway places, true or not true?*' The Admiral shook his head in wonder. '*But go on, Chang, master storyteller.*'

'*The Soong minions arranged for all four dragons to gather in Shanghai, but there was a plot to capture the dragons and so it was decided to send them to Hong Kong, where they would be safer.*' Chang paused and stared at The Admiral, The One Eyed Woo. '*This is the important part of the story, so listen, Admiral.*'

'*Listen? Look at my hands,*' he held them before him. '*They are trembling. How could I not listen!*'

'*The dragons were placed on a junk . . .*'

'*The Silver Cloud,*' The Admiral could not contain himself. '*So the story is true! By the Gods, it is true! It sank in the ocean somewhere between Shanghai and Hong Kong. Exactly where was never known. All hands were lost.*'

'No,' Chang murmured. '*I believe the junk probably made it to Hong Kong, where it was boarded and the Golden Dragons were removed. Its crew would have been murdered and the junk sent to the bottom of the ocean. The dragons were packed in the ammunition boxes my informant was paid to bury in the floor of a godown. He was nightwatchman of the godown and a foreign devil enlisted him to help bury the boxes. He kept the secret for ten years, fearing for his life, but recently he became prey to the milk of the poppy and needed money to feed his desire. He came to me for help.*

He said one box was cracked and curiosity got the better of him. He peered inside and saw the face of a golden dragon with eyes that gleamed like deep red fire.'

Silence reigned in the small room above the inn in the village of Hang Hau Tsuen. Eventually it was The Admiral who spoke.

'*Do you know where the dragons are now?'* he croaked.

'*I believe they are still beneath the floor of the godown waiting to be forgotten. They are safe there.'* Chang nodded. '*Impossible to steal.'*

'*Why do you tell me this?'*

'*I need your assistance because it is impossible for me to get my hands on them while they are on land.'* Chang stared at The Admiral, The One Eyed Woo. '*The godown is fifty yards long. To steal them would mean digging up the whole floor to find them. So I will cause them to be dug up for us. I have a plan to destroy the warehouse in which they are kept. The foreign devils will then be forced to move them. They will have to send them to England, where they can be melted down, transformed into blocks and sold.'*

'*I still don't understand why you're telling me.'*

'*They could not do this in Hong Kong or China. People would find out.'*

'*People like the General Ch'iang Kai-shek?'*

'*And Sun Yat-sen's wife, Soong Ching-ling. Her brother Soong Tsu-wen created the Central Bank of China only last year. He is the main financier of the Kuomintang and the dear friend of Ch'iang Kai-shek.'*

'*They are indeed powerful people,'* The Admiral whispered. '*But I still don't understand why you are telling me, Fat One.'*

Tiger Paw Chang sighed deeply. '*Hong Kong is an island, true or not true?'*

'*Most definitely true. I have sailed around it.'*

'*To remove something from an island you must take it across water, also true?'*

'*True.'*

'*Therefore, if the foreign devils are forced to send the*

Golden Dragons across the ocean to England . . .'

'*Aah!*' The One Eyed Woo exclaimed. '*You need a boat!*'

Chang closed his eyes and tried to eradicate the image of hitting Woo on the head with an axe. He took a deep breath and exhaled slowly. '*Yes,*' he smiled. '*And someone to sail it, who would not be averse to attacking the boat with the Golden Dragons on it and stealing them.*'

'*Then you'll need a pirate, true or not true? Fortunately for you I am the finest pirate in the world!*'

'*You have a brilliant mind, Admiral,*' Chang closed his eyes again. '*Fortunately for me.*'

'*Fortunately for both of us, Elder Brother,*' The Admiral grinned.

CHAPTER THREE

Three months passed, during which Richard Brewster settled into life in the Colony. He felt comfortable living among the Chinese, accepting even the violent sub-culture of the Hung societies which abounded in Hong Kong and which he had yet to understand. There was so much he was determined to learn. His Cantonese classes with Quincy continued every evening with a bowl of soup, and his increasing mastery of the language gave him the ability to communicate, and understand the minds of this intriguing race of people.

He began to think less and less of England and his father. Hallowdene became merely some far off place, a blur in his memory. The throb of Richard's life became the sights, sounds and smells of Hong Kong. He was in a vibrant land where life boiled and bubbled, where people smiled and chatted incessantly as they went about their unceasing business. Richard felt wonderfully alive. On the odd occasion when he did think of his father, he felt a strange sense of satisfaction. Binky Brewster had sent his son to Hong Kong to 'make a bloody man of him', presumably to exercise his superiority as an Englishman. Binky would certainly not approve of his son's growing affection for both the Colony and the Chinese. The thought pleased Richard.

As a sergeant, he'd been assigned twelve men and instructed to carry out beat policing duties in the streets immediately surrounding Central Police Station. It was not particularly difficult work; mostly checking or issuing hawkers' licences, mediating in local disputes, and arresting, or at least moving on, those illegal hawkers complained of by shopkeepers.

At four o'clock on Friday afternoon, Richard addressed his squad of men on the parade square in the centre of the station prior to dismissing them from duty.

Central Station was impressive. It was actually four buildings joined at the corners to create a quadrangle. It was a fort, no less, Richard decided. An enormous edifice, three floors high, built of stone in the Victorian style. On the inside, each of the buildings opened onto a verandah surrounding the parade square. The whole atmosphere was one of military correctness, with signs identifying each of the offices such as the Charge Room, the Armoury, the NCO's Quarters, the Canteen, and so on, which one could enter off the square. And on each side of the square a large naval bell hung motionless. These were the station bells to be rung in times of fire or other emergencies.

Richard inspected his men and issued orders for the morrow, returned their collective salute and watched them turn and march three paces before breaking ranks and going to the barred Station Armoury window, to return the batons issued to them at the start of their shift.

His men were a mixture of Cantonese and Wei Hai Wei, or 'men from Shangtung' as they were known within the ranks. The Cantonese were, of course, recruited locally, but the 'men from Shangtung' were an entirely different breed.

The previous year under direct orders from Inspector-General Wolfe, the head of the police force, two senior officers were sent to Wei Hai Wei in the North China province of Shangtung. They recruited men from the area and gave them preliminary training for entry into the Hong Kong Police. Fifty of the tall, burly northerners entered service and soon proved their worth on the streets. Their formidable presence was an effective deterrent against crime.

One Wei Hai Wei man, in particular, stood tall, even amongst his northern contemporaries. Police Constable Lo Shi-mon was a big Chinese at six feet and two inches, and weighed in at fourteen stone. He had a pleasant disposition and an air of invincibility about him. He was also the first PC Richard had ever encountered, the one he'd asked directions of on the first day he'd arrived in Hong Kong. PC Lo had waited for him to faint, then carried him to Central Police Station and dropped him on Inspector McCraw's rattan sofa.

Richard returned his revolver to the Armoury then entered the Charge Room smiling at the memory of his indecorous first meeting with Inspector McCraw. He'd been the butt of many a joke over the incident. Stewart Cameron had suggested Richard had turned the matter of 'sleeping on the job' into an art form.

He wrote an entry in the Crime & Occurrence Book summarising briefly the mundane events of his day's work, officially signed himself off duty, then made his way hurriedly down the main corridor and began running up the central staircase to his room. He was desperate to be free of responsibility, out of the station, and walking in the warm late afternoon air. The sounds and aromas of Hong Kong delighted him more and more and he couldn't wait for them to assail his senses yet again. He looked at his wristwatch. Thirty minutes would see him ensconced with Quincy Heffernan at old Mrs Leung's soup stall, prattling on in Cantonese.

Richard was becoming quite proficient at the basics of the language. On the several occasions he'd used it in the street, the locals' initial shock at hearing their mother tongue come from the mouth of a foreigner had turned to expressions of delight.

Quincy had been right. Their attitude towards him had changed dramatically the moment he'd spoken their language. Cautious looks had turned to beaming smiles and cheerful Cantonese calls of 'Good morning, Elder Brother' came to his ears in every street.

'I say, Brewster,' Sergeant Stewart Cameron stood at the top of the stairs with another Englishman in a sergeant's uniform. 'I'd like you to meet Terrence Delaney,' he indicated the man with a nod of his head. 'Terrence is stationed here at Central, but he's been on secondment in the New Territories for the past few months.'

'I'm pleased to make your acquaintance, Delaney,' Richard replied and shook the hand Terrence Delaney offered.

'Likewise I'm sure,' Delaney replied in a thick Yorkshire accent. 'Boot name's Terrence, or Sergeant Delaney. I don't go in for the likes of surname calling and sooch, oonless it's on parade square.'

'Right you are. Terrence it is then,' Richard said and let go of Delaney's powerful grip. 'A Yorkshireman if I'm not mistaken?' Richard smiled. 'Whereabouts in Yorkshire?'

'I come from the East,' Delaney replied. 'To seek that which was lost in the West.'

Richard knew full well that Delaney was approaching him with a recognition speech from Masonic law. When he'd taken Delaney's hand he'd felt the pressure of Delaney's thumb on his knuckles. It was the handshake of a Freemason.

'Got your directions about face I think, Terrence,' Richard said. 'You've actually come from the West to the Far East.'

'I made a mistake,' Delaney murmured, and the ghost of a grin crossed his face. 'Your father would have understood.'

Richard was instantly on his guard as the shadow of his father fell squarely between them. 'You know him?'

'Like a broother, you might say,' said the big Yorkshireman and he winked at Richard, signalling the brotherhood was that of the Masonic Lodge.

Richard couldn't help but laugh, Delaney was an engaging character. 'Right you are!' he chuckled. Binky Brewster was a senior official in the Grand Masonic Lodge in London and Richard had no doubt that letters had been written by his father to Delaney, asking him to keep an eye on his only son. 'Do you think you'll find that which was lost in the West?' he asked.

'I already have, lad,' Delaney nodded. 'And it has a friend if ever it needs it, if you oonderstand my meaning.'

'I certainly do, Terrence, and I appreciate it, but I can assure you there is no need for concern.' Richard felt an instant liking for this big man, sensing that Delaney would be no man's spy. Terrence Delaney was offering his personal friend-ship and had no intention of reporting to Binky Brewster.

'That which was lost in the West, has found itself in the East.'

'That's my appraisal of the situation also, Richard. No more need be said to those who might enquire.'

'I'm glad to hear it.'

'What on Earth are you two on about?' Stewart Cameron interjected. 'I can't understand a word you're saying.'

'Never mind, Stewart,' Richard patted him on the arm. 'Now if you two will excuse me, I have a meeting to go to.' He pushed past the two men and headed for his room. 'Nice to have met you, Terrence.'

'Are you still coming to the Merchants' Ball tonight, Richard?' Stewart Cameron called out.

'I certainly am, I've got the weekend off. Wouldn't miss it for the world.' Richard yelled back as he entered his room and began throwing off his uniform.

龍

The two men sat side by side on small wooden stools and spoke in Cantonese as they drank their bowls of soup.

'Is your soup good, or not good?'

'My soup is good, Teacher.'

'Today's weather is very good, true or not true?'

'True. Today's weather is very good.'

'This soup is cheap, true or not true?'

'True. This soup is cheap.'

'Do you reside in Central District or Western District?'

'Teacher, I reside in Central district at the police station. I work in Central District and Western district, but my homeland is England. I am an Englishman and I work in Hong Kong as a police officer.'

'What rank do you hold?'

'Excuse me, Teacher. I do not understand.'

'Ha!' Quincy Heffernan exploded. 'Got you at last!' He roared in English and slapped his hand on Richard's knee. 'My word, young Richard Brewster, we'll make an eastern scholar of you yet.'

'What did you ask me?' Richard sighed. 'I couldn't make head nor tail of it.'

'You said you worked in Hong Kong as a police officer and I asked you what rank you hold.' Quincy smiled.

'Say it again?'

'Not today, young Richard. Here endeth the lesson for today, my boy.' Quincy finished the last drop of his soup and pushed the bowl away towards the old soup lady. *'Your soup is very good to eat, Mrs Leung. It is indescribable.'*

'Aaiyah! Mr Heffernan. You speak big words.'

'Did Mrs Leung say "you speak big words"?' Richard asked.

'Yes,' Quincy replied. *'Gong dai wah*, literally means speak big words. It's like saying in English "you are exaggerating" or "you're pulling my leg".' Quincy lit a cigarette and spat tobacco from his lip.

'And you used the phrase, *"mo dak ding"*. What does it mean?' Richard enquired.

Quincy shook his head. 'You've got a damned fine ear for this language, I must say. *Mo dak ding* translates as "no can describe". Indescribable. It's the ultimate Cantonese superlative, if there can be such a thing.'

'So you said her soup was indescribable and she replied that you were a liar, or pulling her leg?'

'Correct!' Quincy exhaled a stream of smoke. 'And that definitely ends today's lesson, all right!' He turned and stared at his young friend. 'Now why don't we converse in our native tongue for ten minutes. How's work?'

'It's fine,' Richard stood up and stretched, then sat on his small stool again. 'It's rather mundane stuff so far, but with all the violence going on in Hong Kong at the moment I don't expect it'll be too long before I'm in the thick of it.'

Quincy blew a smoke ring and poked his cigarette through it. 'These are turbulent times, Richard. Violent times, which you must try to understand. The civil unrest in Hong Kong is being generated from the Central Realms.'

'I'm afraid you've lost me, Quince,' Richard frowned, trying to block out the noise coming at him from all sides as the predominantly Cantonese dock workers went about their business.

'China is where all Hong Kong's problems arise,' Quincy waved his arm expansively. 'Look around you, Richard, and tell me what you see.'

Richard did as he was told and shook his head as he spoke. 'It's not so much what I see as what I hear! Hong Kong has to be the noisiest city in the world,' he answered. 'But I see the Kowloon Mountains, the harbour, boats, shop signs I can't read, and people, lots of very noisy people.'

'Exactly, my boy!' Quincy nodded wisely. 'People. Chinese people. One in four people on the face of this planet is Chinese.'

'So?' Richard shrugged.

Old Mrs Leung placed an ashtray in front of Quincy and he stubbed out his cigarette. 'They are one of the oldest civilised races of people still intact. They go back over three thousand years. The Chinese had grand palaces, art, literature, theatre, a postal system and whatever else you'd care to name, while our ancestors were still living in caves and mud huts.'

'I still don't get the point,' Richard said apologetically. 'What's that got to do with civil unrest?'

'They call their country *Jung Gwok*, that means Central Realms, or Middle Kingdom. They consider themselves to be at the centre of the universe and anyone from outside their borders is a barbarian. A foreign, second class form of human being,' Quincy sipped his tea and lit another cigarette. 'Without boring you with three thousand years of history, picture this,' he blew another smoke ring and watched it slowly disappear. 'In the centre of Peking there is a place called the Forbidden City. In that city sits the Dragon Throne and on it, for thirty centuries, sat the Emperor of China, the Son of Heaven on Earth. Those thirty centuries of totalitarian rule came to an end nearly fifteen years ago, with the overthrowing of the much hated Manchu Dynasty. Dr Sun Yat-sen declared the country a Republic in 1912 and set up a government in Nanking. The Chinese people are now confronted with the bewildering prospect of democracy, or perhaps Communism. The Marxist theories appeal to the lower classes and many of China's intellectuals. And the Soviet Union is making damn sure the groundswell of appeal is fuelled,' Quincy sighed and shook his head. 'The people of China are being bombarded with political ideology in all its shapes and forms. Liberalism, Trotskyism, Confucianism, Marxism, Leninism, Nationalism, Capitalism and every other "ism" you can think of, their heads are spinning. It is anathema to the average Chinese. They've been told what to do for three thousand years and now they have to figure things out for themselves.'

'And they're not doing too good a job of it from what I can gather,' Richard said as he poured them both more tea. 'The Communists and the Kuomintang are at each other's throats one minute and then partners the next, according to the press.'

'Give them time, boy,' Quincy chuckled. 'They are a clever race of people. Eventually order will be restored in China and then look out. They'll scratch and claw their way into the twentieth century and by God, they'll become a force to be reckoned with. A modern, unified China with a strong central government, be it communist or democratic, and a modern well-equipped army, will once again assert itself as the centre of the universe. Until that time arrives, there'll be civil unrest and bloodshed and that civil unrest will continue to spill into Hong Kong.' Quincy laughed out loud. 'There, I'm finally back to my point.'

'Which is?' Richard asked with a grin.

'Hong Kong is, as far as the Chinese are concerned, a foreign enclave full of *gwai lohs*, just like the city of Shanghai in the north. They despise all foreigners, and by foreigners they mean other Chinese as well! Any Chinese unlucky enough not to have been born along the Yellow River, in fact. They particularly despise Westerners and, despite their internal strife, if they can cause foreigners trouble, they'll do so with great delight. Hence, the union trouble being stirred up here at the moment. Especially the Seamen's Union.'

'But Hong Kong is different, surely?' Richard interrupted. 'I know the New Territories is only under lease to Britain for ninety-nine years from 1898, but the island itself and the Kowloon Peninsula is actually British soil, it was ceded to Britain in perpetuity by the Treaty of Nanking in 1842.'

'Don't fool yourself, young Sergeant Brewster,' Quincy stood up. 'Hong Kong will be British only for as long as China is divided by political turmoil. Look at our own country's history. England was under French rule for three hundred years on and off, but is it now? No! Of course it isn't. No country gives its soil away unless it is forced to, and as soon as it has the military might to take it back, it inevitably does.' Quincy placed his crumpled Panama hat on his head and straightened his even more crumpled suit coat. 'That's a lesson in human nature, dear boy, and my final lesson to you for this evening. Your thirst for knowledge is utterly exhausting.'

You're right there, Richard thought. He seemed, lately, to be overwhelmed with a thirst for knowledge. His mind was opening up to all sorts of possibilities and it was his arrival in Hong Kong that had started it all. His years of repression in school, the army, and at home, had combined to squash the natural curiosity he'd inherited from his mother. He'd done as he was told all his life, but now, for the first time he was realising his individuality. He was in a different world and free of constraint. He was determined to seize the day and make it his own, and to do that he needed knowledge.

'I'm sorry, Quincy,' Richard said as he stood up. 'There's just so much I need to know.'

'All in good time, Richard,' Quincy replied and extended his hand. 'I'm always here at Mrs Leung's. Until tomorrow, eh?'

'Until tomorrow,' Richard smiled and shook the older man's hand. '*Joi kin pang yau.*'

'*Joi kin,* young Richard Brewster.'

Richard sat and watched the old scholar walk off through the crush of Chinese humanity on the dockside street. In his hat and fading white suit he was a sight to behold and a fond smile spread across Richard's face.

'*Ho ho yan, hai m hai ah?*'

'*True, Mrs Leung,*' Richard said softly, then more to himself, 'he's a very good man indeed.'

龍

The strains of a Strauss waltz floated magnificently on the balmy evening air as Richard and Stewart Cameron walked up the fashionable Peak Road on their way to the Merchant Ball.

'John Merchant is a well-to-do businessman in Hong Kong. Damned well-to-do,' Stewart said as they neared the massive gates of the Merchant mansion. 'A public servant to start off with, he's risen to the top of Colonial society by simply amassing more money than any of his English middle class contemporaries. How he did it nobody actually knows. Rumours abound that he was in league with the Hong merchants of Canton and was rewarded for the favourable considerations he'd shown to them as a Government employee.'

'Rewarded?' Richard raised an eyebrow.

'Yes,' Cameron chuckled mirthlessly. 'That's how it was described to me, but considering that he was in the Customs Service, the Port Authority, the Import Quota Bureau, and the Office of Public Works to name but a few departments, you can put on that any connotation you like. Anyway, he retired from Government service fifteen years ago, set up an import export business and Bob's your uncle.'

'A well-respected Hong Kong businessman,' Richard offered.

'No names, no pack drill,' Stewart tapped his nose with a forefinger. 'It's not a good idea to speculate out loud about our dear old John Merchant. He's fifty-five and happily ensconced at the top of the social ladder. Prominent member of both the Hong Kong Club and the Jockey Club, owner of the largest private yacht in the harbour, Vice-Commodore of the Hong Kong Yacht Club, what more can one say? His business ventures are diverse and well managed, giving him time to spend hob-nobbing and throwing lavish parties to flaunt his obvious wealth.'

'Certainly obvious, if these gates are anything to go by,'

Richard said as they passed through the two enormous wrought-iron gates emblazoned with the crest of the Merchant Company.

'Wait until you see the house. Objets d'art fill the bloody place and he delights in bringing them to your attention. But the jewel in his crown,' Stewart winked lasciviously, 'is undoubtedly Elanora, his beautiful young Eurasian wife.'

'Really?' Richard enquired politely. The scenario was sounding suspiciously familiar, he thought, as the image of his mother and Hallowdene returned. Elizabeth Ayesha McKenzie had been the pride of Binky Brewster's collection. He was beginning to dread the evening to come.

'Thirty years his junior, old boy.' Stewart prattled on as they walked the drive to the house. 'Elanora Maria Escaravelho Merchant is a Eurasian of incomparable beauty. She was born in Macau, the only child of Don Rodrigo Escaravelho, a Portuguese nobleman, who amassed a fortune trading opium for silver up the Pearl River, and Tang Siu Ling, youngest daughter of the wealthy Tang Kwan-hui, a Hong merchant in Canton. You may have heard of him?'

'Can't say I have,' Richard replied, uninterested.

'Elanora was educated in Europe and groomed by an iron-fisted aunt for an arranged marriage. Apparently, Merchant first laid eyes on her in Macau and was instantly smitten. She was fourteen years old,' Cameron smirked. 'That was the same day she'd sailed for Portugal to complete her education. For four years, until she returned to Macau, Merchant ruthlessly acquired property and business interests over there, then through influential friends, he approached the House of Escaravelho for Elanora's hand.'

'A determined man,' Richard muttered.

'Oh, yes. The story has it, Don Rodrigo was not thrilled with the idea of his only daughter marrying an Englishman,' Stewart chuckled, 'but after having it pointed out that John Merchant was in a position to ruin him, he consented to the union. Elanora Maria Escaravelho cost John Merchant a small fortune.'

The orchestra broke into Strauss' *Tales of the Vienna*

Woods as Richard and Stewart reached the entrance to Merchant House. Groups of people had made their way outdoors to take advantage of the warm night air and Chinese lanterns strung throughout the immaculate front gardens gave the scene a fairytale aspect. As the young sergeants reached the stairs leading to the ornate front doors, they handed their entree cards to one of the two liveried footmen who were busy opening car and carriage doors and assisting the cream of Hong Kong society from their vehicles.

Four enormous bronze elephants greeted the men as they entered the foyer of John Merchant's palatial residence. The four behemoths stood tail to tail as the central piece of a fountain. Water sprayed from their upraised trunks and cascaded over their backs to collect in a marble dish, overflowing into a pond of exotic fish. To Richard, the statue was preposterously ostentatious.

The two men were greeted by a large Indian Sikh resplendent in a turban. 'Good evening, sahibs, the ballroom is on the left of the main hall directly ahead,' the Indian purred and indicated vaguely with his outstretched arm.

'A spot too ornate for me, Brewster,' Stewart Cameron whispered in Richard's ear. 'But what the deuce, eh? Old Merchant puts on a show second to none.'

Richard didn't answer. He was appalled at the garish show of wealth John Merchant's house represented, but at the same time was intrigued with the man and looked forward to observing him first hand. He didn't have to wait long.

'Good evening, Sergeant Cameron,' a small, dapper man called as he came to meet them. 'Glad you could find time to attend my soiree.' He took Stewart's hand and shook it a little over-zealously for Richard's liking.

'Hardly a soiree by my standards, Sir.' Stewart gave a sycophantic chuckle.

'And this must be the newly arrived Mr Brewster,' the little man smiled and extended his hand. Richard took it and felt as if his shoulder was being relocated. 'I must say I've been looking forward to meeting the son of Binky Brewster. John Merchant's the name, pleased to meet you, Sir.'

'And I'm glad to make your acquaintance at long last, Mr Merchant.' Richard replied as he suffered the absurdly vigorous handshake.

'John! Call me John,' Merchant said and broke off the handshake to point towards the main ballroom. 'In you go, you two. I'll catch up with you later, Mr Brewster, and we'll get to know each other, eh? Lady Grayson!' Merchant called and took off in the direction of a man and woman entering the foyer.

'He's a rather good sort, old Merchant, nouveau riche most definitely, but,' Stewart winked at Richard, and steered him by the arm towards the ballroom, 'play your cards right and you'll do very well, if you get my drift.'

They entered the grand ballroom and Richard was again shocked by the opulence. Three massive chandeliers domi-nated the room, each ten feet in diameter and set forty feet apart. A quick calculation suggested the ballroom was fifty yards long. Men in formal attire and women in the latest French fashions swirled around the room as the orchestra, with at least twenty members, played the beautiful Viennese music. Chinese waiters with trays of champagne and hors d'oeuvres moved skilfully among the guests and an air of gaiety filled the room.

'Stewart, darling!' a pretty young woman gasped. Richard watched as his companion was whisked away into the mael-strom of dancers. He took a glass of champagne and found himself a secluded spot near one of the many sets of French windows leading into the gardens. He smoothed the front of his double-breasted dinner jacket and inched an index finger into the collar of his winged dress shirt. Bow-ties and Hong Kong weather, he decided, definitely weren't meant for each other.

It was obvious that this gathering was a who's who of Hong Kong society. Among the honoured guests were Charles McIlvaine Messer, Colonial Treasurer and former head of the Police Force, Edward Dudley Corscaden Wolfe, the current head of the Force with the newly created title of Inspector-General, and a host of senior government adminis-trative officers, registrars, directors and magistrates.

From among the private sector there were bankers, lawyers, company officers, brokers, and even a Chinese mandarin in full regalia with a peacock feather sprouting from his hat, who was in deep and animated conversation with Charles Higgins.

The women present were a sight to behold. Richard lost count of the beautiful ladies in the latest 'flapper' styles, which to Richard's way of thinking was the most sensible female clothing he'd ever seen. The young 'Charleston' girls as they were known, after the latest American dance craze, had taken to wearing their dresses above the knee, during daylight hours at least, and their formal evening wear was merely an extension of the hemline to above ankle length. Sad about the breasts though, Richard mused. Why do they insist on flattening them? Probably the fashion designer had small breasts and created the designs to flatten all the other women in the world so she wouldn't be seen as different. Vanity, thy name is woman. He shook his head and smiled.

'Ah, Richard. Enjoying the ball, are we?' There was no mistaking the sensual purr.

'Good evening, Sir,' he answered as he turned to the smiling face of Charles Higgins. 'I must say, Sir, I'm impressed with Mr Merchant's residence, not to mention the array of beautiful ladies gracing it,' he lied. Richard, despite the beautiful ladies, was not enjoying himself at all.

'Yairs, yairs,' Higgins drawled. 'A handsome young man like you could run riot in a place like this, I dare say, but enough of that.' Higgins concluded by taking Richard's champagne and sipping it. 'Aaah!' He grimaced. 'Champagne, never could stand the stuff! Can't stand the French either for that matter.' He gave back the glass and disappeared.

The evening dragged on for Richard. His initial excitement soon wore off and, after dancing with several rather self-obsessed young women, he found himself once again watching the proceedings from a safe distance. He hated evenings such as this. He'd suffered similar affairs at Hallowdene. Admittedly the surrounds had been more tasteful, he thought with another glance at the garish chandeliers, but the passing parade had been much the same. Normally intelligent people behaving like strutting peacocks, the whole business was so boring and meaningless.

Richard's boredom was, however, shortlived as his eyes fell upon a pretty young woman immediately opposite him across the dance floor. Her red hair was bobbed into the latest style, an Eton crop, and she wore an emerald green evening dress, a simple silk sheath, which failed to conceal a curvaceous body and breasts that refused to be flattened. A single strand of pearls highlighted her throat. She was politely refusing a number of young men asking her to dance.

Richard could not stop staring and eventually she caught him out. He blushed, and her eyes crinkled as the most enchanting smile spread across her face. He felt himself moving towards her, but could not remember giving his feet any such orders.

'May I have the pleasure of this dance,' he heard himself ask.

'You certainly may,' the young woman replied in a lilting Irish accent and she extended her naked arms in expectation.

The next moment, eyes locked, they were swept away on the magic of the music. They circled the room several times without ever breaking eye contact and when the music finished, both were reluctant to let go of the moment.

Richard was suddenly aware that people were staring at them and smiling behind their hands. 'My name is Richard Brewster,' he stammered as the music struck up again. 'From England.'

'Caitlin Maclain, from Ireland,' the girl said, as they began to dance again and were once more lost in each other's eyes.

The music stopped and several speeches were made from the bandstand. Richard and Caitlin stood side by side listening politely as several heavily be-medalled old men in turn praised John Merchant to the skies, and offered the opinion that Hong Kong would be much the less without him. They reminded Richard of the speeches made at Hallowdene by his father's sycophantic minions whenever balls or parties were thrown. When he could suffer it no more, he offered Caitlin his arm and escorted her out through French windows onto a large patio, which looked down over the gardens.

They stood in silence for several minutes, entranced by their fairytale surroundings. The Chinese lanterns all through the gardens bobbed and weaved in the soft evening breeze while the glow from the lights in the harbour below lit up the night sky.

Caitlin made a thorough appraisal of the young man from the corner of her eye as they took in the view. Dark-eyed, olive-skinned and devilishly good-looking, a lock of dark hair hung lazily across his brow and, despite being brushed away several times, it insisted upon returning insolently to its unruly position. Somewhere between five feet ten and six feet in height, the young man had a charismatic air about him, but at the same time she sensed a shyness that was most appealing.

'So, um . . .' Richard began awkwardly, 'you're from, um, . . . Ireland, Miss Maclain?'

'Yes,' Caitlin replied. 'From Kinsale. It's a fishing port in the south of Ireland.'

'Holidaying in Hong Kong, no doubt?'

'No, I'm employed here. I'm governess to Mr Merchant's young son, James.'

'Well!' Richard was unable to disguise his delight. 'A permanent resident! Well, what do you know about that!'

'And what do you do?'

Richard attempted to maintain his smile, but the girl's proximity was unnerving him. She was standing very close and had placed her hand upon his forearm when she'd voiced her question. And there was the most alluring scent of frangipani blossom about her. 'I've been here about six months. I'm a sergeant in the police force, but I'll be an inspector soon.'

'Really?' Caitlin raised an eyebrow in a deliberate attempt to unnerve him even further.

'Well, what I mean is, I . . .'

'You don't have to explain your ambitious nature to me,' she interrupted, provoking his embarrassment even further. 'I think it's good for a man to be ambitious.'

'I'm not ambitious,' Richard said awkwardly. 'I mean I am ambitious, but well, not ambitious in the way you mean. My promotion to inspector is a contractual thing, that's all. According to the Colonial Regulations . . .'

'I'm sorry, Sergeant,' Caitlin apologised. 'I was teasing you. Do forgive me?'

'Oh, yes,' Richard stammered. 'Of course.' Her eyes were the deepest emerald green and the warmth emanating from her smile was irresistible.

Richard's conversational experience with girls was limited. He was not a virgin, he'd lost that claim on a weekend trip to Paris whilst serving in the army, and further trips had ensured his physical knowledge of love-making had developed rapidly. However, his Paris experiences had required little conversation, and had been in muffled schoolboy French. The women in his life to date with whom he'd been required to converse had all been aristocratic young 'things' and he'd found the art of such social conversation insufferably boring.

Caitlin Maclain was another kettle of fish. She seemed, to him, a worldly and mature young woman and devastatingly attractive. Richard Brewster was smitten for the first time in his life and he knew he must make a date to see her again as soon as possible.

'Miss Maclain . . .'

'Call me Caitlin, most people do.'

'Er, yes, Caitlin.' He was beginning to feel a little foolish. 'Very good. Well, Caitlin, I was wondering if . . .?'

'I see you two have met.' Higgins was suddenly standing immediately behind them.

'Oh, yes, Sir!' Richard replied, startled by his superior's appearance. 'Miss Maclain,' he continued, 'I'd like you to meet my . . .'

'We're old friends, Caitlin and I,' Higgins interrupted.

'Really, Sir?' Richard was unable to hide his surprise.

'Oh, yes,' Higgins kissed Caitlin's hand. 'I'm a regular visitor here at Merchant House,' he chuckled. 'We even have a secret, don't we, my dear?'

'You promised you'd never tell a living soul, Mr Higgins.' Caitlin's eyes twinkled.

'I think the secret will be safe with Sergeant Brewster,' Higgins grinned, warming to the game. 'You see, Richard, both Miss Maclain and I know that Mr Merchant's young son James is a right little prat!'

'Now, Superintendent,' Caitlin chided. 'You go too far. I merely said that the boy was inclined to be spirited. He's only six years old. You're a terrible man and that you are!'

Higgins laughed and took her hand in both of his. 'I'm sure you're right, my dear, just as I'm sure you're upset that I've intruded upon your privacy. However,' he raised his hand interrupting Caitlin as she began to protest, 'I have police business to discuss with my young sergeant that cannot wait.'

'I understand, Superintendent,' Caitlin replied apologetically. 'I'll leave you two alone.'

'Tut, tut, tut,' Higgins raised his hand once more. 'First things, first,' he turned to his junior officer. 'Sergeant?'

'Yes, Sir?' Richard answered.

'So you can't accuse me of destroying your private life, would you care to ask Miss Maclain to elevenses on Sunday?'

'Well, Sir . . .' Richard blushed. 'If the truth be known I was just about . . .'

'Very well, I'll ask her for you,' Higgins turned to her. 'Miss Maclain, would you care to take tea with my handsome young sergeant on Sunday morning?'

Caitlin couldn't help but laugh. 'Sir,' she replied in mock aristocratic manner, 'If your handsome young sergeant would call for me on Sunday morning at eleven o'clock, I'd be only too delighted to take tea with him.'

'Very well, then,' Higgins winked at her. 'It's settled. Sergeant Brewster?'

'Sir!' Richard stood to attention. If they were playing a game, he was prepared to join in.

'Have you anything to say?'

'No, Sir. Apart from the fact that I'm looking forward to Sunday morning very much, Sir!'

'Now, my dear,' Higgins said kindly. 'Would you excuse us?'

'Most certainly,' Caitlin replied and curtsied. 'Good evening to you, Superintendent Higgins.' She smiled genuinely at Richard. 'Until Sunday, Sergeant Brewster.' She turned gracefully on her heel and was gone.

'What is it, Sir?'

'Mmmh?' Higgins took a cigar from a gold case and clipped the end off it. 'Too late to go into it now, but we've got a big problem. So I want you out of here immediately and home to bed.'

'Certainly, Sir.'

'All hands on deck, my office, six in the morning.'

'May I ask what the problem is, Sir?'

Higgins lit his cigar and puffed on it for several seconds, before looking at Richard. 'This Colony is a violent place, Richard, and those who serve in its police force must be tough and uncompromising.' Richard didn't reply as Higgins puffed furiously on his cigar. 'I've received information that there's to be a riot tomorrow morning on the Western Docks.'

'A riot? Over what?'

'That's not the point, really,' Higgins purred. 'What you'll be confronted with tomorrow is a politically-motivated act.' He took several paces, then stopped and crossed his arms. 'Since the bloody Ching dynasty collapsed in 1911, the Chinese have been at each others' throats politically. This creates a recurring problem for the Colony. The struggle for psychological dominance between the Communists on the one hand, and the bloody Kuomintang on the other.' Higgins looked about for eavesdroppers and came closer to Richard. 'Currently the Kuomintang rule the roost and the leader of this rabble, dear old Generalissimo Ch'iang Kai-shek, needs to impress the population of China, so he starts sabre-rattling and cursing the British imperialists! That's us, by the way.'

'I think I follow you, Sir,' Richard nodded. 'General Ch'iang gets his supporters in Hong Kong to cause trouble and tells the Chinese that it's all the fault of the British.'

'In a nutshell, Richard,' Higgins purred. 'Then he calls for a full scale boycott of British goods, etcetera, and the only real victims in the whole drama are inevitably Hong Kong's working class, whom he's supposedly trying to help!'

'An intriguing man by the sound of it, Sir.'

'Intriguing?' Higgins sneered. 'Strange more like!' He peered at Richard as if he were observing an alien being. 'Peculiar to say the least, in my opinion. In fact, bizarre is probably a better adjective. Mind you, he's bloody Chinese.'

'Yes, Sir,' Richard muttered stiffly.

Higgins took a few steps away and then turned to stare at his subordinate. 'You realise of course, dear boy, that the Chinese detest foreigners?' Richard could only nod as Higgins built up steam. 'And more to the point,' he continued, 'they utterly loathe we English! They think they're so bloody superior to everyone and yet they can't even get their domestic affairs in order. Never could and never will! Personally, I'm all for a bit more gunboat diplomacy.' He paused momentarily, looked about, then lowered his voice to continue. 'I'm of the opinion that the British Navy should shoot the bejesus out of the Chinese and then let our army swarm over their precious continent and claim the whole bloody lot as part of His Majesty's dominions!' He puffed on his cigar and blew the smoke into Richard's face. 'That'd shut 'em up once and for all! And furthermore, tomorrow morning, if any of those bloody unionists or their dear little triad society friends so much as spit on the footpath I'll order them squashed like ants!'

'Yes, Sir,' was all Richard could think of replying.

'Well, you'd better be running along, Brewster. More of all this tomorrow.'

'I'd, er, better get off home, Sir,' Richard muttered glad to escape Higgins' tirade.

龍

In Sai Ying Poon, the dockside area of western Hong Kong Island, a tall black-clad figure hurried down an alleyway. He followed his moonlight shadow as it scurried furtively between the warehouses. The streets were silent. The workers retired. Rats haunted the silent narrow lanes and watchful eyes, through bamboo shutters, noted all. All but the passing of this silent stranger.

A cat screeched in the night and the tall figure stopped and glanced about before disappearing through a narrow gap between two godowns, as the warehouses were known. Cockroaches crunched beneath his bare feet and the stink of raw sewage assailed his nostrils as he made his way between the two buildings.

Reaching up, he pulled his body through a narrow window, night things brushing his face and arms. He dropped silently to the warehouse floor and crouched, motionless, allowing his eyes to adjust to the soft red light of the moon lanterns hanging twenty feet above his head. He waited until his breathing slowed, then moved stealthily between the rows of produce searching for his next objective.

The trapdoor was beneath a wooden barrel in the north-east corner of the godown, exactly as his master had described. Again he waited, this time a full two minutes, before quietly moving the barrel and lifting the door. He dropped through it and adopted his fighting crouch. Adrenalin surged through his tensed muscles as his senses sought out any possible foe.

Before him, a six feet by four feet tunnel ran through solid rock. He peered through eerie yellow light and saw the steel doorway, not thirty feet away. He approached it warily and knocked five times as his Master had instructed.

An eye appeared at a peephole in the steel door and a voice whispered to him in Cantonese:

'Where were you born?'

'Beneath the peach tree,' the black clad stranger murmured.

'Have you died yet?'

'I have died once.'

'How did you die?'

'By being covered with a yellow quilt.'

'When were you born?'

'On the twenty-fifth day, seventh moon, of the Kap Yan year.'
'Where do you live?'
'On Five Finger Mountain. At the topmost summit. In the house which is the third from right and left,' the stranger said and bowed deeply.

The steel door swung open to reveal the whisperer. He was a big man wearing a black robe and a red headband, from which a silken veil hung, masking his identity. Around his neck hung a red scarf and a white belt adorned his middle. In his left hand he held a large curved sword, but it was his feet that drew attention. On his right foot he wore a normal slipper-like shoe, common among the Cantonese working class, but on his left foot was a straw sandal sole, strapped on with grass twine. He was a senior official of the Man Shing Tong, the most powerful of the Hong Kong's secret societies. It reigned supreme on the Western waterfront.

'Why do you seek out the Lodge of the Man Shing Tong?' the official asked.

'I must speak with your Honoured Master,' the stranger replied. 'I am of the Lodge of the Man Yee On and bear words from my Honourable Master to yours.'

Outwardly the official remained calm, but inside he was seething with anger. How had this messenger from the lowly Man Yee On society got past his outer sentries? The fools! The official was the Red Pole of his society, responsible for its security and he would lose great face in front of his Master. His sentries would pay for their lack of observation.

'We respect the Man Yee On as a society dedicated to the same goals as the Man Shing Tong,' the official murmured. 'You are welcome. My Master will give you audience.'

The stranger bowed and entered the inner chamber of the Lodge. It was a cavern hewn in the rock beneath the streets of Hong Kong Island. He moved between the rows of men dressed in black robes, their faces also veiled, and approached the altar at the far end of the room. The place was thick with the smoke of burning incense and the Master of the Lodge, an obese individual with long fingernails, sat amongst it with a silken veil hiding his face.

'*You honour our Lodge with your presence, Little Brother.*' The Master's voice was deep. '*You are to be congratulated for your stealth and courage in avoiding our watchers. You must be the Red Pole of your Lodge, is this true or not true?*'

'*It is true, Honoured Master,*' the stranger replied. '*I am the 426, the Red Pole of my Lodge.*'

'*You are not Cantonese, Little Brother,*' the Master stood up and adjusted the red robe which only he, as head of the society, could wear. '*You are far too tall. You came from where to Hong Kong?*'

'*I came from the far north, Master. I am from Wei Hai Wei.*'

'*Ah, a man from Shantung, true or not true?*'

'*True, Master.*'

'*Then does it not follow that, as a man from Shantung, you are also a yellow running dog?*' the Master barked.

'*Honourable Master . . .*'

'*You are a lackey of the British Imperialists! You are a despised member of the police, true or not true!*'

The stranger remained silent as the assembled members muttered angrily.

'*True or not true?*' the Master snapped again.

'*Honourable Master, the oath I took as a member of the Man Yee On forbids me from answering.*'

'*You show much bravery, dog,*' the Master sat back down. '*But you are a dog nonetheless. The honour of the Lodge of Man Shing Tong forces me to hear you out. What message do you bring?*'

'*My Master wishes you to know that words on the wind have informed him that tomorrow there is to be trouble on the Western Docks.*'

'*Words on the wind, eh?*' the Master sneered. His head moved slowly on his shoulders and all of the members of his Lodge felt his icy stare. '*I know nothing of words on the wind! Nor do I know what the future holds.*' He pointed a long fingernail at the stranger. '*You tell your Master that whatever occurs on the Western Docks is not his concern.*

It is purely the business of the Man Shing Tong and the pathetic Man Yee On should respect this and keep away!'

'Master,' the stranger insisted, 'to ask this of the Man Yee On is impossible. Several of our members are employed in government positions, and their involvement tomorrow will be unavoidable.'

'Ha!' the red robed leader grunted. 'There, you see! You admit that you are police! Yellow running dog Imperialist lackeys! Snivelling curs of the British shit-eaters!'

'Master, the Man Yee On is but one small society dedicated to the restoration of the true family of Ming upon the throne of the China. Since the Manchurian hordes swept down from the north and took the Dragon Throne from Chinese hands over three hundred years ago, all triads have been secretly working to restore the Ming Dynasty. Surely the Man Shing Tong is no different . . .'

'Do not question the ideals of the Man Shing Tong!'

'Master, I had no intention . . .'

'Our society is pure! We have no spawn of rabid dogs in our ranks. Your Man Yee On is full of policemen. Arsehole-licking servants of the British.'

'Master, I beg you. Discussion of tomorrow's events by our two honoured Lodges can only unite us. Things will be made easier for all. I came here to burn the yellow paper of peaceful discussion with the Man Shing Tong . . .'

'Silence!' the head of the Man Shing Tong rose to his feet. 'You will return to your Master and tell him that we will not burn the yellow paper! And we will hold no discussion with the Man Yee On. And furthermore, if anything occurs tomorrow on the docks and your members interfere, we of the Man Shing Tong will rise as one and destroy your Man Yee On triad forever!' A rousing cheer greeted this statement as the tall stranger's shoulders slumped. He turned and walked through the throng of men, who shouted curses at him and his Lodge.

After the stranger had gone, Tiger Paw Chang lifted the veil from his face and growled at his Lodge members to do likewise. He frowned as he inspected his cultivated nails.

He would have to be wary of the Man Yee On as they were all men from Shantung, and although their society was a small one, the members of it were anything but small.

Tiger Paw knew the tall messenger. Lo Shi-mon was the favoured one of Old Kwan, the *Shan Chu* of the Man Yee On Triad. He was also a police constable. A man to be feared, highly skilled in the martial arts. A dangerous adversary.

'Brothers,' Chang snarled. '*Tomorrow will be a day the foreign devils will not forget!*' He'd been waiting for this opportunity for three months. He'd been asked by the Kuomintang to stir up political unrest and blame the British for it and he knew exactly where he would stage the riot. The plan he had masterminded would centre on the suburb containing the warehouse that housed the Golden Dragons. Those in possession of the statues would be forced to move them, and as they did he would observe closely and calculate the exact moment for the crazy pirate, The One Eyed Woo, to steal them.

'Tomorrow,' Chang continued, '*we will do the bidding of the great patriot Ch'iang Kai-shek. He asks our assistance. We will help the Seamen's Union in their struggle against tyranny. I expect all of you to fight valiantly for the honour of our Lodge!*'

'*For the honour of our Lodge,*' his men roared. '*Overthrow the Ch'ing, restore the Ming!*' they yelled. It was the ancient phrase of the original and highly honourable *Hung Mun* triad society.

Tiger Paw Chang smiled. The fact that the Ch'ing Dynasty of the Manchus had been overthrown made the first part of the ancient phrase redundant, but he encouraged his men to observe tradition and keep alive the old rituals. He understood the primitive power of initiation. He understood the desire of man to belong. History proved that men united in a common cause were far more dangerous than those who stood alone. And that knowledge gave him power. The Man Shing Tong was a professional criminal organisation, a corrupted triad society of which he was now the supreme ruler and he meant to keep it that way.

'*I need two men,*' he said, raising his hand for silence. '*Two men for a special mission tomorrow.*' He watched as many hands were raised throughout the cavern.

He chose two members and they moved to the foot of his chair. '*You two are greatly honoured. Tomorrow you will deliver the gift of fire to the enemies of Ch'iang Kai-shek, those devourers of snot who call themselves the Hong Kong Police!*'

Tiger Paw Chang's grin was one of pure evil as he listened to his men spit oaths and call down the wrath of the Gods upon the hated police. Yes, he mused, tomorrow will be a great day. A great day for me. I will be wealthy beyond all imagining. I will own the Golden Dragons.

龍

Outside in the street, Lo Shi-mon removed the black silk cloth that hid his face. He walked down to the harbour's edge on Connaught Road and stood staring across the water towards Kowloon. He knew that tomorrow he and other members of his Lodge, wearing the uniform of the Hong Kong Police, would receive orders to arrest rioting members of Tiger Paw Chang's Man Shing Tong triad society. The arrests would put the two societies into direct conflict. It would result in a full scale war which the Man Yee On could never hope to win. Not only did they have less members than the Man Shing Tong, but another powerful triad, the Fuk Yee Hing, had formed a loose alliance with the Man Shing Tong for tomorrow's disturbance and would combine with the Man Shing Tong to eradicate his own small triad forever.

Lo Shi-mon looked out again across the darkened harbour to the lights of Kowloon. Tomorrow will be a test of honour, he thought sadly. A test of honour for himself, his men and for his little society, the Man Yee On. But what cost would honour demand? Only the gods could answer that.

Chapter Four

'Paraaade!' the voice of Inspector McCraw bellowed across the formal parade square at Central Police Station. 'Parade, attention!' Simultaneously, a mixture of two hundred Chinese sandalled feet and European leather boot soles crashed on stone flagging and the sound echoed off the walls and died away. Total silence remained, broken only by the low braying of a ship's horn in the harbour below as it signalled its intention to leave port. 'Paraaade! Parade, stand at ease!' Once again the feet sounded as one, silence again enveloped the ranks of policemen. For fifteen minutes no sound was heard except for the intermittent ruffling of the Union Jack, as the odd breath of early morning breeze found it atop the magnificent colonial facade of Central Police Station. Beneath that symbol of British supremacy, the parade, as still as death, awaited inspection.

Richard Brewster stood at the front of his platoon and rocked, almost imperceptibly, back and forth on his heels. It was a trick he'd learned in the army. The slight rocking motion and the flexing of the foot muscles stimulated the blood flow and many soldiers believed it helped avoid fainting. The parade had been formed for nearly thirty minutes and he knew someone would faint soon. He knew what it was like to stand in the ranks for two hours or more, waiting for some self-absorbed commanding officer or other to finish his breakfast before inspecting the men. So he rocked and he flexed, waiting for the inevitable grunt of a man fainting in the ranks.

The sound, when it came, wasn't a grunt, it was a cough

followed by the sound of a body and wooden baton hitting the ground. Richard heard the bark of Robert McCraw's voice ordering the removal of the collapsed man from the square, then there was the smart crack of footsteps from behind signalling the approach of their Commanding Officer.

Superintendent Charles Higgins appeared to Richard's right and marched past him towards Inspector McCraw, the Parade Commander.

'Parade present and ready for inspection, Sir!' McCraw threw a snappy salute and Higgins returned it rather casually.

'Yairs, yairs,' Higgins purred and fingered his moustache. 'Carry on, Inspector.'

'Paraaade!' McCraw bellowed and Higgins winced at the stentorian effort. 'Parade, attention!' Crash went the feet. 'Parade, open order, march!'

Once more the feet crashed and Higgins moved towards the extreme right of the parade. The front rank of Richard's platoon would be inspected first. McCraw followed, skipping once to get into step with his Commanding Officer.

'Morning, Sergeant Brewster,' Higgins drawled. 'Ready for the fracas, eh what?'

'We certainly are, Sir.' Richard saluted as the two senior officers disappeared behind him. He stood at attention for ten minutes as Higgins passed from his platoon to the next, until the inspection was over.

'Very good, Inspector McCraw,' Higgins mumbled and turned to the ranks. 'All officers,' he called in a lazy, off-hand way, 'will meet me in the Mess at the completion of this parade.' He turned back to McCraw. 'Dismiss the men.' He marched off the square as McCraw drew in a mighty breath.

'Paraaade! Parade, close order, march!' McCraw bellowed and the feet crashed. 'Paraaade! Dismissed!' The men left-turned. Crash went the feet, then marched three paces and the men mingled into a disorderly mob, like cows outside a milking shed. Babbling voices rose and NCOs shouted orders as the strict air of parade discipline disappeared on the wind, to be replaced with nervous expectancy.

Although predominantly Cantonese, the rank and file of

the Hong Kong Police were of mixed antecedents. Men from throughout the British Empire and elsewhere stood shoulder to shoulder with Chinese. For ease of recognition and organisation, the Force was divided into separate contingents identified by different collar badges. European police, mostly English, Scots, Welsh and Irish, wore a number preceded by the letter A. Indians, mostly Sikhs and Punjabis 'B', Shangtungese 'D', and White Russians, who'd flowed south after the Revolution, the letter E. Cantonese policemen wore the letter C on their collars, but were also distinguishable by their green uniforms, white leggings and soft slippers.

They formed into casual groups, lighting cigarettes and talking just that little bit too loudly, betraying their anxiety. They knew what was in store for them this day. They knew what was going to happen on the Western Docks. The rumours going around the barracks that morning had all pointed to one thing. A riot. A policeman's worst nightmare. So they stood in their groups and waited for orders.

A group of Chinese, more noticeable than the others because of the height of its members, stood beneath one of the curved arches which formed the front of Central Police Station. They were standing in a huddle, listening intently to the tallest of them as he spoke in a furtive whisper.

'*Brothers,*' Constable Lo Shi-mon hissed urgently in his native dialect of Shangtung. '*We must wait until Brewster Sergeant returns from the officers' briefing. Perhaps our platoon will be on reserve duty. Perhaps we will avoid direct confrontation with the Man Shing Tong altogether.*'

'*And perhaps my mother's arsehole does not point towards the ground!*' said Constable Lee Siu Lau, a big stocky fellow, as he spat contemptuously. '*We are men from Shangtung! The foreign devil officers use us first on every occasion, true or not true?*'

'*True, but our Sergeant is a baby, true or not true?*' Lo Shi-mon replied, desperate to calm his compatriots' rising anxiety. '*He is as yet untested. Perhaps Higgins Superintendent will not risk him in the confrontation.*'

'*You fool yourself if you believe that, Ah Lo!*' The man

who spoke was, in fact, Lo's cousin, Chan Man Long. The two men had grown up together in the Shangtung seaport of Tsingtao. *'Higgins Superintendent will use us first. He always does.'*

'Maybe you are right, Ah Chan,' Lo sighed. *'Perhaps we are in a race that cannot be won, but we are men from Shangtung! We were sought out by the British who asked us for help, and we signed the Big Paper which said we will serve the British and honour demands we do so.'*

'We also swore a blood oath to the brotherhood of the Man Yee On,' Chan looked around him for support. *'If we arrest members of the Man Shing Tong there will be a war and our Man Yee On Society will be destroyed. Surely our first loyalty is to our triad?'* Several of the other Shangtungese in the group nodded furiously, murmuring agreement with Chan.

'Our Master said we must always act according to the Will of Heaven,' Lo pleaded. *'What will be, will be. But whatever happens we must keep our honour, even if it means our deaths.'* He looked at the faces of the men around him and continued, *'We must honour our commitment to the British and if by doing so it causes a war with the Man Shing Tong and the Fuk Yee Hing then what will be, will be! We are the Brotherhood of Man Yee On. We are an honourable society, unlike the Man Shing Tong and their kind who have forgotten why the original Hung Mun triad society was formed.'* Lo Shi-mon made a sign with his left hand, extending his thumb, index and middle fingers leaving the smallest two tucked into his palm. He placed the hand in the centre of his chest and looked into their eyes. *'I am the Red Pole of the Society of Man Yee On! "Overthrow the Ch'ing. Restore the Ming". That is the oath we swore. Well, the Ch'ing Dynasty has been removed from the Dragon Throne, but the fat pig Tiger Paw Chang and others like him choose to forget that the Ming Dynasty has not yet been restored. Greed and avarice, and their new-found wealth in this city where rich men eat fat pork, have turned them to the ways of robbery and murder. They are undisciplined rabble! We are men of honour.*

And without honour we are nothing!' Lo Shi-mon dropped his hand to his side and searched their eyes. *'Whatever happens today, keep your pride as men from Shangtung and maintain the honour of the Man Yee On. Death is a far sweeter fruit than dishonour.'*

龍

'To conclude the briefing, gentlemen. As you all know,' Higgins drawled, 'the law requires a commissioned officer to declare the gathered mob an illegal assembly. That'll be your job, Bertie,' he finished by waving a long wooden ruler towards the rear of the Mess at Bertie Pertwee.

'Right you are, Sir,' Pertwee replied.

'Then, for God's sake, get to the rear of the ranks. We don't want you getting hit on the noggin by a flying cabbage, do we, what?' Higgins smiled and allowed his officers a nervous chuckle. He took great pride in his briefing ability and knew full well the value of a chuckle or two when it came to easing tension. 'The law further states that if the illegal assembly gets unruly and, in the opinion of a commissioned officer, could create a threat to public order, then it can be termed an affray. Inspector McCraw, that'll be your job.'

'Yes, Sir,' Robert McCraw bellowed and Higgins cringed at the volume.

'I've assigned this job to you because I've no doubt in my mind that you'll be heard,' Higgins articulated. 'Probably as far away as Bombay, if I'm not mistaken.'

'Right, Sir,' McCraw reddened with embarrassment as the others laughed.

'Finally, and this is the serious end of things, chaps,' Higgins raised his arm for silence. 'An affray by law becomes a riot if a commissioned officer forms the opinion that injury to persons or property is imminent.' He looked at his men before continuing. 'I and I alone will decide when that moment arrives. Inspector McCraw?'

'Yes, Sir.'

'Once again your stentorian abilities will be required. You will order the crowd in front to disperse and arrange for the banner with the dispersal order written in Chinese characters to be raised aloft in clear view of the crowd.'

'Yes, Sir, I . . .' McCraw paused as if to go on.

'What is it, man?'

'Well, Sir,' he stammered. 'I've taken the liberty of learning the dispersal order in Cantonese.'

'Good God Almighty,' Higgins groaned.

'It is actually required by law that the crowd be directed in both English and Cantonese, Sir,' McCraw finished lamely.

'Christ alive, man! It'll be unintelligible gibberish. Have your sergeant deliver it.'

'With all due respect, Sir,' McCraw growled. 'I've made quite a study of the sentence.'

'Very well, Mr McCraw,' Higgins sighed. 'If you must, but make sure you get that dispersal banner up, because by the time they've translated what on earth you're on about it'll be bloody dark!' He allowed the men a final laugh then silenced them with a wave of his hand. 'That's about it, gentlemen. Any questions?'

'Excuse me, Sir?' Richard Brewster raised his hand. 'I'm afraid I've not been given specific instructions for my platoon.'

'Oh hell!' Higgins exclaimed. 'Terribly sorry, young Brewster. Mustn't forget the new man, eh? Your men of Shangtung would normally be my first line, and I don't want you to take this as a slight on your character, but you're new here and I'd rather you were at the rear.'

'But, Sir . . .'

'But no buts, Sir!' Higgins roared. 'Dammee, Brewster, when are you going to learn.' His eyes glittered insanely for an instant and then he smiled. 'I realise you're keen, boy, but riots are a very dangerous thing. You will march your platoon down Hollywood Road into Queen's Road and take up a position in front of the Western Police Station. Is that clear?'

'Yes, Sir,' Richard replied stiffly.

'If and when the affray disintegrates into a riot, you will disperse your men down Western Street. They will take up positions in all doorways. When the crowd is driven up that

street towards the arrest area, which will be at the intersection of Queen's Road and Western Street, your men will
not allow them to enter buildings. After the drive platoons
have herded the rioters past your men, they will fall in behind
and mop up the stragglers. Are you instructed?'

'Yes, Sir.'

'Would you care to write your instructions in your notebook in case you forget them?' Higgins purred sarcastically.

'That won't be necessary, Sir.'

'Very well!' Higgins turned to the assembled officers. 'That
will be all, gentlemen. Return to your men and instruct them
accordingly. Dismissed.'

As his officers left the room, Higgins called to Richard.
'Sergeant Brewster, a word if you please.' When they were
alone, Higgins placed a fatherly arm about Richard's
shoulder. 'My dear boy, I'm sorry if I sounded a little harsh
in the briefing, but one has to maintain discipline, you do
understand?'

'Of course, Sir.'

'Good lad. Now, with regard to your orders, the two
buildings which run down Western Street and Chung Ching
Lane, which is directly opposite the Police Station, are rather
more important than you might think,' Higgins smiled his
fondest paternal smile. 'Those buildings are godowns which
are packed to the ceilings with valuable merchandise belonging to none other than John Merchant.'

'Really, Sir.'

'Yes. Really. Now I want you and your giants from Shangtung to protect those godowns with your lives. Do you get
my meaning?'

'Loud and clear, Sir.' Richard stared at the blackboard
Higgins had used for the briefing.

'Good lad,' Higgins drawled. 'And just between us, old
thing,' he winked at Richard. 'Some of that merchandise
belongs to me.' Higgins fell silent for a moment, allowing his
meaning to sink in. 'You're dismissed, Sergeant.'

龍

In a shed on a small fishing boat pier on the Western Docks, a stout Chinese of indeterminate age removed a wet label from a beer bottle and placed it in a tray. The tray contained a solution of potassium nitrate and sugar. He then filled the empty bottle with an equal parts mixture of petrol and sulphuric acid, added a quantity of soap flakes and carefully recapped it. Finally he wiped the bottle dry and gingerly replaced the soaking wet label.

With his work completed he stood up and stretched, then moved over to the window and glanced fearfully at the harbour as he carefully rearranged three flat octagonal plates, with mirrors inset at their centres, evenly along the window ledge. The plates, known as *ba'kwa,* were to keep evil spirits from his jetty shed. He prayed that, today of all days, any evil spirits wandering the nether world between heaven and earth would recoil at their own hideous reflections and fly, screaming, far away. He turned, muttering a final incantation, carefully picked up the bottle and went outside.

He looked about furtively, then placed the bottle in a wooden beer crate along with eleven other beer bottles he had painstakingly prepared in the same way. Satisfied that all was in order, he took a red bandanna from his pocket and signalled, by wiping his brow with it, then walked away towards the end of the pier.

He stood looking out across Hong Kong Harbour towards Kowloon. The port was congested with every conceivable type of vessel, but this particular day there was no activity on the harbour. Normally the ocean-going cargo ships were like queen bees lying sluggish in the water, constantly attended by a flotilla of motorised sampans, like drones, which scuttled back and forth from ship to shore, loading and unloading. But not today. Today an eerie stillness gripped the usually bustling harbour. A stillness he could only compare to that frightening time when the eye of a typhoon, from the South China Sea, passes over the city giving a moment of respite before its winds begin with renewed ferocity.

After several minutes he turned and looked back towards the shed. The crate was gone. He caught a brief glimpse of the deadly container, as two young men scurried off the pier with it and disappeared up an alley on the opposite side of Connaught Road.

The man shook his head sadly and heaved a sigh of relief. His work was done, for the time being. The brotherhood of the Man Shing Tong would call again. They always did.

龍

Richard Brewster stood on the front steps of Western Police Station in Queen's Road. Hong Kong had died. Its heart had stopped beating. His wonderful Hong Kong with its smells, sounds, frantic activity and happy, laughing, hardworking people. The silence was unnerving. Shop shutters were closed, doorways had been boarded up and the streets were empty.

Normally the scene was one of bustling activity. Hawkers shouted and peddled their wares, food stalls gave out a thousand different aromas, people haggled and argued and children ran about filling the air with the pure joy of youth. For the first time since arriving in the Colony, Richard was scared. And he wasn't the only one.

The faces of his men were drawn and tense. A dog barked somewhere nearby and forty uniformed bodies stiffened defensively. Somebody laughed nervously and the sound took forever to fade away on the still, heavy air. The silence returned, like a pall of doom.

Richard realised, perhaps for the first time in his existence, that his life could soon be in danger. He'd never had to consider the fact before; during his military service he'd not seen action. Now, here he was, five thousand miles from the safety of his regimental lines, in a silent street in the Orient about to engage in the quelling of a riot. He breathed deeply and slowly, urging his body to relax. His mind chased desperately a quotation he'd first heard in school. 'If you can keep calm, when all about . . .' No. The word wasn't calm. 'If you can keep still . . .' No! Damn it! It wasn't still! 'If you can keep your head . . .' Yes, that was it. 'If you can keep your head, when all about you are losing theirs . . .' Was that it? It sounded right. Who said it? Shakespeare? Browning?

Kipling? Does it matter, his mind screamed? Just keep your head, stay calm and remain focused on the situation.

Richard was determined to overcome fear and meet whatever adversity confronted him. He would do this for himself, not for his father nor anyone else. He would do it for himself alone.

'If you can keep your head . . .' Kipling! That's right, it was Kipling. 'If you can keep your head when all about you are losing theirs and blaming it on you; if you can trust yourself when all men doubt you . . .' Yes, that was it. And how did it finish? Something about Triumph and Disaster being imposters? Was it treat them the same? Yes! Treat them the same and 'yours is the Earth and everything that's in it'. That's it! That's it! I'll make mine the earth and everything that's in it. All I've got to do is keep my head. Please, God, let me keep my head.

To ease his jitters, he considered his geographical position in relation to the expected focal point of the riot. In his mind's eye, Richard stood at the centre point on one side of a square of streets. He stood in Queen's Road facing north towards the harbour, two parallel streets away. To his left, Western Street ran due north down across Des Voeux Road to join with Connaught Road at the harbour's edge. To his right, Centre Street did the same thing. A simple square.

Richard had to admire Charles Higgins' planning. The best generals kept their operations simple, that way order was maintained and nobody became confused. Higgins was adhering strictly to that rule. It was his intention that the crowd be confronted on the north-east corner of the square, driven west along the harbour's edge on Connaught Road, then south up Western Street, where they would be arrested, most conveniently, outside Western Police Station.

Higgins was also observing the unwritten law in crowd control. Always allow an avenue of escape for the unfortunate citizens who may be caught up in events by accident, and also for the more faint hearted of the troublemakers. He had done this by not blocking off Connaught Road to the west. Some of the crowd would spill down Connaught Road, more particularly those at the rear of the mob, the ones trying to avoid confrontation with the police. He would then block off the escape route and be left with 'those who wanted trouble', as he'd described them at the briefing.

'I want them flogged and flung into the compound at the rear of Western Police Station,' he'd roared. 'And we'll sort out the ringleaders at our bloody leisure!'

Richard gave silent Queen's Road a last look and went into the Charge Room.

Higgins was right, Richard had no experience in riot control, or anything else for that matter, but the British army had given him a military logic which, right at this moment, filled him with disquiet.

Richard had made a reconnaissance of Western Street, and had been chilled by a sense of foreboding. It was not actually a street at all, at least not by normal standards. It was more of a stairway. From Des Voeux Road to where he stood in Queen's Road it was a series of stone steps that ran, ladder-like, up from the harbour to the higher ground of Hong Kong Island. It was most definitely not the sort of street in which Richard would choose to confront a mob of rioters.

Richard's other concern was even more ominous. He'd been ordered to place his men in the warehouse doorways. Why? Was it merely to protect goods owned by John Merchant and Higgins himself? If that were so, then it was an order Richard's conscience could not condone. The mere thought of his men being trapped in the coffin-like entrances to the stone godowns as the rioters crushed past them, sent shivers up his spine. He'd immediately dispatched a messenger to Superintendent Higgins to voice his concerns, but as yet the man had not returned.

He sat by the Charge Room telephone that would relay the order to move his men into position. He closed his eyes and prayed it would not ring.

龍

At the intersection of Connaught Road and Centre Street, one hundred and forty policemen stood in ranks facing west.

To their right the harbour waters glistened in the early morning sunlight, to their left, silent buildings seemed to be watching them, while in front Connaught Road, soon to be their battleground, ran away to the western end of the Island. Time stood still.

The front ranks were motionless, feet apart at ease, arms to their sides. With riot shields of heavy woven rattan strapped to their left arms and black batons gripped like swords in their right hands, they stood, frozen, like Roman gladiators.

Inspector Robert McCraw stood beside the front rank of his men and surveyed the empty road. For all of the horror and violence he'd known during times of war, he found himself on this day to be a novice. He'd never experienced a riot and was not looking forward to it. The stillness and the silence worried him not one whit, he'd felt it many times before on the battlefields of France. But this was not a battlefield, he reminded himself. The people he would confront today would be civilians. His men would win this day, of that he had no doubt, but at what cost? He felt uncomfortable. He liked the Chinese.

When he'd first arrived in Hong Kong, several years before, he'd not liked the Chinese at all. They abused every law of human decency as far as his Scots Presbyterian mind was concerned. They were noisy, unwashed heathens. Godless souls lost in the darkness. He'd continued to believe this until a year ago.

Robert had been given the rank of Inspector and the position allowed him certain privileges. He'd moved from the single men's quarters at Central Station and taken a government flat in the Mid Levels, on the side of Hong Kong Island. On his first night in the new premises, he'd nearly died of fright when a young woman had appeared in the lounge room and asked him in broken English, if he'd care to take a bath.

Robert had summoned a sergeant from the station and had him ask the girl what on earth she was doing in his flat. The sergeant had laughed and told him that the girl was his *amah*.

'A saaairvant!' Robert had roared. 'I don't need a bloody saaairvant! Get rid of her, maaarn!'

The sergeant had been horrified. 'No can do, Elder Brother,' he'd replied. 'She have nowhere to go. You frow her out, she die on streets. She haf to beg.'

That had been it. Li Ping, as she turned out to be, had fed him, washed him, pressed his uniforms, done the shopping, cleaned his house and literally taken over his off-duty life. And eventually he'd taken her into his bed.

Robert's life had turned around since that day. Through Li Ping, he'd come to understand the Chinese. He now realised they were no different to anyone else, and above all, they certainly knew how to enjoy life. He loved Chinese food, he wore a silk robe around the house and at thirty-five, he'd finally discovered sex. No more furtive coupling in the dark with women whose faces he couldn't remember. No more the Christian fear of eternal agony for sins of the flesh. How could such a joyful experience be considered a sin?

Li Ping was honest and faithful to Robert. She appeared to worship the ground he walked on, yet at the same time, she was a wholesomely wanton woman who indulged in sex as freely as she indulged in eating and drinking. The whole exercise of living, which she embraced with such joy, had come as a revelation to Robert McCraw. He'd never felt more alive.

Now, as he stood side by side with his Chinese officers his dilemma became all too evident. He lived with a Hong Kong Chinese woman and he loved the Hong Kong Chinese people, but his first loyalty must lie with his men and the law he'd sworn to uphold.

There were no finer troops to be found anywhere. Over the last year, as his attitude had softened towards them, so too had their perspective of him. Initially, they'd received his attempts to instil badly needed discipline in their ranks with an ill-mannered grace, now they saw it as a cheerful challenge of their ability. There was a healthy competitiveness amongst the rank and file at Central Station. The men took to their duties with an enthusiasm not seen in the Colony before, and they wore their uniforms with a pride equal to that of the best British regiments. Robert McCraw knew of the effort they made for him and felt proud. His men would strike today, and they would conquer.

'Here we go, Robbie,' Bertie Pertwee muttered softly, as he came to McCraw's side. 'Round one is about to commence.'

Robert looked down Connaught Road and saw several young Chinese coolies, members of the Seamen's Union, no doubt, he thought. They ambled across towards the Kowloon Wharf & Godown Company Pier, a 'T' shaped affair which jutted out into the harbour. At the same time he noticed a large motorised junk pulling up alongside the pier. It was practically awash. Several hundred young coolies jammed its decks waving banners and placards, and somewhere to its stern a large Chinese drum began a furious rhythm that was immediately countered by the noisy clash of cymbals. The ear shattering din excited the flag wavers even more.

'Dreadful, eh what?'

Robert McCraw hated the way Charles Higgins crept up behind him. 'Sorry, Sir?' he mumbled.

'That cacophony. They believe noise will drive away evil spirits.' Higgins stroked his moustache and listened for a moment. 'Temple drum and cymbals. Bloody awful things,' he drawled and gave Robert a laconic smile. 'They're buggers for noise, you know. Noisiest people in the world, God bless their little heathen souls. It'll go on for a while yet, just ignore it.'

'Yes, Sir.' Robert replied grimly. Was I like Higgins once, he asked himself, so able to dismiss the Chinese as a race of semi-humans? Higgins' vain, imperialistic attitude irritated him. Robert knew these people to be much more than what Charles Higgins tried to paint them as.

'They'll all get orf that bally boat in a minute,' Higgins continued. 'And carry on like monkeys. Throw a few eggs. Harmless stuff. The real troublemakers aren't even here yet.'

'The *real* troublemakers, Sir?'

'Oh yes. I should think so, Robert.' Higgins chuckled. 'And you should have no trouble recognising them. They'll be the ones throwing rocks at you.'

'Thank you, Sir.'

Higgins turned to Inspector Pertwee. 'Give them an hour or so to expend a bit of energy, Bertie, then tell them to go home.'

'Yes, Sir,' Pertwee saluted.

'And Bertie,' Higgins smiled. 'Be irritatingly pleasant when you do, because they absolutely hate it. Carry on,' he said cheerfully and walked off swaggering.

Bertie Pertwee looked at McCraw and raised his eyebrows. 'He loves this sort of thing.'

'I'm fully aware of that, Bertie,' Robert replied.

'He can be a nasty piece of work, you know.' Pertwee dropped his voice. 'If this lot,' he waved in the direction of the demonstrators, 'look like getting too big for their boots, Higgins is just as likely to call up the riflemen and order them all shot.'

'He wouldn't dare, they're civilians. We're not at war.'

'Mark my words, Robert.' Pertwee leaned closer to him, 'Higgins will order them shot like rats in a barrel or my name's not Albert Pertwee. And what's more,' he shook his head, 'he'll not suffer the slightest remorse.'

'Higgins is nobody's fool, Bertie. Even he wouldn't go that far.'

'Oh yes, he jolly well would! And he'll make sure he gets away with it!' Bertie sighed. 'I've known Charlie Higgins for a lot of years. A lot more than you have. He's a gentleman, a scholar and a damn good friend, until his authority is questioned. Once that happens he'll strike like a king cobra. He really can become quite irrational.'

Robert was irked by the 'old school tie' tone in Pertwee's voice, but even more so, his sense of honour was offended. How dare they contemplate shooting civilians and how dare Pertwee discuss the matter in such an off-handed way. They were policemen and therefore honour bound to serve and protect. They'd sworn an oath for God's sake. 'But surely the Laws of Hong Kong . . .' he began to argue.

'Higgins has a brilliant mind,' Pertwee ignored the interruption. 'And he knows the laws of this Colony inside out.

He'll open fire on them just like that,' he snapped his fingers.
'And justify it under the Colonial Security Regulations.'

'Why?' the big Scot was now full of unease.

'Why?' Bertie looked at him and sighed. 'I'll tell you why,
and I say this not a little sadly,' he paused and looked out
across the harbour. 'Because he enjoys it.'

龍

Six-year-old Kwan Man Hop sat at the upstairs window and
watched the young coolies arrive on the junk at Kowloon
Wharf & Godown Company Pier. He'd been sitting there
patiently since six in the morning.

Little Kwan had told his sister he was going to the North
Point Markets to work for Mr Ho, the butcher, in return for
which he'd receive a sizeable portion of pork for the family
dinner table. It was only half a lie. Mr Ho owed him the piece
of pork for work he'd done the previous week. So Little
Kwan would return to his grandfather's house with the meat
and his sister, Wei Ling, would be none the wiser.

He'd been planning his adventure for two days, ever since
he'd heard his grandfather's whispered conversation with
Constable Lo Shi-mon. Little Kwan knew that his grandfather was the *Shan Chu*, the Master of the Man Yee On Triad
and he was pretty sure that the huge policeman was his
grandad's *Hung Kwan*, the Red Pole. Little Kwan wanted to
be a Red Pole one day with the triad hierarchal number 426,
so every time Constable Lo visited his grandfather's house,
the boy made sure he overhead` their exchanges.

Most of their conversation he had not understood because
of the secret words they used, but he'd gleaned that Constable Lo was to seek out a man called Tiger Paw, the Master of
another society and try to make some sort of deal. And also
that the trouble would be at a wharf on the Western Docks
at Sai Ying Pun.

No six-year-old could resist such information. So, at first
light he'd left the house and ran up the street to Hollywood
Road, then hurried west down into Queen's Road and
around the corner into Chung Ching Lane. A brief struggle

with rusty shutter hinges on a disused window and he was inside the stone godown of the Flaming Dragon Import Company at the intersection of Western Street and Connaught Road. He'd climbed the wall ladder and was now happily ensconced in the loft, with a perfect view of the area his grandfather had mentioned.

Across the road, men were gathering and waving placards. Drums roared and cymbals crashed and firecrackers exploded on the ground. A man stood on a barrel and shouted at the crowd inciting them, and all roared approval of his words.

Little Kwan looked further up the street and saw the policemen. They stood in rows with the English officers' metal helmets glittering in the sunlight, set amongst rows of straw conical hats. They didn't move, not even when other junks arrived and more men joined the crowd. Even when a huge crowd came along Connaught Road from the west and joined the others, the policemen still didn't move.

It is going to be a most exciting day, thought Little Kwan, as he placed a piece of *char siu* in his mouth. He'd taken a healthy portion of the thin slivers of pork from his sister's meat cage just before he'd left home. He chewed the meat and washed it down with a sip of sugar cane juice from an earthenware bottle. His excitement grew and his eyes glittered as he watched the crowd get bigger and bigger. Something incredible was about to happen, he was sure of it.

He watched as a group of coolies ran towards the policemen and threw a long string of firecrackers at them, then turned away and swaggered back to their friends. Still the policemen didn't move. All of a sudden, one of them, a foreign devil officer, marched towards the crowd and shouted something. Little Kwan couldn't hear what he shouted, but the crowd laughed and hooted at him, so he went back to his men.

Little Kwan's excitement knew no bounds. This was the best day of his young life. He watched as the crowd of men, now so many he couldn't possibly count them, roared as the man on the barrel shouted. They turned as one and moved towards the rows of policemen. Things began to fly through the air. Eggs! They were throwing eggs at the policemen. Little Kwan inched forward and watched the rows of policemen. They were beginning to ripple. Something was going to happen soon. It had to! He tucked into his pork and drank in small swigs from his bottle, supremely happy in his front row seat.

龍

'Sergeant!' Robert McCraw screamed and Sergeant Greschnev, a tall White Russian, came through the ranks. 'Get on the telephone and warn Sergeant Delaney to standby.'

Charles Higgins pushed his way through the front rank of his men. 'Righto, McCraw,' his eyes were glittering. 'Give them five more minutes to hang themselves, then give the order.'

'Yes, Sir!' McCraw yelled over the top of the screaming mob, then ducked as a half brick flew past his head. He turned as one of his front ranks grunted and fell to the ground. Blood gushed from a cut in the man's cheek.

'Bugger them!' Higgins shouted. 'That's it! Never mind the bloody warning, McCraw. Drive into the bastards! Their fun stops here and now!'

McCraw blew hard on his police whistle. The shrill sound could be heard clearly above the din. His men surged into the demonstrators, batons flailing furiously, seeking revenge for the insults, the rotten eggs and rock throwing they'd suffered for the past hour.

In an instant the mood had changed. The demonstrators had been enjoying themselves. The police will do nothing, they'd been told. *'Have no fear'*, the man on the barrel had shouted. *'The police are paper tigers! Yellow running dogs of the British Imperialists! Cowardly lackeys of the foreign devils!'* But this was not the case. The police were falling upon the crowd like rabid dogs!

A man screamed as a black baton smashed across his nose. Blood spurted over his companions as they turned and ran from the furious onslaught, tripping over bodies in their desire to escape. But many in the crowd produced weapons and went after police blood as the battle began in earnest.

Knives and sharpened files glinted in the sunlight. Bone and cartilage snapped, tissue ripped and men screamed as the first of the baton charges tore into the demonstrators.

Robert McCraw waded into the fray, his black baton striking left and right. One of his men fell and as he hauled the man to his feet, McCraw felt a searing pain in his left shoulder. The hilt of an oyster knife jutted from his tunic. The two-inch blade was embedded to the hilt in the muscle of his upper arm. The man who stabbed him went down under a rain of blows but the police charge faltered.

'Form on me!' McCraw screamed, and the sight of their officer with a knife handle protruding from his shoulder drove the men into a frenzy. They surged forward and straightened line abreast. 'Advance on me!' McCraw screamed at the top of his voice and the onslaught resumed.

龍

In the offices of the Hong Kong Tug & Lighterage Company some distance down Connaught Road beyond Western Street, the telephone rang. Sergeant Terrence Delaney answered it and listened, his strong Yorkshire face a mask of grim determination.

'That's it!' he snapped at Stewart Cameron as he hung up. 'Let's get the men out onto the street, but keep the platoon on the footpath so the buggers can get by.'

Stewart Cameron shouted orders, and his men, forty in number and strewn about the offices, leapt to their feet and ran for the doors that opened onto Connaught Road.

龍

In Queen's Road, Richard Brewster ran down the steps of the police station and shouted to his men.

'Western Street on the double and block off all the bloody doorways!' he screamed as the adrenalin surged through his system. 'Come on, move!' he urged his men.

The platoon ran down the steps of Western Street and took up their positions. Richard stood in the centre of the street. '*Ah Lo!*' he yelled and Constable Lo Shi-mon was at his side.

'No one leaves the street! No one gets in a door! Make sure of it!'

'Yes, Sir!' Lo Shi-mon yelled and ran down the street repeating his sergeant's orders in Chinese.

Richard stood still. He could hear the screaming from Connaught Road and saw people down at the bottom intersection, where Western Street met the harbour. They were running for their lives. He watched, incredulous, as the crowd thickened into a stream of humanity rushing west along Connaught Road.

Delaney and Cameron watched as the crowd streamed past them. Hundreds surged by as the panic gripped them.

'There's the signal,' yelled Delaney and pointed skyward as a bright green flare, fired from a Verey pistol, shot through the air and burst over the harbour.

'Form squad on me!' Cameron shouted over the shrieking demonstrators as he pushed into the throng.

Rattan shields cut through the crowd and forced a wall of police officers across Connaught Road, effectively blocking it off. The crowd turned, looking for escape. They had two choices, the harbour waters or Western Street. The wise ones opted for the water.

'Wheel them left!' Robert McCraw yelled and his men drove the rioters into Western Street and joined ranks with Delaney's platoon.

Crash went the shields. Whack went the batons. Stamp went the feet, as the driving platoons slowly but surely forced the rioters up Western Street.

龍

Richard Brewster was not prepared for the sight that formed before his eyes. Hundreds of Chinese rounded the corner and slowly backed towards him, fighting every inch of the way. He watched steel helmets flash and batons crash. He saw Robert McCraw in the thick of it wielding his baton. Richard blinked in disbelief. McCraw had a knife embedded in his shoulder.

People screamed as Delaney's platoon joined the fray. Those at the rear of the mob turned and began running towards Richard. They were terrified. A wall of widened eyes and shrieking mouths rushed at him. Behind him two arrest platoons blocked the street. Richard was caught in no-man's land, and pure fear hit him in the stomach.

龍

Fear also lanced through Little Kwan as he edged his way into the corner of the loft and hid behind a tea chest. His day of adventure had turned into a nightmare. What he'd witnessed in the street had made his skin prickle with a mixture of worry and excitement, but he'd not felt frightened. His fear had come from another direction. There were two men in the godown.

He'd seen them downstairs on the warehouse floor carrying a crate of beer and a large tin can. He'd watched, terrified, as they poured liquid from the can over the warehouse floor.

Now they stood on packing crates looking out of the high windows down onto Western Street. When he'd first heard them he'd thought, perhaps, they were policemen who'd seen him at the loft window and were after him. But they were not policemen and they were not after him. They were men of the *Man Shing Tong* triad and they were at the windows with beer bottles in their hands.

龍

The fire came from nowhere. One minute Richard was looking down the street at the mob, the next they disappeared in a sheet of flames. He looked up and saw a huge flaming dragon, snarling in the air above him. For one insane moment he thought that the dragon had breathed fire on the fighters below, then he realised it was a wooden carving, an emblem of the Flaming Dragon Import Company, attached by metal struts to a rain water downpipe on the godown wall.

Beside the dragon a face appeared at a window. Richard watched in horror as the man threw a beer bottle down at the melee below. The glass bottle burst against a policeman's head and flames engulfed him. Other bottles followed and the whole street erupted. Fire bombs! Good God Almighty! His mind screamed. The man was throwing fire bombs!

A young woman, her clothing alight, was flung against the godown wall. She screamed as the flames enveloped her, devouring the silk clothing she wore. Richard watched horrified, as the flames leapt from her writhing body to an awning on the godown wall before rushing, with incredible speed, up into the eaves of the building.

Closer to Richard another man appeared at a window; he too held a beer bottle. Richard drew his Webley .455 revolver and fired. The huge bullet hit the bomber in the chest and flung him back inside. An explosion followed and almost instantaneously, flames belched from the high godown windows.

Inside, Little Kwan watched in horror as the man at the window flew through the air and crashed to the floor. The bottle he was holding smashed on the stone floor. A huge ball of flame erupted as the potassium nitrate-soaked label came into contact with the mixture of petrol and sulphuric acid. The added soap flakes, insoluble in the mixture, flew as tiny balls of flame in all directions igniting the liquid the men had poured on the floor. In minutes the godown became a raging inferno.

Fire sprang through the cracks at the boy's feet. He crawled from his position in the loft and out onto the central beam which ran the length of the warehouse. Slowly he made his way along it, the flames reaching up greedily for him.

Outside in the street, with the dreaded fear of fire in their nostrils, the rioters turned and surged over the front police ranks like a tidal wave. Robert McCraw went down in a seething mass of arms, legs, rattan shields, helmets and batons. Fortunately for him, the line of confrontation had reached the intersection of Des Voeux Road.

The crowd bulged to their left. Policemen and barriers blocking Des Voeux Road were flattened as the screaming mass of terrified people burst over them like flood waters and poured westward into the empty road.

In Western Street, rioters and policemen ran in all directions, their instinct for survival overriding all else.

Richard Brewster heard a shrill scream. It was a high-pitched wail of pure terror. He looked up and saw a small boy high above him, at the end window of the godown.

'*Ah Lo!*' he screamed in Cantonese and the big constable was instantly at his side. '*We must get inside!*'

The two men flung their bodies at a door. It burst under their weight and Richard fell onto the warehouse floor. Fires were burning everywhere. He looked up to see a man, his clothing a ball of flame, screaming as he fell from a window ledge. Constable Lo leapt over Richard's body and flung himself on the man, extinguishing the flames with his hands.

'*Get him outside!*' Richard yelled in Cantonese, then got to his feet and ran through the flaming rows of merchandise. At the end of the building on the wall he found a steel ladder. He climbed in the direction of the window at which the boy had appeared.

The child was terrified. Richard found him crouched in the corner of the loft, his knees in front of his face and his bare arms covering his head.

'*Good morning, Little Brother.*' Richard tried to sound casual as he called to the boy in Cantonese. He could feel the flames rising from the godown floor and knew that it would be impossible to go back that way. '*We should leave this place, true or not true?*' he whispered to the boy as he knelt towards him.

'*True, Elder Brother. Definitely true,*' the boy flew into Richard's arms and locked his hands around the policeman's neck.

'*You are Little Kwan, true or not true?*' Richard had recognised the small boy from the Centre Street food stall.

'*True, true!*' the boy coughed. '*You are Litchard, my friend. We go now, Litchard?*'

'*Yes, we go.*'

龍

'Bertie!' Higgins roared. 'Get up to Western Station and break out the fire-fighting equipment.'

'Right you are, Sir!' Bertie Pertwee replied and headed off up Western Street.

'And alert Central Station, North Point and Aberdeen, all available officers, rank and file to stand by for fire brigade duty,' Higgins yelled after him. 'Delaney?' he snapped as he spun around searching for his officers.

'Here, Sir,' the big Yorkshireman responded.

'You and Cameron get the men into some semblance of order!'

'Yes, Sir.'

'I want this bloody crowd under control! And kept clear of that godown.' Higgins shielded his face from the heat of the flames. 'The brigades will need room to work. If this blaze spreads we'll have a hell on bloody earth!'

'By Crikey,' Delaney raised his arm. 'Look at that!'

As Higgins followed Delaney's pointing finger the crowd of several hundred gasped.

At the top window of the godown Richard Brewster appeared. A small boy straddled his back, his arms wrapped tightly around Richard's neck. The crowd watched, their own fears momentarily forgotten, as Richard reached tentatively for the wooden carving of the flaming dragon.

'Someone get a ladder!' Higgins yelled, then watched spellbound as Richard placed his foot in the curve of the dragon's tail.

'Hold on tightly, Little Brother,' Richard hissed through clenched teeth as flames licked at his face from beneath the eaves. He placed his foot on the wooden carving and tested its strength. Satisfied, he reached for the body of the dragon and clasped his arms around it. As flames belched from the window behind, he dropped his body weight onto the curving tail. Below, he heard the crowd gasp, while above, he heard the ominous sound of metal scraping on metal.

'Aiyah! Elder Brother, the dragon is slipping,' Little Kwan coughed, the smoke tearing at his throat.

Richard twisted his neck and looked at the steel struts holding the carved dragon. Christ, he thought. They're not even attached to the building. The strut ends were only steel

clamps bolted around the downpiping that ran from the guttering to the ground.

The huge flaming dragon slipped dramatically. It dropped
several feet then stopped and a huge sigh burst from the
onlookers. All Richard could do was hang on. At least for the
moment they were clear of the flames.

Several explosions rocked the godown as the fire bombs
left inside succumbed to the heat. And the dragon moved
again. Slowly, to the stunned amazement of the crowd, it slid,
metal screeching against metal, down the side of the building
until, with a jarring thud, the dragon's tail met the ground. A
huge cheer rang out as Richard and Little Kwan dropped to
safety, and, not a moment too soon, ran clear of the building.
An agonising groan shuddered through the godown and the
huge roof collapsed inward, sending up a shower of sparks.

Fire is the nemesis of Hong Kong. Its inhabitants knew
from bitter experience the damage it could wreak. Many
times over the years whole areas of the Colony had been
ravaged. Complete suburbs had been razed to the ground. A
port for refugees and the inevitable shantytowns they built,
Hong Kong was a tinderbox awaiting a spark, and the riot
was now forgotten as policemen and citizens alike leapt to
the task of fighting their common enemy.

Fire Brigades arrived from Central, North Point and
Western districts. Police water pumps from Western Station
were set up and sea water from the harbour was drawn from
the mains below Des Voeux Road. The riot was over, but
another battle was starting.

Richard sat against a wall and surveyed the scene around
him. It was a disaster. Charred bodies lay everywhere. People
groaned and called for help. Fire hoses snaked every which
way as water filled the air. Doctors and nurses from the
hospital in Queen's Road attended the injured and body carts
began removing the dead. The heat from the fire scorched the
air and the smell of burnt flesh filled his nostrils. Never had
Richard witnessed such carnage.

'Sergeant Brewster!' It was Higgins. 'Get off your arse,
man! There's a fire to fight!'

'Yes, Sir,' Richard groaned wearily as he got to his feet.

'Regard if you will the burning warehouse,' Higgins murmured. He seemed totally at ease, which to Richard, was nothing short of amazing given the current situation. 'The warehouse I asked you to guard with your life.' Higgins went on. 'It will soon be a stone shell full of ashes.'

'I'm sorry, Sir. There were two men inside, they had fire bombs. There was nothing I could do.'

'Are they dead?'

'I'm sorry?' Richard was nonplussed.

'Are they dead?'

'Who, Sir?'

'Dammit, man!' Higgins snapped. 'The men who were in my godown. Are they bloody well dead!'

'I shot one, Sir.'

'Good man. Did you kill him?'

'Yes, Sir.' Richard saw again the .455 calibre bullet ripping into the man's chest.

'And the other one?'

'Constable Lo got him out, I believe.' He watched as two nurses in starched white uniforms attempted to restrain a writhing, blackened body, then he looked away. 'But the man was badly burnt. Horribly burnt. He was a ball of flame when Lo got to him. I can't imagine he survived.'

'I should damn well hope not!' Higgins turned and considered the operations going on about him. 'Keep clear of the hoses,' he shouted at a young constable.

After what seemed an eternity to Richard, the warehouse fire was brought under control and he took the opportunity to slump against a wall, shocked by the day's events. The sky was a pall of black smoke, and water cascaded down Western Street towards the harbour. Firemen shouted, hoses hissed, and white ambulances with large red crosses painted on them honked their horns indignantly, crawling, ant-like, to and from the scene. Groups of people sat in stunned silence as Catholic nuns, in black habits, offered cups of water and words of kindness.

'Come on, man!' Higgins turned to Richard. 'Snap out of

it! Get your platoon together and up to Western Station. Get them fed, get them cleaned up, and get them back here as quickly as possible.'

'Yes, Sir,' Richard answered automatically.

'And by the way,' Higgins purred. 'That was a very heroic thing you did, rescuing the boy.'

'Thank you, Sir.'

'Just what the force needs, heroes. You and your constable, what's his name?'

'Constable Lo.'

'Yairs,' Higgins drawled. 'You'll both be commended for your actions.' Richard turned to go. 'Just a moment, Brewster!' Higgins snapped.

'Sorry, Sir.' He stopped. He felt as if he was miles away, outside his own body, watching the scene from way up in the clouds.

'Be back here before that fire's extinguished.'

'Why?' he heard himself ask.

'You will surround that godown and guard it until you are relieved,' Higgins brushed ash from his tunic. 'Is that clear?'

'But it's burned to the ground, totally gutted,' Richard watched as the fire brigades doused the flames, slowly getting control of them. 'There's nothing left but the stone walls.'

'I'll be the judge of that,' Higgins caught Richard with an icy stare and pointed at the burning building. 'When that fire is extinguished, if anybody so much as steps foot in the ashes I'll have your guts for garters, Brewster! Do I make myself clear?'

'Yes, Sir!' Richard jumped to attention, the venom in Higgins' voice dragging him out of his lethargy.

'Well?' Higgins roared. 'What are you waiting for? You've been given your orders! Carry them out!'

龍

'I'm terribly sorry, old man, but this is going to hurt.'

Robert McCraw winced as the surgeon removed the oyster blade from his shoulder. 'Bloody Jesus, maaarn,' he growled. 'Do you have no sympathy in your soul?'

'I warned you it may hurt,' came the doctor's indignant reply. 'Now, please sit back down, I have to tamp the wound.'

'In a pig's aaarse!' McCraw yelled as he fell back onto his chair. 'Its not a bloody gunshot wound, why tamp it?' He roared and glared at several constables who were trying not to laugh at his antics.

'It's an oyster knife, Inspector,' the doctor sighed. 'It'll be crawling with bacteria. The wound must be tamped.'

'Get on with it then, you cruel bastard!' McCraw muttered and stuffed the leather cross-strap of his Sam Browne belt between his teeth. The doctor began pushing a treated gauze strip into the wound as the big Scot bit down on the leather strap.

Richard entered the canteen of Western Police Station and despite his aching limbs, grinned as the Scotsman growled through clenched teeth.

'Sassenach aaarrstard!'

'I'm sorry, I don't speak Gaelic,' the doctor said.

McCraw spat the strap from his mouth. 'I said, you're a Sassenach bastard. A bastard Englishman in other words, you butcher!' he growled as the doctor inserted a single stitch in his shoulder to contain the tamping.

'Laddie,' McCraw said when he saw Richard, 'that was a fine thing you did, rescuing that wee bairn from the building.'

'It was nothing you wouldn't do yourself, Sir,' Richard replied, a little embarrassed but secretly pleased by the big Scot's praise.

'I must admit, Mr Brewster, I would have used the stairs.' McCraw grinned. 'Crowd pleasing antics like sliding down a wall on the back of a dragon is a wee bit ostentatious for my liking.'

'I admit I felt like a fool! Must have looked like one too.'

'Not in the eyes of the Chinese, laddie. Well, most of them anyway.' McCraw's voice took on a more serious tone. 'There's talk of nothing else. You rode a flaming dragon through fiery skies, not to mention the fact that you rescued one of their kind. You've done yourself no end of good with the locals, Sergeant. You're a hero.'

All eyes were upon him and Richard felt self-conscious. 'Constable Lo?' he called for want of something better to do.

'Yes, Sir?' As usual the big Chinese appeared from nowhere.

'Ah, there you are. How many of our platoon were injured?'

'Six, Elder Brother.'

'Any serious?'

'PC Singh B1644 is burned, Sir.' Lo indicated a back room door. 'He died. Just now.'

'Christ,' Richard muttered. An image of the tall, be-turbaned Sikh with the perennial smile flashed through his mind. Constable Singh had been a good fellow, always cheerful and enthusiastic. *'PC Singh, married or not?'* he asked, switching to Cantonese.

'Married already, Sir,' the big Shangtungese replied.

'Children?'

'Two.'

Richard looked around the canteen and for the first time noticed just how many injured policemen were there. The hospital further up Queen's Road had been inundated with wounded and it had been decided to set up a casualty area in the police station. The place was now strewn with uniformed men and medical staff. Nurses scurried every which way administering aid and calling for supplies of fresh bandages and ointments.

Constable Lo spoke again in Cantonese.

'I'm sorry?' Richard looked at him. 'I didn't understand, you speak too quickly for me.'

'PC D1650, Chan Man Long,' Lo continued in English. 'He cannot see from his eyes.'

'He's blind, you mean?'

'Blind, yes.'

'He is your cousin, isn't he?'

'Yes, Sir.'

'Anyone else?' Richard felt himself sink into a pit of despair.

'Four other men are burned, but they are not bad.'

'Seven dead from the police ranks, Brewster,' McCraw interrupted. 'Seven good men, and God knows how many civilians. It's been a black day.'

'Inspector Pertwee,' Lo added. 'He says eleven citizens die. Two are women.'

'That makes eighteen dead, and how many injured the Lord only knows. Must be several hundred or more,' McCraw shook his head. 'A black day indeed.'

'Mr Lo,' Richard stretched his aching body. 'Do a headcount of our platoon. I need to know how many can return to duty.'

'Yes, Sir,' Lo saluted and turned away. He was forced to yell in Cantonese to make himself heard over the moans of the wounded and the incessant chatter of the medical staff attending them.

'Christ alone knows why Higgins wants his bloody godown guarded,' Richard said to no one in particular, as the doctor moved on to his next patient.

'Which godown?' McCraw asked.

'The one that was gutted by fire. It's just a stone shell.'

'Why on Earth would he would he give an order like that?'

'My point exactly, Sir. He told me this morning at the conclusion of the briefing that the godown contained property belonging to him and John Merchant. He ordered me to guard it with my life, but now it's been burnt to the ground to continue guarding it seems rather pointless.'

'He's a strange man, that one,' McCraw muttered. 'I've known him for several years but never been remotely close to him. He's a loner and I've never trusted loners.' He stopped abruptly, realising he'd been speaking his thoughts aloud to a junior officer. 'He must have cause, lad, and ours is not to reason why. Make sure your men get some food in their bellies before you report back. And have the doctor take a look at your burns. Get something on them or they'll become infected. First rule in the tropics.'

'Yes, Sir,' Richard turned to go.

'Sergeant,' the big Scot's voice rumbled. 'A moment more of your time, lad.'

'Yes, Sir?'

'Don't return your firearm to the Armoury tonight.'

'But I have to. The regulations state . . .'

'Never mind the bloody regulations,' McCraw lowered his voice as he added, 'the Station Armoury is under my control and you'll do as I say! Is that clear?'

'Yes, Sir,' Richard replied in a whisper. McCraw's conspiratorial tone was obvious, and he was puzzled.

'Today's riot was not a spur of the moment thing, laddie,' McCraw murmured. 'It was a performance put on by a very nasty group of men known as the Man Shing Tong Society and I have it on good authority that the grandfather of the little boy you rescued is in direct opposition to this society.'

'But, what's that got to . . .'

'Shhh! Keep your voice down,' McCraw hissed, looking about before continuing. 'The Man Shing Tong will regard what you did as an insult. Don't ask me to explain, it's all to do with face. It's too bloody complicated for anyone but the Chinese to understand. Keep your firearm on you and watch your back. If anything untoward happens, come straight to me. Do I make myself clear?'

'Yes, Sir!'

'Good. Now get about your business. And one more thing,' McCraw added as Richard turned to go. 'Remember today, Sergeant Brewster. Remember that you survived it. You're alive and that's all that counts in the long run.'

CHAPTER FIVE

Caitlin Maclain's hands trembled as she poured tea into Elanora Merchant's cup. High up near the pinnacle of Victoria Peak, on the balcony of the Merchant House with its magnificent views of Hong Kong Harbour and Kowloon, the two women were sharing Sunday breakfast.

Merchant had had the house built on the cardinal compass points of east and west, facing north. From the balcony one could see, lying forty miles west beyond Lantau Island, the Portuguese Colony of Macau, while fifteen hundred feet below lay the harbour, with the Kowloon Mountains beyond to the north. And the easterly aspect revealed Tathong Channel meeting the harbour waters.

'For Heaven's sake, Caitlin, calm down,' Elanora teased. 'Your sergeant won't be here for at least another hour.'

Caitlin poured her own tea and, to hide her embarrassment, raised the newspaper and read again the graphic descriptions of the 'Western Docks Riot', as it was being called.

Richard's face stared back at her from the front page, and she again admired his looks. The photograph showed him in action fighting the fires in Western Street, the unruly lock of hair across his face and the grim determined set of his jaw reminded her of the heroic statues of ancient Roman generals she'd seen in Italy when she was a girl.

He had telephoned earlier that morning to reassure her that he was unharmed, that he would pick her up at eleven as planned, and he had suggested they take one of the scenic walks around the Peak. He'd sounded so calm and assured on the phone, a fact which had also excited her.

'EIGHTEEN DIE ON WESTERN DOCKS' the news headline screamed, and underneath a photograph of Richard, 'HERO DEFIES FLAMES TO RESCUE BOY'. Caitlin had read the article several times. While she was shocked and horrified by the tragic violence, her heart beat wildly at the thought of Richard in the burning godown.

Superintendent Higgins was quoted as saying Richard would be promoted immediately and highly commended in recognition of his outstanding bravery, and a Chinese constable under Richard's command was to be promoted to sergeant and would receive a Commendation from the Inspector-General of the police force.

'He's a handsome devil, our young sergeant Brewster,' Elanora Merchant smiled and placed her cup on its saucer. 'The photograph doesn't do him justice.'

'Do you think so?' Caitlin adopted an indifferent tone. 'I hadn't really considered it.'

'Oh come now, Caitlin!' Elanora laughed. 'You're trembling like a wet kitten.'

'I am not.'

'Oh yes you are, my pretty maid,' Elanora's almond eyes glinted mischievously. She stood, placed her hands on the balcony and gazed over the panorama of Hong Kong. 'Will you have him on your walk?'

'I beg your pardon!' Caitlin was shocked.

'Will you let him seduce you?' Elanora spun back to look at her child's governess. 'There are secluded places behind the peak. You could pretend to fall and then he would have to come to your aid and . . .'

'Mrs Merchant!' Caitlin gasped, her face reddening.

'Or how about right here?' Elanora continued. 'The right wing of the house is utterly empty. Or the summerhouse, you could take him there and let him . . .'

'I refuse to listen to you!' Caitlin turned stiffly in her chair.

'I'm sorry,' Elanora realised she'd gone too far. She sat down and took the girl's hand. 'I've embarrassed you. Do forgive me.' Caitlin nodded and smiled at her mistress. 'It's just that I envy you so much.'

'You envy me?'

'Certainly.'

'But why? You have everything a woman could wish for. A child, a beautiful home, a successful husband . . .'

'A successful man, yes, but a husband? No, Caitlin.'

'How can you say that?' Caitlin was always shocked by the frankness of her mistress. Elanora Merchant was a forthright woman. And a powerful one. Especially amongst the Chinese population, who revered her. There was an air of mystery about Elanora that captivated Caitlin. The way she disappeared every so often into the poverty-stricken areas of Kowloon and to Portuguese Macau where, according to the Merchant House servants, she paid for, and supervised, a clinic for women in distress. Then the next minute she'd be seen frivolously circulating amongst Hong Kong's elite, the mistress of all she surveyed.

'How can you say that?' Caitlin asked again.

'Because John Merchant doesn't love me.'

'That's ridiculous . . .'

'No, it isn't,' Elanora interrupted. She looked again across the wonderful view, watching a kite, its wings widespread, looking for its morning meal, as it floated on a thermal updraught, a free spirit. 'John Merchant is a collector, Caitlin. He collects beautiful things. Vases, furniture, motor cars, objets d'art . . . me.' She looked at the young Irish girl and nodded sadly.

'That's not true,' Caitlin whispered.

'I'm afraid it's all too true,' Elanora replied. 'He collected me because I am beautiful, physically beautiful. And that is not vanity speaking.' She gave a mirthless laugh. 'I am fully aware of my beauty, my family never ever allowed me to forget it.' She shook her head and smiled ruefully. 'My aunt would often say, "you are a rare beauty, Elanora, you must use it to your advantage", and my father would declare every Sunday morning, "a man will one day pay dearly for your beauty, my darling". And when I went to London, *The Times* described me as one of the most beautiful women in the world.'

'You certainly are,' Caitlin agreed. Elanora Merchant was the perfect balance of East and West, a delicate mixture of the classical and exotic.

'But beautiful to whom?' Elanora exploded with frustration. 'And why?' she raised her hands in a gesture of hopelessness. 'My aunt wanted me to use my beauty to gain power. My father wanted me to sell my beauty for riches. And the journalist from *The Times* wanted my beauty to assuage his carnal desire. He would have given anything to bed me.'

Caitlin was once again shocked. 'But that's terrible . . .'

'Not really. At least he was honest about it. My father saw my beauty as a salesworthy commodity, but he was wrong. Beauty has little true value. What constitutes beauty? That bird?' Elanora pointed at the kite hanging in the warm air. 'That bird is beautiful. The view is beautiful. I am beautiful. So what? Beauty is only what people perceive it to be. It has no value. What does beauty bring to a marriage, for instance? Nothing!' she almost spat the word as she moved again to the balcony rail and stared at the kite wheeling in the breeze. Finally she turned, 'Love makes a marriage,' she said sadly. 'And I am not loved. Admired, maybe . . . but not loved. Nor do I know what it's like to love a man.' Caitlin joined her at the railing and the two women stood in silence, watching the beautiful bird soaring high in the sunlit sky.

'That's why I envy you, Caitlin.'

'Why me?'

'Because you're in love. *Carpe diem*, as my husband is so fond of saying. Seize, the day, my dear.' She seized the Irish girl's hand fiercely as if by way of example, squeezing her fingers. 'Don't let the opportunity slip away.'

龍

'Melt them down?! Melt them down?! Are you out of your mind? You're talking about the Golden Dragons, for God's sake!'

Two floors below the young women, John Merchant paced the floor of his study, an agitated man. He went to the side cabinet, poured himself a large brandy and gulped it greedily. He turned and stared at Superintendent Charles Higgins, seated comfortably in a large leather chair.

'They are priceless,' he hissed at the policeman. 'There are people in this world, rich people, collectors of antiquities, who would pay a king's ransom for them.'

'The game's up, John,' Higgins purred as he puffed on his cigar. 'They've become a liability. They were safely hidden underneath the warehouse in Western for ten years and not a soul in this world knew, except you and me. Our original plan to keep them hidden until everyone had forgotten about them is out of the bloody window. The game's up, laddie . . .' he shrugged. 'The bloody godown is a burnt-out shell. The element of risk has re-entered the equation. To sell them as antiquities is now out of the question.'

'Where are they now?' Merchant asked.

'Early this morning, I transferred them to your number three godown,' Higgins replied. 'They're under heavy guard, but people will soon be wondering just what in hell is in the godown that would warrant police protection. At the moment the locals think the guard is simply extra protection for the docks, given that we've just had a riot, but that excuse won't last forever. That's why I'm telling you, our only chance now is to get them to England, melt them down, sell the gold and get the money into circulation.'

'We'll lose a fortune,' Merchant moaned.

'God Almighty, man!' Higgins snapped. 'How much money can you spend in a lifetime? The eight jewelled eyes alone will fetch the best part of a million pounds sterling!'

'That's not the point.'

'You're quite right!' Higgins leapt to his feet. 'I'll tell you the point! The point is, if the Soong family or, God help us, Ch'iang Kai-shek and his bloody Kuomintang ever find out their Golden Dragons are not somewhere off the coast of China at the bottom of the Pacific Ocean, where legend hath it they bloody well rest, our lives will not be worth a tinker's cuss! That's the bloody point!' Higgins finished, his eyes blazing with a look that Merchant knew only too well.

'All right, all right!' Merchant mopped his sweaty brow with a handkerchief. 'Calm down, Charles.'

'Oh, don't you worry, Johnny m'lad,' Higgins purred lazily as he resumed his seat. 'I'm calm, perfectly calm, it's you who's upset.' He smiled and shook his head. 'I can't understand you. Here you are, as rich as Croesus already and standing to make several more millions, and you're upset because you can't have the best of all possible worlds.' Higgins puffed gently on his cigar. 'You're greedy, Johnny,' he chuckled softly. 'You're a greedy boy, and that you are.'

'Yes,' Merchant took a deep breath and exhaled slowly. 'You're right, you're right. I'm sorry.'

'Oh, no need to apologise to me, old man.' Higgins went to the cabinet and poured a glass from the brandy decanter. He sniffed the fumes from the balloon and looked Merchant in the eye. 'If an apology from you to me was ever warranted, you'd be dead before you could offer it.' The clock on the mantelpiece whirred and chimed eleven as Higgins sipped his drink. 'You do get my meaning, don't you, Johnny m'lad?'

John Merchant could only nod. His throat had seized up. Charles Higgins was the only man in Hong Kong of whom he was afraid.

When they'd first met, Merchant had thought Charles Higgins was a simple man, easily read. A middle class dandy obviously well educated and given to a life of ease. A refined hedonist, who had found a niche for himself in the Colonial Service in dear old Honkers, as Higgins often referred to the Colony.

Merchant had maintained his opinion until, one night, while playing cards in the Hong Kong Club he'd called Higgins a fool. It was an off-hand remark, made innocently during the excitement of the game. In an instant, Higgins' eyes had gone cold and lifeless and Merchant felt like a rabbit caught in the hypnotic stare of a snake. 'If you ever call me a fool again,' Higgins had murmured, his voice as cold as a grave, 'I'll kill you'. Then he'd laughed and resumed playing cards as if nothing had happened.

That had been it, but Merchant knew beyond all doubt

he'd meant it and since that night Merchant had been terrified of the dark creature that dwelt in Higgins' soul.

'Now, we've got to get those statues out of Hong Kong, so don't you think we'd better decide on a plan of action?' Higgins said, swirling the brandy around in his glass.

'Yes. Certainly.' Merchant replied. 'What do you suggest?'

'They must be transported to England as soon as poss–'

'Excuse me, Mr Merchant, I'm sorry to interrupt.'

'Yes, Caitlin, what is it?' Merchant said.

'Good morning, Superintendent Higgins, and how would you be on such a lovely day, Sir?'

'What is it, Caitlin!' Merchant snapped even louder.

'I'm terribly sorry,' Caitlin took a step back, shocked by Merchant's tone.

'It's all right, my dear,' Higgins murmured. 'It's just that you startled us. We didn't hear you come in.' he smiled at her. 'You're as quiet as a mouse.'

'I'm sorry I disturbed you, Mr Merchant, it's just that I'm on my way out and Mrs Mer–'

'Ah, yes!' Higgins interjected. 'With our hero, young Sergeant Brewster . . . Oops,' he chuckled. 'Forgive me, Inspector Brewster. He's been promoted. And well deserved, I must say.'

'Yes, Sir.'

'Well, what is it, Caitlin?' Merchant asked.

'Mrs Merchant ask me to inform you, Sir, she'll be lunching at the Repulse Bay Hotel. With the Ladies' Auxiliary.'

'Right, fine. Is that all?'

'Yes, Sir, thank you, Sir.' Caitlin turned and opened the study door.

'Give my regards to our hero,' Higgins said in a jovial tone.

'I will, Mr Higgins,' she replied and left closing the door behind her.

'God, man!' Merchant mopped his brow with his handkerchief, the room seemed suddenly warm. 'What if she heard us?'

'Wouldn't matter,' Higgins laughed. 'She's in love: in one ear and out the other. Besides, it wouldn't make any sense to her if she did,' he added, as he helped himself to another brandy. 'Now,' he turned to Merchant, 'which of your ships is next to sail? And when?'

'The *Pacific Star*. Six days from now, next Friday,' Merchant answered, still staring at the closed door.

'Nothing sailing any sooner?' Higgins drawled.

'No.'

'Who's the captain?'

'Watling. A good man, been with the Company ten years. Not far off retirement, actually.'

'Near retirement, eh?' Higgins asked. 'Then he's our man all right. You'd better arrange a chat with him, say Wednesday night?'

'I'll have him come to the Company offices in Central.'

'Then the *Pacific Star* it is. I can keep my men at the godown for six days to guard our precious little golden friends without arousing suspicion, then they'll be loaded onto the *Pacific Star* and on their way to dear old England.' Higgins sat back down. 'From then on it's out of our hands. The money will do a tour of the banks of the world and end up in our pockets. What a lovely thought,' he purred. 'Yairs, yairs. What a lovely thought.'

'Amen to that,' Merchant added.

'It doesn't seem like ten years, does it old man?' said Higgins as he stared into the golden liquid in his balloon, and remembered.

龍

Monsoonal rain had swept in sheets across Ice House Street in Hong Kong Central, as Inspector Charles Higgins had dashed up the stairs of John Merchant & Co. House. It was after midnight and a single light burned in the top floor window.

He'd shaken the water from his cape as he'd made his way up the four flights of stairs and knocked on the door.

'It's open,' a voice answered.

John Merchant was seated at his desk, slumped over the blotter. He'd been drinking, a glass and a bottle of navy rum sat before his folded arms.

'Well, how did it go?' Merchant's voice was fuzzy from the alcohol.

'Like clockwork,' Higgins replied, hanging his cape over a chair.

'Really?' Merchant brightened visibly and sat up.

'Yairs.' How I hate weakness in men, Higgins thought. 'Were you worried?'

'No, not at all!' Merchant managed a smile. 'Never expected anything else. That's why I chose you for the job.'

'You chose me because you found out that a cargo of fabulous wealth was being conveyed to Hong Kong and you decided to steal it, but never had the guts to do it yourself.' Higgins sneered. 'You're pathetic!' He pointed at the bottle. 'Why the drink, eh? Were you expecting the police to walk in and arrest you?'

'Listen, Charles . . .'

'No! You listen!' Higgins leant down so their faces were inches apart. 'It's over. The *Silver Cloud* is at the bottom of Tathong Channel and the Golden Dragons are safely buried in ammunition boxes under your godown floor on the Western Docks, exactly as planned.' He stood, disgusted at the drunken individual behind the desk. 'They will stay there until their disappearance becomes a faded memory, is that clear? You will forget they ever existed. The world will forget they ever existed,' he continued, not waiting for a reply. 'As far as the Chinese are concerned the *Silver Cloud* and the Golden Dragons disappeared without trace somewhere out in the Pacific Ocean. If you so much as breathe the words Golden Dragons, you'll die. In fact we'd both probably die.'

'Oh, God,' Merchant groaned and took a swig of rum which brought on a fit of coughing.

'Get hold of yourself, man!' Higgins roared. 'No one in the world knows where those statues are except you and me.'

'Did you . . .' Merchant began and coughed violently.

'Kill them all?' Higgins walked to the window and looked out at the rain. 'Yes. The crew of the *Silver Cloud* are in Chinese Heaven, wherever that is.'

'And the policemen?' Merchant wheezed.

'After we got the statues, I had them take the police launch back to Aberdeen Harbour.' He gave a sigh of resignation, he hadn't wanted it to happen but it was the only plan that would've worked. 'I shot all four of them, made sure they were dead and emptied the ship's armoury into the harbour. I removed our darling little dragons, packed them in ammunition boxes and had them delivered to the godown. Then I set the police launch adrift off Ap Li Chau Island and swam ashore.' He turned and looked at John Merchant. 'Don't worry, they'll find it floating in Lamma Channel and presume it the work of pirates after police firearms.'

'But can we be sure?'

'They've done it before. Only last year in Tai O pirates stole Police Launch Number Three and took all the weapons from its armoury. The Force won't even bother investigating this incident.'

'Good God,' Merchant's eyes widened in horror, visions of bullet-riddled bodies filling his mind. 'All those dead men.' His hand shook as he raised the glass of rum to his lips and drank.

'Now now, Johnny m'lad,' Higgins' tone was gentle, soothing. 'You're not going to go under on me, are you?'

'What?'

'I said, you're not going to fall to pieces on me, are you?' He placed a revolver on the desk right in front of the shaken man's face.

'What's that for?' Merchant gasped.

'It's for you, my dear fellow,' He brought his face down to Merchant's level. 'Unless you begin to exhibit some fortitude.'

'I don't understand,' Merchant stared at the firearm, mesmerised.

'It's quite simple, John,' Higgins' look was one of pure malice. 'If you don't have the stomach for our little game, you become a liability. A liability I cannot afford. Now,' he went on, his voice becoming harder. 'I'm giving you two options. You can either smarten yourself up and continue playing, or you can remove yourself from the game altogether.'

'You . . . you surely can't mean . . .?'

'That's exactly what I mean,' Higgins smiled and picked up the pistol as he stood. 'Do the honourable thing, John!' he waited, letting his words sink in. 'That is unless you don't have the wherewithal,' he paused. 'In which case,' he placed the revolver muzzle against Merchant's temple and cocked the hammer, 'I'll do it for you.'

'Oh, please, please,' Merchant begged, his eyes squeezed shut. 'Please don't. I'll be fine.' He began to cry. 'Honestly, Charles. I'll be all right.'

'Are you quite sure about that?'

'Yes! Yes! Oh yes, please,' Merchant blubbered as he felt the cold steel against his head.

'They'll remain buried, John,' Higgins said quietly. 'Those statues will remain buried until they are a faded memory. All you have to do is keep your mouth tightly shut.'

'I will! I swear I will!' Merchant sobbed, tears running freely down his reddened cheeks.

'When the world has forgotten they ever existed, we sell the statues to private, and I mean *very* private, collectors, whose own best interests would be served by keeping the existence of the statues a secret still. That's our plan.' Higgins gently scratched the top of the trembling man's head with the muzzle of the gun. 'And it's a good plan,' he said in a jovial tone, as if talking to a child. He uncocked the revolver, moved again to the window and looked out at the stormy night. Rain lashed the window pane and Hong Kong Harbour was all but invisible. Behind him, John Merchant sobbed quietly.

'Now, why don't you go home,' Higgins purred. 'Or better still, go and visit one of those lovely young singsong girls on the flower boats at North Point.' He turned and looked at Merchant. The man was dribbling into his handkerchief. 'Perhaps not, it's rather late. Better to go home to a nice warm bed, eh?' He picked up his cape and walked towards the door. 'Goodnight, John.'

龍

Charles Higgins withdrew his gaze from the brandy in the balloon. 'No,' he shook his head slowly. 'It doesn't seem like ten years at all. What a pity. Those statues were almost a faded memory,' he muttered. 'Most regrettable, very irritating . . .'

'Sorry?' Merchant queried.

'Oh, just thinking out loud,' Higgins drawled. He looked at the mantle clock. Good God, he thought, quarter past eleven. He'd been daydreaming for far too long. He swallowed the brandy, placed the balloon on the side table and stood up. 'I'd better be off.' He took his police cap from the hat stand beside the double doors of the study.

'Right you are,' Merchant opened the doors wide and extended his hand. 'Would you like my chauffeur to drive you down to Central?'

'No, thank you.' Higgins stared at the outstretched hand. 'I'll walk down. It'll do me good.' He ignored the hand and raised his eyes to stare at Merchant.

'As you like,' Merchant tried to avoid Higgins' cold blue eyes. It was impossible.

'Is our course of action perfectly clear to you, John?'

'Oh, yes!' Merchant tried to sound cheerful. 'Perfectly clear old man, perfectly clear.' He was unable to break away from the hypnotic gaze. 'Friday night. S.S. *Pacific Star*. Got it.'

'Good,' Higgins spoke softly, but his tone was full of menace. 'It wouldn't do to have you wander off course at this late stage, would it, eh? Just because of a simple change of plan.'

John Merchant could only shake his head. He stood motionless, watching Charles Higgins walk across the cathedral-like foyer, past the huge elephant fountain, to the front door and exit with a friendly wave of his hand.

龍

In the Sunday afternoon sunshine a young couple sat on a wooden bench outside the office of the Hong Kong High

Level Tramway Company Limited on top of Victoria Peak. The double track of the cable tram, which hauled tourists from Central to the Peak, fell away from them almost vertically, disappearing beneath an arch of lantana vines.

Richard and Caitlin had walked for two hours around Victoria Peak, until, having exhausted all the available paths, they found themselves at the Peak Tram Station, looking down over Hong Kong Harbour.

At the start of their walk, they had discussed the previous day's riot on Western Docks. Caitlin had babbled on, asking questions and 'oohing' and 'aahing' like a schoolgirl until she realised, very suddenly, that Richard was uncomfortable with the topic. She'd looked at his bandaged hands and the sticking plaster on his cheek and felt embarrassed at her insensitivity.

'Oh, how crass of me!' she placed her hand on his forearm. 'I'm sorry, Richard.'

'What for?' he'd asked.

'The topic of conversation. It was utterly tasteless of me.'

'It's quite all right, really,' he shrugged.

'No! No, it's not! I'm truly sorry.'

'It's all right,' he'd insisted.

They'd continued to stroll, and made small talk. They'd discussed their various schools, pets, holidays, favourite places, likes, dislikes and amusements and Richard had been grateful for the common ground, because the nearness of the girl was having a profound effect on him. The hemline of her dress was at least an inch above the knee revealing a perfect set of legs, and her breasts simply would not accept any form of constraint, fighting valiantly against the fashion of the day. She was intelligent and gracious, with a complete lack of pretence.

Caitlin was in a similar state. Richard Brewster was the most compelling man she'd ever met. Besides being polite and courteous, there was an honesty about him that seemed of another age. The last two hours with him had been a revelation to her. Their conversations had revealed a truly fine young man. A sensitive, sometimes shy, yet charismatic, intelligent man. She knew, too, from his behaviour during the riot, that he was a man not afraid to risk his life. But part of him remained a little boy. A little boy who had earnestly confessed to her, not one hour before, that he intended to make his mark on the world and prove himself worthy. Yet worthy of what, or whom, he didn't say.

Caitlin Maclain was confused, and her hormonal response was not helping. When she looked at him, she was overcome by a feeling of lust, which shocked her. And now, as she sat on the bench watching him from the corner of her eye, the words of Elanora rang like alarm bells inside her head, 'That's why I envy you, Caitlin . . . you're in love'. But was she? Was it love, or was it lust?

She looked at the finely sculptured muscles in his forearms and was reminded, yet again, of the marble statues she'd seen in Florence. Richard Brewster was handsome, there was no denying it, but there was something far more compelling about him than his looks. He is no ordinary individual, Caitlin thought, he is a man who will seek his destiny, no matter what the cost, although perhaps he himself does not realise it yet.

Whether her sense of something extraordinary in the man was her own fantasy or not, Caitlin was sure of one thing. Elanora had been right. '*Carpe diem*, my dear, . . . Don't let the opportunity slip away'. Caitlin decided that she wouldn't.

'There's something about you that makes you special, Richard. No, don't interrupt, let me finish.' She had no idea what she was about to say, but she rushed on regardless, 'You're the sort of man other men will follow.'

'Do you really think so?'

'Oh, yes. In Ireland, young men like you spell trouble.'

'How do you mean?'

'You're dangerous.'

'Dangerous?' Richard gave her a quizzical look. 'Dangerous to whom?'

'I don't know,' she said, a little flustered as she stood and looked out towards Lantau Island. 'To kings, to governments, to those in positions of power.' She paused and took a deep breath. 'And to me, Richard.'

He rose and crossed to stand behind her, and the touch of his hand on her shoulder suddenly brought her to her senses.

'Oh, dear!' she gasped. 'Oh, dear, listen to me going on. We've only been acquainted since Friday evening and here I am presuming that . . .' she shuddered visibly. 'Oh, how embarrassing!' She realised she'd been so busy grabbing at the opportunity she'd failed to consider that perhaps there was no opportunity to be grabbed in the first place. Perhaps he had no feelings for her at all.

'If I've upset you . . .' Richard began, placing his hands on her shoulders.

'No, no you haven't upset me one bit,' she insisted with forced gaiety. 'I've embarrassed myself, that's all.' Caitlin turned into his arms and looked him square in the eye. 'I'm not good at affairs of the heart, in fact, I've never been involved in one and this morning I was told, well . . .' she shrugged, '. . . it was suggested to me that I seize the moment and . . . I tried to . . . and I had no right to assume your feelings would in any way match mine and . . .' she took another deep breath, '. . . I'm no good at this, Richard.' She continued staring into his eyes. 'I think what I've been trying to say is, . . . if we're going to have an affair, you'll have to start it!'

'Have you finished?' he whispered.

'Yes, I believe I have.'

'Good. Consider it started,' and he kissed her.

龍

That same Sunday before sunrise, a young Chinese couple had left the village of Hang Hau Tsuen and, after walking to the market town of Piang Shan, they'd followed the hiking track south through tiny villages until they'd reached the pass, which dropped them down into the town of Un-tan. From there they could see across the water, away to the south-east, Hong Kong Island with Victoria Peak soaring bright and clear against the early morning sky.

Earlier, just after sunrise, The Young Captain Wong had greatly impressed the girl by shooting a brace of quail and two blue herons, which he said would be gifts for her grandmother when they arrived in Kowloon. He'd then hidden his rifle and ammunition in a hollow tree trunk and taken from the trunk a coolie's straw hat and padded coat, which he put on. He hunched over and appeared for all the world to the young girl like an old man. It would not be prudent, he told her, for a famous pirate to walk the streets of Kowloon without a disguise. The police would surely take him into custody if he did. Of this he had no doubt.

The couple then walked down another pass to the west until they reached the fishing village of Tai Lam Chung, where the girl consulted a timetable attached to a post on the wharf and told him they'd have to wait for twenty minutes before catching the ferry to Kowloon.

'*It is most fortuitous, my fiancée,*' the girl said. '*The timetable says that sometimes the tides do not allow ferries to stop here at all. We are lucky, true or not true?*'

'*Do not tell me about tides!*' Wong, as the old man, snapped. '*I know all there is to know about tides!*'

'*If you wish,*' she whispered and then looked at him shyly. A grin creased her face, she could not help it. She was bursting with happiness. Happiness at her newly discovered pregnancy and happiness at her impending marriage to The Young Captain Wong who would provide for her child. '*Still, my fiancée, it is most fortuitous.*'

'*Almost as fortuitous as you falling pregnant,*' he growled.

'*Aaaiyah!*' she wailed, but her hand went to her mouth to stifle a laugh. '*How could my small body resist the entry of your powerful seed into my womb?*'

'*Hmmm,*' he considered her words. '*There is that I suppose,*' and he nodded wisely.

'*And how could any woman resist the magnificent gift of* . . .' she let her voice trail off as her hip brushed backwards and forwards across the front of his pants. '*My lord,*' she whispered, '*truly has the largest shaft in all the Central Realms.*'

'*Stop it!*' he roared, then dropped his voice to a whisper. '*I'm an old man!*'

The young woman could contain her laughter no longer. It bubbled up from her soul and she fell to the ground shrieking as tears rolled down her pretty cheeks.

'*Why do you laugh?*' he hissed, but smiled in spite of himself.

'*I'm sorry, Lord . . .,*' she cried, pointing to the bulge in his trousers, '*. . . but you are anything but an old man at the moment. True or not true?*'

'*True, most definitely true,*' he said through clenched teeth, unable to suppress his own amusement. The sight of her rolling on the ground convulsed with laughter, and him with his penis threatening to burst his trouser seams would, he had to admit, be enough to cause mirth in even the unhappiest of men.

'*I'm sorry, Lord,*' she squeaked, as big, fat tears, forced their way through her tightly shut eyelids.

'*How am I supposed to board a public ferry . . .*' he asked, the laughter overtaking him as he indicated the bulging front of his trousers, '*. . . looking like this!*'

'*I'm sorry, Lord,*' was, again, all she could manage.

'*Perhaps I should do this!*' he gasped and placed his bamboo hat over the bulge. The girl could only shake her head in defence as she rocked on the ground. '*Or this!*' He continued as he took his hands away from the hat and it remained suspended in front of his groin.

'*No more,*' the girl pleaded. '*No more, Lord, please!*' she begged as he replaced his hat on his head and collapsed beside her.

Finally, their laughter subsided and they lay on the wooden wharf staring into each other's eyes.

'*I am happy you will marry me, you have given my grandmother and me great face, but I am sad that you have to go away,*' the girl said softly.

'*I will return for you and the child,*' he lied, placing his hand against her flat stomach. '*You must not doubt this,*' he added and a flicker of remorse moved through him. It was a pity he had to kill her, but those were his orders and he would obey. Besides, she'd developed a habit for opium and it would eventually destroy her life and that of any children she would have. The flicker of remorse faded.

'*I do not doubt,*' she answered.

'*After the birth you must stay with your grandmother,*' he said and rose to his feet. The girl also stood up at the sound of someone walking on the wooden wharf.

An old woman approached and settled on a seat near them. She smiled at the couple and spoke. '*Your daughter is very beautiful, Sir. Your house is to be blessed with a grand-child. May the gods grant you a grandson.*'

'*How can you tell? I do not show yet,*' the girl gasped with delight.

'*Such happiness radiates from a woman's eyes only when a child is within her body,*' the old woman replied. She pointed to an approaching ferry and walked off down the pier.

'*Our family secret is revealed, grandfather,*' the girl chuckled to her escort.

'*We will stay at your grandmother's house tonight,*' the man said to her. He picked up the girl's bundle of belongings and his brace of freshly killed birds and, as he did so, his bamboo hat fell from his head.

'*Aiaayah,*' the girl hissed. '*Your disguise.*' She recovered his hat and pushed it onto his head.

'*A curse on disguises!*' he snapped, but raised his hand and made sure the brim concealed his features. '*Disguises are for women and fools! Why the Admiral insisted I wear such stupid apparel, the gods only know!*' He glanced at the old woman now sitting on the far end of the pier. '*I am The Young Captain Wong, not some old man!*'

'*The Admiral insisted you must not be recognised in Kowloon, because it could jeopardise his plan,*' the girl said. '*You said that was the order he gave you.*'

The orders from The One Eyed Woo had been explicit. It had been several months since Tiger Paw Chang had come to Lau Fau Shan with his proposal but word had arrived yesterday that the time of the Golden Dragons had come.

'Go to Kowloon,' The Admiral had said. 'And make sure you are not recognised. Meet with Tiger Paw Chang and learn his plan to steal the Golden Dragons.'

The fact of the girl's unwanted pregnancy had proved fortuitous. The Admiral had announced to all in the village that The Young Captain Wong would marry for the sake of the child and would travel to Kowloon to tell the girl's grandmother of the impending nuptials. It was the perfect cover; even the villagers were fooled.

Once in Kowloon, the girl was to be silenced. Even though she'd been under the effects of opium, she'd been present when Tiger Paw Chang had told his story at the inn.

'Tomorrow I will meet Tiger Paw Chang to discuss business,' The Young Captain said to her. *'After that I will return to the Admiral. Do you understand or not understand?'*

'I understand.'

'You must remain inconspicuous and never speak my name. And I will carry out the orders of The Admiral, The One Eyed Woo.'

'That is how it shall be,' the girl answered gravely.

The small wooden ferry waited for them to board and sounded its new hooter cheerfully as it set course for Kap Sui-moon Pass at the north-east tip of Lantau Island. Once through it, they would sail east to Kowloon Public Pier in Hong Kong Harbour.

龍

Tiger Paw Chang sat on a bench beneath the clock tower on Kowloon Public Pier and gazed at Hong Kong Island, bathed in late afternoon sunshine. A sense of tranquillity filled his obese body, despite the hustle and bustle of hundreds of watercraft going about their business on the harbour before him. He looked again at the clock tower. Five o'clock, time for The Young Captain Wong to meet him.

Tiger Paw Chang insisted upon punctuality. Where was The Young Captain Wong? But he would let nothing interfere with his feeling of well-being on this wonderful Sunday. He wiggled his long fingernails, concealed in the sleeves of his traditional Chinese gown, against the smooth hairless skin of his forearms and sighed with contentment. Soon he would be rich beyond his wildest dreams.

He would divorce himself from the Man Shing Tong Triad Society and live the life of an indulgent mandarin. He would be the model citizen, and give to charities and support the arts as the *gwai loh* did. He would be known as a benefactor to schools, monasteries and churches alike. His wealth would be second to none and he would have great face and be respected by all.

And that's where I will build my mansion, he thought, as his eyes took in the magnificent houses ablaze with the late afternoon sun, dotted around Victoria Peak. Up there where only the best of Hong Kong's wealthy dwell. I will fill it with treasures and servants. Young servants, who will bring me soup made from birds' nests from the caves of Amoy, and bears' paws from the far western mountains, and I will sip the best brandy from the place called France.

And I will drink the blood of innocents, he heard another voice whisper from the darkest recesses of his mind. And you will give me pipes, the voice hissed. Pipes to ease my torment. And Tiger Paw Chang nodded his consent to the demon within and closed his eyes as the joy of anticipation over-whelmed him.

'*Ah Chang, Sir,*' another voice whispered.

Tiger Paw opened his eyes and nodded in welcome as The Young Captain Wong, looking for all the world like an old mendicant, sat by his side on the bench.

'*You are not ageing well, my young captain,*' Tiger Paw said and his fat body began to shake with mirth. '*What happened to the grunting young stallion I witnessed in the village of Hang Hau Tsuen,*' he chuckled. '*Surely you must never copulate again, if this is what it does to your body!*'

'*It is the Admiral's wish that I not be recognised,*' the young man replied.

'*Ah, The Admiral, The One Eyed Woo, he who is most in my thoughts these days. His health is good or not good?*'

'*It is good.*'

'I am glad,' Chang nodded. 'It is better than yours, true or not true?'

'What do you mean?'

'Are you not aware that you are bleeding from the mouth?'

'Am I?' The Young Captain Wong placed his hand on his lips and his fingers came away covered in blood. He felt with his tongue at his loosened teeth. Damn! he thought. What a day he'd had. First, the walk from Lau Fau Shan to Tai Lam Chung with that stupid young girl, then the ferry into Kowloon, then finding her grandmother's hovel in the bowels of the Walled City. Then, less than an hour ago, the blow from the young girl that had hit him in the mouth as he'd thrust his knife at her. She'd caught him by surprise in the act of cutting her grandmother's throat.

'You should go to a tooth doctor in the Walled City,' Tiger Paw Chang said. 'They are the best in all of China.'

'It is not necessary.'

'I can only offer advice. Your wisdom in matters of health does not match your age, old man,' Tiger Paw Chang joked as his body jiggled with mirth.

'Honourable Chang,' The Young Captain Wong muttered through clenched teeth. 'I mean no disrespect, but I am a pirate and although I consider the profession to be a proper one, the authorities do not. My face adorns the walls of police stations and post offices and it is not healthy for me to sit in public places for too long, true or not true?'

Chang giggled and The Young Captain Wong suppressed a great urge to cut off the fat man's scrotum.

Tiger Paw looked across at Hong Kong Island and his smile disappeared, as he saw the pall of smoke still evident from the previous day's fire. 'As a result of the Western Docks riot, the four statues that interest us have risen from the ashes. Do you understand, or not understand?'

'I understand.'

'Look now at the foreign ship that anchors in the harbour.'

The Young Captain Wong followed Chang's long finger-nail and saw a steamship of some 1500 tons. 'She flies the flag of the foreign taipan John Merchant,' he said.

'*My spies inform me, that she is the next ship of the Merchant Line to sail.*' Chang turned to the young pirate, '*On Friday she will sail for the country of England.*'

He was about to go on, but stopped abruptly as The Young Captain Wong shook his head slowly.

'*What is it, my young Captain?*'

'*She's too big,*' Wong replied and looked about before continuing in a hushed whisper. '*I speak for The Admiral, The One Eyed Woo, when I tell you that his junks could never attack a ship that size. Only three months ago, he attacked a Macau Ferry and lost half his fleet. This ship you indicate is five times bigger and . . .*'

The two men fell silent as several people walked by.

'*Do not consider me a fool, Wong!*' Tiger Paw Chang snapped when they were free to resume their conversation.

'*I do not, Honourable One, but . . .*'

'*Then shut up and listen,*' Chang hissed. He took a deep breath and exhaled as he looked out over the water. The harbour was alive with ships of all kinds and he watched them for some time, overcoming his irritation, before turning again to the young pirate. '*You will need only one junk.*'

'*But . . .*'

'*Listen! I will not tell you again.*' Chang's eyes narrowed to evil slits. '*Six of my men of the Man Shing Tong are watching us at this moment.*' He struggled to swallow his anger. '*At a sign from me they will hack you to pieces where you sit. Do you understand or not understand?*'

'*I understand,*' Wong nodded and looked about nervously.

'*That ship is called the Pacific Star,*' Chang nodded in the direction of the vessel. '*She will sail through the West Lamma Channel and she will run aground on the eastern extremity of Wei ling Tin Island, just outside Hong Kong waters.*'

'*Where the Marine Police have no jurisdiction.*'

'*Exactly,*' Chang nodded. '*No one on the vessel must be left alive, that includes anybody who claims to be my agent. The Admiral, The One Eyed Woo, will secure the statues and bring them to Bias Bay, where I will meet him.*'

'*And we will all be rich!*' The Young Captain Wong exclaimed.

Tiger Paw Chang looked at the young man in his old man's disguise. '*Yes,*' he murmured. '*We will all be rich.*'

'*I must return and repeat your instructions to my Admiral,*' Wong whispered and stood up. He was only too happy the meeting was at an end.

'*I have another message for your Admiral,*' Chang said softly and patted the seat vacated by the pirate.

The Young Captain Wong sat back down and looked around. '*What would the message be?*' he asked tremulously.

'*Tell him, the sight of such mythical animals can turn a man's heart to greed, therefore the Admiral should be on guard against his inner demons. Failure to do so would incur the wrath of the Man Shing Tong.*'

'*My Admiral is a man of honour!*' Wong had felt obliged to interrupt, but the glare in Chang's eyes silenced him.

'*Calm yourself, my young sea hawk,*' Chang's voice sent a shiver through the pirate. '*As long as my plans are carried out all will be well.*' He stood, grunting with the effort. '*Go to your Admiral and tell him I look forward to the day soon when we will all be rich. And I will see you again, when I see my legendary golden friends.*'

The Young Captain Wong could only stare across the water as Tiger Paw Chang shuffled off into the circle of his bodyguards.

CHAPTER SIX

On the Monday morning following Saturday's riot, the smell of tragedy wafted through the corridors of Central Police Station. Men avoided each other's eyes, their speech was soft, their demeanour subdued. The usual happy, pre-shift babbling from the Chinese barracks was noticeably absent and the funereal atmosphere that replaced it was oppressive.

Robert McCraw stood on the balcony one floor above the quadrangle and stared down at the members of Richard Brewster's platoon. They shuffled unhappily from the armoury window to the centre of the square where they huddled, sheep-like, awaiting the call to form ranks for inspection. McCraw knew how they felt. Death in the ranks was something all soldiers and policemen experienced eventually and it was a difficult thing to share. The pain felt for lost colleagues was always tinged with a feeling of guilt. McCraw had experienced it many times.

Images of the battlefields of France flickered through his brain, the Somme, Ypres, Verdun. Battlefields scattered with the bodies of young men. The dead and the dying, moaning as they lay in the mud of No Man's Land, desperately clinging to life until the coming of night when their rescue would be attempted. And he remembered his guilt. The fleeting wish that it was him lying out there and not his comrades, and then the overwhelming rush of relief that it was *not* him. It was a terrible emotion. Once experienced, never forgotten. The only thing you can do, laddies, he thought sadly as he looked at the young policemen, is to laugh it off and get on with life.

When Richard Brewster inspected his platoon the full extent of the tragedy came home to him. PC Singh had been killed, PC Chan Man Long permanently blinded, and four others were unable to work because of injury. Two others from his platoon had failed to turn up for duty, but given the horror of the previous Saturday's events, Richard was loath to report them.

'Gentlemen,' he began addressing his men in English, then smiled and switched to halting Cantonese, much to the horror of Lo Shi-mon. '*Yesterday on the streets of Western District, you give me great face. I very much like your very good work.*'

Richard's men shuffled uneasily in the ranks. They glanced at one another and many of the Shangtungese looked at Constable Lo Shi-mon.

Lo was as shocked as the others. This *gwai loh* was different, unlike most of his compatriots, Brewster *Sin Sang* had no sense of class distinction. To him, Chinese, Indian, Russian and European men were equal and for that he was to be admired, but for an officer to use a language other than English on parade was unheard of and Lo was ill at ease.

'*PC Singh is dead,*' Richard continued, '*and PC Chan has no eyes. Therefore, I am unhappy here,*' he placed his hand over his heart. '*Policemen will always be unhappy. Our job is very much danger. Therefore, we must be brothers. Therefore, we must be one family all together, cunt or not cunt?*' he finished and watched his platoon fall to pieces, laughing.

'*Aaaiyaah!*' Lo exhaled.

'Have I said something wrong?' Richard said, helplessly.

'Brewster!'

Richard turned at the roar of his name. 'Good morning, Sir,' he gulped as Robert McCraw strode across the quadrangle.

'You idiot!' the big Scot bellowed. 'Standing Orders forbids the use of any language but the King's English by an officer whilst on formal parade!'

'Yes, Sir.' Richard saluted.

'And furthermore,' his senior officer lowered his voice.

'No matter what language is used, they expressly forbid the use of the word cunt!'

'I beg your pardon, Sir?' Richard was shocked.

'You will not use Cantonese on the parade square. You will address your men in English and your translator, whom I believe is Constable Lo, will translate. Am I understood, Brewster?'

'Yes, Sir.' Richard saluted again.

'Good! Now get this lot into some semblance of order,' he said, indicating the broken ranks of laughing men. Despite his stern demeanour McCraw was secretly pleased. Richard's linguistic blunder had brought a smile to the faces of the men for the first time in two days. God knows, he thought, they could do with a laugh, even if it was at their officer's expense.

McCraw considered the young officer before him. The boy, for that's what he was, had shown great courage the previous Saturday and even more to McCraw's liking, he had shown great consideration for the men under his command. It was the hallmark of a born leader, the big Scot knew, to show initiative and lead by example and Richard Brewster had done just that, but more importantly, after seeing the treacherous stepped street and sunken godown doorways his men were required to protect, he'd shown concern for their safety by requesting confirmation of his orders before placing them at risk.

Robert McCraw was developing a healthy respect for the young Englishman. Richard Brewster was made of the right stuff and would make a good officer, but Robert sensed something far more in the lad. He'd known many officers in his time in the British Army but he'd known few who'd lived up to their rank. Those few had had a special quality about them, an aura, McCraw thought, for want of a better word, that set them apart from other men and he was beginning to sense that aura about Richard Brewster. It was the indefinable quality of a leader that made others follow, unquestioning, like sailors followed a star at night knowing it would lead them safely home.

Young Brewster himself may not realise it yet, McCraw

mused, but the riot had revealed qualities in the lad that, when combined with the responsibility of leadership, could take him to the highest echelons of command.

'Squad!' Richard roared, and his men formed ranks instantly, realising the joke was over. 'Squad, attention!'

'That's better,' McCraw muttered. 'A word of advice, Mr Brewster. Cantonese is a tonal language. The words may sound the same, but they are delivered in different tones and if they're not, the result can be extremely embarrassing. This is especially so with the word *hai*,' he went on, aware of another ripple of mirth through the ranks. 'Which is the positive part of the Cantonese verb "to be". When used in the interrogative sense and intoned correctly, in a low tone with a falling inflection, it asks the question; is this true or, is this so? When pronounced in a high tone with a rising inflection, the word *hai* becomes a crude reference to the female genitalia!'

'Oh, my God!' Richard blushed. 'I'm terribly sorry.'

'Exactly,' the big Scot murmured. 'Now stand your men at ease, I've an order to read.'

'Yes, Sir!' Richard saluted yet again, and yet again McCraw was forced to return the salute.

'For Christ's sake, maaarn! Get on with it!'

'Squad! Stand at ease!' Richard yelled, cringing with embarrassment. 'Stand easy.' He turned to McCraw and was about to salute again, but dropped his arm as he caught the Scotsman's eye. 'They're all yours, Sir,' he finished lamely.

Robert McCraw took a letter from his pocket, turned to the squad and indicated that Constable Lo should translate. 'Gentlemen,' his voice rang through the quadrangle. 'I have, this day, received orders from The Inspector-General of the Hong Kong Police Force that Sergeant Richard Brewster is to be promoted to the rank of Inspector, effective immediately.' A murmur of approval went through the ranks. 'Settle down,' McCraw warned. 'Furthermore, the same order directs that Constable Lo Shi-mon be promoted to the rank of Sergeant, also with immediate effect. That will be all.'

McCraw turned and smiled. 'Well done, lad,' he said and shook Richard's hand.

'Thank you, Sir.'

'And to you, Sergeant Lo,' McCraw continued. 'Congratulations.' He shook the surprised Shangtungese by the hand. 'Both appointments well deserved, dare I say. That will be all, carry on.' He saluted and walked off the square.

The rest of the parade and duty briefing went by in a blur for Richard and, before he realised it, his men had gone off to their duties and he was left alone on the square with Lo Shi-mon.

'Congratulations, Sergeant,' Richard smiled and the pair shook hands. 'Is there a specific word for sergeant in Cantonese, or is it just *Sa jin*?'

'*Sa jin*,' the tall Chinese confirmed. 'English same-same, there is no Chinese word for *Sa jin*. Just *Sa jin*.' Lo grinned. 'I am called *Sa jin* and you are called *Bom Baan*, that is Inspector.'

'Well, in that case, *Sa jin*, I think we'd better get out on patrol, what do you say?' Richard couldn't suppress a grin. He was happy that his Chinese friend had been promoted. It would mean a great deal more money to Lo and give him great face among his peers. And furthermore, he was the right man for the job. Lo Shi-mon was a born NCO, highly esteemed by his fellow police officers, especially the Shangtungese, who were almost obsequious in his presence.

'Yes Sir, *Bom Baan*!' Lo snapped a salute.

'And about our two men missing from parade,' Richard winked conspiratorially. 'I think we'll overlook their absence just this once, eh?'

Lo looked left and right and shuffled his huge boots before speaking. 'Ah, Elder Brother,' he whispered. 'I think the men will not come back.'

'What?'

'I think they maybe run away.'

'Sergeant,' Richard replied sternly, for he could sense immediately that Lo Shi-mon was being evasive. 'Those men are under my command, and yours now, for that matter. They are our responsibility so if there's anything wrong . . .?' He left the question hanging in the air.

'Ah, Brewster *Bom Baan*, I think we cannot talk about it.'

'Really,' Richard said uneasily, it was obvious to him that his new sergeant was uncomfortable. Lo's eyes were averted, searching the doorways and offices surrounding the quadrangle. 'And why is that, Mr Lo?'

'You will not understand.'

'Why do you say that?'

'Sir, all the PCs like you very much. Much more than all other officers. Maybe only McCraw *Bom Baan* they like as much as you. You learn to speak Chinese like McCraw, Sir. This is very good . . .'

'Don't patronise me, Sergeant!'

'. . . but you do not know the Chinese people yet.'

'What's this got to do with two missing PCs?' Richard asked abruptly.

Lo Shi-mon took a deep breath, turned his gaze directly at the young Englishman, and made the most important decision of his life. 'They are not missing, Sir, they are killed.'

'What?'

'Please, Sir,' Lo looked about furtively. 'Tonight you must find your *lo pang yau*, 'Effernan Sin Sang . . .'

'Never mind my old friend Mr Heffernan,' Richard snapped. 'Where are my two missing men?' He was getting angry. What was the man on about? Two men killed?

'Please, *Dai Loh*,' the Chinese hissed and pulled Richard into the shadows of the quadrangle. 'You must learn about the *Hung Mun*!'

'The *Hung Mun*? You mean triad societies?'

''Effernan Sin Sang he will tell you,' Lo's frustration at his lack of English was showing. ''Effernan is expert about the Chinese, I think. He is a teacher of wisdom.'

'Sergeant Lo, I am losing my patience with you . . .'

'No,' Lo's voice was a deep growl. He grabbed Richard by the wrist, causing an excruciating pain to shoot up his arm. 'You must listen, *Dai Loh*, please!'

'What on earth are you two chaps up to?' Both men froze at the voice. It was Bertie Pertwee. 'Brewster? Is that you?'

'Please, *Dai Loh*?' Lo Shi-mon whispered.

'Aaah, er, yes, Sir.' Richard managed to find his voice. His fingers were completely numb.

'Why aren't you out on the streets, man?'

'So sorry, Mister Pertwee, Sir,' Lo interjected. 'I show Mister Brewster *kung fu*, Sir.'

'Oh, right,' Pertwee said jovially. 'Damn good stuff. All that leaping about and gibbering like monkeys, eh what? By the way, Mr Brewster, congratulations on your promotion, good show.' He waved his arm airily. 'Well, carry on,' he muttered, bemused and walked off the square into the Charge Room.

When he'd gone, Richard massaged his wrist and stared coldly at the Chinese. 'I could put you on a charge for that, Mr Lo,' he said flatly.

'Sir, I am sorry.' He looked in the direction of the Charge Room. 'Tonight you see *'Effernan Sin Sang* and I will come with you. There is much danger for us. I cannot tell you the story of the *Hung Mun* in English.' The eyes of the big Chinese pleaded with Richard. 'But you must learn it, for now you are deeply involved.'

Finally, Richard nodded. '*Very well, Sa jin,*' he said softly in Cantonese. '*Tonight. You, me and Heffernan Sin Sang.*'

龍

Sergeant Terrence Delaney had seen most things in his forty-two years. He'd been a coalminer in Yorkshire, raised amongst hard men, and he'd fought for money bare-knuckled in the pubs of many a Midlands town. He'd even been in the Great War on the battlefields of France, but nothing could have prepared him for the sight he'd just witnessed.

He stood outside the cool store of Kam Yuk Meat Importers in Hennessey Road, his face as white as a sheet. Sweat broke out on his forehead and he resisted the urge to vomit, his hands shaking as he opened his notebook to record the event.

Behind him the door crashed open and Stewart Cameron burst into the light of day and vomited his breakfast onto the stone footpath. He gasped and heaved for breath, wave after wave of nausea wrenching his stomach dry, then he fell to his knees and began to cry.

The smell of Cameron's vomit hit Delaney in the nostrils and he fought for control as his own stomach began to spasm. He took a deep breath, held it for a full minute, then exhaled and tried to force the horrendous images from his head. God Almighty! His mind screamed. Why did I have to see that? No one should ever have to see anything like that. His body shook with revulsion as he looked around him at the happy, babbling Cantonese going about their daily business, unaware of what lay not fifty feet from them. What sort of people are you? he wanted to shout at them. What sort of society is this to allow such barbarity?

Inside on the cool room floor, amongst several hundred freshly slaughtered pig carcasses, lay two men. Delaney couldn't tell if they were Chinese or foreign. Their skins had been removed. Completely. Their muscles and tissues remained intact. Their eyes, still in the sockets, staring. Their teeth exposed, grinning in death. All Delaney knew was that they were police constables. Their uniforms lay beside them, and they'd been ritually murdered in triad society fashion.

龍

'I don't like it, Richard,' Quincy Heffernan's hands shook as he poured Chinese tea into three small porcelain cups. 'I don't like it one little bit.'

Richard looked through the door that led out onto the small balcony of Quincy's abode. Quincy lived on the south side of Hong Kong Island. The building which contained his modest second floor flat was one of hundreds of similar stone edifices, jammed together along the channel of water which separated Hong Kong Island from the smaller island of Ap Li Chau. It was known, incongruously, as Aberdeen Harbour. Hundreds of junks and fishing trawlers filled the bloated port. It was said that more than seventy thousand people lived aboard them and rarely did they set foot on land. In the moonlight, the lamps on the vessels created a fairyland scene, warm, silent and peaceful.

Sergeant Lo Shi-mon rocked the first knuckles of his index and middle fingers on the wooden table top in an ancient sign of thank you for the cup of tea. The sign imitated a man on his knees, kow-towing his forehead to the floor in an act of obeisance

'Thank you, 'Effernan Sin Sang,' Lo said politely.

'Not necessary to say thank you,' Quincy replied and placed the teapot on the table.

'Triad societies are dangerous, Richard,' he continued. 'They are no longer the noble organisations they once were. Those days are gone, they are merely the Chinese equivalent of gangsters.'

'No,' Lo Shi-mon interrupted. He placed his cup on the table and spoke rapidly in Cantonese. "Effernan Sin Sang, I am the Hung Kwan, the number 426 of the Man Yee On.'

'Good God!' Quincy gasped.

'What is it?' Richard asked. 'What is Hung Kwan?'

Quincy was silent for a moment. 'Your friend, Sergeant Lo, just told me he is the Red Pole of the Man Yee On Triad Society.' He looked at Richard, clearly shocked. 'Under triad law he could be executed for admitting that to an outsider.'

'Elder Brother,' Lo continued to Quincy, 'You are a friend to the Chinese people. All in Hong Kong like you. You are a secret expert on the history of the Hung Mun Societies. Many years ago my Shan Chu imparted the knowledge of the societies to you and allowed you to remain alive with that knowledge. Have you ever asked yourself why?'

'No,' Quincy replied in Cantonese. 'But I've never uttered a word of the story to anyone. I've kept the secrets to myself all these years.' Quincy was scared.

'You were told because my Master knew that one day we would be in need of your help. One day we would need a foreign devil to explain our Ancient Order, and that day is today. The Man Yee On is in much trouble. My Lodge is true to the ancient ways, unlike the other societies that exist in Hong Kong like the Man Shing Tong and the Fuk Yee Hing.' Lo Shi-mon grabbed Quincy Heffernan by the arm. 'Both these societies have declared war upon the Man Yee On.'

'Oh heavens,' Quincy's voice quavered.

'What's he saying?' Richard interjected. 'He's speaking too fast for me to understand.'

'*The riot on Saturday caused a triad war,*' the big Chinese went on. '*And Brewster Bom Baan is heavily involved. The boy he saved by riding the flaming dragon is the grandson of my Shan Chu and because he saved the boy's life he is now responsible for it, as is the Chinese way. The Man Shing Tong knows this and your friend Brewster is on its death list. As far as they are concerned he is one of us and worse, he has caused them great loss of face.*'

Quincy Heffernan rose to his feet and looked at the young men before him.

'For God's sake, Quincy, what's going on?' Richard demanded.

Quincy could only shake his head. He placed his hand on his forehead and walked slowly about his living room. Never, in all his years in Hong Kong, had he been placed in such an invidious situation. He'd spent his life as a quiet scholar. He'd offended no one and lived what he'd thought was a happy, if solitary, existence. And now, that tranquil life was shattered forever. Quincy realised that the mere fact these two policemen were in his house would embroil him in the evil game they were caught up in. Lo Shi-mon had dragged him into the game without even asking. He studied the faces of the two young men. Richard's bore the look of bewilderment, and Lo Shi-mon's that of a drowning man. Lo Shi-mon had exposed himself. He'd declared himself to an outsider. But why, Quincy's mind asked, why do it? Why not let the young Englishman die at the hands of the Man Shing Tong? He was just a *gwai loh* after all.

Quincy looked at the young Chinese again. '*Why?*' he asked.

'*My Shan Chu is a man of honour, 'Effernan,*' Lo said earnestly. '*This man saved his grandson's life. He must be protected. That is why I am here, my Shan Chu ordered it. Your friend Brewster must have our story. Once he is told the story he will have no alternative but to join our society and enjoy its protection. And you are the only one who can give him this knowledge in his own language.'*

'Look, what on earth is going on?' Richard leapt to his feet. 'I'm unable to understand a word of what's being said. Sergeant Lo is gabbling like a typewriter.'

Quincy looked at the young police inspector and a deep sadness enveloped him. Because of this young man his tranquil existence as a simple oriental scholar was finished. His fate had been decreed. He placed a hand on the boy's shoulder. 'Sit down, Richard,' he said. 'I have a story to tell you. I'm going to tell you the traditional triad society history, as seen through the eyes of the founders. I warn you it is much romanticised for the Chinese are, by nature, prone to allegory, but don't dismiss it as pure mythology, Richard, for it is not. I will admit that it cannot be taken at face value, but then, such is the case with much of history. The history of Christianity, for example, is rampantly allegorical and yet it is widely believed. Anyway, according to the Old Kwan, this is what happened.

'Towards the end of the reign of Ch'ung-chen, in about 1644 or thereabouts, or in our history during the reign of Charles I, the Ming Dynasty of China was rotten to the core. The Emperor was a sexual degenerate. He surrounded himself with sycophants who catered to his every whim in return for Imperial appointments and favours. The internal administration of the Central Realms collapsed. Famine swept the country and the people starved while those few in the Emperor's favour grew fat and rich at the expense of the common man. And encamped outside the Great Wall, the Manchu Tartars from the north awaited their opportunity to seize the Dragon Throne.

'Meanwhile, in the city of Peking, a group of honest Ming officials and citizens formed a secret organisation. The aim of this organisation was to rid the Court of corrupt officials and restore the Dynasty of the Ming to its former glory. Unfortunately the Manchus swept in and seized the Dragon Throne for themselves. They set up Shun Chi as the first Emperor of the Ch'ing Dynasty.

'The covert Ming organisation fled to Fukien Province and became monks in the Siu Lam monastery and that is where the story really begins. The Siu Lam order of monks is better known by the Mandarin name of Shaolin. The Shaolin monastery in the Kaolin Mountains of Fukien is where the original *Hung Mun* Society really began. The Heroes of Shaolin, as these monks became known, practised and further developed ancient methods of combat called *kung fu . . .*'

'*Kung fu?*' Richard looked at Lo Shi-mon.

The big sergeant nodded. '*Yes, Elder Brother, kung fu,*' he replied and Richard remembered the pain he'd experienced that morning when Lo Shi-mon had seized his wrist.

'It is an ancient and very highly developed form of martial art,' Quincy went on. 'The complete knowledge of which is known to very few . . .'

'He knows it,' Richard nodded at Lo Shi-mon.

'Really?' Quincy raised his eyebrows.

'*I have practised the disciplines of Shaolin since I was a tiny boy, 'Effernan Sin Sang,*' Lo replied softly.

Quincy looked at the hands of the big Chinese. The knuckles and edges of his palms were calloused and hard. '*Then you would make a formidable adversary, Lo Sin Sang,*' Quincy bowed his head slightly towards the sergeant. '*Or a valuable friend, true or not true?*'

'*True, 'Effernan teacher,*' Lo replied, as his eyes accepted Quincy's challenge. '*And my loyalty to Brewster Bom Baan is beyond question. It extends beyond death, so do not question it, understand or not understand?*'

'Understand,' Quincy smiled. 'So, let us continue . . .'

He then embarked upon a lengthy tale of war and treachery spanning three hundred years, which to Richard, seemed absurdly complicated. He talked of magical rivers, spirits and dragons and five men known as The First Five Ancestors, and an hour later, his voice seemed to recede into the distance as sleep began to search for control of Richard's mind.

'I'm afraid the story meanders into the realm of pure fantasy around about this point,' Quincy finally shrugged. 'It all gets a touch biblical, if you know what I mean.'

'You must go on!' Lo Shi-mon interjected. 'You tell the story most perfectly accurate.'

'Mr Lo,' Quincy fixed the Chinese with a baleful stare. 'The story of The First Five Ancestors cannot be told in one night. Besides, Mr Brewster has heard more than enough to suit your master's purpose. He is utterly compromised, which is what your master wanted.' Quincy turned to Richard. 'The story continues for hours, Richard, and half of it defies explanation. It is barbaric and ferocious beyond imagining. Suffice it to say it ends with The First Five Ancestors swearing a blood oath to *fan Ch'ing, fuk Ming*. Overthrow the Ch'ing, restore the Ming. Hence the origin of the modern day triad society.' Quincy looked at Lo Shi-mon and fell silent.

Richard shook his head in an attempt to clear his befuddled brain of the hundreds of images Quincy had painted. 'Well,' he said eventually as his eyes focused on the reality, which was Quincy Heffernan's small flat. 'I must say you tell a good story, old man, but I'm afraid the point of it all is lost on me.'

'That's a pity,' Quincy said. 'Because the mere fact that you've heard it is enough to get your throat cut.'

'How's that?' Richard asked as he rubbed his eyes and blinked rapidly.

'You've been compromised, Richard,' Quincy continued. 'You've been told a secret story which should never be heard by anyone who is not a member of a triad society. The fact that your mind wandered through part of it is neither here nor there. Mr Lo has seen to it that your life in Hong Kong will never be the same.'

'That is not fair, 'Effernan Sin Sang,' Lo Shi-mon spoke softly in Cantonese. *'Brewster Inspector's life was destroyed when he rescued the boy. The Man Shing Tong will kill him.'*

'Wait a minute, wait a minute!' Richard snapped. 'Did Sergeant Lo just say someone wants to kill me?'

'I'm afraid so, my lad,' Quincy nodded. 'You shouldn't have rescued the boy during the riot.'

'Don't change the subject! Who is this Man Shing Tong fellow and why does he want to kill me?'

'Not who, what.'

'What?'

'Exactly,' Quincy smiled. 'The Man Shing Tong is a powerful triad society and its members want to slit your throat.'

'Why?'

'Because the police force defeated them last Saturday in a public brawl, and in the middle of that brawl, you had the temerity to rescue the grandson of their worst enemy, causing them to lose even greater face.'

'I'm sorry?' Richard was totally bewildered.

'Yes, well, I'm afraid that won't do,' Quincy shook his head, confusing the young man even more. 'Besides, you've now been told the story of The First Five Ancestors and that makes things far worse.'

'Worse?' Richard could only stare at his white-haired old friend. 'How could it make things worse?'

'By saving the boy, you had one triad society after you. Now that you've been told the story, you might well have every illegal triad society in China after your hide. That is if they discover you know their secret history.'

'But it's a load of old codswallop. A fairy story!'

'It's no different to the Freemasons,' Quincy chided. 'They base their rituals on a load of childish nonsense, do they not? They dress up in infantile aprons and sashes, do they not?' They whisper silly passwords, do they not?'

'I suppose so.'

'Well, then?' Quincy raised an eyebrow. 'The story you have been told, well, enough of it anyway, is the basis for all triad ritual. It contains all their passwords, their secret names, signs and symbols, their dress codes, their initiation ceremonies. Put yourself in their shoes, or should I say straw sandals. What would you do if a foreigner knew the intricacies of your secret political organisation and the traitorous ideals it held for the restoration of the monarchy?'

Richard nodded. 'I see what you're getting at. A once noble political group has turned into a bunch of isolated criminal societies and they all want to kill me because of this ridiculous fairytale you've told me, is that correct?'

Quincy refused to react to Richard's apparent flippancy, recognising it as a cover. The lad had recognised the danger of the situation, he was sure. 'All except for Mr Lo's society, the Man Yee On. They're offering you membership as a means of protection.'

'Do they really take it all that seriously?'

'They're fanatical about it,' Quincy replied bluntly. 'You're as good as dead.'

'What will I do?' Richard's question was rhetorical. His mind was already weighing up the facts. Mention of the Freemasons had brought his father to mind, but he'd instantly dismissed the thought. He would not ask his father for help under any circumstances, he was determined to stand alone, whatever his fate. His first instinct was to run, to take Caitlin and get out of Hong Kong.

'You could take your bold Irish girl and get on the first boat out of Hong Kong,' Quincy said as if reading his mind.

'Run away, in other words?'

'It is one option. Personally, I wouldn't consider it, but it is an option.'

Richard knew it was not an option, because in choosing it he would endanger Caitlin. But what other options were there? Run, or stand and fight, his mind screamed and try as he might he could think of no others.

'*Ha!*' Lo Shi-mon stood up and glared at the two Englishmen. '*Do you think you can just run away? Are you foolish enough to believe that we Chinese live only in the Central Realms? The triads are everywhere! America, Germany, France, Australia! Even your country England!*' He turned on his heel and paced Quincy's living quarters, staring at Richard as he did so. '*Do you believe or not believe that I would help him run away if I thought it would save his life?*' Lo stopped pacing and glared at Quincy. '*Well, ask him!*' he finished with a finger pointing at Richard.

'*I know what you said,*' Richard stood and faced Lo. '*Mei Gwok, Daak Gwok, Faat Gwok, O Jau,* America, Germany, France and Australia and I think you mentioned England as well. The triads are everywhere. *I cannot run, true or not true?*'

'*True, Elder Brother,*' Lo placed his hand on Richard's shoulder. '*If you could run I would help you, but you cannot. They will find you wherever you go. There is no escape, you are caught in the trap you made for yourself.*'

'Sorry,' Richard interrupted by holding his hand in the air, 'I didn't understand the last bit, you speak too fast. You said, "there is no escape", then what?'

'*You are caught in the trap you made for yourself,*' Lo articulated slowly.

'He's saying you are caught in a trap of your own making,' Quincy explained.

'My own making!' Richard's anger got the better of him. 'How did you arrive at that conclusion?' he snapped at the Chinese sergeant. 'All I did was save a little boy's life!'

'That's the problem.' It was Quincy who replied. 'In China, if you save a life, you are responsible for it forever. You saved the grandson of a triad master. In doing so you have embroiled yourself in their bloody business forever.'

'But that's not fair!'

'I agree,' Quincy nodded. 'But I'm afraid the Chinese don't quite see it that way. As far as they're concerned you stuck your nose into a matter that didn't concern you, to wit, the cycle of life and death. You interfered with that cycle by altering a fixed set of circumstances decreed by the gods, in other words you buggered up the natural journey of a soul. So, as far as the gods are concerned, you either cut the boy's throat and allow his soul to continue its journey immediately, or you accept responsibility for the body, which is the temple of the soul, until the boy dies of natural causes.'

'That's utterly illogical!'

'Not to the Chinese.'

'*Effernan Sin Sang,*' Lo Shi-mon said softly. '*Please you again tell the story of Cheng Kwan-tat.*'

'Very good,' Quincy nodded. '*That is a very good idea.*'

'What's a good idea?' Richard enquired.

'Remember Cheng Kwan-tat in the story of Shaolin?'

'No. What about him?'

'He lived in the Shaolin monastery,' Quincy said with the hint of a smile. 'But he was not a monk.'

'So?'

'You live in Hong Kong,' Lo added. 'But you not Chinese.'

'He also joined with the monks to fight a common enemy. Richard, my boy, that's what Mr Lo's asking you to do, join his society for your own safety's sake.'

'I'm not going to join a damned illegal society!' Richard leapt to his feet.

'From where I'm sitting you don't have much choice!' The young Englishman's lack of comprehension was beginning to annoy Quincy. 'You were brought here by a senior triad official,' he pointed at Lo, 'and deliberately compromised. For your own good as far as his triad society is concerned. That's what this little get-together is all about. You know their secrets because they asked me to tell them to you. Now, to their understanding, you have no alternative but to join them and fight for your life! Hence, the offer being made to you by Mr Lo.'

'If you do not fight you will die.' Lo Shi-mon stated flatly. 'It will be a foolish death. A very bad death. The Man Shing Tong will take off all your skin.'

Richard Brewster stiffened as he turned slowly to face his sergeant, realisation dawning on his face. 'Like the two bodies found this morning?' He remembered the looks on the faces of Delaney and Cameron when they'd returned to the station after attending the murder scene. Delaney, tough Yorkshireman that he was, had had a haunted look, and Stewart Cameron had been such a physical and mental wreck, he'd been excused from duty and sent to the doctor.

Lo Shi-mon nodded slowly. 'Yes, Elder Brother. Our men missing from parade.'

'The two things Delaney and Cameron found?'

'Yes, Elder Brother.

'Why didn't you tell me?'

'I tried to tell you after parade.'

Quincy's fist hit the tabletop with considerable force, sending the porcelain tea cups flying in all directions, as he vented his anger upon the foolish young Englishman. 'He could have simply kept his mouth shut altogether and let you die at the hands of Man Shing Tong assassins, like the ignorant *gwai loh* you are showing yourself to be! Now sit down, stop behaving so stupidly and listen for once in your life!'

Shocked by the vehemence of Quincy Heffernan's outburst, both young policemen sat down at the table.

'Richard,' Quincy continued, softly now that he'd gained Richard's full attention. 'As of tonight, your life has changed forever. You are not caught up in some game on the playing fields of Eton! It was foolish of me to suggest you run away, wishful thinking on my part. Lo Shi-mon is right, there is no escape. You are involved, like it or not, in a triad war! They do not stop for a half-time interval with tea and cakes on the lawn. They skin people alive. I've heard tell they can, with a small incision, remove your spleen while keeping you conscious, deep fry it in a wok and eat it before your eyes.'

'That's disgusting.'

'Isn't it,' Quincy agreed. 'Particularly when you consider *you* may well be their next meal. And don't bother going to your English police contemporaries, they won't help you either. They're so ignorant of Chinese society, they wouldn't understand your predicament even if you drew them a picture. And, you can't run away because the Man Shing Tong will find you. I'm afraid you have no alternative, my boy, but to fight them on their own terms, in their own backyard. You will have to kill them, Richard! You will have to kill them, or beat them into submission.'

'There is no option, is there,' Richard whispered, and it wasn't a question.

'You must accept the help Lo Shi-mon and his small brotherhood are offering you. Join the Man Yee On and they will be bound by honour and a blood oath to fight by your side against your common enemy.'

'Yes.' Richard was exhausted. 'Our common enemy.'

'That's right. And, I'm not sure if you're aware of it, but, you have something else in common with the Man Yee On.'

'What's that?' He hardly dared think.

'You're all police officers.'

龍

'*Is it true or not true,*' Richard asked of Lo Shi-mon as they entered the gates of Central Police Station, '*that the Man Yee On is made up entirely of police officers?*'

'It is true, Elder Brother,' the big Chinese sergeant nodded. '*But the Man Yee On is a good society. It is not corrupt like many others.*'

Despite his exhaustion, Richard felt himself smile. '*Is there anyone in Hong Kong who is not in a triad?*'

'*Only foreign devils. All Chinese are connected somehow to a triad, it has been that way for three hundred years.*'

'*I understand.*' He stopped in front of the Charge Room door. '*Goodnight, Sergeant Lo.*'

'*I am glad 'Effernan Sin Sang has made you understand,*' Lo spoke slowly in Cantonese for Richard's benefit. '*We have no choice but to fight for our lives. I am sorry I involved you, but I had no choice, the Man Shing Tong will kill you. It is a matter of face for them.*'

'*I understand completely, Sergeant. Thank you.*'

'*It is not necessary to say thank you. Tomorrow night we must see Master Kwan. I will arrange the meeting.*'

Before Richard could agree, they were interrupted by the Duty Sergeant.

'Excuse me, Sir?' He handed Richard a letter. 'This is for you.'

Richard looked at his name inscribed on the envelope in a very feminine hand and his pulse began to race. He opened the letter and read 'Meet me tonight in the summerhouse at 10 o'clock and may the Devil take us both, C'.

'Will you excuse me, Sergeant Lo?' Richard turned to his companion, but Lo had gone.

Fifteen minutes later, Lo Shi-mon stood in the shadows outside Central Police Station and watched Richard walk out through the main gates.

You are a fool, Englishman, Lo thought, but you are an honest one.

Honesty was the characteristic in Richard Brewster that Lo admired above all else. In the three months since he'd caught the collapsing Englishman and carried him to Central Station, their paths in life had become entwined. The young officer had shown good leadership skill, proved his courage on the Western Docks and even applied himself to learning Cantonese, which few *gwai loh* took the trouble to do. Hong Kong needed foreigners like Richard Brewster desperately, Lo thought. Men who would serve the best interests of the Colony, and serve them honestly. The young inspector had all the qualities required to become a top ranking police officer and perhaps, even the saviour of the Man Yee On society. This made Lo Shi-mon even more determined to protect him on his journey, wherever it may lead them.

He glanced about, furtively, then set off following Richard Brewster up Hollywood Road.

龍

Caitlin Maclain trembled with desire. Richard's powerful body strained as he moved within her. There it is again, she thought vaguely, the tingling sensation in her limbs, a prelude to ecstasy. Suddenly she was washed away in a sea of emotion. Over and over she tumbled, locked in the arms of desire as the sweet ache rocked her senses.

'My God!' she gasped, her brain slowly recovering. 'My God, Richard.' She held him to her, feeling his warm breath caressing her ear. Surely the loss of one's virginity was supposed to be painful, she thought, painful and unpleasant, that's what she'd been led to believe. As the wave of feelings subsided, she pushed him away and rolled on one elbow, a hand across her mouth. 'You can't do this to me. It's not fair!' She rose to her knees and grinned down at him, the fire in her eyes undiminished. 'I now understand the true meaning of wickedness.'

She lay back in his arms and they laughed gently as they kissed. They murmured endearments and shared caresses, and before long they were once again making love, each insatiable for the other.

Finally, Caitlin rose from the bed. 'I could live here in this summerhouse quite happily just waiting for you to come to me every night. I never knew such abandonment was possible.'

He watched her slide her delicate underwear up over her thighs. 'Then why don't you come back to bed and we'll do it all over again,' he murmured.

His voice brushed her like a caress, how she would love to oblige. 'No,' she smiled, 'I must go back to the main house, Mrs Merchant will expect to see me before she retires.'

'Why? She knows where you are. This summerhouse meeting was her idea. You said so.'

'Exactly.' She slipped her dress over her head and let it slide down over her hips. 'But we mustn't abuse the privilege, a certain propriety must be maintained.'

Richard watched her finish dressing. He'd watched his mother dress when he was a boy and the fastidiousness of women never ceased to fascinate him. Caitlin seemed completely composed and in such a short time. Only ten minutes before she'd been writhing beneath him totally abandoned and now she was brushing her hair and adjusting her clothes. She's getting on with the business of living as if nothing has occurred. The thought bemused him. Had his mother Elizabeth ever behaved with such abandonment, he wondered. Try as he might, he could not conjure up an image of his parents coupling, bathed in sweat the way he and Caitlin had just done.

As he dressed, he remembered the girls in Paris. They had loved him with the requisite degree of passion for which he'd paid them in francs, but the ingredient of love had been missing. Caitlin had been equally passionate, but she'd whispered words of love that had caused his heart to burst. She had surrendered her virginity to him, he knew it. And he had surrendered his to her, he thought. He had never loved a woman before. He did now. He loved Caitlin Maclain with every fibre of his being.

Caitlin smiled at him. 'I love you, Inspector Brewster,' she whispered. 'Will you come to me tomorrow night?'

Richard suddenly felt sick as a thought struck him. 'I love you with all my heart, Caitlin, but I can't see you again for a while.'

'Oh?' A stab of fear prompted her. She looked at him as a hundred questions flooded her mind. 'Why? Why can't you see me?'

'I do love you, Caitlin,' he smiled. 'Never doubt it.'

'Are you concerned about our relationship?'

'No, my darling. It has nothing to do with us,' he moved to her side and put his arms around her. 'It's a police matter.'

The events of the last twenty-four hours had suddenly hit him like a steam train. He felt like the joker in a pack of playing cards, Chinese playing cards, the faces of which he didn't recognise. He was caught up in a world of intrigue and deceit he did not understand and his inability to take control of the situation was driving him mad. He was being forced to place his trust in Lo Shi-mon, a man he'd known for barely four months. And he'd been forced to become a member of an illegal secret society. It was an offence for him to even associate himself with a triad, let alone be a member of one. And he'd become the target of assassins, all because he'd saved a little boy's life.

Quincy's words came back to him: 'Your life has changed forever, Richard. You are not caught up in some silly game on the playing fields of Eton! You are involved, like it or not, in a triad war!'

The realisation made him feel angry at himself. In his excitement to see Caitlin it had not occurred to him that he was endangering her by coming to the Merchant House. Somehow, the fabulous mansion on the Peak with its high walls and guard on the wrought iron gates had always seemed impenetrable. But now, as his love for her over-whelmed him, the enormity of the situation finally hit home. Nowhere was safe. And no one connected to him was safe.

'Are you at liberty to speak of it?' Caitlin asked tremu-lously.

'It's simply a police matter, my love.' He moved to the window as he spoke and looked out into the moonlit garden of the Merchant House. He could see the rear of the main house through the trees. 'It's nothing for you to worry about. Remember I love you, and the moment I'm able, I'll come to you.'

'No! Don't go!' She pulled him close. 'You're frightening me.'

'Shhh,' Richard rocked her in his arms. 'You've nothing to be frightened of, Caitlin. As I said, it's a police matter. Nothing to do with you.' He kissed her gently on the cheek. 'And now I must go.'

Caitlin felt him pull away and heard the click of the summerhouse door as it opened and shut. As she watched him disappear through the trees, a chill ran through her body and her mind was filled with a sense of foreboding.

CHAPTER SEVEN

Time has a way of standing still in China.

General Ch'iang Kai-shek stood, hands clasped loosely behind his back, staring out of his office window at the broad expanse of the Pearl River, making its way sluggishly in the heat of day, down to its estuary which meets the South China Sea at Macau. The warm day and the view of the river combined to create in him a sense of tranquillity.

Visions of childhood passed sedately through the General's mind. He saw again another river, near his hometown of Fengwha in Chekiang province. It had seemed to slow in the heat of day, and the small sail craft which navigated that river had done so in a lingering way, as if they wished to nudge the shore and say hello before moving on to their destinations. So too the cargo junks on the Pearl River, inching inexorably closer to their destinations, now gave the impression they would stop, if someone waved, and speak softly of man's futile desire to hurry.

A heat haze spread across the parade square of the Whang Po Military College and down over the town and docks of Whang Po, several miles east of Canton. Errantly known on British Navy maps as Whampoa, owing to mispronunciation by English mariners, Whang Po is an island in the Pearl River. Its docks had once been known as the centre point of the opium trade conducted by the English and other western powers, but now they lay thick with military supplies and sacks of rice needed to fuel the burgeoning Nationalist Army known as the Kuomintang.

A frown crept across the General's brow and the brief

moment of tranquillity vanished. Ch'iang despised opium, almost as much as he despised the foreigners who had introduced it to his countrymen. And for what, he thought bitterly. Tea! A stupid drink that had suddenly, many years ago, become fashionable in the salons of England. The Portuguese, Dutch and particularly the British had introduced the filthy drug to China as a means of controlling the tea trade. They had turned his countrymen into a nation of drug addicts merely to satisfy the desire of the Europeans to drink tea.

Ch'iang Kai-shek turned from the window and looked at the girl lying on his rosewood divan. She was shivering and mumbling incoherently as the effects of the drug wore off. His doctors had kept her in a light opium haze for two days, gently questioning her in the hope of jogging her memory.

'*Well!*' he snapped at the two white coated doctors standing either side of her. '*Has she told you anything more?*'

'*No, Elder Brother,*' one of the doctors stammered. '*The story is locked deep in her mind. She is badly confused. She was full of opium and engaged in the sex act when she heard the story. Furthermore, she was witness to the murder of her grandmother and forced to fight for her life. Such duress has twisted her mind.*'

'*You're telling me she's insane, true or not true?*' Ch'iang picked up a riding crop from his desk and pointed it menacingly at the doctor.

'*She has also been with child,*' the doctor managed to squeak. '*We believe she suffered a miscarriage about the time your agent found her. This, we believe, has driven her mind into a state of wandering from which it may never recover.*'

'*Aaaiiyahh!*' Ch'iang roared. He slapped the crop against his highly polished riding boot.

Ho Shek-min, a former aide to General Ch'iang, and now a KMT agent in Kowloon, had heard the babbling girl while drinking in a tea-house. He knew of his general's long-time interest in the story of the mythical dragons and, although Ho himself thought the story was nonsense, he also thought the general might consider her of interest. The tea-house proprietor had moaned about the fact he did not want the responsibility of caring for an idiot who constantly babbled about murder, pirates and mythical golden dragons and was considering calling the police. Agent Ho had offered to take charge of her and the proprietor had been only too quick to agree.

On the journey to Whang Po, the girl had seemed quite lucid and her story quite convincing, that was until she'd miscarried in his cart. After that Ho simply couldn't wait to get rid of her and had dropped her in front of the Whang Po Military Academy medical office. He'd then reported her presence to the General and suffered such interrogation that he'd wished he'd never become involved. He'd hurried back to Hong Kong as soon as General Ch'iang gave him permission to leave.

'*Get her out of here,*' Ch'iang now snarled to the doctors. '*Give her to the English priests at Gianshan. Tell them from me that their countrymen are responsible for her addiction, so therefore they are responsible for her wellbeing!*'

The two doctors picked up the girl and left, only too grateful to be out of their General's field of fire. Ch'iang Kaishek was not a man to be near when things did not go his way.

The Golden Dragons, he thought, could they still exist? He'd always had doubts about the story of their disappearance. It seemed just too coincidental to him that the ship had foundered at sea, but his spies, try as they might, had never been able to trace even a whisper to the contrary and, as the years went by, he'd reluctantly accepted their fate. And now, this girl's story had stirred the embers of hope yet again.

The General moved in front of a full length wall mirror and adjusted his uniform tunic. He was a dapper man, bald prematurely and his demeanour was one of authority. He was a military man down to his bootstraps. In his uniform of the KMT complete with jodhpurs, Sam Browne belt, riding crop and military campaign medals, he was every inch a General.

Soon, he mused, very soon, my Kuomintang will be ready to move north and unite China under the Nationalist banner as Sun Yat-sen predicted.

Nineteen twenty-six would be the year of the Tiger, the Fire Tiger, and that is what he would become. His artillery would scorch the earth before him and his army would squash all resistance. The peace doves, the warlords, the communists, he would crush them all and build a unified China from the ashes. And by all the gods, if the Golden Dragons still existed and were to be restored to him, what power they would wield. The mere sight of them would cause the world's greatest bankers to fall at his knees with offers of money to finance his war effort. The peasantry, the uneducated superstitious masses, would fall to their knees and worship them. The Golden Dragons would become symbols of the cause. The knowledge of their existence would raise the spirits of every Chinese in the Central Realms and unite them behind him.

He was in a loose alliance with the Communist Party. He needed them to ensure that peace flourished in the south. He could ill-afford to go north and fight with the fear of an uprising at his rear, but he would turn against them when the time proved right. The very thought of communism in China was anathema to him. The doctrine did not suit his people, they were a race of traders. A race of business-minded people who dreamed of procuring wealth to provide security in their declining years. That was the Chinese way. No man alive in China could pursue his dreams under a communist system. Therefore he, Ch'iang Kai-shek, would see to it that Communism did not prevail. For the moment, he courted them and they him, and the Russians courted both sides equally. In fact, he had one in his office at the moment, a Communist International adviser, sent to him by the government in Moscow to help solve his problems.

He adjusted the high collar of his tunic and checked his appearance, then he looked beyond his reflection at the Comintern officer seated in a bamboo chair, swathed in the smoke from his cigarette.

'Well, Major Kruschenko,' the General spoke in clear crisp English. 'Would you care to make your observations on the situation as it stands?'

'Comrade General,' the voice from behind the swirling cigarette smoke was deep and gutteral, the English language delivered with a thick Russian accent. 'Firstly may I say that the whole situation sounds like a fairy tale.'

'I assure you, Comrade Major,' the General spun on his heel and glared at the Russian. 'The Golden Dragons are anything but a fairy tale!'

'Forgive me, General Ch'iang,' the unflappable Russian continued. 'I am a born cynic.' He stood, a tall man powerfully built with a bald bullet-like head, and moved to the window. 'I am Russian. We Russians are sceptical of anything we cannot eat or drink. A story of fabulous golden dragons emblazoned with priceless emeralds and rubies is reminiscent of the stories one hears as a child at bedtime. It is not unlike the stories of our former Tsar and the treasures of . . .'

'Major!' the General snapped. 'I have seen these dragons myself! I saw them with my own eyes. Are you calling me a liar?'

'No, Comrade General,' the Russian turned and stiffened to attention. He realised he'd gone too far while, simultaneously, his mind raced with the visions of golden dragons and priceless gems. 'If you say they exist,' he continued, adopting what he hoped was an obsequious tone, 'then they most definitely do.' Jesus on the cross, his mind gasped, how much must they be worth? And why had his Comintern organisation never heard the faintest whisper of their existence? The organisation was supposed to know everything.

Illya Kruschenko was a realist. His life had taken many turns since he was a boy in the Caucasus. He'd run away with a girl from his village only to be caught by her father who'd sold him to gypsies. The gypsies had taught him to ride, which had led to his forced induction into the Army. He'd attained officer rank through sheer brilliance at horse and had fought in the Great War as a member of the Russian Cavalry.

He'd been perfectly happy with the House of Romanov. The Tsar had paid his wages, enough to keep him supplied with women and vodka, and fighting had been a way of life with him for most of his thirty years. Then along had come Trotsky and Lenin and Marx and a potato field of intelligensia sprouting revolution and his country had turned on its head.

Illya's life turned with it. He'd avoided a firing squad of crazy Bolsheviks by swearing allegiance to Lenin and the cause of Communism and soon found himself a member of the Comintern, an organisation designed to further the aims of international Communism. Eventually, because of his military background and the pure luck of being a Georgian born in the small town of Mercheuili, he'd fallen under the eye of Lavrenti Pavlovich Beria, himself a Georgian from the very same town. Beria, a senior member of the OGPU, the forerunner to the KGB, had taken Illya under his wing.

Beria, a noted plotter and a notoriously skilled organiser of forced labour, terror and espionage, found in Illya the makings of the perfect spy. A total lack of morals, a complete disregard for the sanctity of human life and a lust for women and vodka allowed Beria to turn Illya Kruschenko into not only Russia's top agent, but also its premier assassin.

Unfortunately for anyone concerned with the life of Illya Kruschenko, they failed to remember one simple fact about him. He was first and foremost a survivor.

Now, at thirty-eight years of age, Illya stood before a dapper little general, in a heat affected military academy, five thousand miles from Russia, with visions of golden dragons and fabulous gemstones shimmering before his eyes, wondering if his world had turned again.

'I never really accepted the dragons were lost at sea,' the General muttered, interrupting the Russian's thoughts. 'And listening to this young girl babble about them has stirred something in me, Major. I am convinced she heard something. Not just some old sailor's tale, but something real!' Ch'iang Kai-shek fixed Kruschenko with a fierce glare. 'You will go to Hong Kong and find these dragons for us,' he said, as he moved to his desk and sat down. 'The Kuomintang is not liked by the British authorities and is unwelcome in Hong Kong. You are a foreigner, and can move freely about the

Colony, as they call it. To me it is still part of China as the British will one day find out.' The General lit a cigarette and inhaled deeply. 'It is my most fervent wish that you find the dragons. Be ruthless, let nothing stand in your way.' Ch'iang passed the Russian a meaningful look. 'I am sure you will succeed, you come highly recommended by your superiors in Moscow, Major.'

'Thank you, General,' Kruschenko replied. 'I am the best at what I do. That is not a boast, Sir, it is a fact.'

'This is what we know,' the General stated, handing Kruschenko a file of papers. 'It contains the girl's last address and the name of my agent who first located her. She talks of a pirate called The Young Captain Wong. Pirates are a treacherous lot, Major, they hold allegiance to no one. Spread some money around the Kowloon Docks and you'll soon find this young captain without too much trouble.'

'I'll leave immediately for Hong Kong, Sir,' Illya answered, taking the file.

'I know the idea sounds fantastic, Major, but instinct tells me those dragons are not at the bottom of the ocean, and they represent the work of thousands of Chinese patriots across the world. If you succeed in locating them, you will be rewarded with honour as a true friend of China.'

'Rest assured, Comrade General,' Kruschenko's voice dripped with sincerity. 'If the Golden Dragons exist, I will most definitely find them.'

龍

'Cameron!' Superintendent Charles Higgins' voice boomed off the walls of Central Police Station. 'Inspector Cameron, where the bloody hell are you, man?' Higgins continued to roar as he strode across the quadrangle towards the Charge Room. 'Cameron! Cameron, you idiot! Where in hell are you?'

Stewart Cameron heard his Superintendent roaring even though he had a towel over his head and was drying his ears. Christ alive, he thought as a shiver ran through him, I've never heard Old Higgins roar like that. Quickly his mind retraced the steps of his day searching for anything he may have done wrong. He could think of nothing, except that he was absent from the Charge Room. He was after all supposed to be on duty, but he was only taking a shower. All the senior officers did that occasionally, Hong Kong being the Orient and all that.

'Where's Cameron *Bom Baan*?' Higgins roared again as he entered the Charge Room.

Cameron heard his desk sergeant make a muffled reply and then the Amenities Room door burst open and Higgins stood before him panting like an enraged water buffalo.

'Is something wrong, Sir?' was all Cameron could manage to say as he desperately tried to cover his nakedness.

'Wrong!' Higgins roared. He was apoplectic. 'Wrong! I'll say there's something wrong! You cretin!'

'I say, Sir, steady on. That's a bit strong, what?'

'Did you, Sir,' Higgins voice dropped to a menacing whisper, 'or did you not, Sir, receive a message earlier today from Sergeant Delaney?'

'Er, I'm not sure,' Cameron stammered. 'Let me think.'

'Thinking is a function your brain is incapable of, you imbecile!' Higgins hissed.

'What was the message about?' Stewart Cameron was beginning to sweat profusely; the madness in Higgins' eyes terrified him.

'Did Sergeant Delaney inform this station by telephone that he had caught a man snooping about outside godown number three in Pan Ling Street? The bloody godown I ordered you to surround with a twenty-four hour watch!'

'I'm not sure, Sir,' Cameron mumbled. 'He might have.'

'Might have!' Higgins' face turned purple. 'Might have! He bloody well did, Sir!' Higgins raised the clenched fist, in which he held a crumpled piece of paper. 'Here it is, Sir! Dated today, Tuesday, at 9.15 a.m., Sergeant Delaney rang the desk sergeant and made a report. The desk sergeant wrote it down word for word and delivered it to you. You threw it in your office wastepaper basket where I bloody well found it!'

'It was only a report of some chinky-boy found wandering

near the warehouse, Sir,' Cameron stammered.

'That chinky boy,' Higgins snarled, 'as you so endearingly call him, was a bloody agent for the Kuomintang!'

'Well, how was I to know that?' came the defensive whine.

'It's written here in black and bloody white!' Higgins threw the crumpled report at him. 'You . . . you *retard!*'

'I'm sorry, Sir.' Cameron found himself sinking to his knees.

'Oh, for God's sake,' Higgins sneered contemptuously at the young man crumpled on the floor. 'Get up, man, you're making a complete fool of yourself.'

'Yes, Sir,' the young officer rose unsteadily to his feet.

'When Delaney didn't hear anything back he had no alternative but to let the bastard go. I want him found, do you hear me?'

'But how, Sir?' Cameron whined as he wrapped a towel around his waist.

'That's for you to decide!' The sight of the terrified young man filled Higgins with loathing. 'I don't care if it takes all night! I want him found and brought to my office. Do you understand?'

'Yes, Sir, I suppose so.'

'Stand to attention when you address me!' Higgins voice reverberated about the station walls and the young officer threw his shoulders back and rammed his hands against his sides. He remained that way for a full ten seconds staring straight ahead until his Superintendent finally broke the silence.

'That's better,' Higgins purred, offering the boy a sensuous smile. 'Now,' he murmured, 'be a good lad and get dressed. There's a good fellow. Then it's off to the Charge Room with you.'

Higgins left, closing the door behind him and Stewart Cameron's legs once more gave way.

Richard's initiation into the Man Yee On had been almost farcical in its haste. He'd been expecting a long drawn out

ceremony in which he would struggle with his Cantonese, but
Old Kwan had been far more practical than he'd expected.

'You are Englishman, all right?' Old Kwan had said. 'Englishman is bound by honour, yes?'

'Yes,' was all Richard could reply.

'Will you give your honour to the Man Yee On, even if you
must die?'

'Yes.'

'You say, "I swear" like in the English court,' Kwan had
demanded.

'I swear.'

'You are now member of Man Yee On. Congratulations.'

'Is that it?' Richard felt compelled to ask. 'Is there no
ceremony?'

'Ceremony not for *gwai loh*, only for Chinese. Why you
want ceremony? Is big waste of time. We just have English,
how you say, "swearing in"? Your honour is all that matters.
You are bound to Man Yee On! Man Yee On is bound to
you! All right?'

'I suppose so.'

'Good. Now you eat,' Old Kwan indicated the food on the
table. 'You have *daai sik wooi*, big eating party, you celebrate
by yourself.' The old man chuckled at his joke.

'Will you join me?' Richard felt rather deflated.

'No. I must talk with Ah Lo,' Kwan had replied. And that
had been it. He was officially a member of an illegal secret
society and it had taken less than a minute.

Richard chewed on the succulent quail and smiled appre-
ciatively at the pretty Chinese girl who served him. She was
the sister of Little Kwan and seemed determined to feed him
until he burst.

He looked about the small stone room he was sitting in. It
was the back room of a herbalist's shop, owned by Old
Kwan, the *Shan Chu* of the Man Yee On Triad Society. On a
window sill sat the ubiquitous *ba'kwa* mirrors to keep out
evil spirits, and on a small ledge on the other wall was a
shrine.

Inside the shrine, surrounded by red paper, a small statue

of the fierce-looking warrior god, Kwan Dai, stood glowering at all who entered the room and in his hand he held a long pole with a curved blade on its end. Candles burned next to the little shrine and joss sticks smoked, delivering the sweet perfume of musk into the air. Four rosewood chairs and a table filled the room, a tiny stairway led up to the floor above and a curtain of beads separated the room from the shop in front.

The young woman placed another dish in front of Richard and signalled for him to taste it.

'*Lichard speaks Cantonese, Elder Sister,*' Little Kwan said impatiently as he shuffled inside the small room.

'*Grandfather Kwan told you to watch for customers at the stall outside!*' Wai Ling snapped. '*Your disobedience will cause your downfall one day!*' She threw a cushion at him as he scurried out to maintain his watch.

'*Thank you, Wai Ling,*' Richard smiled at the girl. '*Your food is very good, but I can eat no more.*'

'*It is not necessary to say thank you,*' she replied, then averted her eyes, embarrassed. This *gwai loh* was not like the others she had met. This *gwai loh* had almond coloured eyes and black hair like her. And his skin was a soft golden brown and almost hairless. Perhaps it was burnt off when he rode the flaming dragon through fiery skies, she thought, as she began clearing the food from the table.

Wai Ling continued to watch the foreign devil from the corner of her eye, as he in turn watched her grandfather and the Red Pole, the policeman Lo Shi-mon, talking in soft voices at the other side of the table. Richard Brewster was handsome, of that there was no doubt, and terribly brave to have rescued Little Kwan in such spectacular fashion. She looked again at his soft golden skin and imagined this *gwai loh* hovering over her as she lay in her small bed at the top of the stairs. The thought made her shudder with pleasure. His eyes flicked towards her and the cups and spoons she was carrying rattled slightly in her hands. For one short moment she believed he could read her mind and she blushed furiously and left the room.

Richard shifted his weight from one buttock to the other and looked at his watch. He did not like sitting for long periods and he wished for the umpteenth time that his Cantonese was good enough to follow the conversation taking place opposite him.

He reflected yet again on the circumstances that had led him to this meeting with the master of the Man Yee On Triad Society. How had it all happened? In a matter of a few months his whole life had turned upside down. One minute he'd been in England and now he was in the Orient. He was in a police force. He was in a triad society. He was in love. And he was in the deepest trouble it was possible to imagine. It seemed like the whole world was against him and he had no one to turn to. Not even Caitlin. Especially not Caitlin.

Lo Shi-mon and Old Kwan had been at it for half an hour, during which time Richard had stuffed himself with food. At first as a distraction from the young woman, Wai Ling, whose open scrutiny he'd found embarrassing, then because he'd realised he was starving. He'd forgotten how long it had been since he'd eaten.

'*Elder Brother,*' Lo Shi-mon finally spoke directly to him. '*Our Shan Chu, the honourable Kwan, wishes me to say that he is much in debt to you for the life of the boy.*'

'*Not necessary. Not necessary,*' Richard answered. He was becoming irritated with the snail's pace at which the meeting was progressing. But, if he'd learned one thing in his short time in Hong Kong, it was that you could not hurry such affairs without causing loss of face. Everything with the Chinese was a ceremony.

'*The young inspector is impatient to join our talk,*' Old Kwan said. '*His mind moves at the speed of the rabbit.*'

'*Not true,*' Richard protested self-consciously. It was as if the old man had read his thoughts.

'*You are in grave danger, Inspector. Please forgive an old man who wastes precious time.*'

'*I am in your house, teacher.*' Richard's reply was formal. '*I am your guest and greatly honoured.*'

'*I will waste time no more,*' the old man smiled and

immediately contradicted himself by pouring tea. He slurped noisily from his porcelain cup and nodded wisely at Richard. *'Tea clears the mind, allowing it to operate more efficiently.'*

'It is very good,' Richard sipped the steaming liquid from his cup.

'To die,' the old man went on, *'is without doubt, the greatest of journeys, true or not true?'*

'Excuse me?' Richard's bewildered query was in English.

'Such an experience reveals the answers to all of life's mysteries. Unfortunately, one returns to life in another form unable to remember the answers. And so, in blissful ignorance, one continues turning on the wheel of life. This is foolish, true or not true?'

'True,' Richard replied.

'Why do you say true?' the old man asked.

'Because I didn't understand a word you said except the question, "true or not true", so I answered to be polite. I meant no disrespect.'

'Aaaiyaah!' Old Kwan slapped his knee and roared with laughter. 'I like you, Blue Star!' he continued in English. 'Even your name is good! Lichard Blue Star. You know what is Blue Star in Chinese? Blue Star is *laam sik sing*. Is good name, yes?'

'Yes, thank you.'

'We will kill the Man Shing Tong for you,' the old man stated flatly and sipped at his tea.

'Aaah,' Richard raised his hand like a child asking to be excused from class. 'That's what we should talk about.'

'The Man Shing Tong are evil!' the old man spat, then wiped the remnants of spittle from his thin grey beard. 'It is time they all died!'

'Er, Sergeant?' Richard looked at Lo Shi-mon. 'I think we should speak about this matter. I mean, your er, . . . no our, . . . *Shan Chu*, *Ah Kwan*, is talking about murder. And not just murder, but murder on a rather grand scale.'

'It is the only way, *Dai Loh*,' Lo Shi-mon answered, putting his teacup down. 'We have talked all about it with *'Effernan Sin Sang.'*

'Yes, well, don't you think we should talk to the Man Shing Tong about it? I mean, at least make the effort before we sink into an abyss of wholesale slaughter.'

'Blue Star!' the old man interrupted. 'Did you talk or not talk to the white-haired *gwai loh*, 'Effernan, your teacher?''

'Yes, of course.'

'And you are still unsure of your predicament?'

'Well, I . . .'

'Tiger Paw Chang and his Man Shing Tong brothers will kill you. There is no place for English form of negotiation such as your King Georgie and his parliament are fond of.'

'But Sergeant Lo and I are police officers, for Christ's sake!'

'Ah, yes,' the old man pointed a gnarled finger at the young Englishman. 'Your Jesus Christ. Why you *gwai loh* always talk of Jesus Christ? He was a foolish individual. He say to turn other cheek and look what happen to him! They nail him to a cross! The Roman *gwai loh* soldiers kill him and even his own people say all right! Ha! He was *chi sin*, how you say, crazy in the head.'

'I don't think that's quite the same . . .'

'Same same!' the old man snapped. 'Same same! You will listen to your *Shan Chu*!' he grabbed Richard's forearm with his gnarled hand. 'Two nights ago, your policeman Leung Tse-man return to his home in the north. Is this true?'

'Yes,' Richard replied uneasily. 'He returned to his province to get married, at least that's what I was told.'

'No! The Man Shing Tong kill him in Kowloon.'

'Is this true?' Richard looked at Lo Shi-mon, who nodded. 'Another man lost and still you didn't see fit to confide in me?'

'You never mind confide!' the old man snapped. 'Last night, the Man Shing Tong go to house of John Merchant to kill you!'

'No, they didn't. I didn't see anyone.'

'Because,' the old man pointed at Lo, 'this man, your 426, he stop them!'

'This is true,' Lo said when Richard looked at him. 'They tried to enter the grounds of John Merchant's house.'

'And?' Richard prompted.

'They did not get in,' Lo replied enigmatically.

Richard could only imagine their fate. He'd felt the strength of Lo Shi-mon when they'd argued in the police station quadrangle. 'Did you kill them?' he asked.

'Of course,' Lo Shi-mon replied bluntly.

'Ah Lo follow you last night, to protect you while you play pillow games with your *gwai paw* mistress and ignore your predicament like a stupid Englishman!'

'I should never have gone to her . . .'

'Do not concern yourself with the woman!' Old Kwan interjected. 'She is being watched.'

'By whom?' Richard's fear for Caitlin was overwhelming. If anything was to happen to her . . .

'Two of your policemen are sick, they do not come to work. Is this true?'

'Yes. They reported sick.'

'Not true!' Old Kwan growled. 'They are men from our honourable society of the Man Yee On and they are watching your woman. They protect her while their own families are alone and at the mercy of Tiger Paw Chang's men!' The old man spat again, and again he wiped his beard. He was becoming angry. 'The Man Shing Tong is like the serpent, if you do not kill it, it will bite you and you will die. And so too, we will die! And your woman also! Do you understand this?'

'Yes.' Richard realised his fate was sealed. A fight to the death was all that was left to him. 'I understand,' he said to the old man, as a profound sense of sadness surged through him.

'Good!' Old Kwan muttered and slapped his thigh. 'To kill the snake you must cut off his head. To kill the Man Shing Tong, you must get rid of Tiger Paw Chang and his senior officials.'

'From what little I know of the Man Shing Tong, that won't be easy.'

'Sergeant Lo and I have discussed the matter,' the old man spoke softly and looked at Lo before continuing. 'You have an advantage over them,' he murmured. 'You have something they do not have.'

'What would that be, *Ah Kwan*?' Richard asked.

'The rest of this matter you must discuss with your sergeant,' the old man replied. 'I am weary and need to rest.' He got up, smoothed his long silk coat and flicked his braided queue of grey hair behind his back. 'Please excuse an old man,' he said, and he bowed formally to Richard before disappearing up the small flight of stairs.

The two policemen sat in silence sipping their tea until Richard finally spoke.

'Well, *Ah Lo*, what is this advantage *Ah Kwan* speaks of?' Richard looked squarely into the eyes of his sergeant as he placed his cup on the table.

'Guns,' Lo replied, returning his senior officer's stare.

Richard sat in silence weighing up the implications of that one simple word. Finally, he nodded his head. 'Go on,' he whispered.

龍

The Young Captain Wong could not close his eyes, and yet he was dying. It was confusing him. How could he die if his eyes would not close? And then he remembered the Russian, the man from the country called *Ngoh lo si*. The big bald-headed *gwai loh* had severed his eyelids. That was why he could still see. He had no eyelids to close. I must look strange, he thought.

The Young Captain Wong laughed and pain tore through his body as blood welled up in his throat and ran from his nose and mouth. The pain cleared his mind and he remembered the torture he'd suffered at the hands of the Russian and the men from the Kuomintang.

How had they found him? How did they know about the Golden Dragons? He'd never mentioned them to another soul. He'd returned to Lau Fau Shan, delivered Tiger Paw Chang's information to The One Eyed Woo, and the Admiral had sent him back to the Kowloon Docks to keep a watch on the S.S. *Pacific Star*. It must have been the girl. She'd discovered him cutting her grandmother's throat. He should have killed her first. She'd been skilled in the art of fighting. Her foot had hit him in the mouth, dislodging one of his teeth and she'd escaped through the window and disappeared in the shadowy alleys of the Walled City in Kowloon. He should have killed her first and then her grandmother, but how was he to know? One simple mistake had led him to this ignominious death in a filthy boatshed.

Pain shot through him again. He turned his head and saw a rat chewing at his finger. It horrified him, but there was nothing he could do, the tendons in his wrists, elbows and armpits had been severed along with his Achilles tendons and hamstrings. He could not move a single muscle.

He heard more rats, squeaking and scratching as they moved across the boatshed floor and he whimpered as the fear rose in him. He was going to be eaten alive, just as the *Ngoh lo si gwai loh* had promised.

He saw again the big Russian foreign devil's face as it loomed above him and the glint of the knife as it moved towards his face. 'Where are the Golden Dragons?' the Russian had asked, over and over again. 'You are the young captain,' he'd snarled, as he pinched Wong's eye-lid flesh and pulled it away from the eye socket.

The Young Captain Wong had told them of the Golden Dragons and Tiger Paw Chang, but they hadn't stopped. They'd cut him again and again, asking questions until he'd passed out. And now here he lay, dying in a boatshed in Kowloon.

I should have killed the girl first, he thought, then he screamed as the rats bit into his flesh.

龍

Robert McCraw leaned on the balcony railing of his small government flat and watched the first rays of dawn light the sky over Hong Kong Harbour. It was the one hour in the day when the city truly slept. McCraw knew that by the time the sun crawled into the sky Hong Kong would be awake, its heart beating strongly, and commerce and industry would, once again, be the order of the day.

The big Scot turned and looked at his companions. Sergeant Terrence Delaney sat on the divan, head back, eyes closed, while Richard Brewster, his young inspector, stared into a glass of whisky, his face tired and drawn. It had been a long night for all three.

Richard Brewster had arrived, a nervous wreck, on McCraw's doorstep at ten o'clock, the previous night. Li Ping had ensconced them on the balcony with a bottle of whisky before retiring to her room.

McCraw was fully aware that trouble had been brewing in the young inspector's life and was pleasantly surprised that Richard had sought him out. That was until he'd heard Richard's story and the dubious request which followed it.

'You want me to falsify the Armoury Register,' McCraw had replied, when he finally found his voice. 'So you can use police firearms to start a triad war between the Man Shing Tong and the Man Yee On?'

'The war's already started. I want to put an end to it,' Richard said.

'Why tell me at all, Richard? Why not simply take the weapons, use them and put them back?'

'I thought about it, but . . .' Richard struggled for words, his mind in turmoil.

'But you knew you'd never get away with it, besides which, your honour got the better of you. So you thought you'd tell dear old Inspector McCraw so I'd be ready to duck when the shit hit the bloody fan! Forewarned is forearmed and all that rubbish! Am I right?'

'Something like that, Sir.'

'How very noble of you!' McCraw sneered. 'Straight out of a bloody Boys' Own Album.'

'I just thought that there'd be a public outcry. Everyone would be questioned, including yourself. The Inspector-General, Mr Wolfe, would be hounded by politicians both here and in England, to resolve the matter . . .'

'And let's no' forget His Britannic Majesty the bloody King of England!' Robert McCraw interrupted in his broad

Glaswegian accent. 'Christ alive, laddie! You're in more trouble than a one-legged cavalry officer!'

'It's not a joking matter, Sir!'

'Who's joking!' the Scot roared. 'You enter my house, accept my hospitality and then gently inform me that you're about to embark upon a course of murder and mayhem that'll set this bloody colony on its ear!'

'I'm sorry,' Richard stood. 'I expected far too much from you. I don't know why I even came here, it's just that I'm in a lot of trouble and . . .,' his voice tailed off and his look was one of resignation. 'I'll leave if I can have your word as a gentleman that our conversation is forgotten.'

'Sit down!' McCraw snapped. He pushed his young officer back into the chair and turned towards the railing. 'God save me from English gentlemen,' he sighed. He stood for some time gazing out over the twinkling lights of the harbour below, occasionally shaking his head from side to side. Finally he turned and stared at Richard. 'I won't do it for you, laddie. I'll do it for the two young constables who were skinned alive.'

'Thank you,' was all Richard could say.

'When do you want the weapons?'

'Next Friday night, Sir. At ten o'clock.'

'I suppose you already know who the Armoury officer will be at that time?'

'Yes, Sir. Sergeant Delaney.'

Now it was dawn the following day. McCraw had summoned Terrence Delaney from the night shift and the three men had discussed Richard's predicament.

'Well, Terrence,' McCraw sighed. 'What do you say?'

'I'm all for it,' the Yorkshireman replied. 'I saw the bodies of those two young coonstables. That's enoof for me. Whoever did that deserves to be shot, beside which, we can't let these triad bastards push one of ours around, or the next thing you know they'll think they're roonin' the place and can do as they bloody well please. The way I see it, it's oos or them, Mr McCraw.'

'Right, it's settled.' McCraw pulled a chair up to the

balcony table. 'Now listen carefully,' he said and sipped his whisky. 'At the rear of the Armoury in cabinet number four, there are six handguns. US Army Colts. They're Model 1911A automatics, never been out of the wrapping paper. They're .45 calibre. They'll stop an elephant dead in its tracks. You,' he continued, pointing to Delaney, 'will hand them to young Richard at precisely ten o'clock, and don't let anyone see you do it.'

'Right you are, Sir,' Delaney nodded.

'Now listen, Richard,' McCraw turned his attention back to his young inspector. 'No one but myself and Superintendent Higgins knows of the existence of those automatics. They are not even on the Armoury Register. No one investigating the incident would dream of looking in police stations for .45 calibre automatic weaponry. As far as the public is concerned, we don't have anything like it. Are you both clear about what I've said so far?'

'Yes, Sir,' both men replied in unison.

'Delaney, I will enter the Armoury at precisely eleven o'clock next Friday night and conduct a Weapons Register check. The colts will be recorded as in the Armoury at that time.'

'Yes, Sir.' Delaney nodded.

'You and I will both sign the register, then I will leave.'

'Oonderstood, Sir,' the big Yorkshireman nodded again.

'Good. Now Richard, come hell or high water, I want those weapons back by eleven thirty p.m. You will enter the Armoury, wash the guns in soap and water, oil them thoroughly and re-wrap them in their oil-paper. Then, with Sergeant Delaney, you will replace them in cabinet number four in the same positions as you found them.'

'Got it, Sir.'

'By God, laddie!' McCraw glowered at Richard. 'When Delaney concludes duty at midnight, those firearms must be back where they belong, or else.'

'Understood, Sir,' Richard replied.

'Oh, yes,' McCraw murmured then finished off his whisky. 'There's one more thing. Under no circumstances must you be involved, directly, in the fight.'

'But, Sir . . .' Richard began to protest.

'Silence!' McCraw snapped. 'Use your brain, maaarn! Suppose you're shot? How in God's name would we explain a dead white police officer in the middle of a triad fight!'

'Oh, I see your point, Sir.' Richard's face reddened.

'Exactly, you idiot.' McCraw growled. 'Your cohorts, and don't think I can't name them, will do the business. Your sole job is to deliver those guns and get them safely back to the Armoury, or we're all as good as dead. Am I understood, maaarn?'

'Perfectly, Sir.'

Robert McCraw stood and stretched his arms over his head, then crossed again to the balcony railing and watched the sun begin its climb into the brightening sky.

'Go home, both of you,' he said quietly. 'And say nothing to a living soul. This night's work and the conversations we've had, quite simply, did not take place.'

CHAPTER EIGHT

Captain George Watling was not an easy man to rattle. He'd been a ship's captain for thirty years, ten of those under the Merchant Company flag, and he'd confronted most things that could frighten a man. Typhoons, shipwrecks and pirates had passed his way over the years and he'd dealt with them all to his personal satisfaction. And angry men had never worried him; he'd stared them down with a fierce glare, or fought them with fists, knife and pistol. But that had been in his younger days. Now, as he stood on the after bridge of his ship, the S.S. *Pacific Star*, his hands gripping the white railing as if they would tear it from its bolted mountings, Captain Watling was rattled.

Cargo in the lifeboats. It was against all the rules of safety for ships at sea. And just what that cargo was, he had no idea, nor did he wish to know.

He watched as a police launch manoeuvred its way alongside the *Pacific Star* and a stab of fear went through him as he saw Superintendent Higgins clamber up the Officer's accommodation ladder and make his way towards the bridge.

Cargo in the lifeboats and probably contraband to boot. No halfway decent captain would set sail under such conditions. Why in God's name had he ever agreed to it?

'Unless you do this, you'll never sail a ship in the East again!' John Merchant had screamed, almost hysterical with rage. 'I'll see to it that you're name is mud, from here to Bombay.'

On Wednesday, two nights previously, Captain Watling had been summoned to the private office of John Merchant, his employer. He'd arrived soon after eleven o'clock and been offered brandy, which he'd accepted from Charles Higgins, a senior policeman he knew only by reputation.

In the ensuing half hour, Captain Watling had watched and listened with increasing unease, as John Merchant worked himself into a terrible state explaining that four crates of valuable cargo were to be transferred to the *Pacific Star*. He went on and on about the importance of this cargo being safely conveyed to England.

Captain Watling had remained silent until Merchant suggested the crates be stowed, under cover of darkness, in his ship's lifeboats. It was this preposterous suggestion which had prompted the Captain to politely point out that it would be against all the laws of common sense and safety of ships at sea to do so.

John Merchant's response was that of a man taken leave of his senses. He hissed and spat like a caged leopard as he heaped oaths and curses upon his captain, culminating with the threat that Watling's name would be mud. It was only then that Higgins had gently interrupted.

'There, there, Johnny m'lad,' Superintendent Higgins murmured. 'I'm sure our good Captain Watling will agree to our suggestion if the right inducement is offered.'

Captain Watling had turned to the tall, urbane policeman and looked him up and down with what he hoped was a withering glare. 'Superintendent,' he had growled. 'Nothing on God's earth will induce me to put to sea with cargo in my lifeboats. It is against all the principles of good seamanship. It is . . .'

'Five thousand pounds sterling,' Higgins cut him off mid-sentence. 'Another five thousand pounds as a bonus, if you get the cargo safely to our agents in England.'

'Ten thousand pounds?' Watling gasped. It was more money than he'd ever seen in his life, or was ever likely to see.

'Fifteen,' Higgins purred sensually. 'We'll make it fifteen thousand. No questions asked. No names, no pack drill,' he continued as he crossed to the mantelpiece. He leaned casually against it, lit a cigar and puffed vigorously, taking the extra moment to let the enormity of the amount sink in. 'What say you, Captain laddie? Eh? Eh?'

'I will not pay a captain in my fleet fifteen thousand pounds . . .' John Merchant began to bluster.

'Shut up, John!' Higgins snapped, his voice cutting through the smoke-filled room like a scimitar.

Watling flinched involuntarily. He glanced at Higgins and saw an entirely different animal from the nancy boy he'd been introduced to. For one brief moment he saw the face of a truly evil man. A man to be feared. Then just as quickly a childlike grin appeared on the policeman's face and he reverted to the effeminate fop he chose to portray.

'Just shut up, I say,' he continued softly. 'Look at yourself, man,' and he pointed a lazy finger at John Merchant, 'you're a gibbering idiot. You have spittle on your chin.'

The captain had watched, fascinated, as fear flickered across his employer's face. John Merchant took a handkerchief from his pocket and wiped his chin, then sank back into his office chair, withdrawn, like a frightened child as an awful silence descended, broken only by the ticking of the clock on the mantelpiece.

'Well, Captain?' Higgins finally spoke, his voice a sensuous whisper. 'What say you? With fifteen thousand pounds you could retire to one of those fishing villages in Cornwall and smoke a pipe for the rest of your days,' he chuckled softly. 'You could regale small children with your memories of the sea and build little ships in bottles.'

'And what do you see as my alternative, Superintendent?' Watling asked, somehow aware of the answer. He was doomed and he knew it.

'A slow, lingering death,' Higgins went on, 'brought about by the sheer boredom of sitting in the bar of the China Fleet Club with all the other expatriate drunks the South China Sea has left shipwrecked on Hong Kong's tiny shores. For you, a tragedy of mammoth proportions I dare say, but one you need not even contemplate should you take up our offer.'

Again, only the ticking of the clock on the mantelpiece behind Higgins' head stirred the silence, as the three men stood frozen in their different worlds. The mechanism whirred into life as the hands reached midnight and the chimes began. *One . . . two . . . three . . .*

'Well, seagoing Captain laddie,' Higgins purred. 'What's it going to be?'

Four . . . five . . . six . . . seven . . .

'Cornwall or the China Fleet Club, the choice is yours.'

Eight . . . nine . . . ten . . . eleven . . .

'Cornwall.' Captain Watling whispered on the final stroke of midnight, his resolve now a cracked vessel. He looked again at his silent employer, then moved his gaze to the soft, gentle smile of the policeman beaming innocently at him from beneath the black, glittering eyes of a snake. 'Good-night to you both,' he muttered and hurried from the room.

龍

Yes, Captain Watling knew only too well why he'd agreed to it. That black-hearted bastard Higgins had put the fear of God into him. The man was evil incarnate. Even now as he watched the last of his legitimate cargo being lowered into the aft hold, he could see those black, insane eyes boring into him, goading, challenging, daring his defiance.

The night before, he'd given his complete crew shore leave, then, with his lifeboats manned by a Marine Police crew arranged by Charles Higgins, he'd supervised the loading of the crates from godown number three. Then he'd returned the boats to his ship and ordered them re-slung in their davits.

'Splice the main brace!' Higgins shouted theatrically. 'Man the pumps! And all of those other quaint seafaring terms which so endear you crusty old sea captains to us landlubbers,' he said as he reached the bridge and extended his hand to Captain Watling.

'Good afternoon, Superintendent,' Watling replied, thinking Higgins' hand felt like a wet fish.

'A life on the ocean wave, eh?' the policeman continued as he turned and strutted about the bridge. 'You must love it, eh?' he turned, almost a pirouette, and extended his arms to encompass the decks and rigging. 'Aaah! "I must go down to the seas again, to the lonely sea and sky, and all I ask is a tall ship and a star to steer her by",' he quoted, and inhaled deeply. 'John Masefield, poet and lover of the sea, I do believe.'

'To what do I owe the pleasure of this visit, Mr Higgins?'

'Merely to wish you bon voyage, Captain, and enquire if the fleet is secure.' Higgins smiled, hands on hips.

'I take it you mean the lifeboats?'

'Of course, dear fellow.'

'They're secure. Fore and aft, port and starboard stations.'

'Good, good.' Higgins nodded. 'Now, for your information, Captain, there are four ammunition crates identical to those in the lifeboats and they've been loaded into your rear hold down there,' he said pointing to the deck below. 'If for any reason this ship is boarded by pirates, or anyone else without authority, you will offer no resistance and surrender those crates willingly.'

'I've never surrendered to pirate scum and I never will!'

'My dear Watling,' Higgins sighed. 'If you are boarded, and for all our sakes I hope you are not, it will not be by pirate scum! Rather it will be by scum of a higher order, in fact, rabid Chinese Nationalist scum!'

'Oh my God!'

'Now, now, calm down,' Higgins murmured. 'Surely you must have realised there would be some risk attached to this venture, Captain. No one receives fifteen thousand pounds for nothing, do they, eh?'

'But the Nationalists . . .'

'Will you listen to me, you stupid man!' Higgins snapped. Watling saw the glint of madness in the policeman's eyes and decided to hold his tongue. He would sail for England at full speed, deliver his cargo whatever it was, and be done with the Far East forever.

'If!' Higgins spat vehemently, 'And I say *if*, you are boarded, it will be in Chinese waters by members of the Kuomintang. They will have been ordered to recover four crates and you will allow them to do so!'

'What if they open them?'

Higgins took a deep breath and gazed around the harbour before staring again at the Captain. 'I will stake my reputation on the fact that the KMT officers will not open them. They are notoriously stupid people who will simply recover the crates as ordered and leave your ship.'

'But what if they *do* open them?' Watling asked, his unease multiplying rapidly.

'They will probably have been told that the crates contain property which rightfully belongs to the Chinese Government . . .'

'And do they?' Watling interrupted.

'Yes.' Higgins replied flatly. 'If our little yellow friends do open the crates, they'll find four bone China dragons. The ship's manifest will show they are antique statues on consignment to Sotheby's in London for auction. And, by the by, that's the absolute truth of the matter.'

'And they'll be satisfied with that?' Watling queried.

'Wouldn't you be?' Higgins scoffed. 'A fortune in Chinese antiques rescued from the British imperialists and returned to dear old China?'

'I suppose so.'

'Good. Well, that's it then.' Higgins smiled.

'It would appear so,' the captain murmured. He crossed the bridge to gaze at Victoria Peak, sadness overwhelming him as he realised it would be the last time he would see it. He'd sailed the China Seas for forty years, thirty of those as a captain and in that time he'd come to love Hong Kong like no other port in the world. And now he was leaving, never to see her again. And not leaving under a bright tropical sun, with flags fluttering and a last hurrah. No. He would slink out of the harbour at night on the full tide, carrying God only knew what in his lifeboats. It would be an ignominious exit.

'Something on your mind, Captain Watling?'

'What? Oh, sorry,' Watling answered as his thoughts snapped back to the present. 'I can't help wondering, Mr Higgins, if you're using rare Chinese antiques as a decoy, what in Heaven's name have you got stowed in my lifeboats?'

He laughed, hearing the hollow ring in his voice. 'Just a thought,' he added lamely as Higgins' eyes bore into his.

'A word of warning, Captain,' Higgins' voice was icy. 'If the ammunition crates in the lifeboats were to disappear, for whatever reason, you'd be well advised to disappear with them.'

Summoning his last ounce of courage, Captain Watling straightened his shoulders and looked the policeman in the eye. 'I'll bear that in mind, Mr Higgins.'

'Be sure you do, Captain Watling,' Higgins replied, his voice thick with venom. 'Be sure you do.' Then he smiled disarmingly and gave a salute. 'Bon voyage, my old sea dog Captain laddie. Fair winds and calm seas for all our sakes, eh? Eh?' Then he turned and, whistling airily, made his way off the ship.

龍

At ten minutes past ten on Friday night, Richard Brewster stopped running and strolled casually into the tea shop at the intersection of Hollywood Road and Tin Pang Street. He placed the Gladstone bag he'd been carrying between himself and the wall and ordered a pot of jasmine tea.

What in God's name am I doing? he asked himself yet again, as he looked down at the Gladstone bag leaning so innocently against the wall. He took a deep breath and thought of the two men, skinned alive, then exhaled slowly, willing himself to relax. His moment of truth had arrived. In the next hour his life would change forever. He poured himself tea as the words of Quincy Heffernan came to him again, 'I'm afraid you have no alternative, my boy. You will have to kill them, Richard! You will have to kill them, or beat them into submission.' And old Quincy was right, he had no alternative. He'd reached the fork in the road, and he knew, beyond all doubt which path he had to take.

Richard checked his watch five times in three minutes and was nervously sipping his second cup of tea when Lo Shi-mon, dressed as an itinerant coolie, entered the teashop and sat beside him.

'*It's ten-fifteen sergeant,*' Richard whispered in Cantonese. '*You have forty-five minutes to complete the operation. This bag must be returned to me by eleven o'clock. Understand or not understand?*' he asked pushing the Gladstone bag containing the six Colt .45s towards Lo.

'*I understand, Elder Brother.*' A patina of sweat covered the big Chinese sergeant's face and his eyes glanced furtively about the teashop. He picked up the bag and left without another word as Richard checked his wristwatch yet again.

龍

Chang Cho-su was known as 'The Krait' for good reason. He was of unstable mind and likely to lose control and strike out, like the snake he was named after. He was a big man for a Cantonese, solidly built and had reigned supreme as a bully around the Sai Ying Poon docks for ten years. Everyone knew he was the Red Pole of the Man Shing Tong and, in that capacity, was untouchable, not that anyone had wanted to try.

Since arriving in Hong Kong in 1911, Chang the Krait had enjoyed a successful career, first as a criminal and standover man and then as the Red Pole of a triad society under the auspices of his cousin Tiger Paw Chang, the *Shan Chu* of the Man Shing Tong.

Chang the Krait's fall from grace had been a sudden one. In his capacity as Red Pole, one of his jobs was the security of the Lodge and last Friday night, when the policeman, Lo Shi-mon, had slipped past the guards Chang had so carefully posted and entered the Man Shing Tong cavern, the full wrath of Tiger Paw had fallen upon the Krait. On Sunday morning after the riot, his four guards had had their eyes removed with a hot poker and Chang had been flogged and expelled from the society. His loss of face was complete.

That same Sunday, seething with hatred, Chang had sought out the policeman Lo Shi-mon in the markets on Sai Ying Poon docks and goaded the tall northerner into a fight. The subsequent contest, if it could be called that, proved to be Chang the Krait's final humiliation. Lo Shi-mon revealed himself as a master of the Shaolin arts. The policeman had whirled and spun before Chang's eyes striking at will with both feet and hands, his speed and grace witnessed by the hundreds of people gathered in the markets until Chang had lain prostrate, a bleeding wreck begging for his life.

Chang had never experienced anything like it, he'd been totally defenceless, unable to land even one blow in retaliation. He'd heard, as all Chinese had, of the mercurial fighting skills of the Shaolin priests but it was the stuff of fairytales. Tales told by old men in tea-houses to impress wide-eyed boys as they filled their heads with the legends of the *Hung Mun* societies.

Chang the Krait had learned to fight as a child. He'd studied a form of kung fu known as Saan Da, whose disciples revered the god, Monkey. His childhood friends had learned Wing Chun and Hung Da and other forms of kung fu, but the legendary teachings of Shaolin had been unavailable to them, believed by most to be lost in the mists of antiquity, that was until Lo Shi-mon had revealed his mastery in the markets.

All those in the docks area now held the policeman in awe. Children followed him on his patrols and young men sought him out pleading to be taught the old Shaolin arts, only to be refused with a soft smile and a shake of the head.

Without the protection of his cousin, Tiger Paw Chang, whom he now despised above all others, Chang the Krait was a figure to be ridiculed. People laughed behind his back and pointed him out as the one who'd lost all face.

Revenge, when it came, presented itself from the most unlikely quarter. Two men who said they were from Canton had approached him with an offer of money to betray the Man Shing Tong. It was a lot of money and Chang had bowed deeply to the men and agreed to help them on the condition that Tiger Paw Chang was to be killed during the raid. A bargain was struck and the time and place arranged.

Now, as Chang the Krait stood in the warehouse above the Man Shing Tong's underground cavern, he could almost taste his victory. His dog-fucking cousin Tiger Paw and his cronies in the Man Shing Tong would be destroyed and Chang the Krait would then see to it that Lo Shi-mon, the offal-eating police sergeant, received the blame for their murders.

Four masked men appeared like wraiths to stand before him. Two of them wiped blood from their knife blades, having just killed the Man Shing Tong sentries. The biggest man among them produced a firearm from beneath his coat and loaded it. A strange firearm, Chang noted. He'd never seen its like before.

One of the men, responding to Chang's pointing finger, located a trapdoor and opened it to reveal a ladder, which led to a tunnel below. Chang disappeared down it and the four men followed. He then motioned for silence and rapped on a large steel door.

'*Where were you born?*' a voice from within asked.

'*Beneath the peach tree,*' Chang the Krait replied.

'*Have you died yet?*'

'*I have died once.*'

'*I know that voice,*' the door guardian's voice sneered. '*You are not welcome here, Chang Cho-su!*'

'*Wait!*' Chang's voice pleaded. '*I must speak with the Shan Chu. I have important news. It is vital to the safety of the Man Shing Tong! You know me! I was once your Red Pole. I seek only to restore my honour within the Lodge.*'

There followed a minute of silence before the door bolt was heard sliding open. Chang's victorious smile froze on his face as he turned and saw the big man remove his mask and raise the strange looking firearm. What followed caused even Chang the Krait to tremble with fear.

Major Illya Kruschenko pulled the trigger on the drum-fed .45 calibre machine gun. Two feet of flame burst from the barrel as the bullets cut the door guardian in half. He entered the Man Shing Tong cavern still firing as the others followed. One of the men produced the same type of weapon and they sprayed the cavern within.

'Where is Chang?' Kruschenko asked.

'*Where is the one called Tiger Paw Chang?*' demanded one of the gunmen.

'*Our Master is not here,*' a frightened voice replied.

'The one you seek is not here,' the gunman informed the Russian.

'Ask them where he is.'

A conversation was conducted in rapid Cantonese and the gunman turned to his *gwai loh* superior. 'They say he has left Hong Kong and gone to Daiya Wan on the Mainland.'

'Then we'll leave him a message he cannot misconstrue.'

Chang the Krait fell to his knees, his mouth agape, as he watched the flaming machine guns. Members of the Lodge were torn to pieces. Bodies were flung through the air, blood spattered the walls and men screamed. The huge bullets tore at the walls ripping the silk curtains after passing through the bodies of the men they'd killed.

When the guns stopped, the silence was chilling. Clouds of cordite smoke hung over the macabre scene. Shredded bodies lay everywhere and the moans of dying men were answered by single shots from a revolver. No one was spared, apart from two officials sitting in chairs on the dais, frozen with fear.

'*You will deliver a messsage to the man known as Tiger Paw Chang from General Ch'iang Kai-shek?*' the big Russian's guttural Cantonese rang through the cavern.

Chang the Krait swallowed the vomit rising in his throat and ran. Through the door he went, up the ladder and across the warehouse floor, his ears ringing from the roar of the guns.

The evil deeds Chang had been party to in his life were nothing compared to the wholesale slaughter he'd just witnessed. Even skinning a man alive seemed trivial in the aftermath of such carnage.

As he stumbled through the warehouse, his mind screamed the words Kuomintang! They were Kuomintang! He should have known. He should have guessed.

Chang's plan had been to facilitate the entry of the masked men from Canton to the meeting, let them terrify the Man Shing Tong and murder his cousin Tiger Paw Chang, then blame it on the policeman Lo Shi-mon. But had he known they were Kuomintang, he would never have become involved.

Shaking with fear, he reached the far wall and fumbled with the latch before flinging the warehouse door wide open. A fist hit him in the side of the head and his brain screamed its thanks as it welcomed sweet unconsciousness.

龍

Superintendent Charles Higgins stood on the balcony outside his office at Central Police Station and raised a pair of binoculars to his eyes. The silhouette of the S.S. *Pacific Star* sat on the moonlit waters of Hong Kong Harbour, her boilers building pressure for departure to England. At the top of the tide, she would get underway and his problems would be over. He lowered the glasses and looked at his watch, it was two in the morning. He savoured the moment before turning and entering his office.

'Well, gentlemen,' he purred. 'Tell me about this so called massacre.'

The officers assembled before him included Robert McCraw, Richard Brewster and a somewhat haggard looking Stewart Cameron.

'The call came in just before midnight, Sir.' It was McCraw who spoke. 'Inspector Brewster informed me by telephone of the incident. It took the majority of his watch to seal off the area so I called in Inspector Cameron. His men are handling the general duties.'

'And how many are dead, Mr Brewster?' Higgins asked.

'Thirty-one, Sir,' Richard replied, glancing at McCraw. 'They're all senior members of a triad known as the Man Shing Tong, Sir. We believe the incident occurred at about eleven.'

'How tragic,' Higgins chuckled. 'Have you managed to piece together what may have taken place?'

'Yes, Sir. We had an eyewitness to the account.'

'Had, Inspector Brewster?' Higgins queried.

'I'm afraid he's dead, Sir. His name was Chang the Krait. Sergeant Lo took him into custody and questioned him, but he escaped and fell from the police station rooftop while my men were giving chase.' Richard winced inwardly at the lie. Chang had been questioned all right, and in police custody. Then at Lo Shi-mon's command, two burly constables had thrown him out of a second storey window like a bag of wheat.

Richard had been surprised by his own reaction to the murder, for that's exactly what it had been. He'd witnessed what seemed to him a trivial act when considered against the mass murders of an hour beforehand, and his conscience had accepted it with alarming alacrity. He was momentarily shocked, but with events happening as quickly as they had, he'd soon put it to the back of his mind and got on with what appeared to be more important things.

'Two tragedies in one evening,' Higgins chortled. 'How sad. Still, these triad chappies are given to excessive behaviour. There's always a war going on between one group and another. It's a fact of life amongst the Chinese, wouldn't you say, Mr McCraw?'

'This incident was no triad war, Sir,' the big Scot replied. 'According to Mr Brewster's eye witness, it was a massacre perpetrated by four men.'

'Curiouser and curiouser,' Higgins drawled. 'Just what did your witness see, Inspector Brewster, before his accidental demise?'

'Well, Sir,' Richard answered. 'Apparently four men gained entrance to an underground meeting place of the Man Shing Tong and simply shot everyone in the place then left.'

'That's ridiculous!' Higgins snorted. 'Four men with guns couldn't kill thirty-one triad members without them putting up some sort of fight.'

'It seems they used a machine gun, Sir,' Richard mumbled. 'Two, in fact,' he finished lamely.

Charles Higgins sighed deeply and looked at the three officers standing before his desk. 'Was this Chang the Krait a drug addict or an imbecile?' he asked, his voice dripping with sarcasm.

'Sir,' Richard interrupted. 'The witness described two hand-held shoulder weapons, similar in length to a short

barrel shotgun with what appeared to be cylindrical magazines.'

'There is no such weapon,' Higgins said.

'Perhaps Mr Cameron can shed some light on the matter,'
Robert McCraw interceded. 'He has a formidable knowledge
of the ballistic sciences, Sir.'

'Well, Cameron?' Higgins turned his gaze on the nervous
young sergeant.

'I believe the weapons are referred to as sub-machine guns
or machine carbines, Mr Higgins,' Cameron began hesitantly.
'They fire pistol cartridges, which are magazine fed into a
hand-held shoulder weapon. They were toyed with near the
end of The Great War, Sir. You see,' Cameron continued
warming to his pet subject. 'In an effort to conquer the stale-
mate on the Western Front, a German general, von Hutier
was his name . . .'

'I don't want a bloody lesson on modern warfare,
Cameron!' Higgins interrupted. 'Just tell me how in hell a
Chinaman would get hold of the infernal things!'

'That's just it, Sir, he couldn't,' Cameron replied.

'Then why,' Higgins wiped his hand across his eyes, 'are
we discussing them?'

'Unless, of course,' Cameron went on, enjoying exercising
his superior knowledge, 'that person was a military man.'

'Cameron,' Higgins' voice was a venomous whisper, 'if
you don't get to the point, I'll do something really dreadful
to you.'

'Brigadier General Thompson of the United States Army
invented a .45 calibre sub-machine gun several years ago, Sir.'
Stuart Cameron continued at the rate of knots, the prospect
of Higgins wrath now making him nervous. 'He placed a
prototype with the US Army, and British Intelligence
informed us several months ago that one hundred of these
guns had found their way into the hands of General Ch'iang
Kai-shek.'

Higgins was lost for words, frozen in his chair.

'The Soong family, Sir, clandestinely arranged the shipment
of arms. They're a very powerful family from . . .'

'I know who they are,' Higgins managed to squeak. He cleared his throat and walked to the balcony door before turning to continue. 'Mr Brewster, are you saying the Kuomintang are responsible for this incident?'

'It would appear so, Sir,' Richard snapped to attention. 'The witness also told us that one of the men with the sub-machine guns was a Russian, which would lend credence to his story.'

'Did he describe the Russian?'

'Yes, Sir. He's a big fellow, well built, with a bald head.'

'That will be all,' Higgins said abruptly. 'You can get out now. Get on with the bloody matter!'

'But, Sir,' McCraw said. 'The witness told us quite a bit more.'

'I don't care,' Higgins snapped, grabbing for the telephone on his desk. 'Get out!'

After his officers closed the door behind them a whimper escaped Higgins' lips. 'Christ Almighty, they're on to us. The bloody Kuomintang.' His fingers shook as he dialled John Merchant's private number and prayed silently that the *Pacific Star* would make it out to sea.

龍

'*Kuda ve egyor cha?*' Where are you going, he murmured softly in his native tongue. '*Kuda ve egyor cha?*' Illya Kruschenko stood on the old ferry pier and looked at the S.S. *Pacific Star*. She was raising her anchors.

The Russian major sat on a wooden bollard at the edge of the pier and lit a black Balkan cigar as he watched the big ship carrying the Golden Dragons beyond his grasp.

The young pirate had told him about the vessel, but it had been crawling with Hong Kong police. It would have been impossible for Illya and his men to get anywhere near the treasures, and now it was too late. He would be forced to inform General Ch'iang Kai-shek about the vessel, and it would be boarded at sea and the Golden Dragons recovered. That was not exactly what he'd had in mind for them.

A day earlier, he'd arranged passage for himself and the priceless cargo upon a Russian ship, leaving the following week and bound for Eastern Siberia. He would have sailed north through the Korean Strait and across the Sea of Japan to Vladivostok. Once there, among friends, he would've melted the dragons, hidden the jewels, and taken the gold across to connections in Tokyo for a discreet series of sales. Then to hell with Ch'iang Kai-shek and his Kuomintang. To hell with the Comintern. To hell with Mother Russia. Illya Kruschenko would have been richer than all the tsars.

If only he'd been able to find the fat Chinese known as Tiger Paw. Surely he'd planned a way to get the dragons off the *Pacific Star*. But the fat Chinese had been gone from Hong Kong for several days and his fellow triad members had known nothing of the Golden Dragons. Even as he'd cut the throats of the two officials who'd been spared for interrogation purposes, they'd screamed their ignorance.

Major Kruschenko cursed and threw his cigar into the harbour waters. He wanted those dragons more than life itself. He paced up and down the pier staring at the *Pacific Star* as she moved towards Green Island. Soon she would alter course and travel down the West Lamma Channel to the open sea and it would be there that the man known as Tiger Paw would make his move.

Pirates. Of course. The thought hit him like a lightning bolt. This Tiger Paw fellow would have to use pirates to intercept the ship. Friends of The Young Captain Wong. If only I could stop her before she makes the open sea, he mused. Have her drop anchor until I could get a ship alongside and remove the Golden Dragons. But it was impossible, surely. The man called Tiger Paw had won the game. Illya could not stop her.

The thought struck him. Of course he could not stop her. But he knew who could.

龍

Richard entered the Officers' Mess on the third floor of Central Police Station and studied the lone occupant serving himself a gin and Indian tonic water behind the bar.

Robert McCraw turned and took a long drink from his glass. He didn't particularly like gin, or tonic water for that matter, but it was generally regarded by men who served in the Far East that the quinine contained in Indian tonic water was a defence against malaria. He stared at Richard for what seemed an eternity before he spoke. 'Are the Colts secured in the Armoury?'

'Yes, Sir.'

'Christ only knows what would have happened if your men had walked in on that little triad party.' The big Scot shook his head. 'Those six Colt .45s and their two machine guns blazing away in all directions, God Almighty!'

'Yes, Sir.'

McCraw moved from behind the bar, stood in front of Richard and stared directly at him. 'That is, unless they were *supposed* to walk in there at precisely that time?'

'I don't understand, Sir.'

'Let's drop the Sir business right now, laddie,' McCraw growled. 'Is there anything you've not told me?'

'Not that I know of,' Richard replied. He could sense the anger emanating from McCraw and his brain searched frantically through the events of the day. Could he have missed something? Was there some fact he'd forgotten to mention? Everything had happened so quickly.

'Christ, maaarn!' McCraw roared, then checked himself and dropped his voice to a whisper. 'Do you expect me to believe that on the same night, at the same time we planned to commit mass murder, the Kuomintang, by sheer bloody coincidence, does precisely the same thing to the same bloody people?'

'Yes,' Richard could only shrug.

'Damn it, maaarn!' McCraw crashed his glass onto the bar and it shattered into a thousand pieces, yet never did he break eye contact with his subordinate. 'I don't like being involved in matters I'm not fully cognisant with. Are you sure you told me everything?'

'As sure as I can be,' Richard replied evenly, holding the Scot's glare. 'I delivered the Colts to my sergeant and he set off to complete the mission. He'd no sooner got into position with his men than they heard the machine carbines. They investigated and caught the witness Chang Cho-su who told my sergeant the raid had been perpetrated by Kuomintang agents led by a big bald-headed Russian man. Then they threw him out the window. That's it in total, Sir.'

McCraw gave a sigh of resignation. 'All right, laddie. But the question remains, what's going on? Oh hell, will you look at that,' he gasped, holding up his bloodied hand. He removed a shard of glass from his palm and went behind the bar to the sink. 'I choose not to believe in coincidence, Richard. The intelligence unit of the Kuomintang is a ruthless and dangerous organisation and somehow or other they've become involved in this business and I want to know why. Bugger it!' he cursed as he wrapped his hand in a towel. 'The sooner we find out what's really going on, the better. At least,' he snorted as he moved out from behind the bar, 'your troubles with the bloody Man Shing Tong Triad Society are solved. Once and for all, I'd wager.'

'Yes,' Richard nodded, 'I suppose so, although Tiger Paw Chang hasn't been located.'

'Has it occurred to you, Richard, that perhaps the Man Yee On Triad may just be the nigger in the woodpile here? Could it be that your dear old *Shan Chu* Mr Kwan made secondary arrangements with the Kuomintang to eradicate the Man Shing Tong, just in case your attempt failed?'

'If that was the case, why didn't they wait to see if we were successful or not? It seems a bit silly to have the Kuomintang arrive at precisely the same time for precisely the same reason, wouldn't you say?'

'Point taken, laddie,' the big Scot nodded. 'But all the same, the Kuomintang do not become involved in triad wars unless it's to their advantage. I'm inclined to believe something far more sinister is going on than we are even aware of, as yet.'

'I'm afraid I must speak up regarding the Man Yee On, Robert. They had no need to offer me their friendship or protection, but they did.' In his earnestness, Richard hadn't even realised that he'd referred to his superior officer by his Christian name. 'I believe they've been honest with me and have my best interests at heart. I'm sorry, but my loyalty must lie with them. It's a matter of honour, you do understand?'

Robert McCraw couldn't help but smile as his anger ebbed. He considered the young man standing opposite him. Richard Brewster was a genuine English gentleman, a rare bird indeed who would rather die than relinquish his honour. The boy was in danger of drowning in a sea of trouble and yet he was defending his friends. Robert admired him for it. Robert McGraw was developing a soft spot for young Richard Brewster, despite the calamities his presence seemed to create.

Both men turned their heads to the sound of the Mess door opening. A young sergeant from the Charge Room entered and saluted.

'Excuse me, Ah Sir.'

'At ease, Sergeant,' McCraw said casually, realising the young Chinese was nervous in the Officers' Mess. 'What is it?'

'Mister Higgins say very urgent you go to the House of Merchant on the Peak. He fink there is trouble there, Ah Sir.'

'What sort of trouble?' McCraw asked.

A sick feeling hit Richard in the pit of his stomach. Caitlin, he thought. Oh my God, Caitlin!

As Richard bolted through the door past the terrified sergeant, Robert McCraw grabbed his hat and ran after him.

龍

On board the *Pacific Star*, Captain Watling took a last look at the bright lights of Hong Kong Harbour then turned and entered the bridge. He could smell bad weather coming, a big blow was not far away. In the gloom of the wheelhouse he watched as the coxswain checked the ship's heading by compass then returned to peer intently ahead across the darkening water.

'Alter course to port, Mr Appleby,' Watling heard himself murmur to the coxswain. 'Steer two, zero, zero degrees.'

'Aye aye, Sir,' the young coxswain replied and spun the king spoke handle of the big ship's wheel. 'Altering course to port.'

Watling felt the vessel respond and watched as the north tip of Lamma Island rose high off the port bow.

'Ship's heading is now south by sou' sou' west at two, zero, zero degrees, Sir.'

'Steady as she goes, Mr Appleby, and brace yourself for a nasty night. The sky southward is black as pitch.'

'Aye aye, Sir,' the young coxswain replied.

Watling settled in his captain's chair and allowed himself a moment to savour the intimacy of the wheelhouse. He loved the semi-darkness created by the soft glow of the small light over the chart table and the irridescent glow of the compass face and clinometer in the polished wooden binnacle. He sighed and allowed the throb of the engines to penetrate his thoughts, one last trip they seemed to hum, one last trip. He couldn't resist a smile though. After this one last trip he would retire a very wealthy man.

The sound of Morse Code broke into his thoughts. He listened intently to the insistent tapping from the radio room, his mind spelling out the message as it was being transmitted and his forehead creased into a deep frown.

龍

Caitlin Maclain saw the men enter the grounds of the Merchant House. Unable to sleep, she'd been standing at her bedroom window thinking of Richard when she saw four Chinese, led by a tall bald-headed European, move stealthily across the courtyard towards the main doors. Unsure of what to do, she donned her dressing gown and left her bedroom. Closing the door quietly behind her, she moved off down the hallway of the upstairs west wing towards the bedroom of John Merchant. As she crossed the main hall landing to go to the east wing, she looked down into the foyer. Below her, six-year-old James Merchant stood outside his father's study, a toy rifle hanging loosely from one hand. Light glowed from beneath the study door as young James reached for the knob.

The boy had a habit of roaming at night. Many times Caitlin had found him in different parts of the house. He would walk the halls with his toy rifle and helmet whispering invented stories about tiger hunts and battles.

Caitlin ran down the curved staircase to the marble floor below just as James entered his father's study. She followed the boy through the door.

James was nowhere to be seen, but John Merchant stood behind his desk, the telephone suspended in one hand, a look of fear written across his face.

'John. John! Answer me man, dammit!' Caitlin heard a voice that sounded like Superintendent Higgins bark through the telephone receiver.

Then she heard a whimper to her right and turned. The huge bald-headed man stood at the ground floor balcony doors. One of his hands was clamped over the squirming child's mouth and in the other he held a revolver. Behind him the curtains parted and the four Chinese men entered the room; they were all armed. One moved across to her and placed a knife against her side, while another closed the study door.

'Put the phone down, Mr Merchant,' the Russian said. 'If you value the lives of your wife and child, you will do exactly as I tell you.' John Merchant obeyed the command, too terrified to realise the huge man had mistaken Caitlin for his wife. The Russian moved to Caitlin and pushed the boy against her. 'Keep him quiet, Mrs Merchant, or I'll kill the both of you.'

Caitlin wrapped her arms about the child and stroked his hair. She stared into the face of the big man and realised he would carry out his threat without compunction.

'You will listen very carefully, Mr John Merchant,' the Russian murmured. 'I am an official representative of the Kuomintang sent by General Ch'iang Kai-shek to recover the Golden Dragons.'

'I have no idea . . .' Merchant began.

'Please!' Major Kruschenko raised his hand. 'Do not insult my intelligence by denying they are in your possession. They are presently on your ship, the *Pacific Star*, are they not?'

'No . . .,' Merchant started, then his shoulders slumped in defeat. 'Yes, yes, they are,' he nodded. 'What do you want me to do?'

'You will please pick up the telephone and send a telegraph to your ship. Tell your captain to drop anchor inside Hong Kong waters and await your arrival.'

A tense silence filled the room as John Merchant picked up the phone and dialled his company telegraph office. He passed the message and was about to hang up when the Russian spoke again.

'Tell your office to arrange for your company launch to be at Central Pier in fifteen minutes.'

'My company launch is . . .'

'Do it!' the Russian snapped and Merchant issued the instruction then replaced the telephone handpiece in its cradle.

'I have money in my wall safe,' he began to whimper. 'Take it. It's yours . . .'

'Shut up!' The Russian slapped Merchant across the mouth with his open hand.

What happened then was completely unexpected. The young boy, angered by the violent treatment of his father, broke from his governess and flung himself at the Russian.

'Don't you hurt my daddy!' the boy yelled.

Caitlin reacted by reaching for the child and, as she did so, she felt a searing pain. She gasped and dropped to her knees, a look of bewilderment on her face.

'You idiot!' Illya Kruschenko roared, as he watched the young woman fall to the floor, the knife imbedded in her back. 'Bring the boy!' he snapped to the others. He reached for John Merchant, grabbed him by the collar and flung him towards the balcony doors. 'Hurry,' he boomed, his voice shocking the others into action. 'Get them to the car.'

龍

The Admiral, The One Eyed Woo could not believe his luck. He'd been shadowing the *Pacific Star*, waiting for her to run aground on Wei Ling ting Island as Tiger Paw Chang had arranged, but the huge vessel had altered course to starboard, dropped anchor on the windward side of Cheung Chau Island and lowered her Officer's accommodation ladder. He'd not hesitated, he'd brought his junk, the *China Moon*, right alongside the big ship and his crew had swarmed aboard.

The One Eyed Woo had been prepared for a stiff fight, but the captain and crew of the huge ship had sealed themselves off on the bridge, a new defensive tactic developed by Hong Kong's ferry captains, and sent a Chinese engineer to negotiate with the pirates.

'Oh great Admiral, lord of all pirates,' the terrifed engineer had said. 'I am the faithful servant of Tiger Paw Chang. I was to have arranged for this ship to run aground but . . .'

'Why did the ship heave to?' the Admiral growled. 'Is your captain's penis connected to his forehead?'

'He received a message from his taipan Mr Merchant,' the engineer wailed. 'The captain thought your junk was that of his taipan's, so he lowered the ladder. Then he realised his mistake. He says you should take what you want from the hold, but spare his crew in return for his cargo.'

The Admiral, The One Eyed Woo, threw back his head and laughed uproariously. He looked at the shadowy figures staring at him from the safety of the sealed bridge and gave an exaggerated bow, then he popped out his false eye and waved it around his head.

'What sort of captain are you, Round Eyes?' he roared at the bridge. 'Even with two eyes you cannot tell a pirate junk from your own taipan's, true or not true?'

'Lord of the oceans,' the engineer spoke through trembling lips. 'I must urge you to hurry, because it is true that the boat of the taipan Merchant is coming.'

'Leung jai,' The Admiral called to his first mate. 'Set a man to watch for any approach to this ship.'

'Yes, Lord,' the burly mate replied.

'Now, you, smallest of penises,' The One Eyed Woo leered at the little informant. 'Tiger Paw Chang's cargo. Where is it?'

'Directly below you Admiral, in this hold,' the engineer replied, praying he would be alive to see the sunrise. 'Four identical crates.'

龍

Charles Higgins made sure he arrived at Merchant House after McCraw's men had investigated and secured the place. He walked through the foyer and two young constables snapped to attention and saluted as he crossed the main hall to the study. Richard Brewster was sitting in a chair with his head in his hands.

Higgins was shocked to see Caitlin Maclain, unconscious, being attended to by a weeping Elanora Merchant. Inspector McCraw was on the telephone, apparently to Aberdeen Police Station.

'What in God's name happened?' Higgins said, returning McCraw's salute.

'It would appear, Sir,' McCraw replied, as he hung up the telephone, 'that it's the same men who attacked the Man Shing Tong. Kuomintang agents with a big European in charge.'

'How is she?' he asked indicating the prostrate girl.

'It's not good, Sir,' McCraw answered. 'She's got a knife in her back. I've called for an ambulance.'

'Where's Mr Merchant?'

'Kidnapped.'

'What?'

'Both he and the boy, Sir.'

'Fill me in.' Higgins sighed and moved into a huddle with the big Scot.

Elanora Merchant wiped her eyes and stood up as the ambulance officers arrived. As they ministered to Caitlin, she crossed to Richard and knelt before him.

'Richard,' she whispered placing her hands on his knees. 'Richard, you must listen to me.'

He looked at her through shocked eyes. 'Will she be all right?' He asked. 'Tell me she'll be all right.'

'Richard!' she hissed digging her nails into his forearm. 'You must not mention the Golden Dragons to Higgins.'

'What?' he asked, her sense of urgency dragging him from his despair.

'Caitlin spoke to you of the Golden Dragons, before she passed out, remember?'

'Yes, but God only knows what she meant. She was delirious.'

'Do not mention those words to anyone, especially Higgins. He must not know that you are aware of their existence.'

'I'm not. What are they?' He couldn't seem to come to grips with the conversation.

When Richard had arrived at Merchant House Caitlin had been conscious and while McCraw and his men had searched the house and grounds, she'd told Richard and Elanora what had taken place. Richard had informed McCraw that the Russian had ordered John Merchant to arrange the company junk for their use, but as he was about to mention the words, golden dragons, Elanora had interrupted, insisting that McCraw find her son, and the moment had been lost.

'*Nothing goes on in this house that I don't know of, but explanations are understood more clearly in the light of day, Blue Star,*' Elanora said in Cantonese as Higgins approached them.

'Richard, my boy,' Higgins said. 'I realise this must all be very traumatic for you, what with Miss Maclain injured and all that, but I'm afraid you'll have to go with McCraw to Aberdeen Marine Pier. It's to do with Mr Merchant and his son, their lives are in jeopardy.'

'I'd rather remain with Caitlin, Sir, if that's all right with you?'

'No, it's not all right with me!' Higgins barked. Events were moving too fast, he thought. Did Brewster and McCraw know about the Golden Dragons? Were they aware of the situation on board the S.S. *Pacific Star*? He doubted it, but how could he be sure? And what information had Caitlin Maclain gleaned during the kidnapping? He felt no concern for the wretched girl lying on the floor, but God only knows what she'd heard. From what McCraw had told him, she'd said the Kuomintang had taken Merchant and the boy and were using the Merchant company junk to escape, but apparently no mention had been made of the Golden Dragons. Or of the S.S. *Pacific Star*. Luckily, she was now unconscious, and with a just a tad more luck, he thought, she'd die before she could say anything further.

As for the Kuomintang, they were after the Golden Dragons, of that he had no doubt. But how in hell had they found out about them? Not that it mattered now, he thought. They had taken Merchant as hostage and had probably ordered the ship to drop anchor, a fact he'd confirm by telephoning the telegraph office as soon as he was alone. For the moment, however, he must be seen to be following correct police procedure.

'I'm sorry, Richard, I can't waste time briefing other officers on this matter. I'm afraid it's you and McCraw. John Merchant and his son have been kidnapped and early pursuit is essential. The bloody KMT will want to get them into China, and across the water to the west is the quickest route. Besides, there's nothing you can do for Caitlin, she needs medical attention. I'll see she gets it, I promise you.'

'Yes, Sir.' Richard rose and stared at the inert body of Caitlin as the ambulance men placed her on a stretcher. He looked at the pool of blood where she'd been lying. Rage consumed him.

'This is China, Richard.' He heard Quincy's words. 'You have to kill.' And something snapped. The ability to kill was born in Richard Brewster at that moment. He would kill, all right. First he'd kill those who had dared threaten his love, and then he'd kill anyone else who dared threaten his existence. From this day onward he would live by the laws of the Orient and woe betide anyone who stood in his way.

'I'll go with her to hospital, Richard,' Elanora said, clutching his arm. 'I'll stay with her. You must go and bring my son back for me,' her eyes pleaded with him. 'We must help each other, Richard.'

'Come on, laddie,' Robert McCraw called. 'Police Launch Number Four will pick us up on the south side of the island. We'll head for the western end of Lantau Island. The Kuomintang will want to get into Chinese waters and that's the closest point for them. With a bit of luck we'll get there first. Come on, boy!' he roared impatiently, as he left through the balcony doors.

Richard nodded and looked into Elanora's eyes. 'I'll get your son for you,' he whispered and then, in a voice dripping venom. 'And I'll get the Russian.'

Elanora watched the young Englishman hurry after McCraw and no sooner had he done so than Higgins crossed to the telephone.

'Don't worry, Elanora,' he said, a little too jovially as he picked up the handpiece. 'If anyone can handle this situation, those two can. You go on with Miss Maclain. I'll take care of things here.'

Elanora went into the foyer, a cold fear for her son's life gripping her heart. She took a coat from the wall rack to cover her nightclothes then, as she passed by the study door on her way out, she heard Higgins snapping into the telephone.

'Yes, dammit! Another message to the S.S. *Pacific Star*! Urgent. From Higgins for Captain Watling.'

龍

'*Admiral*,' the first mate of the *China Moon* yelled as he ran from the stern of the S.S. *Pacific Star* to his boss.

'*What's the matter?*' The One Eyed Woo growled, watching the last of the crates settle onto the deck of the *China Moon*.

'*Two ships, Elder Brother. One's closing fast, it's the Merchant Company junk. The other one is Number Four.*'

'The police?' Admiral Woo was surprised.

'*Yes Admiral, she's a good way off, but she's their latest boat, said to be capable of fifteen knots.*'

Curse it, he thought as he ran to look over the stern. That's all I need, the Marine Police. By all the gods in the history of mankind, how did they find out?

The last thing he needed was another run in with the offal-eating Hong Kong Marine Police. It would be the new *gwai loh* commander, of this he was sure. An audacious *gwai loh* commander who'd arranged for his ships to be shot out of the water at their last encounter. An offal-eating, fucker of sows, *gwai loh* commander, who, the Admiral was sure must be an evil spirit re-incarnate, deliberately sent to Earth by some God or other whom the Admiral had inadvertently offended.

'*I don't have time to pray to all of you Gods!*' he shouted into the night sky. '*You are too sensitive! I am just a lowly pirate trying to make a living!*'

The sound of the big ship's anchor winch starting up galvanised him into action. It's obvious that the *gwai loh* captain of this big ship doesn't want an encounter with the police either, he mused, as he ran for the companion way. Perhaps he's had the same misfortune as I. Perhaps the faceless new Marine Police Commander has been sent to Earth to haunt the both of us.

'*Tin Hau protect me,*' he muttered, ushering a prayer up to the goddess of the sea as a sudden foreboding struck him.

'*Cast us off,*' he shouted to his crew, as he followed his first mate down the big ship's companion way. '*The wind tonight has bad joss. The air is thick with spirits and ghosts. Let's get out of here.*'

龍

High above in the wheelhouse on the bridge of the S.S. *Pacific Star*, Captain Watling was experiencing similar feelings. Off his stern quarter the Merchant company junk was approaching at speed and, as if that wasn't enough, a Hong Kong Marine Police vessel was rounding the southern side of Cheung Chau Island.

The first message he'd received from John Merchant had caused a tingle of alarm. It had read: DROP ANCHOR IMMEDIATELY (STOP) AWAIT MY ARRIVAL (STOP) MERCHANT (STOP). Why on earth would Merchant want to come aboard at three in the morning? What could possibly be so important? It could only concern the mysterious cargo in the lifeboats. He wished to God he'd never accepted responsibility for it.

Charles Higgins had been right, the S.S. *Pacific Star* had been boarded before she'd even left Hong Kong waters, although it hadn't been the Nationalist Army who'd boarded her. It had been the mad pirate, The One Eyed Woo. And, as Higgins had predicted, he'd not even opened the decoy crates from the aft hold to check the contents.

Watling paced the deck watching the pirate junk cast off. How could he have been so stupid as to mistake the bloody *China Moon* for his company's junk? They were similar in size and appearance, but he should have been more cautious. He and his crew were lucky to be alive.

'Anchor's aweigh, Captain,' the young coxswain reported.

'Very well, Mr Appleby,' Walting replied. 'I'll take the helm. Have that blasted companionway hauled up and secured, then we'll make for the open sea and stop for no one.'

'What about Mr Merchant's launch, Sir? She's less than five cables off.'

'Never mind the company launch, Mr Appleby!' Watling spun the king spoke of the wheel furiously and thrust the ship's telegraphs forward to full ahead. 'Obey your orders, Sir!'

It was the arrival of the second cable that had caused the sense of foreboding in the captain. It had read: DISREGARD ALL PREVIOUS INSTRUCTIONS (STOP) PUT TO SEA WITH ALL HASTE (STOP) HIGGINS FOR WATLING (STOP), and he was doing just that, despite the launch's imminent arrival and the approach of a police boat which was signalling by Aldis lamp for him to stop.

'Sir,' the ship's Wireless Telegraphy Officer entered the bridge. 'A message from Marine Police Launch Number Four, it reads . . .'

'Make an entry in your log that we were outside of Colony waters when you received the message and could not comply.'

'But, Sir, it's from the police. And they're signalling us by Aldis lamp.'

'I see no such signal.'

'They're astern of us, Sir,' the young officer added.

'Are you questioning my authority, mister?'

'No, Sir,' the young officer replied hastily.

'Then return to your duties and obey my orders.'

'Yes, Sir,' the boy saluted and hurriedly left the bridge.

Captain Watling was nobody's fool. Before long he would be across the western water boundary of Hong Kong and heading for the open sea, beyond the jurisdiction of anyone but himself. As he folded the telegraph messages and put them in his coat pocket for safekeeping, a grim smile creased his face. Like any good sea captain he would carry out his orders explicitly and if he were ever challenged, he would produce the telegraphed orders as evidence. He heard the ship's telegraphs ring full speed ahead and, seconds later, he felt the engines responding. He would make for the open sea, where he alone was master of all he surveyed, and leave the Orient to its own mysterious business.

龍

'It's the *China Moon*,' shouted the coxswain of the Merchant Company junk.

'What?' Illya Kruschenko shouted from the deck railing.

'The *China Moon*. A pirate ship from Lau Fau Shan,' John Merchant yelled over the wind and the screaming engine. 'He's taken the Golden Dragons from the *Pacific Star*!'

'Who has?' Illya yelled, dragging the terrified Merchant into the small wheelhouse perched in the centre of the junk's high poop deck. 'Who has?' he repeated.

'The One Eyed Woo,' John Merchant forced himself to keep calm. He could see a glimmer of hope. The crazy pirate had taken the decoy crates, he was sure of it. He would offer all his resources to assist the Russian in their recovery, and when they were opened he could feign horror at the sight of the bone-china dragons and claim he'd been cheated of the Golden Dragons by some unknown third party. He would then beg forgiveness of General Ch'iang and pay whatever tribute the Nationalist leader demanded.

'The One Eyed what?' the Russian snarled.

'The One Eyed Woo. He calls himself The Admiral.'

'Aaah,' Illya Kruschenko nodded knowingly. 'The Admiral.' He remembered the Chinese pirate, the one they called The Young Captain Wong. Wong had spoken of an Admiral as Illya had cut his eyelids off.

'You know of him?' Merchant said, his hopes rising even more. 'He has the dragons.' He pointed to the junk, which was gathering speed less than one hundred yards away.

The Russian pulled Merchant back out onto the poop deck. 'You are saying the Golden Dragons are on that pirate junk?'

'Yes,' Merchant felt an insane desire to laugh. 'That's right.'

'Then you are of no use to me.' Kruschenko snarled, pushing him back against the railing.

'No,' Merchant gasped, raising his hands. 'Wait. You don't understand.'

'Goodbye, Mr Merchant.' Kruschenko grinned, raised his pistol and shot him through the heart, sending Merchant's body flying over the rails and into the sea.

'Forget the big ship,' the big Russian shouted to the coxswain. 'Catch that junk.' As he moved towards the wheel-house he looked to his left and saw the boy.

James Merchant stood against the stern rail staring in shocked disbelief at the point where his father had disap-peared over the railing. Finally, he turned his gaze upon the Russian. They stared into each other's eyes for what seemed like an eternity, before Illya Kruschenko raised his gun, but there was not a trace of fear in young James Merchant's expression as he faced the big Russian.

The boy has guts, Kruschenko thought, as he watched the child take a deep breath and brace himself for the shock of the bullet to come. But the bullet didn't come. The Russian slowly lowered his firearm and smiled before disappearing into the wheelhouse.

龍

On the bridge of Police Launch Number Four, Crown Sergeant Malcolm Linden watched the junk as it made for the western end of Lantau Island. She was cutting across the wake of a big cargo ship that was heading south west for the open sea.

McCraw turned his attention to Richard. The young man was staring at the junk like a cat watching a mouse. 'There are two hostages on board that junk, Richard,' McCraw murmured. 'Their safety takes precedence over any personal vendetta you may be contemplating.'

'Sir,' a young corporal called to Malcolm Linden as he leapt though the wheelhouse door. 'Sir, it's not the Merchant Company junk, it's the *China Moon*.'

'Ha! How's that for a stroke of luck?' the Crown Sergeant laughed. 'Open the ship's armoury and issue a rifle to each of the crew,' he ordered the young corporal. 'And man the Hotchkiss Gun. I've got you now, you old bugger!' he shouted into the night.

'Got who?' McCraw asked. He was getting angry with both the Marine Sergeant and his brooding Inspector.

'The One Eyed Woo,' Malcolm Linden responded.

'The pirate?'

'I couldn't be sure until now. I've had a man on the bow with binoculars. I thought it was the Merchant Company junk, but it's the *China Moon*. And I'm going to blow him out of the water.'

'You'll do no such thing,' McCraw commanded. 'We're after John Merchant's vessel.'

'Sir,' the young corporal interrupted again. 'The Merchant Company junk is off the starboard quarter. About half a mile.'

McCraw moved to the starboard side of the wheelhouse and looked at the Merchant Company junk before turning to address Sergeant Linden. 'A man and his son are on board that junk over there,' he continued, 'and their lives are in danger. Our job is to rescue them. Any other ideas you may have, such as catching pirates, you'll put out of your head right now! Is that clear?'

'Yes, Sir,' the chastened Marine Sergeant replied.

'And as for you,' the big Scot glowered at Richard, 'I'd suggest you calm down, laddie.' Richard had said nothing, but McCraw had sensed the madness in his anger. 'You are to play no part in this interception. You'll leave it to Sergeant Linden. Understood?'

'Yes, Sir,' Richard answered evenly, his eyes trained on the Merchant junk.

'Keep your eye on the task at hand, laddie, and don't waver.'

'Good God Almighty!' Malcolm Linden gasped pointing through the windows ahead. 'The junks are firing at each other!'

McCraw and Richard looked ahead. In the moonlight, they saw the muzzle flashes of machine guns as the two junks engaged in battle.

龍

The Admiral, The One Eyed Woo, had been watching the S.S. *Pacific Star* make for the open sea when the first burst of machine gun fire had raked his wheelhouse windows, the bullets barely missing him.

'By all the gods!' he gasped as he looked astern, the Merchant junk was nearly on him. He hadn't realised she was so fast.

Outside, on the rear of the poop deck, the pirate's second in command, Leung jai, uncovered the Lewis gun and returned fire. His bullets tore into the superstructure of the Merchant junk and he saw a man drop an odd-looking weapon. Strange he thought, as he continued to strafe the junk, it was a machine gun, a machine gun that fired from the hands. Never before had he known of such a gun.

The One Eyed Woo swung his ship hard to starboard to bring his other machine gun to bear on the Merchant Company vessel. And then he realised, too late, his mistake. She was bearing down on him hard amidships, her engine under full power. Too close, he thought, staring at the huge wooden prow of the junk. She's too fast and too close.

At the wheel of the Merchant junk, Major Illya Kruschenko flinched as the bullets from the pirate's Lewis gun ripped into the woodwork around him. Forward on the bow both of his machine gunners were dead and, to make matters even worse, away to his left a police vessel was approaching.

'Police!' he cursed softly. As if pirates weren't bad enough, how in hell had the police got into the equation.

It should have been a simple operation. Stop the S.S. *Pacific Star*, have Merchant order the removal of the Golden Dragons onto the company junk, then transfer them to the waiting Russian freighter upon which he'd arranged passage and shipment to Vladivostok.

'Damn you all!' he growled in his native tongue as another hail of bullets ripped through the wheelhouse.

He looked down at the wounded coxswain on the floor behind him. They were out-gunned and out-manned, but the thought of losing the prize in the pirate junk drove him to the brink of madness. For once in his life, Illya Kruschenko was unsure of what to do, then the thought struck him like a hammer blow.

'How deep is it here?' he yelled at the injured coxswain.

'About five fathoms,' the man groaned.

Ahead of him, Illya saw the junk heel over and swing to starboard and another Lewis gun opened fire at him from amidships.

'I'll ram her!' he yelled to no one at all.

That's it, he thought, he'd sink her. Five fathoms was only thirty feet. Even if both junks went down it would still be worth it. Lantau Island was close by and he was a strong swimmer. The police would never locate him in the darkness and he could come back and dive for the dragons when it was safe.

He held tight to the wheel and watched as the huge wooden prow of his vessel rose high on a wave, then bore down on the exposed side of the pirate junk.

'He's going to ram her!' Malcolm Linden yelled from the bridge of Police Launch Number Four.

Forward, on the bow Richard Brewster and Robert McCraw watched, horrified. Less then one hundred yards away the Merchant junk reared like a stallion before crashing into the side of the *China Moon*.

Above them at the wheel, Malcolm Linden, hypnotised by what he was witnessing, realised almost too late just how close he was to the disaster. Police Launch Number Four, all one hundred and eleven feet of her, was steaming at full speed towards the junks. The Crown Sergeant swung the wheel hard to port and the big police vessel listed dangerously to starboard as it responded. Hard about she came, her bow barely twenty yards from the side of the stricken junks.

Richard seized the opportunity and flung himself headlong into the foaming waters. He swam for the stern of the Merchant junk, which was precariously low in the water, its bow jammed hard and fast, high on the *China Moon*. He reached the railing, hauled himself aboard and lay gasping for air on the sloping poop deck.

龍

On board the *China Moon*, The Admiral, The One Eyed Woo, roared in fury as the bow of the Merchant junk came over his gunwales and crashed down into the deck of his ship, striking a mortal blow. Several men from the Merchant junk leapt aboard. Around him, the crews engaged in hand to hand combat. With his good eye, The Admiral searched for the motherless dog fucker who'd dared to ram him.

Most of the crews from both ships had dived overboard, knowing only too well that when the ships went down they'd go right along with them.

The Admiral noticed his second in command was fighting with a big *gwai loh* and he knew beyond all doubt that this was the man responsible for his misfortune. He watched the foreign devil pick up Leung jai and toss him over the side. The Admiral screamed his rage and rushed at the man, hitting him full in the body and taking him to the deck.

The One Eyed Woo was first to his feet and unsheathed his knife. He crouched on the listing deck and prepared for mortal combat as the *gwai loh* stood up, but the man was holding a pistol and pointing it straight at the pirate's heart.

Richard Brewster had climbed up onto the bow of the Merchant junk. He was ten feet directly above the Russian and saw him pull the gun. Filled with blind hatred, Richard did not hesitate. With a bloodcurdling scream, he flung himself down on the big man and drove him into the deck.

The Admiral, taken by surprise, watched fascinated as the big bald-headed *gwai loh* was first to get to his feet. The giant's eyes searched quickly for his lost firearm, but could not find it, so he crouched and rushed at the uniformed policeman.

Richard saw the Russian charge. He knew that he faced his final moment, that the giant would squash him like an ant. Then his hand fell upon cold steel. A marlinspike. He gripped it hard.

As the big Russian reached his full momentum, Richard drove himself forward embedding the vicious spike into the shocked man's stomach.

He struggled to his feet and watched the giant stagger past him. Their eyes met for a brief moment as Major Illya Kruschenko toppled over the rail into the churning sea. Richard turned to confront the one eyed pirate.

'*You're under arrest,*' he said.

'*I'm what?*' The One Eyed Woo grinned at the policeman, then laughed out loud. '*At last I meet a foreign devil who speaks my tongue and he turns out to be not only a policeman, but an idiot as well!*'

Richard looked around, recognising the ridiculousness of the situation, and he too laughed. An odd laugh, with a manic edge that seemed to issue from someone other than himself. The world had finally gone mad. He continued to laugh, along with the Admiral The One-Eyed Woo, both men howling their insane mirth at the night sky. And then a huge explosion caused all thought to stop.

龍

'She's blown her tanks!' Malcolm Linden yelled at Robert McCraw.

Fifty yards from the stricken junks, the crew of Police Launch Number Four watched in horror as flames belched from the bowels of the *China Moon*. The timbers of both ships groaned in agony as they commenced their final journey to the bottom of the South China Sea. In a final act of revenge, the *China Moon* was taking the Merchant junk down with her.

'Stand by to take on survivors,' Crown Sergeant Linden called as he moved into the wheelhouse and took the ship's wheel.

Robert McCraw's eyes searched the waters for any sign of Richard Brewster, as the two junks slid beneath the waves. 'Where are you laddie?' he whispered. 'Where are you?'

龍

Richard regained consciousness to find himself floating on a piece of decking. Strong hands were shaking him roughly. '*Wake up, devil!*' a voice whispered in Cantonese.

He looked about and realised he was on a makeshift raft with none other than the one eyed pirate, and young James Merchant was lying unconscious beside him.

'*Aiyaa!*' The One Eyed Woo grunted. '*I have no time to waste, devil.*' He grinned inanely at Richard. '*The bald one would have killed me with his gun. I owe you a life, so here it is,*' he indicated the boy. '*I must swim for mine. Your sow-fucking friends will pick you up soon. And next time we meet I truly hope your penis is dripping small flowers.*' With his closing reference to venereal disease, he gave a final mad grin and pushed off into the wild black waters.

龍

Richard Brewster awoke, weak and slightly delirious. He stared around the sanitised hospital ward. Through the curtained window he saw heavy rain falling. He felt no pain, until the memory of Caitlin returned.

'Caitlin.' He whispered her name out loud. Caitlin, he had to see Caitlin. But where was she? An operation. Yes, that's right. He could remember, in his delirious state, Elanora had said something about an operation.

'Caitlin!' He struggled out of bed, this time calling her name loudly, and upon hearing his cry, a young nurse entered the ward.

'You must rest, Mr Brewster,' she said, trying to get him back into bed.

'Caitlin Maclain,' he mumbled. 'I must see Caitlin Maclain.'

'Miss Maclain is in a post-operative ward, Sir. You can't see her.'

'Is she all right?'

'She survived the operation, but you can't possibly see her,' the nurse replied sternly. 'She's gravely ill.'

'How long have I been here?'

'Two days, Mr Brewster.'

'I've got to see her. Get me something to wear.' He summoned all the strength and authority he could muster as he gave the young nurse her orders. 'Get me something to wear or I'll go to her in this gown!'

The girl saw the pain and worry in his eyes and relented. She found his uniform and helped him dress, then assisted him to the post-operative ward.

He saw her through a window, sleeping peacefully, her hair awash across the pillow, and on her face the faintest hint of a smile. He'd known her only one week, but his love for her was so strong it seemed a lifetime.

As he moved closer to the window, a doctor, unaware of his presence, slowly pulled the white bed sheet over her face then crossed himself for the repose of her soul.

龍

Elanora's servants found him later that night in the grounds of the Merchant Mansion. He'd walked, delirious, all the way up the Peak Road in a monsoonal downpour and stood beneath Caitlin's bedroom window until he collapsed.

By the time Elanora got him into bed he was burning up with fever. She called George Phillips, her private physician, and physician to the Governor of Hong Kong no less, then sat on the huge staircase in her night attire, too tired and too worried to care what anyone might think.

'Well?' she asked the doctor, after he concluded his examination and stood staring down at her from the stair landing above. 'Will he be all right?'

'I can't say, it's out of my hands,' he replied as he walked down to join her on the landing.

'What do you mean? You're a doctor!'

'Mrs Merchant, Inspector Brewster has an acutely high fever. There's nothing anyone can do. He'll either survive it, in which case he'll slowly get well, barring the onset of pneumonia, or it will kill him.'

'What about taking him back to hospital?'

'They can do no more than I can, I'm afraid. In fact I think the move would probably kill him.'

'Damn it!' Elanora snapped. 'He saved the life of my only son. What about medicines?'

'I've given him quinine, it'll help fight the fever. I've left instructions with your *amah* to administer it to him every four hours.'

'I'll do it, she's an idiot!' Helplessness was making Elanora angry. 'She'd probably poison him.'

'Apart from that,' Doctor Phillips sighed. 'There's nothing for you to do except keep him warm, watch over him and pray.'

'Well, I certainly know how to do that, doctor,' she replied sarcastically, 'I spent most of my formative years in convents.'

'I'm a Catholic, too, Mrs Merchant.'

The doctor's benign smile brought to mind the self-righteous priests and nuns Elanora had been surrounded by as a girl. They'd constantly reminded her of her 'heathen' blood and urged her, for the sake of her mortal soul, to embrace their glorious God.

'Well, I'm not!' Anger finally burst from her. 'And you are wrong to assume so!'

'I do beg your pardon,' he replied rather stiffly.

'I'm afraid I was unable to take the leap of faith required, Doctor. I could never accept the Resurrection, it is to my Chinese mind a foolish notion, invented to frighten ignorant *gwai loh* into a religious belief that defies logic. Thank you for calling so promptly, Doctor Phillips. Goodnight.'

龍

The sounds, sights and smells of Hong Kong assaulted Richard's senses. Quincy Heffernan offered him a bowl of soup that turned into a pit of hissing snakes. He rode a fiery dragon through bright blue skies that suddenly turned to black, as the dragon turned and breathed flames on him. Hordes of men stripped of their skins chased him through the dark alleyways of Kowloon. The skinless men became thousands of Chinese running, screaming, up the steps of Western Street threatening to crush him to death against the godown walls. Machine guns and pistols opened fire all around him and he ran towards the open spaces of Victoria Peak, where the vision of Caitlin Maclain beckoned to him. Then he saw the huge, bald-headed Russian approaching her, a gleaming knife raised in the air. She was unaware of the Russian's presence. She was laughing and waving to him as he struggled up the side of the mountain with all its trees turning into triad members who slashed at him with their choppers. He killed them as they appeared, but the more he killed the more appeared and the Russian was getting closer and closer to Caitlin.

'Caitlin! Caitlin!'

It was three in the morning when Richard began scream-ing. Elanora sat bolt upright in the chair by his bed where she'd been dozing. She reached for the quinine and water and with his head in a vice-like grip she forced the liquid through his clenched teeth.

After several minutes of frantic wrestling he fell asleep again and Elanora sat watching him shiver with the fever. His teeth chattered and he threw his bedclothes off and his body gleamed with sweat.

She remembered being a child in Macau where several times she'd had fevers herself. Fevers in one form or another were commonplace along the South China coast, especially in the unsanitary, heat affected Portuguese colony of Macau. The little port was a melting pot for sailors from all over the world and they invariably brought diseases with them, usually during the insufferable heat of summer. Typhoid, dengue, smallpox, cholera and other plagues had all wreaked havoc on the population at one time or another.

Elanora smiled sadly at the memory of her dear old *amah*. The woman insisted that the spirits which dwelled within a fevered mind could be drawn out of one body and into another. The old crone would strip naked and lie hugging Elanora to her, all the while muttering incantations to the devils lurking in Elanora's feverish body and when Elanora recovered, the *amah* would rush about the Escaravelho house claiming victory over the evil ones.

Elanora was never quite convinced of the old witch's remedy, but she was sure the semi-awareness of a warm body enfolding her own gave comfort and security to her delirious mind.

Who really knows, she thought. Her strict Portuguese Catholic upbringing had insisted she scoff at the complex oriental world of spirits and mythology, but her Chinese heart, inherited from her mother, told her otherwise.

She looked at the delirious young policeman and her Chinese heart won out. Richard had suffered a great shock with the loss of Caitlin and his tortured mind would be searching for her, unwilling to accept her death. If she could let him hold Caitlin in his arms, maybe the knowledge that he was embracing her would ease his torment and give him the strength to recover.

Her decision made, Elanora locked the door and stripped off her night attire. She quickly got in beside the sick young man and pulled the covers over them. Wrapping her arms around him, she whispered sweet words in his ear each time he mumbled. And as the monsoon rain howled outside, she whispered too the old incantations to the spirits of the air, calling upon them to exorcise the devils that tortured the body and soul of Richard Brewster.

BOOK TWO

FLIGHT

CHAPTER NINE

Hong Kong, 1933

Chan Man Lam was late. He pushed his way through the Saturday night crowd in Sa Po Road Kowloon, cursing all the gods of time and distance for making him late to this most important of meetings.

'*Buy this duck,*' an old hawker lady shouted in his face as he crossed Carpenter Road. She grabbed Chan firmly by his shirt front with one gnarled hand while the other thrust the live bird in his face.

'*I don't want a duck,*' Chan snapped as he tried to free her grip on his shirt.

'*Everyone wants a duck!*' she cackled back at him. '*One cannot live without ducks! Ducks are the essence of life! Without ducks there would be no Peking Duck! True or not true?*' she asked thrusting her face into his.

'*I don't know,*' Chan growled, still trying to break free.

'*Then again,*' she went on, breathing garlic into his face. '*Perhaps you prefer pork.*' The old crone let go of him momentarily, bent down and stood back up. '*Buy this pig,*' she cried pushing a squealing young animal into his face.

'*I don't want to buy a pig!*' Chan yelled. Seizing his opportunity to escape he ran up Tung Tsing Road.

'*I wouldn't sell you one anyway,*' the old crone screeched after him. '*You'd only fuck it if I did!*'

Chan Man Lam kept running up Tung Tsing Road past the quack dentist shops and apothecaries, pushing his way through the throngs of happy Saturday night revellers until he encountered, on his left, the Walled City of Kowloon.

He looked about furtively then disappeared down a dark alley into the bowels of the infamous fortress.

The Walled City was whispered about by everyone who'd ever visited Hong Kong, a den of iniquity, a home for every villain on the South China coast, they whispered. The Walled City, owned by many, governed by none.

Originally a small, insignificant fort, it had been built by an emperor long ago to display the imperial flag of Peking in the remote wilds of Southern China. In 1847 it had been rebuilt in order to keep a watch on the British across the harbour on Hong Kong Island. It had six watchtowers, walls fifteen feet thick, a garrison of several hundred soldiers and was presided over by a third-ranked mandarin appointed by the emperor of the day.

When the British signed a ninety-nine year lease over the New Territories in 1898, sovereignty of the tiny city became a political dilemma never quite solved by either side. Nobody, in Hong Kong at least, really understood who governed it, so it was politely ignored. As the years rolled by it was simply referred to as the Walled City for want of a better name.

Not far from the Kowloon Aerodrome and virtually on the border separating British Kowloon and the New Territories, the Walled City became the haunt of misfits and villains. A maze of narrow lanes and alleys, gas pipes and illegal electric wires, a rabbit warren filled to the brim with the worst guttersnipes and criminals the burgeoning port of Hong Kong could offer. It was, in short, a disgusting slum, so much so that even the rats refused to live in it and by 1933, its human population had dwindled to several hundred.

Chan Man Lam made it, puffing, to the *ya'man*, the original administrative office in the centre of the tiny city. A glow filled the windows and he knew the ceremony had started as he tapped three times on the front door.

'*Your heart is what colour?*' a Cantonese voice from within asked him.

'*My heart is blue,*' Chan replied.

'*Your soul is what colour?*'

'*My soul is golden.*'
'*Your master is who?*'
'*The Golden Dragon.*'
'*He has how many brothers?*'
'*Four.*'
'*His brothers came from where to here?*'
'*From the four foreign cities.*'
'*They brought what with them?*'
'*They brought the truth.*'
'*And their eyes are which colours?*'
'Red, blue, green and white,' Chan finished, and the big black door opened to him.

'*You're late,*' the door guard whispered to him. '*The ceremony is about to begin. You'd better sneak around to the left and make sure the Red Dragon doesn't see you.*'

Chan Man Lam bowed his thanks to the guard and made his way around to the side of the hall. He stopped at the end of a block of raised wooden seats and nudged the man sitting on the end to make room for him. He climbed up, sat down and took a blue headband from his pocket and tied it around his forehead. The sign on the headband, a single chevron, indicated his low rank in the secret society.

Chan surveyed the scene before him. His block of wooden seats was one of three, each filled with men, forming three sides of a square, the fourth side being a raised dais on which sat the *Shan Chu* of the secret Triad. The Golden Dragon, as he was known in the lore of the society, and, along either side of him, sat the four Coloured Dragons. Chan had never before seen all five masters gathered at the one time, and the collective power they exuded sent a chill through his small frame.

The Honoured First Five, like all the other dragons in the room, were dressed in ordinary clothes, the only references to rank being their blue headbands. The *Shan Chu*'s bore the pips of a Chief Inspector, as did that of the big redheaded *gwai loh* next to him; the other three bore the insignias of Crown Sergeants.

Constable Chan knew them well. The Grand Dragon was none other than the famous *gwai loh*, *Blue Star*, who, with the four men, had founded the *Gam Loong Tong*, the Society of Golden Dragons, in the year of the Fire Tiger, 1926.

To the right of Blue Star sat the *gwai loh* McCraw, known as the White Dragon. The big man from Scotland was the head of all dragons stationed in Hong Kong Island, and beside him sat the *gwai loh* pirate killer, Malcolm Linden, Blue Dragon of the Marine Police.

To the Grand Dragon's left sat the Red Dragon, Lo Shi-mon, iron-fisted ruler of Kowloon District and warlord of the society, and next to him sat Terrence Delaney, the Green Dragon of the New Territories.

The sight that excited Chan most was the statues. Four golden dragons, one guarding each corner of the square. They sat three feet high and, in the candlelight, their eyes glowed the four famous colours, ruby red, sapphire blue, emerald green and diamond white.

In the middle of the square two young men stood facing the *Shan Chu* and twenty feet in front of them was a flat box roughly ten feet square, six inches deep and full of fine sand.

Constable Chan felt his excitement rise as the young men bowed to the *Shan Chu*. He knew what was in store: it had been talked about in the ranks for the last two weeks. Tonight, the young men would be inducted into the society.

They were special, these two young men, because they were not policemen. The Golden Dragon himself had made the exception that they be allowed to enter the ranks of the secret society of policemen. They were skilled in the arts of Shaolin and would serve as enforcers, he'd announced. Tonight, as part of their initiation ceremony they would perform the twelve principal disciplines.

Chan Man Lam felt very privileged. He had been chosen by the other members of his Lodge to represent them at this ceremony. He was to witness the events and report back to his small branch of the Society of Golden Dragons in the New Territories. It had been whispered among the initiated that Lo Shi-mon, the Red Dragon, had been instructing the boys for years in the secret arts of Shaolin, and tonight they would perform the ancient rituals.

Blue Star raised his hand and the room fell silent, then Constable Chan heard a noise that made his hair stand on end. It was coming from the two young initiates as they emptied their lungs of air then breathed in again and hissed like dragons.

As Chan continued to watch, the two young dragons, for that was surely what they were in Chan's eyes, began to move in perfect harmony. Their hands flashed and their feet struck the air as they went through a series of furious movements his eyes could barely keep up with. He watched awestruck as they spun through space like winged demons only to land, so softly and continue their mesmeric dance.

On and on they went, the sweat pouring from their bodies as their minds summoned up the gods of the spirit world. First the tiger appeared, then the mantis, crane, rat, monkey and snake, all of them answering the call of the young men. Then suddenly, so suddenly that Chan gasped, the two young dragons fell still. The air seemed to crackle as they sensed the approach of danger. Four men armed with bows and arrows appeared on either side of the dais. They began firing, their arrows aiming straight for the bodies of the young fighters, but as Constable Chan winced, the arrows were caught in mid air by the young men.

A roar of approval from all present greeted this spectacular finale until, with one wave of his hand, *Blue Star* silenced the room. Hissing and spitting, the young dragons moved towards the dais. They walked with a strange, disjointed gait across the box full of sand, then knelt at the foot of the Dragon Throne and Chan Man Lam's jaw dropped in amazement. Where the two boys had walked on the sand, there appeared not one footprint. Not one grain of sand had been disturbed.

Lo Shi-mon stepped forward and bowed deeply to the man seated above him on the Dragon Throne.

'My Lord, Golden Dragon,' Lo intoned. *'Please accept these humble gifts from me, your servant.'*

'Mark them as mine,' Richard Brewster replied. *'From this day forward they will be known as The Dragons of Shao-lin, in honour of your ancient teachers, Lo Shi-mon.'*

'*Your will be done, Lord,*' Lo Shi-mon murmured, and he signalled an official standing at a coal brazier next to the dais.

'*Dragons,*' Richard's voice rang out through the hall, as he addressed the assembled company, '*bear witness to the ceremony.*'

The official drew a branding iron from the brazier. The brand was the image of a snarling, five-toed dragon glowing white hot. He carried it, with great ceremony, towards the two supplicants.

Thirteen-year-old James Merchant watched as the iron burned into the flesh of his upper right arm. His nostrils flared at the smell of his burning skin, but his mind divorced itself from the trauma and he remained calm.

Kwan Man Hop, too, watched in silence as he was branded a dragon. His mind was in a place of peace, he stood on the edge of a tranquil lake listening to the wind rustle through the trees along the shoreline

'*These men have been marked, My Lord,*' Lo Shi-mon continued. '*One on the right shoulder and one on the left so they may stand facing north to your throne with their brands concealed. It is for you alone to order them to turn away from each other and face the south, whereupon their marks of honour will be exposed, revealing them to be the defenders of our Noble House and the enforcers of your will.*'

Richard had inwardly flinched as he'd watched the iron burn into the boys' flesh. He had not wanted the branding done, but Lo Shi-mon had insisted, explaining that the rank and file of the society would accept the boys more readily if they displayed courage on top of their fighting skills.

'*Red Dragon,*' Richard said, standing to address the assembled company. '*The Society thanks you for these two honoured members who have joined our ranks tonight. Their skills will be of great value to us.*'

He stepped down from the dais and walked to the centre of the square, where he gazed about at the faces of his men. He saw predominantly Chinese faces including members from his original Shangtungese platoon and, sprinkled among them, Russians, Sikhs and Punjabis, several other British, a Canadian and a young Australian.

Richard and Lo Shi-mon, along with McCraw, Linden and Delaney, had started with the original core group of the Man Yee On. They'd renamed the society and slowly, but surely, begun to recruit more members. It had not been difficult; the men of the Hong Kong Police were a desperate bunch. The *gwai loh*, in particular, had drifted to Hong Kong from all parts of the globe, some running from the law, some from persecution and others from broken love affairs or disintegrated families. The offer of a fresh start with a new 'family' had been seized by all with both hands. Like their local counterparts, the foreigners embraced the idea of having somewhere, or someone, to turn to for advice and assistance. After all, the Hong Kong Government offered them no such conditions.

'Gentlemen,' he said. *'Seven years ago the four dragons you see, one guarding each corner of our Lodge, were delivered into the care of the Honoured First Five by a secret benefactor who encouraged the Five to form a society for our mutual protection.*

'They were dark days. As one of the Honoured First Five I can tell you, they were dark and dangerous days . . .'

Dark and dangerous days, Lo Shi-mon let the phrase wander through his mind. Dark and dangerous, he thought, was an understatement.

Lo sat in his Red Dragon's chair and looked at his friends seated on the dais alongside him. Robert McCraw, Malcolm Linden, Terrence Delaney. And as Richard addressed the brotherhood, Lo's mind wandered back to that fateful night, eight years before, when it had all started.

龍

Elanora Merchant had been at the hospital when Lo Shi-mon had arrived with Richard Brewster and her son, James. The boy had been wrapped in a blanket and appeared not to recognise his mother as she'd thrown her arms about him. The medical officer had informed her that James was in shock and, after allaying her initial fears for his wellbeing, he quickly took the lad away for further examination.

'How's Caitlin?' Richard managed to ask. He too, was wrapped in a blanket and Elanora noticed that he was shivering violently.

'Not good, Richard,' she replied. 'The knife pierced her kidney.'

'Can I see her?'

'Not yet.' Elanora put her arms around the young inspector and sat with him on a bench. She could barely hold him, he was shaking so badly.

'*Ah Lo,*' she snapped briskly in Cantonese. '*Your Elder Brother needs attention, get someone immediately!*'

'*Yes, Elder Sister. At once, Elder Sister,*' Lo Shi-mon hurried off. He knew better than to disobey the Merchant Mistress.

Among the Chinese communities in Macau and Hong Kong, Elanora Merchant was known and loved for her compassion and generosity. She was not dependent on her husband's great riches and gave freely of her time and money to help the poor and destitute. She'd set up several schools and assisted in the creation of small businesses. She had also set up halfway houses for young women, and an obstetrics clinic in Macau bore her family name.

But money and power were known to go hand in glove, and Elanora Merchant was no exception. Lo Shi-mon was fully aware that if someone was foolish enough to make an enemy of the Merchant Mistress, they would encounter a formidable adversary. He had heard stories. Rumours abounded concerning the Merchant Mistress, and not all of them were pleasant. She could be utterly ruthless if her authority was challenged.

As the big Shangtungese sergeant searched for a nurse, it occurred to him that the beautiful Merchant Mistress had not once asked after her husband's welfare. Did she know he was dead? Did she know she was a widow? And not just a widow, Lo thought, but as of tonight one of the wealthiest widows in Asia.

'Thank you for my son's life,' Elanora whispered, trying to rub warmth into Richard's shivering frame with the coarse blanket. 'I am forever in your debt.'

'I k-k-killed him, Elanora,' Richard stammered, his teeth chattering with the cold that consumed him. 'The Russian. I d-d-drove a marlinspike through his guts.'

'Good.'

'But I'm afraid your husband is d-d-dead. I saw his body on Police Launch Number Four. He was shot through the heart.'

'That is also good.'

He stared at her wordlessly, his whole body shaking as the cold reached into the deepest part of his being.

'Here is a nurse to help you,' Elanora said as Lo Shi-mon arrived with a young woman. She assisted him to his feet. 'Go with her.'

The nurse took Richard by the arm and led him away while Elanora and Lo Shi-mon stood watching.

'*He will be all right, Elder Sister,*' Lo assured her. '*Blue Star is strong. True or not true?*'

'*True, Ah Lo,*' Elanora murmured in her mother's tongue. '*He is very strong. And he will need to be even stronger to defeat the Man Shing Tong, is this not also true?*'

Lo Shi-mon did not know where to look. With one simple question she had put him in a precarious situation. Here was not some ordinary woman whom he could tell to mind her own business. Here stood the Mistress of the House of Merchant. '*Elder Sister,*' Lo began. '*My honour is in jeopardy.*'

'*I know everything, Sergeant,*' Elanora interrupted. '*Am I not the Merchant Mistress! I have spies and informants in every house from Macau to Peking! Do you think the business of the Hong Kong Police or your pathetic triad society, the Man Yee On, can be kept secret from me?*'

'*No, Elder Sister,*' Lo Shi-mon replied. '*Please forgive me, Elder Sister.*'

'*The child-defiling piece of shit Tiger Paw Chang is still alive!*' Elanora hissed. '*And while he lives, Sergeant, our friend Blue Star is not safe. True or not true?*'

'*True, Elder Sister,*' he looked about, fearful of their being overheard.

'*I want that fat son of a lame whore slaughtered!*' Elanora went on regardless of several nurses passing by, and Lo could see the anger glowing in her eyes. '*I want him and anyone remotely connected to him disembowelled and fed to the dogs, Sergeant! Understand or not understand?*'

'*I understand, Elder Sister.*'

'*While he lives the Man Shing Tong also lives, weakened though it may be. I want you to spread the same message my spies will spread. Blue Star is not to be touched!*'

'Aaah, there you are, Elanora,' Charles Higgins purred, hoping that he sounded like a grieving friend.

'Hello, Charles,' Elanora replied, reverting to English.

'I'm afraid I have some bad news, my dear.'

'I know,' she replied. 'John is dead. Richard told me.'

'You have my deepest sympathy,' Higgins murmured, all the while his eyes appraising her as a cat would a mouse. 'Where's Richard, my dear?' he asked placing a hand on her forearm.

'He's not well. They took him in there.' She indicated the set of double doors.

'Then if you'll excuse me, I'll leave you to your grief,' he intoned obsequiously and walked off.

'*That is another of Blue Star's enemies,*' Elanora whispered as Higgins disappeared through the swinging doors.

'*Higgins Superintendent?*' Lo Shi-mon asked incredulously.

'*Do you doubt my word?*' She glared at him.

'*No, Elder Sister.*'

'*If you are Blue Star's friend, you will watch Higgins carefully, Lo Sergeant.*'

'*I will do so.*'

'*Good. Now I must go to my son.*' Her face softened as she smiled at him, a smile of complicity. '*You and I, Lo Shi-mon, have business to discuss, and it must be soon. Between us I hope to place Blue Star in a position where he will not be challenged.*'

'*I hope for that too, Elder Sister,*' Lo nodded.

'*Excellent!*' She clapped her hands together. '*I will summon you, Lo Shi-mon Sergeant,*' then spun on her heel and headed for the swinging double doors.

Six weeks passed before the summons occurred.

龍

Lo Shi-mon walked to the Merchant House high on the Peak Road. Several times he stopped and looked down on the panorama that was Hong Kong. He rarely had the opportunity to see it from the Peak. He was Chinese after all and the Peak was the domain of the rich. The harbour below was dotted with ships from all nations, old junks sailing sedately among them, and ferries rushed busily between the island and Kowloon.

One day perhaps I will be rich, Lo mused, one never knows what the gods have in store. He passed through the ornate iron gates of the Merchant House and was challenged immediately by one of the ground staff who demanded to know his business. Lo identified himself and was taken to the summerhouse in the rear gardens.

Richard Brewster was sitting on the summerhouse patio sipping tea. To the Shangtungese sergeant, who had not seen him since the night he had chased the S.S. *Pacific Star*, he looked drawn and weary. Lo knew that Richard had discovered Caitlin dead and that he'd staggered to the Merchant House in a storm where the Merchant Mistress had found him. Richard owed his life to the woman.

'*Ah Lo,*' Richard forced a smile, dragging his mind back from the night he'd spent with Caitlin in this very same summerhouse. '*Today's weather is good, true or not true?*'

'*True, Elder Brother,*' Lo replied. '*It is almost as good as your Cantonese. If I were a blind man I would swear I was talking to a mandarin of great rank.*'

'*You can thank the Merchant Mistress for that, we have spent many hours together during my convalescence and she refuses to speak English to me.*'

'*The Merchant Mistress is wise. She makes you practise because she knows that when you master the language you will more quickly be able to separate your friends from your enemies.'*

'Yes, she is wise,' Richard agreed. *'She is also mysterious. She told me to expect you, and asked that we meet her here at the summer house. Only the gods know what it all means.'*

Lo Shi-mon could see Elanora Escaravelho Merchant approaching across the manicured lawns from the main house. Gliding like a rain cloud low over a restless sea, he could never remember her looking more beautiful. But there was something else, something different about the woman that Lo Shi-mon could not identify until she stopped in front of him, bowed and then turned to look upon Richard Brewster.

'Good morning, *Ah Lo. Have you eaten or not eaten rice today?'* It was a common greeting among Chinese to ask whether or not a person had eaten breakfast, based on the assumption that if they had then they were obviously in good health. But, even as she made her enquiry to the big sergeant, her eyes were devouring the young Englishman.

'I have eaten already, *Elder Sister,'* Lo replied automatically, but he was shocked. Elanora's desire was obvious. It is written all over her face, he thought, and he wondered whether there was a liaison between the Merchant Mistress and his young inspector. But when he looked at Richard Brewster, the young man appeared not only unaware of the adoration in her eyes, but had barely noticed her arrival.

'Hello, Elanora.' Richard turned. 'I'm sorry, I was miles away.' His smile was pleasant. 'Now what's all this mystery? What on Earth could be so important that you require not one, but two of Hong Kong's finest to meet with you in your summerhouse?'

Lo could see she was hurt by his casual response. The glow faded from her eyes and she crossed to the patio doors.

'I'm sorry, this place will hold painful memories for you, Richard, but it is essential we meet here.' She went into the summerhouse, and the two policemen followed her.

'I have a story to tell you both,' Elanora pulled the dust covers from the furniture and bade them sit. 'Please remain

silent until I've finished as the tale is a rather complicated one
and will take some time.'

'All this mystery,' Richard said with an attempt at levity.
'Really, Elanora, it's very theatrical.'

She ignored him, sat in an armchair and began her story.

The two policemen sat, and Elanora told them her tale of
intrigue, murder and betrayal. At first, Richard tried to interrupt only to be silenced by a wave of her hand or an impatient
stamp of her foot. On she went, rising from her seat, pacing
the summerhouse floor, as she spoke of her husband's greed,
the treachery of his police friend, a one-eyed pirate and a fat,
evil paedophile. She told of a young Englishman who rode a
golden dragon through fiery skies and mentioned the great
Generalissimo Ch'iang Kai-shek and a psychopathic operative
from the Russian government and four fabulous golden
statues. She fought back tears as she spoke of the murder of
her friend Caitlin Maclain, and told of her relief at the sight
of her son, alive in the hospital. When she finally fell silent,
she sat back in her chair and stared intently at Richard.

But Richard said nothing. It was Lo Shi-mon who spoke.
'Higgins has a lot to answer for,' he said.

Elanora could only nod as she waited for Richard's
response, but still Richard said nothing, his face an unread-
able mask.

Throughout his recuperation, the ache of his love for
Caitlin had haunted Richard. He'd heard the lilt of her voice,
and the vision of her face had been with him constantly. The
copper halo of her hair, the cream of her Irish skin, but above
all, the light in her beautiful green eyes. Mischievous,
wanton, teasing him with her love. The senselessness of her
death had come close to driving him mad, but he'd known
that he must put it behind him. Caitlin had simply been in the
wrong place at the wrong time, killed by a Chinese person
unknown during the commission of a criminal act. At least
that's what he'd told himself; it was a way to stay sane.

Now, having heard Elanora's story, forcing himself to
listen quietly and objectively, analysing each piece of information, one man had become the focus of Richard's

thoughts. It had been Charles Higgins who had set in motion the chain of circumstances that had led to Caitlin's death. Higgins' greed and treachery had murdered Caitlin, as surely as if Higgins himself had been holding the knife.

'Higgins. Charles Higgins,' he muttered when he could finally bring himself to speak. 'Charles, Superintendent laddie boyo Higgins.' Elanora and Lo exchanged a concerned glance at the venom in his voice. 'I'll see him dead for this. I swear on my mother's grave, and on the grave of Caitlin Maclain, that he'll pay with his life for what he's done.' He rose from his seat. 'I'll cut his black heart out and . . .'

'No!' Elanora also stood. 'I did not nurse you back from the brink of death so you could waste your life in an act of childish revenge!'

'He was responsible for Caitlin's death and he'll pay!'

'You will listen to me carefully, Richard.' Elanora could see the hatred welling inside him and she knew, for all their sakes, that she must force him to control it. She must make him realise the danger of letting it run, unchecked. 'You must not allow your emotions to override rational response. It's time you stopped thinking like an Englishman! You live in China. Start thinking like a Chinese!'

'But Caitlin . . .'

'Caitlin is dead!' Elanora continued her assault. 'She was stabbed in the back and she died!'

'Yes,' Richard snapped coldly. 'And I hold Charles Higgins responsible.'

'He is not your principal enemy!' She felt her own anger rising. 'He is merely a pawn in the game. Can't you see that? He is of no significance! Now sit down and control yourself.'

Richard stared at her and Elanora glowered back forcing her will upon him. Finally they both sat, and silence ruled the room.

As Lo Shi-mon looked at Elanora, an image formed in his mind of the hawks, floating on the thermal up-draughts around Victoria Peak. They were proud, beautiful and graceful to behold, but when a quarry appeared, they calculated the exact angle of interception and killed swiftly and without remorse. Lo realised that Elanora, like a bird of prey, had been sorting through the evidence for weeks and calculating an attack on Richard Brewster's enemies that would be swift, remorseless and final.

'The Merchant Mistress is right, *Blue Star*.' Lo Shi-mon finally spoke. 'You must listen to her.'

Richard gave a curt nod. 'Very well. So, Elanora,' he said, turning to her warily. 'Tell me what you think it is I should do.'

'Tiger Paw Chang is your number one enemy. He is the one you must destroy first. He is in hiding while he restores his forces, but he will come after you eventually, Richard. Do not wait. Strike first.'

'This is good advice, Elder Brother,' Lo Shi-mon agreed. 'Chang lost great face when his Lodge was attacked. If he does not retaliate he will be seen as weak and his own men will turn on him.'

'I understand what you're both saying,' Richard said as he rose again and started distractedly pacing the room. 'More wholesale killing. You Chinese talk about murdering people like other people discuss a walk in the countryside.'

'*Aaaiiiya!*' Elanora wailed angrily as she stood and confronted him. '*Two tigers cannot live on one mountain, Blue Star!*'

'What?' Richard halted, confused, he couldn't understand her rapid Cantonese.

'You must strike, Richard! You have been told this before, am I not right? When will you learn? *Two tigers cannot live on one mountain!* I'll say it in English,' she slowly repeated. 'Two tigers cannot live on one mountain!'

'One tiger can simply leave the mountain, Elanora.' Richard felt overcome by a sudden weariness, and he lowered his head into his hands, defeated; Binky Brewster's words echoed in his mind, 'Let's hope Hong Kong will make a man out of you.' Richard had hoped so too. He'd been so confident, so eager to make his mark in Hong Kong

Elanora recognised his defeat. She was getting nowhere, she thought. She must use a stronger approach, but how far should she go?

Lo Shi-mon could sense the frustration in the Merchant Mistress. He knew what she was fighting for. Despite her great wealth and position, she was a woman alone in a city of men. She needed a champion to protect her and her son. And if Richard Brewster was to be that champion, she needed to place him in a position of power. Lo Shi-mon had no doubt she would do so, despite the weakness the Englishman was showing. Which was after all understandable, Lo thought, following the death of Caitlin Maclain.

'This is not England, Richard,' Elanora started again, gently this time. 'It is China. You must learn to live by our rules or you will not survive.' She looked at the big sergeant who nodded agreement. 'Think of Caitlin,' she said. 'Think of the beautiful girl you've lost forever. Think of the life you two could have shared. The children she would have borne you.' Her voice was seductive now. 'Think of her beautiful white body, and the night you spent making love in this very room. Did she whisper, "I will love you forever, Richard" as you held her in your arms . . .'

Lo Shi-mon watched, fascinated as the Merchant Mistress carefully placed the seeds of controlled revenge in Richard's brain.

'. . . Think sensibly, Richard,' Elanora continued softly. 'If you wish to avenge Caitlin's death, as I know you do, you must evaluate carefully, plan meticulously, and then execute with complete finality. Surely you can see that?'

'You're right!' Richard's defeat and brief bout of self-pity was replaced by a new sense of purpose. He didn't care that his reaction was no doubt that which Elanora had intended. Every word she'd spoken had been the truth, and he would play the game the Chinese way. 'Of course you're right. I'll kill them,' he said evenly, 'I'll kill them like I killed the Russian. I'll slaughter Tiger Paw Chang and every last one of the Man Shing Tong, and I'll kill them all for one reason.' The revenge that welled in him was calculated now. 'They took the life of Caitlin Maclain!'

'That's it,' Elanora urged. 'Avenge your lost love. But use wisdom and cunning to achieve your desire. You must do it dispassionately, Richard. You must not allow emotion to cloud your vision. That is the way here in China. *True or not true, Ah Lo?*'

Lo Shi-mon could only nod his reply, the words were stuck in his throat. He knew what the Merchant Mistress was doing and was lost in admiration. She must be aware, Lo thought, that when the killing began she would lose *Blue Star* forever, yet she had not faltered. She loved the Englishman, he was sure, but if the death lust overtook *Blue Star*, as it was bound to, his heart would be blackened for all eternity. He would be incapable of returning her love. Tread softly, Elder Sister, Lo Shi-mon wanted to whisper. You have awoken a sleeping dragon, but as yet, you have only a timorous hold on his tail.

'Do we know where Chang is?' Richard asked.

'In the pirate haven of Lau Fau Shan,' Elanora answered. 'He and the Admiral are no doubt licking their wounds.'

'I'll kill Chang first, and then I'll kill Higgins,' Richard said.

'No,' Elanora said. 'Higgins must remain unharmed.' Richard was about to interrupt but she cut him off. 'Stop thinking emotionally,' she continued. 'You have Higgins in the palm of your hand! Use him.'

'How?'

'He will officially approve a police raid on Lau Fau Shan. He will sign the order for you to achieve your revenge on Tiger Paw Chang.'

'Excellent! I'll kill him after the raid.'

'No! Higgins must remain alive.'

'Why?'

'I have it on good authority that Higgins will replace Mr Wolfe as Inspector-General of the Police Force.'

'But if that happens I won't be able to kill him for years!'

'Think,' Elanora coaxed him. 'The Chinese way, remember? When Higgins is made Inspector-General you will control him like a puppet.'

The woman was brilliant, Lo Shi-mon thought. She was so far ahead of them both. *'Elder Sister is right, Blue Star. The power would be yours.'*

'The power to do what?' Richard asked.

'To be the *Shan Chu* of a new triad,' Elanora declared.

'*Aaaiiya!*' Lo Shi-mon exclaimed. '*You have the wisdom of ten thousand buddhas!*'

'Are you suggesting,' Richard interrupted. 'That we form an illegal secret society and that I be the grand master?'

'Exactly,' Elanora replied. 'Use what is left of the tiny Man Yee On triad to create a new, powerful society.' She looked briefly at Lo Shi-mon who was nodding furiously. 'Its members will accept you without question. Avenge the death of Caitlin Maclain, nurture your hatred for Charles Higgins and surround yourself with a bodyguard of men you can trust, your policemen of the Man Yee On. That is the Chinese way. Only then, with total power, will you be truly able to control your destiny.'

'Think of it, Elder Brother,' Lo Shi-mon whispered, as he joined Elanora in the seduction of the Englishman. 'Total power. It would mean a better life for all of us. You could rule Hong Kong.'

'The organisation is already in place,' Richard said, his mind racing with possibilities as he paced the floor. 'Just imagine! Hundreds of trained men throughout the colony! And they're already in uniform!' He laughed out loud. 'It would be the most powerful triad in Hong Kong. All we'd need is a few trusted senior men like McCraw and Delaney to get it up and running and there'd be no stopping us.'

'It would be a truly wonderful thing, *Blue Star*,' Lo Shi-mon said. 'An honourable society for the welfare of all policemen, which would serve and protect the people of Hong Kong.'

'And inside that society, Richard,' Elanora added, 'you would be safe from harm.' She looked at Lo Shi-mon. He offered her a smile, which sealed their conspiracy.

'You will need money,' Elanora continued. 'I can supply that, subject to it being repaid with interest, of course.'

'That's very generous of you,' Richard said.

'But the loan carries conditions.'

'And what would they be?'

'My son must be placed under the protection of your triad.'

'That shall be my first order,' Richard replied. 'Your life and the life of your son James will be under the eternal protection of the society. It shall be a blood oath.'

'Thank you, Richard.'

'You said *conditions*, Elanora. State the others.'

'There is only one other.'

'And that is?'

'That I be allowed to name your new society.'

'By all means. What do you suggest we call it?'

'How about the Society of Golden Dragons,' Elanora said as she walked across the room and pulled a white dust cover from an oval rosewood table to reveal a sight that made them gasp.

The two men stood frozen in wonder. Four Golden Dragons stood snarling, side by side. Each three feet tall, they glowed in the half light from the window shutters, their eyes ablaze with the fabulous stones, ruby red, emerald green, sapphire blue, diamond white.

'Beautiful, aren't they?' she murmured.

It was a full minute before Richard found his voice. 'You stole them?' he asked.

'Yes,' she smiled. 'I know my husband's telegraphic codes. The secret codes to which only the captains of his ships have access. The day after his unfortunate death, my dead husband telegraphed Captain Watling to offload the crates at sea, far from any prying eyes. I'm sure Captain Watling was only too happy to oblige. Several of my trusted servants from Macau took a small ship to a meeting with the S.S. *Pacific Star*. I arranged four substitute crates to be exchanged for the originals and I can just imagine Higgins' face when he got the telegraph from his agents in London stating the crates contained nothing but worthless rocks.' She laughed.

Lo Shi-mon joined in her laughter. The image of Higgins staring at the telegram, jaw agape, eyes bulging with shock and disbelief, then the apoplectic rage that must have ensued, delighted him.

'They're magnificent,' Richard crossed to the table to examine them, as Elanora sat down and looked at Lo Shi-mon.

'*Your husband was a fool to tell you of their existence,*' the big sergeant whispered, sitting beside her.

'*If a woman does not love a man, Ah Lo, the man is helpless in her arms, true or not true?*'

'*Very true, Elder Sister.*'

'*Unfortunately, Sergeant,*' Elanora looked at Richard. '*The same rule applies in reverse.*'

Lo Shi-mon followed her gaze to the young man inspecting the statues. He was surprised that she had chosen to confide in him. Was it a ploy to strengthen their alliance? Was she attempting to manipulate him by revealing her intimate feelings for *Blue Star*? If so, her tactics had once again succeeded. She had deepened the bond of loyalty between them, for Lo Shi-mon, too, had great affection for the Englishman.

Lo felt a deep sorrow for the Merchant Mistress. If the future followed the dark and dangerous course they had plotted, her love for *Blue Star* would be the first casualty of this war.

龍

Dark and dangerous days, Lo Shi-mon thought, as he watched the last of the society members leave the *ya'man* and vanish into the night. But he and Richard Brewster had survived. No, not just survived, they had formed a society so powerful it now ruled Hong Kong.

Between the three of them, under a cloak of utmost secrecy, they had removed the precious stones from the statues and had the gold melted down into ingots. Then with the unwitting help of the Merchant Company accountants, Elanora had introduced the gold in small amounts into the banking system and scattered their wealth to the four corners of the Earth. The four statues used at ceremonies were fakes.

As Lo had expected, Richard Brewster was a born leader. The role of *Shan Chu* had become second nature to him. He recruited Robert McCraw, Terrence Delaney and Malcolm

Linden to assist in the administration and appointed Lo Shi-mon as the Red Pole, or enforcer. He had worked out an itin-erary for them all to follow and the society had developed rapidly.

Financially too, Richard had proved his worth. With the helpful advice of Elanora he'd made clever business decisions regarding the investment of society money and built a benev-olence chest that saw all members were looked after in times of trouble. But Lo's premonition that Richard's heart would harden had also proved correct.

On several occasions when things had not gone his way, Richard had shown a cold detachment. Lo Shi-mon had watched as the acquisition of power had seduced the young inspector. Richard Brewster had used standover tactics and threats on a number of occasions and reconciled their use by saying it was necessary for the Society's good. And he had killed. Swiftly and remorselessly in acts of pure revenge, to assuage the pain and guilt he felt for the untimely death of Caitlin Maclain.

Slowly but surely, in Richard's mind, Caitlin's death and the circumstances surrounding it had grown out of all pro-portion and now coloured his every action. Lo Shi-mon had witnessed his friend's transition from an idealistic young Eng-lishman into a ruthlessly brilliant *Shan Chu*.

Lo Shi-mon had also witnessed the rise in fortunes of McCraw, Delaney and Linden. When Richard had first approached them, they had needed little persuasion to join the Society, realising the benefits to be had from it. But, along with Richard they had invested money at various times and as a result had increased their own fortunes tenfold.

Lo himself had taken money over the years, but never for personal gain. He had given it away to those less fortunate, or donated it to charities and local orphanages. He had little need for money, his frugal upbringing and years associating with the monks from Shaolin monastery had freed him of the desire for material wealth. There were times over the last eight years, he had to admit, when the thought of riches had entered his mind and dreams of a great house and servants to do his bidding had tempted him, but those moments had been rare. He had a rice bowl, a change of clothing, four walls and a roof to shield him from the elements, and he genuinely desired nothing more.

As long as the *Gam Loong Tong* remained a source of welfare for overworked and underpaid policemen and their families, Lo Shi-mon didn't care what fortunes were made, or by whom. Besides, he could hardly take the moral high ground. Had he not thrown Chang the Krait out of a second storey window of Central Police Station? Had he not conveyed threats, on *Blue Star*'s behalf, to various businessmen in Hong Kong, warning them of the dire consequences they'd suffer if they dared operate against the Society's interests? Of course he had. He was as morally corrupt as the others. And he had sworn a blood oath to be loyal and would remain so until his death.

Lo Shi-mon had no idea what the future held for him, but he had chosen his path. He would walk with the Dragons and together they would face whatever the gods decreed.

'Ah Lo, may I have a moment of your time?'

Robert McCraw's voice brought him crashing back into the present. 'Certainly,' he replied.

'Has Richard mentioned London to you at all?'

'London?' Lo Shi-mon, looked perplexed.

'Yes, London,' McCraw replied. 'I've had a notion in my head for some time and I've spoken of it to Richard. He's of the opinion we First Five should meet and discuss the prospect of opening an office there.'

'It is a good idea,' Lo nodded. 'Our businesses here in the Colony are thriving, we are making so much profit that it is sometimes embarrassing to meet the eyes of our bankers. A nest in the heart of the British Empire would be invaluable to us. A very wise business move indeed.'

'You old fox! I thought you'd approve,' McCraw laughed.

'Approve of what?' Richard asked as he joined them.

'The idea of an office in London,' McCraw replied.

'It's time we expanded, Ah Lo,' Richard patted his friend on the shoulder. 'Our interests in the Colony are secure, but this place is only a tiny part of the British Empire. I've been meaning to speak of it with you but have not had an opportunity. Delaney and Linden are all for it.'

'Then it is unanimously agreed, Elder Brother,' Lo smiled. 'We will sneak silently into London like the Emperor's assassins and before anyone is aware of our presence we will have control. Is this not the way you see it?'

'It will require a great deal of thought,' Richard said as he waved for Delaney and Malcolm Linden to join them. 'It's not a move to be made lightly.'

'Is this the London thing?' Linden asked as he moved to Richard's side.

'Yes, Malcolm,' Richard nodded. 'Have you given any more thought to my request?'

'I have.'

'And?'

'My loyalty lies with the *Gam Loong Tong*. If it serves the Society of Golden Dragons for me to reside in London, then I will do so without hesitation.'

'I knew I could count on you, Malcolm,' Richard clapped an arm around the Marine Sergeant's shoulder.

'However,' Linden raised his hand, 'I reserve the right to return when our Society's business interests are established and secure. Hong Kong is my home and the Dragons are my family.'

'You'll be welcomed with open arms,' Richard replied.

'So, Malcolm laddie,' Robert McCraw said. 'You're to be our man in London.'

'King George's man,' Richard corrected with a smile.

'Now you've lost me entirely,' the big Scot looked puzzled.

'Gentlemen,' Richard grinned and indicated the Marine Sergeant. 'Meet the new Superintendent of the London Port Authority.'

'You're not serious, laddie!'

'A brilliant move,' Lo Shi-mon said. 'A brilliant move indeed it is, *Blue Star*!'

'It's taken three months of lobbying and bribery,' Richard went on. 'But I've been at it since you first gave me the idea of opening offices in London, Robert.'

'But, Richard,' Terrence Delaney interrupted. 'How can Malcolm be our company businessman in England if he works for Customs?'

'He won't be our businessman in England, Terrence, he'll be our watchdog.' Richard replied. 'In his official capacity, he'll have control of all vessels and cargoes in and out of the Pool of London.'

'Smuggling without fear of prosecution,' Lo Shi-mon smiled.

'And he'll be able to keep an eye on our new business representative in England,' Richard added.

'If Malcolm is not to be our business representative, Elder Brother, then who is? We must choose with great care. Have you anyone in mind?'

'I have already appointed him, *Ah Lo*.'

The four men were surprised. Their *Shan Chu* normally consulted them before making major appointments.

'As Golden Dragon I am ultimately responsible for the wellbeing of our Society and its members, do you not agree?'

'Of course, Elder Brother,' Lo replied. 'You are the *Shan Chu* and your word is law.'

'You've made a decision, Richard,' Robert McCraw interjected. 'None of us will challenge it. If that's what you're getting at?'

'I thought long and hard before I chose this man and I'd like you all to consider the decision on its merits before you start screaming obscenities at me.'

'Och laddie!' McCraw moaned. 'Will ye no get on with it? Nobody will scream at you, for God's sake. Who have you chosen?'

'Charles Higgins.'

'Jesus Christ, maaarn! Are you out of your bloody mind?!'

CHAPTER TEN

Richard Brewster sat on the upstairs balcony of the Merchant House high above the teeming harbour of Hong Kong. Despite the fact that it was Sunday the sheet of blue water separating Hong Kong Island from Kowloon was a hive of activity. Sampans, tugboats and barges barely avoided each other in their efforts to service cargo ships, small ferries shuttled passengers to and from ocean liners, larger ferries made their way relentlessly across the expanse of water and among it all, several ancient Chinese junks sailed sedately westward, unbothered by the frantic activity.

The mournful sound of a ship's horn called Richard's attention from the pages of *The South China Morning Post* and he gazed down at the scene far below him. The S.S. *Dunfermline* had hoisted its Blue Peter, the fluttering pennant pronouncing its imminent departure for England. He looked at his watch and realised sadly it would soon be time to take the boys down to Queen's Pier or they'd miss their ship.

He'd known for several years that this day would come, but the knowledge didn't make the parting any easier. Elanora had cried all night, and the house servants had been moping about dolefully for the past week. Ah Poh, the boys' *amah*, had done her best to prevent their departure with a series of ominous declarations. Firstly she'd stated that the boys had contracted typhoid and, when this had been dismissed by Elanora with a derisive snort, the old *amah* had claimed that a snake had come to her in her dreams and warned her not to let the boys travel. When the mistress had once again dismissed her foolishness, Ah Poh had declared that, before her very eyes, she had seen a kite take one of the house cats, an ill omen of the direst kind. And finally, in desperation, the old woman had threatened to kill herself if the boys left Hong Kong. Elanora had been forced to scold Ah Poh severely and, ever since, the old *amah* had been wandering about the house, scowling and muttering and, when the mistress wasn't looking, lavishing every known treat upon the two boys.

Richard's thoughts went back to the previous night in the Walled City. James and Lee had surprised even him. Lo Shi-mon had been instructing them every day without fail for eight years in the legendary martial art form. Every morning at six o'clock he would call for them at the Merchant House and run them across the wilds of the Peak until they were exhausted, then he would drill them relentlessly on the lawn behind the summerhouse.

They'd been six years old when their training had started and Richard smiled as he remembered the two sleepy-eyed little boys wandering down the tiled driveway of the house to meet Sergeant Lo. He remembered the horror on Elanora's face when she'd first seen them return from their morning run exhausted and barely able to stand. And how she'd protested when he'd informed her that they would be subjected to the same treatment every day of their lives. For a week or two Richard believed she might even put a stop to it, but she never did. The Chinese part of Elanora knew the benefits the boys would reap from the instruction of Lo Shi-mon.

At fourteen years of age, James Merchant and Lee Kwan Man Hop were tough, resilient and forthright with maturity and intelligence far beyond their years. They were boys whom any parent would be proud to have. But, Richard thought, they were not ordinary boys. As of last night, James and Kwan were members of the Society of Golden Dragons and that made them anything but ordinary. To the Society and to Richard, in particular, they were a pair of lethal weapons created carefully and patiently over a period of eight years by Lo Shi-mon as a strike weapon, to be used only at Richard's discretion in times of direst adversity.

Elanora had no idea that her son and ward had been initiated. The burns of the dragon brands on their shoulders had been carefully concealed from her, and the boys were setting sail for England in approximately two hours. It would be a long time before they would return to Hong Kong.

Richard had felt a pang of guilt at the ceremony the previous night; it had been his idea to have the boys trained. He had struggled with the idea at first, remembering the traumatic experiences of his school days and the loathing he had later developed for military discipline. Adherence to strict discipline, Richard knew, could have a desensitising effect on young minds. Did he have the right to subject the little boys to a regimented code of ethics far stricter than any he himself had experienced? After all, they were not even his children. But Elanora had made it clear that she wished him to take an interest in their futures. 'They have no father,' she had said. 'And I would greatly appreciate your occasional assistance and advice, until I find them one.'

Finally Richard decided the disciplines Lo Shi-mon would impose upon the boys would aid their survival, and protect them from the bullying and racial prejudice they would encounter in a public school obsessed with the rules of the British class system. Now he was glad of his decision. James and Lee would cope, adherence to strict discipline had become second nature to them. They would make the transition to life at Gladstone School for Boys with ease.

Lo Shi-mon had initially been reluctant to undertake the boys' instruction. When Richard had added that James and Kwan would undoubtedly return as men to Hong Kong and eventually be principal players in both the Society and the Merchant Company, Lo Shi-mon had been quick to see the wisdom behind his commanding officer's plan.

'We will not live forever, Ah Lo, true or not true?' Richard had said.

'True, Elder Brother,' Lo had replied. 'And the discipline the arts of Shaolin imposes upon its students makes them the finest of adversaries in battle and the most astute of men in business. I will train their minds to focus and their limbs to strike.'

And so it had come to pass.

Kwan Man Hop, the small boy Richard had rescued from the burning godown, had been taken into the Merchant House at Richard's suggestion by an eternally grateful Elanora. The care of a child was small payment indeed to the man who had saved the life of her son. The boy's grandfather Old Kwan had been beside himself with pride and excitement when the proposition had been put to him. For his grandson to work in the house of the Merchant Mistress would ensure the boy's future and provide great face for the Kwan family.

At first the young Kwan, who called himself Lee – which he insisted was short for Lee'chard as he called Richard – was destined for a future as a houseboy and a butler, but the boy's irresistible charm had quickly endeared him to Elanora. She recognised in him the perfect companion for James. Lee Kwan was not only beguiling, his intelligence and ability to learn was undeniable, and Elanora was determined to see him properly educated and placed in a position to achieve. She arranged to become his legal guardian and from that day on, Lee Kwan had gained all the rights and privileges shared by James and the other well-to-do children of the Colony. He'd been educated privately with James by the finest tutors including Quincy Heffernan and the two had become inseparable companions. Both boys had been well tutored and now it was time for them to attend boarding school in England to complete their education, hence, Richard's arrangements for them to sail on the tide aboard the S.S. *Dunfermline* for England.

'Mother!'

Richard was startled from his reverie as James burst onto the balcony. 'Don't scream, James,' he chided. 'You sound like all the devils in hell.'

'Sorry, Sir,' the boy apologised. 'But have you seen Mother?'

'She's downstairs attending to your luggage.'

'Thanks.' James leapt over the balcony rail like a cat. It was three floors to the gardens below and Richard's heart momentarily jumped.

'Damn it!' he growled, but by the time he'd made it to the balcony rail the boy had disappeared. He should have known no harm would befall the lad. For years both of the boys had been scaling the house walls like monkeys. It was all part of their training. Lo Shi-mon had taught them well.

'Where's James?' Lee asked, his head appearing over the balcony rail.

'Didn't you pass him on the wall?' Richard queried sarcastically. 'He went down as you came up.'

'Thanks.' Lee disappeared.

'Come back here at once!' Richard roared, and the boy's head slowly reappeared at the rail. 'Go and get James. I want to talk to the both of you.'

'Yes, Sir,' Lee stared at his *Shan Chu*. He knew they were in trouble, Richard rarely yelled.

'Now!' Richard said and, as the boy began to disappear, he added. 'Not that way! Use the stairs, boy! You're not a monkey!'

'Yes, Sir!' Young Lee sprang onto the verandah and walked quickly through the doorway leading to the main staircase.

Richard smiled despite himself. It was impossible to stay angry with the boys. They were good lads and he loved them in his own way, although the emotion of love, for Richard, was little more than affection. Richard was incapable of loving anyone. The death of Caitlin Maclain, the years of violence and the ways of the Orient had changed him forever. Richard Brewster had become a cold man. His smile faded as he reflected upon his own past. Nine years in Hong Kong had changed him drastically, and he knew it.

To the colonial social set Richard Brewster was a simple police inspector who held the heart of a wealthy woman, but to those who knew him well he was a very different proposition. To them, he was no longer a sensitive, idealistic young Englishman. That innocent had disappeared forever, to be replaced by a dragon. A powerful, dangerous and at times, malevolent dragon who would stop at nothing, including murder, to achieve his goals. *Blue Star* they knew, could be benevolent when necessary, and indeed charitable when required, but *Blue Star* ruled his world and theirs with fierce eyes and claws of steel and if they dared transgress, he would breathe upon them the fire of extinction.

Richard had, at first, been unaware of the changes taking place within him. He'd met the girl of his dreams, only to have her stolen away and, with that loss, a light had gone out in him, to be replaced by a dark force that craved revenge. And revenge had been swift in coming. He'd murdered, coldly and dispassionately and, as he had, he'd felt the joy of retribution. It was only then he'd realised the different man he was becoming, but there was no turning back. He'd charged onward seeking power. He'd bullied, cajoled and threatened as he built a society that formed a wall about him, from within which he developed his lust for control.

He had most certainly changed, Richard thought, and he wondered briefly whether Binky Brewster would think for the better.

James and Lee burst onto the balcony with their usual energy and stood before him. The sight made him smile and his demons momentarily retreated.

'Boys,' he began. 'I was going to speak with you both when we boarded the vessel, prior to your departure, a sort of a farewell speech, but I think the time is ripe for me to speak now.'

'Yes, Sir,' they answered in unison.

'I have been your friend for many years and now I am your *Shan Chu*. It is as your *Shan Chu* that I now speak. You are going far away to England to attend school and there are some things I want you both to do while you are there.' The boys nodded. 'Firstly, and this is an order, you will allow no one to see your skills of Shaolin . . .'

'But . . .' James began.

'Be silent, James,' Richard raised a hand. 'I'm telling this to you for your own good. People in England will not under-stand your ways. They are ignorant of the ways of the East and ignorance breeds fear, as Master Lo must have told you many times. Most people there have never witnessed, are not even aware of, the teachings of Shaolin. Your skills will frighten them and you two will be outcasts as a result. Do you understand?'

'Yes, Sir.'

'You will watch and copy the ways of English boys. If you have cause to fight, as I've no doubt you will, you will do so in the childish manner of schoolboys.'

'You mean we have to roll around in the dirt like babies?' Lee interjected, horrified.

'Exactly. Unless your lives are threatened and you have no other avenue of escape, you are never to display your skills. Furthermore you will use your mind techniques to keep your spirits at peace and to confound the teachers with your ability to learn. I expect nothing more than the highest academic achievement from you both. If you get homesick, as all men do, you will have each other for comfort. Guard each other with your lives and keep your secrets for that which they were created, the Society of Golden Dragons. Speak Cantonese or Portuguese only in the strictest of privacy. Observe and draw knowledge from all that you witness. Learn the ways of the English until you are as one with them, because it is the English you will have to deal with as men.'

'But I am English . . .' James interjected.

'Here in Hong Kong that may be the case, James, but there is much racial intolerance in England. There are some in England who will not accept you.' He studied the boy's olive skin, the slight almond shape of his eyes, the touch of the exotic he'd inherited from his mother. It was eminently attractive, but it would alienate him from English school-boys. 'And you even more so, Lee,' Richard continued, turning his attention to the young Chinese. 'You will be reviled on occasion because of your foreign blood. Do not let this trouble your spirit. Turn to each other for guidance and forgive those who curse or malign you, for it will only be their ignorance which occasions it. You will both maintain regular correspondence with Elanora and your letters to her will bear no complaint. You will also keep regular correspondence with me, your *Shan Chu*. You will tell me of all your adventures so that I may be aware of how much you are learning.'

'Finally, you will at all times uphold the honour of the Golden Dragons. I want you to swear to me now that you will obey me and do all I have said. You first, James.'

'I swear by the Five Dragons that I will uphold their honour and obey your words,' James intoned solemnly.

'Now you, Lee.'

'I swear by the Five Dragons that I will uphold their honour and obey your words,' Lee whispered with obedient haste before shifting his gaze to the doorway behind Richard, signalling that someone was very close at hand.

'Ah, there you are.' Elanora stepped out onto the verandah. She fought back the tears that threatened to fall and produced a radiant smile. 'It's time to leave, boys. Your baggage has been put in the car and Ah Poh and the other servants are waiting on the front steps to say goodbye.'

'Right, lads.' Richard stood. 'Your great adventure is about to begin. Let's get down to the docks, I've arranged a Police Launch to ferry you to the *Dunfermline*.'

'Fantastic!' James whooped and the two boys scooted for the stairs leaving the adults to stare sorrowfully at one another.

'It has to be, Elanora. They need to experience England and come to grips with it, or they'll never survive what's in store for them.'

'I know,' she replied. 'Let's get it over and done with.'

Richard watched her go and he stood in silence for a moment. What a strange partnership theirs was, he thought.

Richard had great respect for Elanora, both as a woman and as a business partner, but in many ways she remained a puzzle to him. She could be inscrutably Chinese one moment, then when the Portuguese in her took over, a virago, fiery-tempered and unreasonable. She could be a witty, charming sophisticate on the one hand, and on the other a ruthless martinet, impervious to the feelings of those around her. She could mother the boys to the point of absurdity, then, when duty called, dismiss them into the company of the servants and barely speak to them for days. She could transform herself from wealthy socialite to superstitious peasant whenever the occasion arose, being equally at home dining on pheasant with the Governor, or a bowl of fish head soup with her crazy old *amah*, Ah Poh. Elanora Escaravelho Merchant was, in short, an enigma.

Two things, however, remained constant in Elanora: her loyalty and her brilliant business mind. Her loyalty was unquestionable. Richard knew she loved him, it was patently obvious, but he simply was incapable of returning it. He had never professed his love and never intended to. He did, however, love her mind. When it came to business, Elanora had no peer.

At first the two had found great pleasure in setting up the society and organising its treasury. Richard remembered the long days spent here on this very balcony scheming and planning the distribution of the gold ingots, which had once been the statues. Elanora had been his tutor in the fascinating and complicated world of Hong Kong economics.

He remembered also the various balls, official functions and parties he'd escorted her to and the looks of envy on the faces of all the eligible bachelors in the Colony as he led her onto the dance floors. And he remembered vividly one night in particular, four years ago.

龍

The party had been a tedious affair, another of the many summer shows thrown by various dignitaries and wealthy merchants for no other reason than to flaunt their wealth and position in the Colony pecking order. Richard and Elanora had arrived home at Merchant House late, Richard quite the worse for wear after having uncharacteristically drunk too much champagne.

The car had pulled up at the front entrance and he'd leapt out to open her door.

'Your residence, my princess!' he declared, taking her hand as she stepped out onto the tiles. 'My humblest thanks for the privilege of escorting you to the ball,' he gave a mock bow.

''Til the morrow,' and was about to climb back into the car.

'Don't go,' she said. 'Come inside for a drink, there's something I want to tell you.'

Thinking it all a little mysterious, Richard found himself sitting on a sofa on the upstairs verandah looking over the fairytale vista of Hong Kong. Elanora had disappeared, and a sleepy-eyed houseboy served chilled champagne and caviar, before he too surreptitiously disappeared. Richard poured two glasses and looked down at the twinkling lights.

'I hope champagne's all right,' Elanora said, reappearing silently.

'Fine by me,' he grinned, the effects of the alcohol making him feel foolishly light-headed. He looked up at her. She'd changed her clothing. She wore an embroidered Chinese silk gown over a diaphanous negligee, and her hair was piled loosely up on her head, held by a jade comb. The effect was stunning.

'I don't want you to go home tonight, Richard,' she said.

'Elanora . . .'

'I wish to say something. Please let me inish.'

'Very well.' The pleasant effects of the alcohol suddenly began to wane.

'I'm in love with you. No, don't interrupt,' she said as he started to protest. 'I've been in love with you since the first night I saw you. It was right here in Merchant House, the night you met Caitlin . . .' She faltered and looked down at the harbour. 'It has taken me a long time to find the courage to say this, and to find the right moment to say it. I know how much you loved Caitlin, but Caitlin's been dead for a long while and you cannot mourn her forever.'

'I can't love you, Elanora.' It was a blunt statement, he suddenly felt stone cold sober. 'I can't love anyone. I will not expose my feelings like that again, to you or anyone else.'

'I've learned to accept that.' Her voice was stronger now as she turned to look directly at him. 'But the fact is, I'm in love with you, and I always have been. It was Caitlin who won your heart, I know. But Caitlin has been dead for four years, the same length of time I've been a widow, and my feelings for you are as strong as ever. Stronger. I don't expect you to return them. My love is unconditional.'

He felt confronted, the woman was offering herself to him, but didn't she realise it was beyond his capability to love her? He'd said so, but she appeared not to believe him.

'I desire you, Elanora, what man wouldn't? You're one of the most beautiful women I've ever laid eyes on. But I can't . . .'

'Then desire will do. I meant what I said. My love is unconditional. Given the way I'm dressed that should be obvious.' She placed her hands on the balcony rail and once again stared out at the night. 'I am standing in front of you practically naked and I am humiliating myself. I am yours to do with as you wish. I want to love you and, in return, I will take whatever affection you care to offer. You can leave and our friendship will continue as if this conversation never happened. Or,' she turned, her eyes daring him, 'you can take me, right here and now. The choice is yours.' She let the silk gown drop to the floor.

'I will never love you.' He crossed to her.

'I know.' She pushed the straps of the negligee from her shoulders. 'Do with me whatever you wish.' The negligee fell around her ankles. 'I am yours, *Blue Star*.' She stepped from the folds of material into his arms and kissed him deeply.

He finally pulled back and stared into her eyes. 'Unconditionally?'

'Unconditionally,' she replied.

'Go to your bedroom,' he said. 'Lie on your bed and wait for me.'

Elanora obeyed. She walked to the end of the verandah, to her bedroom doors, then disappeared inside without a backward glance.

Richard breathed deeply, trying to keep his emotions in check. He was angered by the lust that burned in him. Damn it! Why couldn't their relationship have remained as it was? He'd been aware in the past of Elanora's looks to him. He'd known how she felt, but he'd never shown any sign of returning her feelings. He had no desire to love or be loved. He'd satisfied his male desires, infrequently, by going to the flower girls on the sampans in North Point and that had been enough for him. But now the thing he'd dreaded most had happened. Elanora had declared herself and to scorn her love would destroy their relationship. He had to admit that the thought of making love to her had crossed his mind on many occasions, but he'd kept his distance not only for both their sakes, but also for the sake of the Society. Now things would change forever. Elanora was a magnificent woman and her frank declaration had set him on fire. He wanted her.

He filled their glasses with champagne and walked slowly to her bedroom doors. Elanora saw him silhouetted against the night sky. He approached the bed and handed her a glass. She sipped from it, placed it on the side table, pulled the jade comb from her hair and fell back against the silk coverlet, her long black hair cascading over the pillows.

Richard sipped his own drink, placed the glass alongside hers and began to undress slowly, Elanora's eyes following his every move. Then she parted her legs and offered her arms up to him.

'Unconditional,' he said softly.

'Yes,' she breathed. 'Unconditional.'

龍

Richard smiled at the memory of his seduction as he folded the newspaper and tucked it under his arm. He would read it on the drive down to the docks. He walked along the corridor to the main staircase, which led down to the foyer. Over the past four years, while maintaining his single room in Central Police Station, he had spent much of his off-duty time up at the Merchant residence enjoying the family atmosphere Elanora created for him and the boys.

The fact that they were lovers was never mentioned in society circles. As far as the citizens of Hong Kong were concerned, Richard Brewster was merely the lucky sod that got to escort the beautiful Elanora Merchant to official functions. No one would dare suggest otherwise and risk incurring the wrath of the Merchant Mistress, or Inspector Brewster for that matter. For a simple police inspector,

Mr Brewster seemed to exert an inordinate amount of authority at times, but no one dared question why. To ask a question like that would be dangerous, very dangerous indeed.

Dangerous. He smiled again, considering the word. Everything in Hong Kong was dangerous, that was what he loved most about the place. One false move in business could prove fatal, and not only in business, he thought. Pleasure too, had its moments. Even his relationship with the beautiful Merchant Mistress was dangerous. They were both strong willed, independent people drawn together, initially, by a mutual need for protection, and now comfortably co-dependent upon each other. But their relationship sat on a knife's edge. The delicate balance of power they shared was forged by trust, and if that trust were ever broken, Richard knew both of their worlds could collapse around them. Dangerous? He smiled again. Oh yes, most definitely dangerous. But nothing he need fear as long as he maintained the status quo.

Elanora's advice to Richard had been invaluable as he'd forged ahead in his police career and slowly inched the Golden Dragons to their position of power. It had been her idea for the Society to start a welfare fund for policemen in financial trouble, or with family distress, and the move had been a stroke of genius. 'Help them, Richard,' she had said. 'Help them and they will help you. Love them and they will love you.' Covertly, the First Five had let it be known that there was a group to which distressed policemen could turn for assistance and, as a result, their recruitment of members into the Society flourished. Of the four thousand odd members in the Hong Kong Police in 1933, nearly six hundred were Dragons.

They'd recruited cautiously. Slowly but surely they'd chosen their members and shrouded them in the heaviest cloak of secrecy. 'No colour, no creed' and 'We look after our own' had been their recruitment slogans. They'd come from all quarters, Europeans, Indians, Russians, Chinese and others had covertly, silently, filled the ranks of the Society and set up an intelligence network through every station in the Colony. Daily they'd grown stronger until, after seven years, the Society of Golden Dragons was powerful in Hong Kong, and yet, so secret had their rise been, that they were still barely known to anyone outside their ranks. They were but a puff of smoke in the darkest recesses of Hong Kong's subconscious.

Richard walked down the curved staircase to the grand entrance hall of Merchant House. As he passed Elanora's office, the image of Caitlin Maclain lying in there on the floor, bleeding, flashed through his mind. Then his thoughts flew to the Russian he'd killed with a marlinspike. He also saw the hideous, grinning, face of the old pirate, The Admiral, The One Eyed Woo. It all seemed so long ago and yet . . .

'Come along, Richard, my love,' Elanora called to him from the front doors. 'Or we'll miss the Police Launch.'

He shook the images from his mind and walked through the front doors, towards the sounds of excited laughter from James and Lee. Elanora was waiting on the front verandah. He pecked her comfortingly on the cheek before joining the boys at the car.

Elanora watched him stride towards the motor vehicle, the touch of his lips on her cheek still lingering. He moves like a cat, she thought, so fluid, so self-assured, so aware of his surroundings and ready to confront whatever may occur. She felt herself flush at the thought of his body moving over her as they made love. All the time she'd known him her passion had never waned. She still desired him, and her love for him had deepened with each passing year. If only he could love her in return.

Unconditional. The word echoed forlornly in her mind. She'd waited patiently for nearly four years, hoping that Richard's affections would meet hers, and during that time she'd guided him, coerced him, encouraged him and goaded him into becoming the man she believed would control her future. Even before they'd become lovers she had sought to change him. 'Think like a Chinese, Richard. Do not allow your emotions to override rational response,' she remembered saying so long ago. Now, all these years later, she realised that she had aided in the creation of a heartless man, and in doing so she had lost the one thing she desired most, the gentle boy who, at first sight, had stolen her heart.

Elanora blanched at the memory of her attempt to seduce him. She had humiliated herself, begged for his love, and when it had not been forthcoming, she'd taken his body in consolation. She'd hoped, given time, her love and attention would place her in his heart, and she had indeed been rewarded with his affection, friendship and trust. But never his love. Finally, she'd been forced to acknowledge to herself that his heart would remain cold forever. The only thing she could be sure of was that he was incapable of loving anyone else. He did not have the capacity for it.

Elanora was trapped in a situation which she knew was, in many ways, of her own making, and she had accepted the fact, allowing Richard, remote as he was, to become the central figure in her life. But there was a further element which remained of constant concern: the influence he exerted over the boys worried her deeply. James and Lee simply adored him and looked upon him as their father. It was what she had wished for, but now, with their enemies defeated, she had hoped they could settle into a loving family. But the Richard she had helped mould was seduced by power and she was fearful of the future and what it held, both for herself and for the boys. Again, it appeared, she had created her own trap.

James and Lee were waving impatiently and she joined them at the car, disguising her fears behind a radiant smile.

龍

The former Hong Kong Police Superintendent, Charles Higgins, adopted what he hoped was an amiable grandfather's expression and smiled at the two young boys seated opposite him as he commenced his evening meal. To his left sat the captain of the S.S. *Dunfermline*, a bearded giant of a man with glaring black eyes, and to his right Miss Spencer-Price, a spinster returning to England after six months in the Orient visiting her only brother, a Jesuit priest.

James Merchant and the young Chinese Lee Kwan

unnerved Higgins. He couldn't deny it. In their formal black tie dinner dress, displaying perfect table manners, they looked for all the world like two little angels. They already had Captain Townsend and Miss Spencer-Price beaming at them like doting grandparents, completely unaware of what vicious little killers these two precocious boy-men could become if provoked. Higgins, on the other hand, was only too aware of their unusual abilities.

That morning at six, Charles Higgins had gone to check on his two little proteges to make sure they were well tucked abed only to find their cabin empty. Panicking, he'd searched the ship from stem to stern and found them on the uppermost deck between the funnels hissing and spitting like feral cats as they moved through the most intricate martial arts movements he'd ever seen. Charles had stood mesmerised behind a wooden container of life preservers, as these two seemingly innocent youths had performed the most beautiful, ballétic sequence of dances he'd ever been privileged to witness. Faster and faster they moved until they seemed to blur into one image and then they'd stopped, turned as one and stared him straight in the eye.

He remembered his boyhood, staring at a big cat in the London Zoo, and he recalled his father's instruction at the time, 'The secret is to show no fear my boy. If he smells your fear he'll be on you in a flash'. That same fear had swept over him then as the young men stared at him. He saw again the eyes of that tiger in the London Zoo, and they seemed to say to him, 'You mean nothing and will not be missed.'

Sweat had beaded on Charles' forehead despite the strong morning breeze and he'd mopped it away before waving to the boys casually and hurrying to the safety of his cabin.

'Christ on the Cross,' he'd muttered to himself as he reached the safety of his quarters. 'What sort of children are they?' He'd known the answer, however, even as his lips had formed the question. He'd seen part of that dance before. Eight years before, to be precise.

龍

Charles Higgins had hummed an obscure tune from a Gilbert & Sullivan opera as he'd sat down to his breakfast in the back garden of his residence above Repulse Bay on the south side of Hong Kong Island. He was rattled, a feeling he'd not experienced often in his life. He dismissed his *amah* and tried to read the *South China Morning Post* but his mind would have none of it. What could possibly have happened to the Golden Dragons?

Sunday mornings were normally special to Charles, it was the one time he set aside for himself and refused to let the business of the Hong Kong Police Force interfere with his life. But since receiving the telegraph from London the previous Friday, he'd been badly worried. Three months had passed since the *Pacific Star* had sailed and all had seemed right in Charles' world until the arrival of that bloody cable.

The crates had contained rocks! Bloody rocks! How could it have happened? He'd supervised the loading of the damned things onto the *Pacific Star* himself. It was just not possible. Watling must have done it. Captain bloody Watling. Charles would not have believed the man had it in him, but it must have been him. No one else knew. Well, Charles would know soon enough. He'd wired his agents in London. They could be trusted to interview dear old sea dog captain laddie Watling. Charles would soon know where his dragons were and have them recovered. In the meantime, all he could do was wait for another telegraphic message, and the waiting rattled him.

He noticed a movement in the bushes along the back wall of the garden. He stared at a particular bush for perhaps ten seconds before he realised he was looking at a man dressed in black who seemed to materialise from the plant.

'Who the Devil are you, Sir?' Higgins had growled, but the masked man, a Chinese, had remained motionless. 'Do you realise whose property you're trespassing on?' He growled again, and the man had moved slowly towards him.

As if in a dream, Higgins watched the man. He seemed to glide like a ghostly apparition until he was no more than

three feet from Higgins, who suddenly realised he'd uncon-
sciously sat back down on his chair. The man's arms began to
move with the wonderful grace of a bird. Or was it a snake?
Higgins was mesmerised. He'd never in his life seen such
menacing beauty. In a blur the man's fist flew into Higgins'
face. He knew the blow would have killed him had it struck
home. It stopped an inch from his nose and then the man's
palm opened to reveal a tiny statuette.

'What do you want?' Charles managed to whisper, but the
man remained silent. He placed the little ornament on the
table next to Charles and, in the blink of an eye, the man had
back-somersaulted three times and cleared his bloody garden
wall. Actually leapt clean over the damned thing. The whole
episode had been astonishing and obviously meant to be
interpreted as a threat. And the look in the man's eyes had
been one of pure hatred.

Charles stared down at the tiny statuette; it was an intricate
gold carving of a dragon, perfect, in minute detail. Its lips were
curled into a snarl and its tiny claws tickled Charles' palm as
he picked it up to inspect it. A golden dragon, he frowned, a
golden dragon. And then the inference struck home.

'A golden dragon!' he heard himself whisper. 'Oh Christ!
Oh Christ no!' The bloody Kuomintang was onto him. Panic
gripped his body and bile rose in his throat. 'Dear God!' he
nearly cried the words out. 'They've connected me to the
bloody statues.' Then he stifled his voice. But how could
they? His brain screamed. John Merchant, yes, but not me,
surely? There was nothing to connect him to the dragons as
far as he knew, but what if he'd slipped up somewhere? The
Kuomintang. Christ, I'm a dead man.

He rang Aberdeen Police Station and ordered police
guards to man each of the walled entrances to his residence.
He closed all of his doors and sealed himself in the library,
and placed his service revolver on the desk. The little golden
dragon had been a warning. The Kuomintang would come
for him as sure as day follows night.

Locked in his library he paced throughout the day trying
desperately to figure out where he'd gone wrong, all the

while listening for the noise of intruders as fear poisoned his reasoning.

How could they possibly know? He kept asking himself. He and Merchant had been so careful. Nobody knew we had them, he thought, nobody could possibly have known. But then again, how did one explain the Russian and his killers? They were Kuomintang. But they attacked the pirate vessel. They never went near the *Pacific Star*. They had Merchant order it stopped, but they never boarded it. Damn it! The rising panic was stopping him from thinking straight. He'd put the dragons on the *Pacific Star* himself and they'd turned to rocks by the time they arrived in London. It must have been Watling.

It was late in the evening by the time Charles Higgins recovered his self-possession. He had planned his answers to the Kuomintang when they confronted him, as he knew they would. Perhaps, after all, they were guessing, and if this were the case he would simply talk his way out of it. But if they *did* know, then he had decided upon a course which would assure his safety. The Kuomintang would not kill him if they thought he still had the dragons in his possession, or at least under his control. He would tell them this was so, and he would offer to return the statues. It was a stalling device, and at all costs he must retain his composure until he could make good his escape.

'*Sung jai?*' He unlocked the library door and called for his houseboy, he needed a drink. '*Sung jai!*' Where was the stupid boy? He pulled back the heavy curtain from the window and looked out into the deepening night.

'Good evening, Charles.'

'Christ Almighty! Brewster! What on earth are you doing here? Is something wrong? Have your men caught an intruder?'

'There'll be no intruders to this house tonight,' Richard Brewster stepped into the light of the library, Robert McCraw by his side. 'You can rest assured of that, Charles. We've given your servants the night off.'

'You've what? Has something come up? An emergency?' The men's dour expressions were making him uneasy. Sergeant Lo Shi-mon entered the room and their eyes met.

Charles knew those eyes. 'You!' he gasped. 'You were the man in my garden this morning.'

'Sit down, Charles,' Richard Brewster's voice was full of menace. 'We're all going to have a long chat.'

'About what?' Charles sat heavily in his library chair.

'On the night John Merchant was kidnapped and murdered,' Richard began, 'you sent a coded telegraphic message to the *Pacific Star*. Why did you do that, Charles?'

The interrogation lasted two hours, at the end of which Charles Higgins was a broken man. They had him in their grip forever. Under the withering stare of the big Chinese sergeant Charles had confessed to everything. They were intelligent men and slowly but surely they'd unravelled the whole scenario and left Charles Higgins an empty vessel. A cracked cup.

Since that fateful evening, Charles had come to recognise that Richard Brewster was a ruthless man and much to be feared. How had such an extraordinary change occurred?

Charles had been delighted by the arrival of the bright-eyed boy fresh from England, seeing him as a lad ripe for the plucking, one to be moulded into a corrupt subordinate who would serve whichever purpose he, Charles Higgins, chose. Richard had, however, taken corruption to a new level altogether. Richard Brewster had formed his own secret triad society for God's sake. The man had achieved power beyond Charles' wildest imaginings. He was acutely intelligent, and vicious in the extreme when the need presented itself. This was brutally apparent when the horrific raid had been launched on Lau Fau Shan.

Richard had burst into Charles' office one spring morning with Robert McCraw and a marine sergeant in tow.

'This is Sergeant Linden from Marine Division,' Richard had unceremoniously announced.

'Good morning,' Linden said, and Charles noted the distinct lack of the word 'Sir'.

'Aaah,' he drawled, annoyed but confronted by the deliberate show of disrespect. 'Another of your confidants I assume, Mr Brewster?'

'That's right.' Linden gave a malicious grin, Richard didn't even deign to reply. 'A very close confidant,' he added.

'You're required to sign these orders,' McCraw threw a sheaf of papers onto Charles' desk.

'Required?' Charles raised an eyebrow.

'That's right!' McCraw said. 'Required!'

'May I ask what they are for?' Higgins fingered the papers.

'A raid on the pirate enclave at Lau Fau Shan,' Richard replied. 'We believe opium is being stored there.'

'Don't be ridiculous. Old One Eyed Woo may be a pirate, but he'd no more have opium in Lau Fau Shan than fly to the moon.'

'We have it on good authority,' Malcolm Linden said. 'We've also been advised that we'll meet with heavy resistance when we hit the village, so part of that plan you'll sign endorses the use of cannon fire from Police Launch Number Four to soften the place up.'

'Cannon fire!' Higgins was genuinely shocked. 'You can't do that! It'll be murder!'

'I agree with you,' McCraw grinned. 'But if they're your direct orders, we can do naught but obey them.'

'I see,' Higgins replied. 'So that's how you intend to play the game, is it? I'm to be made the scapegoat if anything should go wrong.'

'Don't you think it's a bit far down the track for you to be concerned with illegal police procedures?' Richard sneered. 'You're a hypocrite, Charles, the sound of you making moral judgments makes me want to vomit! Now sign the bloody orders!'

Higgins signed each page of the orders without further objection and handed them to McCraw.

The other two men left the office, but Richard turned at the door. 'Oh, there's one other stipulation.' There was a pleasurable edge of malice to his tone. 'As this raid is your idea, I think it's only fitting that you accompany us on Launch Number Four tomorrow morning as our indomitable leader. You wouldn't want to miss the destruction of the last pirate enclave upon British soil, would you? After all, it is your plan.' He waved the sheaf of papers mockingly. 'Who knows,

Charles, you might even get a commendation from the King.'

Police Launch Number Four hove to three hundred yards off the sleeping village of Lau Fau Shan just as the sun commenced its steep climb into the eastern sky. Charles had been on deck for at least half an hour when he suddenly realised it was the morning of Good Friday 1926.

Charming, he thought to himself, utterly charming. A good day for whom, he wondered? Certainly not for the poor buggers now asleep in the village of Lau Fau Shan.

He sipped the cup of hot tea provided for him by a steward and watched the men, mostly Wei hai Wei from Shantung, squatting on the deck waiting for the order to take to the boats. They were predominantly men from Brewster's own platoon led, he noticed, by that evil Chinese Sergeant, Lo Shi-mon. He pitied those in the village when that lot got among them.

The boom of cannon fire almost made him drop the cup he was holding and he watched in awe as the first in a line of five junks moored at Lau Fau Shan pier erupted in a sheet of flame. A direct hit to its fuel tank no doubt, he thought. More cannon fire from Launch Number Eight astern saw another junk spew flames from its guts and before long all five boats were afire. Higgins heard men screaming and then, quite distinctly, he heard the sound of machine gun fire coming from the other side of the village.

'Delaney,' Richard said as he gave the order for his men to go ashore. He stood directly behind Higgins. 'He's got a squad of men on the land side. They moved into position overnight from Tai Lam Chung. I must say, Charles, your plan has left nothing to chance.'

'Do you intend killing the women and children too, Richard?' Higgins asked.

'I'm afraid not, Charles,' Richard replied caustically. 'I leave the murder of women to men like you.'

'I don't rate in your category, Brewster. What you're condoning here is nothing short of genocide.'

'I disagree. I am merely ridding Hong Kong of a rat infestation. The men in that village are the worst scum on the South China coast. We'll all be well shot of them. And you might like to know, this village is also home to the last remnants of a triad society called the Man Shing Tong.' Richard patted Charles on the shoulder and indicated a waiting boat. 'Care to go ashore for a little sport, old man?'

The carnage in the street was all too evident. Men lay dead and dying in front of the old shop and the inn. The wreckage from the exploding junks had flown in all directions killing man and beast alike and a thick pall of smoke hung, fog like, in the still morning air.

The women and children had been herded into a group around the huge tree in the centre of the village. They were pathetic to see. Some women were in shock, others stared at the intruders, while children cried at their feet. Some sixty men had been arrested and were chained together at the end of the street awaiting orders to march to the nearest police station.

'The fat one?' Richard asked Sergeant Lo. *'Here or not?'*

'Here, Elder Brother,' Lo replied. *'Delaney Sergeant caught him trying to escape in an ox cart on the western road.'*

'Bring him to me.'

'We found the Admiral,' Robert McCraw yelled loudly to Richard as he came out of the inn door.

'I don't want him harmed,' Richard replied.

'He's dead,' McCraw added.

'I said I wanted him taken alive!' Richard snapped.

'He's been dead a while, laddie,' McCraw gave a surreptitious wink. 'The old crone inside said he drowned in the bath. I'd say it was a heart attack.'

Richard held McCraw's glance for a moment, then nodded his acceptance.

An ox cart appeared at the end of the street being driven by a young police constable and in it sat the trembling bulk of Tiger Paw Chang. The ox dragging it along snorted as the cart moved up the street and stopped beneath the branches of the tree. A number of the women and children moved away, some remained, staring at Chang with unveiled hatred.

'Strip him off and tie him to the tree.' Richard ordered and the fat man was dragged from the cart and thrown onto the dusty street. His clothes were removed and he was strung to the tree by wrists and neck. A young constable started to remove the knife that lay strapped to Chang's left forearm, but Richard stopped him.

Sweat poured down Tiger Paw's forehead and ran into his eyes. He squinted at his captors and made several gurgling noises in his throat.

Richard moved close to the fat man and stared at him. *'Today marks the death of the Man Shing Tong,'* Richard declared. He looked at the eyes of the women around the tree, bright with expectation, then said loud enough for all to hear. *'It is my opinion that you owe something to the village of Lau Fau Shan, Tiger Paw Chang. Therefore I have decided that you must be responsible for feeding the village dogs. Do you agree or not agree, fat one?'*

'I agree,' Tiger Paw Chang managed between gasps for air.

'It won't be for long,' Richard said, and he removed Chang's knife from its arm scabbard and slit the fat man's stomach from one side to the other. Tiger Paw Chang screamed horribly and stared down at his entrails as they slithered in a bluish red mass to the ground between his feet. *'You'll be dead by nightfall.'*

An old woman sitting several feet from the tree began to cackle. She lifted up part of the exposed intestine and offered it to a mangy dog by her side. The animal whined pathetically and sniffed at the offering before taking it in his mouth. Several of the other women who'd watched the disembowelment began to laugh aloud and were soon joined by others. Before long all the women in the village were laughing and pointing at Tiger Paw Chang who was screaming in horror at the sight of the dog eating him alive.

Richard Brewster had been wrong with only one detail, Tiger Paw Chang had not lasted until nightfall. The image of the man's agony had remained with Charles Higgins forever.

龍

Charles breathed deeply and took a gulp of his red wine.

'I must say the food is absolutely delicious, Captain,' Miss Spencer-Price commented. 'Wouldn't you agree, Mr Higgins?'

'Yairs, yairs. It certainly is, my dear lady,' Charles drawled. 'My compliments to your chef, Captain. You're a lucky man. Isn't he, young James?'

'Very lucky, Sir,' James Merchant concurred, his eyes burning into Charles' brain.

Feral! Charles thought, and he shivered involuntarily. The bloody boy's feral. He looked at Lee Kwan who was silently eating his meal. They're just children, he told himself. Yet he knew without doubt that with one word from Richard Brewster this pair of little innocents would rip his heart out and eat it in front of him. He wondered idly what Miss Spencer-Price would think if he told her what was going through his mind. She'd shit in her bloomers! The thought made him smile, and he gave an involuntary chuckle.

'You're in exceptionally good spirits this evening, Mr Higgins,' the Captain remarked.

'And why not, Sir?' Charles replied as he wiped his chin delicately with his napkin. 'My life in the Orient is over. Having retired as Inspector-General of the Hong Kong Police, I'm finally going home to take up a new position as head of the British office of Dragon Import & Export.'

'A very powerful position indeed, if I may make so bold, Sir,' the Captain replied.

'Yairs, yairs,' Charles grinned affably. 'I dare say that is so, but what I'm really looking forward to is watching my two young charges here grow into honourable manhood. I've been charged by none other than Mrs Elanora Escaravelho Merchant to serve as guardian to her two lads as they discover the mysterious world known to we English as the public school for boys.'

What Charles failed to add was that the Devil incarnate, Richard Brewster, had also had his little say. Richard had told him in no uncertain terms that if any harm befell either of the boys, Charles' life would be forfeit. Charles was forced to smile. As if anything short of trench warfare could possibly harm those two.

'I've wanted to take your life for eight years, Charles,' Richard had said to him in that cold, calculating way of his, just before the ship departed Hong Kong. 'Every day for eight long years I've wanted to cut your throat. The only reason I spared your life was at Elanora Merchant's request. She said you'd be useful and so you have proved to be. You served the Dragons well, especially after we arranged for your promotion to Inspector-General, and I've no doubt you'll continue to be equally useful in your new position as our representative in London. Be that as it may, I want to impress upon you just how valuable these two lads are. The Society has invested a fortune in their training as future leaders and cannot afford to lose them. Please be aware if either of the boys comes to any harm whatsoever, I will have you butchered, Charles. Butchered slowly, clinically, until you beg for an end to it and welcome death with loving arms.' Charles knew he meant every word.

'You've gone as white as a sheet all of a sudden, Mr Higgins,' Miss Spencer-Price remarked. 'I do hope the food hasn't disagreed with you?'

'On the contrary, Madam,' Charles resurrected a smile. 'I was just momentarily overawed by the importance of my charge. It is my job to provide these boys with the utmost care and attention, call me a soft old fool if you will, but sometimes the thought that anything could possibly happen to them terrifies me.'

'Oh, Mr Higgins,' Miss Spencer-Price chuckled. 'I'm sure you'll provide them with a happy and safe environment. I've no doubt you're a good and kindly man.'

'You can be assured of that, Madam,' Charles nodded furiously as the mental image returned of Tiger Paw Chang tied to the tree. 'I shall love them as my own, for without them, my life would not be worth living. And there's an amen to that!'

CHAPTER ELEVEN

James Merchant licked the blood from his lip and stared sullenly at the boy in the boxing ring opposite him. Kenneth Wiggins was a fat, useless school bully who definitely needed a good punch in the mouth.

'I know what you're thinking, James,' Lee whispered in his ear as he wiped the sweat from James' brow with a towel. 'And you must forget it.'

'Just once!' James hissed through his bruised lips. 'Just once I'd love to drive my fist into his fat guts and make him vomit all over his dear old bum boy, Geoffrey Coussins.'

'It is not permitted. Our *Shan Chu* made us swear, remember?'

'At times like this, Lee, how could one possibly forget?' The bell sounded for the commencement of the final round and James stood, resigning himself to another couple of punches to the face. The other boys in the gymnasium were enjoying the fight. They cheered raucously, dutifully supporting Wiggins, as they'd been told to do by Coussins, the Head Boy.

James made sure he avoided eye contact with Kenneth Wiggins because eye contact revealed defiance and James needed Wiggins to continue believing he was afraid of him. The fat boy grinned and circled the ring slowly, his fists raised, and James watched his flat-footed movements and the airy-fairy way the bigger boy waved his gloves about, mimicking the style of English boxers. Disgust welled in him at the thought of another humiliation at the hands of Wiggins, and he was getting bored now with the orchestration of the fight, it was too easy choosing which punch he would allow to make contact. Wiggins hadn't hurt him at all until James had been caught napping and one punch had landed and split his lip. Instinctively, he'd been about to retaliate, until he'd heard Lee laugh from his corner of the ring. The sound had brought James to his senses, just as Lee had intended it should. Keep your wits about you, and keep up the pretence, the laugh reminded him. Now, as the fat boy swung at him, he muttered, 'Here we go again.'

James and Lee attended Gladstone Public School for Boys as irregular boarders, staying at the school from Monday to Friday and spending the weekends by special arrangement in London at the residence of their uncle Charles Higgins. And for a full three years now, Geoffrey Coussins, the Head Boy of their form and now Head Boy of Gladstone, together with his fat bully Kenneth Wiggins, had caused James and Lee whatever trouble they could.

It had started from the moment they'd arrived at Glad-stone. In the quadrangle of the old school on the very first day, James had had an unfortunate run in with Geoffrey Coussins. It had been a simple accident in which James and Lee had bumped into Coussins and caused the boy to drop his books. James had actually stooped to help the boy recover his spilt belongings and, in doing so, he'd stepped on Coussins' favourite fountain pen, breaking it in half.

Coussins' reaction to the accident had been extraordinary. He'd called James 'a bloody half-breed' and swung a punch at his head. James had reacted instinctively, stopping the punch with a defensive block, which snapped Geoffrey Coussins' arm like a twig. In the ensuing fracas, as other boys gathered round and goaded the two into more fighting, a teacher arrived and dragged them both off to the Dean's Office.

James had feigned tears in front of Dean Sheppard and said he could offer no explanation. He'd merely been fright-ened, he said, and he'd raised his arm to ward off the blow, and then he'd heard Coussins cry out in pain. The ruse had worked and James had avoided any further trouble over the incident, but he and Lee Kwan had discussed Richard Brewster's advice and orders, and, for three years now, had been the whipping boys of their form and for the older boys at large.

Lee Kwan had copped the worst of it, due to his Chinese appearance and the slight accent to his English which, try as he might, he found impossible to eradicate. Of medium height with jet-black hair and bright, intelligent almond eyes, Lee wore his 'foreign-ness' with an air of pride that had annoyed the schoolyard bullies from the outset. Not once had Lee retaliated, and James was in awe of his blood brother's self control. Not only had Lee endured his un-provoked beatings, he'd accepted the blame for things, which James, in a welter of temper, had occasioned. When James had smashed open Geoffrey Coussins' dormitory door with his fist, intent on killing the boy, who was fortunately not there at the time, Lee had gone to Dean Sheppard and owned up to the offence, saying he'd committed the act with a fire axe. Had it not been for the intervention of their uncle, Charles Higgins, Lee would have been expelled from Gladstone.

Later, when James asked Lee why he had stood in his place, Lee had simply replied that James had been in no fit state of mind to receive the punishment, that he would have rebelled and done something he'd have regretted. Lee, on the other hand, had not been upset and was therefore better suited to absorb whatever punishment was forthcoming.

They had shared their burden as brothers-in-arms, each looking out for the other and their mutual love, in the face of all Gladstone could throw at them, had bound them even more closely. They were regarded as foreigners, not only because of their oriental appearance, but because they remained apart from the mainstream of school life, preferring each other's company.

Both boys had carefully kept the brand of the dragon on their shoulders concealed from all. It had been Lee who had been most inventive in this deception. During the compulsory swimming lessons, he had convinced the sports teacher to let him and James swim in their white, short-sleeved, sports vests. He had informed the gullible man, 'with great respect', that it was a social sin in Chinese society for young men to be seen bare-shouldered until they'd reached eighteen years of age.

Lee was also the top scholar in each of his three years thereby carrying out his *Shan Chu*'s instructions to succeed academically. James, on the other hand, maintained good grades in all his subjects, but was not the scholar Lee had proved to be. He was 'a capable student' as his term report cards invariably stated, but Lee knew only too well that James' energy and interests lay not in the pursuit of academia, but in other directions.

Lee was aware that James had been sexually active as a twelve-year-old in his mother's household in Hong Kong. In fact, Lee thought it an act of Providence that they'd left Hong Kong when they did, because none of the young female servants at Merchant House had been safe from James' nocturnal wanderings. Not that they'd wanted to be.

Like many Eurasians, James was an extremely handsome boy. Taller than Lee, he had inherited his mother's devastating good looks, her olive Portuguese skin and almond eyes, but his colouring and hair had been tempered by his father's blood. With an unruly mop of dark brown hair, and the complexion of a well-tanned Englishman, James was fatally attractive to women. James Merchant was a man trapped in a schoolboy's existence. He disliked Gladstone intensely and longed for the time when he could return to Hong Kong and take over the Merchant Company. He couldn't stand the childish banter of his classmates. They raved about which team would win the Football Association Cup or which 'dish' they preferred among the current crop of Hollywood screen beauties, and James found it all very tiresome. He wanted to be in the South China Sea fighting the pirates who attacked the Merchant Shipping Line vessels. At seventeen, he wanted power and influence. And he wanted women. By God how he wanted women. It seemed to James the most tragic thing of all that, having discovered the unparalleled delights of the female body and what he could do with it, he was now denied such pleasure. Until recently anyway.

He'd spent his time at Gladstone School for Boys acting

like a frightened child, taking beatings from effeminate nancy-boys and studying Greek and Latin which he despised and would never have any use for. But his time would come. One day soon, he told himself.

As James clumsily dodged another sissy punch from Kenneth Wiggins, he cast a glance at his brother, Lee. Lee was shaking his head imperceptibly, so James gave him a conspiratorial wink and continued to wrestle foolishly with the bigger boy's bulk.

'Go on, Wiggles, finish him off!' Geoffrey Coussins yelled from the fat boy's corner. 'Give the little prat what for!' His high-pitched effeminate squeal grated on James' eardrums.

Thankfully the bell went to end the 'punishment' contest as Geoffrey Coussins had declared it, and James turned wearily towards his corner. He shrugged, gave a tired smile to Lee and Kenneth Wiggins punched him straight in the back of the head. James fell to the floor dazed, but as his senses returned, anger burned in his chest. He raised himself on one knee and looked again at his corner for support, but Lee was laughing fit to kill himself. Damn him! James couldn't help but smile too. Lee was a true brother. And the smartest friend he could wish for.

'Thank God it's Friday afternoon, eh *Sai Loh*?' James said in the change rooms as he pulled off his boxing gloves.

'Shhh!' Lee glanced about warily at James' use of Cantonese. 'And don't call me Little Brother. I am only three days younger than you.'

'That still makes you my little brother.'

The three days difference in their ages had been a long-standing bone of contention between them. Lee hated the fact and James loved it. Apart from the literal meanings of the two Cantonese phrases, *sai loh* and *dai loh*, meaning younger brother and elder brother, *sai loh* was a term of address to an inferior in the social order and *dai loh* was a term of great respect. This fact stuck in the throat of Lee, and was a never-ending source of amusement to James, and it was probably the only thing the two young men had ever argued about in the decade their lives had been intertwined.

'It's the birthday of our new King Edward VIII this weekend,' James said as he took the towel Lee held out to him.

'He won't be king for much longer if the newspapers have their way,' Lee replied. 'They are painting him as a wilful and irresponsible fool because of the American woman, Mrs Simpson. He has the government in crisis and I am with the editors. The man is a fool.'

'Who cares?' James laughed from behind the towel. 'It means we get Monday off. And that means an extra night in London.'

'Aaah, I see,' Lee grinned. 'An extra night in the arms of your beloved, eh?'

'Hardly my beloved,' James looked about furtively, making sure no one was listening. 'But a very modern young woman, Lee. A very modern young woman indeed!'

'I'm sure she is,' Lee murmured.

'Better get a move on, *Sai Loh*, don't want to miss the train to London.' James dived into one of the shower cubicles, and Lee smiled as he picked up the boxing gloves and headed back to the gymnasium. James Merchant was incorrigible, absolutely incorrigible.

James had been sneaking out of Charles Higgins' house on Saturday nights for the past three months. He had a girl-friend in Chelsea and nothing on earth could stop him from going to her. Lee had urged him to stop before he was caught, but James would have none of it. Wild horses, Lee knew, couldn't keep James away from women. Not that Higgins would do anything about it anyway. Charles Higgins appeared to be putty in their hands. He would simply pat them on the head and tell them to be good boys in the future.

As he put the boxing gloves into the locker, Lee thought about 'Uncle Charles'. Always benign, always avuncular, Charles Higgins had looked after them ever since the day they'd set sail on the S.S. *Dunfermline*, hence the reason the boys called him Uncle Charles. Charles himself approved, and it sounded right. But Lee could sense an undercurrent of fear in the man. Charles was, for some reason, afraid of the

two of them. At first Lee had thought it was because he'd discovered them doing their formal exercises on the top deck of
the ship not long after they'd sailed for England, but now he
suspected there was more to it.

Occasionally over the years James and Lee had been
woken by the man's screams in the middle of the night and
when they'd gone to him to see if he needed help, he had
simply shaken his head. 'Just dreams, lads,' he'd said, wiping
the sweat from his brow. 'Just dreams that can frighten an
old man. Now back to bed with you both.'

Charles Higgins knows things, Lee thought, as he closed
the locker door. Lee had been thinking about the situation a
great deal lately. Charles knows things about Hong Kong
that even James and I don't know, he thought, and the
memory of them terrifies him. It was puzzling, too, that the
man wasn't a member of the Golden Dragons, yet he was
their representative in London. Just where did Charles
Higgins sit in the scheme of things? Lee wondered. And why
did he scream in his nightmares?

龍

The summer heat in Hong Kong was oppressive. The tem-
perature hovered near the hundred-degree mark and the
humidity made the air sticky.

Robert McCraw got out of a rickshaw, gave its owner a
coin, and flexed his shoulder muscles trying to get air down
the back of his shirt where it stuck to his skin. He entered the
cool stone edifice of James Merchant Company Head Office
in Ice House Street, and took a deep breath, stretching his
arms out wide as the wind from the ceiling fans chilled the
sweat patches in his armpits.

'*Good afternoon, Elder Brother,*' the ancient foyer porter
said, handing McCraw a damp face towel. '*Today's weather
is very hot, true or not true?*'

'*True,*' McCraw growled. '*Very penis true!*'

The old porter cackled at McCraw's suitably dirty remark
in Cantonese as he shuffled over to the elevator, pulled back
the wooden door and opened the brass safety cage. McCraw

entered the lift and the old man followed him, closing the cage and door and pushing the big bronze lift lever to the third floor mark.

'*Mr Wing, all your sons are good or not good?*' McCraw asked politely as the elevator ground its way upward.

'*Good, good good.*' The old man nodded happy to be in conversation with the powerful *gwai loh* who spoke his native tongue so well. Wing Mun liked the big Scot. Several years before, one of Wing's sons, a constable in the police force, had got into a bit of trouble and McCraw had fixed the matter very quietly, therefore saving Wing Mun great face.

'*My second son is enjoying his life in the Marine Police,*' Wing said as he opened the elevator. '*Thanks to you, his life is without trouble.*'

'*Tell him I watch him,*' McCraw replied, stepping out into the third floor corridor. He walked towards a door marked Strictly Private. It had been a simple statement which had cost McCraw nothing, but it would give the old man great face when next he talked to his son.

Richard Brewster sat behind a desk beneath a portrait of Elanora Escaravelho Merchant. He looked up as Robert McCraw entered the office.

'Sorry to call you in, Robert,' Richard stood and offered his hand, 'but the matter can't wait.'

'That's all right, laddie,' the big Scot replied as they shook.

'I've decided on a course of action, but I will need your help.'

'What in God's name is *he* doing here?' McCraw exclaimed as he saw the old man.

'He's part of the solution.' They both looked at the old pirate sitting in a chair behind the office door.

The Admiral, The One Eyed Woo, regarded the policemen with his good eye, the other rolling crazily in its socket. He smiled at McCraw as he lit the cigar Richard had given him. It was a cigar from Cuba. Where Cuba was, The One Eyed Woo didn't know, but it must be a wonderful place if they could make superb cigars like the one he was lighting, he thought.

'*Red hair means you have fire in your testicles!*' The Admiral blew cigar smoke at Robert McCraw. '*You have much red hair, Mak Law. Therefore must it not be so that you masturbate often!*' He gave a loud cackle.

'*May your mother's breasts give forth green slime, you old fucker of pigs,*' McCraw replied, but he couldn't help grinning, he liked the old pirate.

'*Aaaiiiyaah!*' The Admiral cried. '*Your Cantonese is better than excellent. Mak Law! Truly you have a gift for description second only to me, may your penis join with your forehead!*'

'*I should never have agreed to help fake your death in the village of Lau Fau Shan,*' McCraw growled. '*If it had not been for Blue Star here, you would have been gutted like Tiger Paw Chang and fed to the dogs.*'

After the village raid, Robert McCraw had reported the death of The One Eyed Woo aloud, for all to hear. In fact, the old pirate had been sent a warning by Richard two days beforehand and had been in Macau when the raid took place. McCraw hadn't liked letting the old bugger off the hook, but the Admiral had saved Richard's life and that of the Merchant boy during the *Pacific Star* incident, and Richard had been adamant he should be spared.

The Admiral The One Eyed Woo realised, after being approached by the big sergeant from Shangtung called Lo, that his time as a pirate was up. At first he'd ranted about the destruction of his village and the imminent attack on his junks, but when given the offer of a new life in a village north of Macau and a bag full of gold, The Admiral had reconsidered. He owed his men nothing, they were pirate scum just like him, and one day soon he would have been knifed by a pretender to his throne anyway and fed to the sharks. Why not take the offer and live out the rest of his life in peace? Besides, he had two young sons in school in Canton and he had them to consider. *Blue Star* had been honourable and paid him handsomely in gold, enough to live well on, and the last few years had been good for him. He had a fine new boat in which to sail with his sons and a new young wife who cooked superbly and kept him amused in bed. All of these things served to keep him young at heart. And if occasionally he returned to his old ways at the request of *Blue Star*, whom he knew was none other that the *Shan Chu* of the *Gam Loong Tong*, well, what of it? What could be wrong with piracy sanctioned by the Hong Kong Police?

'*You two can be rude to each other on your own time,*' Richard intervened. '*I want our business settled and Admiral Woo out of the Colony before people start saying they've seen a ghost.*'

The business to which Richard referred would hopefully put an end to a nasty situation that had been developing over the past year. Malcolm Linden had sent a report from London about an independent Member of Parliament who had been asking some very serious questions regarding the importation of goods by a company called Dragon Import & Export. Sir Herbert Billings, MP, had informed the House that he'd received anonymous information that all was not well within the Port of London Authority. He'd suggested that favouritism was being shown to certain importers and that corruption was rife among the Authority staff. As the months had passed, a groundswell of opinion had arisen among some politicians, which was moving inexorably closer to a Royal Commission of Enquiry. Charles Higgins and Malcolm had done all they could to dampen the flames of suspicion, but both were urging more positive action from Richard before things got out of hand.

Several months previously, news had been leaked to Malcolm that a witness was prepared to give damaging testimony against the company known as Dragon Import & Export. The witness was apparently a well-known government official from Hong Kong, and Sir Herbert was awaiting his arrival in England. The whole matter had been handled with the utmost secrecy. The London Metropolitan Police, through Scotland Yard, had identified the witness to the Hong Kong Police and arrangements had been made for his transportation to London.

Inspector Richard Brewster had been put in charge of the covert operation by the Governor of Hong Kong personally. Richard had communicated with an Inspector Lawson at Scotland Yard using a code, and the name of the witness had been supplied to him. The man was to be transported to Singapore aboard the private yacht owned by the Governor of Hong Kong, and from Singapore he would take passage aboard a ship bound for London.

'What's his name?' McCraw asked Richard in English.

'Stephen Hemmings.'

'The Englishman from Customs & Excise?'

'The same,' Richard nodded.

'He lives up near Jardine's Lookout.' Robert McCraw poured himself a brandy from a cut glass decanter and looked through the window down into Ice House Street. 'Couldn't he simply have a fall or something?'

'We can't touch him in Hong Kong.'

'So you intend, I take it, to let this madman,' he pointed at Woo, 'loose upon a yacht owned by the bloody Governor of Hong Kong?'

'*Speak Cantonese!*' The One Eyed Woo exclaimed as he headed for the brandy decanter. '*My English is not good.*'

'*Sorry, Woo,*' Richard reverted to Cantonese. '*We were saying there is a certain foreigner who will sail aboard the Governor's yacht tomorrow night and we would like him silenced.*'

'*Why do you English drink from such stupid vessels?*' The Admiral growled his annoyance as he buried his nose in a brandy balloon. '*I have only one eye. I cannot see the rim of the glass and therefore I spill the brandy! These are foolish cups!*'

'*Here,*' Richard handed him a teacup from the sideboard.

'*This is very good porcelain.*' Woo examined the fine china admiringly, then he poured the remains of his brandy from the balloon into the cup and gulped it down. '*This brandy is from the place called France, true or not true?*'

'*True,*' Richard replied. '*Have some more,*' he topped up the pirate's cup. '*And have a look at this photograph.*'

The One Eyed Woo squinted at a photograph of Stephen Hemmings. *'This is the foreigner you want silenced?'*

'Yes, but it must be done far to the south. Sail down off the coast of Indochina before you attack, it must look like the work of foreign pirates. I want no connection made between the sinking of the Governor's yacht and Hong Kong.'

'I know the Governor's yacht,' The Admiral said. *'It is a fast yacht. Its engine can do ten knots at least. I will never keep up with it in my boat as I would have in my old China Moon.'*

'There is a boat impounded in the Marine Police dockyard which has twice the speed of the yacht,' Robert McCraw said. *'It was taken from Formosan pirates just last week. I will arrange for it to be stolen and delivered to you.'*

'Can I keep it?'

'No, you bloody well can't!' McCraw snapped in English, exasperated.

'Did he say no?' The One Eyed Woo asked Richard.

'Yes, Woo,' Richard smiled. *'And he's right. You will have to sink it.'*

'Why is it every time we meet, Blue Star, a boat gets sunk?' The old pirate shook his head. *'There must be some god you can pray to and have this rectified. It is destructive, true or not true? There will be no boats left to sail if we keep meeting.'*

'Ha!' Robert McCraw hooted. *'The old thief's got a point there!'*

'You'd better go, Elder Brother,' Richard patted him on the shoulder. *'McCraw will be in touch with you. And make sure no one identifies you when you leave the building.'*

'Who would believe I am The Admiral, The One Eyed Woo,' the old man said, *'even if I told them? Without a ship beneath my feet and a pistol in my hand, I am just an old man.'*

When the pirate had gone, Robert McCraw poured another brandy for himself and one for Richard and sat in a large leather chair.

'You've taken rather drastic measures, if you don't mind me saying so, laddie.'

'This is China, Robert,' Richard sipped his brandy. 'And

drastic measures are necessary. There's too much at stake to allow someone to bring it all crashing down around our ears by shooting off his mouth to the British Parliament.'

'Maybe you're right, Richie my lad, but the Governor's yacht?' McCraw shook his big head. 'Jesus Christ, maaarn! There'll be bloody hell to pay.'

'The Hong Kong Government will buy a new yacht, and no one will give a damn about Stephen Hemmings. He'll be killed by South China Sea pirates, an occupational hazard for anyone living in the Orient.'

'I suppose you're right. But he's only part of the problem. What do you intend to do about the bloody Sassenach MP, Sir Herbert Billings? He's the real fly in the ointment.'

'I don't think he'll trouble us for much longer,' Richard smiled knowingly. 'Poor old Sir Herbert is about to suffer a nightmare. A nightmare filled with images of dragons. Little dragons. *Siu loong*, as the Cantonese say.'

'Little dragons?'

'Didn't you know, Robert? Little dragons are the most dangerous of all.'

龍

The train pulled into St Pancras Station and had barely stopped when James and Lee leapt to the platform and headed for the street. James as usual led the way, always impatient to be somewhere else, while Lee raced behind him, dodging among the throng of people, and wished he could amble slowly through the beautiful red brick station and take it all in.

St Pancras was Lee's favourite building in the whole world. It looked like the castles of old that he'd seen in the drawings of his childhood storybooks back in Hong Kong. He had only to pause for one second and look around to feel the whole of English history wrap itself about him like a dragon's breath. But not this evening, he thought, as he held his straw boater to his head and hurried to catch James.

They arrived breathless out on the street and there, double-parked at the taxi rank, was Charles Higgins' silver grey

Bentley. The boys opened the back door and threw themselves inside.

'Hello, Thomas,' James said to the chauffeur as the car pulled out into traffic. 'How's good old London Town been treating you?'

'Not too badly, Master James,' the cockney driver replied. 'And 'ow abaht you and Master Lee? 'Ow's life in the country?'

Thomas Smith had served in the Great War and the ensuing years had seen him down on his luck. Three years ago, however, a man named Malcolm Linden, a bigwig from the London Port Authority, had called upon him with an offer of employment.

'I don't know nuffink abaht boats,' he'd told the man.

'You served in The Great War, didn't you?' Linden had asked him.

'For King and Country, Sir,' Thomas had nodded proudly. 'What abaht it?'

'Did you know a Regimental Sergeant Major from the Black Watch?'

'I did indeed, Sir, S'ar'nt Major McCraw! The finest man what evah lived! Saved my life, he did, at the bleedin' Somme. We 'ad some right old times together, we did. All froo France!'

And now Thomas Smith lived in a ground floor flat in 'bleedin' Belgravia', as he called it, one of the most exclusive suburbs in London. He was a chauffeur to a toff called Charles Higgins, the boss of a company called Dragon Import & Export and it was all thanks to Robert McCraw, a Scot who'd saved his live at the infamous Battle of the Somme. All Thomas had to do in return was a little bit of spying on old Mr Higgins, harmless stuff really, and guard the two young lads now seated in the back of the Bentley with his life. A job he found extremely pleasant because he adored the two boys. He secretly regarded the boys, or young men as they now were, as his own. They were good lads right enough.

'Never mind about life in the country, Thomas,' James said to the chauffeur. 'Good old London Town's the place for a man like me.'

'I see,' Thomas replied. 'Orf to Chelsea again are we, Sir?'

James was caught off guard. 'I've not the slightest idea what you're talking about, Thomas.'

'A partickaler young lady by the name of Sally Beacham, Master James.' Thomas smiled knowingly at James in the rear view mirror. 'Young Irene the maid is in the habit of takin' elevenses at a small tea house in Chelsea, Sir. You can't keep nuffink a secret from 'ouse servants, especially in bleedin' Belgravia.'

'Miss Beacham and I are barely on speaking terms, Thomas.'

'Yes, that's the impression young Irene got, Sir. As she tells it, speaking is ab'aht the only fing you and the young lady don't do.'

'Cripes,' James said. 'Does Cook know about it?'

'No, Sir, I've sworn Irene to secrecy . . . for the moment. But you know Mrs Daley, nuffink escapes our Cook for long.'

'Let's face it,' Lee interjected. 'Your little game's up, James.'

'No good's gunna come of that partickaler liaison, Master James. I fink you should give the little lady a miss. Mark my words, if Mr Higgins gets so much as a whiff of what you're up to, you'll be d'an the plug hole or my name's not Thomas Smiff!'

'Oh come on, Thomas,' James winked at Lee. 'Be a sport.'

'Mind you,' Thomas continued. 'If someone stays up late wiv 'im playin' chess and he fills hisself wiv port, as he's a mind to, there's no way he'd be aware of what anybody got up to, would 'e? After 'e's 'ad a drop of the doin's you could let a bomb orf in bleedin' Belgravia an' 'e wouldn't know nuffink abaht it, would 'e?'

'That's the ticket, Thomas!' James exclaimed. 'Lee here loves nothing more than a game of chess, isn't that right, *Dai Loh*?' he said, clapping Lee on the shoulder.

'As you called me Elder Brother,' Lee smiled. 'I don't see how I can refuse.'

'Are you gonna climb down the aht'side of the ah'se again, Sir?' Thomas asked. 'Because, if you don't mind me sayin' so,

I fink that's all a bit unnatural, if you know what I mean?'

'It's the only way to get out safely, Thomas,' James replied. 'If I use the stairs I might wake up Irene, or worse still Cook! If Cook thought there was a burglar in the place she'd scream the house down.'

'I take your point, Master James, but it's a bit of a worry all the same. Climbin' abaht like that should be left to monkeys and such. It don't 'alf make me shiver when you scrabble d'an the walls like you do.'

'Leave the worrying to me, Thomas,' James answered, settling back into the plush upholstery of the Bentley. 'You just make sure you're asleep by midnight.'

The big car weaved its way through the Friday night traffic and turned right into Shaftesbury Avenue. It stopped momentarily at Piccadilly Circus amid the throngs of people scuttling across the famous intersection and the sounds of honking car horns, then continued along Piccadilly towards Constitution Arch, beyond which lay the suburb of Belgravia and home.

'Good evening, Master Lee, Master James,' Irene said as she took the boys' bags and coats from them. 'King's Birthday weekend, Sirs, London will be lively, that's for sure.'

'Good evening, Irene,' James replied. He watched her as she hung up their coats and moved up the stairs with their bags. She was a pretty young thing, he noted yet again.

Irene had been nearly fifteen when Charles Higgins had employed her, along with Mrs Daley the cook, from an exclusive agency in Mayfair. It had been shortly after he and the boys had arrived in London, and both women had been in the employ of the late Duke of Bexley and had come highly recommended. When James first laid eyes on Irene, he'd lusted after her for several months as he had his mother's servants, until Irene had put him straight. She was in the employ of Mr Higgins, she'd told James, and had no intention of losing her job. Besides, she'd added, James was only a baby.

'Oh, I'm sorry,' Irene turned on the stair landing. 'Correspondence has arrived from Hong Kong, Thomas. But this time it wasn't addressed just to you, but also to Master James and Master Lee. And it didn't come in the post either. It was delivered by an oriental gentleman. He left a small parcel as well. I put them in your room, just like always.'

'Does Mr Higgins know?'

'No, he's been out all day.'

'Well done, girl.' Thomas turned to the boys. 'I fink we'd better adjourn to my room, gentlemen.'

龍

The big Bentley slipped down Fulham Road through Chelsea, the purr of its engine barely audible. It was after one o'clock on Saturday morning as Thomas drove towards Richmond with James Merchant and Lee Kwan as his passengers.

Thomas Smith's letter of instructions from Robert McCraw had been explicit. Take the boys to Richmond and find a property called Stawell Manor. Drop the boys wherever they request and take instructions from them as to where and when they should be picked up for the return journey to London. It seemed innocent enough, but Thomas was no fool, the tension in the car was palpable and he knew something serious was afoot.

The boys had also received a letter and after reading it, they'd spoken very rapidly to one another in Chinese. Normally the sound of his two lads chattering away like monkeys made him smile, but when they'd burned the letters in the library fireplace, including his from Robert McCraw, Thomas had noticed a distinct change come over the proceedings and was in no doubt with whom the authority lay.

'I'm afraid there'll be no sleep for you tonight, Thomas,' James stated. 'We'll leave at midnight and Mr Higgins is to be kept completely in the dark. Am I understood?'

'Perfectly, Sir.'

'Lee,' James continued. 'I think you should entertain Uncle Charles with a game of chess as Thomas suggested.'

'You mean get him drunk,' Lee replied.

'Exactly. He is to know nothing of what transpires tonight.'

Thomas Smith had no idea what took place in that meeting after he'd been dismissed, nor did he care, his twelve years in the British Army had taught him to obey orders without question. They had also taught him to recognise a born leader, and James Merchant had that unmistakable aura about him.

'Would you excuse us please, Thomas?' James had asked politely, but his tone had been unmistakable. The implication had been 'you're dismissed'.

'Certainly, Mistah Merchant,' Thomas had heard himself reply. Mistah Merchant he'd called the lad, not Master James, but Mistah Merchant. Well, there you go.

Thomas peered intently at the road ahead. God knows what they're up to, he thought, but I'm involved in a small way and that's how it should be. Besides, Sa'rn't Major McCraw had asked for his help, hadn't he? By letter no less. All the way from Hong bleedin' Kong. And if Robert McCraw wanted his help, Thomas thought, then Robert McCraw would get his help. Any bleedin' time he asked for it.

As the car approached Putney Heath, the tingle of excitement Thomas felt was replaced by one of apprehension when he looked in the rear vision mirror. James and Lee had donned black clothing, including black hoods, which covered all but their eyes. Those eyes caught his in the mirror and a chill ran through him. Those eyes did not belong to the boys he knew. Those eyes put the fear of God into him.

No conversation transpired until ten minutes later, when the car had passed around Richmond Park and headed west over a bridge. On the left loomed a sign that read, 'Stawell Manor Private Road – Trespassers will be Prosecuted'.

'This will do us,' Lee said and Thomas eased the big car onto the grass verge of the road.

'Give me ten minutes,' James said to Lee and he disappeared. Thomas hadn't even heard the door open and close, but he caught a glimpse of a dark figure leap over a six feet high wrought-iron gate and vanish into the trees.

'Might I ask what's . . .'

'No, Thomas.' Lee's voice was cold and remote. 'Let the silence and the darkness sharpen your wits. You will function more efficiently and your assigned task will become easier.'

After what seemed an eternity to Thomas, James' face appeared at his window, scaring the poor chauffeur witless.

'The time is thirteen minutes to two, Thomas,' James said. 'Return to this spot at exactly two thirty. If we are not here to greet you, go home.'

'But what . . .'

'But nothing!' James hissed softly. 'Lee? Let's go.' Within seconds both boys were gone.

Thomas sat in the Bentley on the dark country road and his imagination ran riot. He was unnerved. Whoever those two men were, they were not his boys, his lads. There was an air of malevolence about them which made him thank the Lord he was on their side.

'Bleedin' hell,' he whispered to himself as he fired the big car's engine to life. Thomas Smith had no idea what was going on and he didn't want to know, but he felt very sorry for whoever lived in Stawell Manor. He checked his watch and drove several hundred yards down the road before switching on the headlights.

龍

The squirrel didn't move, it sat frozen on the limb of an oak tree and watched the two dark shadows beneath it move slowly through the bushes. When they'd disappeared, the squirrel twitched its nose sniffing for the scent of the strange animals, still unsure of itself. The animals were mankind, of that it was sure, but not like the mankind it was used to, the shuffling noisy creatures that disturbed its daily routine, these two moved more like animals of the forest, sure of themselves, confident, silent. They were hunting.

The low growl of a guard dog caused the squirrel to forgo its dash for the safety of higher branches, once again it stiffened and waited. The big black dog crept forward into the moonlight beneath the tree where it was joined by its mate.

They were stalking the mankind, but the squirrel could sense uncertainty in the pair, they were tentative, unsure. Then one of the mankind appeared before them. It crouched low to the ground and gave a noise from its throat, a sort of humming noise that confused the dogs. One of the big black monsters whined pathetically and then both dogs lay down and rolled on their backs. The mankind approached them, stroked their bellies, and fed them something from its hand.

After a minute or more, the squirrel watched the mankind stand up on its hind legs and move off after its mate. The black dogs remained where they lay, asleep. The squirrel took its chance and scurried up the trunk of the tree, where it paused for a moment to watch the mankind pair cross the lawns towards the big house. Then it headed for its hollow and safety. They were strange, the mankind, and dangerous, especially when they were hunting.

Stawell Manor, a magnificent example of Jacobean architecture with its late Gothic and Palladian motifs, sat solid and forbidding in the bright moonlight. A huge stone portico dominated the front entrance where, in days gone by, coaches and horses had negotiated the circular driveway and stopped beneath its arches to deliver lords and ladies.

James and Lee made only a cursory examination of the main entrance. Huge doors made of solid oak refused them entry. At the base of the crenellated side wall of the portico, Lee stopped and pointed upwards. James nodded and looked up to the battlements, high above. He nodded in return and both of them began to climb. They were shielded from the moonlight as they made their way up to the crenelles atop the wall. Once there, they pulled themselves through the equidistant stone battlements and crouched low.

The top of the portico was a large patio area, which embraced the complete front of the manor at first floor level. Double doors were featured in pairs all along the front, while above, the windows of the second and third floors of the manor stared down at them with the stern expression of a schoolmaster. Who are you two, and what are you doing here? the house seemed to ask.

James crossed quickly to one of the sets of doors and peered through. Inside a circular balcony stretched to the left and right as far as he could see. He set to on the door lock and had it defeated in seconds. He opened the door, motioned to Lee to join him, and the pair moved silently inside and closed the door behind them.

James looked down over the balcony into the huge entrance hall of the manor. Black and white tiles covered the floor and led to an enormous fireplace that dominated the lower half of the wall opposite him. Ancestral portraits and paintings of hunting scenes hung in grand array and suits of armour stood, silent sentinels lit by bright moonlight from the first floor balcony doors.

Lee watched James' shadow flit across the wall opposite as he moved left along the balcony, then right to the far corner to stand above the staircase which led down to the tiled floor below. James signalled that all was well and Lee joined him, together they continued along a corridor, moving deeper into the interior of the manor.

They moved silently, effortlessly, searching each room on either side of the hallway, looking for the man with the iron-grey beard. The man whose photograph had been included in Robert McCraw's letter. Room after room yielded dark antique furniture, heavy brocade window drapes rich in silver and gold weave, Persian carpets, porcelain from the Orient and objets d'art. But in none of them was the man with the iron grey beard.

At the end of the second of the main corridors, they froze. Along a secondary hallway a door latch had clicked. Motion-less, they watched a young woman cross the hallway and enter another room. Several minutes passed then they heard a toilet flush and the young woman returned to her room.

Cautiously, they approached her door. James reached for the handle, but Lee shook his head. He pointed to the door opposite and James nodded. They crossed the hallway. James opened the door and slipped inside the room. There in the bed, bathed in moonlight from the open window lay the man with the iron-grey beard.

James looked back through the partially open door and signalled to Lee, who joined him, handing him a small bottle. Silently, James approached the bed. He stood over the man for several minutes listening to the pattern of his breathing. It was deep, he was snoring gently, rhythmically. James removed the liquid dropper from the bottle, instantly placing his gloved thumb over the open top of the bottle to avoid any fumes, and reaching forward, he carefully squeezed the small rubber bubble of the drop dispenser. A tear of liquid fell on the sleeping man's top lip.

The reaction was almost instantaneous. Just two rhythmic snores, and then the man's body stiffened. His eyes sprung open and stared directly into James'. His face drew into a grimace and he clutched at his heart. His whole body lifted from the bed as if electrified, then fell back to lie still. The eyes of Sir Herbert Billings MP stared back at James, lifeless.

James returned the dropper to the bottle, secured the top and placed the bottle in a small pocket on the leg of his black trousers. He looked around the room quickly out of habit and then rejoined Lee who was keeping watch in the corridor. The pair moved carefully, retracing their footsteps to the main hallway and to the door through which they'd entered. They quickly relocked the door and climbed back down to the base of the portico. James landed first and moved towards the lawn and the safety of the trees. He wanted to be away from the place. The death of the man with the iron-grey beard had disturbed him.

'That'll be far enoof,' a heavy Yorkshire voice said, as the butt of a gun hit James in the side of the head.

Stunned and dizzy, James looked up into the face of a big man dressed in a heavy trench coat with a hat pulled down over his eyes. He was aiming a shotgun at James' midriff.

'If you've done 'owt to ma' dogs, young'un, I'll be havin' you for . . .' They were the last words the man ever spoke as Lee's foot hit him in the throat crushing his windpipe. The man dropped the shotgun and fell to his knees clutching at his neck and Lee drove his fist into the back of his head snapping his spine.

'Where did he come from?' James struggled to his feet.

'You should have sensed his presence.' Lee was annoyed. 'If you'd been alert we could have avoided him, now our situation is compromised. What do we do?'

'Take him with us,' James said. 'And the dogs too.'

'What?'

'If we leave the body, they'll know someone's been here and the police will be called. If the gardener, or gamekeeper or whatever he is,' James pointed at the man on the ground, 'disappears with his dogs, so what? Gamekeepers are like gypsies, they disappear all the time.'

'Right,' Lee nodded. 'What about Thomas?'

'Thomas will say nothing,' James replied with confidence. 'He's McCraw's man first and foremost. Besides, he's implicated in the affair now whether he likes it or not. I'll take the man, you get the dogs. Bring their bodies to the main gate, and cover your tracks.' Lee slipped silently away into the night. James felt his face. His fingers came away covered in blood.

龍

James sat in the library while Dr Foster Robbards sewed four stitches under his left eye along the cheekbone. Upon his return, James had donned his pyjamas and stained them with his blood. It had been a worried Charles Higgins, still quite the worse for drink, who had rung the doctor.

'Sorry,' the doctor said as James winced. 'Nearly finished. I'm afraid you'll be left with a nasty scar under this eye, young man. Sleepwalking in a house full of staircases is not a healthy sport, I'm sure you'll agree?'

'How's it all going?' Charles Higgins said as he entered the library followed by Irene the maid, carrying a silver tea service on a tray. 'Irene's arranged a spot of tea for us.' He looked at James and raised his eyebrows suggesting the tea had not been his idea.

'Not for me, old boy,' Dr Robbards remarked much to Charles' relief, as he applied a plaster bandage to James' face. 'It's nearly four in the morning and I've got surgery in a few hours.'

'Yairs, yairs.' Higgins drawled. 'Of course, old man, how silly of me. Mustn't hold you up, eh? Irene will show you to the door.'

'Rest and more rest,' the doctor remarked jovially, as he snapped shut his medical bag and took his coat from Irene. 'And no more sleepwalking, my lad. Your Uncle Charles will have to put a damned tether on you and that'd be no good, would it?'

'I'll see to him, Robbards,' Higgins declared as he escorted the doctor into the front hallway. 'Good night and thanks again, old man.' Higgins closed the double doors of the library and turned to face James.

'How are you feeling, James?' he asked, hoping he sounded suitably concerned. Personally he couldn't have cared less if the boy had broken his neck, but he remembered Richard Brewster's threat of reprisal should any harm befall James or Lee. Even the fact it was an accident wouldn't deter Richard.

'Calm down, Uncle Charles,' James murmured. 'It's just a cut and I've been well attended to. Sleepwalking of all things, would you believe it?'

No, Charles thought, I would not. He was well aware of James's nocturnal visits to young women and had considered warning the boy of such scurrilous behaviour, but the lad was seventeen after all and Charles didn't like the idea of talking intimately about sexual matters to anyone, let alone James Merchant. He had turned a blind eye, deciding that if James' mother ever found out about her son's exploits, he could simply plead ignorance. Now, however, he could not possibly accept James' lame excuse of sleepwalking. The boy's nocturnal wanderings had, this time, resulted in injury. They were placing him in danger, and any danger to James Merchant was a double danger to Charles Higgins. It had to be stopped.

'Can I be of any further assistance?' Irene asked after she'd returned to pour James a cup of tea. She put the pot down and looked at him, concern written all over her face. 'Your poor eye,' she exclaimed, putting her hand to his cheek. 'Are you in pain?'

'That will be all, Irene,' Higgins snapped. 'Go to bed.'

'Yes, Sir,' the girl replied not taking her eyes from James. The boy has become a man, she thought. In a matter of only a few hours, James Merchant had become a man. She knew he had not fallen down the stairs. When she'd heard the crashing noise and had found him at the foot of the stairs, the blood on his face and in his hair had already been dry. He'd been out, she was sure of it. Probably to visit Sally Beacham in Chelsea, but something else had occurred. James was different. A confrontation, perhaps? She felt a power emanating from him that caused her knees to weaken. 'If there's anything I can do for you, Mister Merchant, please don't hesitate to call me.'

'I'll call, don't you worry,' James replied, still not breaking eye contact. 'Mister Merchant' she'd called him. He detected subservience in her, not that of a house servant, but of a woman to a man. Irene was his for the taking, and he felt an overwhelming urge to take her right there on the floor.

'Goodnight,' Irene whispered softly. 'And goodnight to you, Mr Higgins.'

'Yes, yes,' Higgins answered impatiently as she left the room.

When she'd closed the door, Charles got up and went to the mantelpiece. He took a meerschaum pipe from the rack beside the elaborately decorated ormolu clock and busied himself lighting it. James casually sipped his tea and said nothing.

Finally Higgins spoke. 'James, my boy,' he began awkwardly, 'I'm not much good speaking about matters of a sexual nature . . .'

'I beg your pardon, Uncle Charles?' James interrupted.

'I know you went to Chelsea tonight to visit a young lady by the name of Beacham . . .'

'Did I?'

'Yes, you did. Don't try to deny it, James. You can't keep secrets from me, you know.'

He knows nothing, James thought and inwardly heaved a sigh of relief. He'd seen the light of suspicion in Charles' eye earlier and had been expecting an interrogation, but Charles was making it easy for him. It was to have been his intention to confess of his liaison with Sally Beacham and claim he'd been attacked while returning from Chelsea, then beg Charles not to inform his mother in exchange for better behaviour in the future. 'I'm sorry, Uncle Charles,' he replied contritely. 'It won't happen again, I promise. I've behaved foolishly and with complete disregard for your guardianship. Do forgive me.'

'Well, er, James,' Higgins stammered; he had not been expecting such apologetic behaviour, especially from James. 'Thank you for the respect you've shown. I had expected some defiance from you, I must admit, but you've proved yourself a gentleman. We'll say no more on the matter, shall we? Eh? Eh?' He was delighted things had gone so smoothly; the thought of discussing the act of sexual intercourse with young James Merchant had been most abhorrent.

Now I must get old Uncle Charles to bed before Lee and Thomas returned, James thought. 'You won't say anything of this to Mother then, Uncle?'

'Of course not, James. But do bear in mind, speaking man to man, it's not the dalliance that worried me, but rather your physical safety. Roaming the streets of London in the dead of night is damned dangerous as you discovered this evening, to your peril. Promise me there will be no recurrence of this errant behaviour and we'll let sleeping dogs lie.'

'You have my word, Uncle.'

'Good lad.'

'I wonder if you could offer me some advice?'

'About what?' Charles suddenly felt uncomfortable.

'The sexual act itself, Uncle. I mean to say, if I'm going to be married some day, my wife would need to be satisfied on a regular basis, and I have little experience of anything other than the odd adventure, so to speak. I need to learn about sexual technique and I wondered . . .'

'Not now, lad.' Oh, how positively ghastly, Charles thought. 'Not now. It's practically daybreak!'

'Of course, Uncle Charles. Do forgive me again. Perhaps

some other time would be better. Why don't you go off to bed? I'll sit here for a while and finish my tea.'

'A much better idea, lad. Some other time.' But not in my life time, thank you very much, Charles thought as he tamped out his pipe and put it back in the rack. 'I'll just shuffle off to bed, if that's all right?'

'Of course, Uncle.' James suppressed a laugh. 'Good night.'

After he'd gone, James sat in the library, and reflected on the night's events. He'd blundered badly by not observing the gamekeeper. The whole mission could have been a shambles by morning with police crawling all over Stawell Manor, but he'd had the presence of mind to clean up and was not unduly worried. He knew no pathologist on earth would detect the poison he'd administered to Sir Herbert Billings. It had been supplied by a Chinese apothecary in Soho, no doubt an expert in the oriental art of poisoning. The bottle had been delivered, by hand, anonymously to the Belgravia house, along with the letters from Hong Kong.

The death of Herbert Billings had disturbed James deeply. He had not liked what he'd done, but his *Shan Chu* had demanded it of him, and not to carry out an order was, to James, unthinkable. He was bound by oath and honour, and however distasteful the task may have been, not to carry it out would have been unforgivable in the eyes of the Society of Golden Dragons. He had done his duty, but it was the way in which he'd had to do it that did not sit well with him. Assassination was an act he could not warm to. It was cowardly. He'd much prefer to kill a man while looking him in the eye, giving the man a chance to fight for his life. There was honour in that. There was no honour in what had passed tonight.

James tried to assuage his guilt with the knowledge that Sir Herbert Billings was a fool. The MP must have realised how inflammatory his speeches had become. The man had been given veiled warnings on several occasions, yet he'd still insisted in carrying on his crusade.

'Did everything go as planned?' he said aloud in Cantonese.

'Exactly as planned,' Lee answered as he stepped into

James' view. '*What gave me away? Was it the door handle? Or my breathing?*'

'*I can smell the dogs on you,*' James replied. '*Did you get rid of the bodies?*'

Lee sat down behind Charles' desk and put his feet up on it. He looked at James, considering him for some time before he spoke. '*Did you know or not know that parts of the Thames River contain quicksand? I did not know. Apparently there is a very famous pit built into the rear of the Embankment near Limehouse. Thomas says it was built several hundred years ago and is maintained to this day for one specific purpose. Providing you have the money to pay the keeper of the trapdoor. It is something worth remembering, true or not true?*'

'*True,*' James replied.

'*The killing does not sit well with you, brother, true or not true?*'

'*True.*'

'*Billings was a bad man, he deserved to die.*'

'*What makes you say that, Lee?*'

'*He was a supporter of the Japanese Government. They are militarists of the worst possible kind. Since they seized Manchuria in 1931 and put their puppet emperor on the throne it has been obvious what their intentions are. If they have their way, all of China will eventually be under Japanese rule. Billings was their strongest ally in the British Parliament and as such he was an enemy of China. I am overjoyed that he is dead.*'

'*Be that as it may, Lee, I still do not think it is right to kill a man in his sleep. It was cowardly.*'

'*It was necessary,*' Lee said sternly. '*We obeyed our Master's orders. It is not for us to question his methods or his motives.*'

'*I question nothing!*' James said, getting to his feet. '*But assassination is the act of a coward and I swear I will never do it again.*'

'*You may be ordered to do it again. Would you disobey the Society?*'

'I will kill again if I am ordered, but any man I kill will be looking into my eyes when he dies, understand or not understand?'

'Understand.'

'I am going to bed.' James crossed to the library doors. *'I suggest you do the same. Good night, Lee, and thank you for being my brother.'*

'It is not necessary to say thank you,' Lee replied as his brother closed the door.

As James passed Irene's door on the second floor landing he noticed it was ajar. He pushed it open silently and saw the girl lying in her bed.

Irene was not asleep. She stared at him. She'd known he would come. She felt the power emanating from him. The boy was gone. The man had come.

James closed the door gently, moved to her bedside and stood looking down at her.

'Something terrible happened tonight, didn't it?' she whispered.

'Yes,' James pulled back the bedclothes.

'You were involved in something terrible, weren't you?' She lifted up her nightgown.

'Yes.'

'Sally Beacham said you were the Devil. She said you make her do things. Things she can't help doing. She's in your power, isn't she?'

'Yes.'

'Are you going to make me do them?' Irene was breathing in soft gasps now.

'Yes,' James whispered as he loomed over her.

'Are you the Devil?' she whispered, reaching for him.

'Yes,' James answered as he embedded himself in the warmth of her.

'You're the Devil,' she moaned as he moved within her. 'You're the Devil. I knew it.'

'Yes, Irene,' James murmured. 'I'm the Devil and you belong to me. Just like Sally.'

'Yes. Yes,' the girl groaned. 'Oh yes. Oh yes. Oh yes!' she

hissed savagely, rhythmically, as she bucked beneath him.

James purged himself within the flesh of the girl, and as she writhed frantically, the image of Sir Herbert Billings slowly but surely dissolved from his mind.

Chapter Twelve

Richard Brewster sat sipping Chinese tea on the balcony of Quincy Heffernan's flat as night settled quickly over Aberdeen Harbour, a narrow stretch of water on the south side of Hong Kong Island. The Harbour separated the small island of Ap Li Chau and Hong Kong Island by only several hundred yards. A solid mass of floating junks bobbed gently in the warm evening air and as the night deepened, thousands of lanterns began to glow from the junks and sampans making the sight, rather squalid by day, appear like a fairyland picture in a child's storybook.

Quincy's hair, Richard noted, was now snow white and he had a slight tremor in his hands. He's getting old, Richard thought. He'd seen Quincy less and less as the years had passed and a guilty feeling crept over him. The man had befriended him when he'd first arrived in Hong Kong. He'd taught Richard Cantonese and given him sensible advice when he'd been in trouble.

And how have I repaid him? Richard asked himself. By ignoring him. By allowing him to grow old without even noticing. And why have I ignored him? Richard felt the guilt pressing on his shoulders like a stone weight as the answer shook his conscience. Because Quincy Heffernan had maintained his core values of honour and integrity, whereas Richard had knowingly, and deliberately, divorced himself from those same values he'd once held so dear.

'How long have you lived here now, Quincy?' Richard asked the old scholar as he watched him pour the last of the tea from an antique Chinese pot.

'Thirty-eight years,' Quincy replied, putting the teapot onto the table and sitting opposite Richard. 'Nearly two-thirds of my lifetime. I came to the Orient as a callow youth of twenty-six in 1898, the same year Britain leased the New Territories from China.'

'Do you have any regrets?'

'Everyone has regrets, Richard,' Quincy smiled. 'A French-man might boldly state, *non je ne regrette rien*, but in truth he won't really mean it. The French love nothing more than to wallow in an ocean of regret and talk of their *affaires d'amour*, or their damned inevitable *affaires d'honneur*. Everyone in the world has regrets, Richard, you of all people should know that.'

'Me? Richard scoffed. 'I have no regrets, Quince old man. Not a one.'

'Then why are you here?'

'What?'

'Never mind,' Quincy stared at him. 'Have you ever taken another man's life, Richard?'

'You know damned well I have. On more than one occasion.'

'And you don't regret it?' Quincy raised an eyebrow.

'I've had no choice.' Richard's reply was defensive.

'You had a choice in Lau Fau Shan.'

'What do you mean?'

'You disembowelled a man who was tied to a tree, did you not?'

'He was a paedophile! Scum of the worst kind! Anyway, how do you know about it?'

'This is Hong Kong, Richard, remember, and I speak sixteen different Chinese languages. And don't try to change the subject. You had a choice, did you not?'

'I suppose I did,' Richard looked sternly at the old scholar.

'And do you regret your actions?'

'In hindsight, perhaps I was wrong, but . . .'

'In hindsight you were most definitely wrong! Life is a series of choices, my young *pang yau*. You chose to come to Hong Kong. You chose to rescue a boy from a burning building. You chose to give your love to a woman who died. You chose to murder a defenceless man in Lau Fau Shan. All *your* choices, Richard, and the very word choice, by definition, means options. In life, you choose one option and forgo another, thereby giving yourself cause to wonder as your life progresses, whether the choices you made were correct. When you get older and hopefully wiser, you realise that some of the choices you made were wrong, *ipso facto*, you have regrets. *Quod erat demonstrandum,* my dear boy. Mind you, a life lived without cause for regret would be no life at all, it would be a dream utterly devoid of emotion and therefore too absurd to contemplate.'

'Thanks for the philosophy lesson,' Richard drained his cup and stood to lean against the balcony rail. 'But that's not why I came here.'

'Yes, it is, Richard.' Quincy rose and took the teapot into his small flat to refill it. 'It's precisely why you came here,' he called over his shoulder.

'Really?' Richard followed him into the tiny sitting room.

'You only ever come to see me when your conscience is troubled, and that occurs less and less these days, isn't that so?' Richard did not reply. 'Now that you're a force to be reckoned with, am I right?' Again Richard did not reply.

Quincy lit the gas burner beneath the kettle to re-heat the water. 'These days, I'm the only person in your world you can't intimidate. Hence, you come to me when you're guilty of something because you know I'll say exactly what I think of your behaviour. I analyse your actions, then you apply my analysis to whatever it is you've done wrong and somehow you twist my philosophy to assuage any guilt you are feeling. In short, Inspector Brewster, I give you absolution.'

'My philosophical genius and father confessor, eh?'

'Don't patronise me, Richard. I know you better than you know yourself. I remember vividly that warm evening on the docks in Sai Ying Poon, when a young Englishman shared a bowl of soup with me and asked me to teach him Cantonese.'

'Mrs Leung's *daai paai dong*,' Richard smiled at the memory of the old lady and her soup stall.

'I remember how innocent you were in the ways of the world, Richard. And I remember how quickly that innocence died when you got into trouble with the Man Shing Tong.'

'Tiger Paw Chang was the *Shan Chu* of . . .'

'Yes,' Quincy interrupted. 'I know. And he was the same defenceless man you disembowelled at Lau Fau Shan in a fit of white rage.'

'He deserved it!'

'Don't get angry, it will serve no purpose. As I said before, you cannot intimidate me.' Quincy lifted the re-heated kettle onto the sink and poured water into the teapot. 'You came here to seek absolution for something either you or that despicable society of yours has done.'

'That's not fair . . .'

'Isn't it?' Quincy interrupted. 'Remember it's me you're talking to, *pang yau*. You formed that society to protect yourself from your enemies, did you not?'

'Yes, but . . .'

'But now your enemies are vanquished, *true or not true*?'

'For the time being, yes.'

'Then why have you not dissolved the society? It should be a matter of honour to you.'

'Damn it, man! It's not that simple!'

'I'm sure it's not,' Quincy's voice was even. 'Why don't you just admit the fact that you're depressed? Your conscience has, momentarily, caught up with you and you're feeling guilty, or perhaps even ashamed of your behaviour.'

'I'm not ashamed of my behaviour.'

'Of course you're not.' There was a mocking edge to Quincy's tone now. 'The *Shan Chu* of the *Gam Loong Tong* is never ashamed of his behaviour, the *Shan Chu* of the *Gam Loong Tong* is a hard and ruthless man, utterly shameless, and seduced by power and avarice.'

'Is that what you think, Quincy?'

'Yes, I do, but he's not completely beyond redemption. Let's go outside.'

They returned to the balcony and Quincy poured the tea. 'The remnants of the young Englishman I met ten years ago is ashamed, and he's come to use me as a sounding board in the hope that what I say will assuage his guilt, and in the process, cheer him out of a bout of depression. And if that's all I can do for the moment, then so be it,' he smiled fondly. 'Why don't you just say what's on your mind, eh?'

'That's just it, Quince,' Richard stared morosely at his teacup. 'There are so many things on my mind at the moment I don't know where to begin.'

' "Begin at the beginning, the King said, gravely, and go on 'til you come to the end: then stop." '

'What?'

'Lewis Carroll, *Through the Looking Glass*. Did you ever read *Through the Looking Glass,* when you were young?'

'My mother read it to me when I was little, I didn't understand a word of it.'

'You're not supposed to. It's nonsense. Deliberately and brilliantly created, but nonsense nonetheless. What else would you expect from a mathematician?'

'A what?'

'Dodgson was a mathematician.'

'Who?'

'Charles Dodgson, Lewis Carroll's real name. He lectured in mathematics at Christ Church College, Oxford. Before my time, I might add, but I met him as an old man on several occasions. Strange chap, always photographing young girls with whom he seemed to empathise particularly. He died the very same year I came to Hong Kong.'

'Did he ever explain why he wrote rubbish?' Richard couldn't help smiling. He loved it when the old academic reminisced.

'Oh, it's not rubbish. It is nonsense most certainly, but nonsense in its purest form. Dodgson was an academic *in extremis*. A classical scholar and a moralist, he would have loved you.' Quincy chuckled mirthlessly. 'He was totally unsuited to the world outside his college gate. I believe he saw it as an ugly place full of sorrow and pain and so he turned his back on it completely and in his spare time wrote nonsense. But I believe his nonsense verse was his way of raging at a world he didn't like.'

'How do you mean?'

'"Twas brillig, and the slithy toves did gyre and gimble in the wabe;"' Quincy quoted, '"all mimsy were the borogroves, and the mome raths outgrabe". What does that conjure up in your mind, Richard?'

'Evil and darkness,' Richard shrugged. 'Mangrove swamps and snakes.'

'There you go!' Quincy declared. 'That's not what it does to me. To me and many others it elicits images of fairies and moonbeams and elvin dancing. I read it as whimsical nonsense written to delight wide-eyed children.' The old man was warming to his theory. 'Most of his writing is just that, delightful and whimsical nonsense! But I believe Charles Dodgson suffered acute bouts of depression, not unlike you, Richard. I saw it in his eyes the moment I met him. In his darkest moments I'd wager he had visions of unspeakable horror, and so twisted was his rage that his pen formed words his tongue could not articulate . . . The man was mad.'

'Are you suggesting I'm mad?'

'Oh, no.' Quincy patted his young friend's arm, a companionable gesture. 'But you struggle with your world, just like Dodgson and when it gets the better of you, you come to your old father confessor and pour your heart out.'

Richard inexplicably reached over and touched Quincy's hair. ' "You are old Father William, the young man said, and your hair has become very white. And yet you incessantly stand on your head, do you think at your age it is right?"'

'Ha!' Quincy laughed delightedly and took up the quote. '"In my youth, Father William replied to his son, I feared it might injure the brain; but now that I'm perfectly sure I have none, why, I do it again and again". Damn you, Richard, I thought you said you couldn't understand Lewis Carroll, now here you are quoting him for all the world to hear!'

'I remember that verse very clearly,' Richard joined in the old man's laughter. 'The image of old Father William standing on his head always made me laugh.'

'Just like it's doing now, eh?'

Richard studied the old scholar affectionately. 'You're a crafty old fox, aren't you?'

'Not me, Richard. Charles Dodgson.' Quincy picked up the teapot. 'You should recite one of his silliest passages out loud every day. "Take some more tea?"'

'Lewis Carroll again, right?'

' "I've had nothing yet, Alice replied in an offended tone, so I can't take more. You mean you can't take *less*, said the Hatter: it's very easy to take *more* than nothing".' Quincy finished quoting and poured more tea. 'Enough of Lewis Carroll. Now that I've made you laugh, tell me, what's ailing Richard Brewster?'

'Well, for a start, Elanora wants to bring the boys home from England.'

'But what about their education?' Concern was evident in Quincy's voice: he had always held secret hopes that the boys might go on to achieve high academic success, especially Lee Kwan. 'They're about ready to enter university, aren't they?'

'Next year, yes.'

'What's got into the woman?'

'It's not what's got into Elanora, I wish it were that simple, it's what's got into the boys that has her up in arms.'

'For instance?'

'Well, in James' case it's his sexual proclivity. He's matured awfully quickly. Elanora says that, according to our *amah*, he was sexually active here in Hong Kong before he left, and he's been at it with a vengeance these past three years in London. He's been involved with several young women that we know of.'

'I must say that doesn't surprise me,' Quincy nodded. 'I suspected James was involved in that sort of behaviour as a twelve-year-old, when I tutored him at the Merchant House. Surely Mr Higgins can take the appropriate steps to correct the boy's behaviour?'

'Charles Higgins has no control over James whatsoever. Besides, we are not dealing with your average seventeen-year-old boy, Quince, we have an adult on our hands whether we like it or not.' And an assassin, Richard thought, but he could hardly tell Quincy that. 'James is no ordinary young man,' he continued. 'I don't want to chop his legs out from under him just as he's learned to stand on them, if you know what I mean?'

'But his education must be completed.'

'That's where you come in, my friend. I wish you to tutor both boys again upon their return.'

'I would be honoured to take over their academic instruction, Richard, but as for controlling James . . .' Quincy's snow-white eyebrows were raised in comical, but genuine, concern. 'If Charles Higgins can't control him, I most certainly won't be able to.'

'I can,' Richard said bluntly.

'Mmmnh,' Quincy studied him. 'I'll just bet you can, too. What hold do you have over that boy, Richard?'

'What on earth are you talking about? I have no hold over him.'

'I know you too well, you have a hold over everyone. That's how you operate. Is that boy beholden to you in some way? Or both of them for that matter?'

'Don't be ridiculous, Quince!'

The realisation suddenly hit Quincy. 'You've got them mixed up in that infernal Society of yours, haven't you?'

'You're letting your imagination run away with you,' Richard said dismissively.

'Don't treat me like a fool.' Quincy stared across the table at him. 'I've watched those boys grow up. I've seen them playing together. They are highly skilled in a specific form of *kung fu* that is unmistakeably *Shaolin*, and I have no doubt it was taught to them by Lo Shi-mon, the Red Pole of your Society. Am I correct?'

'They are not members of the *Gam Loong Tong*,' Richard looked the old man directly in the eye as he lied.

'Very well,' Quincy paused for a moment, then nodded thoughtfully. 'I'll take your word on that. So now explain to me why an intelligent woman like Elanora would want her son James brought home from England, thereby terminating his education and threatening his future chances in life, all because of a matter as inconsequential as his sexual dalliances?'

'I hadn't considered that,' Richard lied again, but this time he looked away. The question had been plaguing him. Quincy was right, Elanora had been acting strangely of late and her demand that the boys be brought home for such a superficial reason had concerned him deeply. Had she learned of their membership of the society? Or worse still, had she learned that he'd used them to assassinate Sir Herbert Billings? He doubted it. She would have flown at him like a tigress had she known of either matter.

'Perhaps,' he continued, 'it's simply maternal concern that's motivating her. She's a woman, isn't she? She thinks with her heart.'

'Or perhaps,' Quincy ventured as he poured more tea, 'she feels she has no control over them while they're in England?'

'What do you mean by that?' Richard demanded defensively.

'Oh, nothing really,' Quincy knew he'd hit a nerve. There was trouble brewing between Richard and Elanora, trouble that could prove catastrophic. They both wanted control over the boys, Quincy thought, and their fight for that control could destroy them both. In her own way, Elanora was as powerful as Richard. Although Quincy barely knew the woman, he sensed it. It was difficult not to in a woman like Elanora Escaravelho Merchant. And Richard? Well, Quincy knew Richard better than Richard knew himself. Quincy had recognised both Richard's strengths and weaknesses from the very outset. He'd sensed in the young lad who had so quickly responded to, and embraced, the mystique of the Orient the fact that he could fall prey to its seduction. He'd also sensed the power of commitment in the boy, and he'd prayed that his commitment would follow a righteous path. But Richard's lust for power had consumed him. So too had his self-justification. Richard was convinced that the *Gam Loong Tong* served a noble purpose, and Quincy knew there was nothing he could say to persuade him otherwise. Now it appeared he had involved the boys in the society's nefarious activities. Quincy didn't approve at all.

'When does Elanora intend to bring the boys home?' he asked, simply, sticking to the immediate subject at hand. The power struggle between Elanora and Richard was none of his business, he thought.

'December, it would appear. They'll be here for Christmas.'

'She shouldn't bring Lee home. He should go to Oxford. The lad has a gift. He is a natural student with a brilliant intellect. I've already written to Christ Church College on his behalf. He'll be accepted, Elanora has my word!'

Richard was shaking his head even as Quincy spoke. 'We overlooked one thing, my friend.'

'What's that?'

'England and the bloody English.'

'What about them?' Quincy appeared genuinely puzzled.

'Lee's developing a nasty case of Anglophobia and the longer he stays in England the worse it will become. Eventually he'll return to Hong Kong hating the lot of us.'

'That's sad. I thought he was happy there.' The old man shook his head, concerned. 'His school results attest to that. No one could scale to such academic heights if they were not happy at school.'

'His letters over the last year tell his grandfather Old Kwan and sister Wai Ling a different story. His resentment of everyone in England, excluding James, is evident. And what's of even more concern, particularly to his grandfather, is the fanatical Nationalism which has become more and more evident in his letters. He's obsessed with Ch'iang Kai-shek and the political situation in China. He continually asks for information concerning the Japanese military build up in Manchuria, or Manchukuo as the Japanese insist it be called. And he repeatedly expresses his disgust at Pu Yi, the emperor the Japs installed in Mukden.'

'Poor old Henry Pu Yi, eh?' Quincy shook his head. 'The last Emperor of the Manchus. He's merely a pawn in a game of international politics. I feel sorry for the man.'

'Well, as far as the bloody Japanese are concerned he's the Emperor of China!'

'He's merely a puppet. They're using him to give legitimacy to their so called State of Manchukuo in the eyes of the international community, but it won't work.'

'Well, I wish someone would tell Lee that,' Richard snapped. 'He's of the opinion their propaganda is working and he's got the idea that there will be war between China and Japan. He wants to return to China and fight with the Nationalist Forces. Have you ever heard of anything so stupid?'

'He's right about a war. It's inevitable.'

'Surely you don't believe that?'

'Oh yes, I do.' Quincy said firmly. 'I believe there'll be war in Europe too, despite Neville Chamberlain's attitude of appeasement towards Germany. Our dear old crusty, stiff upper lip Chancellor of the Exchequer is trying to douse a flame that won't be put out, because Adolf Hitler is as mad as a March hare. He's espousing the fact that the Germans, well, the white Aryan stock at least, are a master race destined to rule the world, and Chamberlain patting him on the head and telling him to calm down won't do a bit of good. Hitler sees Europe unified under Nazi control and nothing short of a good punch on the nose will stop him. And Japan views Asia in much the same way. Lee is right, war between China and Japan is inevitable.'

'Japan's economy couldn't sustain a war with anyone, they're broke. The Crash of '29 and The Depression flattened them and they don't have the resources to recover.'

'All the more reason to fight a war, wouldn't you think, Richard? History is awash with monarchs and governments who started wars simply to manipulate public resentment away from themselves onto some foreign enemy, thereby easing the pressure created by their own ineptitude on the home front.'

'But Ch'iang Kai-shek's Nationalist Army is twice the size of Japan's. Emperor Hirohito would be a fool to take on such a task.'

'It's not Hirohito you have to worry about, he's just the emperor. It's the *samurai* classes who rule Japan.'

'Well, whomever,' Richard shrugged. 'They'd be fools to try it.'

'They did it before in 1931, and got Manchuria out of it, what makes you think they won't do it again and this time take the whole country?'

'Ch'iang Kai-shek could conscript ten times the army he has now if needs be. The Japanese would be up against an impenetrable wall of human beings. They'd never succeed.'

'Richard,' the old scholar placed his hand on his young friend's arm, 'Ch'iang's army is a disorganised rabble. The Japanese Army is quite the opposite.'

'I don't agree with you, Quince.'

'Do you know the Japanese word *bushido*?'

'Yes,' Richard said. 'It's a form of Japanese martial art.'

'Oh no, it's not. It's much more than that. *Bushido* is a way of life, a code of honour, which is practised by the Japanese *samurai* or warrior class. To meet death in the service of the emperor is the greatest honour a *samurai* can achieve in his lifetime. Adherents of this ethic will unflinchingly disembowel themselves in front of witnesses if they believe they've failed to meet their military obligations. *Bushido* is woven into the fabric of Japanese culture, it extends throughout all social classes. So believe me when I tell you, my boy, that the Japanese Army will go through the Nationalists like pork through a goose, or my name is not Quincy Heffernan.'

'Well, to hell with them . . .' Richard was about to continue, but he glanced at his watch. 'Oh, my God, I have to go,' he said guiltily. 'Elanora invited me to dinner.' He looked distractedly at the twinkling harbour of Aberdeen for a moment. 'My main concern in this affair is for young Lee. What do I do about him, Quincy?'

'Try to put yourself in his shoes, Richard,' Quincy also stood, and he placed a gentle hand on the younger man's shoulder. 'What would you do at seventeen years of age if England were being threatened by a foreign power?'

'I'd join the army and fight,' Richard replied without hesitation. He once again looked out at the harbour, but this time his gaze was not distracted. He saw the mass of junks strung together on the waters below, and he imagined the thousands of Chinese on board, going about the business of living. It was a floating microcosm of China. 'Yes,' he said. 'I'd join the army and fight.'

'Exactly. And that's just what Lee will do. So if that's what's been troubling you, rest assured there is nothing you can do about it, it's out of your hands. You are absolved of guilt. On that score in any event.' There was fondness in the old man's eyes, but censure in his tone. Quincy wasn't going to let his young friend off the hook entirely. Besides he liked to have the last word.

As he drove back around the Island from Aberdeen, Richard reflected on his evening with Quincy Heffernan. The old scholar was nobody's fool and, despite the man's obvious affection for him, Richard had sensed a disapproval in Quincy he'd not known before.

He truly believes I'm beyond redemption, Richard thought. And yet it was at his suggestion I started the Society that turned me into what I am. It was all well and good for Quincy to sit there in bloody judgment upon him, but looking back over the years, Richard could not see what other option there had been. And what else was it Quincy had said? Dissolve the Society? It was a good organisation. A benevolent organisation that had helped many people over the years, didn't Quincy see that? Of course he'd done things he wasn't proud of, and yes, he'd gutted that fat pig Tiger Paw Chang, but so what? It was all for the greater good.

The Society of Golden Dragons was now a powerful affiliation of policemen in a colony that cared nothing about their welfare. The Society had helped suffering families, put food upon their tables and money in their hands. What was wrong with that? Children of policemen had received health care and basic education, whereas before they'd had nothing. How in God's name could he dissolve an organisation like that?

Richard started to feel angry. He and the others had fought long and hard to make the Dragons a force to be reckoned with. He now had power and influence and more money than he'd ever need, and he'd be damned if he was going to give it all up. What was it Quincy had called it? A matter of honour? Well, honour be damned! Quincy could go to hell. And so could Elanora for that matter.

He thought of Elanora waiting patiently for him at Merchant House. What was she up to? What did she know? The woman had spies everywhere, including England. Why did she want the boys brought home? Had she found something out? Did she think she could release them from his influence? They'd sworn a blood oath to the *Gam Loong Tong*. They were under his control and nothing she could do would alter that fact. But he knew she would find out eventually, and the issue would shatter their relationship into a thousand pieces. Richard did not relish the thought of a war with Elanora.

龍

The sun sat on the western horizon, a huge crimson ball, glowing, shimmering softly in the coastal mist over Hainan Island in the Gulf of Tongkin, as The Admiral, The One Eyed Woo, stopped the massive diesel engine and set the boat to drift. The craft he sailed was truly a wonderful ship. A Formosan junk for all intents and purposes, but with a western-style 'v'-shaped displacement hull, which allowed the huge diesel engine to push her through the water at sixteen knots.

The One Eyed Woo sat on the railing of the poop deck, lit a cigar and gave himself a minute's respite to appreciate the beauty in the western sky. He was nearly three hundred miles south by south-west of Hong Kong and pirating once again. He looked at his twin sons moving about the main deck and prayed to the gods that this trip would excite their interest in piracy.

They were good boys, strong and healthy, but their singular lack of interest in piracy bewildered him. He'd taught them to kill when they were five years old by having them cut the heads off ducks and they'd shown a real aptitude for it, but when they'd found out that the same thing could happen to them if they followed in their father's footsteps they'd declared a sudden disinterest in his profession.

Their mother was to blame, Woo thought, when she gave them those stupid *gwai loh* names, Napoleon and Wellington, saying they were great foreign warriors. He should never have allowed it, but he loved oral sex and she was the best flute player he'd ever known. The boys had set their hearts on becoming businessmen. Businessmen! The thought of it made him spit. He'd had to drag them from the land by their necks and make them come on this voyage with him.

Mind you, he'd had them educated to get on in the world, and he had to admit that they made more money working than he ever had out of piracy. Especially out of the brothel they ran in Lau Fau Shan. It had been a stroke of business genius when the twins had killed the former owners and started running it themselves. He was very proud of them for that. The Admiral was of the opinion that everyone should have a bit of criminality in them in order to survive in a cruel world. But he still wished they had at least a taste for piracy.

Well, perhaps this trip would change their minds. Soon he would order them to raise the large red battened sail, which would push them slowly, south east into the path of the Governor's yacht. He'd overtaken the yacht during the night and had maintained full speed to reach the Gulf of Tongkin. Hainan Island was the southernmost province of China and south of it the gulf water was the domain of French Indochina. In French waters he would destroy the Governor's yacht and the whole business would be blamed on the pirates who operated out of Da Nang and Hue on the Indochina Coast.

'*Hoist the sail, boys!*' The Admiral yelled to his sons down on the main deck, as he shifted the tiller to starboard. He would have no trouble intercepting the big yacht, he knew it would come out of the night lit up like a floating lantern at the Festival of the Dead. The previous night when he'd overtaken it, he'd been shocked at the amount of light she gave under running. Her white hull, all seventy feet of it, reflected the lights from her portholes and wheelhouse and the Admiral could not help but ponder on the stupidity of a skipper who would run the South China Sea lit up in such an obvious fashion. The idiot even had festoon lights glowing, lighting up the full shape of his vessel. The man deserved to be taken by pirates and The Admiral, The One Eyed Woo, would be only too pleased to oblige.

The old pirate nodded for his mate, *Ho jai*, to take the tiller and went forward and looked again at the weapons in their boxes. He had never seen such weapons before. Three boxes lay open in the fo'c'sle and in each was a gleaming new German MG34 machine gun. *Blue Star* had supplied the guns and explained they were called Mausers. The One Eyed Woo chuckled at the thought of such an absurd name. Beside the guns, shining bronze in the last rays of sunlight, lay boxes of 7.92mm ammunition. The bullets were set into a belt, which fed into the breech of the gun and one could fire the gun all day at a furious rate, all one had to do was keep changing the belts.

He climbed back to the poop deck and sniffed the evening breeze, happy to be on the sea with a fine ship beneath his feet. Life is good, he thought. I have a valuable ship that I will keep, despite *Blue Star*'s wishes, and sell it in Macau. I have three machine guns that spit bullets at a rate of twelve hundred per minute, that I will also keep. My twin sons are with me and hopefully getting a taste for the noble art of piracy. I have many Cuban cigars, and *Blue Star* has none because I emptied the large box in his office. And I have a rich *gwai loh* yacht to burn and plunder.

'Ha!' Woo laughed at his coxswain. '*Ho jai, my testicles are bigger than that orb,*' he pointed at the huge crimson mass of the sun as it began to drop behind the horizon. '*True or not true?*'

'*True, Lord of the Sea,*' Ho jai replied. '*Your sperm could block the Pearl River.*'

'*That is also true,*' Woo cackled. '*And with my new guns, which the Germans call mouse catchers, I once again control the South China Sea! Would you like, or not like, a cigar?*'

'*I would like a cigar very much, Admiral.*'

'*You can have one of the shit-tasting cigars I get from India, Ho jai.*' The Admiral took the tiller from his coxswain. '*They are in my bedding, but do not touch the Cuban cigars or I will feed you to the sharks. Cuban cigars are only for Admirals and other such notable people.*'

'*Thank you, Lord.*' The coxswain scampered down the stairs to the main deck.

'*Giving a Cuban cigar to you,*' the old pirate yelled after him, '*would be like giving a sweet cake to a pig!*'

The rustle of the battened sailcloth as it caught the breeze caused Woo to gaze aloft.

'*Wu Loong!*' He called to the mischievous black dragon of Chinese mythology. '*Are you in the air, my villainous friend? There is a fat white duck on the pond tonight and I'm going to pluck it!*' He felt the pressure on the tiller in his hand and laughed out loud when, as if in answer to his call, a gust of wind turned his vessel towards the darkening east.

龍

Captain James Moore, Captain of the M.V. *Ulysses*, the official yacht of the Governor of Hong Kong, hated nothing more than bad seamanship. A former Captain in the Royal Navy and veteran of the Battle of Jutland, James Moore adhered to the naval adage that 'a fool at sea, a danger be'. The idiot in charge of the fishing junk three hundred yards off his starboard bow was just such a fool.

'Damn the man!' Captain Moore exclaimed to no one in particular as he looked through his binoculars at the Formosan junk. 'No navigation lights whatsoever, not even a masthead light. How these people survive at sea is beyond me!'

'She's making weigh, Sir,' his coxswain said. 'Sail up, but under engine power at about six knots and holding her course.'

'Could be a pirate vessel out of Da Nang, Sir,' the Captain's Master at Arms said. 'Shall I break out the weapons?'

'Ha!' the Captain snorted. 'No need to panic sergeant, she'll not get within a country mile of us. She'd be far too slow. Coxswain,' he said lowering his glasses. 'Thirty degrees to port and full ahead if you please.'

'Aye aye, Sir,' the coxswain replied as he turned the ship's wheel. 'Thirty degrees to port and full ahead, Sir.'

'Steady as she goes.'

'Steady as she goes, Captain.'

'Apologise to our passengers in the main saloon,' the Captain said to his sergeant. 'Sorry for the abrupt change in course, no need for concern and all that, eh what?'

'Aye aye, Sir,' the Sergeant at Arms replied and went off to do his Captain's bidding.

'Should have had the Sar'nt-at-Arms break open the armoury and put a couple of shots into his decking,' Captain Moore joked to his coxswain. 'That'd wake the bugger up. Teach him to flap about at sea without his bally navigation lights on, eh?'

'That's right, Captain. That'd teach him what for,' the coxswain forced a laugh, but in reality he was wishing the festoon lights of the M.V. *Ulysses* were turned off. Their vessel was lit up like a Christmas tree in the most dangerous stretch of water between the polar caps and Captain Moore seemed to have no regard for pirates whatsoever. He looked astern and the hackles rose on his neck. There she was, sitting in their wake and she seemed to be getting closer. Shocked, the coxswain realised the junk had dropped her sail and was gaining on them rapidly.

'Er, Skipper?' he muttered.

'Mmmh? the Captain grunted as he perused a map spread on the chart table before him, paying little attention to his coxswain.

'Ah, er, Skipper?' the coxswain repeated.

'Mmmh?' The Captain's eyes remained glued to the chart as he sipped honeyed tea from a large tin mug.

'Er, that junk, Sir,' the coxswain stared at the dark mass crossing their wake.

'Mmmh?'

'She's gaining on us.'

'Mmmh, what was that?'

'That bleedin' junk, Sir!' the coxswain roared losing his nerve altogether. 'She's bloody well gaining on us!'

'What?' the Captain turned as the coxswain's words sunk in.

'She's hard on our stern quarter!'

'Good God Almighty!' The Captain hit the alarm bell on the cabin wall above the chart-table. An electric bell began to shrill loudly as James Moore raised his binoculars to focus on the junk astern.

He saw a small light like a torch beam flicker in the darkness and he thought, for one split second, it might be a muzzle flash. Then a 7.92mm bullet smashed through the right binocular tube, entered his brain and blew the back of his skull off.

The coxswain saw his Captain's brains splash across the chart table and screamed as the wheelhouse began to disintegrate around him. Hundreds of rounds from the three German machine guns tore through the superstructure of the vessel and filled the air like angry hornets.

A burst of ten or more caught the coxswain across the midriff and ripped his body in half.

In the opulent main saloon, which opened onto the quarterdeck at the stern of the vessel, Stephen Hemmings heard the staccato rattle of machine guns. He looked astern and saw the dark shape of a junk barely twenty yards from the stern rail of the M.V. *Ulysses,* and he dived down the companionway to the accommodation deck below, just in time to avoid the stream of shells that tore through the saloon doors.

On the poop deck of his junk, The One Eyed Woo cackled madly as he heaved the tiller amidships to take station abeam of the stricken yacht. His son, Napoleon, altered his line of machine gun fire to the water line of the bigger vessel, his aim searching for the engine room. The bullets did their work, and great chunks of the yacht's hull flew in all directions, as the ship heaved and slewed towards the junk, sea water flooding her below decks.

'*Aaaiiiyaah!*' The Admiral screamed, and he heaved the tiller hard to port as the big yacht's hull yawed towards him. The two ships ground against one another, then sprang apart like lovestruck whales. The Admiral's junk continued to starboard a full three hundred and sixty degrees and came up hard astern of the stricken yacht. The One Eyed Woo cut his engine and eased up behind his prey.

The M.V. *Ulysses* was dead in the water, listing badly to starboard as the merciless sea surged through her hull. People screamed and flames shot up into the night sky. A lifeboat was launched and many on board, including several women, leapt into the water and clung to its sides. Three of the crew jumped off the port bow with lifebuoys around their waists, and a man in formal evening dress clung precariously to what was left of the wheelhouse.

The Admiral, The One Eyed Woo eased his junk alongside the yacht as his good eye searched for the man whose photograph he held in his hand. Ignoring the screams of his victims, thrashing for their lives in the sea, The Admiral focused on a man afloat in a lifebuoy just off the yacht's starboard bow.

'*Get me that man!*' the pirate growled.

Wellington Woo, the elder by ten minutes of the Admiral's twin sons, grabbed a gaff hook from the scuppers of the junk and reached over the weather rail towards the man his father had pointed out. As the junk eased past the man, Wellington Woo skewered Stephen Hemmings through the throat, and with the help of his brother Napoleon, hauled him aboard and dropped him on the deck.

The Admiral engaged his engine to slow ahead and the junk drifted off several hundred yards from the yacht. He then reverted to neutral and, as the junk bobbed to a stop, he went down onto the main deck and looked at the dying *gwai loh*.

Stephen Hemmings lay in a pool of blood staring up at a mad one-eyed man. The gaff hook had entered Stephen's neck and come out through his right eye and, as he gasped his last breaths, he wondered idly if he too would have a false eye like this man's.

'*You killed him!*' The Admiral yelled as he hit the elder twin in the head with his huge fist. '*Why did you gaff him through the head, you idiot? Couldn't you have hooked his coat?*'

'*He's the one you wanted dead, isn't he?*' Wellington Woo cried as he held onto his stinging ear. '*He's the one in the picture Blue Star gave you!*'

'*I was supposed to kill him!*' The One Eyed Woo roared.

'*Well, you're too late, old man,*' Napoleon the younger twin said as he wrenched the gaff hook free from Stephen Hemmings' head. '*The important thing is he's dead! At least I think he's dead.*' Napoleon leaned down and pushed his finger deep into Stephen Hemmings' eye socket. '*Yes, he's dead,*' he declared. '*This is what Blue Star wanted, true or not true?*'

'*Neither one of you will ever be a good pirate!*' Woo declared as he turned his back on the annoying screams of the people two hundred yards astern in the water.

'*I don't want to be a pirate!*' Napoleon said.

'*Neither do I!*' Wellington added.

'*Aaiiyaaaah!*' The Admiral, The One Eyed Woo was stunned. What was wrong with them? How could anyone not want to be a pirate? Especially anyone related to him by blood. It was unthinkable.

'*I want to work for Blue Star,*' Napoleon continued, emboldened by the fact that his father hadn't hit him. '*I want to work in an office and wear fine suits of clothes. I want to be a boss in the city of Hong Kong where rich men eat fat pork.*'

'*You want to be a fat, soft-bellied taipan in Hong Kong, true or not true?*' Woo asked as he shook his head in disbelief.

'*True,*' Napoleon replied.

'*Where's the romance in that?*' Woo cried. '*Where's the danger, the action, the adventure? Look here,*' he growled as he dragged Napoleon to the running rail. '*Does that excite, or not excite you?*' He pointed to the catastrophe in the water as the M.V. *Ulysses* slowly sank beneath the waves. '*What about you?*' he asked turning to the elder twin, who shook his head and dropped his eyes to the deck. '*Well, what do you want to do for a living?*'

'*I want to join the Hong Kong Police,*' Wellington muttered.

'*Aaaaaaaahhh!*' The Admiral roared at the night sky. '*Aaaaaaaaahhh!*'

'*Here, have a cigar,*' Ho jai said. '*You're upset, Lord of the Sea.*'

'*Wouldn't you be?*' The Admiral snatched the cigar from his First Mate's outstretched hand. '*Where did you get this?*'

'*From your bedding, Great Dragon of the Oceans. I took only one.*'

'*How would you feel if your sons betrayed you?*' The One Eyed Woo angrily bit the end of the cigar and spat onto the deck.

'*They have not betrayed you, old friend,*' Ho jai said softly. '*We are too old, you and I, for piracy, and your sons are too smart. Soon great naval ships of the English and others will come and destroy us all. Piracy is no longer safe and the twins show good judgement to consider work in other fields of endeavour. Do they not already run the finest brothel in Lau Fau Shan? They are educated thanks to you, Great Lord, and they should put what they've learned at school in Canton to good use.*'

'*Maybe you are right, Ho jai,*' The Admiral sighed heavily as he lit his cigar and blew out a long trail of smoke. '*You are too old, and I am nearly too old. Piracy is fucked! It has been sodomised by progress! Perhaps we should sell this fine ship in Macau and go home with the profits, and our necks, while we've still got them, true or not true?*'

'*True, Emperor of all the Seas!*' Ho jai declared. '*I could buy a new wife in Macau and you could buy a second one, or a third, or even a fourth, and we could fuck ourselves to death! Good or not good?*'

'Good!' Woo laughed. '*More than good! Excellent! Do you know what else . . .*'

'Help! Help us!' An English voice interrupted, calling pitifully in the darkness.

The Admiral looked over the railing down into a lifeboat full of survivors from the M.V. *Ulysses*. *'Indochina is that way,'* Woo pointed into the darkness. *'Manila is the other way.'*

'You've got to help us,' a man shouted up to him.

'You're lucky I've decided to retire as of now!' The Admiral yelled down to the boat. *'Go away, you sucker of your sister's swollen clitoris!'* He picked up the body of Stephen Hemmings and carried it to the railings. *'And take this bag of dog shit with you,'* he snarled, throwing the dead body down into the lifeboat onto the screaming occupants. Then he noticed the waterproofed wallet that had fallen from Hemmings' pocket onto the deck, and he picked it up. Perhaps this will be of interest to *Blue Star*, the Admiral thought, as he made for the poop deck.

龍

Richard parked his car and ran up the front stairs of Merchant House. A storm was brewing in the night sky, and it would break soon. A servant took his hat and coat and he made his way to the dining room. Elanora was already seated at the dining table.

'I'm sorry I'm a little late, dear, I had tea with Quincy.' Richard kissed her cheek and sat opposite her at the big oval rosewood table.

'No matter,' Elanora replied. She rang a small silver dinner bell and a servant appeared with a soup tureen. 'How is Quincy? It's ages since I saw him last.'

'He's well,' Richard busied himself rearranging the napkin that had been placed across his lap. 'He sends his love.'

'That's nice,' she answered, not looking at him.

Richard appraised her from the far side of the table. She sat, rigidly beautiful, and raised a spoonful of soup to her lips. Her *cheung saam*, green and gold, was split either side from ankle to thigh, her hair, piled loosely on her head, was held in place by her favourite jade comb, and she wore lipstick of the deepest red gloss. It was rare for Elanora to wear makeup. On the occasions when she did, it was an unmistakable signal she wanted him to stay the night. But this time it was different. The tension in Elanora was unmistakable.

'Is there something bothering you, dear?' Richard asked. 'You seem a little distant this evening.'

'It's nothing,' she replied. 'I booked a long distance telephone call this morning from the Company office to James and Lee, in London.'

'Really?' Richard prepared himself for the onslaught to follow.

'When I reprimanded James for his unseemly behaviour, he replied: "Oh, Mother, for heaven's sake" and laughed at me.'

'He's not the little boy you once knew, Elanora, he's a young adult with modern ideas.'

'Be that as it may,' she replied tightly. 'I will not tolerate insolence from my son.'

'What was your response?'

'I ordered them both home immediately the school term finishes.'

'And what was James' response to that?'

'He responded with a question,' Elanora lowered her soup spoon and stared directly at him. 'He asked me if I'd discussed the matter with you.'

'Me?' Richard feigned surprise. 'What on Earth's it got to do with me?'

'Obviously a great deal.' There was steely silence before she continued. 'Since the telephone call I've thought of nothing else the whole day.' She hesitated, then the words came out as an accusation. 'You have a control over those boys that I, as their mother, find disturbing.'

She knows, he thought. She's found out the boys are members of the *Gam Loong Tong*. 'Then, Elanora,' he said reasonably. 'Let us discuss it.'

Elanora had always found Richard's calm self-assurance unsettling, and this time more so than ever. She hesitated again. Waiting for him to arrive, she'd been so sure of what she was going to say, the discussion had been so clear in her mind, but now the moment had arrived she was an emotional mess. She knew her feelings were purely instinctive and she knew, with his typically male logic, he would refute whatever she said at every turn. He would tell her she was overreacting. He would laugh condescendingly as she struggled to articulate her emotions.

'Both James and Lee,' she began, knowing the words would not come, 'regard you, whether you like it or not, as their father.'

The tension that had been building within him began to dissipate. She doesn't know, he thought thankfully. 'And I'm greatly honoured that they do so, my dear.' He sipped his wine.

'I, too, regard you as their father.'

'Elanora . . .'

'I know, I know,' she interrupted clumsily, feeling inept. Her mind searched for the essence of the discussion she'd started, but her resolve was rapidly diminishing. Something is wrong, she wanted to scream, something is wrong between us. But what is it? Even as she asked the question, her mind answered. I don't know! I don't know what's wrong but something is wrong!

Did she want a commitment from him to her and the boys? Did she want more control of her own destiny? Did she want him to love her? Did she know what she wanted at all? Or was she simply awash in a sea of inexplicable emotions? Ask him something, anything, her mind screamed. 'It's just that the telephone call with James went badly,' she stumbled on getting further and further away from the essence of her emotional trauma. 'I became unreasonably angry and broke the connection. He seemed so old, Richard. He sounded so adult . . .'

'As I said before, my dear, James is no longer a little boy.'

'I know. He made that point himself during our conversation. That's when I became angry and terminated the call.'

'Would you like me to book a trunk call to James tomorrow?'

'Would you?' She gave a wan smile. 'Assert your authority, Richard, for my sake. I want them home.' Elanora realised the moment had passed. 'I want to share the experience of family, and I want you here to share it with me,' she finished lamely.

'I will always be here for you, Elanora, as I will be for the boys.' Richard spoke gently, aware of the struggle that had transpired within her. She'd failed miserably this time, he thought, but he knew the 'unconditional' arrangement they shared was nearing its end. Elanora was not the kind of woman to surrender. Eventually he would have to give more of himself. How to do so and keep the upper hand was the question. The trick, he knew, was to keep her off guard.

As the evening progressed Richard pondered his dilemma. He kept the conversation light-hearted and, slowly, Elanora relaxed. Several times he caught her looking at him and when she finished eating and delicately dabbed a napkin to her lips, the desire had returned in her eyes.

Elanora rang the bell for the servants to clear the table, then without speaking, stood and offered him her out-stretched hand. Richard took it and she led him through the house to her bedroom. Closing the door behind them, she kissed him deeply.

Their lovemaking was intense, and in a complete role reversal Elanora took control from the outset. She's playing the game again, he thought. She led him to the brink of ecstasy and kept him there. Finally, she sat astride him, her hands on his shoulders, her jet-black hair cascading around his face. Their eyes locked as she controlled his desire with her hips, until it became a battle of wills.

Richard fought for control as she moved on him. He fought against his body's need for release until he saw doubt appear in Elanora's eyes and knew he was gaining the ascendancy.

'Tell me you love me, Richard,' Elanora hissed through clenched teeth. He reached up and, placing a hand on her cheek, smiled into her eyes. He was in total control.

'Say it,' she hissed again. 'Damn you, Richard, say it!' She was reaching the point of no return. 'I love you, Richard.' Her orgasm was seconds away. 'Tell me you love me,' she pleaded.

Richard smiled again, awaiting the moment. He placed

both hands on her cheeks and with her climax a breath away he whispered, 'I love you.'

The tropical storm, which had been gathering over Hong Kong, broke with a violent intensity. Thunder boomed, lightning cracked and the bedroom was momentarily flooded with white light.

Richard watched Elanora's eyes, wide with the shock of recognition, as the power of his words and the power of her orgasm joined with the elements to shatter the night.

Long after the storm had abated and Elanora slept in his arms, Richard pondered his audacious move. She'd begged him to say the words before, at the height of their lovemaking, but he had never committed himself, and afterwards she'd always laughed it off. Unconditional, she'd said, and unconditional it had been. But now, his calculated confession of love had changed the relationship. He wondered if his gamble would pay off.

It was only a matter of time before Elanora learned of the boys' induction into the Society, and that knowledge would strain the relationship to the hilt. But if she believed he loved her, would she risk losing the love she'd fought so long to gain by challenging his control over her sons? He thought not. Elanora would be furious, of that he had no doubt, but strong as she was, Elanora was a creature ultimately ruled by her heart, and now she had his confession of love.

And he did love her, Richard thought, as he listened to the gentle rain following the storm, so far as he was capable of loving anyone. He hadn't lied. She is my closest friend and confidante, he reasoned, and I feel a great affection for her. Isn't that a form of love? He stroked her nipple as she slept. I might even marry her, he thought. Yes, why not? A marriage proposal would be the *coup de grace*, it would quell any future opposition immediately.

Elanora stirred in his arms. Marriage would give him complete control over her and the boys. He smiled in the darkness as she awoke to his caress and reached for him. But he would save the proposal for now. He would not use his trump card until it was absolutely imperative.

CHAPTER THIRTEEN

Private Waan Lok-pui ran for his life down the Street of Heavenly Joy towards its junction with Wing Po Square. He stopped and dived into a doorway as the whine of a heavy artillery shell signalled yet more trouble for him, as if he did not have enough. A huge explosion erupted behind him and flames engulfed an abandoned military truck not fifty yards from his shelter. Stone and metal fragments tore into the wall next to his head and smoke filled the street as he bolted across to another doorway on the opposite side of the street and tried to peer through dust and smoke, searching for the command post he'd been sent to find.

What, by all the gods, was he doing in Shanghai, he asked himself, not for the first time. He was a farmer from a small village north of Canton and never in his life had he expected to find himself in the north of China in the late autumn of 1937.

'*You must fight for your country,*' the recruitment officer in Canton had said to him. '*Unless every son of China fights for General Ch'iang Kai-shek and for the new Republic we will never know freedom.*'

It had all seemed so simple then and quite romantic to a farm lad. He had joined the Nationalist Army and been trained at Whang Po near Canton and his parents and brothers and sisters had been so proud of him in his new uniform. The mayor of his village had invited him to tea and sweet cakes and told him the whole village was proud of their son and would pray every day for his safe return. Leung So-Lai, the prettiest girl in the village, who would not look at him before, had offered him conversation and a walk in the

forest, which had proved to be the most wonderful experience of his life. He had touched her breasts and she had
brushed his member with her knee and who knows what else
might have happened if his sisters had not followed them and
giggled at their dalliance.

But nobody had told him he would have to fight the *Lo
Baat Tau*, the Turnip Heads who were at this very moment
trying to kill him with cannons. He was told he would be
fighting the Communists who were trying to take over The
Middle Kingdom, a rag-tail lot who would turn and run at
the first shot fired. How was it then that he now found
himself in the City of Shanghai fighting the Japanese?

According to his lieutenant, several months earlier in July
on the Marco Polo Bridge in Tientsin near Peking, some idiot
had taken a shot at a Japanese soldier and because of this the
Turnip Heads had attacked the Chinese fort of Wanping and
blown it to bits.

'*Does anyone know the name of this idiot?*' Waan Lok-pui
shouted to no one in particular as his nerves jangled at
another explosion behind him. '*Could this idiot not be
located and forced to apologise to the Turnip Heads?*' Waan
yelled as he bolted down the street hoping to find the
command post. Another blast behind him, but much closer,
lifted him off his feet and flung him through the air. He
landed with a thud in a pile of bricks and heard someone
grunt beneath him.

'*Get off me, you fucker of pregnant sows,*' a voice growled
and Private Waan rolled onto his side with the assistance of
a shove from the hands belonging to the voice.

'*I don't know his name!*' Waan shouted. '*If I did I would
surely tell you.*'

'*Whose name?*' The older soldier lying next to him asked.

'*The idiot who fired at you on the Marco Polo Bridge!*'
Waan exclaimed.

'*What are you talking about?*'

'*Are you Japanese?*' Waan asked in return.

'*Do you still have testicles?*' the seasoned campaigner
grinned at Waan.

'*I believe so,*' Waan replied feeling his groin.

'*Then I'm not a Turnip Head,*' the soldier roared. '*If I was, I'd be roasting your testicles over a fire by now anticipating a fine lunch.*'

'*What's going on out there?*' a voice demanded from inside the nearby bombed-out building.

'*I think we have a deserter on our hands, Sir,*' the soldier yelled through a large hole in the wall, into the interior of the building.

'*I'm not a deserter,*' Private Waan cried. '*Has a disease eaten your brain? Deserters do not run towards the enemy! They run away from the enemy! True or not true?*' he yelled at the grinning old soldier.

'*That is providing one knows where the enemy is,*' the soldier replied. '*Therefore allowing the deserter to make a logical decision about the direction in which to run.*'

'*Shoot him!*' The order came from within.

'*Yes, Sir!*' the soldier yelled.

'*Wait!*' Waan cried. '*I'm not a deserter! I carry a message from Headquarters for Captain Lee Kwan. I'm looking for the forward command post in Wing Po Square.*'

'*Well, you've found it,*' the soldier declared as another heavy artillery shell exploded in the street. '*Do your orders include a message of congratulations for Private Soong? Perhaps a personal message from General Ch'iang congratulating me on my meritorious service to the Nationalist cause and relieving me of my military obligations so that I may return to my village in Hunan and resume my peaceful life as a brick-maker?*'

'*No.*'

'*I did not think so.*'

'*Is Captain Lee Kwan here?*' Both men ducked their heads as yet another shell exploded.

'*He is the one who just ordered you shot. Why don't you crawl inside through that hole and see if he's changed his mind.*'

'*Tell me,*' Waan asked, '*is he or is he not, the famous young Captain Lee Kwan who goes among the enemy ranks at night and kills them in their sleep?*'

'He is indeed,' Private Soong said proudly. 'And he brings their boots and socks back to us so we will not have cold feet now that winter is nearly upon us.'

'Aaah!' Waan exclaimed. 'He is the most popular topic of conversation at Headquarters. They say he is only a boy, but his adventures are told by all. It is said he can move among men and they don't know he is there. Is this true or not true?'

'True, little brother. Our Captain is a man to be feared. The Japanese have a price on his head. It is said they will pay ten thousand taels of silver for him dead or alive. He has killed so many Turnip Heads they believe they are fighting two different armies, The Nationalists and Captain Lee Kwan!'

'Is it true or not true that he is schooled in the arts of Shaolin?'

'True! I have seen him fight.' Several shells exploded demolishing a building, opposite where the two men lay. 'There was much hand to hand combat in this area when we got here,' Private Soong shouted, shaking the dust from his hair. 'But now the Japanese only fire their cannons at us. None of them come here any more in person, because the Captain terrifies them so much, they shit in their pants! I have never seen a more dangerous individual than my young Captain. I am his closest friend and adviser, but if we were not at war, I would not wander within five miles of him. Mind you,' the soldier laughed, 'while we are at war I would not wander five feet from him.'

'Private Soong!' the voice yelled over the roar of the incoming shells.

'Yes, Sir!'

'What's going on out there?'

'The deserter is not a deserter, Sir! He is a messenger from Headquarters.'

'Then send him in here, you idiot!'

'Yes, Sir!' the soldier replied. 'Well, my friend, are you ready to enter the lair of the dragon? I warn you, be careful what you say or you might just get eaten up!'

Private Waan nodded a reply and looked into the dark,

dust-filled cavern. He took a deep breath and moved into the gloom as another shell screamed into the street.

The inside of what had once been an apothecary's shop was rubble. Old rosewood cabinets, which had once lined the walls, lay smashed all around and several wounded soldiers lay on blankets, tended by their comrades. A young boy in a captain's uniform sat at a rickety table poring over a map of the city as Private Waan approached him and saluted. Good Heavens, Waan thought, he's younger than I am.

'Who are you?' Lee asked without looking up from his map.

'Private Waan Lok-pui, Sir, 81st Army, 104th Division, Communications Unit, stationed at Army Headquarters in Tangli. I have a message from Colonel Chung, Sir.'

'Colonel Chung?' Lee Kwan looked up, immediately interested. 'Do you mean Colonel Chung Shek-mei? General Ch'iang's Chief-of-Staff?'

'I don't know what he does, Sir, but his name is Colonel Chung Shek-mei.'

'And what is the message, Private Waan?'

'Your unit is to withdraw from this suburb, Captain, and dig in around the Jade Garden Monument on the western edge of the suburb of Tangli. You must hand over your command to your second-in-charge and report to Headquarters immediately, Sir.'

'Private Soong!' Lee Kwan yelled, frightening the daylights out of poor Private Waan.

'Yes, Sir?' Soong coughed as he came in through the dust and smoke.

'Where is my second-in-command Lieutenant Foo?'

'At the barricade in Ping Fan Road, just around the corner on the other side of the square. They are under heavy fire, Captain. Worse than us.'

'Get over to him and tell him to withdraw to the Jade Gardens and dig in,' Lee Kwan ordered as he strapped on his Sam Browne belt and holster. 'Help him inform all NCOs.'

'Where are you going?'

'I've been ordered to HQ.'

'Then I must go with you. It is General Ch'iang Kai-shek's order.'

'You will do as you are told, Soong! I should not be long. I will meet you at the monument outside the garden gates. Tell Foo to set up our HQ there, it will provide good protection.'

'Yes, Sir!' Private Soong shouted over the noise of the shelling as he turned and made his way back into the street.

'Excuse me, Captain?' Private Waan said, as he watched Lee Kwan pick up a machine gun and stuff several magazines of ammunition into his belt. *'What will I do?'*

'Return to where you came from, Private.'

'I'm not sure where that is, Sir. I'd rather come with you.'

Lee Kwan stopped and looked at the soldier. *'Did you say you are in Communications?'*

'Yes, Sir, I am a radio operator.'

'Good, I need one. Pick up that gear,' Lee said pointing to a pile of radio equipment. *'And follow me. Consider yourself under my command.'*

'Yes, Sir!' Private Waan said happily as Lee gave orders for the removal of the wounded. He had a sudden feeling that his war, at least, had taken a turn for the better.

龍

Captain Lee Kwan sat in the Orderly's Room in a corridor opposite the office of General Ch'iang Kai-shek's Chief-of-Staff, his chopsticks clacking madly as he stuffed food into his mouth. He was ravenous, realising he'd not eaten in nearly forty-eight hours, and the Colonel's Orderly had kindly offered him a bowl of noodles.

The building taken over by General Ch'iang had been, until recently, the offices of the City Elders and it was a magnificent edifice. The doors and windows were of oak and polished silkwood and the floors were beautiful examples of tiled Ming mosaic patterns. The furniture throughout, including the table he ate from, was rosewood, elaborately and painstakingly carved by master craftsmen. The desk in front of him was similar to the one he'd often sat at in

Merchant House, when he and James had done school work under the patient eye of Quincy Heffernan.

Lee smiled. He'd loved the years he'd spent at Merchant House with James and Elanora. When the Merchant Mistress had taken him under her wing and become his official guardian his whole world had changed. He'd received the best education possible in Hong Kong and had had three years at college in England and he knew for certain that, but for his education, he would not be an officer in the Nationalist Army. Lee Kwan had much for which to be thankful.

A frown creased his forehead as he remembered the previous Christmas of 1936. Had it been only eleven months ago, it seemed like eleven years. He wondered what Elanora and Richard were doing right at this moment, as he sat eating noodles in the City of Shanghai. He hoped they'd sorted out their feelings for each other and were happily together; Lee knew only too well Elanora's mercurial mood swings and how unsettling her anger could be.

Elanora's attitude had, at first, been one of understanding when he had announced his intention to join the Nationalist Army. Her Chinese side accepted his desire to go to his homeland and do what he perceived to be the right thing. She was sympathetic, she said, but, as he was after all only seventeen, it was unthinkable. Perhaps when he was older. When Lee announced he was resolved to join the fight, with or without her consent, the mother in her had taken over. She'd flown into a rage, calling him disloyal and ungrateful, and she'd turned to Richard for support. But Richard had sided with Lee. Elanora had immediately stopped her ranting and, for what seemed like an eternity, she'd stared at Richard. Then she'd walked slowly from the room, defeated. Lee had never seen her broken like that. It was then he realised all was not well between the two people he looked upon as his parents. And there was worse to come. The straw that broke the camel's back was Elanora's discovery of the secret he, James and Richard had been keeping from her.

It had happened just after New Year's Day when he and James had been training in the summerhouse. He remembered vividly how Elanora had burst in on them all smiles and lace.

'There you are my darlings . . .' she'd begun, but her smile had frozen as she'd stood staring at the brands on their respective shoulders.

'Good morning, Mother,' James was fast. He flicked a towel over the brand on his arm. It was instinctive, both boys had learned over the years to hide their dragon brands from all. But he was not fast enough.

'What?' Elanora had been stunned, unable to believe that she'd seen the symbol of the *Gam Loong Tong* burned into the flesh of her son's upper arm.

'I said, good morning, Mother,' James reiterated as Lee folded his arms across his chest, placing his palm over the identical mark on his shoulder.

Lee knew she'd seen it. Her boys had been marked as servants of the Golden Dragons.

'Oh, yes, good morning, James,' she recovered her equilibrium and laughed, a brittle, false attempt at gaiety. 'I'm sorry I burst in on you like that. I just wondered where you both were . . . it's nothing. No matter.' She laughed, again very unconvincingly. 'I thought we might have lunch on the balcony, but I've just remembered something I have to do.' She spun on her heel and walked out.

'Christ on the Cross!' James had muttered the phrase so often used by Charles Higgins. 'The cat's out of the bag now, Lee.'

When they'd first returned to Hong Kong, Richard had told them that Elanora was still unaware they were members of the *Gam Loong Tong* and they were to keep the secret until he deemed it appropriate to tell her. It would have been a simple task, were it not for the brands on their shoulders. They had been inducted into the dragons the night before they'd left for England and Elanora had had no time to notice the scars. But, as Lee had warned Richard, now they were once again under Elanora's roof, keeping the secret for any length of time would be difficult. His warning had proved correct.

Lee had been disappointed in his *Shan Chu*. Richard had erred in judgment for the first time in Lee's eyes. Not informing Elanora had been a foolish tactical error. Or had it been? Lee wondered. Perhaps his *Shan Chu* had merely been awaiting the inevitable. Perhaps he had wanted Elanora to discover the secret herself?

'He can't say I didn't warn him,' Lee had said to James. They had dressed hurriedly and gone to find Richard, but unfortunately Elanora had found him first. The boys stood on the stone flagging outside the study and listened to the disastrous exchange.

'How dare you!' Elanora had burst through the study doors and confronted him.

'How dare I what?' Richard replied.

'Don't treat me like a fool!' Elanora hit her fist against the mantelpiece, furious. 'Did you seriously believe I wouldn't find out?' Richard remained silent. 'I will ask you this question only once and I warn you to think carefully before you answer, because a war between us would do neither of us any good.' Elanora crossed to the desk where he sat, placed both palms on the top and leaned towards him. 'Are my two boys sworn to the Society?'

'Yes,' Richard stared right back at her.

'Damn you, Richard!' She swiped the desk clear with her arm, sending pens, books and a tea service flying across floor. 'You stole my children!'

'Don't you think you're being a bit melodramatic?'

'You are their *Shan Chu*, are you not?'

'I am.'

'I have seen the brands on their shoulders! They are bound to you and the Society by blood oath, are they not?'

'That's correct.'

'Well, I won't have it, do you hear me?' she screamed. 'I won't have it!' Hysteria was getting the better of her, she fought for control. 'I had my suspicions for some time, Richard,' she said, trying to keep the tremor from her voice. 'But I chose to ignore them. My heart would not believe that you would have the temerity for such an act.'

'One of the first conditions you stipulated when we formed the Society was that James should be placed under its protection . . .'

'Under its protection, yes,' Elanora interrupted. 'But never a member of it. I've seen the brands on their arms. They were only boys! Little boys, too young to understand what they were getting involved in, and you scarred them for life, Richard . . . in more ways than one.'

'Without the protection of the Society, those boys will be like lambs in a slaughterhouse.'

'I will not have those boys as members of a triad! I will not have it!

'Think like a Chinese, remember?' Richard said coldly. 'This is Hong Kong, Elanora, or have you forgotten?'

'They are my children, or have *you* forgotten! I warn you, Richard, if you exert any further authority over those boys' lives before they are old enough to choose whether or not they wish to accept it, you'll regret the day you ever set foot in Hong Kong!'

'Are you threatening me, Elanora?'

'If I must, yes!'

'Very well,' Richard rose and straightened his coat. 'I can assure you that I will do nothing to stop the boys from doing as they wish. You have my word on it.' He walked past her, out of the study into the main foyer and opened the front door.

'If you walk out that door, Richard,' Elanora said, following him into the foyer. 'Don't bother coming back.'

'Good day, Elanora.' He closed the door and left Merchant House.

Lee and James sat on the balcony rail outside and stared at each other in shocked silence as they listened to Elanora crying.

龍

Lee Kwan finished his noodles and pushed the bowl away. He hoped things had been repaired between Richard and Elanora, he loved them both deeply. And he hoped James had curbed his wilful behaviour and was not adding to their problems.

He stood up and stretched his aching limbs then crossed to the window and looked down into the street. The sight he beheld was a sad one. Refugees from the city's east filled the street making a steady flow towards the western suburbs of Shanghai. They'd been displaced by the rampant Japanese Army and had nowhere to go but west, in the hope of finding food and a safe haven in which to rest momentarily before they were forced to move on again.

Lee's hatred of the Japanese consumed him. They'd instigated the war in Tientsin by faking an attack on themselves on the Marco Polo Bridge and blaming it on the Chinese. They were blatant militarists intent on subduing all of Asia under the rule of the indulged Emperor Hirohito. Lee had studied their expansionist programme while at college in England and he knew their goal. They would not stop until someone met them head on and sent them back to their islands to think again.

As he watched, down in the front courtyard wounded soldiers, in rows on straw mattresses, were being tended by a depleted medical staff, while in the street more and more refugees streamed west, realising there was no hope for them in Shanghai.

The battle for Shanghai had been going on since August. It was now November and Lee doubted the Chinese forces could hold out much longer. They'd fought valiantly against the better equipped and better trained Japanese, giving up the city, street by street, in bloody conflict, but Lee knew the end was in sight. Although the Chinese outnumbered the Japanese by ten to one, they'd stood little chance against Hirohito's Imperial Forces and there was no doubt in his mind that Shanghai would fall. It was only a matter of days.

'*Excuse me, Elder Brother,*' the Orderly said as he re-entered his office. '*Colonel Chung will see you now.*'

'*Thank you, Private,*' Lee said as he put on his cap. '*And thank you for the noodles. It is a kind man who offers his food to others, especially in times like these. May Heaven smile upon you, Little Brother.*'

Lee crossed the corridor and entered the office of Colonel Chung. He stood to attention, saluted smartly and awaited instructions.

'Captain Kwan,' the elderly Colonel stood and walked around his desk to greet the younger man. 'It is an honour to make your acquaintance at last.' He extended his hand. 'I have heard much of your exploits in the streets against our adversaries. You set a fine example for others to follow.'

'Thank you, Sir.' They shook, and Lee sat down in the chair the Colonel indicated. 'But we are losing the city, street by street. I'm afraid our efforts to hold Shanghai are not enough to stop the Lo Baat Tau.'

'Ha!' the Colonel laughed at the disparaging term. 'But you must admit, my valiant young Captain, that their heads, which are truly shaped like turnips, make excellent targets! True or not true?'

'True, Colonel,' Lee smiled.

'You are ordered to leave Shanghai,' the old Staff Officer said as he sank wearily into his chair and placed his hands flat on his desk.

'But, Sir, . . .'

'I know how you feel, Captain,' Colonel Chung interrupted. 'I'm sure your arguments would be commendable and your idealistic notions on war noble in the extreme, but I've heard them all before from other young men and I can assure you they would fall on deaf ears. I have been fighting China's wars since I was a boy and I can tell you, right here and now, that death before dishonour is a foolish philosophy to a professional soldier, unless he happens to be Japanese, but I have no time to waste explaining why. All I will say is, you are too valuable for us to lose in a conflict in which defeat is inevitable, so be quiet and listen.'

'Yes, Sir,' Lee said, sitting stiffly on the edge of the leather chair.

'Our Leader, General Ch'iang Kai-shek, whom you have met, I believe?'

'Yes, Sir. In Whang Po Academy in February when I was training.'

'*General Ch'iang is most insistent that nothing happen to you and I agree with him. You are a valuable commodity to the Nationalist cause, not only because of your undoubted fighting skills, but because of your impeccable education in Hong Kong and England and your skill in languages.*' The Colonel rose and went to the window, where he stood for some time gazing at the sad scene below before turning back to Lee. '*Shanghai is merely a battle, Captain Kwan, a battle we have already lost, but the war is a different matter entirely. This war with Japan will be long and bloody and many difficult situations will arise, which will need fine young men like you to attend them. General Ch'iang needs you and others like you close by his side for the worse times to come. Understand or not understand?*'

'*Understand, Sir,*' Lee nodded. He'd seen the pain in Chung's eyes as the old man had turned back from the window.

'*General Ch'iang has already left Shanghai,*' the Colonel sat and pushed an envelope across the desk towards Lee. '*Written orders in our Leader's own hand. You are ordered to join him in Nanking immediately, where you and other young men with exceptional skills will be under his direct command. That is all, Captain Kwan. You are dismissed.*'

'*Yes, Sir,*' Lee stood to attention and saluted. He picked up the envelope, and marched to the door.

'*Captain,*' the old soldier called after him.

'*Sir?*' Lee turned at the open door.

'*The Japanese have once again made the mistake of trying to subjugate China. History seems to have taught them nothing. They have once again trodden on the tail of a sleeping dragon that will come slowly from its slumber and roar at the heavens, then it will vent its anger on those who dared disturb it. The dragon needs men like you, Captain Kwan. You will be rewarded with honour. I wish you good luck, young man.*'

'*Thank you, Elder Brother. I wish you good luck also,*' Lee replied and left the office.

Lee Kwan walked down the steps of the old administration building into the throng of humanity jamming the street. The scene was one worthy of Dante's *Inferno*. Through the drifting dust and smoke from the artillery shells pounding the city to the east, the wounded moaned, the refugees cried aloud and ambulances and military vehicles honked their horns demanding clear passage. People called out names of lost loved ones hoping they would materialise out of thin air. Several anguished screams could only mean that death had come to a loved one in that street of pain.

Lee heard his name being called and searched the street for a face he knew. He saw Private Waan, the young radio operator, waving at him from across the street and with him stood Private Soong, Lee's old retainer.

Soong had been with Lee since he'd graduated from the Whang Po Military Academy. The old Private had been seconded to him by a General Staff Order for some obscure military reason Lee had never quite understood. Soong, on the other hand, understood the order only too well. It had come directly from General Ch'iang Kai-shek and it said if anything happened to Captain Kwan, Soong's own life would not be worth living. The old fellow had done his level best to make sure he carried the order out.

Lee waved back, acknowledging the two men, and pushed his way into the mass of people. He forced his way through crying old women, past shell-shocked soldiers, ignoring children begging for help.

'*What are you two doing here?*' he demanded.

'*Elder Brother,*' Private Soong began. '*We did not even get time to dig in at the Jade Gardens before we were overrun by Lo Baat Tau.*'

'*Where is Lieutenant Foo?*'

'*He is dead, Sir,*' Private Waan said. '*The whole unit was slaughtered. The Japanese will take the city by nightfall, Sir. They are swarming like bees everywhere north, east and south of here.*'

Inured as he had become to the death that surrounded him, Lee felt sickened by the thought of the loss of his men. '*Soong jai,*' he clapped his man on the back, there was much to be done. '*I have been ordered to join General Ch'iang in Nanking. You arrange transport for us, can or cannot?*'

'*Can, Elder Brother,*' the old soldier replied with a

sardonic grin. *'I'd fuck the Emperor of Japan if it meant we'd get out of Shanghai in one piece, but that will not be necessary.'* He pointed down the side street to a Ford military truck. *'A palanquin with wheels just for us, my Emperor!'*

'You old rogue! Where did you get it?'

'It has been in my family for many years, Elder Brother. I walked all the way to Hunan to borrow it from my father.'

'All right, all right! I should have known better than to ask. Let's go.'

'What about me?' Private Waan asked.

Lee looked at the young private standing forlornly in the street. *'Well, you cannot go back in there,'* he said, pointing at the Headquarters Waan had left that morning. *'Or you will be dead by night's fall. Do you still have my radio transmitter?'*

'Yes, Elder Brother. It is in the truck we stole, I mean the one Private Soong borrowed from his father in Hunan.'

'Well, you'd better come with us,' Lee set off at a pace down the street towards the truck.

'Truly you are of noble birth, Captain Kwan!' Private Waan cried with relief. He began running after his hero. *'May all the dragons in the Celestial Kingdom, presided over by the Son of Heaven, surround you and protect you from the Turnip Heads and any other evil adversaries you may encounter in your long and fruitful life! May you have many children and fifty concubines to sap your prolific loins of their . . .'*

'Shut up and get in the truck!' Lee yelled.

As his newly found Captain got in the passenger side and slammed the door shut, Private Waan threw himself into the back of the vehicle and sat there grinning stupidly as Private Soong engaged the gears and moved off down the street. They inched slowly westward eventually entering the foothills of Wing Po, and Private Waan's good humour ebbed from his body as he watched the City of Shanghai being ceremonially disembowelled.

龍

The heat in the Inn of Heavenly Joy was stifling. A large fire roared in the main fireplace and the tables were packed with soldiers desperate for one night of drunken forgetfulness before their forced march to Nanking continued on the morrow. They drowned their sorrows for comrades lost in the fighting at Shanghai and made boasts of what they would do to the Japanese forces daring to contemplate an attack on Nanking, the ancient and sacred capital of China. Outside, the night was near freezing with winter only days away, but inside, in the hot fetid air of the tavern, the soldiers found brief respite and solace in drink, good company and songs of happier times.

Lin Li watched from the bar as several of the soldiers began an arm-wrestling competition and she knew from experience that it would be the start of trouble. Though only seventeen years old, Lin Li was used to hard men and hard times. She'd grown up as an innkeeper's daughter and knew only too well that when men began to flex their muscles it would not be long before a fight started.

Lin Li felt a rush of cold air as the inn door opened and three more soldiers walked in. The first at the bar was a private, no more than a boy, small in stature, and he was followed by another private, an old man, battle-scarred and grumpy who Lin Li picked for a southern Cantonese. There was something about the third man, or boy more like, Li thought, as he approached the bar, something authoritative in his bearing.

By all the heavens, she thought, shocked. He's an officer. A captain according to his uniform, but he's only a baby. He's not as old as I am, she mused, as the young man placed his hand on the bar top.

'*Mandarin? Cantonese?*' the young man asked her.

'*Take your pick, my mother's from the south, my father's from the north,*' Lin Li replied.

'*What food do you have for three hungry soldiers?*' the older private asked her.

'*There is a soup of fish with noodles, but that is all we have because of the war and my father charges excessively for it.*'

'*Business is business,*' Soong laughed. '*Three bowls of your soup and a bottle of good wine to warm our bodies.*' He threw some coins on the bar top.

Over near the fireplace a table overturned and two men snarled at each other. A fight began but was soon broken up by other soldiers and the inn settled down again.

'*Frightened men behave foolishly, Elder Brother,*' Soong said to his Captain, noticing that the young officer was looking intently at the men who'd been arguing. '*Foolish behaviour is good for them. It will make them forget the Japanese, at least for one night.*'

Lee Kwan shrugged carelessly and nodded to a table being vacated at the far end of the room. As the three men moved towards it a hand reached out and grabbed Lee's arm.

'*Where did you steal the officer's uniform, boy?*' The sergeant who spoke was drunk and he eyed Lee with a vicious glare. Lee placed his hand on the man's neck, squeezed and the man fell unconscious, his head cracking on the top of the table at which he sat.

'*He's had too much wine,*' Lee remarked casually to the man's friend and continued to walk to the table they'd spied.

'*How did he do that?*' Waan hissed at Soong as they sat at the table, but old Soong just smiled and shook his head as if to say, 'don't ask'.

'*Three bowls of ridiculously expensive soup,*' Lin Li said as she placed the steaming bowls in front of the men. '*And here is your bottle of wine. Don't complain to me about the quality of it, because it is all we have!*'

'*I'm sure it will be excellent,*' Lee replied.

He was a beautiful young man, Lin Li thought, and she felt a brief shock as her eyes met his. It was as if, for one second, his mind was reading hers. He is a strange one, she thought. '*Was the drunk correct?*' she asked. '*Did you steal that uniform from a dead officer?*' She felt foolish the moment the question had passed her lips, but something in her had compelled her to goad him.

'*I have never stolen anything in my life,*' Lee replied softly. '*Why are you trying to upset me? What has made you angry, Little Sister?*'

Lin Li stood paralysed, frozen to the spot as the young man's gaze seemed to bare her soul.

'*What did you do to my Sergeant?*' a rough voice demanded.

'*Does your mother's vagina taste good, little boy?*' another voice added.

Lin Li backed away. She knew the beautiful young man would be bashed and she wanted to warn him to run far away, but she couldn't speak.

'*Stand to attention when you address a senior officer,*' Lee said to the two angry soldiers now standing in front of his table.

'*You're not an officer,*' a third drunken soldier sneered as he joined his two friends. '*You may be a fucker of goats, but you're not an officer.*'

Lin Li watched horrified as two of the men lunged at the young captain. In a blur, the boy moved. He came up from the table and struck one man in the face, then he spun through the air and hit another with his heel. The third protagonist could only stare as Lee's fist hit him in the sternum, and he collapsed unconscious to the floor.

The inn was silent as fifty or more soldiers watched Lee Kwan go back to his seat and start eating his soup. He sipped cautiously at the hot liquid, then looked up as if suddenly aware of being watched.

'*I am the senior officer in this tavern and you will all listen to me carefully. My name is Lee Kwan, Captain Lee Kwan.*' A ripple of recognition went round the room at the mention of his name, but Lee did not bother rising from his seat to take advantage of it. '*I am in the service of General Ch'iang Kai-shek, as are all of you. My companions and I are on our way to Nanking to fight the Japanese, as are all of you. So save your anger for the enemy and think of the harm you will do to him. And while you do so, consider also the harm that may befall you . . .*' he paused and his eyes roamed the room, '*. . . for such is the nature of war. Enjoy yourselves while you can. And enjoy the company of your comrades in arms, while it is still yours to enjoy. Now, someone see to these men.*' Lee resumed eating his soup and slowly the noise of camaraderie restored itself to the inn, while the three fallen men were roused and dragged away.

Lin Li looked at her father who was looking at the baby boy officer with wide-eyed amazement. The old innkeeper turned his gaze on his daughter and a big grin split his face. He motioned her over to the bar and leant to her ear.

'*Our baby officer is a mighty dragon, true or not true, daughter?*'

'*Not true,*' Lin Li sniffed haughtily feigning disinterest.

'*A boy like that who is already an officer and with those fighting skills surely must be of noble birth,*' her father snapped at her. '*Make sure he and his companions get whatever they want and do not charge them, it is not often we get people of his standing at our inn. Prepare a bed for him in the special guestroom upstairs and tell his friends they may sleep in the stable. Tell him also it would give your father great face if he would stay in our humble house as my special guest, free of charge.*'

'*Have you gone mad?*' Lin Li asked. She knew her father to be a miser at the best of times and for him to use the words 'free of charge' meant he was temporarily unhinged.

'*Do as you are told, daughter!*' the innkeeper hissed. '*And prepare him a hot bath when he is ready to retire tonight.*'

'*A bath!*' Lin Li was astounded.

'*Yes! A bath!*' her father replied acidly. '*And get in it with him if he asks you to!*'

'*I would rather die!*' she gasped.

'*That can be arranged,*' her father said flatly. '*Come here.*' He dragged her behind the bar into the small tap-room, that housed the barrels of wine. '*Daughter, you have known since you were born that the day would come when I would get rid of you. You are a useless mouth! A girl child! It would be different if you were a son, but you are not, and therefore you are useless to me! Understand or not understand?*'

'*Understand,*' Lin Li whimpered.

'*Good!*' her father gripped her by the shoulders. '*That boy officer out there is a rare commodity in our world. Did you hear him speak to those ruffians? He is educated and obviously from a wealthy family, therefore he will have honour, that stupid sense of behaviour that only the rich can afford. You will allow him to take your virginity tonight...'*

'Father!' she was horrified.

'Listen to me,' the old man growled. *'Tomorrow morning I shall confront him and declare that he has shamed our house and he will be bound by his honour not to forsake you. I will demand compensation for your lost virginity, and further demand that he meet the cost for a male servant to replace you. He will be caught up in our net like a fat golden carp!'*

'Father,' the girl sobbed. *'Please don't make me do...'*

'Shut up, girl! You will do as I say, or tomorrow night you'll sleep in the snow where I should have put you on the night you were born. It is time you paid me back for all the years I've suffered your uselessness. Understand or not understand?' The girl remained silent, her head bowed. *'Understand or not understand?'* Her father repeated the question ominously and the girl slowly nodded her head, unable to meet his eye.

'Excuse me, my good Captain.'

Lee looked up into a fat cheerful face set upon a rotund body. The man spoke Mandarin, but his accent was pure Cantonese, he was definitely a southerner from the Pearl River. A trader and scoundrel no doubt, Lee thought, as he noticed the man's fine silk gown and delicate sandals.

'I could not help but hear that you are on your way to Nanking,' the man said. *'I am heading there myself on business and wondered if we might have a conversation regarding that fine old city?'*

'You come from where in the south?' Lee asked slipping into Cantonese.

'Aaah, it is good to hear my native tongue spoken so beautifully,' the man sighed and sat down, uninvited at the table.

'Save your flattery for fools,' Lee said to him. *'You come from where in the south?'*

'I meant no disrespect, Elder Brother,' the man replied warily.

'My Captain asked you a question, fat boy!' Soong snarled. *'And I too would be interested to know the answer. Your face seems familiar to me.'*

'*I was born in Canton, my good Captain,*' the chubby merchant said, not looking at Soong. '*But my business interests have required me to move about frequently. I have lived in Hong Kong and Macau at various times in my poor, wretched life.*'

'*What is your name?*' Soong demanded.

'*My humble name is Feng Chan San and I am at your service, my Captain.*'

'*You are the merchant who was sentenced to death for stealing Army produce in Shanghai, true or not true?*' Soong said, pointing an accusative finger at the man.

'*Oh, that unfortunate incident,*' Feng chuckled. '*It was a simple case of mistaken identity. When the Governor of Shanghai realised the error his agents had made mistaking me for a common thief, he apologised personally and allowed me to leave.*'

'*After you covered his palm with silver, true or not true?*' Lee asked, staring straight into the man's eyes.

'*Half true, Elder Brother,*' Feng Chan San shook his head sadly.

'*Half true?*' Lee asked, raising an eyebrow.

'*He also demanded my truck and two new wives I'd recently purchased. I ask you, Captain, who was the real thief in the unfortunate affair, me or that sow-fucking, pig's piss-drinking, son of a lame prostitute and timid licker of men's shafts, the Governor of Shanghai?*'

'*That's a harsh appraisal of a man in a high position,*' Lee laughed. The scurrilous merchant was engaging company, if nothing else.

'*Well, perhaps he doesn't drink pig's piss, I tend to exaggerate,*' Feng smiled mischievously. '*But as for the rest, I have hard evidence that he is so inclined! And his mother's vagina gives off a smell that reminds residents of Shanghai that they export fish!*'

The reclusive Private Waan sprayed a mouthful of wine over everyone at this remark and the whole table fell to fits of laughing.

'*This is Private Soong and Private Waan,*' Lee introduced his men.

'*Feng Chan San*,' the merchant replied. '*Known from Peking to Canton as Four Fingers Feng*.' As he extended his hand towards Lee, the three soldiers could not help but notice that Feng's left forefinger was missing. '*Some say I picked my nose too much as a child. Others say it is still stuck up the arse of a whore in Hong Kong, but the truth is, it simply did not grow. Perhaps some goddess kept it as a sexual aid and at this very moment is fingering herself in the Celestial Kingdom!*'

When their renewed laughter finally subsided, Lee noticed the serving girl, Lin Li, standing by his side. She leant down and whispered in his ear then, after attempting a smile, she moved to the bottom of the stairs leading to the sleeping quarters above the inn, smiled again, shyly this time and went upstairs.

'*If that was not an invitation, my name is not Four Fingers Feng*,' the merchant whispered theatrically to Lee.

'*We have been invited to stay the night*,' was all Lee said and the frown on his face did not call for any further discussion on the matter.

'*And you go towards Nanking tomorrow?*' Feng asked.

'*Yes, if our truck holds out*,' Soong answered. '*It is not a good truck.*'

'*The roads between here and Nanking are jammed with soldiers and refugees*,' Feng said. '*Your truck will be useless. The roads are impassable.*'

'*How do you travel, Ah Feng?*' Lee asked.

'*I go into the city of Suchow tomorrow and will take the train to Nanking. I have arranged a first class compartment and you and your companions are welcome to join me, Captain Kwan.*'

'*That is most kind of you, Ah Feng, but our truck will see us through*,' Lee replied.

'*If the Captain will indulge me for one moment*,' Four Fingers Feng continued in an obsequious tone. '*I believe it will take you two weeks to reach Nanking by road. If you travel with me, you will be there in two days.*'

'*I do not perceive you as a man driven by patriotic fervour,*

Ah Feng,' Lee said quietly as his eyes fixed on Feng's. 'Therefore I must ask why it is you wish to assist three humble soldiers on their journey to a city which will in all probability turn into another Shanghai?'

'That is impossible. Nanking will be an impregnable fortress against the Japanese.'

'Simple geography says otherwise, Feng.'

'How so, Captain?'

'The Yang-tse River approaches Nanking from the south west and curves around the west and north of the city, then runs east to Shanghai. Do you know the game of snooker, Ah Feng?'

'It is a game played on a table by the foreign devils in Shanghai.'

'Consider Nanking as the corner pocket on the table and the Yang-tse River as the edge of that table, then imagine three separate Japanese armies as snooker balls rushing with considerable speed at the pocket?'

'Nanking will become a hell on earth,' Four Fingers Feng whispered.

'Logic suggests there is no other outcome, and so I return to my original question, why are you so eager to help us get to Nanking?'

'You are a Captain in the Nationalist Army, it is my duty . . .'

'Three Fingers Feng,' Lee interrupted.

'Four Fingers Feng,' the merchant corrected.

'At the moment,' Lee went on. 'But if you continue to talk to me as if I am an idiot, you will become known as Three Fingers Feng and then Two Fingers Feng, understand or not understand?'

'I understand completely.'

'How long is it since you spoke the truth?'

'Just before I became a Christian.'

'You are a Christian?' Lee was surprised. 'Which faith do you follow?'

'The one with Jesus in it,' Four Finger Feng's face was a mask of piety.

'Ha!' Lee's hoot of laughter was genuine as he leaned over and took Feng's deformed hand in his own. The immediate pain was excruciating, it caused Feng to stiffen with shock. *'Listen to me carefully, Four Fingers Feng,'* Lee said. *'You have spent too much time in the company of idiots and as a result of this, you have formed the foolish opinion that you are clever.'* Lee increased the pressure on the merchant's hand. *'Look into my eyes, Feng, and tell me what you see.'*

'I see a very, very clever man, Elder Brother,' Feng hissed through gritted teeth.

'Well done, Little Brother,' Lee released the man's hand and placed it on the table top. *'Now tell me truthfully, why did you seek out our company and offer us assistance?'*

Four Finger Feng's hands shook and sweat beaded on his chubby cheeks as he stared into the eyes of Lee Kwan. What manner of boy is this, he asked himself as his mind raced to the only possible conclusion it could make. He has the eyes of a dragon. A very dangerous dragon. Whatever you do don't lie, his brain shrieked, or you're a dead man.

'I have a warehouse in Nanking full of medical supplies,' he blurted out. *'I need a contact in the Army who can put me in touch with the right authority to sell them to.'*

'Ah, the truth at last!' Lee said. *'That wasn't so hard, was it?'*

'No, Elder Brother,' Feng shook his head and tried to smile but the expression only served to remind the others of one suffering from constipation, and they exchanged a glance of amusement.

'And you think the Captain's your man, do you?' Soong sniggered. The merchant had singled out the only incorruptible man Soong had ever met. The Captain would now ascertain the address of the warehouse then drag the man outside, shoot him stone dead and leave him in the snow.

'I am most definitely his man,' Lee declared, and Soong turned to stare at Private Waan in amazement. *'And do not think you two will be left out of the profit sharing,'* Lee said as he smiled at the two Privates. *'Four Fingers Feng,'* he declared, rising from the table. *'Destiny has brought us four*

together this night. We will humbly accept your offer of a ride to Nanking and assist you in your business when we arrive.'

'That is most excellent,' Four Fingers Feng beamed at the young Captain.

'I happen to be a trusted member of General Ch'iang Kaishek's personal staff,' Lee whispered to the fat merchant, then announced loudly, *'I'm off to bed men. I'll see you all in the morning.'*

When Lee reached the top of the stairs, he was confronted by the forlorn figure of Lin Li, standing in the hallway holding a fresh towel in her arms. Lee noticed as she bowed towards him that she'd washed and changed her clothes and the smell of incense hung in the air.

'This is your room, Elder Brother,' Lin Li said quietly and she opened a door for him to enter. *'Your bed is freshly made up,'* she followed him into the room. *'And I have prepared a hot bath for you.'*

A large tub of steaming water sat in the middle of the room, and the raised double bed with cushions and a quilt reminded him that he hadn't slept in a decent bed for months. The window was open to the night air, but with the combination of the steam and the heat from a glowing brazier of coals in the corner, the room was cosy.

Lin Li immediately approached her husband-to-be and began unbuttoning his army tunic.

'That will not be necessary, Little Sister,' Lee said, staying her fingers at his throat with both his hands. *'You may go now.'* He drew her hands away, took her by the shoulders, turned her towards the door and gave her a gentle push.

'I wish to stay,' the girl whispered, turning back to face him.

'What is your honourable name?' Lee asked formally.

'Lin Li,' the girl replied. *'And I want to stay.'*

'Very well, Lin Li,' he replied. *'You may stay if you wish, but I suggest you turn your back for propriety's sake, because I intend to enjoy this bath whether you are here or not.'*

'Thank you, Elder Brother.'

'Perhaps we can discuss Japanese troop movements,' Lee suggested sarcastically as he undressed. *'Are you aware, or*

not aware, that General Nakajima's 16th Division has crossed the Yang-tse River at Paimou Inlet and is heading for Changshu just to the north of here?'

'*I was not aware of that, Captain,*' Lin Li knelt on the floor with her back to him.

'*Well, you should be.*' He placed his foot timorously into the scalding water. '*And so should your father.*'

'*I shall inform him at first light, Elder Brother, and thank you for the information.*'

'Oh God!' Lee groaned ecstatically in English as he sank into the hot water. He rested his head on the edge of the tub and closed his eyes, the steam rising around his face.

'*What is the matter?*' Lin Li turned to him, concerned.

'*Nothing,*' he sighed.

'*You made a strange noise,*' the girl said. '*Is the bath not to your liking?*'

'*The bath is very much to my liking.*'

'*Do you wish me to scrub you?*' Lin Li asked, becoming bolder by the minute. '*I have washed my brothers for years, it would not concern me.*'

'*I will just soak for a while and you may talk to me.*'

'*About what?*' the girl asked, squatting next to the tub. '*I know nothing about the Turnip Heads, as a matter of fact I have never even met one.*'

'*Well, you soon will. General Matsui Iwane's 9th Division is heading straight for Suchow.*'

'*Are they truly as horrible as people say?*'

'*They are not nice,*' Lee answered. He felt very sorry for this pretty young girl. What sort of life must she have had? And what sort of life would she have in a couple of days when the Japanese swallowed up Suchow? '*Is your father truly unaware that the Japanese are only days from his doorstep?*'

'*He says he does not care.*'

'*Then he is a fool. I have heard tell that General Nakajima is a sadist and that the Japanese soldiers are very cruel to civilians. You want to hope General Matsui gets here first. He will be the lesser of two evils, because he is ill with the blood-water disease in his lungs.*'

'*My father is an innkeeper, Captain Kwan,*' the girl replied. '*Innkeepers do not care who drinks their wine as long as they have the money to pay for it and father says the Japanese are rich.*'

'*Lin Li,*' Lee looked at her. '*The Japanese soldiers are violent and evil. You must tell your father to get away from here and take you with him.*'

'*My father cares nothing for me,*' the girl said casually as she picked up a bar of soap and a scrubbing brush and went to immerse them in the bath water.

'*There is no need for you to scrub me,*' Lee said gently. '*I have an idea why you are doing it and it is not necessary.*'

'*I want to do it,*' Lin Li replied, looking him straight in the eye. '*You are filthy, you know? Your uniform smells like a pigsty, I will wash it for you. How long is it since you washed?*'

'*Your father put you up to this, true or not true? And tomorrow morning he will demand money from me, also true?*'

'*True,*' Lin Li said. '*But I will tell him nothing happened.*'

'*Nothing is going to happen.*'

'*But I want it to happen. You are the nicest boy I ever met and it would be a great honour for me to give my virtue to you. The Japanese will only take it if you do not.*'

Lee gave up the argument as the scrubbing brush raked his neck and back. Lin Li's other hand was busy splashing water on his chest and with each stroke, she managed to find the tip of his penis, which was dutifully responding.

'*No more!*' he gasped after several minutes of exquisite torture.

'*There is much more,*' Lin Li said. '*I know what happens between men and women, the walls of this old inn are thin and worn. We should now go to the bed and you should lie on top of me, or get behind me. That is how my father copulates with women, the same as dogs, but most other men I've watched get on top of the women.*'

'*Get me a towel,*' Lee said as he grabbed the girl's hands and held them in his own.

'Yes, *Lord!*' Lin Li broke free and scurried to do his bidding.

'*And do not call me Lord! I am not your Lord! My name is Kwan Man Hop . . .*'

'*The same as the fabled swordsman?*' Lin Li asked as she handed him a towel.

'Yes,' Lee stood up in the tub, wrapping the towel around him, '*but people call me Lee.*'

'*The same as me!*' Lin Li gasped, clapping her hands together. '*I am Li and you are Lee! We were meant to couple. It is the will of the gods.*'

'*Nothing is going to happen.*'

'*But I want it to happen! And so do you!*' Lin Li declared as she pointed at the prominent spike, obvious beneath the towel.

'*Nothing is going to happen, Li.*'

'*You will not have to marry me, if that is what worries you.*'

'*Marry you? Whatever gave you that idea?*'

'*My father said that because you are of noble birth, after you deflower me your sense of honour will require that you marry me to save me from public shame.*'

'*Aah, I see. It is not only money he is after, but a son-in-law to take you off his hands, true or not true?*'

'True,' Lin Li lowered her gaze to the floor. '*If I do not succeed in making you my husband by morning, my father will cast me out into the snow. I am a useless mouth. Understand or not understand?*'

'*I understand,*' he said. '*But your father is right. My honour will not let me shame you.*'

'*Do you not find me attractive?*' the girl looked up at him with eyes full of sorrow. '*Is it my imperfection that disappoints you?*' She pointed to a mole an inch above the edge of her mouth.

Lee smiled down at her. '*You are very attractive, Lin Li, and that imperfection you are worried about is considered a sign of great beauty in countries of the West. The most beautiful women in England and France paint a black dot on their face to make people believe they have a mole such as you have. It is true,*' he nodded in reply to the girl's questioning look.

'*My father says it is a sign that I was an unwanted child.*'

'*Your father is an idiot!*' he snapped. In the morning, he decided, he would break the man's neck. It would save the Japanese the trouble.

'*Will you marry me, please?*' Lin Li asked in a whisper as a tear trickled silently down her cheek.

'No.' He took her hands and sat her on the bed beside him. '*But I will help you. I want you to pack your belongings and be ready to leave in the morning. I will take you to Nanking and find you some work. In Nanking, perhaps you can make a fresh start in life, good or not good?*'

'Good!' Lin Li exclaimed. 'Very good!'

'*Now you must leave, I need some sleep. It has been a long time since I slept in a bed and I intend to enjoy the luxury of it.*'

'*May I stay here, please?*' Lin Li pleaded, reaching her hands out to him as he began to protest. '*I will be quiet, I promise. And I will leave you alone to sleep.*'

'*I do not think that is a good idea, Li.*'

'*Do not send me away, I beg you, my father will suspect something, I know it. And perhaps in the morning you could tell him you are taking me away to marry me?*'

'Ah ha,' Lee agreed. '*I see your point. Very well, you may stay here, and in the morning I will tell your father that I will marry you in Nanking.*'

'*And will you tell him you are rich?*'

'Very well,' he smiled. '*I will tell him I belong to the richest family in the city of Hong Kong where rich men eat fat pork. Good or not good?*'

'Excellent,' Lin Li cried out in delight. '*Truly excellent!*'

龍

'Happy New Year, son.'

'Happy New Year, mother.'

Fireworks lit up the sky over Hong Kong and as ocean

liners, ferries and cargo ships of all nations sounded their horns, people cheered and hugged each other in the streets and sang raucously, the sentimental song of friendship and regret, *Auld Lang Syne*. As the words of the song drifted across the lawn from the ballroom, Elanora and James sang along and when they finished, James hugged her close. 'Happy New Year, Mother,' he whispered into her hair.

High on Victoria Peak, Elanora Escaravelho Merchant kissed her son James on the cheek, surreptitiously wiped a tear from her eye, then turned to gaze at the fireworks on the harbour below. The image of Richard Brewster rose before her eyes, and the pain of their separation claimed her yet again.

Nineteen thirty-seven had proved to be the worst year of her life. She and Richard had been estranged for six months until Robert McCraw had virtually dragged them together for what he had described as 'sanity's sake'. The business and financial affairs of both the Merchant Company and the Society had become a tangled mess, ignored by them both.

In June, McCraw had insisted they meet in the Merchant Company offices to 'sort matters out' and they had done so. The meeting had not been pleasant at first, but as they'd progressed through the items on the agenda of business the old familiarity had settled upon the three of them and after four hours, they'd parted on amicable terms, at least as far as business was concerned. Fortnightly meetings had continued since then, even laughter at an occasional joke had occurred, but neither Richard nor Elanora had ever broached the subject of their personal relationship.

'Let's hope 1938 will be a happy and prosperous year for us all,' she remarked, a little too cheerfully. She turned back to James for an answer, but he was crossing the lawn to re-enter the ballroom where many of Hong Kong society's fairest young women were gathered in celebration. She couldn't blame him, he was young and life should be lived to the full at his age. Why spend New Year's Eve with your mother when the thrills of youth beckoned from within a ballroom?

James had been the rock on which she'd leaned throughout the year. Since his return from England, he'd undertaken tutorage from Quincy Heffernan, as arranged by Richard, and he had surprised all with his application. He had also started work three days a week in the Company offices and, at his own instigation, he'd started on the bottom rung of the ladder. He had moved through successive departments teaching himself the business from the ground up and Elanora had been truly impressed by his ability to learn. According to her spies, however, James' appetite for young women had not waned, it had increased. But he had assured her she would never have cause to question his behaviour, and he had remained true to his word.

Elanora watched him fondly as he entered the ballroom. Heaven help whichever young woman he focused his charms upon tonight. She leaned on the railing and concentrated once again on the view, her thoughts turning to her other boy. How she missed him! By all reports, Lee was in Nanking and she feared for him, desperately. Nanking was under siege by the Japanese and she'd heard nothing from him for several months. He'd written to her regularly from the Military Academy in Whang Po, but since his transfer north to Shanghai, she'd had no word, and her fear for his safety grew daily.

Elanora had tried every maternal wile from rage to tears to stop him from enlisting, but he'd been utterly determined, and when Richard had sided with him on the matter, she'd known that she'd lost. She had hated Richard at that moment. On reflection, she had realised that Richard's reaction had been based upon sheer common sense. Lee had been immovable and Richard had known it, so why give the boy the added grief of separating from his family on bad terms? Richard had been right in that instance, and she was prepared to forgive what she had momentarily seen as betrayal. But there had been a far greater betrayal she could never forgive. He had stolen her sons. He had taken them into the *Gam Loong Tong* and secured their allegiance forever. The boys were no longer hers.

Richard, she thought, and she gripped the railing as her anger and her love for him welled in equal proportion. He had torn her in half with his actions. But over the past six months, since their business meetings had started, she had noted a change in him which, try as she might, she could not ignore. He'd been courteous and kind whenever they'd met, and the looks she'd frequently caught from him had displayed an affection signalling something far deeper than they'd previously shared. Was it possible he'd mellowed during their separation? Had he realised what he had lost? Did he now harbour thoughts of genuine love for her? She wanted to believe it was so. She couldn't help herself, she desperately wanted to believe he loved her. But she would never ask him. She would never go to him. He would have to come to her.

'Happy New Year, Elanora,' Richard said from behind her. She gripped the railing even tighter in an attempt to quell the surge of excitement that rose in her.

She turned. He was silhouetted against the light emanating from the ballroom. 'And the same to you, Richard,' she replied evenly. 'How are you?'

'As of this moment,' his smile was warm in the light from the harbour below. 'I'm in paradise. I'm with the Merchant Mistress, the most beautiful woman in the South China seas. Perhaps even the world.'

'Don't play games, Richard, it's beneath you.'

'It's true. I have never seen a woman more beautiful than you are tonight.'

She gave a wave of her hand, dismissing the remark. 'What brings you here, tonight of all nights?'

'Us, Elanora.'

'Us?' She laughed mirthlessly. 'There is no "us", Richard. You made sure of that.'

'Now you're playing games.'

'How dare you come here and speak to me of "us"?'

'Because if I don't, I'll lose you forever and I couldn't bear that.'

Elanora stood frozen. It was as if the world had stopped spinning. She stared at him, not daring to believe what she'd heard. Was he playing games with her again? Or had what she'd hoped for finally happened? 'I will not be broken again, Richard.'

'I understand.'

'You took my love for granted and shattered the trust we shared.'

'I was a fool.'

'Yes, you were.'

'And I'm here to apologise if you will allow me.'

'On your knees?' She regretted the remark as it left her lips. Part of her wanted to fight, but the sight of him was weakening her resolve.

'Don't mock me, Elanora. I will go only so far.'

'I'm sorry,' she said softly. She found herself staring at the young Englishman she'd first seen all those years ago and the anger ebbed from her.

'May I continue?' he asked.

'Yes.'

'A young Irish woman loved me, years ago,' he said. 'But she died. And for the last twelve months I've had trouble remembering her name.'

'Oh, Richard, don't,' Elanora whispered. 'Her name was Caitlin.'

'That's right, it was. I met her in this very house nearly thirteen years ago. And that same night a beautiful Eurasian woman came into my life . . .'

She held her breath.

'Her name was Elanora. And the depth of her love for me was unfathomable. I never knew until recently how much she loved me . . .'

'Her name was Elanora?'

'That's right. I took her love for granted for many years and finally through my own stupidity I lost it. So I came to the same house tonight to see if she is still here.'

'Her name was . . .?'

'Elanora. If you see her will you tell her something for me?'

'Of course I will.' Her voice was a whisper.

'Tell her I love her.' Richard began walking back across the lawn, then stopped and spoke over his shoulder. 'Tell her my life in Hong Kong, or anywhere else for that matter, will be nothing without her love. Tell her I want to marry her.' He kept walking towards the lights of the ballroom. That's it, he thought, you've played your last card. If she doesn't declare her hand before you reach the ballroom, you've lost. He kept walking.

He was barely five steps from the ballroom doors when she called out.

'Richard.'

He stopped.

'She's right here. Why don't you tell her yourself.'

He smiled, and walked back to her.

龍

'Good morning, Annie,' James said to the newest young member of the household staff as she arrived in the upstairs drawing room with his newspaper. She's a beauty all right, he thought, straight from the rice paddies, in awe of her opulent surroundings and ripe for the plucking.

'Good morning, Master James,' the girl replied. 'Here your newspaper, Sir.'

'Here *is* your newspaper,' he corrected her.

'No, is *your* newspaper,' she replied and James gave up. He was lost in admiration for his mother's patience when teaching English to the servants. God forbid he should ever have to do it.

'*The Merchant Mistress is where?*' he asked in Cantonese.

'*Your mother is on the balcony . . .*' Annie replied.

'*Thank you.*' He took the newspaper from her out-stretched hand.

'*. . . with her lover,*' she finished with a conspiratorial smile.

James gave a puzzled frown. 'Really?' he said, reverting to English, and he strode to the balcony. His expression changed to one of delight. 'Mother,' he gasped in mock horror. 'Whatever have you been up to?' The answer was patently obvious, he thought, as he grinned at Richard and

Elanora, my guess is they've been at it all night!

'Good morning, James,' Richard stood and offered his hand.

'Good? It's delightful, Sir,' he shook the proffered hand vigorously. 'And Mother, you are positively glowing.' An understatement if ever there was one, he thought, as he leaned down to kiss her cheek. James had seen the very expression his mother now wore on many a woman's face, and he knew what it meant only too well. And as for his *Shan Chu*, the black circles under his eyes said it all. My God, but they must have been at it like rabbits.

'Good morning, darling,' his mother replied.

'I must say I could not have asked for a better start to the new year. It's so good to see you both together again. You should never be apart.'

'And we don't intend to be,' Richard said. 'I've asked for your mother's hand in marriage, James, and she's accepted. I do hope her decision meets with your approval?'

'It most certainly does. Congratulations, Mother.' He kissed her again, boisterously this time. 'And to you too, Sir,' he shook Richard's hand again. 'I'm so happy for both of you, and for myself.' He couldn't wipe the grin off his face. 'I've wished you two would marry since I was a little boy. What a shame Lee won't be here to see it happen.'

'He will be,' Elanora said.

'It was the one condition your mother set,' Richard added. 'She wants Lee back home and so do I. I've sent Lo Shi-mon, this very morning, to fetch him.'

'He won't come.'

'What on earth makes you say that?' Elanora asked.

'I know him better than anyone and I can tell you now, he won't come.' He registered his mother's worried expression, and sat beside her. 'Mother,' he continued gently. 'Lee is Chinese.' He glanced up at Richard for support. 'More Chinese than anyone I know. And I can tell you quite frankly, although he'll be as delighted as I am at the thought of your marriage, he will not return from China until the war with Japan is over.'

'But he must . . .' Elanora began.

'You're upsetting your mother, James,' Richard said firmly. 'Lee will do as he is told and return home with Lo Shi-mon, I'm sure of it.'

'Not in this instance, *Dai Loh*,' James shook his head. 'Not even *Ah Lo* will convince him.' He addressed his mother. 'Lee is a grown man, Mother. His heart is in China and that's where he'll stay. You know in your *own* heart what I'm saying is true, don't you?'

Elanora shook her head in denial. 'No. He will come home to me.'

Richard interjected. 'Lee will also come home because the war with Japan is going to embrace Hong Kong and we must prepare for it. He's smart and will realise he's needed here.'

'Embrace Hong Kong?' Elanora's look was one of disbelief. 'Japan will withdraw, Richard. They cannot afford the cost of a protracted war with China, and they would certainly not dare invite the wrath of the British Empire. The war will never reach us here in the south . . .'

'Get your head out of the clouds, woman!' Richard snapped involuntarily. 'Oh, I'm sorry, Elanora, how rude . . . But damn it, girl,' he continued with equal exasperation. 'The war *will* bloody well reach us, make no mistake about that. And when it does Hong Kong must be ready for it. As it stands at the moment we couldn't defend ourselves against a flock of sheep! Decisions need to be made and plans formulated if the Colony is to survive. Lee will know that and he'll come home. Lo Shi-mon will make him understand.'

'I'm sure Richard's right, Mother,' James stroked his mother's forearm. He didn't agree with his *Shan Chu* at all, but then perhaps Richard was only attempting to comfort Elanora. 'I'm sorry for destroying the happy atmosphere. Lee will come home, I'm sure of it.'

Richard was not attempting to comfort Elanora at all. He wanted both James and Lee Kwan in Hong Kong as much as Elanora did, but for his own purposes. He'd been intending to send Lo Shi-mon to Nanking anyway, and the condition she'd imposed on their marriage had given him the perfect excuse.

He breathed in the morning air, enjoying a feeling of deep contentment. He'd played his trump card and won. Elanora would marry him thereby making him the boys' stepfather and guardian. His control, over both her and his little dragons, would be absolute. All he needed was the return of Lee Kwan to complete his coup. Lo Shi-mon's orders were inviolate. Lee Kwan was to return to Hong Kong. His *Shan Chu* demanded it.

CHAPTER FOURTEEN

Lee Kwan buried himself in the pile of rotting corpses as the Japanese soldiers passed within feet of him on their nightly patrol along the wall outside Hanchung Gate. When enough time had passed, he pulled himself free of the putrid pile of flesh and began dragging aside other corpses that he'd used to cover the entrance of a tunnel he'd dug beneath the Nanking Wall. He stopped several times to spit the bile from his mouth as chunks of decaying skin and muscle slid free from the arms and legs of the corpses he was manhandling. Eventually, he uncovered the entrance he was searching for and the twisted face of Private Soong appeared, gagging at the overpowering stink of long dead Chinese soldiers and civilians.

'Hurry, Elder Brother,' Soong said as he gagged yet again, stomach bile dribbling down his filthy face. *'I cannot stand it!'*

'*Shut up,*' Lee hissed, and he pushed one of the last two cartons of medical supplies down the hole into Soong's waiting hands. *'I sometimes wonder if it is not better up here with the dead. At least they don't moan and complain like you, Soong jai. Turn around and start crawling!'*

It had taken Lee and Soong eight days and nights to dig the tunnel. It was more like a rabbit's warren than a tunnel, thirty-five feet in length and just wide enough for one man to crawl through at a time. Laboriously, they'd scraped out earth and rocks and propped the tunnel up with whatever pieces of wood they'd found in Ginling College and other institutions in the International Safety Zone. Bits and pieces of tea chests and the backs from a number of chairs were all that stopped the mighty wall above from crushing them and Lee knew it was only a matter of time before it collapsed entirely. The Nanking Wall, by some strange law of physics, was tolerating them. Perhaps it admires our audacity, Lee thought. Or perhaps the Wall, too, had seen enough pain and sorrow in Nanking and was offering its help in the only way it could; by letting two tiny human beings crawl beneath it.

The Nanking Wall, built by Hung Wu the founding emperor of the Ming Dynasty in the 14th and 15th centuries, was twenty-one miles long, stood forty feet high and twenty feet thick, and its thirteen gates were the only entrances to the City of Nanking. It surrounded the old city completely and many residents had believed it would save them from the Japanese invaders.

And it should have, Lee thought grimly as he pushed the final carton of medical supplies through the tunnel, right on the heels of Private Soong, if it had not been for the appalling incompetence of General Ch'iang Kai-shek and his dithering sub-commander General Tang Sheng-chih. Between them, Lee believed, the two generals had had ample time, men and resources to create a formidable defence, but they'd only managed to set the scene for a military catastrophe.

General Ch'iang Kai-shek had left the city with his wife and advisers as soon as the Japanese had attacked, leaving General Tang with strict orders to 'fight to the death'. Only one day after Ch'iang had departed, members of the International Safety Zone Committee negotiated a ceasefire with the Japanese, and Ch'iang, when informed of the offer, had refused it. He could have withdrawn his whole army without a shot being fired, saving countless thousands of lives, at least temporarily. Inexplicably, three days later, Ch'iang had ordered General Tang to retreat from Nanking. Lee, who had been present when the order had arrived, could not believe his ears. Only three days after the chance of an orderly withdrawal had been ignored, Ch'iang had ordered a retreat that could not possibly be carried out with any military precision. General Tang had seized the opportunity given to him by Ch'iang, and deserted half a million of his countrymen, leaving them to the mercy of the Japanese. He had ordered the retreat, which had turned into a rout.

No, not just a rout, Lee Kwan thought, as he crawled through the tunnel, an unmitigated disaster. He had witnessed the chaos at the enormous Yichang Gate, which led through the Wall to the wharves in the dockside suburb of Hsiakwan and the boats that were the only means of escape across the Yang-tse River. The Yichang Gate, or the Water Gate as it was also known, was jammed with men and vehicles, so much so that it was impassable and he'd watched men make ropes from their trousers and shirts and try to lower themselves down the outside of the Wall. Hundreds fell to their deaths. On the docks in Hsiakwan it was worse. Men fought and clawed each other for seats in the boats, while others clung to the gunwales crying and screaming. Thousands died in the icy waters as they tried to swim for the western shore and others killed their comrades, as they fought over any object that would float and support their weight.

Lee had travelled to the Yichang Gate with General Tang, and witnessed the horrific events from the comfort of a big black sedan car, until finally, he could stand it no more. He'd got out of the car and decided then and there that he'd rather die than take part in what he saw as a shameful and cowardly retreat. He'd glared at General Tang, slammed the car door and forced his way through the tide of human suffering making its way to the docks.

Private Soong and Private Waan, who'd been walking behind the vehicle, had taken one look at their Captain's face and both had known precisely what had transpired. Without a word and barely a glance to each other, they had turned and followed him. Lee's heart had swelled with pride as the two soldiers had walked with him, silently, back into battle.

How many Japanese he'd killed that night Lee could not remember. He'd slaughtered them with bayonet, hands and feet. Street by street, lane by lane, silently, covertly, he and his two faithful men had killed, and Lee's savagery had numbed his brain. All three were drenched in Japanese blood and Private Waan, who'd never killed a living creature in his life,

let alone a man, was crying softly when they found themselves staring at an American flag outside Ginling College in
the International Safety Zone.

龍

The hatred Lee felt for the military incompetence displayed
by General Ch'iang Kai-shek and General Tang Sheng-chih
burned in him, giving him the strength to push onwards and
overcome the mind-numbing fear of being buried alive
beneath the Nanking Wall.

Ahead of him, he heard Soong, who had crawled out of the
tunnel on the other side of the wall, loudly gulping the putrid
night air into his lungs. Lee pushed frantically towards the
glimmer of night sky as a terrible fear of the tunnel collapsing surged through him.

'Jesu! Jesu!' Soong exclaimed in Latin as he lay on the dead
bodies outside the tunnel entrance. Several of the nuns at
Ginling College had been trying unsuccessfully to convert
the old soldier to Christianity and, having picked up the
name of the son of the Christian god from them, he abused
it mercilessly.

'Shhh,' Lee hissed, collapsing briefly beside his comrade. 'I
hate crawling through there too, but there's no need to tell
the whole Japanese Army the location of the tunnel!'

Dead bodies lay everywhere, piled six deep all the way
down the laneway that led to Hanchung Road, from where
the two would make their final dash to the International
Safety Zone.

'Move!' Lee whispered urgently as he hauled corpses over
the tunnel entrance. One of the dead bodies, a girl no more
than ten years old, had a shaft of bamboo protruding from
her vagina. Lee removed it before laying her lifeless frame
over the others. He turned and followed Soong and, together,
they crawled over the hundreds of rotting dead.

At the intersection of the laneway and Hanchung Road,
Lee paused and looked westward at the huge arch that was
Hanchung Gate. Several Japanese soldiers stood around a
drum with a fire in it. They were smoking cigarettes and

stamping their feet to ward off the freezing night air. Lee pushed Soong forward. They'd be all right as long as they remained hidden crawling along behind the piles of dead, which lined Hanchung Road.

Three hundred yards from Hanchung Gate stood the gate of the German Embassy, and once through it they would be safe, but this last stretch was the part Lee disliked most. The Japanese had used kerosene and petrol in an attempt to incinerate the hundreds of dead bodies in Hanchung Road and they'd run out of the fuel. The corpses were half roasted and smelled even worse than the putrefying flesh he'd had to endure elsewhere along the route. As he crawled eastward, the meat from the corpses squelched beneath his hands and knees until his whole body was smeared with half-cooked human flesh.

Two Germans wearing red and white armbands of the Nazi swastika opened the embassy gates as Lee and Soong rushed across the road and fell inside the compound, clinging desperately to the priceless boxes of medical supplies covered in the slime of human remains.

While Lee lay on the cobblestones gasping for breath, another German came down the steps of the embassy, crossed the courtyard and stood smiling over him. The man was completely bald and wore circular horn-rimmed spectacles and he also sported a swastika on his arm.

'Well done yet again, my young friend,' the man said softly in English with a heavy German accent. 'My men will take those,' he gestured to the boxes Lee and Soong were clutching to their chests. 'You are a brave man, Lee Kwan, and a true son of China and my letters to the Fuehrer Adolf Hitler and members of the international press will ring with your praises, I promise you.'

'I'd rather intervention by the nations of the west, Mr Rabe,' Lee answered.

Despite the German's political predilection, Lee Kwan admired the man standing over him more than most men he'd met. John Rabe was an unlikely hero. A German businessman who had lived and worked in Nanking for thirty

362   THE TIME OF THE DRAGONS

years, he was not only a German national and therefore an
ally of Japan, but leader of the Nazi Party in Nanking. His
efforts against the Japanese, as head of the International
Safety Zone, had saved thousands of Chinese lives. When
most other German citizens had left Nanking, Rabe had
decided to stay because he felt responsible for the safety of
his Chinese employees working for the Siemens Company of
which he was in charge. They maintained the turbines in the
city's main power plant, the telephones and clocks in every
government ministry, the alarms in the police stations and
banks, and the indispensable X-ray machine at the central
hospital. John Rabe was determined to protect them.

During the Japanese bombing before the occupation of
Nanking, he had been the main instigator for the establish-
ment of the International Safety Zone. Made up of an area of
two and a half square miles inside the Wall of Nanking, its
borders were lined by white flags and sheets marked with the
Red Cross symbol, and by the time the city fell, it was a
swarming 'human beehive' of 250,000 refugees.

The Japanese behaviour in Nanking became more obvious
and more bestial after the city fell. Thousands of women
were raped and murdered, old people and children were shot
or bayoneted in the streets and countless thousands of
Chinese prisoners of war were taken to secret locations all
around the city and executed. John Rabe became more
incensed as the days passed. He worked tirelessly writing
letters of protest to Hitler and sending details of Japanese
atrocities to the world press, while at the same time doing all
in his power to help the sad mass of humanity crowded
within the Zone.

Lee had witnessed the atrocities first hand. He'd seen men
buried to their waists and then, still alive, torn to pieces by
the Japanese's vicious guard dogs. He'd watched from a
rooftop, horrified, as hundreds of captured Chinese soldiers
and civilians were used for live bayonet practice by the
invaders. He'd even witnessed two Japanese officers carry
out a contest to see which of the two could behead, with a
sword, one hundred Chinese POWs in the quickest time,

while other Japanese officers and troops stood about laughing and gambling on the outcome of the contest.

'I'm afraid you must leave the safety of the embassy, Lee,' John Rabe instructed. 'Take your friend, go out through the rear entrance and get back to Ginling College. You will be needed tonight to watch over the women folk. The Japanese soldiers are bound to try and enter the Safety Zone to kidnap more young girls for their brothels. And wash yourself down with carbolic soap or you will have every disease known to man flowing through your veins.'

'Very well,' Lee lifted himself wearily to his feet. *'Come along, Soong jai.* Goodnight, Mr Rabe, and make those medical supplies last as long as you can, the stocks are dwindling.'

'How much longer can we keep on receiving them, Lee?'

'What's left is still in the ruined temple on the edge of Mo Chou Lake outside the Hanchung Gate, but the Japanese patrols could discover them at any time and there's every likelihood that the tunnel could collapse, so . . .' Lee shrugged.

'Well, just make sure that tunnel doesn't collapse while you and your friend are in it, ja?' The German tried to sound cheerful, but his heart wasn't in it. He knew the grave dangers Lee and Soong faced every night to get the medicines and that sooner or later it would end with the collapse of the tunnel and possibly the deaths of these men. 'You are a brave young man, Lee Kwan, and so too is your friend, Soong. Go my boy, and may God be with you.'

'Thank you, Mr Rabe, and goodnight to you.'

'Oh, and by the way, Lee,' Rabe called after him.

'Yes, Sir?' Lee turned back.

'Happy New Year.'

'What?'

'Happy New Year,' John Rabe repeated as he looked at his watch. 'It's just past midnight, so that makes it 1938!'

'Happy New Year to you too, Mr Rabe.' Lee called in reply.

'Ja. Happy New Year,' the German said to himself as he watched the boy walk into the shadows of the darkened embassy.

Lee and Soong made their way back to Ginling College, trudging wearily through the several streets that made up the International Safety Zone. All about them thousands of refugees lay in the streets and in burnt-out houses, existing on rats and cockroaches and whatever rice was rationed out among them by the International Committee, and The Red Cross. People lay dying, dirty, diseased and lice-ridden, exposed to the freezing night air, and they stared with glazed expressions at Lee picking his way through them. They didn't know that he was called, by the *gwai loh* on the International Safety Zone Committee, 'The Angel of Nanking'.

As the two men entered the college doors, Minnie could smell them from fifty feet away, where she stood at the door to her office. Lee stopped in the hallway and gave her a haunted look.

'God protects his angels,' she said softly in the silent hall, then she inclined her head, indicating he should go upstairs to the wash girl.

Minnie smiled at old Soong who stood forlornly in the hallway watching his captain climb the staircase.

'*Dragons of the Celestial Kingdom cannot die, true or not true?*' Soong asked, and his tired eyes asked for her agreement.

'*True, Ah Soong,*' Minnie replied in Cantonese. '*And you are also one of those dragons. You will truly live forever, my friend, in the hearts of your countrymen. You and your captain. Now go and wash.*'

'*Goodnight, Elder Sister,*' Soong said.

'*Goodnight, Elder Brother,*' she replied respectfully, and she watched him shuffle off towards the rear of the building.

'Minnie?' Lee called to her from the top of the stairs.

'Yes?' she turned back from her office door.

'Happy New Year.'

'Oh my God, is it?'

'As of one hour ago.'

'Happy New Year, Lee.'

Lee Kwan walked slowly to the end of the first floor hallway and entered the laundry. He passed several copper tubs and a series of sinks and opened the door to a smaller room, entered it and closed the door behind him

Wilhelmina Vautrin, or Minnie as most people called her, was an American schoolteacher who'd left her home in Illinois as a young woman and made a life for herself in her adopted homeland of China. She was head of the Education Department and dean of studies at Ginling Women's Arts and Science College and one of the very few foreign women who'd refused to leave the city prior to what was being referred to as 'The Rape of Nanking' by the international press.

Minnie was a tall, handsome woman of fifty-one years with a shock of long dark hair streaked with hints of grey. As a young college graduate, she'd joined the United Christian Missionary Society and had been living in China for over twenty years. She spoke fluent Chinese in any number of dialects, had a noble heart, and the courage of a lioness. Many times since the fall of Nanking, she'd risked her own personal safety to rescue others, particularly young women, from the rampant and vicious Japanese soldiers, causing the Chinese to name her 'The Living Goddess'.

With most of the faculty members having fled the city upon the approach of the Japanese, Madam Vautrin was now acting head of the institution. She laboured to prepare the campus for female refugees and assisted with the evacuation from the city of countless wounded soldiers. To disguise their identities, she burned their military papers and uniforms in the college incinerator. Under her direction, furniture was moved into attics, safes were emptied, dormitories were cleaned and valuables were wrapped in oilpaper and hidden.

By the second week of December when the city was under complete attack, Minnie Vautrin opened the gates of Ginling College to women and children. Each day, from eight o'clock in the morning until six in the evening, she would stand at the college gates and accept refugees. By the night of 15 December, two days after the fall of Nanking, when the Japanese soldiers were at their bloody worst raping and killing civilians in an orgy of violence, three thousand, mostly young women and children, were crammed into Ginling

College grounds. On that same night, as despair washed over her, an angel drenched in blood had come to Minnie Vautrin.

'I have come to offer what help I can,' the young man had said as he entered her office.

The soldier had turned out to be Captain Lee Kwan and Minnie had thanked God for His gift of the young officer every night since.

Late that same night Minnie had questioned the boy, for that's all he was, a child of seventeen or eighteen dressed in the uniform of a captain in the Kuomintang. At first she'd not believed he could possibly hold a commission, but he'd shown her his written orders directing him to join General Ch'iang Kai-shek's personal staff. Then, as the night proceeded into the small hours and she'd incinerated the Army papers and uniforms of her young captain and his two companions, she'd learned that Lee spoke Mandarin, Cantonese, English, French, Portuguese and Latin. He'd been educated in Hong Kong and Britain and was quite an authority on Japanese history and customs. But the greatest gift he'd brought to the Zone was not discovered until several nights later when she'd had Lee and the other two medically examined by Dr Wilson.

Dr Robert Wilson had arrived at Ginling College at 11 o'clock in the evening after completing a mammoth surgical stint at the University Hospital. He'd looked drawn and exhausted, but he'd come at Minnie's request.

Wilson, a skinny, balding, bespectacled man, had been born in Nanking and raised by a family of Methodist missionaries. After graduating from Princeton University he had returned to China, and when all other doctors in Nanking had finally fled, he had remained, for the city of his birth and boyhood held a special place in his heart, alongside the love he had for the Chinese people.

'Your English is excellent, Lee,' Wilson had remarked as he held a stethoscope to Lee's back. 'Where did you study it?'

Lee spoke openly and easily with the doctor, and after Wilson announced him healthy, the two had became engrossed in discussion, enjoying each other's company. And then Wilson had complained of the lack of medical supplies in Nanking and the frustration of his attempts to have the Japanese supply any.

'I know where there are medical supplies in Nanking,' Lee had said.

'There are no medical supplies in Nanking.' Minnie Vautrin's interjection had been abrupt. 'If there were I would know of them.'

'There is a man called Four Fingers Feng, who has a warehouse full of medical supplies, if he hasn't sold them to the Japanese already.'

The following day, through the chaos and killing in the streets of Nanking, Lee somehow managed to find Feng and, after a brief one-sided discussion, the merchant accompanied him to the International Safety Zone Headquarters at Number Five Ninghai Road.

In front of John Rabe, Dr Wilson and other founding members of the International Safety Zone Committee, Four Fingers Feng had offered a fortune in medical supplies for the treatment of refugees and not asked for a single penny in return. It was a most magnanimous offer, greeted with warm applause by all concerned except Minnie Vautrin, who stared suspiciously at Lee Kwan after it was made.

Every night since, Lee had disappeared into the darkness and invariably came back with medicines which he delivered to Robert Wilson, and every night, as Minnie Vautrin worked tirelessly among the refugees, she had anxiously watched the clock praying for his safe return. Minnie knew that the supplies lay hidden well outside Nanking. One night when Lee did not return, she'd expected the worst until he entered her office at dawn and told her that he'd moved the remaining supplies into a bombed-out temple on the edge of Mo Chou Lake, just outside the Wall. In case anything happened to him, she would know where to find them, he'd explained.

Minnie was aware that, with his old companion Soong, Lee had dug a tunnel under the Wall beside Hanchung Gate directly opposite the lake. Apart from all the other seemingly impossible tasks he performed, Lee would go regularly to the lake to collect medicines and would return to Ginling College stinking of death and decay. And each night, when he returned, he would go straight to the wash girl's room and she would bathe him.

龍

Lin Li stared up from the mattress upon which she lay. She looked thin and worn, but Lee noticed her hair was freshly washed and shined jet-black as it flowed over her shoulders and down the centre of her back. She wore a clean cotton dress that Minnie Vautrin had given her.

'Are you well or not well?' he asked as he took off his stinking clothes. He always asked the same question upon his return, although he knew there would be no reply. Lin Li had not spoken since he'd found her two weeks earlier, lying prostrate on the steps of Nanking University Hospital.

God! Was it only two weeks? Lee asked himself. It seemed a lifetime ago.

龍

On 1 December when they'd arrived with Four Fingers Feng at the Nanking Shanghai Railway Station, Captain Lee Kwan had approached an officer he'd known well in Shanghai. The Major, a doctor, had told Lee he could employ Lin Li at the University Hospital and accommodation would be found for her. Lin Li had agreed and, in high spirits, had left with the doctor after arranging to meet again with Lee in a few days when she'd settled in.

She had been given a bed of her own on the floor of an enclosed verandah of the hospital and a clean white smock to wear while she toiled each day cleaning the hospital wards. She shared the verandah with a number of other girls and although the work was long and tiring, she'd settled into a routine and was quite happy to be on her own and employed. Even a city under the threat of invasion was a better option than her father's inn. And the friends she made, very quickly, were all country girls like herself who'd come to the city under similar circumstances. At night they would sit huddled together on the verandah for warmth and they'd talk and giggle as they told stories of their various misfortunes, until the Triage Nurse would come and scold them for their noise.

Lee had not visited her as arranged and at first she'd thought he might have been injured or killed, until one afternoon, she'd seen him travelling in a big shiny black car. One of the other girls had said that the man in the car with Lee was General Ch'iang Kai-shek, and Lin Li realised that Lee must have important work to do and she'd scolded herself for being selfish. Why would an important officer in the Kuomintang come to visit a simple wash girl? She had been foolish to believe it in the first place and she'd decided to forget her beautiful young officer. But each evening, alone in her bed, her thoughts were filled with images of Lee Kwan, her champion.

Late on the night of 14 December, the Japanese soldiers had entered the hospital. Lin Li had watched, horrified as they shot and bayoneted wounded Chinese soldiers in their beds and smashed furniture and machinery throughout the wards. She'd been one of fifty wash girls rounded up at gunpoint and herded into the central courtyard. What had happened to her was only a vague memory, now deep in the darkest recesses of her mind. She had been raped over and over again by the Japanese, then thrown, unconscious, bleeding and bruised into the corner of the courtyard.

Lin Li had awoken several times during the night, but had no idea where she was. The smell of blood and vomit filled her nostrils and she'd drifted back into unconsciousness. In the morning, she'd gained consciousness and become aware of a heavy weight pressing on her back and she'd struggled to free herself. Eventually, when she'd managed to stand, she saw that that she'd been lying beneath a pile of dead bodies. Her friends, the other wash girls. All of them had been shot or bayoneted. Lin Li had been overlooked in the killing spree, the soldiers having thought her already dead.

She'd staggered into the hospital and somehow walked through a crowd of Japanese officers in the foyer without being given a second look. A young officer had called out to her and when she did not respond, he'd raised his pistol and shot her. The bullet had grazed her skull rendering her unconscious. She'd come to her senses as the old woman carried her, with the strength of a man, into the Safety Zone. The old woman's face looked strangely like that of Lee Kwan. She'd vaguely recalled seeing the American flag flying on the flagpole in front of the building they'd entered.

Inside Ginling College, Lin Li had watched the moving mouths of Lee Kwan, in his old woman's disguise, and a tall foreign woman. Both of them had been speaking to her, but she'd been unable to respond. The *gwai loh* had jabbed her with a needle, which made her sleep, but when she'd awoken, her ability to speak had escaped her. She was mute, and she realised that she was now destined to spend her life silently reliving that terrible night.

Lee Kwan came to visit her every evening, but as much as she wanted to speak with him, she could not. On the third night, she realised that, although she could not speak, her sense of smell remained unimpaired. Lee stank of blood and decay and Lin Li knew the smell only too well. She could not have her wonderful Captain smell like that. With that smell on him, he would be living in hell, just as she was destined to do. The awful realisation struck her. Her demons were outside Ginling College and they were seeking her, and each night Lee Kwan went out to do battle with them in order to keep them from finding her. And from raping her again. This is why he comes to me with their decaying flesh all over him, she told herself. She knew immediately that she must wash him to keep him safe.

Tonight, as she did every night, Lin Li rose from her mattress and, as her Captain stood silently watching her, she undressed him. Following the simple ritual she'd developed for his protection against the demons, she took his clothes to the laundry outside her little room, boiled water in one of the big copper pots and soaked them. Then she washed and rewashed his body until it was clean.

It is the least I can do, she reasoned, for the only man who has ever cared about me and who protects me from the demons every night. I will wash him every day and every night for the rest of my life if need be.

He was her Captain Lee Kwan. He was her anchor, her traumatised mind managed to convey to her, her one tenuous hold on sanity. Without him, she knew madness would come and she would be left all alone to sink into the world of the demons forever.

Lee breathed slowly and deeply as she bathed him, the sickly stink of Nanking, despite Lin Li's efforts, still in his nostrils. The city is a nightmare, he thought, a hell on earth strewn with thousands of unburied bodies. People were saying as many as two hundred, perhaps even three hundred thousand people had been killed. Lee knew that deep trenches, dug weeks before by Chinese soldiers as defences against Japanese tanks, were being used as mass graves. On his nightly travels he'd seen the Japanese throwing bodies into the trenches and forcing Chinese POWs to shovel dirt onto their comrades, before they in turn suffered the same fate. But thousands of dead remained, rotting in the streets.

Typhoid and cholera were rife, new cases being reported every day and the International Safety Committee had ordered anyone found showing signs of the diseases to be thrown out of the Zone. It was cruel but necessary, and Lee felt sorry for John Rabe and his foreign friends who'd been forced to issue such drastic orders.

Lee saw his life as a wheel that turned full circle every twenty-four hours. The repetition of his days culminated each night with a trip through the tunnel and back, then a ritual washing from Lin Li. When would it ever end?

Early one morning, about two weeks later, he was in the basement completing his daily hour of concentrated Shaolin disciplines, when the door swung open and Minnie Vautrin came down the stairs carrying a box of bloodstained bandages for the incinerator.

'Good morning, Lee,' she said, putting down the box and opening the burner door. 'There's someone here to see you.'

'To see me?' Lee was surprised. 'Who is it?'

'I'd say it's your 426,' Minnie replied knowingly.

'My what?' He feigned bewilderment.

'Don't patronise me, Lee,' Minnie gently admonished him. 'I've lived in China for many years. That one up in my office is a senior official in a triad society or my name's not Wilhelmina Vautrin.'

'I'd better go upstairs,' Lee muttered.

'Not so fast, young man!' Minnie stopped him in his tracks. 'Your self-proclaimed friend up there could be anyone, a Japanese spy for all I know, so I'm not taking any chances.' Minnie pulled a .455 calibre Webley revolver from her large apron pocket and waved it under Lee's nose. 'If he's not who he says he is, use this!'

'There won't be any need for that,' Lee smiled and pushed the hand holding the gun down by her side. 'I can take care of myself.'

'Not with the likes of this one,' Minnie shook her head emphatically. 'Judging by the size of the calluses on his knuckles, I'd say he's been punching rice bags since the day he was born.'

'Why don't I take a look at him first?'

'That's a good idea,' she nodded. 'And I'll be right behind you with this!' She waved the gun around again for effect and then headed for the stairs.

The man smiled at Lee, then placed his palms together and bowed politely.

'Lo Shi-mon! What on earth are you doing in Nanking?' Lee asked as he threw his arms around his old friend and teacher.

'More to the point,' Minnie interrupted. 'How on earth did he *get* into Nanking?'

'My friend is a resourceful man, Minnie.'

'Your friend,' Lo Shi-mon agreed. 'And also your brother-in-law. And *you* will soon be an uncle.'

'No!' Lee exclaimed, delighted. 'That is wonderful news. I always hoped you would marry Wai-Ling. It was something I wished for when I was little. And she is with child you say?'

'It will be born in the spring. April.'

'Excellent news. Minnie?' Lee turned to the tall American woman. 'This is Lo Shi-mon and he is from my home, so there is no need to shoot him.'

'Shoot me?' Lo raised an eyebrow.

'Call me overcautious,' Minnie put the gun back in her apron pocket, 'Nanking has that effect on people. I'm pleased to meet you, *Ah Lo*. We'll get acquainted later, for the moment I'll leave you two to talk. But be careful Lee, the *Lo Baat Tau* have a habit of bursting in here unannounced.'

'Waan is in the garden keeping watch as always, Minnie. He'll warn us if they come near.'

Minnie nodded and left.

'*How is Blue Star?*' Lee asked eagerly in Cantonese. '*And James and Elanora?*'

'*Blue Star sent me to get you, Lee.*'

'*What is wrong?*'

'*It is a trivial concern compared to what I have seen in Nanking,*' Lo said. '*Never in my life before have I witnessed such madness. I have read things in the Hong Kong papers and heard rumours, but nothing could have prepared me for what I have seen in here.*'

'*If you multiplied what you've read, heard and seen by ten thousand you still would not realise the horror of this place. The Turnip Heads are the most vicious soldiers in the world and my hatred for them has turned me into a butcher. I work at night for the "Goddess" Vautrin getting medical supplies, but the madness of killing runs thick in my veins and I kill for pleasure.*'

'*I came through the city last night, Lee,*' Lo Shi-mon said as he sat on a settee and shook his head sadly. '*And I understand your anger and distress, but to kill for pleasure is the first step down the pathway to insanity. Human beings tend to move in the direction of their thoughts. If the mind is dominated by hatred it can only lead to greater hatred. Revenge leads to more revenge. Killing leads to more killing. True or not true?*'

'*I don't know any more.*'

'*Have you forgotten the teachings of Shaolin?*'

'They do not apply here in Nanking. Nothing applies in Nanking except death! Besides, do not the teachings of Shaolin say assist the unfortunate, protect the weak and fight those who seek to oppress others?'

'You have done enough, more than enough. You must leave here with me for your own sake, Little Brother. You have seen too much too soon and it has made you ill. You must rest and restore your spirit, then return later and take up the cause of China with renewed vigour.'

'I might leave Nanking eventually, Elder Brother,' Lee sat beside the older man. 'But I will never leave China. The Middle Kingdom is at war and I am Chinese, I cannot leave. You have witnessed the distress of our countrymen. I cannot possibly leave.'

'The Merchant Mistress is terrified something will happen to you, Lee. She struck a deal with Blue Star, which requires that you return to Hong Kong with me.'

'In this college alone,' Lee said, rising to prowl the office restlessly. 'There are three thousand women and children and each night as many as fifty young girls are kidnapped by the Japanese and taken to brothels. In the Zone itself, there are over a hundred thousand sick and starving and I alone can get them medicines while the stocks last. Every night I kill Japanese near the boundaries of the Zone, hoping it will dissuade others from entering it.' Lee stared at Lo Shi-mon. 'If you can give me a reason strong enough to ignore these things and return to Hong Kong, I will do so without further discussion.'

Lo Shi-mon was silent for some time. 'I cannot,' he finally answered.

'You see my predicament. I cannot return to Hong Kong,' Lee sat behind Minnie Vautrin's desk. 'Not while one Japanese remains on Chinese soil,' he said. 'My loyalty to the Society of Golden Dragons is strong within me, but I will not let it override my love of country. Is that not why the original Hung Mun societies were created?' he leaned forward and looked earnestly at Lo. 'Were they not created by men who loved China and wanted to rid it of the invaders from the north? Is that not the very basis of the teachings of Shaolin? Overthrow the Ch'ing, Restore the Ming! I am in the very city where Hung Wu founded the Ming Dynasty and it is crawling with invaders! True or not true?'

'Enough. All you say is true,' Lo Shi-mon quietly answered. 'You have put your case very eloquently. I cannot argue with you, my concern is only for you, while yours is for a greater good. You speak like a true man of the Ming and I am proud to know you, Kwan Man-hop. Part of me feels I should stay with you, but I cannot, my loyalties lie in the south. I am not a man of the Ming. I am not a man of China. I have known the Middle Kingdom under the Ch'ing, I have seen it under Republican rule and I have read its history well and I cannot love it like you, Lee.'

'How can you say that, Elder Brother?'

'Because I was born a Chinese of peasant stock and I know how it feels to fall on my hands and knees and put my forehead in the mud. I never knew freedom until I travelled to Hong Kong as one of the Men of Wei Hai Wei, recruited by the Hong Kong Police, and lived in the city where rich men eat fat pork. In my youth I saw Imperial oppression and I have observed also the tyranny of warlords and the fanaticism of the Kuomintang. And before that for hundreds of years, long before the Ming, the Middle Kingdom has known no peace. It is either attacked from without or torn from within and its people have known nothing but war and subservience. I have no passion for China as you do. I live in a city run by crazy foreigners and the even crazier Cantonese, where I bow only if I wish to show respect. I am not ruled by a family with a certain birthright, or those with an army at their back to enforce my subservience. I have the Society of Golden Dragons and I live in the small house of your grandfather with my wife, your sister Wai-Ling and I can do and say what I please. And my children will have those same rights.'

'Thomas Jefferson would have loved you,' Lee said in English.

'Who is this foreign devil you speak of? Does he live in Hong Kong?'

'No,' Lee laughed. He stood and walked around to the front of the desk. *'He was an American.'*

'The Vautrin woman is an American, true or not true?'

'True,' he perched on the edge of the desk. *'The Americans are passionate about the rights of the individual, Elder Brother. They have a law that says all men are created equal.'*

'What more can be said? It is the best law there could possibly be.'

'Perhaps,' Lee acknowledged. *'Perhaps when this war with Japan is over, China can have that law too. That's another reason why I must stay, Ah Lo. Understand or not understand?'*

'I understand, I will convey your thoughts to Blue Star, but he will be very angry.'

'My loyalty to the Golden Dragons Society cannot be questioned, but my country is at war and I must fight. If Blue Star were a young man in my position, he would make the same decision I have made, do you agree or not agree?'

'I agree, Little Brother,' Lo Shi-mon nodded.

'Even the fact that he saved my life, by riding a dragon through fiery skies, will not make me return until this war is over. Tell him I said that, Ah Lo.'

'I will tell him.'

'Blue Star is an Englishman, he will understand. The English have fought many wars over the centuries to protect the sovereignty of their little nation and I am doing no less for mine.' Lee clapped his friend on the back. *'Do not worry, Ah Lo, I will write letters for you to take back to Hong Kong to Blue Star and Elanora. They will explain why I am unable to return.'*

'I am not going back to Hong Kong,' Lo Shi-mon stated flatly. *'Not immediately.'*

Lee looked at his teacher for several moments then smiled. Any discussion of Lo Shi-mon's thought processes on why he'd decided to stay would be a waste of breath. With anyone else he would raise an argument in protest, but Lo Shi-mon had made a decision and Lee knew if he attempted to debate the matter, he would be told to mind his own business.

'*Then I must find another way of delivering the letters,*' Lee said finally.

'*You will find a way,*' Lo replied. '*You are resourceful.*'

'*Right,*' Lee could think of no reply. '*Well . . . you must tell me all about Hong Kong and how things are with Blue Star and Elanora.*'

'*Blue Star and the Merchant Mistress are to be married.*'

'*That's wonderful news!*'

'*The Merchant Mistress wants you to be present at the ceremony.*'

A mental image of his beautiful guardian came to Lee's mind, he was happy for her. '*We both agree that is impossible, Ah Lo, but the thought of their marriage fills me with happiness. Elanora will accept my absence,*' he grinned. '*Now tell me more. What of James and the Society?*'

'*For a bowl of rice, Kwan Man-hop, I will tell you everything you wish to know.*'

'*Ha!*' Lee slapped his thigh. '*Come to the kitchen, old friend, and I'll see what I can do.*'

龍

Darkness was beginning to settle over Nanking by the time Lee and his new brother-in-law had talked themselves to a standstill. At intervals throughout the day, they'd been joined by Minnie Vautrin and old Private Soong for *yam cha*, when tea and bread had been shared and much had been discussed. Lee had written letters to Richard Brewster and Elanora, and the two were once again alone, discussing Lee's nightly dash for supplies, when the doors burst open and a terrified Lin Li staggered through them into the old parlour. Trembling, she stared at Lee, her eyes imploring him for help.

'*What is it?*' Lee asked, but the girl turned and lurched back out of the door.

'*Waan jai!*' Private Soong declared from the hallway as Lee and Lo Shi-mon followed Lin Li out of the room. '*The Japanese Military Police have kidnapped Waan jai.*'

'Lee!' Minnie Vautrin yelled, racing in from the back garden and nearly knocking Lin Li over. 'They've got Waan!'

I sent him to watch over Lin Li while she hung washing in the back garden. They were Kempeitei, obviously after Lin Li. She escaped into the kitchen, but by the time I got out there they were through the gate and into Chungshan Road. Waan must have tried to intervene, so they took him.'

Lee ran out through the kitchen into the rear yard. A washing basket lay upturned and clean clothing was strewn about the garden.

'*There is blood here,*' Lo Shi-mon said as he knelt near the iron gate built into the high stone wall, which, in more peaceful times had guaranteed security. '*And look!*' He pointed at the open gate. The lock had been forced until it had broken free of the stonework.

Lee dropped to his knees beside Lin Li who was pawing in the dust and smearing dirt on her face. '*It's all right, Little Sister,*' he said softly to the deranged young woman. '*They are gone. No one will hurt you.*'

'*Come with me, Lin Li,*' Minnie Vautrin gently raised the girl to her feet, put her arm around her and escorted her to the kitchen door.

'*Instead of yelling for help, the fool tried to protect the girl himself,*' Lee said.

'*He is young, Captain,*' Soong replied. '*He feels he does not contribute. He always asks if he can come with us to collect the medicines and I always say no. He feels inadequate.*'

'*There is much blood on the stones near the gate,*' Lo Shi-mon said. '*I fear your friend has been wounded badly, unless the blood is Japanese and I doubt that.*'

'*I told him so many times to be careful!*' Lee shook his head in exasperation.

'*I told him too,*' Soong nodded. '*But sensible advice is wasted on the young. He was careless and got himself kidnapped.*'

'Well,' Lee gave a shrug. '*We'll just have to kidnap him back!*'

'*Aaaiiiyaah!*' Soong put his hands on his head and spun around on one heel. '*Why did I know you were going to say that?'* Soong shook his fists at the sky as he called on the troublesome black dragon of Chinese mythology. *'Wu Loong, you black son of a slut! This is your doing! May you copulate with the Whores of Hell and lose your penis!'*

'The Kempeitei will have him in their guardroom,' Lee said to Lo Shi-mon, ignoring the ravings of old Soong. *'It's just down Chungshan Road where it meets Chungyang Road.'*

'With all due respect, Elder Brother,' Soong pleaded. *'You are talking about the Kempeitei Headquarters!'*

'So?'

'Military Police Headquarters!'

'So?'

'It's full of Military Policemen!'

'Don't worry so much, Soong jai.'

'In fact, it's very full of Military Policemen!'

'They will not be a problem, Soong.'

'I would go so far as to say it is an infestation. The building is infested with Military Policemen.'

'It is not your concern, Soong!' Lee snapped at the old soldier to shut him up. *'You will not have to go there. Good or not good?'*

'Not good,' Soong said indignantly. *'What's wrong with me?'*

'Shut up, Soong,' Lee turned to Lo Shi-mon who was inspecting the damaged gate.

'First we must secure this gate,' Lo said.

'It's a bit late for that,' Lee replied bitterly in English. 'The horse has already bolted.'

'That does not mean the horse will not return,' Lo argued softly in English. He saw the pain and anger in Lee's eyes and added reassuringly. 'It will be night soon, Lee. When it is dark we will go together and get your friend. But I fear we may be too late.'

'Then I'll get his body back. I won't have him put into a mass grave or fed to the dogs. I won't let those bastards torture him and adulterate his body in some sick ritual for their amusement.'

'If that is what it takes to ease your pain, then that is what we will do,' Lo said. *'Bear in mind, Little Brother, for*

whatever revenge you achieve tonight, someone will suffer reprisal tomorrow. That is the way of the conqueror and the fate of the vanquished.' Lo Shi-mon looked Lee directly in the eye then walked off towards the kitchen door.

They found the body of Private Waan Lok-pui not one hundred yards from the rear gate of Ginling College. It was naked, riddled with bayonet wounds and the penis had been severed and stuffed in his mouth.

Another two hundred yards on the opposite side down Chungshan North Road, the Japanese Kempeitei Headquarters was lit up like a Christmas tree. It was a three-floored, triangular building, shaped by the angled intersection at which it stood. Light flooded from every window and Soong had not exaggerated the number of soldiers and Kempeitei inhabiting it.

Lee looked up from the mutilated body of his young friend and stared at the headquarters with hate-filled eyes, he was trembling with fury, every fibre of his being screaming for retaliation.

'Revenge is not the answer,' Lo Shi-mon placed a hand on Lee's neck.

'Then what is?' Lee asked bitterly, trying with little success to control his rage.

'There is no answer to war, just as there is no answer to inhumanity of any sort. We came to recover the body of your friend Lee and we have done so. Let us take him back to the College and see that he has a decent burial.'

'No!' Lee would not be thwarted. *'I will kill every Japanese I can find tonight.'*

'And tomorrow, other Japanese will come and kill your friends,' Lo said, his voice soft, but his hand tightening considerably on Lee's neck until the young man winced at the pain. *'Control your anger, Little Brother. Let the pain I am inflicting wash away your thoughts of revenge.'*

'Aah!' Lee gasped, trying to squirm free of the older man's grip. *'I'm going to kill every Kempeitei in that building,'* he hissed through gritted teeth, at the same time sinking to his knees as paralysis overtook the muscles down his left side.

'*Still your mind,*' Lo murmured. '*Allow reason to take hold of your thinking process.*'

'*They deserve to die,*' Lee mumbled as unconsciousness crept over him.

'*I agree,*' Lo said firmly and he let go of the young man's neck.

'*What?*' Lee asked, the blood rushing back to his brain.

'*I agree with you that they deserve to die, but I do not believe you should murder them. It will make their generals order reprisals against those in the Safety Zone.*'

'*I am sorry, Teacher, I do not understand. A moment ago you were . . .*'

'*Tomorrow morning,*' Lo interrupted. '*If the Japanese discover that a large number of their comrades in the Kempeitei have been murdered, there will be big trouble, true or not true?*'

'*True, but . . .*'

'*Tomorrow morning, if the Japanese discover that their whole Military Police Unit died during the night, that would be another matter. True or not?*'

'*You mean . . .*'

'*I mean if there was a terrible accident, a tragedy of immense proportions, it would cause much consternation and grieving among the Japanese, but it would not call for reprisals against those in the Safety Zone.*'

'*Like if the place burnt down?*' Lee asked.

'*Or blew up,*' Lo pointed between the buildings opposite. '*Do you understand, or not understand, the meaning of that sign?*' Lee looked in the direction Lo was pointing, and there stood a string of railway carriages with signs painted on them that any soldier, of whatever nationality, could not help but identify. The carriages were munitions trucks.

'*Let us give your friend respect,*' Lo said. '*We will take his body to the American woman. She has a kind heart and I know she will ensure that he travels to his ancestors with dignity.*'

龍

The North China Railway line that runs south from Nanking for a thousand miles, to Canton and Hong Kong, lay not two hundred and fifty yards from the Ginling College rear gate. It began its winding journey down along the Yang-tse River from the port suburb of Hsiakwan, less than a mile north of Ginling College. It ran parallel with Chungshan North Road and crossed Chungyang Road, right where they intersected, immediately outside the former railway construction building used by the Japanese as headquarters for the Military Police.

The two disciples of Shaolin sat on a rooftop fifty yards from the police building observing the comings and goings of the police patrol units and other activities fifty feet below, in the railway compound that served as barracks and offices. For two hours, after they'd carefully broken into one of the munition carriages, they transported kegs of Japanese gun-powder, hand grenades and three-inch mortar shells up onto the roof. For another hour, they'd walked back and forth across a steel gantry, used in peacetime to support a travers-ing crane and which now stood idle and rusting at the end of the yard, to the top of the police building. They'd moved stealthily, like black cats, all over the roof of the Kempeitei building, depositing the explosives in the eaves and wherever they could hide them.

'We have just created the biggest firecracker Nanking will ever see, Elder Brother,' Lee whispered to Lo Shi-mon. 'Now how are we going to set it off?'

'We will not have to,' Lo replied.

'Please, do not confuse me. It is freezing up here on this roof.'

'We will be asleep in our beds. The explosion will wake us up tomorrow morning and we will rush out into the street, shocked and confused.'

Lee stared at his companion. 'I am confused right now.'

'The Turnip Heads will set it off for us.'

'Now I am perplexed, Ah Lo. The experience is the same as being confused.'

'Observe, please,' Lo pointed down into the yard below.

'Japanese soldiers?' Lee asked cynically.

'No,' Lo pointed again. '*An incinerator.*'

'Aaah,' Lee murmured. '*I am enlightened, Elder Brother. Forgive me for doubting your wisdom in matters of death and destruction. Please continue.*'

'*A steel plate covers the top of the furnace and my nose discovered it has often and recently been used for cooking. On top of it sits a large urn full of water. What is the first thing a soldier desires on a cold morning?*'

'Hot *water*,' Lee answered. '*To make tea and wash the sleep from his eyes.*'

'*Soldiers rise early, usually about six o'clock, true or not true?*'

'*True.*'

'*For the water to be boiling when they rise, one soldier will be under orders to light a fire beneath it at about four o'clock, when all the other soldiers will be inside the building asleep, true or not true?*'

'*True.*'

'So,' Lo Shi-mon continued, and Lee smiled at his cunning. '*Notice how high the furnace chimney rises up the side wall of the building, it nearly reaches the wooden eaves of the roof. Observe that those eaves are burnt black from the flames that spout each morning from the chimney. I am surprised the building has not burned to the ground before this!*'

'*So all we have to do is get the flames from the chimney to reach the explosives!*'

'*Exactly!*'

'*How do we do that?*'

'*We block the downpipes and fill the gutter beneath the eaves with petrol, then we drench your happy-jacket and dangle it from the gutter into the top of the chimney.*'

'*Why my happy-jacket? Why not your cotton shirt?*'

'*In war, Little Brother, some sacrifices must be made,*' Lo patted Lee on the back.

'*We don't have any petrol. There is no petrol in all of Nanking.*'

'The Japanese have petrol,' Lo pointed into the floodlit compound at a row of army vehicles parked against the far wall. '*I will get the petrol and meet you on the roof top.*'

'*It's bright as day down there, Ah Lo, you will be seen by the sentries.*'

'*Have you forgotten all I taught you?*' Lo Shi-mon's glare was censorious. '*When a man looks, what does he see?*'

'*The eyes only see what the brain expects to see,*' Lee automatically recited the Shaolin principle he'd been taught since childhood.

'*When covert movement is necessary, what do you do?*'

'*Become as one with the elements around you.*'

'*And . . .?*'

'*Be black as night, or white as light. Wear the environment as a cloak.*'

'*Perhaps these lessons have become simple children's rhymes now you are a big man?*'

'No, *Teacher!*' Lee could feel the scorn emanating from the older man. '*That is not true!*'

'*Then show respect.*'

'*Yes, Teacher,*' Lee replied, humbly.

'*Good,*' Lo nodded. '*Now calm your mind and concentrate.*'

The two men stood and stepped out onto the steel gantry that stretched across the railway compound. Like wraiths they moved easily across it while, just fifty feet below, bored Japanese soldiers stood on sentry duty, completely unaware of their existence.

They paused in the darkness directly above the sloping tiled roof of the main building and Lo Shi-mon pointed to the guttering above the incinerator chimney and pushed his two clenched fists together, indicating they would meet there soon.

Lee nodded acknowledgement and dropped to his haunches to wait as Lo Shi-mon continued along the gantry to a point directly above the row of parked army vehicles. Lee watched his teacher drop silently onto the roof above the vehicles, then onto the top of a truck and onto the ground. He continued to watch in awe as his mentor moved, quite openly, towards two sentries who were guarding the trucks.

Although he was in clear light, the sentries were unaware of his presence until he stood in front of them. Then before the shock of an intruder appearing before them out of nowhere could sink in, they both lay lifeless on the ground.

Lo Shi-mon pulled the two dead soldiers into the shadows behind the truck. He looked about quickly, counting fifteen sentries at other strategic points within the compound, none aware of what had occurred. He gazed up into the darkness looking for Lee on the gantry, but the boy was an apt pupil, Lo could see nothing but the dark steel structure against the night sky. Satisfied, he took a bayonet from one of the dead sentries and moved towards his next target, a soldier asleep on a chair beside a stack of five-gallon jerry cans.

Private Akiro Takada of the Motorised Regiment, 16th Division, Japanese Imperial Forces closed his eyes and willed his mind back to his small village on the island of Honshu. He saw the fishing boats bobbing alongside the wharf and the sun sparkling off clear blue water. He saw his children at play on the foreshore and his wife's hands at work repairing fishing nets, strung out to dry in the warm afternoon breeze. Then he heard the hiss of air as it left his lungs and a roaring came into his ears. He opened his eyes and realised that his throat had been cut. Why? He wanted to ask the man who stood in front of him, but the roaring noise increased, then stopped.

Lo Shi-mon looked up from the dead body. A sentry was staring directly at him from thirty feet away, a puzzled expression on his face. Lo held the dead Japanese in his seated position, leaned over the body and beckoned to the sentry, who approached casually, unaware of the danger.

'Takada, you old fool,' the sentry said, walking up to his comrade. 'Got yourself a Chinese to suck your cock, have you?'

Lo Shi-mon turned with the speed of a snake and struck the sentry under the nose, driving the cartilage into the man's brain, killing him instantly. He caught the soldier's body and moved back behind the truck, dropping the dead Japanese with the other bodies, then looked out apprehensively from under the truck. There was no outcry from within the compound, but Lo Shi-mon sat frozen for a full two minutes before he moved again.

Thirty yards further along the wall stood a large fuel tank on a trailer. Lo donned the Japanese sentry's helmet, slung a rifle over his shoulder and crossed back to where Akiro Takada sat slumped in his chair. He picked up a jerry can and walked slowly through the shadows to the petrol tank. Opening the spigot, he gazed about casually as the jerry can filled. Several sentries looked directly at him, but no one challenged him, because the eyes only see what the brain expects to see.

High in the darkness, Lee Kwan watched the drama being played out below. And he watched with amusement, despite the danger of the situation. He could see Lo Shi-mon quite clearly, and yet the man appeared invisible to the Japanese soldiers. A master of Shaolin was at work.

Lo Shi-mon picked up the jerry can full of petrol and walked back along the row of trucks until he was next to a steel stanchion which, when he climbed it, would bring him up to the main roof not far from where Lee sat, immediately above the incinerator.

Minutes later, Lee watched as Lo scurried across the roof beside him before daring to whisper, '*Black as night, white as light.*'

'*A simple trick,*' Lo whispered in return. '*Only to be used against simple minds.*'

'*I have blocked the downpipes at each end of the roof and the fuse is in position,*' Lee said, pointing to the ripped remains of his happy-jacket tied around the guttering and extending in a thin strip down into the incinerator chimney.

Lo Shi-mon nodded, pleased with his pupil. He drenched the happy-jacket with petrol then upturned the jerry can and watched the gutter fill with petrol.

龍

Minnie Vautrin awoke to the sound of fire alarm bells ringing not far from the College. She glanced at her watch: it was five fifteen in the morning. She dressed quickly.

Private Soong stood in the hallway outside her office, while young women from the College gathered in the parlour, huddling together, fearful of what the sound might be.

Minnie raced down the stairs. '*What is happening, Ah Soong?*'

'*I have looked from the roof, Mistress,*' the old soldier replied. '*It appears the Japanese Military Police Building is on fire.*'

Lee Kwan, Minnie noticed, was conspicuous by his absence. Usually, at the first sign of trouble Lee would be up and on guard, but in this instance he was nowhere to be seen. Minnie was filled with a terrible foreboding.

'*Where is Lee Kwan?*' she snapped at Soong.

'*I don't know, Mistress.*'

'*Well, find him,*' she said fiercely. '*And his friend Lo Shi-mon.*'

The first explosion, when it came, was the loudest noise Minnie Vautrin had ever experienced. She heard the back windows in the College imploding, she watched books fly from bookcases, standing lamps crash to the floor and framed pictures fall from their wall hangings. The whole building trembled for several seconds as dust and mortar from the ceiling showered down over everything.

Minnie shook her head, trying desperately to clear the ringing from her ears. Throughout the college, women and children ran screaming in all directions and Private Soong was running around in circles with his hands over his ears shouting 'Jesu! Jesu!' for all he was worth. Another explosion caused the front doors of the College to fall off their hinges onto the front verandah. 'Jesu! Jesu!' Private Soong yelled, dropping to his knees.

Amid the chaos and confusion, Minnie looked up to the first floor landing and saw Lee Kwan and Lo Shi-mon.

'What in God's name have you done, Lee?' she whispered.

龍

General Matsui Iwane, Supreme Commander of Japan's China Expeditionary Force, sat astride his chestnut stallion and surveyed the ruins of the Military Police barracks and offices. There was nothing left but a pile of bricks crowned with the twisted steel girders of a traversing crane, which had stood over the compound. It is a sign, he thought, a sign from Heaven. His over-zealous officers were being repaid for the atrocities they'd committed in the name of the Emperor, atrocities he did not have the power to prevent.

Matsui, ostensibly in command of the Japanese Army, had in fact lost control of his forces with the arrival in Nanking of Prince Asaka, a cousin to the Emperor Hirohito. Asaka had aligned himself with General Nakajima, Commander of the Japanese 16th Division and as a result, the bestial, perverted Nakajima, with the apparent consent of the blood royal, had ordered the mass murder of tens of thousands of prisoners of war and equally as many civilians. Matsui had been powerless to intervene.

We have been punished for our sins, Matsui thought as he stared at the devastation. He coughed into a handkerchief and felt red phlegm from his tubercular lungs spill onto his chin.

'Colonel Tagawa!' Matsui said loudly as he wiped away the offending spots.

'Sir,' the colonel approached the general's horse and saluted.

'What is the body count?'

'Three hundred and thirty-nine so far, but we're still counting, Sir.'

'Have you completed your investigation?'

'It was simply a fire, General Matsui,' the colonel replied reverently. 'It started at the incinerator on the side of the building and spread quickly to the sleeping quarters and then into the Armoury. It would appear that the men of the Kempeitei had been stockpiling explosives. Soldiers have a habit of doing that, Sir. The Armoury exploding must have set them off as well causing the devastation you now see, General.'

'So it was an accident, is that what you're saying?'

'Yes, General.'

'Then inform General Nakajima and Prince Asaka of your findings and tell . . .'

'I have already done so, Sir.'

'You've what!' Matsui snapped.

'Prince Asaka is of the royal household, Sir,' Colonel Tagawa replied. 'I was ordered by General Nakajima . . .'

'Very well,' Matsui said. 'Now, if you will, convey my best wishes to the Prince and the General and say that I concur with your findings and will say so *officially* in my report to Tokyo. The incident was nothing more than a tragic accident, and there will be no reprisals against the Chinese.'

'But, Sir . . .' the Colonel stuttered.

'There will be no reprisals! That is an order!' Matsui roared, bringing on another cough. 'Just this once, Colonel, there will be no reprisals, do you understand?'

'Yes, Sir!' the Colonel saluted smartly.

'There have been enough reprisals,' General Matsui said, as he turned his horse and allowed the animal to pick its way through the scattered debris from the explosion. He thought briefly of his men caught in the blast, and then his eyes fell on the hundreds of rotting Chinese corpses littering Chungyan Road. 'There have been enough reprisals to haunt us forever,' he muttered to himself. 'And when what has happened here is revealed to the world, Japan's shame will be complete.'

CHAPTER FIFTEEN

The Latin Club is an absurd name for a Hong Kong night-club, James Merchant thought idly to himself, as he sat at his usual table with his usual friends drinking his usual cocktail. It was Saturday night and he and his friends were 'howling', which was the latest expression from the States that any young, 'with it' socialite used when going out for the evening. He looked around the table of eight. They were dressed to the nines, the men in white tie and tails and the women in the very latest evening gowns from Paris. They were all laughing a little too gaily and imbibing a little too freely in their bid to be noticed as the wild and willing young jazz set of Hong Kong.

The jazz band was excellent, but James couldn't say so. They were Chinese musicians and, to his friends' way of thinking, only second rate impressionists of American jazz. The piano player, in particular, played in the style of the great Albert Ammons, James' favourite boogie and blues man, but he doubted his friends would even know the black musician's name. And the Chinese female vocalist was sensational. She was singing in faultless English and was good as any of the American girls he'd heard on record.

He looked across the table at Winifred Constance, his current girlfriend as far as Hong Kong society was con-cerned. She winked at him and pursed her lips in a kiss and James smiled back with a distinct lack of enthusiasm. Winnie was a stupid, empty-headed girl, who irritated him in the extreme. She'd been born in Hong Kong, the only daughter of a well-known colonial banker and was terribly, terribly

English. Winnie spoke no Cantonese, despite having lived in the Colony all her life, apart from three years of finishing school in Geneva, and she talked of nothing but 'home' as she called England. James let her intimate to her friends that they were 'a couple', but he did so for one reason only. Winnie was becoming an expert at fellatio.

When he'd first escorted her to the Merchant Company Ball, James had discovered, in the summerhouse of his mother's home, Winnie's sexual frustration. She was a virgin on the verge of exploding. She'd gone crazy as his fingers had brought her to a tumultuous orgasm, but she'd flatly denied him sexual gratification. In a perverse act of revenge, he'd pretended he was genuinely interested in her. He knew beyond all doubt that Winnie intended to be a virgin on her wedding night, so he'd wooed her and taken her to parties and slowly but surely led her to believe they were intended for one another. He drove her into sexual delirium at every opportunity and never once sought anything from her in return. Then, as he'd anticipated, one night, drunk on orgasms, Winnie had suggested she 'relieve' him, to use her word for it. James had feigned ignorance in matters sexual and Winnie had shyly suggested that they experiment with one another for their love's sake. James had shyly agreed.

Their sexual encounters left Winnie more besotted with him than ever. Never had she known such wicked, yet harmless, bliss and she applied herself diligently, loving James' groans of encouragement and adopting every tentative suggestion he proffered. He was her love slave, she decided, and she determined to keep him under her spell until he could not live without her ministrations and begged her to marry him. James Merchant was the most eligible bachelor in the Colony and she had him right where she wanted him. In the meantime, their blissful sexual encounters could continue unabated.

James caught Winnie's eye and the message he transmitted across the table was unmistakable to her. She smiled at him seductively, recognising his proposal, but hoping to put him off for an hour or so while she soaked up some of the racy glamour of the club. Then the familiar fire started between her legs. The mere thought of his hands on her made her tremble. The titillating knowledge that within minutes she'd be groaning in ecstasy caused her heart to flutter, and she licked her lips, staring back at him through half-closed eyes as he rose from the table.

'Not leaving already, are you, old man?' Dougie Withers, one of James' few close friends said. 'A bit early, isn't it, old thing?'

'I'm just going outside for a bit of fresh air,' James replied, never once taking his eyes from Winnie's.

'Think I might join you,' Dougie started to rise. 'Bloody hot in here, eh?'

'That won't be necessary, Doug,' James placed a hand on his friend's shoulder and Dougie, sensing something was afoot, allowed himself to be gently forced back into his seat.

Winnie watched James move through the nightclub to the curtained doorway, which led backstage. He turned and gave her a look before disappearing.

'Will you excuse me for a moment?' Winnie said distract-edly. She stood, her legs barely supporting her weight. Her knees trembled and she felt the rush of heat between her thighs intensify as desire overwhelmed reason.

'Off to the powder room?' her friend, Jane Onslow asked.

'Yes,' Winnie answered breathlessly. 'Would you order me another drink, Jane?' She registered the smirk behind the glass as Jane sipped her cocktail demurely.

'Don't want any company, I suppose?'

'No, I'll only be a moment.'

'I wouldn't bet on that.' Jane licked the moisture from the rim of her glass lasciviously and gave Winnie a knowing look.

Jane Onslow knew full well what was going on. After all, she played the same game with James Merchant now and then. Unlike Winnie, Jane had realised very quickly it was just that to James Merchant. A game. James was a sexual animal, he radiated sexuality and Jane had been unable to resist him. She still couldn't, but she knew there was no future with

James Merchant, for her or any other woman. She continued to play the game with him, however, for her own sexual pleasure. No one could play the game quite like James.

Backstage, James stood in the half-light of the wings and looked out at the jazz band. He'd tipped the stagehand to disappear for ten minutes and he waited behind some packing cases for Winnie to arrive.

'Are you completely and utterly mad?' Winnie gasped as she joined him. 'Let's go outside into the alley, this is too public, James.'

In answer, James grabbed the girl and forced her against the packing cases. He kissed her passionately and felt her instant response. God, how I love women, he thought. He had Winnie right where he wanted her. She was helpless. Slowly, he raised the hem of her skirt, his fingers moving with the skill of an expert.

'Oh, James,' Winnie gasped. 'We can't, not here.' Then she groaned as her legs opened allowing him access.

On stage, the beautiful Chinese girl was singing 'Love Me Or Leave Me' and as she worked the room, her eyes caught a movement in the wings. A handsome young man stared at her from behind the band's packing cases. He was gazing at her, pure lust in his eyes, and the energy flowing from him made her falter momentarily with her lyrics, bringing a glance of surprise from the band leader.

Winnie leaned against the cases and closed her eyes. The soft caress of James's fingers was turning her body into liquid fire. Feelings of ecstasy flooded through her and she bit her lip to stop herself from calling his name out loud.

Shirley Wong sang 'Love Me Or Leave Me' like she'd never sung it before, the young man's gaze all but burning her skin with its intensity. Her uncle, the bandleader, realising something special was going on, took the song into a third chorus.

James stared at the beautiful young singer. His eyes undressed her until she stood naked on the stage, in his mind he laid her down on the floor and entered her. He imagined himself thrusting into the warmth of her and he felt her cling to him, groaning ecstatically.

Winnie Constance's knees gave way at the force of her orgasm and she sank to the floor. She struggled frantically with James' trouser buttons until his penis sprang free. She stared at it, mesmerised, took it in her hand and greedily engulfed it with her mouth. With her free hand she sought herself and massaged roughly. Orgasms began to hit her almost instantaneously. She grunted her lust around him, and as he ejaculated, another orgasm shook her body into a state of bliss.

The young man closed his eyes and for a moment his face held an expression of pure ecstasy, he opened them and his smile touched Shirley Wong's very core as she reached the end of her love song. She held the last note, wringing it out for as long as she could, shocked at the physical effect the young man was having on her. She staggered and held onto the microphone stand as the nightclub patrons fell momentarily silent, then instant applause broke out and the audience rose to its feet, cheering and whistling her performance.

In the wings, Winnie Constance gathered herself together and glanced about furtively before announcing to James that she'd see him back at the table.

Shirley Wong came off the stage to thunderous applause and stopped in front of the young man.

'*Will you meet me tonight?*' James asked.

'*Yes,*' she said.

'*Where?*' His eyes didn't leave hers.

'*Anywhere you say.*'

'*Star Ferry terminal, two o'clock.*'

The girl nodded as her uncle and the other jazzmen came into the wings, chattering all at once and patting her on the back. Shirley Wong stared at the curtain through which the young man had suddenly disappeared. He was a coloured wolf, of that she had no doubt, and her body hummed with desire.

龍

It was late that same evening as Richard Brewster ran across Ice House Street through the drizzling rain to the front doors of the Merchant Company Building. He hated Hong Kong winters, but thank God February was coming to a close and soon the warmer weather would return. He leapt up the stairs and burst into the front foyer showering the ancient night porter Mr Wing with rainwater as he pulled his trench coat from over his head, swirled it in matador fashion and folded it over his arm.

'Goo' evenin', Blue Star *Sing Sang*,' the old porter gabbled in his personalised form of Chinglish, as Richard called it. Mr Wing was extremely proud of the King's English he'd butchered regularly for fifty years. 'Merchant *tai tai*, she no here!' he announced emphatically.

'Mrs Merchant is not here,' Richard corrected the old man and realised instantly he'd landed himself in trouble.

'I know!' the old man declared. 'I jus' tell you dat.'

Richard squinted at the wall for several seconds and prepared himself for the war of logic he was about to encounter. 'She is somewhere else?' he asked, silently kicking himself for not simply asking where Elanora was. Conversations with Mr Wing unnerved him. When he tried to talk with idiot simplicity he only made things worse. If he spoke in Cantonese, Mr Wing would lose face because he'd opened the conversation in Richard's mother tongue. The fact that they could converse in fluent Cantonese was no longer an option.

'Of course! I am here, you are there,' Mr Wing pointed at him. 'But Merchant *tai tai* must be somewhere else! How can it be otherwise?'

'Where is she?' Richard asked.

'She come back *yat goh jung tau*. She say you must waaaiii' here for her,' he sang the verb.

'She'll be back in one hour?' Damn it, he thought, I've done it again.

'I know!' Mr Wing declared emphatically, regarding Richard as if he were an idiot.

'Is anyone else here?' Richard asked, meaning McCraw, whom he'd called to attend the meeting in Elanora's office.

Mr Wing looked around the empty foyer and wondered whether Richard was temporarily insane. But he was polite, he smiled and said nothing.

'I mean is anyone upstairs?' Richard sighed.

'*Ho doh yan!*' Mr Wing replied, happy to have a sensible question to answer. 'Many people, *Dai Loh!* Merchant Company people they do *gung fu*. They do work. All day, all night! They do commercee,' he nodded, pleased to be able to use his new word. 'Commercee' meant work, he'd recently discovered, although why two words were needed for the same thing he had no idea. He felt very sorry for people who had to learn English. Fortunately it wasn't a problem for him, he'd been speaking it for fifty years or more and understood its complexities.

'No, no, no,' Richard smiled politely. 'Is anyone in the Merchant *tai tai's* office?'

'Mac Law,' the old man said.

'Thank you, Wing *Sing Sang*,' Richard said. 'I will use the *sing gong gei*. Go to first floor.' God Almighty, he thought as he crossed to the elevator, he's got *me* speaking Chinglish now. Wing Mun smiled in return and bowed slightly. He watched his friend *Blue Star* go to the 'up down machine' as Chinese logic demanded the elevator be called. *Blue Star* must be drunk, he thought. The 'up down machine' is already at ground level, which, Chinese logic demanded, was the first floor. So, how can *Blue Star* take it to the first floor when it is already at the first floor? Sometimes, Wing thought, *Blue Star* appears to be very stupid, especially when he speaks in his native tongue. But he is rich and powerful. How can a man become rich and powerful if he is stupid? The Gods in Heaven bestow their gifts upon mortals in the strangest ways.

Richard smiled as he stood in the elevator. East would never meet West, he thought, not completely. He'd been in Hong Kong thirteen years and the converse logic of the two colliding cultures never ceased to amaze him. Hong Kong was an anachronism, a place apart, which simply didn't care what the rest of the world thought of it. It went on through fire, rain, feast and famine, engrossed in the business of commerce, or 'commercee' as old Wing Mun pronounced it.

He closed the doors and the safety gate, then pushed the lever and, as he began the interminable wait until the machinery decided to operate, he thought, not unkindly, of his father. Old Binky Brewster was gravely ill. The telegram he'd received that morning from Geoffrey Brewster, his cousin in London, had said 'come at once' and that telegraphic phrase meant only one thing. Well, it's about time, old boy, he thought. Seventy-five was a good innings. Many a man would be glad to have experienced three quarters of a century.

Richard was aware of his imminent inheritance. There was a lot of money somewhere in England, and a large estate, both of which would soon be his, and the thought of it annoyed him. The last thing he needed was money, he had already amassed more than he'd ever need, and then there was Elanora's wealth to boot. All his inheritance would mean was more financial headaches. Fortunately, his father had retired and sold most of his assets in newspapers, mining companies and the textile manufacturing industry, so for Richard it would only be a matter of controlling the family estate.

He had seen his father only twice in the intervening thirteen years since he'd been thrown to the wolves of the Far East. The first time had been in 1929, when Binky had demanded he return to discuss the family fortune, which had experienced a hiccup during the Wall Street Crash. He'd gone home, had a fearful argument with his father at Hallowdene Manor, and left the next day. The trip had achieved absolutely nothing. The second occasion had been a dinner party. Two years ago, Binky had passed through Hong Kong on a cruise liner in the company of some young widowed duchess whose name now escaped Richard's memory. The old villain had been sowing the last of his wild oats, Richard recalled with a wry smile of amusement. He and Elanora had dined with the old man and his young duchess, aboard the cruise liner on Hong Kong Harbour.

龍

'Your woman's a rare beauty, boy,' his father had declared as the two of them stood on the stern promenade deck of the vessel, smoking cigars before joining the women at dinner.

'By Christ there's nothing like a cross-breed for good looks,' Binky slapped him on the back and looked out across the harbour.

Richard studied his father's profile. Binky had aged a great deal in the nine years since their last disastrous meeting at Hallowdene. His hair and moustache were snowy white and his hands trembled uncontrollably. Binky Brewster had become an old man. The bluff exterior was still there and the booming voice, but Binky had finally grown old.

'I don't suppose we're likely to see each other again, Richard,' his father said.

'No,' Richard replied, 'I don't suppose we will.'

'I never liked you as a boy, you know? You were soft. You were weak, like the runt of a litter.'

'No, I wasn't.' Richard kept an even tone determined to avoid an angry exchange, but what his father said next knocked the wind right out of his sails.

'I know that now, lad,' Binky looked his son straight in the eye. 'I realised it the moment you told me to go to hell at Hallowdene and stormed out.'

'I travelled all the way to England to discover you'd lost a measly ten thousand pounds on the New York Stock Exchange. What did you expect, my condolences? Ten thousand pounds wouldn't cover your yearly cigar bill.'

His father laughed. 'I thought it was more.'

'You had me travel half way around the world, thinking you were a penniless wreck on the verge of suicide. I was not amused.'

'I wanted to see you,' there was a softer tone to Binky's voice. 'I wanted to see how you'd turned out. Whether or not my gamble had paid off. And I was glad to see it had.' He looked his son up and down. 'Hong Kong has been the making of you.'

'I've been lucky,' Richard said.

'Hmmm,' Binky puffed on his cigar. 'Perhaps. But from the information I've received, over the last several years in particular, you seem to have an inordinate amount of money and influence for a public servant. And not only in Hong Kong, but in London too. A company with which your name has been associated has been the subject of parliamentary debate on more than one occasion. Does the name Dragon Import & Export ring any bells with you?'

'Have you been spying on me, Father?' Richard smiled humourlessly.

'Surely a father has the right to enquire after his only son's welfare?'

'I wouldn't have thought you cared enough to bother.'

'You stand to inherit a lot of money when I die, Richard.'

'I don't want, or need, your money.'

'So it would seem. Dragon Import & Export is making money hand over fist by all accounts. Are you sure you've nothing to do with it?'

'I have never heard of Dragon Import & Export.'

'Ha!' Binky snorted. 'By God, I'd hate to meet you across a boardroom table, boy. But fair enough. I lost the right to know your business many years ago. I'll not intrude now.'

Richard wanted the conversation ended. 'Shall we join the ladies?'

'Not just yet,' the voice was suddenly old. 'I have something to say.'

'Then say it, Father.'

'It's no accident I'm aboard this ship. When I learned Hong Kong would be one of its ports of call I booked passage. I allowed people to believe I was making a fool of myself chasing after the young woman we're to dine with, but the truth is, I viewed it as one last opportunity to see you.'

'It's a bit late in the day for hearts and flowers, don't you think?' Richard said coldly.

'I'm dying, Richard.' It was a matter of fact statement. 'I have a terminal form of cancer. The doctors say I have a year or two left and I wanted to clear the air between us.'

'I'm very sorry.' It was all he could say. He looked at the old man and felt a twinge of emotion. Was it pity? He couldn't properly define it.

'I don't want your pity,' his father said as if he'd read Richard's mind. 'I just want your attention. I'm not going to apologise for being a bad father, what's done is done. I wanted you to know that I loved your mother very deeply, despite what you may have thought. And her death was the most traumatic event in my life. I decided then and there that I would never allow myself to love anyone again. And that included you. No, let me finish,' the old man said as Richard attempted to speak. 'You reminded me so much of her that I couldn't bear to look at you. So I threw you into boarding school and ignored you. I should have loved you, Richard, I know that now, and for failing to do so, I apologise.'

'Your apology is accepted, shall we join the ladies?'

'You're a cold one, aren't you?' Binky stared at his son.

'Yes,' Richard replied stiffly. He was feeling anything but cold, his emotions were in turmoil, he wanted his father to go away.

'That's what's been on my mind since our last meeting at Hallowdene,' Binky continued. 'I realised then that you'd become hard and remote, just like me. And I wanted to tell you, face to face, you understand . . .?' He didn't wait for a reply. 'There is no need to be that way, Richard. It doesn't make you a man. You were born with a soft and gentle nature, just like your mother, and I should have nurtured that in you. Instead I pushed you into military service, then sent you to the Orient to fend for yourself. And now, God knows what you've become. I have no idea.'

'And I'm afraid you never will, Father,' Richard said. 'But I would like to say thank you. For what, I'm not quite sure, but thank you, anyway. It was decent of you to come all this way and say what you did. Your words were brief, but eloquent, and I know they came from your heart, so . . . thank you,' Richard smiled at the old man. 'And now I really think we should join . . .'

'Just one more thing,' Binky interrupted. 'You are my sole heir, Richard, and although I know you're not interested in my money, I'm afraid it will be yours whether you like it or not. Do with it what you will. But I would ask one favour of you?'

'What is that?' Richard threw his cigar butt overboard.

'Hallowdene,' Binky too, threw his cigar over the railing.

'I'm afraid I've ignored it. It's now a bit of a mess. I'd like you to restore it after my death. It's been in our family for generations and I'd like to think it was well maintained. It's all I'll ask of you.'

'Consider it done,' Richard said.

'Will you always stay in Hong Kong?' Binky asked as they walked through the saloon door to join the women.

'Yes,' Richard replied. 'Hong Kong is my home.'

龍

And she always will be, Richard thought, as he stepped out of the elevator cage into the first floor hallway. How was it Charles Higgins had described Hong Kong? 'She's a wildcat,' he'd said. 'A slut of the first water. Learn her ways and, above all, show no fear, then she's yours. You can make her your mistress.'

'My mistress,' Richard said aloud and his thoughts flew to Elanora. 'And my wife to be.' He gave a short laugh. Elanora had always symbolised Hong Kong to him. Her capricious mix of East and West was the very epitome of the place. And now he was marrying her. Hong Kong had become more than his mistress, he thought with a smile. Hong Kong was about to become his wife.

Richard suddenly realised he was looking forward to his marriage, and to being a proper husband and father. Father, he thought fondly, as he considered James and Lee. Yes, he was looking forward to being a real father to the boys. Although, he corrected himself, the boys were certainly not boys any more.

James Merchant was fast becoming a businessman. He was smart and ruthless, and Richard was sure that, when he'd learned to control his libido which, like most young men his age, was currently out of control, he'd no doubt become *tai pan* of his family company and rule it with an iron fist. He would one day prove a greater asset to the Society than Richard had ever imagined.

And Lee. Lee Kwan had travelled a long way from the little boy in the burning godown. He was an officer in the Kuomintang fighting a war against the Japanese. When a letter from Lee had arrived, postmarked Hankow, stating he would not return to Hong Kong, Richard had expected to feel anger, but the eloquence of Lee's argument had moved him. The Dragons would have to do without Lee for the time being.

It seemed to Richard only yesterday that the boys had been climbing all over the walls of the Merchant home like little monkeys. Had it really been thirteen years since Lo Shi-mon had taken them under his wing? What an idea that had been, Richard congratulated himself. Lo Shi-mon had made no idle boast when he'd said he could turn them into warriors; the boys were the most powerful weapon in the Society's arsenal, he thought proudly.

Richard was visited with occasional pangs of guilt when he thought of Sir Herbert Billings, MP and the fact that he'd ordered his two *siu loong* to murder the man when they were barely seventeen years old. But was it really guilt, he wondered, or was it fear? He recalled with great clarity Elanora's explosion when she'd discovered the boys were members of the Society. She would become positively incendiary if she knew they had murdered upon his command. But that was what Lo Shi-mon had trained them for after all, Richard reasoned. They were assassins. They were sworn to the Society of Golden Dragons just like him. Billings' death had been necessary, vital, to the Dragons' continued existence, and so he'd been eradicated, it was as simple as that.

Sir Herbert Billings, Richard mused as he walked towards Elanora's office. The damned man wouldn't go away, at least the damned enquiry he'd started wouldn't go away. He felt in his coat pocket for the waterproof wallet which had been delivered to him that very morning.

'Hello, laddie,' Robert McCraw's voice boomed. 'You're late, it's gone ten o'clock and I'm afraid I've taken to Elanora's port.' He waved a glass of the fortified wine in front of Richard's nose.

'Don't mind if I do,' Richard hung his coat on one of the wall pegs in the office and headed for the sideboard. 'It would appear Elanora's running late, Robert.' He poured himself a port from the decanter. 'I'm afraid we'll just have to be patient,' he said, raising his glass to the big Scot. *'Yam sing!'* He drained the glass in one gulp and poured himself another.

'Och no, laddie,' the Chief Inspector shook his head. 'I'm too wise to fall for that *yam sing* business. *Yam jing* is my motto, just a sip. Never a full glass in one go.'

'You're getting old, McCraw,' Richard laughed. 'What's the matter with you?'

'Wine makes the world spin slower and the head spin faster, laddie. When you reach my age you'll no doubt agree with me and until then you can suffer alone.' He sipped his port. 'Well, what's so important that you've dragged me out on a wet, miserable Saturday night such as this? I could have been at home curled up with my *amah*.'

'Why don't you marry Li Ping?'

'I've asked her, but she won't agree to it. She thinks it'll turn her into a *gwai loh*. And don't try to change the subject. What trouble have you got us into this time?'

Richard pulled the waterproof wallet from his inside pocket, threw it onto Elanora's desk and crossed to the gas fire burning in the grate.

'What's that?' McCraw asked.

'That is a wallet full of personal papers in the handwriting of Stephen Hemmings.'

'Where did it come from?'

'His dead body,' Richard said, drying his trouser cuffs at the fire.

'That was eighteen months ago, how come they've turned up now?'

'That crazy old pirate just remembered he had them,' Richard said. 'His younger twin Napoleon delivered them to me this morning. And you're not going to like what they suggest.'

'And just what do they suggest, laddie?'

'Sit down and I'll tell you,' Richard indicated a large leather chair.

Elanora arrived at her office just before one in the morning. Richard and Robert McCraw had enjoyed several drinks and were chatting idly when she entered. She offered her apologies for being late, and then gently kissed Richard.

'I'm sorry about the news of your father, darling,' she said.

'Is your father ill?' McCraw asked.

'Gravely,' Richard replied.

'I'm sorry to hear it.'

'Don't be,' Richard shrugged. 'I've had little to do with him for years. And besides, it may prove a blessing in disguise.'

'How so, Richie lad?'

'I'll tell you later.'

The three got down to business and, over the ensuing hour or so, sorted out company and Society matters, then Richard produced the Hemmings papers and the two men sat in silence as Elanora read them.

'Well, we have a mole in the organisation,' she said finally, leaning back in her office chair. 'And it has to be someone in London . . .'

'I'm inclined to agree,' Robert McCraw said. 'But who, in London?'

'. . . That is of course,' Elanora added, 'if these papers are genuine.'

'Oh, they're genuine all right,' Richard looked out of the office window at the light rain drifting over Hong Kong Harbour. 'The One Eyed Woo wouldn't lie. He might be an old villain and a cut-throat, but he's not a liar.'

'Where did he get them?' Elanora asked.

'He didn't offer that information,' Richard replied evasively, with a glance at McCraw. 'His son Napoleon merely said that his father thought I should see them. Where Woo got them is anyone's guess, but there's no doubt they were written by Stephen Hemmings. The handwriting's been checked and the wallet even has the initials S.H. branded into the corner of it.'

'It struck me at the time as more than a coincidence,' Elanora said smugly, alternating her gaze between the two men. 'That Stephen Hemmings disappeared, along with the Governor's yacht, just when he happened to be going to

London to give information to a parliamentary committee.'

The men once again exchanged a glance, which did not go unnoticed by Elanora. 'Then, all this time later, right out of the blue, his private papers are delivered to you two, of all people, by the son of a pirate. How curious,' she smiled. 'Now let's get back to the problem at hand, shall we?'

'The mole in London,' McCraw declared, happy to change the subject.

'It has to be someone in London,' Elanora nodded. 'Hemmings admits in his notes that he had no idea which of our ships were allowed Customs entry into the Pool of London without inspection. And yet, Sir Herbert Billings claimed Hemmings was his original source of information when he named the ships in Parliament. This could not possibly have been correct.'

'Which means someone else told Billings the names of the ships,' Richard added. 'Someone who had access to Malcolm Linden's private files at the Port of London Authority.'

'Perhaps it was Malcolm himself?' Elanora suggested.

'No,' Richard was quick to disagree. 'I'd trust him with my life. Malcolm would never betray the Society of Golden Dragons.'

'Malcolm's a good man, Elanora,' Robert McCraw added. 'Honest and trustworthy.'

'I know, I know,' Elanora said. 'I just thought I should offer a name. In fact, any name, before I state the obvious one!'

Richard and Robert glanced at each other. 'Charles Higgins!' they announced simultaneously.

'Oh, well done!' Elanora exclaimed with a touch of condescension. 'Now one more question springs to mind.'

'And what is that?' Richard queried stiffly. Elanora appeared to find the whole business amusing.

'It's for Robert, actually,' she turned her gaze upon the big Scot.

'What would that be?' McCraw asked, enjoying Elanora's performance. He'd not seen her so animated for a long time. She was positively glowing.

'Can you remember, Robert, the name of the idiot who put Charles Higgins in a position to betray us in the first place?'

'It was him!' Robert McCraw pointed instantly at Richard.

'All right! All right!' Richard snapped. 'You two have had your little joke! The point is, what are we going to do about him?'

'No,' Elanora said. 'The point is, what are *you* going to do about him?'

'What do you think!' Richard glared at her.

'I think,' Elanora replied, raising her eyebrows at McCraw who was struggling to suppress a hoot of laughter. 'You'll fly off to London in a fit of juvenile rage and kill him!'

'That's exactly what I intend to do!' Richard was furious with both of them and even more furious with himself for allowing Elanora to bait him.

'Oh, Richard,' she sighed. 'You're such an adorable fool! When will you ever learn?'

'I'll cut his traitorous heart out and . . .!'

'Wrong,' Elanora almost sang the word.

'I've wanted to kill him for years!'

'Wrong! Wrong! Wrong! You stupid man!'

Richard stopped his theatrical posturing and scowled at her. 'If I remember correctly, it was actually your idea that Higgins work for the Society in London when he retired.'

'It most certainly was not,' Elanora looked to McCraw for support.

'I'm afraid he's got you there, lassie,' McCraw said.

'Well, be that as it may, it was only an idea. It was you,' she pointed at Richard, 'who sent him.'

The exchange was becoming childish, and the hint of a smile betrayed itself on Richard's lips. 'You're absolutely right, and I offer my humblest apology,' he said finally.

'Is that offer unconditional?' she asked.

'Completely,' Richard nodded, sharing the private joke.

'How about a drink on the strength of it all?' McCraw moved to the decanters on the bureau by the fireplace. 'We can toast your coming nuptials.'

'Make mine a Cognac,' Richard said.

'Mine too,' Elanora answered. She looked at Richard, sitting like a schoolboy in a headmaster's office, fingers locked in his lap as he watched McCraw pour the drinks. She wanted to brush the unruly lock of hair from his eyes and hold him in her arms.

He caught her gaze and held it. And, as he did, something happened to Richard. His feelings for Elanora suddenly hit him like a hammer blow. He felt a great rush of affection for her. She's thinking only of me, he thought. She really loves me. And the thought made him inexpressibly happy.

'We'll drink to your health,' Robert McCraw said as he handed around the drinks. 'That is before we decide who gets to kill that Sassenach bastard Higgins.'

'No one's going to kill Higgins,' Elanora stated, tearing her eyes from Richard's. She found his gaze distracting and she needed to concentrate. 'Let's get one thing straight from the outset, no one kills Charles Higgins,' she reiterated. 'It's too dangerous, we don't know what other information he may have imparted or to whom.'

'By Christ, Richard,' McCraw said urgently. 'She's right. You'd better away to London *jik haak,* laddie! And I don't just mean quickly, as they say in *Gwang Dung wah,* I mean bloody quickly! You've got to find out just what that bastard's been up to and straighten matters out before we're all for the drop! He's had over a year. Christ alone knows what he's been up to.'

'Robbie's right,' Elanora agreed. 'You must leave for London the day after tomorrow on the Flying Boat Service.'

'Yes,' Richard said. 'And you must come with me, my darling. Charles is nobody's fool, he'll smell a rat if I suddenly turn up in London without informing him of my arrival, and we have the perfect excuse of my father's illness. We'll arrive unannounced to visit Father, then when Higgins is least expecting it, I'll have the truth out of him in thirty seconds.'

'Did you no' hear what your lassie said, laddie? What if he has accomplices? Allies?' McCraw interrupted. 'You've got to ascertain not only what he's done and for whom, but whether he's done it alone. Has he set up in business for himself? How fat are his bank accounts compared to Dragon Imports? How much information has been passed to the Scotland Yard Enquiry?'

'Robert's correct, Richard,' Elanora said. 'There's a mountain of investigation to be done before we can accuse Charles. And we must make sure that, when we do, we have all the facts.'

'How could I have been so stupid as to trust Charles Higgins?' Richard groaned.

'Don't blame yourself, Richard,' Robert said. 'If Malcolm Linden didn't suspect anything why should you? Besides there's always the slim possibility he's not the mole at all.' McCraw rose and took his coat from the wall peg. 'Well there's little else to discuss, except to wish you good luck,' he shook hands with the two of them. 'I'm sure you'll take care of the matter, laddie,' he said to Richard. 'And don't worry about things here in Hong Kong, I'll see that all runs smoothly.' He turned at the door. 'I'll bid you both goodnight and a safe journey.'

When McCraw had gone, Richard put an arm around Elanora. 'It's time we went home too, my darling, it's nearly three in the morning.' He desperately wanted to make love to her.

龍

The girl was dead! He couldn't believe it. The girl was dead!

'Bugger it! Bugger it! Bugger it!' It was early morning as James hurled his Norton motorcycle along Causeway Bay Road towards Wanchai, and he cursed into the wind. How had he gotten himself into such a situation? 'Bugger it! Bugger it! Bugger it!' he cursed again, braking the big bike to avoid a rickshaw, then once more giving it full throttle.

It had been her idea to go to Shaukiwan when they'd crossed the harbour to Hong Kong Island on the ferry. Shaukiwan was a seedy little bay area past North Point on the edge of Lai Yi Mun Pass, the eastern entrance to Hong Kong Harbour. Shirley had explained that her aunt had a small house there in Po Wuk Street where they could be alone together. James had been all for it, and he'd taken her there on his motorcycle through the pouring rain. He hadn't realised until later, when he was drunk on *mou toi* wine, that Shirley was a *doh yau,* and by that time he couldn't have cared less.

James had never used opium before: he'd been sternly warned against it by Richard and Lo Shi-mon. But the girl had been irresistible, naked beneath her slinky silk chemise, and he'd gone along with her game.

The experience had been indescribable, one of sexual delirium, as Shirley Wong, under the influence of the drug, had abandoned herself. She'd led him through a series of sexual exercises he could not have imagined possible. He'd been besotted; he couldn't get enough of her. Finally, exhausted, he'd drifted into a state of insensibility brought about by the opiate. He'd come to at about six o'clock, awoken by the first rays of sunlight filtering through the bamboo curtains, and he'd felt a sticky substance along his flank. It was blood! The girl lying beside him was drenched in blood!

At first he'd panicked, scrambling into his clothes, about to flee the place, then he'd managed to control his rising fear and examine the girl. There were blood-engorged leeches on the insides of her thighs, and small cuts on her breasts and stomach. It appeared to James that she'd smeared her body with her own blood, until he noticed small nicks on his own torso and nipples, and flashes of memory returned to him. The two of them writhing on the bed, smearing blood between their bodies as they coupled, lost in a cloud of drug-induced lust. Then he saw the razor on the floor next to the bed and panic finally got the better of him.

James had fled the silent house. He'd wheeled his Norton as far as Shaukiwan Road, then taken off, not knowing where he was going, driven by the urge to get as far away from Shirley Wong's dead body as he could.

He slowed the bike as he approached Kings Road, pulled over to the side and stopped. He let his head fall forward onto the handle bars and fought to gain control of his whirling brain.

'Bugger it,' he cursed his stupidity. How had he allowed himself to be dragged into such a situation? She was a *doh yau*. A bloody drug addict! He should have dropped her like a hotcake when he'd realised, but oh no, he'd had to go on. He'd had to go that one further step towards perversity. 'You bloody fool,' he said loudly, suddenly realising what he had to do. He turned the bike around and headed back towards Shaukiwan.

He drove more sedately along the still wet road, the chill winter wind on his face awakening his senses. He thought of the four people in his life who mattered most to him. They would expect him to do what he was now doing, he told himself. His Mother, Richard Brewster, Lee and Lo Shi-mon would all expect him to act with honour. No life was worth living without honour. He would return to the house and have the police summoned, and he would take whatever was coming to him like a man. His stomach churned at the thought of the shame it would cause his mother and the anger it would draw from Richard and Lo Shi-mon, but he knew it was the only thing to do.

He turned the bike into Po Wuk street and drove along the little bayside road to the girl's house where, to his amazement, he found Shirley Wong sitting on a fishing trap with her aunty, who was brushing the girl's hair.

'Good morning,' Shirley Wong said as he dismounted his cycle and approached them.

There appeared to be nothing wrong with her. James' head spun with a mixture of relief and disbelief. He looked at her clothes but could see no blood, and apart from a weariness in her eyes, no doubt brought about by their night of debauchery, she seemed quite well.

'Good morning to you,' he replied.

'*He is seeing things,*' Shirley's old aunty said in the fishing folk dialect of Chiu Chau, which James couldn't quite understand.

'What did she say?'

'In Cantonese you would say *waan gok*,' Shirley replied.

'Hallucinations?' James asked. 'She thinks I'm hallucinating?'

'It happens to people, the first time they use the milk of the poppy. My aunt said that you took off out of her house as if all the devils of hell were at your heels. She thinks you must be having pictures in your mind. The after-effects can last for several days.'

'Oh, no. I'm fine,' James shrugged trying to appear nonchalant.

'Do you remember last night?' Shirley purred wantonly as she closed her eyes and let the morning sun warm her face.

'Yes, of course, it was wonderful,' he replied. 'How could I ever forget it?'

'My aunty says you are *sik long*, a coloured wolf,' the girl said and the old lady cackled lasciviously nodding her head at the phrase, which roughly translated meant sex maniac.

'How would she know?' Richard asked uneasily.

'She watched us,' Shirley replied.

'She what!' He was horrified at the thought of the old crone spying on them.

'She said that after we took the drug we coupled for two hours,' Shirley continued. 'Apparently we were like dogs in heat. My aunt believes that your desire was to eat your way into my vagina and never come back out. She said you were disgusting. The act of oral sex to her is abhorrent.'

'*Sik long! Sik long!*' The old crone cackled.

'All right, all right,' James said turning away embarrassed. He squinted against the glare of the morning sun and looked out at the sampans and fishing boats moored in the bay. But, as he watched them, they all caught fire and began to sink. He blinked, shook his head, then looked again and all appeared normal.

'She is right,' Shirley said. 'You are a coloured wolf. Only a coloured wolf could do to me what you did last night when I was singing. The feeling was so overpowering my juices ran down the insides of my legs and I reached the state of sexual bliss on stage. I had to change my underwear after you left.'

'Really,' James looked at her askance, developing a suspicion that the girl wasn't quite right in the head.

'I told my aunt but she does not believe me. She would like to observe the occurrence. Would you do it again now?'

'I can't do it at the drop of a hat,' James said, thinking of Winnie on her knees working desperately to make him ejaculate, a fact of which Shirley Wong had been unaware. 'The circumstances have to be just right.'

'Was it my beauty that made you do it?' the girl asked. She still sat with her eyes closed and her face to the sun as her aunt brushed her hair. 'Or was it my beautiful voice?'

'I have to be going,' James said. There was definitely something strange about the girl. To say that she was beautiful was an understatement, but he was suddenly convinced that, mentally, she wasn't all there.

'My aunt is worried that, because I took your penis into my throat, I may become pregnant in the breasts.'

Then your aunt is crazier than you are, James thought. 'I don't think that is biologically possible, Shirley,' he said.

'When will I see you again?' she asked.

'I don't think I'll be down this way for a while,' James replied as he walked towards his motorcycle. 'I rarely have a reason to come to Shaukiwan.'

'You will be back,' the girl chuckled huskily.

'What makes you say that?' he asked as he got astride the Norton.

'You are a coloured wolf,' she replied. 'My aunt says you need to feed on my vagina, it is the only food that will satisfy the craving of a coloured wolf.'

'You're crazy. Goodbye!' He kick-started the bike.

'You have the madness in you, James,' the girl yelled, finally looking at him. 'The sex madness of the coloured wolf.' She grinned. 'You will be back.'

He gunned the throttle and took off down Po Wuk Street.

'*Sik long!*' He heard the old crone yell after him. '*Sik long!*' She yelled again and cackled like an old witch. The sound sent shivers down his back.

龍

Elanora Merchant heard her son climbing the central staircase of Merchant House. She'd been awake for an hour, reliving the events of the previous night. Richard had made love to her with a bitter, sweet desperation and she knew without doubt, as her body had accommodated him, that he loved her at last, even if he didn't know it himself, yet. She could have wept with happiness.

She looked at the clock over the fireplace. It was nearly nine in the morning, they hadn't arrived home until well after three. James had been out all night, she realised. She removed Richard's arm from where it lay across her stomach and crept silently out of bed. She pulled on a silk peignoir and went out into the hallway as James reached the top of the stairs.

'Are you aware of the time?' Elanora asked sternly.

'Keep away from me!' James gasped as he saw Shirley Wong at the top of the stairs.

'I *beg* your pardon!'

James blinked rapidly and the vision of the drug-addicted singer transformed itself into the figure of his mother. 'Oh. Good morning mother,' he said.

'Are you all right?' she asked, concerned.

'Yes, of course,' James attempted a laugh, but he knew his mother had detected something in his appearance and was staring at him suspiciously. He walked past her down the hallway towards his room.

'Come back here at once,' Elanora's voice was like the crack of a whip.

'Yes, Mother?' He walked back to her trying desperately to avoid her gaze. She was aware of something, but just what, James didn't know.

'Look at me,' she demanded.

'What is it?' he asked as he obediently looked at her.

'Oh my God!' his mother gasped and put her hand over her mouth. 'Richard!' she screamed. 'Richard! Oh my God! Richard!'

James saw Richard Brewster stumble through his mother's bedroom doorway into the hall, a sheet wrapped around his naked body.

'What is it!' Richard exclaimed, blinking in an effort to focus; he'd been fast asleep.

'Look at his eyes,' Elanora said, stepping back from her son.

Richard did, and James saw his *Shan Chu*'s face flush with anger.

'*The eyes of the Ox,*' Elanora cried in Cantonese. James' pupils were dilated in the extreme.

'What is she talking about?' James asked, bewildered.

'Get out of that mess you're wearing,' Richard indicated James' dishevelled clothing. 'And meet us in the study.' He returned to Elanora's bedroom, leaving mother and son staring at each other.

'What is it?' James asked.

'You fool!' Elanora declared. 'You stupid young fool!' James had never heard his mother speak to him that way, and he gaped at her, shocked. 'Do as you're told!' she ordered, then followed Richard into the bedroom.

Thirty minutes later the three of them sat in the study. Silence reigned, broken only by the twittering of a flock of starlings on the lawn outside, enjoying the morning sunlight and the worm hunt brought about by the previous night's heavy rain. The three of them had been sitting in silence for a full quarter of an hour, upon Elanora's instruction. They were waiting for something, James thought, but for what? He had no idea, and he dared not ask.

He heard a car pull up at the front entrance to the house. There was several minutes of rapid Cantonese, muffled by the big study doors and then Ah Poh, the *amah*, entered with an old Chinese man carrying a hessian sack. The housekeeper bowed formally to Elanora and gave James a look of dread before leaving the old man with them.

'*It was good of you to come, Mr Ho,*' Elanora said to the old man.

'*You are most welcome, Merchant Mistress,*' the old man replied as he spilt the contents of his sack onto the study desk. James looked at them in amazement. Spread across the desk was a variety of different plants and jars full of creams and oils, and a freshly killed chicken, which dribbled blood onto the writing blotter. *'Is this the boy who took the foreign mud?'* the old man asked, pointing at James.

'Yes,' Elanora replied, the embarrassment of her admission plain. She turned to her son. *'This is Mr Ho, a herbalist and master of the ancient sciences. He does our house the great honour of attending to its needs at short notice. He is a busy man and much revered in the community. You will pay respectful attention to him, answer his questions truthfully and do as he instructs.'*

'Yes, mother,' James bowed to the old man.

'Did you ingest it, inhale it or have it injected into your body?' Mr Ho asked James.

'I inhaled it,' James answered, aware that there was no point in denial.

'That is good!' the old fellow declared. *'But I must be sure you only chased the dragon. You are sure you did not eat the dragon or allow it to bite you, true or not true?'*

'I do not understand,' James said.

'Did the smoke of the poppy appear as a dragon suspended in the air before your eyes?'

'Yes.'

'And you chased the tail of the dragon through the air, breathing it in through a tube?'

'Yes.'

'Were you given anything to eat?'

'No.'

'Take off your clothes,' Mr Ho said.

'What?' James asked, nonplussed by the request. 'All of them?'

'You heard him,' Elanora snapped. 'Take off your clothes immediately!'

James did as he was told and stood nakedly self-conscious in front of his mother, as Mr Ho studied his body for needle marks. 'I was not injected with anything if that's what you're trying to ascertain,' he said.

'He stinks of the sexual juice of women,' Mr Ho declared as he inspected James' body.

'Mother, I . . .' James began.

'Shut up, James!' Elanora's voice cut him off icily.

Mr Ho shook his head in the direction of Richard, then looked at James. *'Get dressed,'* he quietly instructed, and he turned to his pile of jars and herbs. *'Have you ever taken opium before?'* he asked.

'No,' James answered. *'Never! I swear!'*

'Are you being visited by ghosts?'

'I have been seeing things that cannot be true. I suppose you could call them ghosts.'

'For how long do they visit?'

'Only for a few seconds. When I blink they go away.'

'Then their power is weak. You have been a foolish boy, but you are not the first. Drink this,' the old man handed James a glass of liquid. James fastened his trouser belt and stared at the evil looking concoction.

'I'm not drinking chicken's blood!' he said, disgusted at the thought.

'The chicken is a gift for your mother's kitchen,' the old man explained. *'Drink this potion I have prepared,'* he said again, waving the glass under James' nose.

'Do I have to?' He looked at his mother.

'Drink it!' Richard Brewster roared as he rose from his chair. 'And I hope it makes you as sick as a dog!'

James took the glass and downed it in one gulp. He had never tasted anything so vile in his life. He gagged and brought the liquid up all over the study floor.

'Drink again,' the old man said handing James another glass full. *'And hold your breath until it reaches your stomach.'*

James did as he was instructed and managed to keep the potion down. *'What does it do?'*

'It will clean your blood of the remaining poison from the poppy,' Mr Ho said as he put his various potions and plants back into the sack.

'You will be well rewarded for your services, Mr Ho,' Elanora said to the old man.

'My reward is to serve the Merchant Mistress,' he replied. *'My reward is to rid the young Merchant's blood of the*

poison of the poppy so he may become Big Boss of your Noble House.' He turned to James. '*You have Chinese blood in your veins, young Mr Merchant as do your mother and I. Be sure you keep it clean of poisons and inherit your position of power honourably, for the sake of all Chinese people in Hong Kong.*' He looked at Elanora, who nodded in reply.

'James,' she said. 'Close your eyes, remain still and try to show some humility.'

James did as he was told.

'*You have brought shame on your mother,*' the old man said, and he slapped James across the face. James flinched at the blow but remained still. '*You have brought shame upon your friends,*' the old man hit him again and still James did not move, but he felt himself flush with embarrassment. '*You chased the dragon and in doing so jeopardised the future happiness of many poor people who depend on the Merchant House to sustain them,*' the old man hit him again, and this time a sense of humiliation overwhelmed James as he closed his eyes. '*You are a coloured wolf in danger of becoming an addict to the juice of the poppy. You are a disgrace to your Noble House.*'

James stood rigidly to attention until he heard the old man leave. When the study doors clicked shut, he opened his eyes and stared at his mother. There were tears in her eyes.

'I'm sorry, mother . . .' James began.

'Mr Ho said all that needed to be said,' Richard interrupted. 'The subject is closed, but that does not mean it will be forgotten, James, not for a long time.'

'By either one of us,' Elanora added. 'Now go and sleep off your night of debauchery.'

James obediently turned to leave, the potion causing a wave of tiredness to flood through him.

'There's one more thing, James,' Richard added. 'Your mother and I are travelling to England by air. We leave tomorrow, and you will be coming with us.'

'England!' James exclaimed. 'I will not require watching, Richard, I promise! I realise I've made a mistake and you both have my word it will never happen again.'

'Enough!' his *Shan Chu* roared. 'You will do as you're told, *Sai Loh*!'

James was terrified. Richard's body had suddenly swelled to an enormous size. He'd sprouted wings and horns, and fire gushed from his nostrils. Richard had become a dragon.

'You will do as you are told, *Sai Loh*,' the dragon intoned, its voice guttural, malevolent. 'Do you understand?'

James shook his head, then blinked and saw Richard again. 'Yes, *Dai Loh*,' James heard himself say. 'I understand, *Dai Loh*.' He fled to the summerhouse to perform his Shaolin disciplines. He needed to sweat. He needed to purge the drug from his body. Never, he vowed, never would he touch opium again.

CHAPTER SIXTEEN

When Richard, Elanora and James arrived in London, Malcolm Linden met them at Victoria Station with the news that Binky Brewster had died the previous night. Weary from their journey and saddened by the news, they decided to stay at the company house in Belgravia and travel to Hallowdene the following day.

Charles Higgins was taken aback by their unannounced arrival but, upon hearing the news of Binky Brewster's death, his response was overtly sympathetic.

'My dear Richard,' he declared. 'I cannot begin to tell you how sorry I am. If there is anything at all I can do, please don't hesitate to ask.'

'Thank you, Charles.' The very sight of Higgins made Richard's blood boil but, aware of this fact, Elanora immediately came to his aid.

'How kind of you, Charles,' she purred, taking Richard's arm and squeezing it solicitously. 'It is most upsetting for Richard, as you can imagine. He travelled all the way from Hong Kong to see his father, and to miss him by just one day . . .' She let her voice trail off.

'Yairs, yairs,' Higgins intoned at his obsequious best. 'It's tragic. Damned tragic. He'll be interred at Hallowdene, I dare say?'

'Yes,' Elanora replied.

'I knew Binky very well in the old days, you know . . .'

'No, I didn't,' she interrupted, fearful of the request she assumed he was about to make. 'We've decided the funeral will be a very private affair. You understand, of course?'

The thought of Richard burying his father with a weeping Charles Higgins at his side was too hideous to contemplate. Richard would probably kill him at the graveside.

'I understand completely, my dear,' Higgins replied. 'But may I send a suitable floral tribute to express my grief?'

'Of course.'

'Good.'

They all fell silent for a moment.

'Well,' Higgins said finally, 'I had Irene make up your beds. The third floor apartment is always kept ready for your arrival, Richard. And James,' he turned to the young man. 'Your old room is just as you left it.'

'Thank you, Charles,' James replied flatly.

No Uncle? Charles thought. And no more a boy, either. James Merchant was now a strapping young man, and a damned handsome one to boot. Then again, he mused, James always had been a good-looking boy.

'Don't go to too much trouble, Charles,' Elanora said. 'We'll be going to Hallowdene tomorrow, there's much to be done.'

'It's no bother, I assure you. And will you be returning to Hong Kong after the funeral?' He fervently hoped the answer would be in the affirmative.

'My father's affairs have to be sorted out, Charles,' Richard replied. 'And they will be complicated to say the least.'

Damn it! Charles thought. 'Well, I'll leave you three to your grief. You look very tired, Richard, a good night's sleep will do wonders for you. And once again, dear chap, you have my deepest sympathy.'

龍

Hallowdene, the ancestral home of the Brewster family, sat on a hill in the County of Surrey near the town of Redhill and, from the rear gardens, the low lying hills and forests which formed the estate afforded spectacular views. Built in the 16th century as a priory, it had housed for over two hundred years the Sisters of the Order of St. Jude, until

Richard Brewster's great-great-grandfather had bought the estate from the Church of England.

Colonel Sir Charles Hughthorpe Brewster had served the English Crown with distinction and, after losing his foot to a cannonball at the Battle of Waterloo in 1815, he'd settled in Surrey, bought the priory, taken a wife and bred prolifically. Bingham Edward Brewster, known as Binky, Richard's father and fourth Brewster heir, had inherited Hallowdene and nurtured it lovingly, assured by the knowledge that his only son Richard would one day take over the running of the estate. With Richard's departure to the Colony of Hong Kong, Binky Brewster had left the estate for the comfort of his house in London and Hallowdene had fallen into disrepair.

Now, in accordance with his last request, Binky Brewster was laid to rest in the yard of the estate's private chapel. The funeral was attended by Richard, Elanora, James, Richard's cousin Geoffrey and several of Binky's business associates. A few locals also turned up to pay their respects, but most of the tenant farmers stayed away. That particular day was a market day and life had to go on, they all agreed. In truth, they had little time for old Binky. He'd shown a token interest only in both the estate and their welfare since he'd moved to London, and they'd eventually given up on him.

The night after the funeral, Richard wandered alone through Hallowdene Manor, and memories of what now seemed another life flooded back to him. The enormous kitchen conjured up images of chaos; the frantic preparation that attended the banquets of which his father had been so fond, busy house servants with no time to chat. And the long, lonely corridors. How clearly he recalled meandering through them, pretending he was in search of adventure, but more often than not simply seeking the companionship of one of the servants.

The longer he wandered, the more the house manifested in Richard feelings of sadness for the lonely little boy he'd once been. Hanging on the walls, the portraits of glowering ancestors that had once filled him with dread now seemed dull and lifeless. Hallowdene Manor had become the Brewster family mausoleum, cold, silent and uninviting.

Several days later, Richard, Elanora and James returned to London, James to his room at the Belgravia House and the delights of Irene, and Richard and Elanora to the suite of rooms he had booked for them at the Dorchester. Richard had several meetings with Malcolm Linden, setting the investigation into Charles Higgins in motion, then he sat back to admire Elanora at her glorious best.

Elanora Escaravelho Merchant's unsurpassed beauty and wealth, it was true, drew invitations to balls, premieres, garden parties, horse races and gala charity events. She was feted by all and hotly pursued by the press. She was the toast of the town and, for a month or so, she revelled in it, but the Elanora Richard knew soon planted her feet firmly back on the ground. She announced over breakfast one morning in their suite that she was sick of London's social set. She was sick of its lords and its ladies, she said. Sick of its earls, barons, duchesses, Knights of the Realm and, most of all, she was sick of its Members of Parliament. She would give anything, she said, for a bowl of boiled rice and an ear full of honest conversation. Richard agreed with her wholeheartedly and they moved back to Surrey that same afternoon.

Upon full inspection, the forlorn state of Hallowdene Estate shocked Richard and, recalling the promise he'd made to his father, the desire to restore the family estate to its former glory consumed him. He worked tirelessly, day and night. He held meetings with the tenants and employed new staff, and his vitality and commitment, coupled with the fact that he appeared to have an endless supply of money, stung the tenants and locals into action. By the end of May, Hallowdene was a sight to behold. The ancient priory, with its ivy-covered walls and mullioned windows, once again gleamed resplendent, restored for all to admire.

Hallowdene's crowning glory was, however, Elanora. Like Richard, she devoted herself to the task, employing new household staff, including two Chinese women from London as cooks, and her mere presence gave fresh life to the manor.

She was a constant topic of conversation in the local town, where she was regarded as nothing short of royalty. Tenant farmers who'd not been to the manor house for years suddenly began turning up to pay their respects and to offer advice to Richard on the operation of the estate.

Richard was happier than he'd ever believed possible. Even the matter of Charles Higgins had solved itself, at least temporarily.

Charles had requested leave of absence, to take what he described as a long overdue trip abroad. With Richard and James in England company business was in safe hands, he'd said heartily, and Richard had been only too happy to grant his request. While Charles was away on the Continent, Malcolm Linden and James would be able to snoop into his affairs with far greater freedom.

Parliamentary interest in Dragon Import & Export had waned since Richard's arrival. It did not surprise him. Politicians were only able to ask questions if they had information, he thought, and a spy within any company would obviously go to ground upon the arrival of its owners. Such had been the case. If Charles was the 'mole' they were seeking, and in Richard's mind there was little doubt of it, his decision to go abroad only pointed the finger of suspicion more squarely at him.

The investigation into Charles Higgins continued in his absence, but Malcolm and James could find nothing concrete with which to challenge the man. It became obvious to Richard they would have to remain in England for quite some time. The realisation did not upset him.

At Hallowdene, his relationship with Elanora was blooming. He found himself inventing reasons to be in her company, seeking her out at the oddest times, feeling the need to touch her. They made love frequently, and when they did, Richard experienced a depth of tenderness he'd not known before.

His affection for Elanora had changed. Richard was in love, and the sudden realisation shocked him. He loved her. How could he have failed to recognise it? She was no longer his trump card, it horrified him to think that he could ever have considered her so. He loved her. And not for her beauty, he realised, he loved her for the memories he shared with her. For the trials and tribulations they had suffered together, the trust they had developed, the true friendship that now blossomed like a rose. For the first time in his life, Richard recognised the true depth and capacity of his emotions. Caitlin Maclain had been a youthful infatuation compared to the love he now felt for Elanora. He needed to tell her. He needed to thank her for all she had given him and tell her that he loved her.

He sought her out and discovered her on the patio at the rear of the house. She was cutting flowers for the dining room arrangements, the rolling hills of Surrey forming a backdrop for her beauty. He walked up quietly behind her and put his arms around her waist.

'I love you,' he whispered, taking in her fragrance.

'I know,' Elanora closed her eyes.

'No, you don't understand,' he said. 'I really love you.'

'I know,' she repeated as she turned into his arms. 'I understand, Richard. Now go away.'

'What?'

She kissed him deeply. 'I understand. Now go away, I'll see you at dinner.'

Richard looked into her eyes, they were brimming with tears. 'I love you,' he said again, and he left her alone.

Elanora looked out over the lush English countryside for several minutes. Then she sat on the small stone patio wall and wept. She wept for Richard, tears of relief that he had finally discovered his ability to love. Then she wept for herself, tears of pure joy, until she was unable to weep any more.

Richard and Elanora were married at Hallowdene Manor in the first week of September 1938. They exchanged their vows in the small chapel on the estate with James and Geoffrey Brewster the only family in attendance, and Malcolm Linden acted as Richard's best man.

They honeymooned in Paris, dining by candlelight in romantic restaurants and spending the nights locked in each other's embrace. It was a week of wonderful, selfish foolishness, which ended all too quickly and they returned to a sombre England. In London, as in Paris, the talk was of nothing but war.

War with Germany was becoming more and more a likelihood as each day passed. Germany was on a military footing, with arms and machinery being manufactured at an alarming rate and, despite Prime Minister Neville Chamberlain's declaration to the press . . . 'I believe it is peace for our time . . .', Britons, to a man, were feeling decidedly uneasy. The horrors of the Great War were still fresh in their minds. It had been only twenty years since Britain had lost a generation of young men fighting the Germans and the fear of another war gripped the population.

To Elanora, the thought of war was cause for great apprehension. She lived in constant fear for Lee who was still fighting in China. She had had no word from him since the letters she and Richard had received informing them he was moving from Nanking, and daily she prayed for his safety. War was, to Elanora, as to any mother with a son in service, an abomination. Then, one Saturday afternoon in late November, James arrived at Hallowdene Manor.

Richard was in the back garden discussing a stockbreeding programme with his estate manager when he saw James riding up the road to the house on his motorcycle. He called Elanora, knowing how the visit would delight her, and together they stood at the front steps of the house as James drove up. They watched as he alighted and pulled the leather helmet and goggles from his head. Then, he removed his leather riding coat.

'Oh, my God,' Richard whispered as Elanora's hand flew to her mouth.

'Hello, Mother. What do you think?' James turned around to show off his new Royal Air Force uniform.

'What have you done?' Richard asked as he walked towards the young man.

'What I've wanted to do since Germany annexed Sudetenland and formed the alliance with Austria,' James replied, with a touch of aggression. He knew his enlistment would draw a heavy response from Richard and he was prepared for the fight.

'You bloody fool . . .'

'Don't call me a fool . . .' James started to retaliate, but he was cut short by a wail from his mother as she ran to him.

'Take it off!' Elanora screamed, pulling at his new blue tunic. 'Take it back and tell them you've changed your mind!' In her head was the image of James lying dead on a battle-field, his bloodied body entangled in the burning wreckage of an aircraft.

'Mother,' James protested.

'Elanora,' Richard said. 'Get a hold of yourself!'

'No,' she screamed, tearing again at James' uniform. 'I won't have it. I won't allow it.' Richard took her by the shoulders and turned her, struggling, towards the front doors.

'I'll speak to you later,' he said. 'After dinner.' And he glared at James as he took Elanora inside.

Elanora sat, white-faced, on the sofa in Richard's study and stared through the open window as Richard poured after dinner brandies for himself and James. She had declined the offer of cognac and Richard glanced at her momentarily as he handed a drink to his stepson. She'd not spoken through-out the meal, picking at her food between bouts of wringing her napkin and fitfully touching her hair.

'Thank you,' James took the brandy. He watched Richard move behind the sofa and place a hand on Elanora's shoulder before sipping his cognac.

'Well,' Richard began. 'You've evidently committed yourself?'

'I have,' James inwardly heaved a sigh of relief. He knew by Richard's tone that the battle was already won. After the initial shock of discovery, his mother and Richard had obvi-ously discussed his RAF enlistment and realised there was nothing they could do about it. He congratulated himself on having the foresight to wear his uniform to Hallowdene for the visit. The shock tactic had worked.

'Don't you think it might have been courteous to have discussed it with your mother and me before you acted?'

'Some decisions in life must be made alone. I believed this was one of those decisions.'

'But you could have discussed it with us,' Richard said evenly.

'I thought about it, but I knew you'd try to stop me.'

'Of course we would have, but the decision would have remained yours. We'd hardly have locked you in your room.'

'No,' James gave his stepfather a wry smile. 'You'd have used all of your considerable influence to have my enlistment refused.'

'Do you really think that?' It was Richard's turn to smile.

'I know it. I know how you think, because I think exactly the same way.'

'Do you now?' Richard raised an eyebrow.

'You made sure of that when I was seven,' James replied and he saw the smile fade from Richard's face.

'Just what is it you do in the Air Force?' Richard asked archly.

'At the moment I'm in Basic Training, learning to salute,' James flicked a mock salute. 'That kind of thing, you know the drill. But I'm going to fly, eventually. I've been granted an RAF Short Service Commission. I'm to report to Flying Training School in January.'

'How could you do this to me, James?' Elanora snapped, finally breaking her silence. 'You have behaved recklessly with total disregard for your safety and the future security of your family. How dare you!'

'You allowed Lee to go and fight in China,' James responded. 'And he was only seventeen.'

'That's different,' his mother retaliated.

'How? Lee is Chinese. He went to fight for his country. I'm English. Can't I do the same?'

'England is not at war,' Elanora sat bolt upright and glared at her son.

'Ha!' James scoffed. 'Not yet, Mother, but you can bet it will be before too long.'

'That's enough, young man!' Richard intervened. 'There'll be no more talk of war. Your mother doesn't need to hear it. She is concerned for your safety and that sort of talk will only add to her anxiety.'

'Forgive me for saying so,' James said, 'but that's not like you.'

'What do mean?' Richard asked.

'I can understand your concern for mother's feelings, but surely you of all people would have to agree that war with Germany is inevitable. I thought you might even suggest we sit down, the three of us and discuss the issue. You must admit there's a lot to be discussed. Hong Kong, the Merchant Company, the needs of the Society and, last but not least, Dragon Imports and our wayward Uncle Charlie.'

Richard looked at his stepson with new eyes. Since leaving Hong Kong, almost a year ago, James had matured considerably, he thought. The lad had kept out of trouble and applied himself conscientiously to his work at the offices of Dragon Imports, virtually taking over in the absence of Charles Higgins.

Charles Higgins! The mere thought of the man triggered anger in Richard. They'd been careful in their investigation. Charles was holidaying, blissfully unaware of his perilous situation. It had become apparent very early on that he'd been photographing documents in Malcolm Linden's office and passing the information to someone, but to whom he was passing it had been another matter, entirely. Every avenue they had taken had led to a dead end.

Richard and Malcolm Linden had discussed the matter and decided to await Charles' return from abroad. Then, false documents concerning Dragon Imports' shipping and cargo details would be planted regularly for Charles to discover in the hope he'd make a mistake.

'The lad's right, Elanora,' Richard said to his agitated wife. 'We do have a lot to discuss. James has joined the RAF and there's nothing we can do about it. No use crying over spilt milk, my darling. But we can talk. We can make plans for the future. That there will be war, I have no doubt, but it will be here in Europe, not in the Far East. Perhaps I can arrange for James to be posted to the RAF in Hong Kong, where he'll be out of harm's way.'

James looked at his stepfather and shook his head vigorously, but Richard signalled him to be quiet. Elanora looked up, a glimmer of hope in her eyes.

'Could you arrange it?' she pleaded.

'I can certainly try,' Richard flashed a further look of warning to James.

'Would you be happy with that?' Elanora smiled hopefully at her son.

'I'll go wherever the RAF demands, mother,' James replied. 'My duty to England comes first. If the war reaches the Far East, so be it. It doesn't matter where I fight, as long as I fight.'

'Oh, that's splendid,' Elanora wiped her eyes before smiling at them both in turn. 'Now!' she said briskly, 'James is quite correct, we must discuss the Company and Charles Higgins.'

Richard and James exchanged a glance of amusement. Elanora, ever mercurial, was now in the mood to talk business.

龍

Lee Kwan wiped his chest with a cloth and pulled on his thick coat to ward off the late autumn chill in the air. He'd completed two hours of Shaolin exercises and disciplines and now sat on a log and took in the view of the province of Szechwan spread below him like a quilted eiderdown.

The side of the hill he sat on formed a series of rice paddies falling away to the main road below and, beyond that, to the Yang-tse River, then south towards the province of Kweichow. To the south-west, in the far distance beside the river, he could just see the outline of Chungking, the city Ch'iang Kai-shek had declared the Nationalist capital of China.

Stretched along the road, as far as the eye could see, was a seething mass of refugees, slithering like a serpent inexorably towards Chungking. The river, too, was busy. Another

serpent, Lee thought, boatloads of refugees were motoring,
paddling or sailing their way towards the city of hope, a last
refuge from the Japanese Imperial Army.

Lee's heart swelled with love and admiration for these
eastern refugees making their way to Szechwan, yet anger for
their situation seethed in him. Scholars and poets, intellectuals and businessmen, farmers and laymen, all had given up
everything they owned to move west, away from the
Japanese. Academics too, from the eastern universities, had
loaded carts with the contents of their libraries and school-
rooms and followed the population to continue educating in
small villages under difficult conditions. He admired their
stoicism and their ineffable belief that one day things would
return to normal, that the Japanese would leave the Celestial
Kingdom. Yet, at the same time he despised them for the
sheep they were. How could they endure tyranny with such
forbearance? How could they suffer oppression without
striking out at their oppressors? What bizarre part of the psychological make up of the Chinese, as a race, had allowed
them to tolerate cruelty, persecution and domination by
emperors, war lords and foreign powers? They constituted
one quarter of the world's population, why couldn't they
stand up for themselves?

What will happen to you this time? Lee thought, as he
watched the never-ending human tide move below him. The
Japanese have taken possession of the whole eastern half of
your country. They've set up puppet governments in Peking,
Nanking and Canton in the south and they talk of 'Greater
Eastern Asia', the philosophy of *Wang-tao*, in which all the
peoples of Asia will live together harmoniously under a
beneficent Japanese administration. You can't possibly
believe that, there can be no harmony with the Japanese.
Why don't you turn on them and fight?

Lee plucked a piece of straw grass from beside him and
chewed on it. His countrymen in the east were already
starting to believe in *Wang-tao*. How could they? After what
happened in Shanghai and especially Nanking, how could
they possibly believe the Japanese propaganda? They will kill

and subvert! He wanted to scream it out to the stream of misery below, and he rose to his feet.

'*Look at me when I speak to you!*' he yelled, spitting the grass from his mouth. '*I am up here on the hill! Can you not hear me? You must fight and kill them until there is not one Japanese left standing on your soil!*' He raised his arms to Heaven, then sighed as his voice was carried away on the wind. He sat down again. What was the use, he thought.

A rattling noise startled him. He turned and saw Lin Li standing on the steps of the abandoned farmhouse they'd occupied, banging a spoon on the base of a cooking pot. She looked beautiful, her jet-black hair shining, a smile lighting her face.

Lee waved in acknowledgment of her call to breakfast and stared after her as she re-entered the house. She had changed greatly. So had they all, for that matter, he thought.

Much had transpired in Lee Kwan's life in the year of 1938.

He had been forced to leave Nanking. His actions in blowing up the Kempeitei Headquarters had been severely frowned upon by the International Safety Zone Committee. It was Minnie Vautrin who had been given the job of telling him he must go.

龍

'I did not vote against you, Lee,' Minnie Vautrin said as she sat down on a bench in the back garden of Ginling College. 'Neither did Doctor Wilson or Mr Rabe, but most of the others were furious. Your actions could have destroyed all they've accomplished.'

'There have been no reprisals,' Lee answered. He was folding the freshly-washed bandages that Lin Li was handing to him from the clothesline.

'That is not the point and you know it,' Minnie declared.

'I know. I'm sorry,' he looked at her. 'So, they want me to leave.'

'They are frightened, Lee. They fear another outburst of anger from you will bring Japanese reprisals against the

Safety Zone. And they are right to think that way. The anger in you is palpable, I can feel it from here.'

'When must I leave?'

'Tonight. The Committee has formulated a plan for your escape.' Minnie stood and opened her arms to him.

'Tonight? That soon, eh?' He gave a wry smile as he walked into her embrace.

'I shall miss you,' she crushed him to her ample bosom. 'You came to us in our hour of need, Lee Kwan, and I, for one, shall never forget you. You will always be, to those who suffered here, "The Angel of Nanking".'

'What's this?' Lee stepped back and held the American at arm's length. 'Tears, from Wilhelmina Vautrin?' He smiled. The tears were openly running down her cheeks. 'Why Minnie, as my guardian was wont to say, you're nothing but a big cry-baby.'

'Oh shush,' Minnie mopped at her face with her apron. 'Get a move on now, you've got plans to discuss with your brother-in-law Mr Lo and you'll have preparations to make . . . And here,' she pulled a large signet ring from her finger and pressed it into Lee's hand. 'You may be in need of money so take this, it belonged to my father and it's pure gold . . . Take it!' Minnie insisted as he began to protest. 'Your journey won't be an easy one. Simply getting out of Nanking will be difficult enough, what with four of you travelling together.'

'You mean three,' Lee corrected her.

'I mean four,' Minnie said flatly and her eyes shifted to Lin Li at the clothesline.

'She can't possibly come with us!'

'I'd like to see anyone try to stop her,' Minnie answered. 'You're her only connection with reality, Lee. Without you she'll lose her sanity completely.'

'Rubbish!'

'She was raped, and she was shot. And you appeared from nowhere and rescued her. You are her saviour, Lee.'

'I was simply in the right place at the right time,' he shrugged. 'It was pure luck.'

'What really happened is not important. It's what she thinks happened that matters. Come here and sit down,' Minnie sat once again and patted the bench beside her. 'What little I know of psychiatry leads me to believe that Lin Li is struggling with what happened to her, and in some way you have become the focal point of that struggle. If she loses contact with you, she may well lose contact with reality forever.'

'So you're saying I'm responsible for her?'

'Unfortunately for you, yes,' Minnie replied. 'As I said, I'm no psychiatrist, but I believe Lin Li could possibly recover from her experience given time. Time, a secure environment, and you . . .'

'I can't give her a secure environment,' he interrupted. 'I don't even know where I'm going! Besides which, we're in the middle of a war, or had you forgotten?'

'No, I hadn't forgotten,' Minnie said sternly.

'I'm sorry. Forgive me.'

'Lee, honey . . .' The American took his hand in hers. 'You are Lin Li's security. It won't matter to her where she is, in the middle of the Sahara Desert, or taking tea at Buckingham Palace as long as she is with you. Don't you see? Without you she will lose her fight.'

'All right,' Lee sighed. 'You win. I'll take her with me.' He looked at the young Chinese girl. Lin Li picked up her basket of washing and started walking towards the kitchen door, then, suddenly, she stopped and gave him a quizzical look. He nodded at her. And she offered him a glorious smile before disappearing inside.

'You see!' Minnie exclaimed.

He did.

'She smiled,' Minnie squeezed his hand. 'That's the first time I've ever seen her smile.'

It was in the freezing early hours of Saturday 15 January that Lee, along with Lin Li, old Soong and Lo Shi-mon left Nanking. Going by way of Lee's tunnel under The Wall, they reached the Yang-tse River by sunrise, where the German John Rabe of the International Safety Zone Committee had arranged for a boat to ferry them to Anhwei province some miles to the south.

Disillusioned with Ch'iang Kai-shek and his Nationalist Army, Lee had decided to return to Hong Kong and find an alternative way to assist his ailing country, but he had first to gain his release from the army. And so a plot had been hatched. Members of the International Safety Zone Committee would spread the word that the courageous Captain Lee Kwan had been killed fighting the Japanese. They had procured him false papers in the name of Fong Kip-mei, a scholar from Nanking University, and Doctor Wilson would officially inform the Nationalist Army that Lee was missing and presumed dead.

龍

As Lee walked up the hill to the old farmhouse he looked at the gold signet ring on his right hand and thought of Minnie Vautrin, and that evening in the garden behind Ginling College when Lin Li had first smiled at him. Lin Li smiled all the time now. Had it been nearly a year since they'd left Nanking? So much, so very much had happened since.

The northern and eastern provinces had fallen like dominoes as the year had progressed. First Hopeh, then Shantung, Shensi, Kiangsu, Anhwei, Chekiang, Honan and Hupeh. The Japanese tide was slowly flooding west. The city of Canton in the south had fallen only a month ago in October and at the same time the city of Hankow, not five hundred miles east of Chungking, had fallen too.

The four had spent the summer in Hankow and it had been a good time for them despite the growing food shortages and the increasingly hot weather. It had taken them nearly three months, most of the spring, to cover the three hundred miles from Nanking to Hankow. Life had been difficult and, at times, dangerous. On one occasion they'd had to fight off bandits in a mountain pass, and on another, while avoiding a group of Nationalist deserters who were waylaying people on the main road, they'd had to climb several steep hills and hide in a dry river bed overnight. They'd stopped in villages and towns for several nights at a time, watching the locals packing in preparation for their flight from the advancing Japanese invaders, and it was in one of these towns that Lee had entrusted his letters to Richard and Elanora into the care of two soldiers travelling to Canton. The soldiers had assured him they would send them on at the first opportunity.

When they'd finally reached Hankow, the four had found an abandoned house in the Street of Heavenly Peace and lived out the summer in reasonable comfort. Old Soong scoured the city each day for firewood, Lee and Lo Shi-mon foraged successfully for food, although at times they had to steal it, and all the while Lin Li cooked and washed for them. It was in Hankow that Lee first heard the news of his own death.

In the company of Old Soong, he went one night to the Inn of the Four Clouds. Listening to itinerant travellers was the only way of gathering any intelligence of the war. This particular night they eavesdropped on a group of Nationalist soldiers and Lee found the conversation bizarre.

龍

'The Dragon of Shanghai, he was known as,' one young soldier said. 'And do you know why? It was because he killed one hundred Turnip Heads in one afternoon!'

'That is nothing,' another declared. 'In Nanking, in one night, he killed two thousand men with the help of a Shaolin master!'

'Two thousand men in one night?' an older soldier sneered. 'That is not possible!'

'It is true!' a fourth soldier added. 'They blew fire from their mouths onto the Kempeitei building and it exploded. I heard this story from a sergeant in the 457th Brigade, who heard it from an officer in Ichang, who was told it by a foreigner who was in Nanking when it happened. It was this same foreign devil who said Captain Lee Kwan was dead.'

'The foreign devils,' the first soldier interjected, 'called him The Angel of Nanking.'

Old Soong chuckled madly as he listened to the soldiers' tales. *'Ha!'* he nudged his captain in the ribs. *'It seems your little trick has worked, Elder Brother. Next they will write songs of praise to your memory. Maybe that old devil General Ch'iang will order a medal to be sent to your family.'*

'Let us hope not,' Lee shuddered at the thought of Elanora receiving written news of his death. He wished he could inform her of the ruse he'd perpetrated, but he could not risk contacting her for fear of exposing the fraud. And the thought of this led him to another far more sickening realisation. He realised he could not return to Hong Kong. He was too well known in the Colony. His faked demise would soon be discovered by the Kuomintang and he would be posted as a deserter. Lee cursed himself. How stupid he had been.

Lo Shi-mon would tell Elanora the truth. Lo intended to return to Hong Kong by train from Hankow, but that would not be possible until the following month, because parts of the railway line had been destroyed by Japanese bombing.

Lee and Soong left the inn and walked down Ma Tai Lane to the Street of Heavenly Peace, Lee pondering his latest predicament and Soong still cackling at the joke. As they entered the house, Soong roared the news to all and sundry.

'Captain Lee Kwan is dead!' he yelled into the two rooms the four shared. *'Captain Lee Kwan, The Angel of Nanking is dead!'* A deafening scream from the back room rent the air.

Lin Li had been tending to a pot of soup simmering over the open fire in the back room when she heard Soong's pronouncement. Captain Lee Kwan is dead, she heard the old soldier call and her heart rose into her mouth.

'Nooooooooooo!' She felt the scream begin in the base of her being. It roared from her very soul, up through her diaphragm, past her vocal chords and out of her mouth. The demons from Nanking who lurked on the dark edges of her consciousness fled in fear at the sound. Like a death knell it rang through the rooms and out of the windows into the warm night air. Lin Li could not stop it, the scream would not be denied, it went on for an eternity until she staggered

into the front room and saw Lee Kwan standing there telling Soong to shut his stupid mouth.

The scream stopped as Lin Li's brain registered the truth. *'Lee Kwan,'* she cried out. *'Lee Kwan!'* She rushed to him, threw her arms about his neck and clung to him, trembling, as her fears abated. He picked her up in his arms and took her to her bed where he lay her gently on the quilt, brushing his hand over her brow, murmuring shushing sounds. Her fingernails bit so deeply into his flesh they drew blood. She stared wildly at him as he soothed her until, finally, her eyes closed and she fell into a deep, restorative, mind-healing sleep.

'You idiot!' Lee berated his old retainer when he returned to the front room.

'I thought she was deaf and dumb,' Soong declared.

'I have told you many times she is not deaf! True or not true?'

'True, true,' Soong answered. *'And now we know she is not dumb either, her scream nearly burst my eardrums! What a voice! She could wake the dead with that scream.'*

'You are right!' Lee exclaimed. In his panic at her terror, Lee had not realised. *'She screamed. By all the gods, she screamed.'*

'I am sorry I frightened her, Captain,' Soong apologised.

'Do not be sorry,' Lee grabbed old Soong in a bear hug, lifted him up and spun him around the room. *'Your stupidity has done Lin Li a great service.'*

'Really?' His Captain was squeezing the life out of him. *'Then if that is so, Elder Brother, why are you trying to kill me?'* he wheezed.

Lo Shi-mon burst through the front door. *'What was that scream?'* he asked, alarmed.

'I think it was a miracle,' Lee replied as he set old Soong back on his feet.

Lin Li slept for nearly fifteen hours and when she awoke, Lee Kwan was at her side with water and a wet towel to wipe her brow. She threw herself at him and clung like a frightened child, spilling the water all over her quilt.

'Oh! I so'ee,' she gasped, and the shock of hearing her own slurred voice startled her. She pulled back and stared at Lee.

'*It's all right,*' he replied with a smile. '*You have come back to us. Your journey is over, you are safe now.*'

'*I can spee . . .*' she whispered.

'*Yes, you can speak,*' Lee brushed the hair from her eyes. '*But do not try to for the moment, you must lie back and rest. I will get another cup of water for you.*' He wiped the spilt water up with the towel and went to fetch another cup full.

Lin Li lay back and stared around the room. Her mind searched for the demons she knew must still be dwelling on the edge of her consciousness, but she found only peace. Her mind was still. She conjured up the memories of that awful night in Nanking Hospital, but still the demons did not appear. She watched the horrific images pass through her mind and all she felt was sadness. Sadness for her friends who'd been raped and killed. Sadness as she watched her own body being violated. And then happiness, when Lee Kwan's face appeared above her as she lay on the hospital steps.

Lee returned to her bedside and offered the water to her. She took it and sipped it slowly all the while staring into his beautiful eyes.

'*You 'ere old 'oman,*' her voice slurred the words.

'*That's right, I was an old woman,*' Lee replied. '*You remember, do you?*'

'Yes, I 'emem'er.'

'*I always dressed as an old woman when I went through Nanking by day. I was dressed that way when I found you on the hospital steps.*'

''ank you,' she smiled.

'*Do not talk any more,*' he said, taking her hand. '*You must go slowly. Your tongue and face muscles are weak because you have been unable to use them. That is why your voice sounds strange. As your muscle strength returns so will your power of speech.*' Lee folded up a wet strip of leather and handed it to her. '*I want you to put this in your mouth and chew on it,*' he said. '*It will exercise your mouth and throat muscles and make them stronger. And I want you to hum too, because it will exercise your vocal chords. Understand or not understand?*'

'*Mmmmnnnhhh!*' Lin Li hummed, nodding vigorously as she bit into the leather.

The weeks passed and summer set in with a vengeance. The heat became unbearable in the streets of Hankow. June turned into July and news of the war became of secondary importance as the populace braced itself for water rationing and began praying for rain. Lin Li's voice soon came back and during the long hot days and shorter stiflingly hot nights, Lee delighted in her return to the land of the living.

Often on those hot sticky nights, sitting on the front steps desperate for the hint of a breeze, each would catch the other's covert glances. Secret smiles were exchanged and furtive touches ensued, until Lo Shi-mon, sick of watching them carry on, was forced to act.

'*I have five yuan,*' he declared to Soong one hot evening.

'*Where did you get money from?*' Soong asked.

'*I stole it.*'

'*Only an honest man would say that, Ah Lo,*' Soong replied.

'*Let us go to the Inn of the Four Clouds,*' Lo jumped to his feet.

'*Five yuan will not go far between four of us.*'

'*Then you and I will go on our own,*' Lo signalled Soong with his eyes, but the old soldier failed to read the message.

'*That wouldn't be fair to . . .*'

'*Put your shirt on,*' Lo ordered.

'*Yes, Sir!*'

When they'd gone, a tense silence filled the air. Lin Li sat mending a hole in the elbow of Soong's only other shirt and Lee Kwan concentrated on repairing the sole of his boot, which was all but hanging off. Both were keenly aware that they were alone, together, and the situation was causing considerable discomfort.

'*Will I boil water for tea?*' Lee asked.

'*We don't have any tea,*' she replied.

'*Oh.*' The silence returned with a vengeance.

'*Ah Lo meant for us to be alone,*' Lin Li said, finally.

'*Yes.*'

'*What should we do?*'
'*I do not know.*'
'*We should not waste the time he has given us.*'
'*No.*'
'*Lo Shi-mon has been very gracious.*'
'*Yes.*'
'*He is a wise man, your teacher.*'
'*Yes.*'
'*Remember that night at my father's inn . . .*'
'*Yes, I do.*'
'*. . . when you refused my offer?*'
'*Yes, I remember.*'
'*Would you refuse the offer again?*'
'*No.*'
'*Even though I am no longer a virgin?*' Lin Li's eyes looked for an honest reply.

Lee looked at Lin Li. He realised how difficult the moment was for her and how brave and forthright her question, and he realised, in that instant, that he loved her.

'*You are still a virgin,*' he replied. '*I know this for a fact. Do you think I have not kept an eye on you all this time we have been together? If you had lost your virginity, I, Lee Kwan, would know of it.*'

'*You are kind, Lee Kwan.*' Tears stung her eyes.
'*And you are good, Lin Li.*'
'*Will you take my virginity?*'
'*It would be an honour I would cherish forever.*'

龍

And an honour it had been. Lee would never forget that night. The night when they had both ceased to be virgins. He remembered her surprise when he had told her that he had never slept with a woman, and he smiled at the memory as he stooped to enter the old farmhouse.

Lin Li was seated at the table with Soong. She was ladling hot soup from a pot into three wooden bowls. There were only three of them now, Lo Shi-mon having left from Hankow. Lee grinned from ear to ear as he sat down to eat.

'*What is so funny, husband?*' Lin Li asked, smiling back at him.

'*Nothing, wife,*' he replied, spooning the hot liquid into his mouth. '*I had a surge of great happiness. There was no reason, it just happened.*'

'*I too have these surges of happiness,*' Lin Li patted her distended stomach. '*It is your son growing inside my womb who causes such feelings. Perhaps he transmits them to us both?*'

'*I am sure you are right, Lin Li,*' he grinned again. '*And perhaps it is this farmhouse on top of this hill that makes him transmit such thoughts to us. I have not been this content for a long time. Perhaps it is my destiny to live on a hill in Szechwan with my beautiful wife and child.*'

'*Your destiny lies in Hong Kong, Captain,*' Old Soong muttered without looking up from his soup. '*You know in your heart this is true.*'

'*I cannot return to Hong Kong, Ah Soong,*' Lee cast a worried look at Lin Li. '*The Kuomintang will discover my lie and seek me out.*'

'*The Kuomintang Headquarters is in Chungking not ten miles from here, Elder Brother,*' Soong said. '*Can we not go to there and explain that the news of your death was false? They would welcome you back as a hero.*'

'*And where do I tell them I have been for the past year?*'

'*You tell them that you were injured by a bomb in Nanking,*' Soong put down his spoon and ignored his soup.

'*For a whole year?*'

'*You tell them you forgot who you were,*' Soong suggested eagerly. '*You tell them that you suffered the war disease of forgetfulness and that you have only now remembered. It happens to soldiers all the time.*'

'*And what will you tell them you've been doing for the past twelve months, Ah Soong? Will you tell them that you were blown up by the same bomb, and that you too forgot who you were?*'

'*It is vaguely believable, Elder Brother.*'

'*Ha!*' Lee hooted. '*They would shoot you!*'

'*I am sorry, Captain,*' Old Soong looked sadly at his young comrade. '*I am not a smart man. I was only trying to help. You must sort this problem out or it will follow you forever. One day the Kuomintang will find out and you will be a fugitive for the rest of your life.*' He gave a philosophical shrug. '*Unless, of course, they catch you.*'

'*Is this true, husband?*' Lin Li's face was as white as a funeral shroud.

Lee stared at the remains of his soup. '*Yes, wife, it is true. Damn you, Soong,*' he muttered. '*Couldn't we have discussed this in private? Lin Li is with child and has enough to worry about without you frightening her.*'

'*Don't you dare blame Ah Soong!*' It was Lin Li's turn to explode. '*He is your most trusted friend. He speaks from his heart to you and you curse him. It is not honourable!*'

'Damn it! Damn it! Damn it!' Lee stood and walked to the front door.

'*And don't talk English! We do not speak English! You are being rude!*'

Lee leant against the doorway and stared down at the worn stone steps of the farmhouse. How many feet had climbed up and down them to wear them down like that, part of his mind wondered? How old were they, three hundred, four hundred years? Maybe a thousand? Who had carved them? Who had cut them from the hillside and placed them where they now were? An ordinary man, he supposed. An ordinary man, long ago, had built this stone house with loving care to provide shelter for his family. All this ran through Lee's mind as he sought to divorce himself from the conundrum he faced. What to do, his mind asked itself over and over. What to do?

'*Come and sit down, husband,*' Lin Li said quietly. '*We must discuss this problem. All of our lives are at stake, including your unborn son's.*'

'You are right, Lin Li,' he turned back to them and sat down. '*I have been stupid. I did not anticipate the consequences my actions would cause. It all seemed so simple in Nanking. How could I have believed I could escape the Kuomintang?*'

'The answer to our problem is simple enough,' Lin Li said. 'But it could be dangerous for you, my husband.'

'You mean go to Chungking?' he asked.

'They will not doubt your word, Captain,' Soong said. 'No one would dare to suggest you deserted. You are a legend among the troops in the Kuomintang.'

'Tell them you were gravely ill for many months,' Lin Li added. 'Tell them you had the disease of the mind known as soldier's sickness, just as Soong suggested.'

'And what then?' Lee looked at his wife. 'I will be re-inducted into the army and posted to . . . only the gods know where.'

'We will deal with that when it happens,' Lin Li reached out and took his hand. 'First you must undo the mistake you made in Nanking. Other matters will take care of themselves.'

'I cannot leave you alone. You are carrying our child.'

'Ah Soong will stay with me and this farmhouse will afford us shelter. We will be safe.'

'No!' Lee declared. 'I could be gone for a long time. The Turnip Heads are already in Hankow. You cannot stay here. They will come this way to attack Chungking.'

'But there is nowhere else for us to go.'

'Yes, there is,' Lee looked at his old friend. 'Soong?'

'Yes, Elder Brother?'

'You will take Lin Li south-east to Changsha in Hunan Province. The Japanese army has not reached there yet. You will take the train south to Canton, then you will take a boat down the Pearl River to Hong Kong.'

'The Japanese have taken Canton.'

'But you know Canton very well, you once lived there, true or not true? You should be able to avoid them there and find a boat to sail you to Hong Kong.'

Old Soong nodded his head slowly. 'It is possible. But it is a thousand miles to Canton, it is a long journey you propose for us, Ah Lee.'

'Not as long as mine, old friend,' Lee squeezed his wife's hand. 'Not as long as mine.'

龍

'Good evening, Charles.'

'My dear fellow!' Charles Higgins exclaimed. He leapt to his feet as Richard Brewster entered his study. 'And James,' he said as James Merchant followed his stepfather into the room. 'My, my, but you do look resplendent in your uniform. This is a pleasant surprise.' Higgins shook hands with both men and sensed immediately that something was wrong. 'What on earth could drag you away from Hallowdene on such a fearfully chilly winter's night, Richard?'

It had taken a long time to catch Charles Higgins out, and their final discovery of the cold, hard evidence had proved ludicrously simple. Richard had been discussing Society business with Robert McCraw by telephone in Hong Kong and had bemoaned the fact that the investigation into Higgins was going nowhere. McCraw had suggested Richard talk to Thomas Smith, the company chauffeur, and the walls had come tumbling down.

Thomas Smith had proved to be more than a simple chauffeur. The old soldier and friend of McCraw had provided the simple link they'd been searching for between Higgins and the associates of Sir Herbert Billings. Thomas had produced the logbooks of the company car, and there in the pages which he'd assiduously written up each day, was the evidence Richard needed.

The books showed that Charles had made regular visits to a house in Richmond over the previous two years. There, on the first Monday of every month in The Coach and Horses Tavern, he met with the Reverend Keith Marshall, the shepherd of local Methodist souls. Malcolm Linden had tailed Marshall and discovered that Marshall, in turn, kept a regular appointment every first Wednesday of the month with George Carmichael, a Customs Officer, on the Victoria Embankment, not far from the Houses of Parliament.

The rest of the case had been a matter of simple surveillance and patience. Several trusted agents of the Dragon Import Company had pieced together the chain of evidence Richard had needed and now poor old Charles and several of his cronies were for the drop. Richard relished the thought of confronting Charles Higgins. He would make him sweat then put him to the sword, slowly.

'We have something to discuss, Charles,' Richard said coldly. 'Something very important.'

'Of course, my dear fellow,' Charles felt a shiver of anxiety run up his spine. 'But do have a seat. Can I get you tea?' They both shook their heads. 'Brandy, then? It's definitely brisk enough for it.'

'Lock the doors, James,' Richard said.

'Lock the doors?' Charles queried. 'My word, Richard, this must be important.' A sick feeling began to churn in the pit of Charles' stomach. They were on to him. He was certain of it. But how, in God's name, had they found out? He'd been so careful.

Charles watched as James locked the doors then crossed to the window behind the desk and pulled the drapes. It was James who really terrified him. James had that hooded, feral look in his eyes that Charles had always feared, the look of that tiger in the zoo. I'm to be his next meal, he thought. Stop it. Keep calm, he urged himself. Find out what they know. It may not be that bad. Quick thinking and the odd lie might see you extricate yourself from all this. Damn! If only James would stop staring at me.

'It's a life and death situation, Charles,' Richard said as he sat at Charles' desk.

'Really?' Charles heard himself ask.

'Yes,' Richard's gaze was malevolent. 'My life and your death.'

'What on earth do . . .' Charles began to bluster.

'I told you years ago, that if you ever betrayed me I'd kill you.'

'Betrayed you?' Charles gulped. 'I haven't betrayed you, Richard.'

'James and I attended church this afternoon.'

'Oh really? You went to church?' What the hell was going on, he thought.

'Yes,' Richard smiled coldly. 'A quaint little Methodist church in . . . where was it again?'

'Richmond,' James said.

'I don't see where this is all leading, Richard,' Charles feigned ignorance. 'First you talk of betrayal and then you go to church. What on earth . . .?'

'The church was empty,' Richard continued. 'Except for the reverend. I believe you know the Reverend Keith Marshall? Tall skinny chap, ex-Oxford, quite a decent county cricketer in his day, or so he told us.'

'I can't say I've heard of him,' Charles coughed nervously. They had him all right.

'That's strange, considering you've been paying him regular visits for the past couple of years. They stopped while you were on the Continent, but they started again upon your return. Regular as clockwork.'

'Yairs, yairs,' Charles drawled, adopting his confident air, buying time. 'All right, Richard, very good, very good, you've caught me. I've been a naughty fellow. Why don't we put our cards on the table, eh? Eh? Just what did the jolly old reverend tell you?'

'He told us everything, Charles,' Richard glared at his former superior. 'And then James killed him.'

'And not before time, dare I say,' Charles tried to smile, but the knot in his stomach grew tighter as he imagined just what James, who was now standing right beside him, might have done to Keith Marshall. 'Nothing worse than a crooked priest, wouldn't you agree? The very worst form of hypocrite, a crooked priest.'

'It was a heart attack, Charles, if that's what you're wondering,' Richard said. 'Brought about by a blow to the chest. It leaves a tiny bruise, hardly noticeable.'

'Yairs, yairs. Young James' doing, I imagine?' Charles was beginning to perspire heavily.

'George Carmichael from the Ministry for Customs and Excise has precisely the same bruise,' Richard said. 'He's lying in the morgue as we speak, probably alongside the Right Honourable Tyler Winslow MP who, unfortunately, fell down the stairs outside his office in the houses of Parliament this morning, and snapped his neck in the process.

People say accidents happen in threes Charles, but I think they happen in fours.'

'Meaning me, I take it?' They know it all, he thought. They've cleaned up everyone associated with the affair and now they've come for me. 'I'm to be the fourth, am I?'

'Charles the Fourth,' Richard said. 'The man who would be king, eh Charles? Well, your tilt at the throne was unsuccessful.' His lip curled in a sneer. 'Kill him, James.'

'I'm afraid it won't be as easy as that, Richard.' Terrified as he was, Charles forced himself to remain composed. He still had the ace up his sleeve, the escape route he'd kept open for emergencies. And this was definitely an emergency, he thought as his eyes flickered to the young fighter pilot who was about to kill him. 'You didn't think I'd get involved in this little, *contretemps*, shall we call it, without including an escape clause, did you?'

'Nothing on earth will stop your execution this time, Charles,' Richard said.

'Really?' James' hand was reaching for him, he could already feel the power in the air between those fingers and his throat. 'How about four golden dragons with fabulous gemstones for eyes? White, blue, red and green, does that ring a bell?'

'Don't touch him, James!' On Richard's command, the hand fell short of Higgins' throat. 'Spit it out, Charles!'

'I know who got them, Richard,' Charles straightened his tie and brushed back his silver hair with his palm. He walked over to the sideboard and began pouring himself a brandy, but his hands were shaking as he realised just how close he'd been to Eternity.

'Go on,' Richard said.

'It wasn't all that hard when I put my mind to it. Cheers,' he said and sipped from his glass. 'I must admit, at first I was utterly flabbergasted. Yairs, yairs, when I heard that the crates had arrived in London filled with rocks I was so shocked it took me a year to recover. However, when I eventually calmed down and was able to give the matter some thought, it came down to a simple process of elimination.'

He looked at Richard. 'It had to be someone as close to John Merchant as I had been, someone with total access to both his business and private life. It was the beautiful Elanora, was it not? It couldn't have been anyone else, although I must say the discovery surprised me greatly.'

'It would appear, Charles,' Richard said softly. 'That like so many other men who see nothing but her beauty, you greatly underestimated Elanora.'

'Yairs,' Charles shrugged philosophically. 'Yairs, yairs. By God but she's a magnificent woman! She's a match for any man on the face of the Earth. You're a lucky fellow, Richard, if you'll permit me to say so.'

'Forgive me if I appear a little slow in this matter,' Richard answered. 'But what makes you think this particular piece of information will save your worthless neck?'

'Oh, that's easy,' Charles drained his glass and poured another. 'In the event of my death, a letter will be delivered to the Military High Command of the Kuomintang now barracked in Chungking. It's addressed to Generalissimo Ch'iang Kai-shek, the little yellow monkey who's trying, clumsily I might add, to defend China from the Japanese hordes. I'm willing to bet he'll be only too delighted when he finds out who stole his pretty golden statues.'

Richard said nothing, but silently he was cursing Charles Higgins. And Charles knew it.

'He'll want them back, of course,' Charles was gaining confidence by the second. 'Generals need armies. Armies need weapons. Weapons cost money. Lots and lots of money. Yairs, yairs,' he grinned over the rim of his glass, 'I would say dear old Generalissimo Ch'iang will most definitely want his little statues back. That is, of course, if they still are statues and have not been melted down into more convenient and far less conspicuous shapes, like ingots? But then again, I don't suppose it will matter to Mr Ch'iang as long as he gets his gold back, or its equivalent value in cash.' He began to relax, knowing that he'd won. 'And, dare I say, given today's gold prices that would be a princely sum of money.' Charles feigned a look of concern. 'Why, Richard,' he chuckled. 'You've gone quite green!'

'I should have killed you years ago.'

'I know,' Charles said gently, with the benign tone of a father talking to a child. 'But you didn't, did you? And now, you're going to leave my house and go back to your jolly old hockey sticks and polo ancestral seat in Surrey and forget all about tonight. And remember, my death will cause the greatest catastrophe for your family and friends that you could ever imagine. It is in your best interests to keep me alive and happy.'

'We could always have you pick up the phone and retrieve the letter,' James said softly. 'I'm sure I could convince you to do that.'

'The letter has been attested by a notary public and deposited in the Bank of England.' Charles quelled his shiver of fear as he looked at the young man. 'I couldn't retrieve it if I wanted to. You have a choice, it seems,' he said, turning to Richard. 'Use the time you have left to prepare your defences before, God willing, my death by natural causes, or kill me now and have the Kuomintang all over you like a pack of rabid dogs.'

Damn you, Charles, Richard thought, but once again he didn't say it.

'Yairs, yairs,' Charles smiled. 'I know what you're thinking, my dear fellow. They're an unforgiving lot the KMT, aren't they, eh? Eh?' He chuckled again, actually enjoying the moment.

'It's a Pyrrhic victory you've won, Charles,' Richard said finally.

'Pyrrhic, you say? How so, Richard? Pyrrhus defeated the Romans but suffered heavy losses. I've defeated you and suffered no loss at all. Might I suggest you re-read your history books.' He placed his palms together, fingertips beneath his chin. 'Now, if you two will excuse me I'm having smoked salmon for supper. Will you kindly leave my house?'

'Your house?' James queried. 'Aren't you forgetting something, *Uncle* Charles?'

'And what might that be, young man?' Charles didn't like the boy's tone, but he sniffed haughtily anyway, sure of his ground.

'This house, is jointly owned by Dragon Imports, of which Richard is the Chairman of Directors, and The Merchant Company, of which I am the heir apparent. If anyone should leave, it should be you. Wouldn't you agree, Richard?'

Richard simply nodded.

'Ah, I see,' Charles laughed. 'My Pyrrhic victory, eh? You're going to throw me out of my home. Tut, tut,' he said as if speaking to a recalcitrant schoolboy. 'Come now, you're behaving like a child, Richard. Can't you simply yield like a gentleman? Admit that I've bested you and be gracious in defeat? Eh? Eh?'

'When I spoke of your Pyrrhic victory, Charles, I meant just that. You have won your life, but that is all. You will get out of this house while you still can. And I suggest that you get out of England. If you do not, I shall see to it that you are ruined financially, shunned by your friends, and provoked by your enemies.'

'I don't think you will, Richard.' Charles began backing away from the madman but froze as he felt James' hand against his back.

'If it costs me a million pounds, Charles, I swear to you that you will become a man without a face, an outcast, a pariah!'

'Melodrama does not become you, dear boy,' Charles murmured. 'Now tell your assassin here to let me pass.' He eased his glass onto the sideboard, extricated himself from between the two men, straightened his clothes and unlocked the study doors. 'You're angry, Richard. When you calm down you'll realise my position is inviolate while that letter remains in the vaults of The Bank of England. When it is eventually delivered I'll be dead and therefore beyond your grasp entirely. Face it, Richard, I've won,' he gestured with a theatrical wave of his hand. 'The house is yours, but the victory is mine.' With a mocking bow, Charles Higgins turned and left.

'You've got to give the fellow credit.' James remarked. 'It's checkmate.'

'*May he spend Eternity in the fangs of Wu Loong,*' Richard muttered in Cantonese.

'It's a nice thought, I'll agree,' James said. 'But I rather hope he has a very long life before he meets that old black dragon. Because when he does, and that letter is delivered . . .'

'I know,' Richard said. 'When Charles meets the dragon, we meet the Kuomintang.'

BOOK THREE

BATTLE

CHAPTER SEVENTEEN

Central China, 1940

February snow was falling heavily across the parade square of Kuomintang Headquarters in Chungking as Captain Lee Kwan mounted the front stairs of the building and stood stamping his feet and huffing clouds of steam into the night air.

'Good evening, Captain,' the uniformed sentry said. '*Chungking is the coldest place in the world tonight, true or not true?*'

'True, soldier,' Lee Kwan returned the young soldier's salute. '*The best thing you can do on sentry duty is ignore the cold and dream of some place warmer.*'

'*I know just the place, Captain Kwan,*' the soldier grinned. '*My wife has such a place.*'

'*Well, dream of that,*' Lee smiled. It was the basic response of a soldier at war. Give me a place to rest and forget for a few hours that I am a soldier, a place where I can be simply a man, or where I can cry out my fears like a child. And that place, for most men, was in the arms of a woman. Lee patted the sentry on the shoulder. '*Dreams keep you warm, little brother, take it from one who knows. Dreams of my wife and child have kept me warm for the past year.*' His dreams of Lin Li might have kept him warm, he thought as he entered the front doors of the building, but his waking hours had been fraught with worry for her safety.

Lee had been stationed in the mountain village of Chung Si for twelve months. It was a broken down military outpost in the far west of Sikang Province, and he had been sent there after his re-instatement into the Army. His explanation of his whereabouts throughout the year of 1938 had been accepted by a military tribunal, but with some scepticism. His rank was restored to him, but the Kuomintang had made sure 1939 was a year he would never forget. A year in which he would have time to reflect upon his devotion to the Nationalist cause, while his re-education was conducted.

The time spent in the remote mountain area of Sikang, completely cut off from the outside world, had nearly driven Lee insane. If it had not been for his Shaolin teachings he sometimes wondered if he would have survived the isolation. He'd honed his skills every day, concentrating with all his will to shut out his worry at the fate of his wife and child. To this moment he had no idea of the fate of Lin Li and Old Soong. Had they made it to Hong Kong? Were they safe? Was he a father and if so was his child a boy or a girl?

He would find out soon enough, he thought. He was back from the wilds of Sikang, back from his year of penal servitude and he would find out as soon as it was humanly possible.

Upon entering the building, Lee took off his military greatcoat and looked about. Scattered around the huge reception area were groups of officers, pawing over maps and talking animatedly about whatever part of the winter war they were engaged in. Several men of lower rank busied themselves at a tea urn, distributing welcome cups to those about them. A young private bowed and took Lee's coat from him.

'Well, well. If it isn't the legendary Captain Kwan,' a sarcastic voice remarked. 'Back from service in the west.'

'Good evening, Major Yip,' Lee said, studying the man who approached him, hand extended. Major Yip Mei-hun, known as 'The Weasel', was Liaison Officer on General Ch'iang Kai-shek's personal staff, and a man for whom Lee Kwan felt a distinctive dislike. Yip was a schemer and dissembler of the worst kind who valued nothing in the world above his own welfare and comfort. Rumours persisted that he'd deserted his post at Tangli Headquarters in Shanghai, and that many valuable documents, which Yip should have personally destroyed, had fallen into Japanese hands. Nothing could be proved, and Yip remained on the General's personal staff, where he made sure he was indispensable as a paper clerk, chief spy and rumour-monger.

'*Welcome back, Captain. I do hope 1940 will prove a more pleasant year for you than 1939,*' Yip said as he shook Lee's hand.

'*Pleasant? Europe is in flames, Major, and China is being torn apart. I do not think 1940 will be pleasant for anyone.*'

'*I have no interest in what the foreign devils do to each other in Europe,*' Yip announced to the whole room. '*But while you were stationed in the wilds of Sikang the United States of America cancelled its trade treaty with Japan. That means no raw materials for the Turnip Heads. Their war with us will grind to a halt.*'

'*If you believe that, Major, you do not know your enemy. And if you do not know your enemy, you cannot fight a war.*' Lee returned the major's handshake a little more forcefully than was necessary, Yip suffering the pain in silence. '*And speaking of war, how goes your own war, Major?*' He decided to rub salt into the wounds, knowing only too well that Major Yip was a man who avoided conflict like a dog avoids a bath. '*Fought in any decent engagements lately?*'

'*Not much is happening at the moment, Captain,*' Yip smiled coldly. '*The Japanese seem to have gone into their shells for the winter.*'

'*Lucky for them, or you would have taught them a lesson. True or not true?*'

'*True,*' Yip replied through clenched teeth. He couldn't stand Captain Lee Kwan. He couldn't stand heroes, full stop. Heroes like Lee Kwan with their foolish acts of bravery raised the benchmark by which all other soldiers were judged. Heroes like Lee Kwan made the chances of being killed in war far more likely for everyone about them. Heroes like Lee Kwan, to Yip's way of thinking, should be shot before they got everybody else shot.

'*Can you tell me why I have been summoned?*' Lee asked.

'*I could,*' Yip answered. '*But General Ch'iang's Chief-of-Staff must see you first. I believe it is called privilege of rank.*'

He is in his office.' Yip pointed to a set of beautifully carved wooden doors in the far corner of the foyer.

'*I thought the Chief-of-Staff had gone with General Ch'iang to Yenan to negotiate with the Communists?'*

'*Aiyaah!*' Yip exclaimed. '*You have been out of circulation for a long time, haven't you, Captain?'*

'*General Ch'iang is wise to negotiate with the Communists,'* Lee replied. '*Mao and his fanatical comrades have the support of the masses. True or not true?'*

'*Shhh!*' the major looked about him to see if their conversation had been noted before glaring at Lee. '*Talk like that is bordering on treason, Captain. Please do not include me in such conversation.'*

'*Our Army's behaviour towards the people is becoming more and more fascist every day, Yip!*' Lee declared loudly, causing several soldiers to look up from their conversations. '*The peasants in the fields are beginning to compare the behaviour of the Kuomintang with that of the Japanese Army. Some citizens are even suggesting Japanese rule may be the lesser of two evils.'*

'*Your words are seditious!*' A young lieutenant interrupted Lee's outburst. '*You should not utter such things! You should not even think such things!'*

'*What did you say?*' Lee turned on the lieutenant. He stared at the young officer, who was wearing a red and green patch on his tunic indicating he was a member of the Propaganda Unit.

'*I said,*' the lieutenant's voice was tinged with disdain. '*You should not even think such thoughts.'*

'*It is my inalienable right to think,*' Lee glared at the young man. '*And indeed to say, whatever I wish! The preservation of that right is the reason I wear this uniform!*' Lee advanced upon the young officer. '*It is the sole reason I am engaged in fighting this war. Your uniform indicates that you are in the Propaganda Unit, little boy,*' he sneered. '*Would I be correct in saying you are one of the eaters of pig excrement who are going about telling the local population to stop thinking? Perhaps you can enlighten me on this subject.*

Is it true an order has been issued by General Ch'iang demanding that freedom of thought be suppressed? Or was the peasant who told me that he had been ordered by the Army to stop thinking just making a joke when he asked me how to do it?'

'*You are being facetious, Captain,*' the young officer retorted.

'*With such an absurd order being issued, how can I be anything else, Lieutenant?*' Lee queried. '*Can you please explain to me just how the Army intends to suppress thought? The only way I know to stop a brain from thinking is to put a bullet through it! Do you intend to shoot people who disobey this order? And please explain also how you determine who has disobeyed the order? How can you tell who has stopped thinking and who has not?*'

'*The order does not suggest that people literally stop thinking,*' the young lieutenant was angry at being called 'little boy' in front of his fellow officers, yet he was unnerved. He knew only too well the identity of the Captain glaring at him. '*But your outburst this evening leads me to question just where your loyalties lie, Captain Kwan.*'

'*And the mindless obedience to orders of profound stupidity, which you and others like you display, Lieutenant, leads me to question the very same thing!*'

'*That is treason,*' the young Lieutenant gasped.

'*What is treason?*' The voice was one of authority. Lee turned and saw Colonel Chung, the staff officer who'd ordered him to leave Shanghai. Chung was standing in the arch of the open doorway to his office.

'*Sir, Captain Kwan just declared that he is no longer loyal to the Nationalist cause,*' the young lieutenant said. '*Everyone in the room heard him.*'

'*Captain Kwan is merely obeying orders, Lieutenant,*' Colonel Chung said, motioning Lee to join him. '*Our Supreme Commander's orders. It is a game our Commander plays to keep people on their toes. He has one of his officers talk a little treason here and there to see if anyone responds inappropriately to it.*'

'*The young lieutenant,*' Lee said loudly as he joined Colonel Chung, '*is rabid in his support of the Nationalist cause, Colonel. I highly recommend him, Sir . . .*'

'Good! Good!' Colonel Chung ushered Lee into his office.

'*. . . as another of the mindless young men who will lose us the war,*' Lee hissed as Colonel Chung closed the door behind them.

'*Your tongue will get you beheaded one of these days, Ah Lee.*' Lee followed the Colonel to his desk as Chung circled behind it. '*Did a year in the wilderness teach you nothing? You have been out of touch for too long. Things have changed.*'

The office door opened and Major Yip stepped inside. He carefully closed the door and positioned himself beside it. Lee stared at Yip for a moment before turning back to Colonel Chung with a look of enquiry. Chung simply shook his head and sat down.

Lee heaved a sigh of resignation and muttered under his breath. '*Thank you for what you just did, Colonel. I went too far, I know it, and what you said got me off the hook. But that young lieutenant and those of his ilk make me sick to my stomach. Are there no real soldiers left in the ranks?*' He glanced at Major Yip, keeping his voice low so that the detestable man couldn't hear. '*Are they all fawning propagandists, spouting meaningless phrases like "suspend free thinking" as they attempt to re-educate the masses? And what does that mean, "re-educate the masses"? The "masses", as these damned propagandists so callously call their countrymen, were never educated in the first place, so how can they be re-educated?*'

'Well,' Colonel Chung interrupted sarcastically. '*It would seem your own re-education was a great success.*'

'*I was treated like a village idiot for twelve months, Colonel,*' Lee's anger at his enforced isolation and the stupidity of his 're-education' was evident in his voice. '*I was made to read absurd literature espousing the Nationalist cause and ordered to recite aloud mindless metaphors and ridiculous positivity slogans written by the Propaganda Unit. Fortunately my love of country is strong and remained intact, but the gods alone know what that sort of treatment could do to someone with less strength of mind. The war is not going well, Sir, and if the Army continues this re-education rubbish . . .'*

'Captain Kwan!' Colonel Chung cut him off in mid sentence, then lowered his voice. *'There are many times when I feel just as you do, but I am a soldier first and foremost. I keep my opinions to myself.'* His eyes fell momentarily on Major Yip. *'And you would do well to do likewise.'*

'Besides . . .' Lee paid no heed, pacing the Colonel's office as he began his tirade in earnest, louder this time. *'What good is education to a starving man? Can he eat it? Can he feed it to his children? Can he burn it to warm his house when the winter snows threaten his existence?'*

'Captain!' Colonel Chung stood, smashing his fist upon the desk.

Lee stopped at the sound, realising how indiscreet he had been. He was expounding his political theories perhaps to the wrong man, and certainly in the wrong place. *'I beg your pardon, Colonel Chung,'* he said self-consciously. *'Inactivity does this to me, Sir. It's been a year since I returned to uniform. A year of enforced idleness, and this harsh winter, have allowed me to think too much.'*

'We have all suffered the same winter, Captain,' Major Yip said from his position near the door.

Both men stared at Yip for a second but neither spoke. Chung sat behind his desk. *'You are not alone in your opinions, Lee, but idleness is a professional soldier's worst enemy. It gives him time to dwell upon things other than war, and when he does so, he is of no use to his regiment or his country. Do you understand or not understand, Captain?'*

'I understand only too well, Colonel,' Lee said. *'For I have had much time to dwell upon the whereabouts of my wife and the safety of our child whom I have never seen. I have not heard from her since she left for Hong Kong in December of 1938. It is now late February 1940 and I do not even know where she is.'*

'She is in Hong Kong at your guardian's residence,' Major Yip had edged a little further into the room.

'*You have news of her?*' Lee could barely contain his excitement.

'*Your wife arrived in Hong Kong in March last year and was taken into the House of Merchant by your guardian, Elanora Escaravelho.*'

'*Is there any further news? She was pregnant and very near her time.*'

'*No news of that nature, Captain,*' Yip replied. '*But you will be able to find out for yourself in a few days.*'

'*I do not understand.*'

'*With all due respect, Colonel Chung,*' Yip said softly as he approached the desk. '*I think it is time you left us alone.*'

'*Yes, of course.*' Colonel Chung replied stiffly. He stood and straightened his tunic. '*Forgive me, Captain Lee, but I am a soldier and orders are orders.*' He crossed to the door and opened it. '*Major Yip has a mission for you, the details of which General Ch'iang did not see fit to impart to me.*'

Lee watched, embarrassed, as the old soldier left the room closing the door silently behind him. Major Yip, smiling like a well-fed crocodile, made a show of seating himself at the Colonel's desk.

'*We are going on a mission,*' Yip took an envelope from his pocket and tossed it across the desk to Lee. '*Here are your movement orders.*'

'*We?*' Lee said, picking up the envelope.

'*That is correct. We fly out of Chungking tomorrow. We will be in Hong Kong by Friday.*'

'*Hong Kong?*' The mention of Hong Kong caused Lee's heart to miss a beat. He was going home. To do what, he had no idea, nor did he care. He would see Lin Li and his child.

'*On a mission, Captain, just you and I,*' the Major continued. '*A mission so important General Ch'iang refused to commit the details of it to paper. Instead, he sent me here from Yenan, entrusting me to convey his orders to you personally.*'

Lee struggled to pay attention, but in his excitement it was difficult. I will see Lin Li and my baby, he thought. And Elanora and Richard. It seemed an eternity since he'd seen

Elanora and Richard. And James, he thought eagerly. I will see my brother James.

龍

'Rise and shine, Sir. Come along, it's nearly five a.m.'

The Airman Orderly's voice dragged Flight Lieutenant James Merchant from his sleep. He sat up and looked around the hut, then focused his attention on the young man offering him a steaming mug of tea.

'Thank you, Thompkins,' he managed to mumble. His sleep had been fitful, filled with visions of aerial combat, of exploding fuselages, of wings falling, flaming towards the earth, of German aircraft flashing past him and tracer bullets flashing through the night sky. His dream had not been a nightmare, he realised, it had simply been his mind expressing his frustration. Once again he found himself engaged in the act of killing without personal confrontation.

To James Merchant, aerial combat was not heroic. It was not gallant, as he'd expected it to be. It was anonymous. He flew in a machine and destroyed other machines, then informed his Squadron Intelligence Officer of their shapes and sizes when he landed. A consummate pilot, he enjoyed the technique of aerial combat, the feeling of being at one with his machine. But there was no honour in the actual killing. He felt like a kitchen maid told to swat flies.

'Your wingman, Sir, Flight Sergeant Beckham,' the orderly said softly. 'He thought you might like a cup of tea before flight check, Mr Merchant.'

'Very thoughtful of the sergeant,' James replied. 'Very thoughtful of you both, I must say.' He stood and clutched the mug of tea.

The hut was cold and, as the orderly left the room, James hopped from one foot to the other trying to avoid the chill from the concrete floor.

He dressed quickly, leaving his pyjamas on for extra warmth. Even though it was the end of summer, the air at twenty thousand feet was freezing. Over the top of them, he pulled on Irvin trousers, a woollen sweater, thick fleecy flying boots, a scarf and his Irvin jacket. Then, picking up the mug of tea, he left the room. He had flies to swat.

He hurried across the wet grass to the line of Spitfires, dim silhouettes in the half-light, sitting silent, dangerous, awaiting the first rays of the sun. With their noses pointed high at the horizon they seemed, to James, animated. War birds sniffing the air, hoping for a scent of their enemy.

'Morning, Dickie,' James called to his wingman. Richard Beckham was already climbing into the cockpit of his Spitfire to begin the pre-flight check James had made mandatory. A lot of pilots who'd passed through 806 Squadron had neglected the simple exercise, to their peril.

What the newspapers were calling the Battle of Britain had dragged on through June, July and now August of 1940 and James had seen many young pilots come and go. They were mostly just crosses in the ground now, their faces faded from his memory. The only ones to survive the aerial slaughter had been the cautious ones, men who left nothing to chance, even the simple exercise of a pre-flight check before taking to the air and the madness of the dog fight.

Dickie Beckham was James's third wingman in as many months and James was determined to give him every possible chance of survival. He insisted they fly between sorties practising their turns, sweeps and battle tactics in the hope of becoming a unified pair who thought with one mind and fought with one purpose.

So far so good, James thought. He slid into the cockpit of his fighter and began the daily ritual of the pre-flight check. He ticked off the instruments one by one: petrol tanks full; tail trimming wheels neutral; airscrew fine pitch; directional gyro set; leather helmet and goggles hanging on the reflector sight with oxygen and radio–telephone leads connected. Everything was ready for a quick getaway.

And so began another dangerous day in the life of Flight Lieutenant James Merchant.

At ten past seven that morning, James was in a dreamless sleep in a deck chair outside the Pilot's Ready Room when the air-raid siren began its mournful wailing. How the hell had that happened, he thought. Normally it was the shrill ring of the dispersal telephone that scrambled the pilots into action. The Germans must have somehow avoided the British radar facilities.

Instantly, James was on his feet and running as the sound of the siren was drowned out by another sound he knew only too well. He halted briefly in his dash for the Spitfire to look up at the Stuka diving towards the earth. The Junkers Ju 87B, or Stuka as it was known, with its massive cranked wings, spatted undercarriage and screaming sirens was the picture of evil incarnate. He watched the plane release its bombs, then pull out of the dive and begin a lumbering climb to the relative safety of high altitude.

James reached his Spitfire as the bombs exploded into the Parachute Packing Hall, not fifty yards to his right. He leapt into the cockpit. The big Rolls-Royce Merlin engine, already started by the ground crew, growled impatiently as his crewman shouted above the noise.

'Your 'chute, Sir, you've not got your parachute on!'

'No time,' James yelled in reply. 'Besides, I don't need one, Peters, I'm bullet-proof, didn't you know?'

'It's just as well, isn't it? Down one for me, Sir, it's my birthday,' Sergeant Peters grinned as the fighter plane taxied across the grass gathering speed rapidly. He leapt to the ground, dodged the tail-wing, crossed himself and sent aloft a hasty prayer as he watched Flight Lieutenant Merchant soar skyward.

'Hey! What abaht this then?' Corporal Seddens said in his thick Cockney accent as he joined Sergeant Peters. He held up James' parachute. 'What's he fink 'e is, bullet-proof?'

'That's just what he said.' Both men started to run for the bomb shelter. 'And I wouldn't be at all surprised if he is!' Peters yelled. 'He's a born killer, is our Mr Merchant!' They dived headlong together into the sand bagged entrance of the shelter.

It had been a complete panic take-off, Spitfires darting about all over the field, and James had been lucky to get clear and into the air. At fifteen thousand, feet he levelled out and realised he was alone. Well, not alone exactly, he thought, as he looked at the swarm of German Messerschmitt 109s all around him. Without friends.

He wheeled and soared among them hauling his skittish craft through steep turns, then diving and wheeling upwards again in the bright sunlight. His training in the ancient arts of Shaolin took over his mind and body. *Relax,* he heard Lo Shi-mon's voice whisper inside his head. *Let your mind take control of your body. Use your senses, detect the threat, choose the correct response, strike, withdraw, defend. Detect the next threat. Strike, withdraw, defend. Detect, strike, withdraw, defend. Relax, Little Brother.* He felt a soft, sensual thrill as his body relaxed more and more, until the aircraft became an extension of his being. His body became a conductor of impulses from the brain to his hands and feet, and his aircraft became a dragon, screaming through the sky, venting its wrath upon all who dared challenge it.

An Me109 screamed below his right wing not fifty feet away, another approached him from the left. He saw the orange spit of its cannons and felt his craft spin hard right as he watched the tracer bullets pass harmlessly behind him.

Another Messerschmitt appeared in his gun sights, and he stuck to its tail like a limpet as it twisted and turned to escape him. He closed to within forty yards before opening fire with a terrific blast from his guns. The Messerschmitt exploded into flames and James was forced to fly straight through the debris. As luck would have it, a lumbering Stuka sat before him like a plump pigeon. Once again he opened fire from close range and blew it out of the sky.

He gave his craft full throttle and surged skyward, climbing up through the clouds to rejoin the fight, but there was nothing to be seen. All of sudden it seemed as if the whole episode had been a dream. The sky was empty, devoid of all but James and the early morning sun.

'Sorry I'm late,' a familiar voice rang in his ears through the radio-telephone. 'I had a bit of trouble getting up.' James grinned and waved as his wingman Dickie Beckham drew alongside his wingtip. The boy waved back and stuck his thumb in the air.

'I'm afraid you've missed the party, Dickie,' James said through the radio–telephone. 'There's only you and me and the sun up here.'

'I arrived just in time to see you shoot down two Jerries, Sir. I've never seen anyone fly a Spitfire quite like that. Well done.'

'Cut the chatter and identify yourselves please!' The voice of the 11 Group Controller snapped across the airwaves.

'11 Group, this is 806 Squadron,' James replied, 'Yellow Section, Merchant and Beckham but we're it, I'm afraid. Our strip's a burnt-out mess, looks like we're the only ones to get aloft.'

'806 Yellow Section,' the controller drawled. 'Northolt Airfield under heavy attack, proceed and engage.'

'Roger, Wilco, 11 Group,' James answered. 'You heard him, Dickie, Northolt. Let's go. And remember your training, don't leave my side, stay on the sun side of me and fly low so I can see you without squinting.'

It didn't take long. No sooner had they spotted the smoke billowing up from Northolt Fighter Base than they were engaged in a dogfight. There must have been at least fifty planes in the sky. Spitfires, Hurricanes and German 109s and 110s were spinning and twisting through the sky like angry hornets. James picked his mark, a Me110 and tailed it move for move. The Messerschmitt 110 with its poor acceleration and wide turning circle made it no match for the Spitfire and the pilot eventually went into a steep dive. James dived after it and reduced his range until he opened fire at less than fifty yards.

'You got him, Leader. He's going down!' Dickie Beckham screamed through the R/T.

James watched the German aircraft burst into flames then hauled hard on the stick and his powerful Spitfire surged towards the sun and the safety of high altitude.

'Are you still with me, Dickie?' James asked above the constant stream of German and English babble through the R/T as aircraft from both sides continued their deadly duels.

'I've got a 109 on my tail,' came the terrified answer from young Beckham. 'I can't shake him, James.'

Below him and away to the left, James saw his wingman diving towards the earth with the Messerschmitt hard on his tail. He dived in pursuit at full throttle, willing his craft to make even more speed. He watched horrified as the German opened fire. The tracer bullets flicked through the sky like a serpent's tongue, finding the fuselage of his wingman's plane.

James brought the 109 into his sights and fired, but from three hundred yards he had no hope of diverting the German's attention. Beckham's plane began to smoke and he watched the young man bail out as the German kept firing, until Beckham's Spitfire exploded.

Madness overtook James and he chased the 109 pouring cannon fire into it. So intent was he on destroying the German he was unaware of the danger behind him. Another Me 109 opened fire and black smoke poured from the engine cowling of James' plane as 20mm cannon shells ripped into it. The 109 he was firing on burst into flames in front of him and his world turned black as he flew into the explosion. He heard metal crashing against his craft, then the sky cleared and he watched flames creeping from the engine as his Spitfire headed for the ground.

Immediately James fought to pull the plane from its dive. He hauled back on the stick with all his might and slowly brought the nose up, but he was in serious trouble. He cut the engine, pulled back the cockpit canopy and then realised he had no parachute. Fear hit him like an express train. It was a new, and unwelcome, experience, he was not accustomed to fear. The altimeter read four thousand feet and dropping, he was still losing altitude. He knew his only chance of survival was to land.

'Drop the flaps, keep the nose up,' he muttered to himself as the countryside came up to meet him. 'Five hundred feet to go,' he hissed, struggling to keep the plane flat. There was the sound of an almighty crash as the Spitfire flew between two trees and the wings were shorn clear off. The fuselage rocketed over a fence and into a paddock full of cows, killing several of the beasts. It bounced into the air twice, then tore on like a runaway train for a hundred yards, before crashing over a bank of earth and coming to a halt in a dam full of terrified ducks.

James struggled from brief unconsciousness. He knew immediately that his nose was broken, but he appeared otherwise, uninjured. Considering the odds he'd been faced with less than five minutes before, he could only sit in the cockpit and laugh for all he was worth. The shearing off of the wings had lessened the chances of cartwheeling, and the dam water had saved him from incineration by extinguishing the engine fire. How the engine had not exploded on impact was beyond him. He'd had an impossible escape and he knew it.

'You lucky bastard,' a voice called from his left. He looked across to see a farmer standing on the edge of the dam holding a shotgun. 'If you'd been a Jerry I'd have shot you to compensate for my losses.'

龍

Lying on the straw in the back of a tractor cart being driven slowly up a long driveway, James stared at the now empty sky. He forced the pain he was feeling to the back of his mind and wondered at the madness of war. Not thirty minutes before, he'd been in the sky fighting for his life and now he was lying in a hay cart with the smell of fresh cut grass around him, contemplating the approach of autumn.

'Here we be,' the farmer said as the tractor came to a halt. 'The Manor.'

'Another one!' A female voice exclaimed as James got out of the cart. 'That makes two in one day!'

Beneath the portico of a stately English mansion stood a young woman about James' age, a butler, and three uniformed housemaids. The young woman stepped forward and took his arm.

'Come along,' she said. 'Let's get you inside, there's a doctor here treating one of your lot already. He's got a broken ankle. Are you injured? Apart from your nose?'

James appraised the beauty before him. A genuine English rose, he thought. A vision. Tall, the sun picking out soft lights in her long, brown hair. Green eyes in a patrician face. And a voluptuous body that contradicted the aristocrat she appeared to be. James was rendered speechless. The young woman was unbelievably sensual and he was overwhelmed with desire. It was always the same when he killed. After the kill, he felt an irresistible urge to lose himself in a woman's arms. And this time, with such a woman in such close proximity, the urge was unbearable.

The girl knew it too, he could tell. His dark eyes pierced hers and he watched her redden with embarrassment, but she forced herself to stand up to his scrutiny. She was aware of his desire, he knew it. Was she answering the call? he wondered. He could almost feel the heat of her sexual energy.

'You're beautiful,' he whispered.

'And you're delirious,' she laughed, but James knew he'd made a connection. 'Jenkins,' she turned, flustered, to her butler. 'Get this poor chap in to Doctor Weatherly.'

They entered the huge entrance hall. The floor was a chequerboard of black and white marble and an enormous fireplace dominated the wall in front of him. A shiver of recognition went down his spine.

'Are we in Richmond?' he asked the butler.

'We are indeed, Lieutenant,' Jenkins answered. 'This is Stawell Manor, home of the late Sir Herbert Billings, perhaps you've heard of him?'

'I don't believe I have,' James replied cautiously. 'And the young lady?'

'Miss Katherine Billings. Sir Herbert's niece and heir.'

'James!' Beckham cried out from the large divan he lay on while being attended by Doctor Weatherly.

'Hello, Dickie, you made it, I see?'

'My word, Sir! I parachuted into a hedgerow. Almost landed on that young lady standing right behind you. Broke my ankle. How about you?'

'A broken nose, I believe.' James tentatively touched his nose, and winced from the pain.

'No doubt about it, I'd say,' Dickie chuckled. 'Judging from the blood all over your face.'

'Come into the kitchen, Lieutenant,' Katherine Billings ordered. 'And I'll clean you up a bit. Perhaps when the doctor's finished with young Sergeant Beckham, he can have a look at you?' It was a question and the doctor glanced up wearily and nodded.

Katherine sat James at the kitchen table and busied herself getting a bowl of warm water and a cloth. 'Mr Dreyton, my stock manager, tells me you killed half of my livestock,' she said. James didn't reply, and she was aware of his open admiration as he watched her. She rabbited on about stock and dams and aircraft and the war until, finally, she ran out of things to say and stood in front of him, silent and self-conscious, meeting his gaze.

James took the bowl and cloth from her and wiped the blood from his face. Then, placing the bowl on the table, he pulled her to him. She didn't struggle. He kissed her long and hard before releasing her.

Katherine stood silently for a moment, regaining her composure, then she hit him across the face with the flat of her hand. Fresh blood gushed from his nose.

'I won't apologise,' he said.

'Nor will I,' she replied. 'If I were a man I'd have hit you even harder.'

He reached for the cloth and dipped it in the water, wiping his face and stemming the trickle from his nose. Then he sat at the kitchen table.

'I've had one hell of a day so far, and it's not even lunchtime. I killed four men this morning, and nearly bought it myself. Then I saw the most beautiful woman in England. I won't apologise for my actions,' his eyes were once again undressing her. 'I'm on fire, Katherine.'

'Then we'd better put you out,' she said, and she picked up the bowl of bloody water and poured it over his head.

James stood, laughing loudly. 'Well, you certainly did that!' he spluttered.

Katherine watched him, her hands gripping the table's edge behind her, as he walked to the kitchen door.

'I'm stationed at Fighter Command, Tangmere,' he turned and grinned at her. 'There's a dance on Saturday night at the local hall. I would desperately like you to come to that dance.'

'You've just treated me like a common tart, Lieutenant. What makes you think that . . .'

'Do you know how many times a human being experiences true passion in one lifetime?' His smile was cheeky this time. He was daring her, she knew it. 'Don't deny yourself that experience, Katherine. Come to the dance.'

'Don't be ridiculous. I've only known you five minutes.'

'That's irrelevant.'

'I don't even know your name.'

'It's James, James Merchant, and yours is Katherine Billings, how do you do. There you are, we're now formally introduced, I'll see you on Saturday.'

Katherine held her breath as she watched him leave, then she sagged against the table. He wasn't the only one who was on fire.

'Oh God,' she murmured, her body tingling with excitement. Damn him. Who did he think he was? She could still feel the touch of his mouth on hers. She ran her tongue over her lips, tasting his blood as she did. Go on, you liked it, the demon in her urged. I did not, her moral outrage protested. His behaviour was disgusting, that's why I hit him!

'Oh! I hit him,' Katherine gasped at the memory of the blood spurting from his nose. Her behaviour in that particular part of the episode had been unforgivable. 'Lieutenant!' she called as she ran from the kitchen colliding with him in the corridor outside.

'Yes?' James said as she crashed into his arms. He tried to kiss her again.

'Stop it!' She twisted her head away.

'Will you come to the dance?'

'No! . . . No, I won't.' Once more she gathered her composure. 'You must see the doctor. It would be unchristian of me to have you leave this house without your injuries being attended to.'

'I'll see the doctor if you'll come to the dance.'

'Oh! Will you be serious!'

'I am serious,' he eased her gently against the wall, his face close to hers. He lowered his hand to her chest and felt her heart beat. 'I've never been more serious in my life. Feel your heart, Katherine. It's racing just like mine.'

She stared back at him for several seconds, then, shocked by her physical response, she broke free of his embrace. She had never experienced such wanton desire in her life. She was flooded with an urge to pull him to the floor and give herself to him right then and there.

As if to save her from her own confusion, James broke the moment. 'God,' he said, placing his thumb and forefinger over his nostrils. 'God, but that hurt.'

Katherine found herself laughing. 'Then see the doctor, you stupid boy!'

'If you'll come to Tangmere on Saturday night.'

'Perhaps I will,' she pushed him away. 'And I'll make a complaint to your CO about your offensive behaviour. Now go and see Doctor Weatherly.'

龍

Air Vice-Marshal Keith Park dropped into a heavy leather chair in Dowding's office in Whitehall and stared at a hanging photograph of the King as Dowding droned on.

'So I wrote back to the bally fool and said, apart from the question of discourtesy, I must point out the lack of consideration involved,' Dowding was saying. 'I have had four retirement dates given to me and you are now proposing a fifth! Damn it, Keith! Don't they realise we're involved in the gravest battle in the history of the British Isles! At this very moment in the skies above England . . .'

Park feigned attention as his superior's words jumbled into one long, dull, monotonous hum. Air Chief Marshal Sir Hugh Dowding, Commander-in-Chief of Fighter Command and Park's immediate superior, was boring him witless. Fortunately for England, however, this verbose, difficult, self-opinionated man knew more about aerial warfare than anyone alive, and for that Park admired him greatly.

Rapidly approaching sixty years of age, Dowding was a tall man with thinning hair and a sharp beakish nose. An eccentric and a loner, he found it difficult to make friends and easy to make enemies. Churchill respected him, but couldn't stand him. Everyone at the Air Ministry detested him.

'Have you heard one word I've said, Keith?' Dowding's voice dragged Keith Park from his reverie.

'I'm sorry, Sir?'

'You haven't, have you?'

'I'm afraid not, Hugh,' Park said. 'I'm still angry about the matter of Flight Lieutenant Merchant. I'm sorry but I can't help it. I can't afford to lose a man like him. I've had over eighty pilots killed and forty wounded in the last nine days alone. And now I get an order to . . .'

'Why don't you ring up the Prime Minister and ask him to rescind it, Keith?' Dowding snapped uncharacteristically.

There was a knock at the door and a young WAAF officer entered.

'Air Marshal,' she said. 'Flight Lieutenant Merchant is here, Sir.'

'Good. Send him in. Thank you.'

James entered the office and saluted smartly.

'Lieutenant Merchant,' Dowding said, walking from behind his desk and offering his hand to James. 'I'm Air Marshal Dowding and this is Air Vice-Marshal Park, your Commanding Officer, I believe. How do you do?'

'I'm pleased to make your acquaintance, Sir, . . . I mean, Sirs,' James said. He felt out of his depth as he stood in the oak-panelled office with England's greatest minds on air warfare. And to make matters worse, he had no idea why he was there. His nose began to throb and he placed his fingers tentatively on the sticking plaster holding it in shape.

'How's the nose progressing, lad?' Keith Park asked.

'Er . . . broken, Sir. I mean it was, now it's fixed,' James replied.

'Good show last Wednesday morning, Merchant,' Dowding offered as he sat behind his desk and picked up James' Record of Service. 'I've read your wingman's report on the matter, he seems to think you're a hero.'

'I don't think so, Sir,' James replied.

'Well, I do,' Dowding said. 'And so does Air Vice-Marshal Park. He's recommended you for the Distinguished Flying Cross and I've endorsed the recommendation and submitted it to Cabinet so you'd better bloody well get used to the idea.'

'Yes, Sir. Thank you, Sir.'

'Your Squadron Leader says you're the best pilot he's ever seen, Merchant,' Park added.

'I wouldn't say that, Sir.'

'Stop being so reluctant, boy!' Dowding growled. 'How am I going to explain you to the press if you continue to be reluctant. A reluctant hero. There can be no such thing in my book! It's a contradiction in terms.'

'Excuse my bluntness, Sir,' James replied. 'But have you summoned me here merely to tell me I've won a medal? Other chaps are notified in writing, or they find out from the noticeboard in the Pilot's Ready Room.'

'You shot down four enemy aircraft on Wednesday morning . . .' Dowding began.

'But that's not uncommon, Sir, I've . . .'

'On one sortie, it's *extremely* uncommon,' Keith Park interrupted. 'Now shut up, Lieutenant, and allow the Air Marshall to continue.'

'Yes, Sir.'

'Those kills,' Dowding went on, 'were confirmed by Flight Sergeant Beckham and two other pilots from Tangmere, who also saw you shot down while trying to rescue Beckham. Adding those four to the six enemy aircraft you've destroyed on previous occasions makes a total of ten kills. Only a handful of men have achieved that total, and most of them are dead. The Prime Minister wants you to remain alive.'

'Why, Sir?' James asked.

'Call him an old softie,' Keith Park's voice dripped sarcasm.

'That'll do, Keith!' Dowding shot him a warning glance. 'Whether you like it or not, Merchant, you're a bona fide war hero, an "ace" fighter pilot with a DFC to prove it. You are therefore relieved from active duty immediately and will report to the Office of the Prime Minister on Monday morning at nine o'clock sharp.'

'What for?'

'To sell war bonds!' Keith Park snapped. 'And I for one am bloody well against it! I cannot afford to lose experienced . . .'

'As I was saying,' Hugh Dowding silenced his Vice-Marshal with a glance. 'You will work directly from the PM's office. You will travel wherever you are ordered, to whatever city, town, or hamlet in Britain, and you will parade yourself in front of the local inhabitants and smile, in order to raise money for the war effort.'

'Sir, I'm a fighter pilot!'

'No, you're not,' Dowding snapped. 'You're a war hero! That's why you've been given a bloody medal! I thought I'd just finished explaining that to you. The Prime Minister needs a war hero and you're it, Merchant! Do you understand?'

'Yes, Sir!' James replied.

'Good,' Dowding sighed. 'Now, am I correct in assuming you have no further questions on the matter?'

'I have one, Sir.'

'Why is it I'm not surprised? Well, lad, what is it?'

'Did my mother have anything to do with this?'

'Your mother!' Dowding exclaimed.

'Did my mother arrange my transfer to the Prime Minister's Office?'

'Not unless she's married to the King of England.'

'Very well, Sir. I've no further questions.'

'Excellent,' Dowding raised an eyebrow to Keith Park. 'Perhaps we can adjourn to my club. I'd like to buy you dinner, young man.'

龍

It was ten-thirty at night when James arrived at the house in Belgravia. The place was in darkness as he let himself in by the front door. He made his way to the study in the dark, not wanting to wake up the staff, but he should have known better. By the time he'd turned on the study light, Cook stood on the stairway landing with a torch in her hand, its beam illuminating the pyjama-clad figure of Thomas Smith, the Cockney chauffeur, armed with a double barrelled shotgun.

'Why, Mister Merchant, Sir!' Cook exclaimed. 'Whatever are you doing here so late. Shouldn't you be at Tangmere? And what have you done to your nose?'

'It's nothing. I'm sorry, Mrs Daley, I should have warned you I was coming. I was summoned to Whitehall this afternoon then stayed in the city for dinner. I decided to kip here for tonight.'

'White'all, Sir?' Thomas broke the breach of the shotgun and lay it on the hall table. 'Nuffink wrong I hope, Mista' Brewster?'

'Ha!' James scoffed. 'On the contrary, Thomas, it seems I've won the DFC.'

The announcement of the award caused quite a stir. Mrs Daley, after 'oohing' and 'aahing' for several minutes, went off to make a celebratory supper of cucumber sandwiches and to get a bottle of the best champagne from the wine cellar, while Thomas, a military man through and through, shook James' hand until he thought his shoulder would dislocate.

'You're an 'ero, Sir!' Thomas enthused. 'A bleedin' certified 'ero! I said to Mista' Richard and your muvver that you had the makin's of a fine man. Why, even when you was climbin' abaht this very 'ouse like a monkey, you and Mista' Lee, I knew even then that you was marked for greatness, Sir! You have my deepest congratulations indeed.'

And so it was that James found himself ensconced in the study by a roaring fire with a supper of cucumber sandwiches and champagne and no one to share it with, Cook and Thomas having excused themselves and left him alone. That's how things are done in Belgravia, he thought, the very centre of the British class system. Everyone knows their place in the pecking order. Everyone knows how to behave on every level, except emotionally.

He was aware that Thomas and Mrs Daley had, over the last seven years, become very fond of him, as he had of them, and yet the class distinction between them remained. He was the master and they were the servants and, although they could barely contain their delight in his award, their show of affection had been brief and correct. They'd resumed their stations, and James wished that they hadn't. He needed a woman, but failing that, he needed to talk. He needed to talk to family. He needed to talk to someone who cared for him.

The battle for air supremacy over England had taken its toll on him and he knew it. He'd been on the edge for three months risking his life three, four and even five times a day and now that he'd been withdrawn from the battle, the tension that had built up in him needed release.

He had mixed feelings about his withdrawal from combat. The very thought of selling war bonds was an anathema to him, but he'd been ordered to do so, by the Prime Minister, no less, and he would obey. God knows, he thought, he could do with a rest. But selling war bonds?

He had to admit that being shot down had rattled him. He'd escaped with only a broken nose this time, but there would be a next time, he was sure, and he would not be so lucky. What unsettled him most was his loss of composure before the crash. He'd panicked for a moment. He'd never known panic or fear before, and he had not liked the experience. His exposure to Shaolin discipline at an early age had made him strong of mind. Even in battle he felt no fear, always operating calmly, using the mind control techniques he'd been taught. But, during his screaming descent in the spitfire, he'd briefly felt a mind-numbing fear and it embarrassed him. He must practise his disciplines more diligently, he warned himself. Under no circumstances, ever again, must he lose his composure.

James thought of his family and friends in Hong Kong: he missed them, he realised. Richard and Elanora would be there now, he thought, as he sipped his champagne. They had returned to Hong Kong shortly after the confrontation he and Richard had had with Charles Higgins. Lee, too, had returned to Hong Kong. Elanora's most recent letter had informed James that Lee was married with a child. If he was here with me now, James thought wishfully, we'd talk until dawn. We'd sure as hell have some war stories to exchange.

He got up and paced the room, trying to distract himself with objets d'art and the framed pictures on the walls. His mind went briefly to the maid's room upstairs where Irene once waited for him, but she was gone too. She'd joined the WAAF three months ago and her place had been taken by Minerva Pankhurst, a girl of no more than fifteen, who Mrs Daley had found working in Covent Garden.

James's sudden craving for some form of emotional connection disturbed him. Lo Shi-mon had trained both him and Lee to be unemotional, it was the basis for all Shaolin teaching, and he'd never questioned it. But tonight he needed someone to be with him.

He stared at the champagne bottle in its silver ice bucket, a white napkin wrapped neatly around it, and searched for the inner stillness which brought him comfort. Tonight it would not come.

He sipped again at his champagne and ate a cucumber sandwich, then crossed quickly to the desk, consulted the telephone directory and picked up the phone.

'Hello, Stawell Manor,' she answered on the first ring. 'Hello? Is anyone there?'

James was unable to answer. Her voice caught him unprepared, he'd been expecting to hear the butler.

'Katherine?' he managed to ask.

'Yes, this is Katherine Billings, who is speaking please?'

'It's me,' he replied softly. 'I won the DFC.'

On the other end of the line Katherine Billings froze. It was the young pilot, she knew beyond doubt. 'James Merchant?' she asked tentatively. 'Is that you?'

'Yes.'

His voice sounded hollow, defeated, and she realised instantly that something was wrong. 'Is anything the matter, James,' she asked, but he didn't reply. 'Are you all right,' she asked. But again no answer. 'James, are you hurt?' Still he did not reply. 'Please say something.'

'I want to see you.'

'Yes, tomorrow night in Tangmere. I'm looking forward to it.'

'No.'

'Why not?'

'I need to see you now.'

'Don't be absurd. It's eleven o'clock at night.'

'Not in Hong Kong.'

'What?'

'It's six o'clock in the morning, the sun would just be coming up and the harbour would be bathed in sunshine. Have you ever been to Hong Kong?'

'No, I haven't,' Katherine said. 'Have you been drinking?'

'I've never been so lonely in my life, Katherine,' he whispered. 'I mean it. I've never been so alone, I can't put it into words. Can I come and see you?'

'You can't possibly drive all the way from Tangmere in your present state of mind.'

'I'm in London. I could be in Richmond in thirty minutes.'

'It wouldn't be right, James. Not at this time of night.'

'Katherine . . .' he began, but could think of nothing to add.

The silence down the line lasted several seconds as Katherine fought with her emotions. She took a deep breath and asked, 'Where in London?'

'Belgravia.'

'Give me the address.'

CHAPTER EIGHTEEN

Elanora Brewster stretched languorously, the silk sheets of her bed caressing her body, and purred like a contented kitten. She and Richard had made love the previous night with all the urgency and passion of twenty-five-year-olds. She had been aware that her husband's renewed vigour was a direct result of the anger he'd felt during their supper conversation with Hong Kong's military elite, but she couldn't have cared less at the time. And she still didn't. She was exhausted, and joyously so.

She and Richard had attended the All China Theatre premiere of *Lady Hamilton* starring Vivien Leigh and Laurence Olivier. They'd been guests of the new Governor Sir Mark Young, recently arrived from Barbados, and afterwards they'd attended supper at Victoria Barracks in Central as guests of Major-General Kenneth Gracegirdle, Indian Army, Commanding General of the British Forces in Hong Kong.

The premiere had been a glittering affair, Vivien Leigh living up to her reputation as the most beautiful woman in the empire and her leading man, Laurence Olivier, caused the fluttering of many a young colonial woman's heart.

It had been an enjoyable night all round, despite Richard's fury at supper, Elanora thought, as she rose from the bed and examined herself in the full-length mirror by the French windows. A slight bruise on her hip and a sweet ache throughout her body remained as evidence of their passion.

Elanora loved her husband more deeply than ever, and she knew why. Richard Brewster's recognition of his own love for her had changed him. He was not only kind and considerate, for which she was grateful, but he had rediscovered his honour, and with the rediscovery had come a softening of his attitude to power. He still commanded the Society of Golden Dragons with a firm hand, but he ensured it remained a benevolent society, focusing on its members' welfare, and he no longer saw any need for illegal activity in his business dealings. Dragon Import & Export was now strictly legitimate and making very good profits for all concerned.

Elanora slipped on a silk peignoir and rang the bell for her maidservant. She would order a huge breakfast, she decided, she was starving. She opened the French windows, stepped out onto the balcony and breathed deeply of the fresh morning air. Autumn was her favourite season. But when she looked down at the blue expanse of the harbour, her feeling of wellbeing disappeared.

Warships dominated the scene. A British cruiser and several frigates, recently arrived from Singapore, were being busily attended by a flotilla of smaller craft. Hong Kong had been on a war footing for two years, and the very idea filled Elanora with foreboding. The sight of the warships brought back the arguments of the previous evening with frightening clarity.

For two long years the British Empire had been at war with Germany and Italy, with whom Japan was now in alliance. And Japan, not satisfied with occupying most of China, had occupied Indochina unopposed by the French Vichy Government. A fact which had started the previous evening's argument.

Major-General Gracegirdle had been nothing short of bullish about the prospects of defending the colony. 'I firmly believe,' he'd said in his rumbling military voice, 'that the Colony could be used as a base for offensive attacks against the Japanese in China, should they foolishly decide to enter the war as an ally of Germany.' And that was when Richard had erupted.

'Should they decide?' he'd snapped. 'Should they decide! My dear General, Japan has no alternative but to engage in war. We are staring into the face of global conflict because the British Government, in its infinite wisdom, saw fit to impose embargoes on all exports of steel and oil to Japan, and the United States has done precisely the same thing!'

'And high time it did, too,' one of Gracegirdle's senior officers, Colonel Standish, interjected. 'The bally Japs are militarists to a man. There's no doubt about their intentions in Asia, and the sooner we give them a punch on the nose the better!'

'A punch on the nose, Colonel?' Richard sneered. 'Do you honestly believe that we here in Hong Kong could give Japan a punch on the nose?'

'My bally word we could,' the officer sneered in return.

Richard fought to control his irritation. 'Our combined forces in Hong Kong consist of two battalions of British infantry, two battalions of the Indian Army, a local volunteer force, a handful of small warships, two flying-boats and three torpedo bombers without any bloody torpedoes!'

'"Scraps of information, jeopardise the nation, talk about Tiger instead",' Colonel Standish intoned, tapping the side of his nose with a forefinger.

Richard could not believe his ears. The man was repeating an advertising jingle for the locally brewed Tiger Beer. It was the brewing company's attempt to contribute to the war effort by reminding Hong Kong's citizens of the dangers of careless talk.

'You're an idiot!' Richard exploded.

'I say, steady on, Brewster,' General Gracegirdle muttered.

'Do you seriously believe, Colonel, that the Japanese don't know the sum total of our defence capabilities?' Richard ignored the General's attempt at peacemaking.

'They do not, Sir, but they will,' the Colonel replied. 'If people like you keep blabbing military secrets like you just did. They do have ears, you know.'

Richard was halfway out of his seat when he felt Elanora's hand against his thigh. He sat down and wiped his mouth with his napkin, buying time while he tried to calm himself. 'I'm awfully sorry, General Gracegirdle,' he said finally through gritted teeth. 'I'm afraid I let my feelings run away with me. It's just that I'm greatly concerned for the welfare of the colony, given the latest information we've received about the Japanese.' Elanora squeezed his arm and he reacted by turning to the Colonel. 'And do accept my apologies, Colonel Standish, I was out of order.'

'Nerves. Perfectly understandable, old boy,' the Colonel murmured.

'If the Japanese do attack the colony it would be an act of war,' General Gracegirdle said and he nodded gravely at Richard. 'They would incur the wrath of the King and bring to bear upon themselves the full might of the British Empire.'

'The Japanese, General,' Elanora said softly, 'have invaded the Malay Peninsula and are heading for Singapore, surely we must assume they will also attack Hong Kong?'

'My dear Mrs Brewster,' Gracegirdle intoned condescendingly. 'Singapore is impregnable and so too, I believe, is Hong Kong. We are not the fortress Singapore is, but we have the Shing Mun Redoubt as the centre point of a line of fortifications which runs west from Tsuen Wan, along Smugglers' Ridge to the shores of Port Shelter. It then continues south to Junk Bay and from there to the Harbour. I believe that defensive line could hold the Japanese at bay for a long time. At the very least, long enough for our forces to conduct an orderly withdrawal through Kowloon and across to Hong Kong Island where we could defend ourselves successfully until relief arrived from Singapore.'

'Our sea approaches all contain minefields,' a rather stupid young major in Gracegirdle's staff unit interjected. 'And Hong Kong Island has over seventy pillboxes strategically placed all about it. We could defend it until the cows come home provided we've enough food and ammunition.'

'Major,' Richard said evenly. 'Have you ever stopped to imagine what it would be like to stand on Hong Kong Island while it was shelled by a regiment of Japanese artillery from Kowloon Public Wharf?'

'No, Mr Brewster, I have not,' the Major replied dismissively.

'Well, I bloody well have!' Richard snapped. 'Bearing in mind the distance is considerably less than one mile, I can only envisage it being like standing on parade during a hail storm!'

'A colourful simile, Sir,' the Major responded, offering a mock half-bow. 'But I can assure you that the situation will not have occasion to arise.'

'Besides which,' the Colonel added, 'the Japanese are hopelessly inferior to our chaps when it comes to a stoush. They're short-sighted for one thing, it's to do with the shape of their eyes. And for some religious reason they refuse to fight at night.'

Richard could take no more. 'I don't believe what I'm hearing!' he declared. 'If that is what you actually believe, Colonel,' he said, getting to his feet and glaring at the British officer. 'Then all I can say is God help Hong Kong!'

'I beg your pardon?' the Colonel spluttered.

'And I demand you explain that remark!' the young major shouted, also getting to his feet. 'That, Sir, was a direct insult to me, and my regimental colleagues! You will take it back immediately!'

'The Japanese Army is a well-oiled military machine, Major,' Richard replied vehemently. 'Their troops in southern China alone outnumber us by ten to one. They are battle-hardened professionals who've been fighting in China for the last five years. They have the artillery, the motor transport and the air power to flatten this colony in one day! All they need is the bloody orders to do so and we'll be damned!'

'And damn you, Sir!' the young major cursed.

'Here, here,' Colonel Standish added.

'Silence!' General Gracegirdle roared. He glared at the protagonists before continuing. 'I would remind you, Major, Colonel, and you, Mr Brewster, that you are in the Officers' Mess of Victoria Barracks and as such you are guests of the King! You will contain yourselves, Sirs! Not only by virtue of the fact that there are ladies present, but out of respect for our monarch!'

Richard had ranted all the way home to Merchant House and Elanora had sympathised. The attitude of the military was courting disaster, she'd agreed.

It was typical of the British, in her opinion. It was imperial complacency at its worst. From their lofty heights as rulers of the empire, they were making the same mistake they always made: underestimating Asians. The remarks Colonel Standish had made about the Japanese being short-sighted and afraid of fighting in the dark were typical of his ilk. Elanora, part-Asian, had herself been infuriated throughout supper, but she'd managed to maintain her composure and force Richard to do likewise. She'd been glad when they'd left the Barracks.

The maidservant arrived on the balcony with a tea tray. She placed it on the table and prepared to pour. 'That will be all,' Elanora said. 'I'll pour it myself.'

When the girl had left, Elanora poured herself tea and looked out over her beautiful harbour. She worried for Hong Kong. The Hong Kong Chinese were not fools, they knew Japan's intentions. Hong Kong would be attacked, of that there was no doubt and, in her mind's eye, she could see the devastation. Burning buildings, tanks and soldiers scouring the streets killing and raping. Hong Kong would be their next slaughterhouse, just like Shanghai, Nanking and all the other cities and towns the Japanese Army claimed they had 'liberated'.

In June of 1940, the previous year, European wives and children had been compulsorily evacuated to Australia, although some women and their families had decided to remain, and Elanora had realised that Hong Kong was doomed. What to do? The question inflamed her brain. What was the best course of action for her family's safety?

She sighed as she sipped her tea. It seemed to her like only yesterday that she'd been sitting on this very balcony watching her son James and little Lee Kwan playing in the front gardens. Now James was in England, working for Winston Churchill. James was a war hero, a recipient of the Distinguished Flying Cross, and she was so proud of him. Relieved too, that his hero status meant he was no longer in combat, she'd been beside herself with fear when he'd been flying in the Battle of Britain. Richard had told her he'd done everything possible to get James transferred to Hong Kong, but pilots were at a premium, he'd said, and nothing could be done. James had survived, thank God, and soon, Elanora hoped, engaged to be married. She had seen photographs of the girl. Katherine Billings was every bit as beautiful as James had claimed, and she was the niece and sole heiress of the late Sir Herbert Billings MP.

Elanora's Chinese mind believed it was far more than coincidence that her son had literally fallen from the sky into the arms of Katherine Billings. It was the work of the gods. It was meant to be, she'd decided. It was good joss. Sir Herbert, courtesy of Charles Higgins, had caused untold trouble for Dragon Import & Export, but the situation had rectified itself. Sir Herbert had died of a heart attack, she thought thankfully, crossing herself like a good Catholic, and Charles had been dismissed from the Company's service. Yes, the gods were at work with James and Katherine their love would repair whatever bad joss had previously been in the air.

And Lee. She smiled as she thought of her darling Lee, living right here in Hong Kong with his wife and little son. He was now a high official in the Nationalist Army, raising money for the war effort in China. Elanora was happy for him. After hearing the descriptions of Nanking from Lo Shi-mon, she believed Lee had seen enough of war to last him a lifetime, and she was determined he should remain in Hong Kong and become a successful businessman. God willing, she now thought as she looked down on the harbour. They might well be forced to leave, all of them.

Elanora had made arrangements for herself and Richard, together with Lee and his family, to move to Australia if the situation in Hong Kong worsened. She'd purchased a property on Sydney Harbour, and all that was required was an aircraft to transport them. She had transferred several large amounts of money to Australian banks to add to the substantial company investments there.

The only trouble she could envisage was getting Richard and Lee to make the move. Richard had, of late, been ranting about protecting the colony and fighting in its volunteer force, and Lee's passion for China was bordering on obsessive. She would short circuit them both. Somehow. Together with Lin Li, she would find a way.

Lin Li had been welcomed into the Merchant household three years previously when she'd arrived with Old Soong from Chungking. Their journey had been long and arduous and Lin Li, in her advanced pregnancy, had been dangerously underweight, bordering on emaciated, when she and Elanora had first met. Elanora had cared for the young woman and assiduously prepared her for the birth of Lee's child.

After the birth of Kwan Kip-sen, Elanora had arranged for Lin Li to learn English, and had made available a whole wing of the Merchant House as a home for Lee and his family when he returned. She'd also declared herself grandmother to the boy and enrolled him in an exclusive English school in preparation for his education. But, when Lee had arrived in Hong Kong, he had taken his wife and child and set up home in a small flat in North Point.

There had been no ill feeling connected with the move; she understood his need for independence. She even insisted upon purchasing furniture and, much against Lee's objections, supplying an *amah* for the child.

'Lin Li is not a coolie, Lee,' she'd said at the time. 'The child must have an *amah* so that Lin Li is free to pursue her studies.'

Lee, to his credit, had surrendered graciously and, over the past year, Elanora had watched Lin Li grow into a vivacious and socially astute young woman.

'My God!' Elanora said aloud. 'They'll be here for lunch at twelve!' She looked at her watch, rang for her maidservant, issued a dozen rapid orders, then hurried off to supervise the lunch preparations.

龍

Lee Kwan entered his apartment from the back garden. He took a towel from the small cupboard in the hallway and wiped the sweat from his chest as he entered the kitchen.

Lin Li sat at the table attempting to spoon-feed their son, while Old Soong waved a distracting rattle at the child, chuckling foolishly and pulling funny faces.

Lin Li watched Lee move through the room. He had the grace of a jungle cat, each movement sure and powerful, yet economical, designed to preserve energy. Sweat ran from his body, a result of the Shaolin exercises he practised religiously, twice a day.

'*You should bathe quickly, husband,*' she said. '*We are due at Elanora's house at twelve and must not be late.*'

'*I will be ready on time,*' he answered. '*It is you, Lin Li, who should be hurrying. Get the amah to feed the child, that is what she is paid for.*'

'*A child should be fed by its mother,*' Old Soong said.

Lee looked at his faithful retainer. Soong had aged considerably in the three years since he'd escorted Lin Li to Hong Kong. Lee knew Soong had suffered great hardship on the journey and he owed the old soldier a debt he could never hope to repay. Several times on the journey Lin Li had fallen ill and each time Old Soong had cared for her, once risking his life by stealing food and medicine from a Japanese Army barracks outside Canton. Eventually, he'd stolen a boat and sailed the pregnant girl to Hong Kong where he had made contact with Elanora.

'*A child should not be annoyed by foolish old soldiers either,*' Lee said with a grin. '*Do you have or not have, anything better to do?*'

'*My chores are never ending, Elder Brother,*' Soong replied. '*Your amah does nothing but sleep all the time and I am left with all the work.*'

'*Perhaps if you did not couple with her so much she would have more energy?*' Lee quipped. Soong was old, but not that old.

'*Aaaiiyaah!*' Soong wailed. '*How can you accuse me of such behaviour? The girl is a slut who will not leave my manhood alone! If it were not for the fact that I must remain here to ensure your son is properly raised, I would return to the battle front and die with honour!*'

'*If you go anywhere near the battle front you'll be hanged, you old fool! You are a deserter, remember?*'

'*Ha!*' Soong scoffed, but his tone held a deeper meaning. '*If anyone should be wary of the noose it is not me.*'

'*That is enough!*' Lee dropped the banter, glancing briefly at Lin Li, but her attention was devoted to their son. '*I suggest you go and find something to do.*'

Soong obediently rose. '*A man who tries to live with both the tiger and the snake must expect to be bitten,*' he muttered as he disappeared through the door.

'*What did he mean by that?*' Lin Li asked.

'*Who could know?*' Lee replied. '*Prepare our son, I am going to bathe. And keep an eye out for Elanora's driver, she is sending her car for us.*' He crossed to the door. '*Oh, and tell him I must stop at the apothecary's shop in Wu Tau Lane on the way to the Peak, I need to pick up a potion I ordered,*' he said as he left he room.

龍

A bell tinkled softly. Lee closed the door and stepped into the cool darkness of the apothecary's shop. Rosewood cabinets, containing all manner of things from preserved snakes to deer antlers, lined the walls from floor to ceiling. An abacus lay in front of a collection of glass jars and bottles lined up on the service counter, and the door leading to the rear of the premises was adorned with a chart of the human body, showing the lines of energy studied by acupuncturists. The shop smelled of jasmine and rosewood.

An old man appeared through the rear door and bowed to Lee. He wore the traditional Cantonese garb of an apothecary and his queue, an immaculate plait of silver-grey hair, hung down his back to his waist.

'*Have you eaten or not eaten rice, Elder Brother?*' Lee asked politely.

'*I have eaten,*' the old man replied. '*Thank you for enquiring. Is it a pain, or disenchantment with the elements you are suffering?*'

'*I have no ailment. I seek a man.*'

'*Everyone is seeking someone, Little Brother.*'

'*I seek The Prisoner of Nanking.*'

'*Nanking has seen many prisoners.*'

'*The man I seek was first among them for ten years, from the black winter of 1927 to the coming of the Turnip Heads.*'

'*The man you speak of is still considered a communist criminal by some,*' the old man said softly. '*Surely it would not be wise for one so young as yourself to seek out the company of criminals.*'

'*I am not so young. In Nanking I lived a thousand lifetimes.*'

'*And what is your honourable name?*'

'*I am Kwan Man Hop, known as Lee Kwan.*'

The old man stared at Lee for some time before he spoke. '*You are the "Angel of Nanking", true or not true? My wife's family were in Nanking. It is a great honour to welcome you to my humble shop, Elder Brother.*'

'*The Prisoner of Nanking, old man,*' Lee said, taking an envelope from his pocket. '*This must go to him.*'

'*It will be delivered, Elder Brother,*' the old man took the envelope and, in a trice, it had disappeared inside the voluminous sleeve of his gown. '*You have my word.*'

Outside the shop, Lee climbed into the back seat of Elanora's Bentley and sat silently as the chauffeur drove them to Merchant House.

Lin Li turned to him. '*Where is the potion you were to pick up?*' she asked.

'*It wasn't ready,*' he replied without looking at her.

As Lin Li stared at her husband, a sense of foreboding crept over her. '*What did Soong mean when he said "a man who tries to live with both the tiger and the snake must expect to be bitten"?*'

'*Soong is an old fool given to muttering cliches. It is his mode of expression, without them he would be mute. And what he means by them, only the gods could know.*'

They sat in silence for the rest of the drive. Lee lay his head back and closed his eyes, while Lin Li gazed out the window, a worried frown creasing her brow.

龍

Robert McCraw sipped quietly on a glass of scotch as he sat at the boardroom table of the Merchant Company offices. He'd been summoned to Ice house Street at short notice, but he'd been expecting an extraordinary meeting of the Dragons for some time. Gathered around the table were Terrence Delaney, Lo Shi-mon and Malcolm Linden, since returned from London. All were sitting quietly, like Robert, awaiting the arrival of Richard Brewster.

McCraw glanced surreptitiously at each of his old friends and a rush of melancholy swept over him. After more than twenty years, Hong Kong was his home even more than his native Scotland, and these men were his closest friends. His fortune was assured, and the love of his life, Li Ping, closer to him than ever before. But life's experiences had taught him nothing lasts forever. Robert could see the clouds of disaster gathering on his horizon.

He shivered inwardly and drained the scotch from his glass, but the melancholy feeling would not leave him. He knew that the most meaningful, and most enjoyable, part of his life was coming to a close and he knew that Richard Brewster had called this meeting to tell him, and the others, precisely that.

He joined Malcolm Linden at the sideboard and began pouring himself another liberal glass of whisky.

Linden, too, was in a melancholy mood. He was convinced that a Japanese invasion was little more than a few days away, and a wonderful chapter of his life was about to end with it. He would go to the barricades with his friends in a futile attempt to defend the Colony, and God help us all, he thought.

'I've enjoyed my time in good old Honkers, haven't you, Robbie?' Linden asked.

'Aye, Malcolm, I have,' Torrential rain began to lash the windows. 'Nothing lasts forever, laddie, but we've shared a lot of good years, you and I, have we not?'

'We have indeed, Inspector McCraw,' Malcolm responded

warmly. 'Here's to you, my friend.' He raised his glass and McCraw clinked his against it. 'To friendship.'

'Nay, laddie,' McCraw said sadly. ''Tis more than that. To brotherhood, Malcolm.' He turned to Terrance Delaney and Lo Shi-mon seated at the table. 'To brotherhood,' he repeated and they stood and raised their glasses to him.

'To brotherhood,' they reiterated, and as they drank to each other the door burst open.

'Damn it, but I'm drenched!' Richard declared. 'That rain is as fierce as shotgun pellets. Ten yards from the car to the front door and I'm soaked.' He took off his coat and shook it vigorously, drops spraying the room. 'Sorry about the water, gentlemen,' he smiled apologetically. 'Good evening.'

'Like a drink?' Linden offered.

'My word, yes,' Richard answered. 'A stiff scotch wouldn't go astray.' He looked at the solemn faces of his friends and realised he'd interrupted them. 'I'm sorry,' he said, 'I shouldn't have burst in like that, do forgive me.'

'Not to worry, laddie,' McCraw boomed heartily, ''Twas but a maudlin moment and now it's passed. Why don't we get down to the business at hand?'

'Very well,' Richard took the drink Malcolm Linden handed him. 'But might I take this moment to make a toast?' He raised his glass to them all individually. 'You four men are the best friends I ever had. To friendship, gentlemen.'

'Nay, laddie,' it was Lo Shi-mon, mimicking McCraw, and the big Scotsman smiled at him. 'It is more than that, Richard. To brotherhood.'

'What an excellent suggestion,' Richard agreed softly. 'Gentlemen. To brotherhood.'

'To brotherhood,' they chorused in reply.

龍

Lee Kwan walked along the almost empty streets of the Western Docks through the howling rain. He was being followed, he knew it. Two men had been on his trail since he'd alighted from the tram in Central thirty minutes before. It was Major Yip's doing. Yip the Weasel, his superior in

Hong Kong. Yip was onto him. But how, Lee wondered. How had he made a mistake? He'd been pouring money, gathered from wealthy Chinese in the Colony, into the Kuomintang accounts for two years, he'd been commended by Ch'iang Kai-shek personally for his efforts, he was above suspicion. The fact that he'd been delivering equal amounts to the Communists was a closely guarded secret shared by him and Richard Brewster. Yip couldn't possibly know of his duplicity. Had he guessed? Was The Weasel playing a lone hand sending these two men after him? If so, it was a lone hand that was about to get them killed.

Lee dreaded the thought of killing the two men, but he knew he had no alternative. So this is the price a traitor pays, he thought. A traitor must kill those who hunt him. He dismissed the idea as foolish. His decision to defect to the Communist cause had been made for the good of China.

He'd been planning their murders for ten minutes as he'd led them slowly off the beaten track towards several dark, deserted alleyways he knew near Ladder Street. He wondered at the futility of it all. They were just young Kuomintang operatives fighting for a cause they believed in, just as he had done. They'd been sent by Yip to do a bit of spying, in the hope they may discover something with which Yip could discredit him. Lee wondered what they would do if he now turned and told them they had only ninety seconds to live.

He turned into Ladder Street, increasing his speed, and saw the shop awning he was expecting. He grabbed one of its steel supports with both hands and he swung, like a trapeze artist, up and out of sight. The two men were fifty paces apart. Twenty-five seconds would separate their deaths.

The first young agent appeared below him and Lee dropped directly into his path. He hit him in the neck with the edge of his open hand and an expression of surprise was on his face as he died. He caught the body as it slumped towards the stone footpath. Five seconds. He dragged the corpse into the shop doorway. Ten seconds. He propped the body against the door. Fifteen seconds. He waited. Twenty seconds.

The second operative was quick. Lee struck, and the man, slightly older and more experienced than his partner, deflected the blow and moved to retaliate. Lee ducked the blow and struck the man in the chest with his fist, crushing the sternum and driving a rib into the heart. The man thudded back against the shop's brickwork and gasped audibly as he suffered cardiac arrest. Lee's second strike snapped his neck. Thirty seconds.

Lee looked at his watch. He was late. Over an hour late for his meeting with 'The Prisoner' at the apothecary's shop. He moved off quickly into the worsening storm, a crack of lightning illuminating the scene behind him. The second man slid slowly down the brickwork and came to rest on his haunches, his head slumped forward on his knees, the backs of his hands draped over the stone paving. He looked for all the world like an addict succumbed to opium, oblivious to the raging storm.

龍

'Hong Kong is doomed, my friends, and we all know it,' Richard placed his hands palms downward on the board-room table and looked at the faces of his fellow Dragons. 'And so it must follow that our honourable Society is doomed also.'

'I have done as you asked, Richard,' Delaney said. 'The money you gave me has been placed with various members of the Society for safe-keeping.'

'That money is to be used to help our members in the advent of Japanese occupation,' Richard said. 'It should be handed out when and where it is needed.'

'Those are the instructions I passed on,' the Yorkshireman nodded.

'Good,' Richard replied and looked at Lo Shi-mon. 'Ah Lo, have you spoken to our rank and file about the futility of resistance?'

'I have, Elder Brother,' Lo answered. 'They have been instructed that in the event of invasion, they are to remove their police uniforms and burn them. They have been ordered not to resist the Japanese. I've told them they must blend in with the civil population and concentrate on survival until the Japanese have been overthrown and the Society re-established.'

'The idea will give them hope,' Richard nodded. 'That's it, then.'

'There is always the remote possibility the Japanese won't invade,' Malcolm Linden said, but his heart wasn't in the remark. The others looked at him. 'Well, I did say remote,' he finished lamely.

'The Japanese are allied to Britain's enemies, laddie,' McCraw responded. 'War in Asia will draw British troops away from Europe, making things all the easier for the Germans and Italians.'

'And Japan's conquest of Asia will not be unduly threatened,' Delaney added. 'Japan will attack Singapore and invade the Philippines and Britain will be weakened, forced to fight on both sides of the world at once.'

'It makes perfect sense,' McCraw said, 'and Germany and Italy will ensure the Japanese get the steel and oil they need to support their military operations.'

'And at the end of it all,' Richard said, 'Adolf Hitler gets Europe and Emperor Hirohito gets Asia.'

龍

Sheets of rain lashed at Lee Kwan as he turned into Wu Tau Lane and hurried towards the apothecary's shop. He stopped fifty yards short of his destination and surveyed the street. It appeared empty. He stood motionless in the shadows for ten minutes but could detect no one, so he moved up the street and stopped outside the apothecary's door.

It was near midnight and the shop was in darkness. He rapped three times on the door, counted to five and rapped twice more. The light from a candle appeared, followed by the face of the old apothecary, but not a word was exchanged as the old man led him through to the rear of the shop. He opened a door to reveal a set of rickety steps leading down into a small courtyard and below, through the heavy rain,

Lee could see a small wooden shed set against the rear wall. Light was shining through the cracks in its door.

Lee paused outside the shed and looked about him. The old apothecary and his candle were gone and he was alone in the little yard. Suddenly the high stone walls seemed to be closing in on him. He was back in Nanking crawling beneath the city walls terrified they were going to collapse and entomb him, burying him forever with the pervasive stink of rotten human flesh. He could feel the worms against his skin begin their timeless act of consumption.

'*You are late, Kwan,*' Lee spun on his heel at the sound of the voice. '*Why are you late?*' the voice asked. It was coming from the wooden shed. '*Come inside immediately and explain yourself.*'

Lee entered the shed, closed the door and sat, dripping wet on a packing case, leaning his back against the wall. He was shivering noticeably as he stared through a flickering candle's light into the face of The Prisoner of Nanking.

Tao Chu, The Prisoner of Nanking, was a hero to the Communists of China. He was the ultimate professional revolutionary, a man who'd spent time in gaols because of his beliefs. He'd embraced the ideals of communism in 1925 when he'd entered the Whang Po Military Academy, then a joint Nationalist-Communist enterprise created to educate China's young elite and prepare them for 'service to their homeland'. After Ch'iang Kai-shek led his Northern Expedition to quell the 'northern warlords', the unnatural alliance between Communists and Nationalists had been strained to breaking point and, in 1927, General Ch'iang had ordered the arrest of all Communist cadets at the Academy. This had included Tao Chu. It was largely a formal exercise and Tao Chu had escaped the loose security and headed for Hong Kong. From there he had wandered through various parts of China assisting in Communist plots and uprisings until finally, in 1933, he'd been arrested in Shanghai and transferred to Nanking under sentence of death. The sentence was reduced to life imprisonment and he'd remained in Nanking until the Japanese invasion of

1937. Since then, he'd operated as a guerrilla leader within the Communist Army and had been involved in many clandestine operations raising funds to support the Communist military machine.

Lee had made Tao Chu's acquaintance while he'd been in exile in the far west of Sikang Province. He had been unaware that the older man was a Communist. Tao Chu had been posing as an itinerant farm worker while recuperating from a wound received during a guerrilla skirmish against the Japanese. The two had struck up a friendship of sorts in the local inn where a very lonely and unhappy Lee Kwan had spoken of his doubts concerning the political direction of the Nationalist cause. In the winter of 1940, when Lee Kwan had been appointed to his fundraising position in Hong Kong, Tao Chu had been sent by the Communists to convert him. Lee's conscience had been the catalyst. That, and his profound love for China, had given him no choice but to embrace the Communist ideology.

'Why do you tremble, it is only rain?' Tao Chu asked. He nodded the answer. 'It is the high walls, Lee, you are reminded of Nanking, true or not true? This is a problem many suffer and it never goes away. You must learn to control it in your mind.'

'Yes, Prisoner,' Lee respectfully replied.

'And please do not call me by that name, I do not like it. Mao Tse-tung conferred that title on me and I am not happy with it. Many people suffered far more than I in the prisons of Nanking, and for many more years. Mao has a penchant for giving people titles. Like "The Soldier", "The Writer", "The Speech-Maker" and "The Mayor". His motives are entirely selfish, he cannot remember the real names of people. The problem is, the titles stick in the minds of the masses.' There was a sense of resignation in Tau Chu's voice. 'And before you know it you are part of Chinese Communist folklore. My name is Tao Chu.'

'I understand, Elder Brother,' Lee replied.

'Now,' Tau Chu, went on. 'Why are you late?'

'I was followed.'

Lee recounted the events of the previous two hours in detail and, when he'd finished, Tau Chu sat silent for quite some time.

'*It had to happen,*' the older man said at last. '*No one can keep secrets forever, not even we Chinese and we are especially secretive by nature, true or not true? How long do you think the Kuomintang has been aware of your duplicity?*'

'*I do not think they are aware. I have been extremely careful. I believe Major Yip is conducting a personal vendetta against me. He is a fool, jealous of my standing with our superiors and he wants to discredit me.*'

'*Then you have been very stupid,*' Tau Chu said sharply. '*Why did you not behave in a normal fashion? Visit a friend for the evening, and dispel Yip's suspicions? Why kill the two operatives? You have now confirmed his suspicions, true or not true?*'

'*Espionage is not one of my strengths, Tau Chu,*' Lee stood his ground, refusing to be intimidated. '*I have no potential for lying, understand or not understand?*'

'*Yes, yes,*' Tau raised his hand defensively. '*I understand. I am sorry, young Lee Kwan. I have fought a subversive war for so long now, I sometimes fail to remember that some men are driven by honour above all else. It is a fine human quality, but it belongs on the battlefield. A spy with a sense of honour would have a very short lifespan indeed.*'

'*A spy like me, you mean?*'

'*You need spy no longer, Little Brother,*' the Communist said. '*The reason I arranged this meeting was to tell you just that. Our Communist 4th Army has gathered intelligence, which leads us to believe Hong Kong will be invaded before the foreign devils' Christmas. There will no more gathering of money from our sympathisers, they will flee the Colony. They are fleeing as we speak.*'

'*Richard Brewster will not flee, and neither will his foreign police colleagues,*' Lee countered.

'*Then they will die at the hands of the Japanese,*' Tao Chu said bluntly. '*Have you spoken or not spoken to him of what happened in Nanking?*'

'I have spoken many times. But they say Hong Kong is their home, and that they will defend it with their lives if necessary.'

'Who can understand the British?' Tao Chu shrugged. *'Please convey the thanks of the Communist Party to Richard Brewster. The money he has provided through you has been gratefully received. If we can assist him in any way, he has only to ask.'*

'He would not ask,' Lee shook his head. *'But there is a way in which you could possibly assist him. There is a man in England called Charles Higgins, a former Hong Kong police-man, who holds a sword above Richard Brewster's neck. If there is anything that can be done to remove this threat, I would be eternally grateful. As would Richard Brewster's wife, the Merchant Mistress.'*

'Tell me more.'

Lee did, but was careful to speak only of the letter and who it was addressed to. He explained the letter would prove harmful to Richard Brewster if it was ever delivered, but never once did he disclose what the letter pertained to.

龍

Richard looked around the boardroom table at each of his friends. Time was running out for them all. The Japanese would arrive any day now, he was absolutely sure of it.

'As you know,' he said quietly. 'The statues we use in our ceremonies are imitations, the originals were melted down years ago and the gold was converted to cash, but the precious stones from the eyes remain.'

'They are probably worth more than the gold,' Terrence Delaney added.

'I've had them placed in a Swiss bank vault in Geneva,' Richard continued. 'And there they will remain until such time as the global conflict we are about to experience is resolved. One way or the other.'

'If it is ever resolved,' Malcolm Linden said solemnly.

'All things must pass, laddie.' Robert McCraw patted Malcolm's shoulder. 'All wars end, people pick up the pieces and life continues. It's only a matter of time.'

'Robert's right,' Richard said. 'Peace will come again to Hong Kong and when it does the Society of Golden Dragons must be restored. Hopefully one of us, if not all of us, will survive what is to come. And whoever does so, must redeem the dragons' eyes from *Sui Si lan*,' he concluded, using the Cantonese for Switzerland.

'God knows when that will be,' Malcolm Linden commented.

'When Hong Kong is once again under British Rule,' Richard explained. 'Banque Suisse Geneve has explicit instructions regarding the release of the gems. The first instruction is that they cannot be released unless Hong Kong is under British Rule. And the second instruction is that a conversation with the claimant must take place in Cantonese. The conversation must be word for word as written in the instructions held by the bank, and it must be certified correct by at least two senior officers of the bank.'

'And that conversation is?' Robert McCraw asked.

'It is started by the bank's interpreter rapping his knuckles on a table top three times and asking the question: *your heart is what colour?*'

'*Ha!*' Lo Shi-mon interjected. '*Very good, Elder Brother. The redeemer of the eyes must answer the questions that grant him entry to our society.*'

'Correct,' Richard said. '*My eyes are blue . . .*'

'*Your soul is what colour?*' Lo Shi-mon prompted.

'*My soul is golden,*' Richard answered.

'*Who is your master?*' Malcolm Linden asked with a grin.

'*The Golden Dragon!*' Robert McCraw declared.

'*He has how many brothers?*' Richard continued the incantation.

'*Four!*' the others chorused.

'*His brothers came from where to here?*' All five men continued as one voice. '*From the four foreign cities. They brought with them what? They brought the truth. And their eyes are which colours? Red, blue, green and white!*'

'Very good, laddie!' Robert McCraw added. 'But a lot of men know those answers. Shouldn't there be more questions?'

'There are,' Richard replied, and he continued in Cantonese. '*What was the gift of Lo Shi-mon?*' he asked.

'*Gift?*' Delaney looked puzzled.

'*What was the gift of Lo Shi-mon?*' Richard asked again.

'*The Dragons of Shaolin,*' Lo Shi-mon answered.

'*Why do they face north, shoulder to shoulder?*'

'*To conceal their identity,*' Delaney answered, remembering the night James Merchant and Lee Kwan had been branded during their induction into the society.

'*Why do they face south?*' Richard asked.

'*To defend our Noble House,*' Malcolm answered.

'*And what is their gift?*'

'*A little dragon carved from gold!*' Robert McCraw triumphantly exclaimed.

'Exactly!' Richard replied in English. 'And the answer to that last question is known only by we five in this room, and our young Dragons of Shaolin themselves.'

'And what of my two students?' Lo Shi-mon asked. 'Are the young dragons themselves to be made aware of the eyes in the bank in *Sui Si lan*? Are they to be told how the eyes can be retrieved?'

'That is a matter for we First Five to decide,' Richard answered. 'As it stands, the Society of Golden Dragons has five chances of surviving. To tell the young dragons would make it seven chances.'

'Aaaiiiyaah!' Lo exclaimed. 'The number seven is *ho choi*.'

'Lo's right, laddie,' McCraw nodded. Over the years Li Ping had instilled in him a healthy respect for Chinese superstition. 'The number seven is lucky. We'd be inviting all the bad luck in the world down on our heads if we chose to ignore it.'

'Malcolm?' Richard asked.

'Seven's all right with me,' Linden replied.

'Terrence?'

'As you said yourself, Golden Dragon,' the big Yorkshireman replied. 'Seven is better than five.'

'We're agreed then!' Richard finished. 'I'll instruct James and Lee. Seven to one are the odds.'

Outside in the storm, a flash of lightning lit up the night sky, then several seconds later heavy thunder rumbled.

龍

'Don't move,' the voice whispered as Lee crossed the floor of the apothecary's shop towards the front door. 'Not one muscle, Lee Kwan, or I'll shoot you dead where you stand.'

Lee spun around and froze at the sight of a Luger pistol, exposed momentarily by a flash of lightning. The muzzle was pointing at him from the shadows, and Lee knew the voice of the man who held the pistol.

'Good evening, Major Yip,' he said in English. 'Fancy you being out on a filthy night like this.'

Yip ignored Lee's sarcastic tone. 'If you move I'll pull this trigger.'

'If I move,' Lee replied softly. 'You won't know about it until it's too late.'

'You're a traitor,' Yip declared.

'And you're a coward,' Lee answered. He could smell Yip's fear. 'Therefore I'm intrigued.'

'Intrigued?' Yip had to ask.

'Yes. I'm intrigued as to why a coward like you would be doing your own dirty work when you have any number of minions to do it for you.' As Lee spoke, he began the process of slowing his heart rate and preparing his mind to control the shock that the bullets from the German automatic would create when they hit his body. He allowed his senses to focus on the muzzle of the gun and brought all his powers of concentration to bear on the threat that would burst forth from that 9-mm black hole. At the same time, the part of his brain which was trained to attack made precise measurements of the distance separating him from his target, and the various directions from which that target could be approached and struck.

'Detecting treason is hardly dirty work, Captain,' Yip tried to sound confident, but even with the Luger in his hand he was frightened.

'Unless of course your work is of a more mercenary nature?'

'What do you mean by that?'

'Excuse me for smiling, Major,' Lee replied, buying time as his brain continued to assess the situation. 'But you're not expecting me to believe you've become a patriot, are you? Not at this late stage in your career?'

'You've been supplying money donated to the Nationalist Cause, to the Communists . . .'

'Have I now?'

'Yes,' Yip said quickly. 'And probably keeping some for yourself too.' He was terrified of Lee Kwan. Why in God's name had he ever allowed things to come to this? He should have simply informed on Lee, but greed had overtaken him. He'd felt sure he could make money for himself, and rid the world of a traitor at the same time. All he needed to know was how Lee had been diverting the money, then he would simply divert it to himself. But now the moment of confrontation had arrived. Now he was in this dingy little apothecary's shop, during this filthy storm, and the eyes of a dragon were staring hungrily into his, he was terrified beyond reason. He was shaking so much he could barely hold the Luger. He must pull the trigger, he thought. He must escape into the night before he was devoured. Damn the money. He must pull the trigger and run.

'And now you'd like your share, am I correct, Major?'

'You're a traitor, Captain.'

Lee watched the Luger muzzle wander erratically in Yip's trembling hand. 'A traitor? To whom?' he asked. He knew this pistol, he'd handled it himself on several occasions. The ammunition in the weapon was old, very old, its muzzle velocity would be less than 600 feet per second, extremely weak by handgun standards. He decided on his course of action.

'To China, that's who,' Yip snarled, his nerves at breaking point. 'You think you're such a hero, don't you? Well, you're not! You're nothing but a traitor to your country.'

'Oh, no, that's where you're wrong,' Lee eased Minnie

Vautrin's large gold signet ring from his right middle finger and held it between thumb and forefinger. It was the ring given to him in Nanking. 'A traitor to the Nationalists maybe. A patriot to the Communists probably. But a traitor to China? Never!'

'What have you got in your hand?' Yip's voice was a terrified squeak. 'Show me.'

'This,' Lee held up the signet ring, his left arm outstretched. 'It's for you, solid gold. A down-payment.' He calculated the distance between the heavy gold ring and the muzzle, less than two feet, and without hesitating he thrust forward, jamming the flat face of the ring hard over the pistol muzzle. Then he flicked his right hand towards Yip's face, causing him to flinch and pull the trigger.

The bullet roared from the gun, smashing the ring from Lee's hand and dislocating his finger. The deflected missile flew past him, embedding itself in the door frame, but by then Lee's right hand had flashed out, and his fingers closed like steel around Yip's throat shutting off the supply of oxygen to the lungs, and blood to his brain. Lee's left hand closed over the pistol, his grip making the automatic's mechanism inoperable.

Yip released the Luger, struggling briefly as his brain registered that he was passing into unconsciousness. But this was not unconsciousness, his brain suddenly screamed. This was the void from which there was no return. This was death!

Lee hastened the death. Dropping the Luger, he struck Yip with a blow to the back of the neck, snapping it like a twig, then released his grip on the throat and let the dead body slump to the floor.

'*We'll dispose of the body,*' Tao Chu said. He'd been about to shoot Major Yip when Lee had struck with the speed of a snake, and made his intervention unnecessary. '*There will be many questions asked by the Kuomintang, you must make sure your alibi is irrefutable.*'

Lee winced as he took hold of his forefinger and relocated it with a sudden jerk, then looked at Tao Chu and the old apothecary who was staring, mesmerised by the dead body. He nodded, went to the shop door and opened it.

'*Goodnight, comrade,*' he said, as rain lashed at him through the open doorway.

'*Goodnight, comrade,*' Tao Chu watched the door close against the storm. '*I will see you again, Lee Kwan,*' he said softly. '*In better times.*'

Chapter Nineteen

It was midnight when James unlocked the front door of the house in Belgravia. As he entered the hallway, he heard the sombre chimes of the grandfather clock on the first landing above, and let himself into the study, closing the doors behind him. A fire burned brightly and sandwiches, thoughtfully left by Mrs Daley, sat next to the brandy decanter on the sideboard. He sank into a large leather chair and stared blankly into the flames. The events of the last twenty-four hours had exhausted him.

The day had commenced well enough with his Shaolin disciplines in the cellar. He'd been working vigorously for nearly an hour, concentrating harder and harder as he progressed through each movement, a fine patina of sweat covering his body, when he'd been interrupted by Katherine's voice, calling from the hallway. He'd quickly donned his silk robe and headed upstairs.

'Hello, darling.' She'd kissed him passionately.

'What are you doing here at this hour of the morning?' he asked when he'd recovered from her onslaught.

'It's such a bright sunny day,' she replied. 'Even though it's freezing. I decided I'd take the whole day off, and the night too,' she added seductively. 'And drive up to London and devote myself entirely to you.' Her last remark was delivered with such a suggestive undertone that James couldn't help but smile.

'I see,' he answered, leading her into the study. 'And just what type of devotion did you have in mind, young lady?'

'What I have in mind, sir, is anything but ladylike.'

'Well,' he said, undoing his robe. 'Since you've driven all the way from Richmond I suppose it would be rude of me to refuse.'

'James!' At the sight of his half-naked body, Katherine looked about furtively. 'The servants! Mrs Daley! Close your robe before . . .'

'Lock the doors, Kate.'

'I was joking.'

'No, you weren't. Admit it.' He let the robe fall. 'Lock the doors. Now!'

'James . . .'

'Lock the doors, Kate.'

God, what's become of me, she thought as she locked the doors with trembling fingers and turned to him. The urge was so strong, she could feel her blood pulsing. She felt like a bitch on heat as he walked slowly towards her.

Sexual desire was Katherine Billings' worst enemy, it made a fool of her at every given opportunity. She'd been easy prey, James had known that she would be from the moment they'd first met. Young and innocent as she was, he'd sensed a sexuality begging to be awakened. And he'd done just that.

On the very first night when she'd come to him at Belgravia she'd given herself to him so willingly that even James had been surprised. He had presumed he would seduce her that night, certainly, but in his emotional state at the time, he had expected, indeed wanted, some preliminary discussion.

'You're on fire, Katherine,' he'd said. He could feel it the moment he touched her. 'Well, I suppose we'll have to put you out.' And that had been that.

In the months that followed, Katherine's defences had crumbled entirely. And, as curiosity in her newly discovered taste for sex gathered momentum, James had moulded her into the perfect bed partner. Now, fifteen months into their relationship she was deeply in love with James and besotted with his body.

The Katherine Billings James knew when she was not engaged in sexual congress was quite another animal.

Reserved, gracious, intelligent, well educated, resourceful and more than socially acceptable. Katherine was, for all intents and purposes, the perfect woman for James. That he would marry her he had no doubts. The fact that he didn't love her did not enter the equation.

James Merchant could not love, the capacity seemed to have escaped him. Somewhere between the killing of Herbert Billings and the war, he'd lost, or forgotten, what love represented. He'd become aware of the fact and accepted it but, in a bizarre and direct ratio, his need to have women love and desire him had increased.

As a twelve-year-old in his mother's house, he'd quickly discovered the need in women to be told they were loved, and he'd learned to articulate the words they wanted to hear. It had been a game, and he'd enjoyed it, possibly waiting for the day when he might understand it. But to James, now, the concept of love between a man and a woman had drifted beyond understanding. Unlike duty or honour, ideals he could perceive, love had become unquantifiable, intangible, until finally, he'd dismissed it from his consciousness as unreasonable.

The need of a wife was another matter, however. James would soon be twenty-one and when the war finally ended he would need a wife to give him children and to play hostess at his table. A wife who was loyal, trustworthy, honourable and shrewd, a woman in whom he could confide and consult on business matters, and Katherine Billings was just such a woman. She was a bona fide member of the British aristocracy and would make the perfect wife for him in Hong Kong, and he had no intention of losing her. The fact that he'd murdered her uncle was neither here nor there, as long as she remained unaware of the circumstances of Sir Herbert Billings' death, the matter was not worthy of consideration.

It was ten in the morning, James had donned his uniform and Katherine was upstairs bathing after their encounter on the study divan, when he heard the front doorbell ring.

Mrs Daley opened the study door. 'There are two Chinese gentlemen here to see you, Sir.'

'Any idea what they want?' James straightened his tie and pulled on his Air Force tunic.

'Not a one, Mister Merchant. Very inscrutable types they are, Sir.'

'Show them in, Mrs Daley, but interrupt us in ten minutes, would you? I have to go out,' he indicated the telephone. 'I've been summoned to Whitehall, it could be good news.' James had already forgotten that Katherine, upstairs bathing, was anticipating their day together.

'Very well, Mr Merchant.'

The men were Cantonese, James noted as they entered his study. '. . . five feet five to five feet seven, dark hair, brown eyes, speaks *punti* – colloquial Hong Kong Cantonese – wanted in connection with . . .'. He smiled at the recollection of police descriptions given to the Hong Kong newspapers of any Chinese offender wanted for crimes in the Colony. The description was a standing joke in colonial society. But then, how else could a westerner describe a Cantonese?

'*My name is Captain Chou, Elder Brother,*' the five feet seven one said. '*I am a representative of the Communist Liberation Army and this,*' he indicated the five feet five one, '*is Mr Laai, a member of the Party Committee and representative of Mao Tse-tung.*'

'*There is nothing like a mystery, true or not true?*' James said. '*What can I do for you, gentlemen?*'

'*We will not take up your time,*' Mr Laai began. '*We are to report to you that an investigation was conducted at our request, into all dealings between the Bank of England and the former Hong Kong Inspector-General of Police Charles Higgins. This investigation revealed the existence of a letter.*'

'You got into the Bank of England!' In his astonishment, James had burst into English. '*Sorry. I did not mean to interrupt, but are you saying you gained access to private information inside the Bank of England?*'

'*True, Elder Brother,*' Chou said.

'*How is that possible?*'

'*There are two ideologically opposed armies in the Central Realms,*' Laai continued. '*And both are fighting the Japanese.*

When the Japanese are driven from their country, and that will happen one day, those two armies will fight each other to the death.'

'Two tigers cannot live on one mountain,' James offered.

'Very good, Elder Brother,' Laai inclined his head in a gesture of respect. *'The British Government also knows this, but they do not know which tiger will win. Therefore, they must offer encouragement and assistance to both, for one day they will need the winner's friendship.'*

'In order to maintain their trade agreements and territorial possessions, true or not true, Mr Laai?'

'Your grasp of the political ramifications is excellent,' Laai smiled. *'I have been instructed to give you this.'* He handed James an envelope marked with the coat of arms of the Bank of England. *'A dragon in Hong Kong desired the recovery of this letter, its retrieval was achieved through diplomatic protocol.'*

James opened the letter and read it quickly. *'Do you know if there were any copies made of this letter?'*

'Only the cook knows what's in the pot,' Captain Chou replied.

'I am sorry, please explain?'

'The only person who can answer your question,' Captain Chou replied. *'Is the person who wrote the letter.'*

'Then I suppose I must ask him,' James shook hands with both men. *'Thank you, gentlemen, you have been of great service.'*

Both Chinese gave a nod of respect and departed, leaving James to ponder the situation.

The death of Charles Higgins was a matter of great consideration. Unlike the death of Sir Herbert Billings, which had been an assassination based upon a need to protect Dragon Society business, Charles' death was a far more serious matter. What if a copy of the letter existed? And what if it was delivered to the Kuomintang? Richard's life, and the life of Elanora, would be in grave danger.

James knew Charles Higgins only too well, he'd lived with him for three years, and he'd stake his life on the fact that another copy of the letter existed. Charles would have created an identical letter immediately after informing Richard of the original held in the Bank of England. That was the way Charles' mind worked. He would have made a copy and entrusted it to someone with the same instructions, to post it after his death, for no other reason than to have the last laugh. Charles always had to have the last laugh, even if it was from the other side of the grave.

Katherine caught him in the hallway as he was putting on his greatcoat.

'James?' her voice was querulous. 'You're not going out, surely? I've taken the day off especially to spend it with you.'

'I'm sorry, darling. I'm required at the Ministry ASAP. It's urgent.'

'But James . . .'

'There's a war on, old girl,' he called as he opened the front door, 'I've been summoned to Whitehall, I'll telephone you as soon as I'm clear and we'll make a night of it, all right?' Before she could answer he was gone.

The taxi pulled up in Whitehall and James got out. He paid the driver and stood looking at a street filled with wind-buffeted Londoners, most in military uniforms hugging satchels or attache cases and scurrying between various offices, ostensibly carrying on the nasty business of war. Tough, resilient people, he thought affectionately, indomitable people not unlike the Chinese.

As he entered the Ministry he glanced skyward, grey was quickly replacing the blue. So much for Katherine's beautiful day, it would be bucketing down within the hour.

Three flights of stairs and four corridors finally led him to the office to which he'd been summoned. He entered and bowed with mock sincerity to the young woman behind the desk.

Lieutenant Cynthia Penfold R.N., currently on attachment to the Air Ministry, smiled knowingly. 'Flight Lieutenant Merchant, oops, sorry, Squadron Leader Merchant now, isn't it? Nice of you to drop in even though you're an hour late for your appointment.' James started removing his greatcoat.

'And don't bother undressing, Squadron Leader, it won't get you anywhere . . .'

'What if I lock the door . . .?'

'Don't be disgusting,' Cynthia Penfold said. She adored James Merchant and their titillating conversations. He always made her laugh with his suggestive asides and there was no doubting his sexuality, he exuded it. It was her rule never to mix business with pleasure, but when James appeared on the horizon she invariably had second thoughts. 'Group Captain Hadden-Smythe is not here, you've missed him.'

'Cynthia . . .' James purred seductively as he leant across her desk.

'Lieutenant Penfold to you, Squadron Leader.'

'How do I love thee, let me count the ways . . .'

'Behave yourself! . . . Here.' She handed him an envelope marked 'FOR YOUR EYES ONLY'. 'These are your orders. You've finally hit the jackpot, you're posted to Far East Command. You are to report for duty in Hong Kong at 0800 hours on the fifteenth of December, that's a week from now, so you'd do well to stop flirting and get on with your packing.'

James tore open the letter and read furiously. He was going home! After three applications for transfer, Churchill had finally relented and released him from the circus of public engagements. No more village fetes, no more sad-faced war weary people, gathered to hear him express the Government's gratitude at their meagre contributions. No more stuffy dinners with barons of industry, desperate to show their patriotic fervour with large contributions to the Government coffers. No more reiteration of his exploits in the Battle of Britain as it had become known. He was going home.

'These orders are marked for my eyes only, Lieutenant,' James said with mock severity. 'How did you know the contents, are you a Nazi spy?'

'I typed them out, you idiot!'

'Will you have dinner with me before I depart?'

'I will not.'

'Oh, come on, Cynth. We've been through a lot together, you and I.'

'The sort of fraternisation you have in mind is frowned upon by the brass.'

'Cynthia,' James tapped the epaulettes on his tunic indicating his rank. 'I am the brass. How about I make it an order?'

Cynthia Penfold stared into the depths of his dark, dark eyes, God but he's a handsome man, she thought. Did she dare? No, she decided, she definitely did not.

'I'd rather die, James,' she said.

'Well, we can't have that, can we?' he smiled. 'Perhaps when I return you might want to rethink the proposition. We'll take a cup of kindness some day, eh? For auld lang syne?' Then he smiled again and was gone out the door.

'For auld lang syne,' she repeated, her words hanging in the still office air. Damn this war, she thought, it had already claimed one man she loved. 'Take care of yourself, James,' she said to the open door.

龍

An evening fog, a real 'pea souper' as Londoners called them, enveloped James Merchant as he stood on the Victoria Embankment opposite the public gardens, and wrapped his coat collar firmly about his ears. Through the mist, he could barely make out the inky black water of the Thames below him. Winter had officially arrived in London and James dearly wished himself back in the Orient. Well, not long now, he thought. Just one short week, and he'd be in Hong Kong.

Thomas Smith, James' chauffeur, had traced Charles Higgins to his latest address. 'He lives in "The Stables", Sir,' Thomas had informed him. 'Apartment 42 accordin' to my informant 'oo shall remain nameless.'

The Royal Horse Guards Apartments was in Whitehall Place around the corner from the Ministry James had attended that morning, barely a stone's throw from the Houses of Parliament. James knew the building well, he'd attended several parties there thrown by a young socialite he'd dallied with just before war had broken out. A daughter of affluent parents who indulged her every whim, she'd thrown her soirees while her parents were out of the country. And what soirees they'd been. Champagne had flowed freely, oysters consumed by the dozen, and James had inevitably been the last guest to leave, finally staggering from her bed into the daylight like a lost mole.

'Thank you, whatever your name was,' he murmured as he crossed the Embankment. 'You've made my mission a doddle, old girl.'

Heavy fog hung over the gardens as he entered and moved wraith-like through the trees. Reaching the apartments' ivy-spattered stone wall, he climbed effortlessly to an open first floor window and slipped through it.

He found himself in an empty hallway, apartments leading off either side. He remembered the layout of the place very well: at the end of the hall there would be stairs leading down to the main foyer and up to the floors above. Barely a minute later, he'd reached the fourth floor undetected and was standing in front of Apartment 42. He paused, listening attentively for a full ten seconds, before deftly picking the lock.

Bingo, he thought as he took in the oriental furnishings and wall hangings, just the sort of décor Charles would surround himself with. He breathed slowly and deeply, taking control of his system as he moved through the dark apartment. The only light source came through a door which was slightly ajar. James pushed it open gently, but the face he encountered was not that of Charles Higgins.

A young woman offered him a beautiful smile. She lay on a double bed and stared straight at him while a fat man in his sixties, whose face James could not see, grunted over her in the act of copulation. The man was most definitely not Charles Higgins. This man was sixteen stone at the very least, with a posterior the size of a Clydesdale horse.

The young woman, probably an expensive prostitute, James thought, lifted her arm from the old man's back and waved with her fingers. James put a finger to his lips and the girl nodded her understanding and blew him a kiss. God only knew who she thought he was, but she obviously believed he had every right to be there. He blew her a kiss in return, waved and left the apartment as silently as he'd entered it, carefully closing the front door behind him. James knew she would not be able to identify him, his face had been in half shadow, which was fortunate for the girl and her Clydesdale, he thought.

Bad intelligence, he inwardly cursed. Bad intelligence always resulted in a bungled operation. He decided to leave the building through the front door like a departing guest, he'd check the correct address and apartment number before returning. But, arriving at the stairwell, he was just in time to see the back of Charles Higgins as he disappeared up the stairs to the next floor. Well, well, well, James smiled, if that's not the luck of the Irish. He followed discreetly and watched his prey unlock the door to Apartment 52.

James moved swiftly. Reaching Higgins as the door opened, he struck with a blow to the neck and Charles crumpled to the floor unconscious.

Charles Higgins had no idea where he was at first, he only knew that he was very cold. As his vision cleared, he saw that he was in his living room, strapped tight in an armchair, and a figure was standing in front of the fireplace. Were his eyes playing tricks, or was the figure naked? Yes, by God, it was! His gaze moved up the lean, fit body and he tried to focus on the shadowy face. Then he saw it, flickering in the light from the gas fire, a scar on the upper arm. The scar looked for all the world like a snarling dragon. Recognition dawned and his blood turned to ice.

'Good evening, Charles,' James Merchant's voice touched him like an Arctic wind. 'Do forgive the nudity, but I can't afford to get any blood on my clothing, I have places to go when I leave here.'

'What in hell do you want?' Charles tried to sound authoritative, but his voice came out a croak.

'The truth will do.'

'About what?'

'Lots of things, old boy, lots of things.' James crossed the floor and leant down into Charles' face. 'You've been a bad man, Charles. For a good many years you've been a bad man and now it's time for you to repent your sins. You need to speak to God, Charles, and I'm here to facilitate the meeting.'

'Now just you listen here!'

'First things first,' James placed a small object in Charles' hand.

Charles looked down at it, and his heart leapt into his throat. It was a tiny golden statue of a dragon. He'd seen its like once before.

'You're about to join a very elite group, Charles, this little fellow is the harbinger of death, he's the official messenger of the Society of Golden Dragons. He was presented to you some years ago, in Hong Kong, remember? It was meant as a warning for you to mend your ways, but you didn't heed that warning did you, Charlie old boy?'

'Have a care, James,' Charles commenced his bluff. He hadn't tripped up anywhere, had he? If so, when? How? 'If anything should happen to me . . .'

'And it will,' James interrupted. 'Rest assured that it will, Charles. This time . . . it will.' He squeezed water from a wet towel he'd taken from the kitchen and draped it over his shoulder.

'The letter I placed . . .'

'Ah, yes, the letter. Let's talk about the letter,' James took out a pocket-knife and opened the blade, it flashed momentarily in the gas firelight.

'The letter is in my private box in the Bank of England, James, and if you so much as lay a finger on me, it will go straight to the Kuomintang.'

'The Bank of England has no such letter, Charles.'

'Don't be ridiculous, of course it has!'

'Oh no, it hasn't,' James held the letter up with his thumb and forefinger, allowing Charles enough time to register its authenticity before tossing it back onto the chair beside his clothes. 'Not any more.'

'How could you have it? It's not possible. It was in the Bank of England.'

'Let's just say you became a pawn in a game of international politics.'

'You're talking rubbish.'

'I'd hardly call the British Government's interests in the Far East rubbish.'

'You're bluffing! Show me that letter again.'

'This is not a game of cards at the Hong Kong Club, Charles!' James pushed the naked man's head back against the chair. 'In this game you bleed if you bluff.' He placed a hand firmly over Charles' mouth and with one movement, sliced a six-inch wound across his forehead.

Charles felt no pain. It was shock that made him attempt to cry out, but the hand over his mouth allowed only a muffled grunt to escape through his nostrils. He saw James remove his hand and wipe the blood from it onto the wet towel. Then blood rushed into Charles's eyes, blinding him. He felt it dripping onto his chest, running over his abdomen and down between his legs; he was drenched in blood. He gasped for breath and swallowed blood. He was gagging and retching, choking on his own blood.

James took Charles' hand, slashed open the veins in the wrist and watched blood pump out onto the floor. Charles spluttered, regaining his breath a little, and James looked at him. He was finding torture distasteful. Why couldn't he, just once, find a genuine adversary, a legitimate enemy of the Golden Dragons, look him straight in the eye, and fight him in an honourable contest? There's no honour in what I'm doing, he thought. But it had to be done. If he didn't get the information, which he knew Charles had, Elanora and Richard would die.

'You're going to die, Charles, unless we stop that bleeding.'

'You bastard,' Charles managed to sputter through bloodied lips.

'And I will stop it, if you tell me where the second letter is.'

Charles tried to spit, but only succeeded in dribbling. 'What second letter,' he gurgled.

'Don't make me do this, Uncle,' James placed his hand

over Charles' mouth and pushed the point of the knife into his nipple. 'I know you well,' he continued as Charles snorted blood over his hand. 'There is a second letter somewhere and you will tell me where it is.' He removed his hand.

'It's in a place where you'll never find it,' Charles hissed.

'All you have to do is tell me,' James methodically replaced his hand over Charles' mouth. 'And you will, Charles.' He drove the blade deeper into Charles's skin, running the blade under tissue towards the armpit. 'I can assure you of that.'

Charles could only manage a feeble moan through his nose. The pain was intense and the loss of blood was taking its toll.

'"Who'd have thought the old man had so much blood in him", to quote the bard as you're so fond of doing,' James removed the blade and again wiped the blood from his hands and chest with the wet towel.

Charles' lungs sucked in air. 'I know of a priceless treasure,' he gasped. 'It's there for the taking if . . .'

'A priceless treasure?' James sneered. 'Don't insult my intelligence. You can do better than that.'

'Please,' Charles pleaded blindly. He was suddenly terrified of dying. 'The *China Moon*. The One-Eyed Woo's junk. It went down off Cheung Chau. Ming Dynasty treasures. You were there . . .' He lapsed into unconsciousness.

James clamped his hand over the slit wrist stopping the blood flow. He didn't want the old villain dying before he revealed who had the letter.

'The letter, Charles, remember the letter?' James said, gently slapping the bleeding man back to awareness.

'I'll never tell you . . .' Charles moaned.

'Then let me guess,' James went on. 'You'd have to leave it with someone you trusted to post it, right? A friend, perhaps? But then you haven't got any friends, have you? You're *persona non grata* in London. Richard saw to that.'

Charles was fading fast and he knew it. The pain was excruciating and he realised that it was time for death. I'm dying, he thought. I'm dying, but I'll have my revenge when the letter is posted.

'What about a relative?' James said loudly.

Charles' mind was jolted back to the present. His body jumped, startled, twitching, and he tried desperately to clear the mist of blood from his eyes. The bastard, he thought. He knows. He probably knew before he arrived. This torture is a mindless game to him. He's known all along, and he's having fun watching me bleed.

'Have I touched a nerve, Charles?' James whispered, kneeling beside Higgins, placing a hand on his knee. 'You do have relatives don't you, Charlie boy? I met them several times. Your sister Agnes and her daughter in Battersea.'

'Noooo . . .' Charles groaned. He was mortally weak. 'Don't hurt her, please . . .'

'So, Aunt Agnes has been looking after it all this time.' He released the pressure on Charles's wrist allowing the blood to flow again, then slit the other wrist. 'And I'll just bet she doesn't even know what it's about. She'll probably give it to me, her dear little James, if I tell her you sent me to collect it for you.'

Charles felt the knife puncture his eyeball but he couldn't seem to care, he was drifting towards a distant black mass. It was a mountain, he thought, or a cliff face.

'It's over, Charles,' he heard James say. 'You're going to meet Wu Loong.'

'Wu Loong?' Charles whispered, he couldn't think properly. The black mass before him was taking shape and he was fascinated, watching it uncurl.

'The Black Dragon,' James' voice was coming from far away.

Black Dragon? Charles watched the mountain rise up before him and realised it was a dragon, a black dragon breathing fire at him. Wu Loong! His mind registered the Black Dragon! Oh Christ, help me, his mind screamed as Wu Loong's eyes, blazing with evil, fell upon him.

James struck the knife handle with the heel of his palm driving it deep into Charles Higgins' brain.

龍

'Battersea, Thomas,' James said as he climbed into the back seat of the Rolls-Royce. He'd taken his time after killing Charles. He'd availed himself of the bathroom, showering and dressing, then, before silently leaving the building, he'd watched the letter burn to ashes in Charles' fireplace.

'Somewhere specific, Sir?' Thomas Smith replied as he engaged first gear and moved the car cautiously along the Embankment. The fog had thickened making his job rather difficult.

'Do you remember Agnes Higgins, Charles Higgins' sister? You took Lee and me to her house a couple of times when we were schoolboys.'

'I certainly do, Sir. A sour ol' tart if evah I met one, if you don't mind me sayin' so, Sir. Had her young daughter Mavis livin' wiv 'er. She had a kid to some geezer 'oo ran orf and left her cold.'

'That's right, but it's old Miss Higgins I need to see, Thomas, I'm afraid I have got some bad news for her. And by the way,' he nestled further into the luxurious leather seat, 'the apartment number was 52, not 42.'

'Sorry abaht that, Sir. I shall 'ave a word in my informant's ear. Can't afford mistakes like that, can we?'

'No, we can't,' James murmured. The act of killing Higgins had had the usual affect on him. He wanted sex. He wanted desperately to go to Belgravia and embed himself in Katherine. But following this killing, he was experiencing something else too. Depression. And he couldn't analyse why. He'd served his *Shan Chu* faithfully, and in doing so had also probably saved his mother's life. Furthermore, the world was finally rid of Charles Higgins, and would be a better place for it. Was it because there was no challenge in killing Charles? Yes, he thought, perhaps it was simply that. He saw again Charles' lifeless body slumped in the chair. He saw again the gas flames from the fireplace reflected in the pools of blood. And he saw again the flickering image of the little golden statue in Charles' open, bloodied hand. He dismissed the images from his mind and concentrated on his desire for Katherine's warm body.

The car crossed Waterloo Bridge and air-raid sirens began their doleful moans. Thomas pulled the car up in Nine Elms Lane as bombs began to fall on the City of London.

'Jerry's out in full force again, Sir. He don't let up, does he?'

'No, he doesn't,' James agreed. 'They're flying blind tonight. The fog's obscuring their targets and they're dumping their bomb loads indiscriminately.'

They sat silently in the car as chaos erupted around them. Several bombs exploded in the Thames nearby.

'Shouldn't we find an air-raid shelter, Mistah Merchant?'

'You're not afraid of a few bombs, are you, Thomas?' James chided, as more explosions erupted across the river in Chelsea.

'If you think we'll be orright here, Sir, that's good enough for me,' Thomas answered.

The foggy night was lit up with the red glow of incendiaries, and the fire of burning houses, and soon the sky was dissected by anti-aircraft search light beams desperately trying to seek out the elusive enemy above.

Three fire engines rushed past, their bells clanging furiously.

'They'll be goin' to the Battersea Power Station and the Gas Works,' Thomas remarked with a nonchalance that belied his fear. 'The Jerries don' 'alf give that joint a goin' over. Every night it seems. I shouldn't wonder if it's just a big 'ole in the groun' by now.'

They sat, not speaking for fifteen minutes as bombs rained down on the beleaguered city. Then the all clear sirens sounded and Thomas started the big Rolls-Royce engine.

'Miss 'Iggins' 'ouse, sir?'

'What?' James stirred from his reverie. His mind had been wandering the Peak of Hong Kong Island. He'd been playing hide and seek with Lee, secreting himself in the sub-tropical foliage and staring up breathlessly at the azure blue sky. 'I'm sorry, Thomas, I was miles away.'

'That's all right, Sir. I asked if you'd still like to go to Miss 'Iggins' 'ouse. Judging by the glow down that way it might be a bit risky.'

'Drive on,' James replied. 'I must get to her house, it's important.'

龍

'You don't want to drive that Roller in there, mate,' a fireman pointed down the street as he shouted through the window at Thomas. 'It's Hell's bleeding kitchen at the moment.'

James looked through the car windows at the scene before him. The street, of more than thirty terraced houses, was a blazing inferno. People were screaming and wailing, and firemen's orders went unheard in the cacophony as hoses criss-crossed the cobblestones firing streams of water on the houses in a futile attempt to douse the flames.

Both men alighted from the Rolls-Royce and stood looking on helplessly.

'The Higgins 'ouse is done for, Sir, it's right in the middle of all that.'

'Yes. Wait here a moment,' James ordered and walked into the street.

A small boy about five or six years old stood watching the madness unfold all about him. He dropped the teddy bear he'd been holding and turned his desperate face towards James and watched him approach.

'What's your name, son?' James asked.

'Jeremy. Are you God?' the boy replied.

'No.'

'Are you an angel?' the boy asked, noticing the wings on the man's hat.

'No.'

'The dragons ate my Mum. I was sleeping at my friend's house but I heard the dragons coming, I heard them screaming and Mr Ogden tried to make me stay, but I ran away and when I came home the dragons were here,' the boy sobbed and pointed a trembling finger at the flames engulfing his mother's house.

James took the boy in his arms and stood up. 'I'll look after you,' he said. 'I know where you'll be safe.'

龍

The clock struck two in the morning. James stood up, stretched, reached for the lamp switch on his desk and with a gesture of finality turned it off.

He'd taken the boy to the Sisters of Mercy in Earl's Court and made arrangements for his care. The Sisters had assured him the boy would be correctly identified and if no relatives were located they would notify the proper authorities and he would be fostered to a responsible family.

James was not happy at being unable to locate Charles' letter. But Mrs Higgins had had possession of it, he was sure and, as her house had been razed to the ground, the chances of Ch'iang Kai-shek, or anyone else, ever receiving it were nil.

He switched off the hall lights and climbed the stairs, thoughts of Charles Higgins' bloody death increasing his need for Katherine with each step.

She was asleep. Her bedside lamp was on, and the book she'd been reading had slipped from her fingers to the floor. James picked it up, placed it on the side table and stood looking at her face in the soft glow of the lamp.

Images of Charles' bloodied and mutilated body filled his mind as he stripped off his clothes, and pulled back the bedding. The only way to rid himself of the images was Katherine. He placed his hand between her legs and softly caressed her until she moaned and her eyes opened. She stared up at him and smiled.

龍

At three o'clock in the morning on 8 December 1941, on a street in the suburb of Battersea the fires were finally extinguished and thirty-five chimneys stood in a row, like blackened gravestones to the memory of those who'd died there.

龍

In apartment number 52 of the Royal Horse Guards Apartments the clock struck five in the morning. As the chimes called the hour, the last drops of blood dripped from a lifeless body onto a Persian carpet. Into the pool of blood, a tiny golden dragon slipped from the man's hand and lay twinkling in the firelight.

龍

At seven o'clock in the morning in the house of the Sisters of Mercy, the little boy awoke in a strange bed. The ceiling was very high above him and the walls had coloured windows with pictures on them. One of the pictures showed a pretty lady with a little baby in her arms. The lady looked like his Mum. Slowly but surely the tears welled in his eyes and ran down his cheeks as the realisation of what had occurred dawned in his child's mind. His Mum was dead, and so was his granny.

One of the winged ladies came to him and sat by his bedside. She had a pen and pencil set and a little notebook, which she opened and rested on her lap. She took his hand and held it softly with her fingers until his tears stopped.

'Can you tell me your name?' she asked.

'Yes, Miss, it's Jeremy, Miss,' he whispered forlornly, 'Jeremy Charles Higgins.'

龍

At eight o'clock on that same morning, 8 December 1941, in a far distant time zone, the 38th Division of the Japanese 23rd Army crossed the Shum Chun River from China and invaded the British Crown Colony of Hong Kong.

CHAPTER TWENTY

Richard Brewster fired his machine gun down Shaftesbury Avenue to the intersection of Regent Street then ran into Pall Mall. He scrambled over the dead and dying bodies of British and Japanese alike until he reached Robert McCraw.

'We've got to get out of here, Robbie!' he shouted over gunfire and explosions. 'The Redoubt is lost, the Japanese are swarming all over it.'

'Back through Shaftesbury Avenue is our only hope, laddie,' McCraw replied, referring to the tunnel Richard had just come from.

Shing Mun Redoubt on Smugglers' Ridge was a series of fortified bunkers and gun emplacements, which was supposed to have arrested the Japanese advance on Hong Kong. The men of the garrison who manned the Redoubt had named its various tunnels after streets in London, much to each other's amusement at the time. The Redoubt was the mainstay of the British defensive line and they'd lost it in two hours. Hundreds of men on both sides had died horrific deaths.

Japanese soldiers swarmed throughout the narrow, claustrophobic corridors of concrete as Richard and Robert McCraw fought their way back along Shaftesbury Avenue. They reached a set of stairs where a sign read 'up to Trafalgar Square' and, together, they scrambled up the steps, climbing over the dead bodies that were strewn in their path.

Then they were out in the night air. They'd made it onto the top of the Redoubt. But the enemy was everywhere. Robert McCraw dodged a lunging bayonet and shot his attacker in the face. Richard shot another Japanese, then felt himself grabbed from behind, a bayonet heading for his throat, but McCraw shot the man wielding it.

'Run, laddie!' the big Scot screamed and he pushed Richard towards the edge of the concrete Redoubt.

Richard felt McCraw's huge fist hit him in the back, then he was hurtling through space, the Scot hurtling alongside him. They fell twenty feet into a tangle of bushes and lantana vines.

As they regained their breath, they heard Japanese voices to their left and right, and, with a nod to each other, they charged headlong down Smugglers' Ridge. For several hundred feet, they tumbled and slid, crashing into stunted trees and bushes and rocks, until they came to rest in a small ravine. Scratched and bleeding, Richard scrambled to the top of the far side, his eyes frantically searching the way ahead. Then he rolled back into their shallow retreat and came to rest against McCraw's enormous frame.

'There's only one way to go, Robbie,' he whispered. 'And that's straight down towards Kowloon. We've got to stay ahead of the Japs.'

'You'll be going on your own, lad.' McCraw grunted in pain. 'My leg's busted good and properly.' He pointed to the broken femur bone protruding from his upper left leg. 'I'm done for, laddie, and it's no use us both being caught.'

'I'll carry you!'

'Don't be ridiculous, maaaarn!' McCraw growled.

'But . . .'

'I'll hear no more from you, Richard! I'm out of ammo, give me your pistol and get out of here.' The big Scot raised his arm. 'Here's my hand. Good luck to you, laddie.'

Richard shook his friend's hand and placed the pistol in it. He tried to speak but the words wouldn't come. Then they heard Japanese voices high above them and he nodded to Robbie and disappeared over the edge of the ravine.

The 38th Division's intelligence was brilliant. Before the war, the Japanese community in Hong Kong had contained a host of spies. Even the friendly, and very popular, barber in the Hong Kong Hotel had turned out to be a Japanese naval commander. The photographs and maps of the British military installations and defences, which the barber and others had supplied to Tokyo, were stunningly accurate.

Untrained and ill-equipped British forces crumbled beneath the onslaught of the battle-hardened veterans of the Sino-Japanese War. Within twenty-four hours the 38th Division had secured the New Territories, scaled the heights of the Kowloon Mountains from the North and swept down onto Shing Mun Redoubt, Smugglers' Ridge and the rest of the British defensive line. They slaughtered any who offered resistance and chased those in retreat down the mountain slopes to Kowloon Peninsula. After only four days, the Japanese Army massed on the Kowloon waterfront and prepared to attack Hong Kong Island.

Their Air Force commanded the skies above. The Japanese had attacked the British RAF units at Kai Tak airport completely destroying them. Now, as their comrades of the 38th Division watched, dive-bombers, with the flag of the Rising Sun emblazoned on their fuselages, began systematically bombing the island's waterfront suburbs of Wanchai, Central and Sai Ying Pun.

No sooner had the bombing runs ceased than Japanese artillery units on the Kowloon Peninsula began firing murderous fusillades across the harbour creating total chaos. Soldiers and civilians alike ran screaming for their lives. Horses, escaped from the bombed out Jockey Club stables in Happy Valley, maimed and streaked with blood, ran in blind panic through the streets adding to the nightmarish scene. Buildings crumbled and fires raged unchecked. And all the while the song *Home Sweet Home* boomed across the harbour from Japanese loudspeakers in Kowloon, interspersed with exhortations in Japanese accented English, 'Give up and the Japanese will protect you! Trust in the kindness of the Japanese Army!'

The Japanese shelled Hong Kong Island for five days. Then, on the night of the eighteenth their first troops landed at East Point and, commandeering every available vessel, the main body was shipped straight across the harbour. They swarmed over the island from north to south in a direct line fighting their way through Wong Nei Chong Gap, effectively cutting the island in two. Finally they turned east and west and ended all resistance. The invasion had taken seventeen days.

The War Cabinet in London had been advised that, even if the New Territories and Kowloon were lost to the Japanese, Hong Kong Island could hold out for four months. But Hong Kong Island had held out for just over a week.

龍

On the morning of 19 December, an ancient junk with a crimson lanteen sail glided slowly away from Hong Kong Harbour heading west, seemingly unaware of the war that raged around it. Japanese fighter-bombers filled the air above, racing through the heavy black smoke rising from Wanchai and Central, and all about, boats of every shape and size, from military landing craft to junks and sampans commandeered by the invaders, ferried more Japanese troops across to Hong Kong Island.

Lo Shi-mon, with his wife and son safely below deck, stood on the deck of the junk and watched with astonishment. It had been only ten days since the invasion of Hong Kong had begun, he thought. His eyes were drawn to five British motor torpedo boats from Number Two Flotilla as they rounded Green Island from Lamma Channel. The boats raced into the harbour at full speed with all guns blazing. They tore into any vessels containing troops and fired on them mercilessly until their ammunition was expended, then two of the boats were shot out of the water while attempting to ram larger vessels. It was reckless bravery at its most glorious.

Several miles astern of the junk, the old Royal Navy river gun boat, *Cicala*, under the command of her one armed captain John Boldero, returned fire at the Japanese Artillery units in Kowloon with her three inch gun, while at the same time, she harried and attacked the invasion flotilla crossing the harbour.

Lee Kwan, standing beside Lo Shi-mon, peered through binoculars searching for the Merchant House beneath the Peak. He could see black smoke billowing skyward from the area where the mansion was situated.

'Thank God the family left when they did,' he said.

Lo Shi-mon could only nod in response as he watched the carnage unfold before him. His heart was with Richard and Malcolm and the others whom he knew would be locked in mortal combat with the invading Japanese. They'd be fighting along the waterfront of Central and retreating through the streets of Wanchai, creating what resistance they could in a brave but futile attempt to protect the island.

Lo shook his head sadly. Was it barely a week ago he'd spoken to Richard and tried, in vain, to argue against his foolish code of British honour?

'*Their army is too powerful, Elder Brother. You know this,*' Lo had argued. '*They have taken the New Territories and Kowloon in four days. You were at Shing Mun Redoubt when it fell. The Turnip Heads took it in two hours. And now they are mounting their artillery units in Kowloon not one mile from here! They will blow Hong Kong Island off the face of the earth.*'

'*That is not the issue, Ah Lo,*' Richard replied.

Lo had found his friend in Victoria Barracks. He knew Richard had been with the Hong Kong Volunteers up on Smugglers' Ridge and he had gone to the barracks to enquire of Richard's whereabouts, or indeed to discover if he had survived the initial attack. The two men had embraced like long lost brothers and found a quiet place to recount their experiences.

'*I heard gunfire not long after I left the ravine,*' Richard said as he finished his explanation of events on Smugglers' Ridge. '*I would say McCraw is dead, Ah Lo, and may the gods be kind to his soul.*'

'*He was a good friend,*' was all Lo could say and the two men fell silent.

'*Please do not tell me, Blue Star,*' Lo said eventually. '*That *you will be so foolish as to continue with this war that you cannot win?'*

· *'I have no alternative.'*

'You can come with Lee Kwan and me. We have a sailing junk at Ap Li Chau,' Lo said hopefully. He had arranged the vessel a week before through none other than the sons of The Admiral The One Eyed Woo. Napoleon and Wellington Woo would be waiting with the vessel on Ap Li Chau, an island on the south side of Hong Kong which formed part of Aberdeen Harbour. *'If we sail west through Kap Shui Mun to the Pearl River Estuary, we will be able to escape on the west side of the river. Any fate is better than remaining here awaiting certain death. The Turnip Heads kill indiscriminately, they enjoy it.'*

'I have no alternative,' Richard reiterated. *'I am British, Ah Lo. Britain is at war with the Japanese and I must fight. My honour is at stake and the fate of my home and friends is in jeopardy. Understand or not understand?'*

'I am Chinese. The object of fighting a war is to kill your enemies, not have your enemies kill you. Your reasoning is foolish, Elder Brother. Why stay here and kill only a few Turnip Heads when you can come with Lee Kwan and me and kill lots of them?'

'Just as you are going to fight for China, old friend,' Richard smiled. *'I must fight here, for the British.'*

Lo Shi-mon knew the argument was over. Fate had marked out separate paths for the two friends, and those paths must be followed.

'Will you remember or not remember,' Lo said softly. *'We have The One Eyed Woo's junk at Ap Li Chau?'*

'I will remember,' Richard stood and offered his hand. *'Find Quincy Heffernan if you can, and take him with you.'*

Lo nodded. *'I will not sail until the last moment. Lee and I will watch for you.'* He shook Richard's outstretched hand and bowed slightly, knowing that Richard would not come to the boat, and that it was unlikely he would see his friend again. *'Goodbye, my friend.'*

'Joi kin pang yau,' Richard repeated, then turned and walked away.

龍

Lo Shi-mon looked across the junk's high bow towards Lantau Island and Kap Shui Mun, the narrow channel of water between Lantau's northern tip and the little island of Ma Wan. Once the junk was through Kap Shui Mun they would be reasonably safe. They would sail out into the Pearl River Estuary north of Macau, where the Woo brothers would land him and Lee on the western bank of the Pearl River. He would find a safe haven for Wei-Ling and his son, then he and Lee would head inland, skirting Canton, then north to find the Communist Forces.

Lo had never forgotten the carnage wreaked upon his people by the Japanese in Nanking. As Napoleon and Wellington trimmed the sails to negotiate the Channel, Lo took one last look at the battle raging behind him in Hong Kong, and he allowed the fires of hatred to burn freely, deep within him. He knew now that he must fight, just as Richard was doing, but he would do so on his own terms. He would kill and keep on killing until not a single Japanese remained alive on Chinese soil. And he would survive.

龍

Richard stood in Central Square with the other prisoners and watched, humiliated, as Sir Mark Young, the Governor and Commander-in-Chief, surrendered to Lieutenant General Takashi Sakai of the Imperial Japanese Army. The Japanese flag was raised and all present were forced to bow in recognition. It was the first time a British Crown Colony had ever been surrendered to an enemy.

'Merry Christmas, *pang yau*,' Quincy Heffernan muttered. Quincy had refused his offer of escape aboard the junk, telling Lo Shi-mon that his rightful place was with his countrymen.

'Merry Christmas,' Richard replied as they both watched the Rising Sun fluttering in the breeze. It was Christmas Day 1941.

Richard had fought gallantly alongside Canadian troops in the Battle of Wong Nei Chong Gap. At the height of the battle he'd been badly concussed by a mortar shell and he'd awoken to find himself taken prisoner. Now he stood in Central Square, Malcolm Linden on one side, Quincy Heffernan on the other, witness to Britain's humiliation.

He gazed at the harbour water and saw Elanora. His last sight of her was in the open boat that had ferried her to the Pan-Am flying boat bound for Australia. She was smiling bravely and wiping the tears from her eyes as she waved him farewell.

At least Elanora is safe, he thought. And so were those with her.

'Our family will survive, Richard,' she had said. 'And so will the families of our friends.'

Elanora had taken with her not only Lee's wife Lin Li and their little boy, but Old Soong and Ah Poh, the *amah*, and Li Ping, the devoted *amah* and mistress of Robert McCraw. She had begged Richard and Lee Kwan to accompany her, but both men had steadfastly refused and she'd finally given up.

'Goodbye, my love,' she'd whispered as she clung desperately to him on the embarkation pontoon. 'Promise me I will see you again?'

'I promise, my love,' he'd answered. 'These are dark days, but life goes on and things change. They always do, believe me. Change is inevitable.'

Richard had watched the vessel all the way out to the floating aircraft and he'd waved as the huge amphibious machine took off into the morning sunlight.

龍

The surrender ceremony was over and Richard, Malcolm, Quincy and the others who had been forced to witness it, were marched off, guarded by members of the Kempeitei, along Des Voeux Road to the internment camp on the south side of the island.

'This is it, Richard,' Malcolm said as they walked through the burnt-out buildings of Western. 'We're for it now.'

'I wouldn't be so sure about that if I were you,' Richard

smiled at his friend. 'Circumstances change, Malcolm, they always do.'

As they shuffled along, Richard looked fondly at Quincy Heffernan whose eyes were fixed, steadfast, on the road ahead. He remembered with great clarity something Quincy had once said to him.

'Such is the way of things for a man, Richard,' his old tutor had stated. 'Change is inevitable. The sun rises and sets, the tide ebbs and flows and each season follows in fixed order, of that you can be assured. But for a man there are no such certainties, he is left at the mercy of fickle gods who juggle his fate in their hands and laugh at his litany of woes. He can only take the path he thinks is right and walk it, with the expectation of change and eventual salvation.'

Richard Brewster shivered. Winter had arrived in Hong Kong and he knew *this* winter would last a long, long, time. But spring would come eventually, it always did. He would survive. And the Dragons would rise from the ashes.

BIBLIOGRAPHY

Chang, Iris, 1997, *The Rape of Nanking*, Penguin Books, New York.

Deigton, Len and Hastings, Max, 1999, *The Battle of Britain*, Wordsworth Editions, London.

Empson, Hal, 1992, *Mapping Hong Kong*, Government Information Services, Hong Kong.

Morgan, W.P., 1989, *Triad Societies in Hong Kong*, Government Press, Hong Kong.

Morris, Jan, 1989, *Hong Kong*, Penguin Books, London.

Sinclair, Kevin, 1983, *Asia's Finest*, Unicorn Books, Hong Kong.

Sinclair, Kevin and Kwok-cheung Ng, Nelson, 1997, *Asia's Finest Marches On*, Kevin Sinclair Associates Ltd, Hong Kong.

The South China Morning Post, archival material.

Ward, Iain, 1991, *Sui Geng HK Marine Police 1841–1950*, Hong Kong University Press, Hong Kong.

Also published by Random House Australia

Bruce Venables
The Spirit of the Bush

I looked at the moon in the dark sky tonight and wondered
  if it could see me
An insignificant dot on a planet it gravitates round endlessly

A walk through the poetic mind of 'the Larrikin', Bruce Venables, is a unique experience. Opinions on everything Australian, from philosophy and drought to cricket dwell there.

Now collected here for the first time, the Larrikin's poems are patriotic, funny, sentimental and heartfelt, and pay tribute to the Australian spirit and sense of humour. Venables is a brilliant observer, and weaves his wit, humour and love of his country and its people into scintillating verse in the noble tradition of Henry Lawson and Banjo Paterson.

Judy Nunn
Pacific

Young Australian actor Samantha Lindsay, fresh from her success on the London stage, is thrilled when she scores the lead role in the latest Hollywood war epic, *Torpedo Junction*, to be filmed in the romantic South Pacific islands of Vanuatu. It's the role of a lifetime.

In another era, Jane Thackeray travels from her home in England to the far distant islands of the New Hebrides with her husband, a Presbyterian missionary. Ensnared in the turmoil of war in the South Pacific, Jane witnesses the devastating effect human conflict has upon an innocent race of people. As the winds of war sweep the sleepy island paradise, she meets Charles 'Wolf' Baker, a charismatic American fighter pilot, and Jean-Francois Marat, a powerful French plantation owner. Their lives become entwined in a maelstrom of love, hate, sacrifice and revenge.

On location in Vanuatu, Samantha plays a character based on the life of 'Mamma Tack', a World War II heroine who was invaluable to both the US forces and the New Hebridean natives. Uncanny parallels between history and fiction emerge and Sam begins a quest for the truth. Just who was the real Mamma Tack? And what mysterious forces are at play, reaching from the past to manipulate her life? The answers reveal not only bygone secrets but Sam's own destiny.

From the dark days of Dunkirk to the vicious fighting that was Guadalcanal, from the sedate beauty of the English Channel ports to a tropical paradise, *Pacific* is Judy Nunn at her enthralling best.

Judy Nunn
Territory

Territory is a story of the Top End and the people who dare to dwell there. Of a family who carved an empire from the escarpments of Kakadu to the Indian Ocean and defied God or Man to take it from them. Of Spitfire pilot Terence Galloway, who brings his English bride Henrietta home from the Battle of Britain to Bullalalla cattle station, only to be faced with the desperate defence of Darwin against the Imperial Japanese Air Force.

It is also a story of their sons Malcolm and Kit, two brothers who grow up in the harsh but beautiful environment of the Northern Territory, and share a baptism of fire as young men in the jungles of wartorn Vietnam.

And what of the Dutch East Indies treasure ship which foundered off Western Australia in 1629? How does the Batavia's horrific tale of mutiny and murder touch the lives of the Galloways and other Territorians – like Foong Lee, the patriarch of the Darwin Chinese community, and Jackie Yoorunga, the famous Aboriginal stockman? What is the connection between the infamous 'ship of death' and the Aborigines that compels a young anthropologist to discover the truth?

From the blazing inferno that was Darwin on 19 February 1942 to the devastation of Cyclone Tracy, Territory *is a mile-a-minute read.*

Judy Nunn
Beneath the Southern Cross

'A night of debauchery it was . . .'

Thomas Kendall stood with his grandsons beside the massive sandstone walls of Fort Macquarie. He smiled as he looked out to Sydney Cove, '. . . that night they brought the women and convicts ashore . . .'

In 1788, Thomas Kendall, a naïve nineteen-year-old sentenced to transportation for burglary, finds himself bound for Sydney Town and a new life in the wild and lawless land beneath the Southern Cross.

Thomas fathers a dynasty that will last beyond two hundred years. His descendants play their part in the forging of a nation, but greed and prejudice see an irreparable rift in the family which will echo through the generations. It is only when a young man reaches far into the past and rights a grievous wrong that the Kendall family can reclaim its honour.

Beneath the Southern Cross is as much a story of a city as it is a family chronicle. With her uncanny ability to bring history to life in technicolour, Judy Nunn traces the fortunes of Thomas Kendall's descendants through good times and bad, two devastating wars and several social revolutions to the present day, vividly drawing the events, the characters, and the ideas and issues that have made the city of Sydney and the nation of Australia what they are today.

Judy Nunn
Kal

Kalgoorlie.

It grew out of the red dust of the desert over the world's richest vein of gold. Like the gold it guarded, Kalgoorlie was a magnet to anyone with a sense of adventure, anyone who could dream. People were drawn there from all over the world, settling to start afresh or to seek their fortunes. They called it Kal; it was a place where dreams came true or were lost forever in the dust. It could reward you or it could destroy you, but it would never let you go. You staked your claim in Kal and Kal staked its claim in you.

In a story as breathtaking and as sweeping as the land itself, bestselling author Judy Nunn brings Kal magically to life through the lives of two families, one Australian and one Italian. From the heady early days of the gold rush to the horrors of the First World War in Gallipoli and France, to the shame and confrontation of the post-war riots, *Kal* tells the story of Australia itself and the people who forged a nation out of a harsh and unforgiving land.

'A huge and sumptuous novel . . . absolutely unputdownable. Nunn is mistress of the old-fashioned story we beg to hear.'
Herald-Sun

Judy Nunn
Araluen

He sorely missed Araluen and the vineyards, but that couldn't be helped. One day he would buy a vineyard of his own. One day. In the meantime, he had to make his fortune . . .

Build an empire. Lead a dynasty. At any cost.

From the South Australian vineyards of the 1850s to mega-budget movie-making in modern day New York, *Araluen* tells the story of one man's quest for wealth and position and its shattering effect on succeeding generations.

Turn-of-the-century Sydney gaming houses . . . the opulence and corruption of Hollywood's golden age . . . the New York party set . . . the colour and excitement of the America's Cup . . . the relentless loneliness of the outback . . . Judy Nunn weaves an intricate web of characters and locations in this spellbinding saga of the Ross family and its inescapable legacy of greed and power.

Judy Nunn
Centre Stage

Theatre is a world of illusion. The stars shine on centre stage. But what secrets lie hidden in the shadows? What passions are unleashed when the line between truth and fantasy vanishes?

Alex Rainford has it all. He's sexy, charismatic and adored by fans the world over. But Alex is not all he seems. What spectre from the past is driving him ever closer to evil? And who will fall under his spell along the way?

Madeleine Frances, beautiful stage and screen actress. Years before she escaped Alex's fatal charm, but now she is forced to confront him once again . . . and reveal her devastating secret.

Susannah Wright, the finest classical actress of her generation. Not even her awesome talent can save her from Alex's dangerous charisma.

Imogen McLaughlin, the promising young actress whose biggest career break could be her greatest downfall. She wants Alex Rainford – and she has no idea that he has the power to destroy her . . .

Centre Stage is a tantalising glimpse into the world of theatre and what goes on when the spotlight dims and the curtain falls.